THE GATE

THE GATE

ONDREA KEIGH

ISBN: 979-8-9872442-5-8 (paperback)

ISBN: 979-8-9872442-4-1 (eBook)

ISBN: 979-8-9872442-8-9 (Hardback)

Book Cover by Emily's World of Design

Map by Emily's World of Design

Edited by Laura Ebersole

Published by Lyonsword Publishing

www.ondreakeigh.com/lyonsword-publishing

Acknowledgments

When I started this series, I had never written a book before. It was a massive undertaking that grew from one book to three books, with me learning as I went. But I was never alone. There were many people who helped make this trilogy become a reality, and I am so grateful to everyone who joined me in this adventure!

First and foremost, I would like to thank my Lord and Savior Jesus Christ and my Father God for leading me through this process. This was an undertaking I would never have accomplished if it were not for each thing and person he provided as I went. I have learned so much about faith through this process and will forever treasure the relationships God brought about and deepened at each stage.

I would also like to thank my Mom and Dad, who not only supported me when I decided, practically out of the blue, that I was going to write a fantasy trilogy, but kept me going when I was tired, celebrated with meat every turn, and were the first people to edit these books. I would like to thank my brother Evan, who helped me name some of my favorite characters and worked through the fight scenes with me step by step, literally. I will always treasure those memories. I would like to thank my family as a whole for all they did to help and support me during this process.

It was and always will be a blessing to have them on this journey with me!

I would like to thank Sibella, who took time to walk me through what being an author would take. I think of that phone call regularly and am so thankful for the time she took to help me and the reminders she passed on to persevere and trust God. Thank you to my wonderful editor, Laura, who went above and beyond working on these books. I would not have been able to get them to where they are today if it were not for her and all her hard work! And I would like to say thank you to Emily's World of Design, who designed all three covers and my map. She not only did a phenomenal job on the art, but she was a joy to work with and was so patient with me in my inexperience.

I would also like to thank those who read over these books at an early stage, gave me feedback, and helped get me past roadblocks. Thank you to Jason, who took the time to read these books and give me feedback in the midst of his busy schedule; Lisa, for sharing her horse knowledge to help me make sure Jeb was well taken care of in these books; and to the pastors who preached sermons that answered prayers and helped me get these books finished, right on time!

I really can't thank these people enough. It takes a village to write a book, and the village God gave me is a spectacular one! I am so grateful for each and every person who helped get these books from thought to page and beyond. I look forward to all that comes from this journey, which is just beginning.

To the One who invited me into His story.

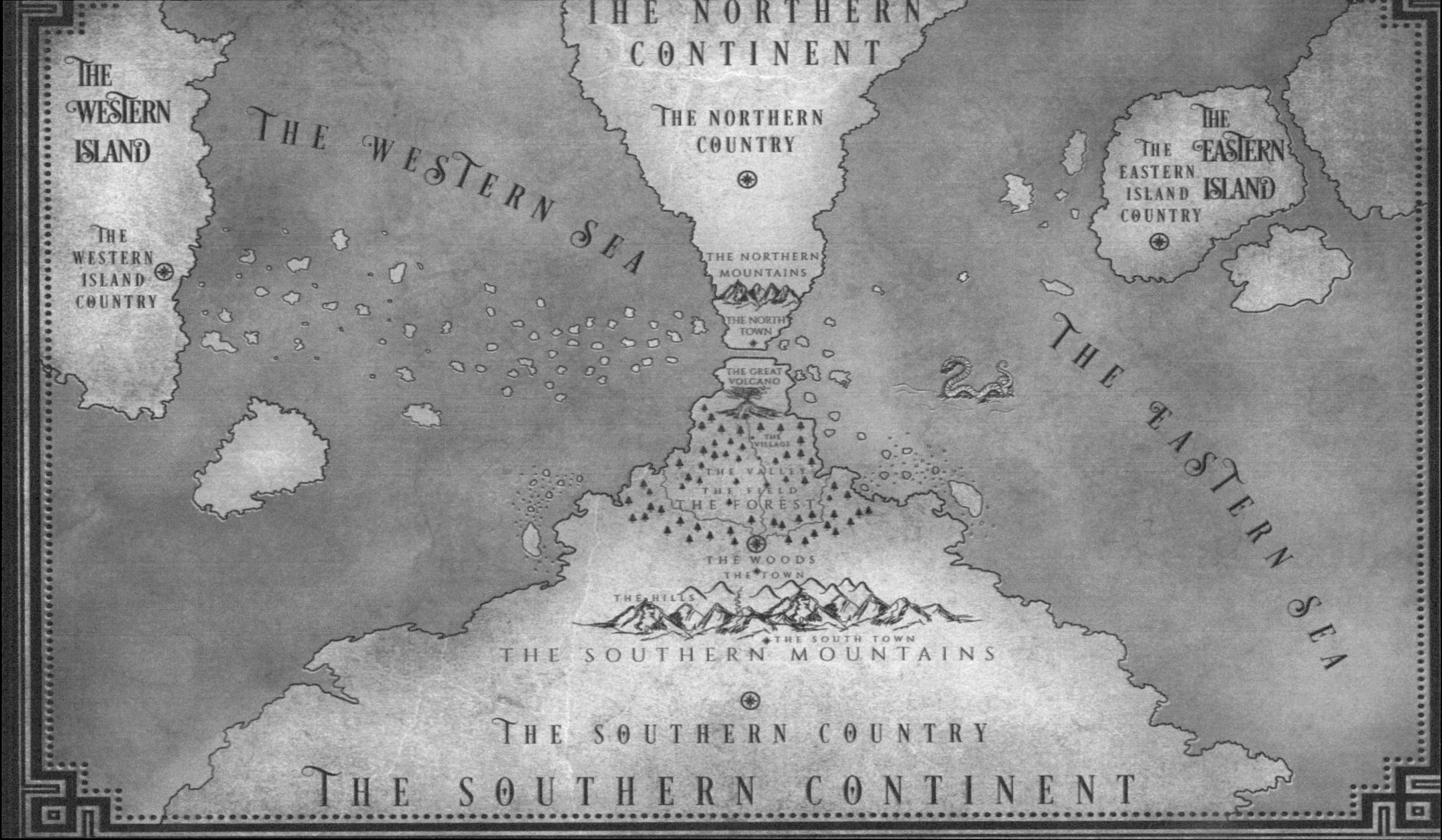

THE EASTERN SEA

THE WESTERN SEA

THE EASTERN ISLAND
THE EASTERN ISLAND COUNTRY

THE NORTHERN CONTINENT

THE NORTHERN COUNTRY

THE NORTHERN MOUNTAINS

THE NORTH TOWN

THE GREAT VOLCANO

THE VILLAGE

THE VALLEY

THE FIELD

THE FOREST

THE WOODS

THE TOWN

THE SOUTH TOWN

THE SOUTHERN MOUNTAINS

THE SOUTHERN COUNTRY

THE SOUTHERN CONTINENT

THE WESTERN ISLAND

THE WESTERN ISLAND COUNTRY

Chapter 1

Light blinded me as I tried to open my eyes, and I snapped them shut at the searing pain from the sun that shone high overhead. Reaching my arm up to block its light, I attempted to wet my dry, cracked lips with my tongue, but it stuck to the inside of my mouth. *Why is my mouth so dry?* I wondered. Desperate to find shelter from the sunlight, I rolled over onto one side, a groan involuntarily wrenching itself from deep in my aching lungs as I did. *Where am I?*

"Benjamin, don't..." I heard a familiar voice mumble in a gruff, tired voice.

"What? Where am I?" I responded hoarsely as someone gently rolled me onto my back again.

I threw my arm up again to block the sun as I registered that whatever I was lying on was moving unsteadily beneath me.

"Benjamin don't roll over. You will fall," warned the voice.

I forced myself to open my eyes, despite the sun's blinding light. Squinting upward, I found myself face-to-face with General Delaney. *Was it his voice I heard? It must be,* I thought. He looked tired and wet. *Wet? Why is he wet?* I wondered as I became gradually aware that I felt wet as well. Suddenly, I noticed the smell of salt in the air, and I began to remember. The dragon attack. The ship breaking apart. Solace.

"Solace!" I bolted upright as I called out to her. But I was faced with nothing but open ocean. We were floating on a piece of wood that I recognized as part of the hull from General Delaney's ship. Raising a heavy hand to shield my eyes, I scanned the horizon, my fingers partially blocking my view. I could see we were surrounded by blue water, which met a partially clouded blue sky on the unobstructed horizon line.

"Ben, careful!" said another voice as someone grabbed me under the arms and pulled me backward.

"Solace—where is she?" I questioned as I frantically looked around, searching for the rest of our ship.

The last thing I remembered was standing on the ship's deck, watching a screaming and crying Solace being held back by Ivan before I was surrounded in fire. Her image was seared into my mind. Her face contorted with fear, tears streaming down her cheeks, one hand reaching toward me as the other tried to pry off Ivan's protective grip.

I broke free from the hands under my arms, and the piece of hull that we were floating on rocked back and forth under my uncoordinated movements. But it wasn't just me that was jostling the large section of wood. Hands grasped my arms again, and I was pulled from the remaining wreckage of our ship and loaded into a small rowboat. I briefly glanced behind me to see a navy galleon ship waiting nearby but quickly turned back to the general.

"Where is Solace?" I demanded, though time spent in the salty water had left my voice raw. "Where are the others?" I added as I scanned the sea around us again, awkwardly trying to stand as I was half pulled, half climbed into the small rowboat. I clambered over the sword and shield, which had apparently survived the shipwreck and were already in the boat, but my mind barely registered their presence. *I need to find the others!* I thought. "We can't leave them!" I said, hearing the desperation in my voice.

The Western Island was nowhere to be seen, and there was nearly no sign of the wrecked ship beyond the piece of hull the general and I had apparently been stranded on, save a few fragments of debris. The ship must have been washed away by the wind and waves, which were now noticeably absent. The ocean around us was calm and flat.

"I..." started the general in a tired voice. "I'm sorry, Benjamin," he said as he tried to hold my gaze. "They are gone."

I looked into his nearly black eyes and saw grief. "What? No!" I contended as I looked back out to sea, not willing to accept the general's pronouncement. "They were—"

"Ben..." the general interrupted me as he placed a tired hand on my shoulder. The others in the boat tried to hold me down to stop me from flipping the craft as I frantically gripped its side to search the water for the others. When the general didn't finish his sentence, I turned to face him. His expression said it all. They were gone and there was nothing I could do about it.

"No..." I whispered as I felt my stomach twist with shock. As the boat set off toward the nearby ship, I sank to the bottom, and everything went numb. The smell of the sea became faint, and the people in the boat seemed to grow fuzzy. Even the feelings of my abrasively salty wet clothes and raw skin faded amidst the sea of anguish that overtook me.

Still sitting in the boat as it was lifted from the water, I felt my mind spinning out of control as it analyzed the recent shipwreck. I played the events over and over in my head, in search of any way the others could have survived. Distracted by my thoughts and numb to everything else, at some point I found myself in a bed in one of the ship's cabins. What pulled me from my stupor was the sound of the general urging his captain to search for the others. Uncertain how long I had been in the bed but faintly aware that my clothes felt dry, I pulled my tired, aching body from the sheets and made my way toward the voices.

"Benjamin," said General Delaney, looking up from where he was slouched in a chair being checked by a physician. "Benjamin, you need rest. We will search for them, but..." He gave me a sympathetic frown as I stood before him, staring blankly, my stomach sour with emotions I dared not allow to surface. "Please, Benjamin, get some rest. We can't do anything in our current state; let my captain do his job," appealed the general.

I felt someone gently guiding me back to my bed, and I yanked my arm from his grip, stumbling slightly as I did. "We must look now! If they are still out there—"

"Benjamin!" said the general, this time in as stern a tone as his raw throat would allow. I fell silent, and he sighed. "I know how much you want to help, but look at yourself. We were floating on that piece of wreckage for three days. It was only by a miracle that one of my navy ships came to find us. My captain will continue to look," he reassured as he locked eyes with me, "but you need rest."

Without another word, I allowed myself to be ushered to my bed, and I sank to its soft, cushioned surface. As the physician covered me with a blanket, exhaustion set into my bones. I closed my eyes, my mouth twisting unconsciously as I held back tears. *They have to be alive,* I told myself. *They have to be alive. The general's men will find them.*

It turned out that we were found only five miles south of the Western Island. The general's crew searched the area and even sent a pigeon to the island to inquire if anyone had washed ashore, but it was no use. A pigeon came back within a day carrying a message that the others were nowhere to be found.

For the next three days, I did nothing. I ate nothing. I drank only when forced. I forgot about the world around me as I fell into a despair I never thought I would feel again. But there it was, strangely familiar. The bottomless pit of hopelessness.

I played the dragon's attack over and over in my mind until I felt I had memorized every detail. Each time I replayed the memory in my head, my feelings ranged from a complete absence of emotion to anger to sorrow so deep I cried until I could not breathe. *They are gone. All of them. Again.*

The general's captain, whom the crew called Captain Arke, had approached me with a loosely disguised look of pity on his face to tell me of the pigeon's message. The islanders had seen no sign of any survivors.

"They are gone. I...I am sorry," Captain Arke had started to say as I sat on the edge of my bed, again refusing the food the physician offered, opting for only water. "We have looked all we can, and this is all we could find." He handed me a small, wet, stuffed bunny toy. It was Yuuki's. "The storms were bad that day."

"The *Lyonsword* must have succumbed to the waves and the dragon as well...I am truly sorry, Benjamin," said the general.

I stared at the floor in silence, my mind somehow blank and filled with regret at the same time. *How is this possible? Everyone, even the* Lyonsword, *gone? Is it even possible for the* Lyonsword *to be destroyed?* But the more I considered it, the more overwhelmed I felt, until I could no longer think straight.

As I sat there, pondering my disastrous circumstances, General Delaney thanked the captain for his help before dismissing him. I felt the general standing in front of me, but I made no effort to look up.

"Benjamin, the crew has spent an entire day searching, and they have not found anything," General Delaney explained. "I have told Captain Arke to head home. We have about three weeks of sailing ahead of us, and there is another storm on its way, so we need to get moving. We will decide what to do once we reach land." After a moment's pause, I heard him turn and walk away without another word.

Home. I let out a heavy sigh as anger filled my bones—a burning anger at the King for letting this all happen. For letting everything be taken away again. From that moment on, time had passed slowly, and now here I was, lost without Solace, my compass, forever.

Three days turned into four. Then five. Then six. All spent in my private cabin the general had arranged for me on the ship. With each day that passed, my sorrow grew stronger, and my anger grew quieter. I wasn't sure who to be angry at anymore. *Can I be angry at the dead? No. They were not at fault. Can I be angry at the animal that killed them? No. It would not understand that anger even if it were here to see it. Can I be angry at myself? Yes. I can.* But I had done that once before, and a part of me was afraid to try it again, for that was a whole different level of hopelessness that only Solace had been able to pull me from. Now that she was gone, I feared that if I let myself fall that far, there would be no one to stop me from plummeting beyond the point of no return.

That brought me to a final thought. *Can I be angry at the King and the Prince of Eeffrayldour?* I spent most of my time trying to answer that one question. I was determined to answer it with a resounding yes. At first, I told myself I should be. I directed all my anger at the eternal beings I could not see. *Maybe they aren't real, and I have just been using them as an excuse to find a purpose in life,* I thought. In moments when I felt they were real, I told myself they had lied to me. The Prince had promised that Solace would become a mighty warrior. She was one half of the Night Rider. Now, she was gone. The Prince had not kept his promise.

But as time went by, I felt my anger begin to slip away. Every time I tried to blame the King and the Prince, something stopped me from fully believing they were at fault. The word "no," not spoken in my own voice but rather in Eyethanoff's. As we battled dark soldiers that day on the Western Island, he had tried to stop me from going to the others, calling out that one word when I ran to their defense. *"No."* The memory interrupted my anger at the eternal beings now deeply intertwined in my life. *What would have happened if I had listened? Would Solace and the others be alive today?* At the time, I had thought Eyethanoff's warning was just a momentary reaction. But now I wondered. *Could he have known what was about to happen? Was that warning intended to protect me and the others? An instruction to stand still and trust that the King could see what I could not?*

Ultimately, I came to the conclusion that the King and the Prince had not failed me, though I was determined to blame them. I told myself that they could have done more. I told myself that they could have instructed Eyethanoff to do more. But in the end, I could not set aside the realization I'd had on the Western Island. They were there—I just couldn't see them. They had a plan—I just didn't understand it yet. It was not their fault. *Maybe they did their part, and I was the one who failed them.* That thought brought me back full circle to the idea that it was my fault. Fear that I was the weak link in this equation gripped my mind and twisted my gut. *Solace would have done better.*

Solace. She would have done this right. Why had the Prince not chosen her to wear the armor? Now she was gone. *Is it even possible to complete this mission without her? With no compass, I am lost in this dark world.*

On the morning of the seventh day, I finally got dressed and left my sleeping quarters. I didn't speak with anyone, but for the first time in days, I felt hungry. I found some food and sat alone, wondering what I was going to do without the others. I had lost everyone once before. Or so I had thought. The first time I lost my family, I still had Ivan and Nadia. This time I didn't. I shook my head at the realization. I had taken Ivan and Nadia for granted. I hadn't lost everything back when Mary and my family had been killed. I had just been unwilling to see what was right in front of me—friends who knew my pain, for they had lost their own family as well. With that thought weighing heavy on my mind, I picked over my food, unable to finish it, and returned to my sleeping quarters. *This time, I truly have lost everything.*

When I entered my cabin, I found myself standing before the sword and shield. I had not paid them any attention since I had come aboard this ship and was unaware of how they had gotten into my quarters. But for some reason, they suddenly held my interest. I stood there, staring at them, as a thought formulated in my mind. *I am telling myself I have lost everything this time. I was wrong before. Am I wrong now?* My father's dying words flowed through my mind like a whisper. *"We fought this battle alone and lost...Choose your friends wisely...Do not fight your battles alone."* I didn't know exactly why those words had come to me. Maybe some part of me wanted to be reminded of what I still had. Things unseen.

I frowned and shook my head. Without Solace, the mission to spread *The Story* and find the armor that could lead us to the Gate was over, or so I attempted to convince myself. *But why would the Prince choose both of us, then let her die?* As I turned my back to the sword and shield, I felt deep down that I didn't truly believe that mission was over. That mission had been much bigger than any one of us. I just didn't want to admit it. I didn't want to face the challenges that lay ahead without Solace.

I left my sleeping quarters in an attempt to distance myself from the armor and headed to find General Delaney. Though I was not yet sure if I could trust him, he had saved my life. For now, I would have to trust him enough to get me safely to land. *It is time to cash in on that break he promised me when this all started.*

The ship's deck was busy as the crew went about their various tasks, but I ignored them, hoping no one would stop to talk to me.

The idea of holding a conversation with a well-meaning, sympathetic stranger sounded more daunting than swimming home.

I successfully navigated the deck without being pulled from the safety of silence and found General Delaney in the captain's quarters discussing plans with his captain. As I entered the room, the general greeted me with too much excitement for me to deal with in my current mood.

"Ah, Benjamin. You are up and about! I heard you ate," said the general with a smile as he grasped my shoulders with his strong, bony hands.

I tensed at his expressive greeting, then nodded. "What port are we headed to?" I asked in a no-nonsense tone, avoiding eye contact.

The general released my shoulders and, ignoring my repressed emotions, gestured to his captain's maps. "We were originally headed for the westernmost port, but Captain Arke and I have decided that the port closer to the Forest's boundary is the best bet," he said.

"Why?" I asked as I crossed my arms and subtly busied myself momentarily by placing my feet exactly hip-width apart.

"It will put us closest to the Town and give us a shorter distance to travel to the Southern Country," he explained. "Plus, according to Captain Arke, it looks like we might avoid some bad weather by changing routes."

I frowned. "Why do we need to get to the Southern Country?"

The general raised his eyebrows in surprise. "To finish the mission," he said, as if it were obvious. "I told you on the island, Ben, finding the Gate can end all our wars with the Great Beasts of the Southern Mountains. We can't give up now."

I shook my head. "I'm done." I stated the words confidently, but something deep down tried to warn me I didn't want to be done. I ignored the feeling as the general began to protest.

"Benjamin," he started, "you cannot stop now."

I took a deep breath and glared at him defiantly. "Back when this all started, you said that after I retrieved the book from Ruth, you would give me a break. I am here to say that, as soon as we reach land, I will be taking leave."

The general's brow creased. "That is no way to speak to your commanding officer," he countered with a hint of frustration in his tone.

I raised an eyebrow. "I am not a soldier in your army anymore," I retorted. "I have not been since the last war with the beasts ended, and you know it. I was—am—simply a hired gun. If you ever want me to trust you again, you will let me go with no trouble," I stated sternly.

I had no desire to play soldier, but I knew the general could technically appeal to the king of the Southern Country to require me to return to my duties during war time. A request the king would most certainly grant since a war was due to start any time now. As a result, I needed to bargain carefully or the general could easily rope me back into his services, permanently, against my will. I stood waiting, hoping I had not been too direct.

The general narrowed his eyes at me. "I know you are dealing with a tragedy...but time is running short," he said in a steady, calm voice. He studied me as he considered my demands, then he finally gave in. "I will give you a week. Then we will be on our way. We must find the last piece of armor if we are going to end these wars with those ravenous beasts forever."

I set my jaw but nodded, reluctantly taking the win. Out of habit, and possibly some kind of twisted rebellion, I stood waiting for the general to release me from his presence.

General Delaney frowned, then his expression relaxed with a faint hint of sympathy, and he waved his hand. "You are dismissed."

With a clipped nod, I turned and left the room. Not knowing exactly where I was headed, I found myself making my way to the bow of the ship, where I leaned against the gunwale. We still had a couple weeks or so before we reached our destination, and I had nothing to do until then except recover my appetite and try not to think about all I had lost.

Over the next few days, I helped the crew with whatever they needed, cleaned my pistols, which had somehow remained on my person during the shipwreck, and wandered about the ship thinking of new things to teach Jeb when I arrived on land. He would conveniently be waiting for my return near the port we were headed toward, as that was near where Captain Bates had planned to land. I could collect Jeb once we docked.

But that thought promptly reminded me that I would have to travel to the Village in the Forest to tell Mrs. Alves that Yuuki was gone. For good. Regret and guilt washed over me as I recalled the day Yuuki had joined our travels. I had been the person tasked with protecting her, and now she was dead. I clenched my jaw and forced myself to hold in the tears that threatened to explode from within.

Suddenly overtaken by an onslaught of emotion, I retreated to my sleeping quarters, and, unable to hold it in any longer, I cried. For the first time since the shipwreck, I allowed myself to remember the people I had lost in detail. Their faces, their personalities, the fond memories all came flooding back and I cried myself to sleep.

Darkness surrounded me, so thick I could not see anything. I felt tired and alone, engulfed by the darkness I had been frantically trying to escape in past dreams. Now I sat in that very darkness, lost and with no energy to fight back. Then I saw it. The mirror from the castle appeared before me, and in it, my reflection. My skin was gray and overshadowed as dark fog swirled around me. Then the mirror disappeared, but my dark image stayed. The dark fog moved in closer and closer until it formed veins that began to burrow their way into my flesh like worms into a corpse.

As fear gripped me, a vein of darkness struck out, aimed directly at my heart. But it hit something hard, and the sound of the vein clanging against metal rang through my dream like a gong. Feeling sluggish, as though the darkness had drugged me, I reached a heavy hand up to my chest in search of what had stopped the vein of darkness, which was now rooting for a new entry point.

As my hand came in contact with whatever it was that had protected my heart, light suddenly poured from the object. It was the breastplate. As I looked down at it in awe, I saw the belt holding it in place, and the shoes appeared on my feet. My gaze abruptly shifted up as the Ice Dragon materialized before me. "Have faith, my friend, for the unseen is a treasure worth believing in."

I looked down again to see the sword in one hand and the shield in the other. The symbol on the shield lit up, its image reflecting light. I searched for this new source of light and realized the sword had lit up as well. The light seemed to come from within it, shining through the words written on its shimmering metal blade.

I looked back up toward the dragon, but she was gone. In her place stood the wooden door. The same door I had seen in the vision on the ship. But suddenly, darkness attacked. Instinctively, I lifted the shield as veins of darkness launched themselves at me like vipers, then it all vanished.

Gasping for air, I snapped awake as sweat dripped down my temples and the sound of someone knocking on a door rang in my ears. My bed sheets were soaked with perspiration, and I forced myself to take a deep breath to calm down. I shivered at the feeling that something was crawling over my skin. I could still just barely feel the armor on me.

The ship swayed, causing the light of a nearby lantern to cast odd shadows across the luxurious room as it swung back and forth in a smooth motion. I took another deep breath and let it out as I glanced at the porthole, wondering what time it was. It was still dark outside.

The knocking came again, and I realized that someone was actually at the door to my cabin.

I climbed out of bed, wiping sweat from my brow as I went to the door. When I opened it, I found one of the ship's crew waiting. "What do you need?" I asked.

"The general would like to speak with you," he said politely.

"About what?" I asked in a tone that was more demanding than I had intended.

"I am not sure. But he wishes to speak with you now," he said, his tone still polite but with a little more force behind it.

With a deep sigh, I nodded. "Thank you. I will be there shortly."

I closed the door and leaned my back against it. I took a deep breath, trying to calm myself, still shaken by the dream. *What could the general need to talk about at this early hour?* Despite the momentary distraction of the odd timing for a meeting, my mind quickly returned to my dream. The loss of my comrades had left me in such a state of shock that I had not realized the dreams might continue. For some reason, Solace's absence made me feel as though the past few months had never actually happened.

Still leaning against the door, my gaze fell on the sword and shield, which were propped up against the wall. The lantern dangled above them, its swaying yellow light illuminating the shield's symbol and bringing back memories of meeting the Prince in the Woods. As I stared at the pieces of armor, my mind wandered to Mary, my first wife. After losing her, I had been lost in deep depression. Depression so abysmal I had not even really known it was there until I met Solace. Now, with Solace gone too, I was back in that abyss once again. I frowned. *No. I am not there.* I had been trying to return to that familiar state of depression, but for some reason I couldn't. *Why?*

Pondering those thoughts, I pushed off the door and began to get dressed. I felt the presence of the sword and shield, as if they were staring at me. The feeling reminded me of the Beast of the Woods. Those piercing green eyes. They had drawn me in, even before I met Solace. That thought made me pause. *Did things really change when I met Solace?* I let my gaze fall to the sword and shield again. *No, things changed when I met Ruth,* I corrected myself as I resumed putting on the clothes that had been provided for me. Then I paused again, looking down at my newly cleaned pistols and recalling the time I had fired one into the air to wake everyone up from the golden ghosts' trance. It had been those green eyes, the Beast's eyes, that had woken me from the stupor. I glanced at the sword and shield again as another correction dawned on me. *Wrong again. Things did not change when I met Ruth. It all started with those green eyes. The Beast sought me out. But why?* As if in response to my question, Ruth's words from what felt like a lifetime ago played in my mind. *"Now that is a good question."*

With a shake of my head, I abruptly broke away from my thoughts and secured the straps of my gun belt around my waist and across my chest. Then I put on a black, hooded cloak before turning and heading out the door, leaving the sword and shield behind.

Chapter 2

I entered General Delaney's quarters to find him mulling over maps, a fresh pot of something warm on the table near him. It appeared he had not fully prepared for the day, as his shirt was still untucked and his jacket was draped over his bed.

I approached him and stopped at a respectful distance. "You called for me, sir," I said plainly.

General Delaney nodded and waved me over without looking up from his maps. "The location of the next piece of armor is still unknown. How did you find the other pieces? Maybe that could help us find this last piece."

His tone was calm, but I knew it thinly concealed demands for my cooperation. I frowned at the fact that the general had apparently forgotten our earlier discussion about me being on leave, but I was not surprised. He was only capable of seeing his own needs. I now knew why I had been so quick to see him as the enemy. He only had eyes for the Town. Not those whom he employed to protect it. However, I found myself wondering if I should help him, as I had nothing better to do. But as I was considering what to do, a red flag seemed to wave in the back of my mind, and I heard Solace's warning words from the night we had boarded General Delaney's doomed ship. *"Don't trust him!"*

Not wanting to deal with the emotions tied to her memory, I shoved her words aside.

My shoulders slouched a bit as I decided I might as well comply with the general's demands, and I explained, "We were not looking for them." I shrugged. "We just found them while we were distributing *The Story*."

The general pursed his lips in thought. "Hmm. Where were you headed next?" he asked, finally shifting his gaze from the maps to me.

"The Southern Country. We were scheduled to meet a contact there, but he is probably long gone," I explained. "I must admit, I don't know what day it is, but we will probably miss him by at least three days due to the shipwreck."

General Delaney nodded. "Yes. You are correct. Our voyage is on schedule, but we must take into account those days we were left adrift. That doesn't mean we can't go there next anyway, though. Do you know the contact's name?" he prompted.

Before answering, I paused, considering all the general had done. He had saved my life, helped me when I was injured and in shock, and commanded the search for the others. But still, that red flag brought on by Solace's words waved in my mind as I considered telling him the plans Captain Bates and I had developed based on Ruth's network. We had planned to meet one of the captain's friends who had been living in the Southern Country for years. But the man had a family. He had gladly committed to helping us get the book to a printer, but he had not signed up to have strangers find out that he was helping in this dangerous fight against the Creature, and I wasn't willing to put him in any danger he hadn't committed to facing. I had evidence that could put General Delaney on either my side or Valdra's side, and I could not bring myself to feel comfortable with divulging certain details to the general, especially those that might put others in danger.

Deciding to hold off on giving away all the information, I shook my head. "Names were not given," I lied. "We had certain people in our group who knew where each contact was located," I said, which was true. Captain Bates and I had decided that not everyone should know all our plans, in case someone was caught. Various people in our group had been in charge of different kinds of details, such as travel routes, escape routes, backup plans, and more. "I was not the one who was told the exact whereabouts of the next contact," I lied again, though I knew I would have to give the general something. "But I could probably point you in the right direction."

The general nodded. "That will have to do for now," he accepted. Then he straightened from leaning over the maps and studied me. "Benjamin, I...I know you wish to take some time," he started, his expression thoughtful as he rubbed his chin.

Here it comes, I thought. *The attempt to rope me into another mission.*

"And I truly understand. But I beg you to reconsider..." he pleaded. When I didn't respond immediately, his expression seemed to darken, and he mumbled, "I could order you to find that piece of armor."

Whether he was talking to himself or to me, I was not entirely sure. I didn't respond.

General Delaney watched me for a moment. Then his expression relaxed, and he added, "But I won't. I know how long you have wanted a break, and I will grant you one. I do require that you help me until we reach land, though. We only have a few more days of travel, so it shouldn't be long," he said with a smile. "And as usual, I will pay you handsomely once we reach home, including what I owe you for retrieving the book from Ruth."

In my current state—tired, untrusting, and annoyed at his self-centered tactics—I was bound to say something that would get me thrown to the sea monsters. So instead, I kept my mouth shut and nodded respectfully. *At least I'll get paid,* I thought.

General Delaney seemed to accept my silent response. "To start with, why don't you show me where you found the other pieces of armor and where you think you were headed to find the next piece," he said, stepping aside and gesturing to the map he had been examining.

I stepped forward and looked over the map and its collection of generically named locations. It showed the two main continents, the Northern Continent and the Southern Continent, bisected by the man-made channel that lay north of the Great Volcano and south of the Northern Mountains. The Town was located near the middle of the map, technically part of the Southern Country and thus ruled by the king of the Southern Country, but rarely referred to as such. For some reason, the Town and the land around it were treated a bit like a country in and of itself, run mostly by General Delaney. The map also displayed detailed depictions of the countries referred to as the four corners of the earth, the Eastern Island Country, the Northern Country, the Western Island Country, and the Southern Country, as most maps did. But this map was more detailed than the type a common sailor might own. This one showed all the little towns in each country, as well as the uncharted lands and various villages near their edges, creating quite a large map of the known world. The king of the Southern Country, who provided the general with most of his resources, had clearly supplied him with a talented cartographer.

As I examined the map, I decided there was no harm in telling the general what we had already discovered. "We found the first piece here, in the Woods," I said as I pointed to a small dot that marked the location of the Woods. The general placed a small figure of a flag on the dot as I continued to the next location. "The second was on the Eastern Island, inside the castle. The third piece was here, in the Northern Country, just outside North Town on the cliffs above the Channel." The general placed small flags on each place as I went. Then I pointed to the Western Island. "The fourth piece was the shield, which I already had, but I didn't use it much until we fought the dragon here in the Western Island Country."

General Delaney nodded as he placed a fourth flag on the dot identifying the Western Island Country. "Just as I thought. The pieces, or something they are connected to, are hidden in the four corners of the earth."

I raised an eyebrow in surprise. "Just as you thought?" I asked. It was true. The armor was located in the four corners of the earth, but I was surprised to hear that the general knew that little tidbit of information.

The general nodded and put his hands on his hips as he glanced over the map. "There was a story I once heard about dragons." He waved his hand dismissively. "They used to hoard treasures. But according to the story, they were protecting some of their treasures from people who would misuse them. Some dragons had special hiding places in the four corners of the earth, though no one knew for sure if the treasures were all in one place or scattered at each corner country. Until now, that is," he finished with a satisfied smile.

I nodded, remembering the Ice Dragon from my dreams and visions. I glanced toward the door as thoughts of the dragon caused my mind to replay the dream I'd had last night. Darkness all around me. Attacking me. Overtaking me. But the armor had still protected my heart. *Since the others died, I have been telling myself I'm alone, but am I really alone?* As I pondered that question, I realized for the first time that this most recent dream had been different from the others. It didn't seem to have anything to do with finding the next piece of armor. *What did it mean? Why was it different?*

"Where were you headed next?" asked General Delaney, pulling me from my thoughts.

I left my own question unanswered and turned back to the map to search for the Southern Country. "There," I said flatly, pointing to the small dot that indicated the Southern Country. "We were headed to the Southern Country, just beyond the Southern Mountains."

The general searched through a pile of maps stacked nearby and pulled out a more detailed one of the Southern Country. "Where exactly where you headed to in the Southern Country?" he asked, spreading it out on top of the one we had been examining.

I leaned forward, placing one hand on either side of the map, and studied the depictions before me. Captain Bates and Lance had been the ones to find contacts, but Dan and Casey had been the only ones besides the contacts who knew the exact locations for the final meetings. I had suggested this strategy because the final leg of the journey would be deep in enemy territory and the chances that someone would be caught were much higher. As an additional safety precaution, Dan had made sure that most of the meeting places were not even the homes of the people we were meeting. Taking all that into account, and the fact that I didn't want to tell the general everything I knew, I decided to go with a half-truth.

"I am not sure, but I do know that we were headed first to that inn," I said, pointing to an inn that was located just inside South Town, a small town nestled against the south side of the Southern Mountains. "I am not sure if we were to meet the contact there or be given directions," I added. Another lie. We had intended to meet someone who would take us from the inn to the actual meeting place. But that person was certainly long gone by now, having been instructed to disappear if we didn't show up to the meeting within the allotted time frame.

"Hmm..." The general rubbed his chin with his boney fingers as he examined that section of the map. "Is there anything in common about each place you found an armor piece that would help us find the right location to search?" he inquired.

Again, I decided I had to give him something, but I wasn't quite sold on telling him that the sword had been the key to finding the other pieces of armor, so I lied again. "The shield. It..." I shrugged. "It drew me to them. To the other pieces," I explained as the image from my dream of the sword and shield in my hands came to mind. *Why did the Beast choose me?* I asked myself again as my thoughts wandered back to my recent nightmare. *And why did that dream last night have nothing to do with finding the next piece of armor? It felt more like...a warning.*

General Delaney nodded. "Okay, then we will use the shield."

I frowned. "Hold on…We?" I asked with raised eyebrows as I straightened from leaning over the maps.

General Delaney looked at me, lips pursed in a skeptical expression, and asked, "Benjamin, are you really going to stand there and tell me that you do not wish to continue with this mission?"

I crossed my arms. "I am done," I said, leaving no room for doubt. Though I was still left with that very feeling. Doubt.

The general nodded. "As I said, I will respect that decision once we reach land. But think about it, Benjamin. With that shield, you would be able to find the rest of the armor—the armor that can show you the solution to our problems. You would have the power to end all this suffering!" he encouraged. The general leaned forward and looked me in the eye. "The place we are headed has been hit by the beasts. The next war is upon us. Captain Arke says when this ship left, it was bad. Imagine what it will be like now," he demanded. "You can stop that." He pointed to my chest but abruptly stopped short of contact. Frowning, as if irritated about something, he put his hand down and said, "Benjamin, just think about it."

As the general concluded his argument, I felt the armor on me. I had felt it ever since I had been woken by that dream, but it suddenly seemed even more present. *Is it calling to the other armor piece?* I wondered. Reluctantly, I entertained the idea of finding the last piece of armor. It was tempting. Something about it brought an image of Solace's bright smile to my mind.

I took a deep breath. "I will think about it," I said simply.

General Delaney nodded with a satisfied expression. "That is all I wish, my boy. Now, I know I woke you early. Go. Eat. I will let you know if I have any other questions. But think on what I have said," he added encouragingly.

I nodded polity before turning to leave. As the door closed behind me, my mind wandered to something Solace had said to me on the *Lyonsword*. *"Have a little faith. It will all work out in the end."* As the memory floated around in my mind, I allowed myself to acknowledge that, for a reason I didn't completely understand yet, I wanted to finish this mission. No matter how hard I tried to return to where I had been—who I had been—before this had all started, I could not. I was not the same person. I had changed. I winced at the thought, though I wasn't sure why, then pushed it from my mind as I headed to find food and a good place to think in peace.

I got food from the cook and found a spot to sit and eat on the deck as the sun rose above the horizon. As I ate, my mind wandered to the adventures I'd had with Solace and the others when we were traveling through the Forest over seven months ago. I had thought back then that my purpose was to help Solace complete her mission. Later, I had been convinced that it was to complete the mission the Prince gave to both of us. Now, Solace was gone, and I was faced with a crossroads. Give up, go home and take that break I had so desperately wanted, then return to life as General Delaney's favorite soldier for hire, or complete the mission on my own, without Solace and the others. *No, there would be no break. The next war with the Great Beasts has started...The Creature would*

remain in control. I shook my head at the thought. *No break is worth that.*

My earlier acknowledgement of what I truly wanted sprang to mind. An acknowledgment that forced me to accept something I had been resisting. Until now, that is. I had no desire to give up. Like it or not, Solace was not here. But my duty was still to the Prince. Sometime between getting attacked by a dragon and learning that it had killed everyone I loved, I had become fully dedicated to the mission the Prince had given me. But ever since I had woken up in the wreckage of that ship, I had been trying to convince myself that I was not dedicated. With Solace gone, I had been struggling to force myself back into the familiar, and oddly comfortable, feelings of self-pity and hopelessness. But now I was certain that I was fully committed to this mission. For if I was not, I would surely be giving up on the Prince in this moment, right now, faced with the chance to get what I had told myself I wanted all those months ago—a break. I had once given up on life because of a similar situation; I had lost everything when my family died. But no matter how much I tried to deny it, things were different now. I was different now. I frowned as I thought about the general's encouragement to keep looking for the armor. *If we can stop what happened to Solace and the others from ever happening again, shouldn't I continue, even though I am only half of the Night Rider without Solace?*

With these thoughts rolling around in my mind, I knew I had to find the general and at least learn what his plan was. I dumped my now empty plate with the cook and went in search of the general again. I found him on the quarterdeck, observing the helmsman expertly guide the ship toward our destination, and I inquired about his plans.

"My plans are to find the final piece of armor, of course," responded the general with a smile.

I frowned. "I need details. If I am going to help you with this, I need to know what we are doing. If we were to die on this mission, then the armor would be lost forever. We are the only ones who know about it."

General Delaney's expression turned thoughtful. "That's a good point." With a deep frown, he contemplated the situation, then said, "Though my plans are sufficient, we should find someone to pass the information on to in case we do perish."

"And what are your plans?" I asked again, redirecting him to my original question.

The general pursed his lips in thought, then began to explain. "You said that the shield led you to the armor pieces. We will take the shield with us and start looking around the area where you believe you were to originally meet your next contact," he said as he began to pace back and forth near the ship's helm.

"But not all the armor pieces were located exactly where the meeting was to take place," I pointed out. "It could be beyond the Southern Country in the Uncharted Forests."

"Yes, but we have no other place to start," explained the general, coming to a halt in front of me.

He was right. We couldn't get much more information without the help of Captain Bates and the crew of the *Lyonsword*. Then I had a thought. "Unless you know where Ruth is now," I suggested. "She originally put together the network we were using. She might know more. When we were on the Western Island, before the dragon attack, didn't you say she was staying somewhere north of the Town?" I asked.

General Delaney nodded. "Yes, near the Western Seaport on the Southern Continent. She was there when I originally left the Southern Country. But she is probably gone by now," he said with a wave of his hand.

"It's a good place to start," I replied, ignoring his excuse. "Before I even began working with Captain Bates, she was the one who originally helped him find contacts. She might not know the exact contacts that the captain chose, but she could at least point us to which contacts live in the area where we are headed," I suggested.

General Delaney nodded again. "You are probably right. I know she has a place near the port we will be docking at." He was silent for a few moments, rubbing his chin in thought. "When we get closer to land, I will have a pigeon sent out. By the time we dock, we will hopefully have a response waiting for us," he finished in a reassuring tone.

Satisfied that the general seemed be genuine in his desire to complete the mission, I gave a short nod, then turned to go.

"So, you are going to assist me?" asked General Delaney, his words stopping me at the top of the stairs that led back down to the main deck.

I had all but decided to help him finish the mission. I glanced down in the direction of my cabin, where the sword and shield remained propped against the wall.

"Benjamin, everything we have worked for is near," said General Delaney as he stepped toward me, angling his head as though trying to get me to look at him. I did, turning back to face him. "All we must do is find this last piece of armor, and it will all be over," he urged. "Then, you and I will be able to end this." As he spoke, he once again pointed to my chest, but then he stopped abruptly, and for a moment I thought I saw anger flare in his eyes. I was distracted from my observations, though, by the same odd sensation from the armor over my chest. This time, the feeling was clearer—it felt as though it was stopping something. My mind drifted to the vein of darkness in my dream and the sound the breastplate had made when the vein hit the armor.

I turned away from the general as the red flag waved in my mind again. "We will see what Ruth says," I replied and headed down the stairs, thoughts of the dream filling my mind.

Leaving the general on the quarterdeck, I went to help the crew and prepare for the end of our voyage. It had been a while since I had been back to the Southern Continent, and part of me was looking forward to it, though, considering the accumulating memories of everything I had lost on that continent, I was not sure why.

During the final few days of our trip, those memories repeatedly led my mind back to the question about the Beast of the Woods. *Why did it seek me out?* Before everything else that happened, it was the Beast of the Woods who had found me. Then, after I met Ruth, I learned that she had apparently picked me as what *The Story* called a Guardian. Not just any Guardian, but the last Guardian. *But I encountered the Beast first. Did it help Ruth choose me?* Then I remembered that the Beast was the King's beast, his messenger of truth. "The Beast" was a name the Creature had given it, as a way to convince people it was evil. But its real name was Adournath, a name I didn't fully know the meaning of but had learned during our watery travels was very similar to that Eeffraylick word for "truth." Back when I first met Ruth, it had seemed like she knew something that I didn't. After I learned of *The Story* and my mission, I simply assumed that she had known *The Story* and had been thinking about choosing me as a Guardian.

The day before we arrived at the Southern Continent, a thought stopped me in my tracks. *Could it be? Is it possible that Ruth did not choose me, but, instead, the King did, and Ruth was simply intrigued by his choice?* The idea that the King was behind it all brought me to another realization. I had learned that the Lion's Sword, the army of the King of Eeffrayldour, had been with me all this time. They had even helped me survive the attack by dark soldiers while we were on the Western Island. The Lion's Sword were invisible to me without the sword's help, but they were here, fighting for me. *Could it be that the King orchestrated all this from the beginning? Was that his role? Was the King the mastermind behind solving this problem of darkness, the Prince simply acting on the King's plan?* I suddenly recalled a part of *The Story* that said the King and the Prince had devised a plan. *Could they have known and chosen me even back then?* I wondered. I knew that the King and the Prince were eternal beings, who, according to *The Story*, knew how to defeat the darkness that plagued this world. But it had never really dawned on me how much the King might have set in motion. *Maybe the King really does have a plan—a plan that is far beyond my understanding.* If that were the case, that meant he had chosen me for this mission before I even believed he was real. My mind bursting with that idea, one thought settled in the forefront. I could not turn my back on this mission now.

As this realization came to full fruition, the family and the life I had gained as a result of the mission seemed like bonuses on a journey I had never fully comprehended until now. A journey that cut through the heart of darkness and revealed the way to light in the midst of darkness—to freedom. Those of us living under the Lie were plagued with a limited ability to see what was truly happening—to see and hear the things of the Unseen Lands.

Standing on the deck of the general's ship, I found myself teetering between my old life and my new life. Solace's words rang in my mind again. *"Have a little faith. It will all work out in the end."* Once again, her words led me in the right direction, and I suddenly knew I had to fully commit to my new life, as I had to my mission. There was no going back. The King had a plan, and it seemed I was part of it. I took a deep breath. *I will not run from my responsibility.* I was a soldier in the King's army, and I had a job to do. A job that would not end in hopelessness. The only job that mattered. A job I would do whatever it took to complete.

With my mind set, I turned to go to my cabin, headed for the sword and shield. I needed to speak with Eyethanoff, and I needed the sword to see him. I needed some guidance as to what to do and how to serve the King. He would be able to point me in the right direction.

As I approached my cabin and opened the door, one of the general's men came up behind me. "The general would like to speak with you," he said, rather abruptly.

I nodded. "Give me a minute," I responded as I started to enter my cabin.

Out of the corner of my eye, I saw the man shake his head and very briefly glance through my open door and back to me. "I am afraid he requested you now," he responded, a bit more urgently. "He is in the captain's quarters."

I let out a sigh and hesitated with the door half open. *I need to speak with Eyethanoff,* I thought. The crewman stepped aside, gesturing me forward. *I guess it can wait until later,* I told myself as I stepped past the crewman, closing the door behind me.

In the captain's quarters, I found General Delaney plotting out a course to the port with the ship's captain and navigator. He glanced up at me as I entered. "Benjamin, I know we just spoke, but your words got me planning, and I wanted to update you. We will be docking tomorrow morning, and the pigeons will be sent out shortly with messages to my soldiers to check Ruth's home near the port. In the meantime, we need to plot a course to each of our destinations, including Ruth's. If Valdra has already reached the Southern Continent, he will be looking for us, and the first place he would search is with Ruth."

I had not thought of that. "Good point. But she has survived this long on her own. I am sure she has some way to protect herself." Ruth had never seemed to worry about agents of the Creature, for, in her words, she was not his to take. *Whatever that means.*

General Delaney shook his head. "I was not actually thinking of her safety," he admitted with a wince. "If we are to finish this mission, we cannot let Valdra get in our way."

"You're a general. What about your army?" I asked, deciding to ignore his disregard for Ruth.

The general nodded. "I have some soldiers. But I am afraid that Valdra has taken charge of many of them."

I raised an eyebrow. *That explains where Valdra got his army,* I thought. "How did that happen?" I asked out loud.

General Delaney gave me an irritated frown. "There is a reason I am usually so hard on those who display insubordination. It is dangerous. I have learned my lesson. I hope you have as well," he said in a slightly warning tone. Clearly, he didn't like me questioning his leadership skills.

I nodded as the red flag waved in my mind again. "Fair enough. But if we are going to succeed, we will need soldiers," I said.

The general's expression softened. "We?" he asked with a smile.

I clasped my hands behind my back and nodded. "I have decided to finish the mission. When we dock tomorrow, I will help you find the final piece of the armor, free the Unseen Lands, and end these wars with the Great Beasts for good."

As the words left my mouth, I felt the armor relax. It was as if something that had been attacking it finally pulled away. The feeling summoned a memory of the moments the general had pointed directly at my chest. The armor had responded in an odd way then, too.

Solace's words rang in my mind again. *"Do not trust him."*

Chapter 3

I EXAMINED THE GENERAL as he stood before me reviewing our travel plans. I had once decided he was the enemy. Then, with no other option, I had boarded his ship with a small amount of evidence that he might not be my enemy. But still, I hadn't fully trusted him, and now there was something in his behavior that just kept raising that red flag.

My mind replayed everything that had happened leading up to my inadvertent reinstatement into General Delaney's employ. The trips in the *Lyonsword* to three of the four corners of the earth. The dragon showing up. Seeing General Delaney on the island. The *Lyonsword* disappearing, along with Lance. The dragon's attack. The memories flipped through my mind like pages in a book as I tried to find anything within them that could tell me for certain that the general was on my side. The dragon's attack had been what motivated me to board the general's ship. Then the ship was destroyed and everyone I loved died.

The memory of Yuuki's stuffed bunny, wet and dripping in my hands, came to mind. At the time, I had been too distraught to really think about it, but now that I did, I realized its appearance just didn't add up. The *Lyonsword* had left before the dragon appeared. It was nowhere in sight during that attack, so it was very unlikely that the dragon had destroyed it. *Could the general be lying to me? I suppose the* Lyonsword *could have shown up to help battle the dragon in the midst of the chaos or after I lost consciousness. And it surely would have been destroyed if that were the case. So maybe he is telling the truth.*

But for some reason, things just didn't seem to make sense. The general had an explanation for everything, but it was all just a bit too hard to believe. Especially the supposed destruction of the *Lyonsword*, a ship with unusual abilities. Come to think of it, when the general had shown up on the island that night, before warning us that Captain Bates was not to be trusted, he told us that he had seen the *Lyonsword* approaching the island. But that didn't make sense. The *Lyonsword* was nearly invisible at night unless you were right in front of it. I knew this for a fact because the first night I had seen the *Lyonsword*, I'd had to get within fifty feet of boarding it before I realized it was a ship. *Granted, at the time, it was inside a dark cave,* I conceded.

However, when we arrived at the Western Island, the *Lyonsword* had docked in a hidden alcove that only Captain Bates and his crew knew about. If he were telling the truth, the general would have either had to find that hidden docking port or catch a glimpse of the ship before it docked, while it was still sailing near the alcove's entrance. But that would have been difficult because the ship had mysteriously arrived at the island much faster than we had thought possible and had not spent much time near the island outside the alcove. The captain would only show the hidden docking port to the general if they were working together, and the only other vantage point of the sea on that section of the shore was at least one hundred yards above the docking port, on the cliffs. At night, viewing it from that distance, there was an extremely small chance that the general could have seen the *Lyonsword*. The options, as I saw them, were that either both Captain Bates and the general were working for Valdra, or the general had lied about everything in an attempt to keep me under control and convince me to help him find the last piece of the armor.

I frowned as I fully allowed myself to begin looking at the general as an enemy again. Then something hit me. As I reviewed the events that had led up to our current tenuous partnership, I realized I could not recall telling the general about the armor. I knew he had read *The Story*, and it told of the armor, but nowhere in *The Story* did it say that the armor would lead to the Gate. I had not told him I had found any of the armor, yet when we first spoke after I had recovered, he had expressed interest in finding the next piece of armor. *How did he know?*

General Delaney must have noticed me watching him because he looked at me with slightly narrowed eyes. "What is it? Is there something we should change?"

I considered my situation. If he was the enemy, and I didn't see how there could be any other explanation, I was trapped on his ship with no backup. It would be best if he didn't know of my suspicions.

I shook my head. "No, sir. Just waiting for a dismissal," I responded, hoping I sounded genuine.

The general nodded. "Of course. You are dismissed," he said with a wave of his hand.

I gave a respectful dip of my head, then turned and left the room.

When we arrived at the docks early the next morning, we were greeted with a response to the general's inquiry about Ruth's location.

"She left five days ago," said the general as he read the note. "No one knows where she went."

I let out a hard breath and allowed a tinge of annoyance to flare within me. *Probably a lie,* I thought. *He probably didn't even send any messages.* "Then we will just have to go with our initial plan," I said, deciding to just play along for now. "We will head to the Southern Country and hope the shield leads us in the right direction," I finished. When the time was right, I would break away from the general and find the last piece of armor on my own.

The general nodded. "I agree. I have placed your things on the cart with the rest of our supplies."

As he spoke, I couldn't help but notice his glance at the shield, which was on my back, and the sword, which was strapped to my side. I had finally gotten a chance to retrieve them from my room, and something about having them with me felt good. The armor felt stronger. But the general seemed to be keeping a closer eye on me now that I had them again. I had noticed one of his men surreptitiously watching me, though it could have just been my paranoid imagination.

"I will need a horse," I said, hoping that would give me a chance to get away.

"You can use one of my soldier's horses," replied General Delaney as he checked his own mount's saddle girth.

I shook my head. "My horse," I said simply. "I know him best, and I trust him."

The general shifted his weight irritably but conceded. "Where is he?"

"The *Lyonsword* was originally destined for this port. There is someone here in town who was supposed to have him and the other horses waiting for us when we arrived. I will retrieve Jeb while you finish setting our travel plans in place. I suggest we send a scout ahead to make sure we are not stepping into a trap by going to the same inn I was originally intending to visit," I said, hoping my attempt to seem helpful would ease the general's mind and prevent him from sending someone with me to retrieve Jeb.

The general nodded. "Good idea. When you return, we will be ready."

With a nod to the general, I set out into the small port town to find a friend of Mrs. Alves who had been tasked with watching over the supplies I and the others would have needed when we returned from our ocean voyage. Leading up to the day we left, we had stayed in the Village, knowing Valdra would probably not look for us there as he had no idea we had grown close with the villagers. Last time we were there, we had managed to get out quickly enough to keep him off their trail. So, we had returned and used the Village as our base of operations. We had asked Mrs. Alves to make sure our things were sent to the port town so we would not have to travel all the way to the Village before heading to the Southern Country to finish the mission. I had never met the man who was to be put in charge of our belongings, but Captain Bates had told me where he lived in case things went wrong.

Well, things had gone wrong, and I very much hoped the man still had Jeb.

I arrived at the man's house to find that he was outside working in his garden and, thankfully, had not sold Jeb. Apparently, the captain had prepared for a few different potential problems and had told him to hold on to our supplies for at least a month before getting rid of anything.

"Captain Bates paid for the stable before he left," said the man when I inquired about the horses and supplies. "Your horse is there. When the captain stopped by to get his things, he said to hold on to it until he could retrieve it."

Surprise coursed through my veins. "Wait," I commanded, holding a hand up before he could continue. "The captain came to pick up his things?" I asked.

The man nodded. "He was here three days ago. He took everything except the bay named Jeb and his tack. Said he had crew that could use the others but that the bay horse was special, and he didn't think anyone else could ride it...Something about the horse not moving for anyone but its owner."

Hope attempted to erupt within me, but I held it back a moment longer. "You are sure it was him? Captain Nathaniel Bates?" I clarified.

The man nodded again. "Oh yes, I would know him anywhere. It was him," he said with a smile.

I was right! The Lyonsword *wasn't destroyed. General Delaney was lying. The captain is alive! He has to be!* And if he was, that meant Yuuki was most likely alive too. And not only that, but there was a good chance the general was lying about the captain's allegiance to the enemy. My spirits lifted, and I grinned. "Thank you! Where are the stables located?" I asked.

"Just go down this street and take a left. The stables are part of an inn there," he explained.

"Thank you for your help. Were you paid?" I asked, forgetting in my excitement that he had already said he had been.

"Yes, it is all taken care of. I wish you luck on your journey," he replied with one last smile and a tip of his hat.

I nodded. "Thank you!"

I left the man's house at a deliberately normal pace as the morning light began to cast shadows and people went about their daily tasks. I headed to the stables where Jeb was apparently waiting, joy flowing through my body. Then, suddenly, my mood dampened as the armor seemed to respond to something nearby, a subtle pulsating feeling reverberating almost imperceptibly over my body.

I forced myself to maintain my normal pace but glanced casually over my surroundings. Nothing. Yet, I felt as though I were being followed. The feeling was familiar, for I had been followed by an unseen force before. *My dark soldier.* He was watching me; I could feel it. I had not felt the dark soldier's presence since before I had encountered General Delaney on the Western Island. I had to be right; the general was working with Valdra, and they were in league with the Creature, as I had originally thought. The fact that the general had lied about the *Lyonsword* going down, and now the invisible presence of my dark soldier, just confirmed it for me.

The feeling of being followed filled me with a sense of urgency despite my hopeful mood. I needed to find the last piece of the armor, but first, I needed to put some distance between myself and the general.

As I entered the barn, the familiar sound of Jeb's nicker greeted me. I smiled as I entered his stall and rubbed his favorite spot at the base of his mane. "Hey, boy!" I said in a low voice.

I leaned into his affectionate nuzzle, taking a moment to breathe in his familiar smell, mixed with the fresh scent of alfalfa. It felt good to be with a friend. He turned his head to one side, watching me as I looked him over and checked his feet. He seemed well cared for. With little time to waste, I tacked him up.

As I finished putting his saddlebags in place, a small scarf fell from one of the pockets. It was Solace's. She used to tie it around her wrist to hide extra coins when she traveled. I picked it up, re-membering how I had come into possession of the delicate fabric. Before we left the Village to begin our sea voyage, on the night of our wedding, Solace had been showing me how she tied it around her wrist to create a pocket. We had gotten distracted when Ivan came in and told us it was time to leave, and it must have been shoved into my saddlebags instead of hers. I smiled at the mem-ory as I ran my fingers over the silky dark green material and its velvety soft flowery design. Holding it to my face, I inhaled. Her scent hung in my nostrils, and I closed my eyes, her face clear in my imagination. *If the* Lyonsword *was not destroyed, then maybe she is alive too. Maybe the captain came back and rescued them,* I speculated, desperately hoping it was so.

After a moment, I put the scarf in my pocket, covered myself in a thick, fur-lined winter cloak from my supplies, and swung into the saddle. With my new certainty that the general was working with the Creature, I would not be heading back to the port. Instead, I would head south to the Town to see if I could find Captain Bates. Knowing him, he had probably continued on with the mission.

Hopefully, he would be there. Even if the dark soldier reported to General Delaney, I would have a small head start.

I cued Jeb to move forward, and we headed out of the barn in the opposite direction of the port where the general had docked. It was about a week of travel to the Town, and winter had set in, so we would be traveling alone in a beast-infested, snow-covered land. We would need to be careful. As we made our way through the wooded terrain, I kept an eye out for any signs that beasts were nearby, watching for tracks, broken branches, or damage to homes and property. The beasts were large and left a mark on the land that was hard to miss.

As we drew closer and closer to our destination, snow began to fall over the rolling hills and patches of dense trees. Winter was intensifying the farther south we went, making travel more difficult. During the day, Jeb and I did our best to stay away from other travelers. People gathered in groups were sure to attract beasts. At night, Jeb and I camped out under the cloudy skies, a fire keeping us warm. Thankfully, beasts didn't like fire, so as long as I could build one, I was most likely safe at night, though it wasn't a sure thing. The occasional brave beast might venture close enough to cause problems. To make sure I would have enough time to escape, I set up a trip wire with bells. Any large creature trying to get to me at night would trigger the bells, waking me in time to make a hasty retreat. Jeb was trained to stay within this man-made boundary, so each night we hunkered down, our lives seemingly in the hands of a thin string and the small metal instruments, and we did our best to sleep as we listened to echoes of the beasts' vicious attacks in the distance.

When we were finally within a day's ride of the Town, we took a shortcut through a wooded area in hopes that we would remain unseen by humans and predators alike. As we wove our way through the trees, I felt Jeb tense beneath me just before he stopped and nickered at something. I hesitated, pulling a pistol from my belt and placing a cautious hand on the hilt of the sword.

"Easy. It's me," I heard a familiar voice say from the trees to my left, and Lance, astride a horse, pushed his way through the branches, his hands raised.

I let out a heavy breath and holstered my pistol. "Lance, don't do that!" I said with a chuckle as we leaned in for an embrace. "You are alive!" I said with joy.

"That I am, my friend!" he replied with a grin.

"The stable owner said the captain came to pick up the horses, but he didn't say if anyone else was with him," I explained, hopeful about the fate of the others.

Lance's smile faded. "The captain is alive, and so is Yuuki. But the others..."

My heart sank like a rock in a pond.

"They didn't make it," he finished. "The captain thought we would be safer out at sea when some of Valdra's soldiers got too close to finding the port, so we left with the intention of coming back for you all. But then a storm came in and we couldn't get to you in time," he said with a look of sorrow.

I turned away as tears threatened to flow and a flare of anger at the captain's choice rose within me.

"I'm so sorry, Ben," said Lance in a quiet voice.

I took a deep breath and let it out. "Where is the captain?" I asked as the anger withdrew.

Lance gestured in the direction I had been headed. "He's in town. We have been planning on making a trip through the Southern Mountains to meet the last contact. But with that fire dragon out and about, we didn't think we could make it there without more people. Word is, it lives in those mountains, and it was spotted in the area only a day ago."

I grimaced. "Against a dragon, more people would be better," I said, forcing myself to focus on the conversation to get my mind off the fact that I had just been told, again, that Solace was gone. *Let her go,* I told myself.

Lance nodded. "But it's a suicide mission. We have been hard pressed to find people to go with us. With Nadia and Ivan gone, it has been—" Lance stopped, apparently noticing my jaw clench at sound of their names. "I'm sorry," he said with an apologetic wince.

I shook my head. "It's not your fault. What is the captain's plan?" I asked in a low voice.

Lance shrugged. "He doesn't have the armor, so he isn't sure how to find the Gate. He doesn't know if it will help, but he figured he would at least finish taking the book to the last contact. So, he reached out to him, and we were able to extend the meeting date."

"When is it?" I asked, my gaze unfocused.

"Two weeks," Lance said.

I shook my head and looked at him. "We can't wait that long."

"Why?" asked Lance.

"General Delaney. He is here. I made it here on his ship. I can only imagine his reason for not keeping me prisoner or keeping the sword and shield for himself," I said in irritation.

Lance frowned. "Then we will have to warn the captain. Follow me," he instructed.

I nodded as Lance moved out, not wasting any time.

We rode through the trees in silence as I felt myself sinking into sadness once again. Part of me wanted to be happy that the captain, Lance, and Yuuki were alive. And part of me was happy. But the others were dead, and I struggled to keep myself from feeling the pain of losing them all over again. I managed. But only by looking forward to what was to come.

After a few hours, I finally started up a conversation with Lance, who had not spoken, presumably attempting to let me mourn in peace.

"What are you doing so far from the Town?" I asked.

"Looking for Ruth," he explained. "The captain and I split up yesterday to look for her. But I didn't find anything. Hopefully, he found her."

I nodded. "How is Yuuki?"

Lance smiled. "She is well. Eric and the crew stayed with the ship, so she misses them." His expression darkened. "And the others..."

I nodded in understanding. "She was close with Ivan especially."

Lance nodded. "She misses him a lot. But not as much as you and Solace," he said with a small smile. "She will be happy to see you."

I allowed a small smile as well. "I am looking forward to it."

The sound of a beast attacking someone in the distance stopped us in our tracks for a moment. When the sound faded, Lance and

I glanced at each other. I held an index finger to my lips, and we exchanged nods, silently agreeing to remain quiet for the rest of the trip. Picking up the pace, we covered the rest of the ground in pretty good time and arrived at the Town an hour before sunset.

"This way," instructed Lance. "The captain and I agreed to meet back at the Kuzmich Inn."

I took the lead, and we trotted through town, headed for the twins' inn. When we arrived, we stowed the horses in the stables and headed toward the back door.

"You sure he will be here?" I asked as I approached the back porch, glancing at Lance to catch his silent confirmatory nod.

"This place should be crawling with dark soldiers," I commented, more to myself than him as I stepped into the safety of a shadow and peeked in through a small window adjacent to the door. The armor fluttered a subtle warning as if it were echoing my thoughts.

"It was. But they left yesterday," Lance said.

I nodded and put my hand on the doorknob. Then I froze as a realization sparked in my mind. "How would you know if dark soldiers were here?" I asked, beginning to turn. "You can't see them without the sw—" I froze when I came to face Lance. He was holding a pistol pointed at my head, his shoulders slouched in self-annoyance at his slipup.

He shook his head. "I knew something was wrong with that answer the moment it left my lips," he chastised himself.

I stared at him in disbelief. "Lance? What are you doing?" I asked, inadvertently raising my hands to shoulder height.

Lance smiled. "My job." He waved at someone to my right, and I spun to look as Valdra appeared, seemingly out of nowhere. He must have been what the armor was reacting to, not my thoughts.

"Hello, old friend," said Valdra with a grin just before something struck me on the head from behind and everything went black.

The sound of metal on metal rang out as I woke to find myself staring up at a gray sky broken up by what looked like the metal bars of a prison cage. I could feel a carriage rocking beneath me as it was pulled along a bumpy dirt road, the sound of horses' hooves on dirt coming from all around me. For a moment, my surroundings didn't make sense. My memories were hazy. I shook my head but stopped when pain shot through my skull. I sat up, chains attached to my wrists clinking together as I reached up to my sore head and looked around. Sure enough, I was in a prison cage.

As I took in my surroundings, everything came rushing back to me. *Lance!* He had betrayed me and the captain. *But how? Why?* The captain had said he was an old comrade, someone he had known for years. Pain again shot through my skull, and I felt the back of my head. My fingers found the source of the pain and came back wet with a small amount of blood. Someone must have knocked me out from behind when I was distracted by Valdra.

I looked beyond the cage bars and searched for Lance and Valdra, but all I saw were Martecyte soldiers behind and in front of the carriage.

I turned to the nearest soldier. "Where are you taking me?" I asked as I gently dabbed at the wound on the back of my head with my sleeve, trying to soak up any blood that wasn't dried.

The soldier pulled his horse up next to the carriage and frowned at me. "General Delaney's mansion." Then his frown turned to a smile. "We will hold you in his dungeon until he gets what he needs. Then I'm sure you will be executed," he said before spurring his horse forward to end the conversation.

I let out a sigh. *This is just great.* I was right about the general being a double-crossing monster. But I had eliminated Lance as a threat the moment I found out the captain was likely not who the general had hinted he was. I rubbed a hand over my face. *Great! How am I going to get out of this?* When an answer didn't immediately present itself, I checked the chains to see if there was any hope of escape. There wasn't.

Then something came to mind that lifted my mood. If Lance was a traitor, maybe he was lying about Solace and the others. For the second time since disembarking the general's ship, I felt a surge of hope that they might be alive. But then that hope crashed when I realized that Lance would have gotten them all captured or killed. *Let her go,* I repeated to myself.

I frowned. I needed to get out of here and find Captain Bates, assuming he was still alive. Whoever had survived, I needed to make sure they were free of the general and his evil master, the Creature.

I glanced around the cage, looking for any weaknesses, but I found none. The soldiers were all Martecytes, and they had taken my pistols, the sword, and the shield. My eyes searched the train of riders around me and spotted the sword and shield on a rider up ahead. Then I saw who it was. Valdra. He glanced back at me, but to my surprise, he didn't smile. His gaze shifted quickly away before he turned to look ahead again.

Letting out a half grunt, half sigh, I knew I was beaten. I couldn't get out of these chains, nor could I escape the cage. Valdra had the sword and shield, leaving me with invisible armor pieces that didn't seem to do much on their own, and I was unable to see how many dark soldiers were lurking nearby. Even if I did escape, there were about thirty or so Martecytes surrounding me and an unknown number of dark soldiers I couldn't see but knew were there. It was a lost cause. I would just have to wait it out and see what happened. I had escaped a prison once, a long time ago. It was a task I could plausibly accomplish again, especially if the general thought he had the upper hand. Granted, back then I'd had Nadia and Ivan's help. I sighed.

It was only a short ride from the Kuzmich Inn to the general's mansion, so I didn't have much time. With that in mind, I leaned back, making sure to look tired and beaten, but paid close attention to the Martecytes around me. I looked for any patterns I could find and memorized faces, rank, and social status—anything that might eventually come in handy if I were able to escape. I had to find Captain Bates or anyone else who had survived and tell them that Lance was a traitor. There was no guessing what Lance and the general had in store.

Chapter 4

General Delaney was not royalty, but, based on the size of his estate, he could have been mistaken for a prince. He was the resident beast expert. and his military existed solely as a beast-fighting force. He was second in command to this land's king and a highly prized counselor for all kings during wars with the beasts. As a result, the general's mansion was magnificent. It had most definitely been built with castles in mind, as, though smaller than most castles, it had similar architecture. The stone building occupied most of six sprawling acres, surrounded by land he, according to Captain Arke's crew, had only recently acquired. The entire estate was maintained by an extensive and highly trained staff. In addition to the mansion's imposing stone exterior, it had a prison in its basement. But it wasn't just an ordinary small prison. It was actually designed to temporarily hold the Great Beasts of the Southern Mountains, back when some of the general's advisors had believed they could learn the secret to killing the beasts by studying them. As a result, the prison was nearly impenetrable.

When we arrived at General Delaney's estate, we passed through the gate, down the hedge-lined cobblestone drive, and through the spacious courtyard in front of the mansion, around back to the entrance to the general's temporary holding cells.

Valdra and two Martecyte guards unchained me and pulled me out of the prison carriage. I made sure to give them my most disdainful frown as they handed me off to two prison guards. But I noticed they followed close behind as I was escorted toward the main door to the cells. When I passed a haughty-looking Lance, I snarled at him in anger, "What did you do?"

Lance smiled. "I did what got me paid," he responded cruelly. There was no remorse in his eyes. The Lance I had thought I knew was gone. His slightly confused, almost bashful personality had been replaced with nothing but pride and an overdeveloped sense of self-worth that was evident in his uplifted chin and joyful grin at the results of his handiwork.

"You told the captain to leave the Western Island, didn't you?" I accused, knowing the captain wouldn't have gone so far out to sea as to be unable to return and help us.

Lance nodded. "Finally starting to catch on?" he asked mockingly. "I did. See, thanks to a tip, I knew the dragon was going to come, and I knew the only way to get rid of your friends was if we killed them all in one fell swoop," he explained with a smile.

But as he spoke, I saw something in his eyes. Not guilt. There was no trace of that. *Frustration?* Then I smiled. "The captain didn't die, did he?" I asked, allowing a small smile to crease the corner of my mouth as Lance's expression darkened. "You weren't lying when you said he and Yuuki survived," I continued. "Does he know it was you who betrayed us?" I asked, allowing my joy at determining that the captain was alive to taint my question with mockery.

Lance's anger grew and he held up a hand, stopping the guards from taking me any further, but I noted Valdra and his men continued, stopping at the prison entrance. "You think I would be stupid enough to let him find out my real intentions?" asked Lance. "The captain knows nothing, and it will stay that way. For years I have been interfering with the plans he and Ruth had to spread that story." His expression relaxed slightly. "And now that you are out of the way, I can get paid even more!" he finished with a self-satisfied smile.

I frowned. "Well, you have failed then. *The Story* has been spread." Then I had a thought. "If you were so dead set on stopping us, why did you not corrupt the book text when you were helping me load the type for the printing press?" I asked with genuine curiosity.

"I knew you would be too smart for that to work. I knew you would check it at some point, and my gamble paid off when General Delaney decided to come to the Western Island," he sneered with a hint of sarcasm, as if the general's presence on the island had somehow diminished the credit he got for executing his own plans.

"Don't feel too bad, Ben," interrupted Valdra before Lance could start complaining about the general. Valdra had been listening from his position leaning against the doorframe at the entrance to the prison. "Lance here has been our spy since before this thing with you and Solace began," he explained in a lazy tone, his arms confidently crossed.

"What do you mean?" I demanded.

"Lance has been feeding us information on the captain's whereabouts since before you even knew the captain or anything about this supposedly grand mission you've gotten yourself into," Valdra began. "Lance befriended the captain years ago when he first left his service to the western king to pursue *The Story*. Shortly thereafter, we found Lance and reminded him that the captain's intentions were ill-founded and a threat to this world," said Valdra in an oddly plain tone that didn't seem to do justice to what he was saying. "Lance has been helping us ever since," he finished, watching me closely.

Lance smiled. "I have been working with them from the beginning. I was the reason we were captured by pirates in the Eastern Sea," he said with pride.

Valdra nodded but made no further acknowledgement of Lance's self-righteous boast. "I must say, I didn't count on your survival skills, Benjamin," commented Valdra dryly. "Solace pulled you further from your state of hopelessness than I thought she would," he said with a frown as he looked me in the eye. Clearly, he and the general had counted on my damaged emotional state to keep me controllable. "Not to mention the captain's resourcefulness. Based on Lance's account of him, I didn't expect him to pull that stunt in the Channel. It seems Lance downplayed his skills," said Valdra, briefly glaring at Lance. He ignored Lance's open-mouthed look of offense and turned back to me. "After you escaped on the Northern Continent, I knew we had to change tactics."

"That's why you called on the Creature's precious dragon to burn an entire town? Just to get to us?" I growled in anger.

While Lance launched into an answer completely devoid of humility, I tuned him out and watched Valdra as his expression changed. His left eyebrow raised slightly, and he watched me for a moment with an odd, slightly blank expression. Then, cutting off Lance, he said flatly, "Your mission is over, Ben. We win." With that, he turned and led his men, and Lance, away as the prison guards took me to my cell.

As we entered the prison, daylight was replaced by the shadowy, dimly lit interior. I was relieved when the guards took me to a hall of holding cells, not the makeshift interrogation chamber I knew General Delaney had in one of the cells. They secured me in an empty cell and then left without saying a word, the lanterns outside each cell casting shadows of their retreating figures.

I stood in the middle of the cold, spacious cell for a moment and watched the guards leave as I processed Valdra's odd behavior and what I had just found out about Lance. Lance had played us all, and he had done it masterfully. But Valdra's demeanor seemed different from when we had fought in the Channel.

I let out a sigh and sank onto a pile of hay in one of the back corners of the cell. My mind reeled, trying to find a way out of this mess. The only option I had was to try calling Eyethanoff without the sword in my hands. *The sword does help me see, rather than helping Eyethanoff hear*, I thought. *It is worth a try.*

"My, you have changed," said a familiar voice to my left.

Hoping the voice belonged to who I thought it did, I turned, rubbing my chest as the breastplate created a dull ache in my sternum. There, sitting in the cell next to mine, wrapped in an old, brown cloak, was Ruth.

"Ruth!" I exclaimed as I launched myself from the floor and went to the rusty bars that separated us. "I was beginning to believe that you were dead!" I said in excitement at seeing her alive.

Ruth smiled. "No. Not dead. Just waiting," she said.

I gave her a look of confusion. "Waiting for what?" I asked.

Her smile widened. "You."

"Me?" I said, pointing to my chest. "Why me? And why in here?" I asked, glancing around her cell.

Ruth chuckled. "Well, they captured me, and I had no way out. They said you were next, so I figured I would just wait," she explained with a shrug.

It was my turn to chuckle. "Maybe you could call your soldier of light?" I asked. "I was about to give that a try myself before I heard your voice," I explained.

"I am afraid the soldiers of light cannot hear us in here. Too much darkness," she said with a shake of her head.

I tossed my hands in the air. "Great, I guess we are stuck in here, then."

Ruth nodded. "Did you find the armor?" she asked.

"Most of it," I confirmed as I ran a hand through my almost shoulder length, sun-bleached brown hair. "I am still missing a piece, though. I can tell because the sword...It doesn't feel right yet."

"Like it is not yet complete?" suggested Ruth.

I nodded. "With each piece of armor I find, the sword feels stronger, and the armor does too. But it also calls to the missing pieces more," I explained.

Ruth nodded again. "They are all connected. Each piece has a specific purpose, and they build on each other, starting with the belt," she explained.

"So what piece is next?" I asked.

"What pieces do you have?" she inquired.

I thought for a moment. "I have the belt, the breastplate, the shoes, the shield, and the sword," I said, counting them off on my fingers as I listed them.

"Did you receive the sword yet?" she asked.

I considered her question. "What do you mean by 'receive'?"

"You had visions that helped you receive each armor piece, did you not?" she asked.

"Yes." I recalled the visions I'd had during our travels and how I had accepted each piece of armor.

"You must receive them all," she pointed out.

I shook my head. "I have not had a vision of the sword yet," I replied.

"You probably won't receive it until you find the helmet," Ruth said with a distant expression.

"Is that the last piece?" I asked.

She nodded. "It is. Once you have that, then the armor will be complete."

Without the sword and shield near me, the armor's power was faint. But I could feel it. And at Ruth's words, it seemed to flutter.

I must have made an odd expression because Ruth looked at me and asked, "What is wrong?"

I frowned. "The armor...I can still feel it. Though it feels weak without the other three pieces," I explained.

Ruth raised an eyebrow. "What did it do?" she asked.

I shrugged. "It just...I don't know...It fluttered. As if something in our conversation bothered it." I shook my head. "I know that sounds crazy."

Ruth glanced at my chest with a wary expression that she quickly hid, but not before I caught it.

"What?" I asked.

Ruth shook her head. "Nothing."

I frowned. So far, it had turned out that a lot of things didn't work the way I thought they did, and that left me feeling a bit on edge. I watched Ruth. Her expression was worried. That was unusual. Especially for someone who had been so unconcerned about the Creature finding her. I shook my head and leaned against the wall of my cell as Ruth situated herself in her own pile of hay.

"We should sleep," she suggested.

"I am not tired," I responded as I pondered what could have triggered the armor's reaction and why Ruth might be worried.

As Ruth went to sleep, my mind wandered through ideas on how to escape. I had to get out of here and find that last piece of armor.

Sometime after that first night, though I couldn't tell when because my cell had no window, Valdra came to the cell block while Ruth's sleeping form still lay motionless in the corner. He approached my cell, his averted eyes indicating no interest in conversation, and unlocked the door. "General Delaney would like a word," he stated without looking at me.

He waved two guards over to escort me from my cell. We left quietly with Valdra in front and the two guards behind me, watching my every move. We ascended a stone spiral staircase and stopped at the top as the prison door was opened. I lifted an arm to block out the daylight that shone through the windows as we entered a sparsely decorated hall. My eyes adjusted slowly as we drew nearer to the larger windows and more ornate halls further from the prison.

As we entered the general's study, I spotted two guards already flanking the window behind the general and took note that my two guards retreated to either side of the door. General Delaney sat in his high-backed wooden chair watching me, a frown creasing his forehead and his chin held between his thumb and the knuckle of his index finger, as if he were still deciding what to do with me. I recalled a time when I had stood before him free to leave. That time had passed. I had chosen sides, and I would not back down.

As I stopped a couple paces in front of the general, the sound of the door closing behind me drew my attention, and I glanced over my shoulder to find Valdra standing before the closed door, blocking the exit. I turned back to face the general and waited in silence for at least a full minute before he spoke.

"Well? Have you nothing to say?" asked General Delaney.

I glared at him but didn't respond.

General Delaney smiled. "Well, then, I guess I will get straight to the point. You have something I want," he said as he placed his elbows on his desk, bringing his hands together to form a steeple with his index fingers.

"And what might that be?" I asked. "My soul?"

General Delaney chuckled softly. "Not exactly."

"What is that supposed to mean?" I asked, intensifying my glare.

General Delaney's expression darkened. "It means that you have an option. You can give me what I want, or I can take it."

I held the general's gaze for a moment as I tried to think of a way out of this predicament. I had spent all night trying to find a way out of the cell and had come up empty. But now I was outside the cell and free of restraints. I had a mission to finish. So, I took a breath and willed myself to think faster. For now, I would just have to try to draw out this conversation in hopes that I'd have enough time to plan an escape. "I don't know what it is that you want," I said flatly.

General Delaney's eyes narrowed. "I want your loyalty," he said sternly.

I raised an eyebrow. "After everything you have done?" I asked with a chuckle.

The general frowned. "You will bend to my will. I will see to it."

"If you want my loyalty, why don't you tell me your plans? Maybe I will change my mind," I said with a shrug.

General Delaney smiled slyly. "You may think that you are safe because I want something from you. But your friends are not. Until you decide to yield to me, your friends—well, those who are still alive—" he said with a grin, "are in danger." His grin suddenly vanished and his expression turned stiff, his eyes intense. "My soldiers know where they are headed, and when they find them, they will kill your friends one at a time until you commit yourself to me. In the meantime, as I said, you have a choice. Pledge your loyalty to me, or I will take your loyalty myself," he said in a threatening tone before his lips slowly curled into a smile.

"And what makes you think your soldiers will catch them?" I asked, hoping to gauge how close they were to capturing Captain Bates and his crew.

General Delaney ignored my question. "Yield to me," he demanded in a stern but steady tone, his eyes locked on mine.

I frowned and responded in an equally steady tone. "No."

General Delaney's brow furrowed. "I will give you one last chance to do this the easy way. Yield to me!" he growled.

Holding his gaze, I leaned forward slightly and repeated myself. "No."

Suddenly, General Delaney stood so fast that his chair fell over backwards. The green eyes of the Beast of the Woods—Adournath—flashed briefly in my mind as the general's physical appearance faded and began to warp into something familiar. As he transformed, fear spread through my body, overtaking the sudden spark of Adournath's warning eyes.

The general's eyes turned black, an eerie red glow emanating from within, and animal-like horns grew from his skull as claws curled from his fingertips. "Yield to me!" he yelled as he lifted on black fog, seeming to grow until he was twice my height. The room shook at the sound of his voice, and I stumbled backward a few steps until I collided with Valdra, who firmly held his ground and gripped my shoulders, stopping me in my tracks. My eyes wide, I stared at the being before me. It was the dark soldier from my dreams. Other soldiers of darkness I had seen just looked like men—pale, with dark circles under their eyes, but just normal men. He was different from them, though, with his horns, his eyes, and his claw-like fingers. I suddenly knew why.

"You...You're him," I whispered in shock. "You're the Creature," I said, unable to look away.

"That I am, and you will bend to my will," he said with a devious smile.

I fought to regain my confidence, but I realized suddenly that my dreams over the past few months had been warning me that the Creature was coming for me. And here he was.

"Doubt..." said the Creature as he leaned forward, almost floating amidst the fog in front of me. "It is a dangerous thing," he taunted. "I can see your fear casting doubt's shadow in your mind, and in shadow I dwell, no matter where it exists," he said as he stretched his arms out wide in a display of confident authority.

I swallowed hard and attempted to squelch the fear and doubt that were, in fact, darkening my mind. I could feel them spreading like shadows throughout my thoughts.

"No!" I yelled as the Creature came closer.

In response, the Creature sent out veins of liquid darkness, flowing from him, rooting for a place to grab hold of me, just as they had in my dream. Their swirling presence fueled my anxiety, and again, the green eyes of Adournath flickered through my mind like a warning. This time, I forced myself to focus on the image of those green eyes as I attempted to cast the fear from within me, my expression settling into a focused frown.

"You want to take this land, forever trapping the unseen?" I yelled. "You cannot have it, for it is not yours to take! I will defend it to my last breath!" I yelled defiantly.

"And what, pray tell, will you do to keep hold of it?" asked the Creature, his voice seeming to echo from everywhere.

"I will find the Gate, and I will end this!" I shouted with confidence.

"*You* will?" mocked the Creature, as if questioning my capability. "Do you really think you can succeed? You have no idea what awaits you," he announced. "You are just as corrupt as this land, and who's to say that you could even enter into that land of light you are so obsessed with?"

I knew he must be speaking of the unseen kingdom, and for a sickening moment I couldn't think of an answer. But then it came to me. The Creature's tangible existence solidified in my mind the reality of *The Story* and reminded me of what I already knew. The Prince, the King, and all I had witnessed on the seas were real.

"The Prince! The Prince will allow me into his kingdom!" I growled defiantly. It was true. The King and the Prince knew what they were doing. They had a plan to fix this. My job was to complete the mission they had tasked me with completing—to free the unseen.

"Hmm," grunted the Creature as he seemed to retreat into a strange humanoid form, half the Creature and half General Delaney. "That may be the case, but you are too weak to get to the Prince," he taunted. "Face it, Benjamin. I have had control of this story since the beginning. You have no idea what you are up against," he said warningly.

"What do you mean?" I asked, feeling uncertainty overshadow me again.

The Creature chuckled. "You think you are aware of the Unseen Lands. But you have no idea what they truly are! You think you know what is going on just because you have met the Prince and seen some of his soldiers. But you have no idea what is truly happening. I have been in control of your every move, and you were too weak to realize that you were being controlled like a puppet from the beginning!" he announced.

I shook my head. "No! That cannot be. Eyethanoff has come to my aid. The King's sword has been leading the way. My dreams and visions are from the King. He has been leading me, not you!"

"Really?" asked the Creature. "Who do you think allowed you to reach the island countries? Who do you think has been controlling Valdra and preventing him from killing you on the spot? Who do you think allowed you to find all those armor pieces? Who do you think brought that dragon to the island? How do you think you and I managed to be the only survivors of that wreck? So many questions, and here is their answer: I did!" he announced, his voice rising as he stabbed his finger at his chest. "I am going to destroy that gate, and you will lead me to it, whether you want to or not," he finished with a grin, turning his accusing finger on me.

At his gesture, the armor I had with me faintly stirred a warning, reminding me to be careful. I suddenly remembered I had felt it do the same thing in the prison cell when I was talking to Ruth, and I realized something had not been right then. Maybe the Creature had wanted me to speak with her. *Was he listening to us?*

Anger at the Creature's manipulations rose within me. "Why do you need me?" I demanded.

"Because that arrogant king made that oh-so-glorious gate only visible in the light!" he yelled bitterly. "I cannot wield the King's armor," he growled, more to himself than to me. "But only that armor can reveal the Gate's location."

"So, you are just as weak as I?" I taunted, trying to keep my confidence from faltering any further.

The Creature let out a cruel laugh, then leaned close to me and smiled, his teeth outlined in black and pink flesh. "You think I am weak simply because I do not wield the King's power?" He laughed as he began to grow into a whirlwind around me. "I will show you power!" he yelled.

The Creature seemed to morph into a storm, his power flowing around me in the form of veins of black liquid and fog. Like snakes, the veins angled toward me at the Creature's command. I swatted them away, for I had no sword or shield to protect me. Yet, when

I dodged one vein of darkness, another cut me off. It seemed that everywhere I turned, there was one waiting for me.

As my confidence diminished, fear took over like a shadow in my mind, covering logic and right thinking in darkness so I could not access them. Surrounded by the enemy, I turned toward Valdra, ready to thrust past him, but to my surprise, he stepped out of my way, allowing me to exit the room.

I burst from the study and ran for the prison cells. I had to free Ruth and get us both out of here. But when I arrived, all I found was an empty cell. Ruth was not there.

The Creature's voice echoed through the stone halls of the prison. "You have been fooled again. That was me last night. I needed to know the strength of your armor. And now I know. For without the final piece, without the helmet, you are mine!"

Fear gripped me as I realized the depth of the danger I now faced. The armor had tried to warn me, but I had not listened. Again, I had believed what I saw with my eyes and ignored the unseen. But that wasn't all. I had told the Creature, whom I thought was Ruth, the specific pieces of armor I had attained. That meant the Creature now knew which pieces I did not yet have. He knew my weak points and exactly how to exploit them. *Get out now!* my mind screamed.

In desperation, I ran for the nearest door and out of the mansion, headed for the streets of the Town. It was dark outside, the moon half hidden by a cloud, and the streets at the base of the Crescent Hill were empty, save for shadows cast by homes and shops. As I entered the Town, the Creature in pursuit, I searched for someplace to hide from him. The Creature walked through the streets behind me, and I glanced back as I ran. Darkness seemed to seep from him like black water, forming a dark puddle below his feet, providing a place for him to walk in the midst of moonlight.

"You cannot hide, Benjamin," the Creature called as he stalked along the empty streets.

I darted behind a house, taking refuge in the building's shadow. Green eyes flashed through my mind's eye, and I wished with all I had that the sword were with me. I stood there in total silence as the Creature and his soldiers searched the streets around me.

"My shadows are everywhere. And where they are, so am I," declared the Creature. "You cannot hide!" he repeated.

"Then explain to me this: how did your soldiers pursue us over water?" I asked with a genuine spark of curiosity. On the open ocean there were no shadows, save those briefly cast by waves.

Suddenly, a dark soldier materialized within the shadow in which I had taken refuge, his fingers grasping at my arm. My heart slammed against my chest, and I yanked my arm free before darting from my hiding place in search of another. *How can I see it?* I wondered. *I am not holding the sword.*

The Creature laughed. "They can follow you on ships of their own, just as I can. Martecytes are men and women who have joined my ranks, taken by my darkness. For the darkness keeps them from entering your precious unseen kingdom," he sneered. "Once infected with my poison, they either join me or die alone."

Panting and sweating as my heart pounded in my chest, I moved in a crouch to a new dark corner. "That is not it," I said. "I checked the ocean for ships one night, using the sword. I saw no ships. But dark soldiers were there on every step of our journey. Not just Martecytes. How did they follow us when they had no shadows to live in on the water?" I panicked as I wondered if the soldiers of darkness had the ability to summon shadows of their own.

"Ah, but you are mistaken. For my soldiers live in the darkness of night and the shadows of your own past," explained the Creature. "You have no idea what darkness really is, for we need not be confined to simple shadows cast where they are seen."

Goosebumps spread across my body as I recalled the dark soldier—the Creature—showing up in my dreams. Suddenly, another dark soldier appeared next to me. He drew a sword and swung, but I dodged it, leaving that shadow behind in search of a new place to hide as this new information ravaged my mind with fears I wished to banish forever. "You mean in my dreams?" I asked myself in a whisper as I pulled back into a nearby alley.

The Creature laughed. "Dark and light—they exist in places you cannot touch," he responded. "For darkness is more than simple shadow. Like I said, you have no idea how this really works. You cannot win, not without my help. I can teach you, Benjamin. You have more questions. I know, because doubt has created a shadow in your mind, a shadow I can dwell within."

They do not control shadows; they live in them! But not just shadows, I thought as I put the Creature's words together. *Darkness! Deep, cold, complete darkness. Darkness I can see and darkness I cannot.* A shiver ran down my spine. *If that is true, the Creature can reach me no matter where I am, for I am stained with a darkness I am powerless to be rid of.*

I clenched my jaw and squeezed my eyes shut, trying to rid myself of the doubt that grew at the Creature's words. There had to be a way out of this. A way to battle against this creature of darkness. But doubt that the armor was capable of getting me out of this alive seized my mind, for the armor I had was not enough. I did not have all the pieces, and I was not fighting flesh and blood. I was fighting darkness itself.

That thought planted a realization in my mind that shook me to the core. *Shadows! I am hiding in a shadow.* I had been so focused on not being seen by the enemy that I hadn't fully grasped what I was doing. It was so natural to hide in shadows. For the first time, I recognized that all my life, darkness had been my refuge. In battle, I used shadows to conceal me from the enemy while I plotted against them. Even from the time I was a child, shadows had offered me comfort in times of fear. It was like an uncontrollable reflex to recede into shadow when I did not want to be found.

As I began to understand how deeply I depended on shadows, green eyes flashed in my mind's eye, and the belt of armor momentarily lit up. *"Have hope, my friend, for the truth is a treasure worth knowing."* I heard the Ice Dragon's voice in my head repeating those words. I tried to refocus on surviving rather than the distinct possibility that I would not make it out of this alive because I depended on the very thing that could end my life. Darkness.

"I will not give in to you!" I shouted with resolve to the Creature in yet another attempt to eradicate the doubt in my mind.

All was silent for a moment, and then the Creature spoke, his voice filled with confidence. "Oh, but you are wrong again. Do you know the story of Zath?" he asked. "The dark dragon who destroyed your dear family on the seas?"

I struggled to keep myself from asking. I did not know the story, but I knew the Creature was baiting me. I had to focus on finding a safe place to hide.

The Creature continued without my response. "That dragon was once as you are. Noble. Brave. A warrior and protector. A soldier for the King of Eeffrayldour and the defender of his most precious treasure, his people."

I searched the area around me, looking for a shadow that was not taken by the enemy. Maybe if I could find one that was unoccupied, I could stay there until I thought of a better solution. But the Creature's words about Zath pulled me in as I wondered how a dragon of the King had been so corrupted that it would aid the Creature in his evil plans.

The Creature chuckled. "Yes. He was as you are. But still he chose me," he said, seeming to read my thoughts.

I couldn't hold it in anymore. "That can't be. You corrupted him! It was you who turned him away from the King!" I yelled, attempting to convince myself that a dragon could not be persuaded to fight for evil without first being corrupted. *If a dragon was that vulnerable, what chance do I have?*

"Oh, you could say that. But my power only exists where light does not," responded the Creature. "You see, when the people turned on the dragons, the dragons were given human forms to help them hide among those they protected. While in his weaker human form, Zath, once known as Feyerndur, allowed a seed of doubt to form a shadow in his mind. His human form was weak, as you are. A shadow is all I need, my boy, to take what is mine," growled the Creature.

I shook my head in disbelief. *The dragon doubted the King?* "How could a dragon doubt the King?" I asked.

The Creature laughed. "Doubt is a shadow cast by fear, my friend," he explained with glee, his voice growing louder as he drew ever closer, zeroing in on my own voice as I tried to understand his words.

Almost in reflex to what he said, I desperately attempted to push away the fear that had taken hold of me. If I could have, I would have run from my own mind. If the Creature could so easily corrupt the King's dragon, I knew he could corrupt me. *I have to get out of here,* I thought, just as another dark soldier appeared before me. *Run!* my mind screamed.

I sprinted for the edge of town, headed for the Woods, but I was stopped short when the Creature suddenly appeared before me. "How many times must I repeat myself? You cannot hide from me, Benjamin, for I see the darkness in your mind. And darkness belongs to me!" he snarled with a glint in his eye as he reached out with his veins of black liquid. They encircled me, threatening to trap me in a shadow of fear I could not escape. I swatted them away and blocked another of their attacks with my arm, attempting to push through them. But it was no use. There were too many of them. They struck out at me like swarming snakes. Darkness was overtaking me.

The Creature rose, fading from view in a dark whirlwind as his fog unfurled around me. "You have lost!" he announced as he began to encircle me completely with his darkness, a foggy storm stirred up around me as the veins of darkness began restraining me, their touch like massive spider legs trapping me as prey. "You have allowed shadows to fill you—you have taken refuge with me. You will never enter the kingdom of light, for darkness has a hold on thee!" yelled the Creature with glee.

As I realized the Creature was right, his words spread fear even deeper, doubling the shadow of doubt within me until it seemed to take over more than just my mind, claiming my body too. The Creature smiled and swiftly darted behind me. Placing long bony fingers on my shoulders, he whispered in my ear as the veins of darkness slowly tightened around me. "But I can help you," he said as his breath grazed my neck, sending chills down my spine. "You were once my soldier. And you can be again. Just give in. Just let go. I know you want to, for you were mine once, and it is a place you know well. A place where you can find refuge. Take refuge in shadow, Benjamin, for shadow will keep you safe."

As fear that I would be lost to darkness overtook my thoughts completely, I attempted to pull away from the Creature's grip. I struggled to get my arms free, momentarily succeeding before the veins of darkness cinched down even stronger than before. They snaked around me, pinning my arms against my torso.

What made this all even worse was that the Creature was not within me. He was not controlling me. Yet I felt as though darkness commanded me to give in and simply let him rule over me, for I was too weak to win this fight alone. Some part of me was drawn to the shadow, for the Creature was right. If I gave in, this fight would stop. If I let him win, I would be free of this feeling of fear. Free of the stark realization that I was at his mercy. If I gave in, I could take refuge in darkness, as I had so many times before.

"You cannot fight me," said the Creature in a soothing tone. "You have lost," he whispered in my ear.

With that, the Creature clamped down around me. Green eyes briefly flashed in my mind, but they were swiftly replaced by an overwhelming sense of panic. I cried out in anger and pain as I tried to resist the growing shadow within me, but exhaustion took over my mind. I could not keep up this fight. I could not win. There was safety in darkness. So, I gave in. Like ink spilled on a page, shadow spread through my mind unhindered, then everything went dark.

Chapter 5

Pain seared through my temples as I opened my eyes. It took me a moment to recognize what I was looking at, as much of my surroundings were doused in shadow. Gradually, I became aware that I was looking at the ceiling of a tent. *What am I doing here?* I wondered as I tried to remember what had happened. My last clear memory was of bringing the book back to General Delaney. Everything since then was a hazy mess, as if a dark shadow covered my mind, blotting out the details.

I took a slow, deep breath and sat up, realizing that my headache probably wasn't going away any time soon. As I rubbed my temples to ease the pain, I looked around the tent. There was no lighting, so most of it was in shadow, but there was enough morning light pouring in through the slightly open front flap that I could see I was in General Delaney's travel tent. It was beautifully decorated with handwoven carpets, which covered the floor, fur pelts, and two small tables—one for eating and one for maps. The map table was a couple of yards away, and I was sitting on what I assumed was General Delaney's cot, a small collapsible nightstand about a foot away. There was no one in the tent but me.

I rubbed my head again in an attempt to soothe my headache and tried to remember what had happened. I had been sent to kill a man who had betrayed the general and retrieve the book from him. After I discovered that he didn't have it, I ended up finding it with an old lady in the Hills. Then General Delaney had learned from the book that if I killed the Beast of the Woods, the wars with the beasts would be over. That is where things began to get fuzzy. *Did he actually tell me that? Or did someone else tell me that? Maybe it was Valdra?* I could only remember vague details of what had happened since then. I remembered finding out about a gate, though I couldn't quite remember its importance, traveling on a ship, and finding out about some strange armor that apparently had a special connection to the gate, but the details were murky. However, one memory began to grow clearer. General Delany had been there to help me find this armor. I also remembered the shipwreck, helping the general put together travel plans, and arriving back on the Southern Continent. For some reason, I had a clear memory of Valdra showing up to help too. But I could not remember everything. In addition, I felt slightly sick, though I didn't know why. *Maybe it is just the headache.*

Wincing at the pain in my head, I glanced around the tent again, trying to see if anything would jog my memory. Instead, I noticed the sword and shield were sitting nearby, leaning up against the nightstand.

I stood up slowly, continuing to rub my temples, and retrieved the sword and shield. A sensation I knew I had felt before stirred around my body, and I faintly recalled the armor on my chest, along with glimpses of finding the other pieces on our travels. But I couldn't remember where or how I had found them. I frowned at the shield and sword for a moment. They felt odd in my hands, though I didn't really remember them ever having felt differently.

I felt a sensation of the armor's presence, but it was a faint tingling that was barely even noticeable. *Am I just imagining it all?* Noticing that I was already wearing a strap used to hold a shield on my back, I swung the shield over my shoulder and secured it to the strap. I rubbed my chest where I knew the breastplate sat and wondered what it had felt like before my apparent memory loss. *I must not be fully recovered from the dehydration of being in a shipwreck,* I thought. *I must have blacked out.*

Whatever had happened, I figured I would either remember it eventually or I could ask Valdra. I placed the sword in its sheath at my hip and buckled on my pistol belt, which had been left on the floor next to the sword and shield. I pulled out each pistol and examined them, checking to make sure all was in order. The intricate design on the silver inlayed ivory handles shone like they had recently been cleaned. A memory of cleaning them on my travels back from the shipwreck sprang to my mind, giving me hope that whatever memories I had lost wouldn't be gone forever. Returning the pistols to their rightful places, I went in search of the others, glancing at one of General Delaney's maps and nearby notes on my way out. It appeared we were near the Woods, just inside the Forest, and planned to head for the Southern Mountains.

As I left the tent, I was preoccupied with the struggle to figure out why the armor felt so unusual, despite the fact that I couldn't remember what it was supposed to feel like. Over the past few months, as the general had helped me find the pieces of armor, it had grown like a protective shield around me. *That's it! It used to feel...safe...dependable.* But today it felt unstable, as if it were rejecting something. *Maybe my encounter with the dragon on the ship caused it some damage?* I tried again to recall what had happened before I blacked out. Still, all I got were various glimpses that followed a loose timeline but didn't all add up and clearly lacked key details.

Rounding the corner of the tent, I was greeted by Valdra. "How do you feel?" he asked lazily from where he stood, leaning against a nearby tree.

I looked around at our surroundings. According to the map I had glanced at in the tent, we had apparently camped just inside the Forest, which made sense considering that we had docked northwest of the Woods. The distance between that port and here was about a week's travel time, so we must have made camp here with the intention of not stopping in the Town but continuing to the Southern Mountains in search of the last piece of armor.

"Fine," I responded. "When are we leaving for the Southern Mountains?" I asked as I struggled to recall something, though I wasn't entirely sure what I should be recalling. It was as if something about my surroundings had jogged a memory, but one I could not access.

Valdra's eyes narrowed for a moment. "Soon. Just need to tear down the tents," he said, sounding tired.

Noting his tone, I looked at him, wondering what could possibly be wrong. He was looking a little paler than usual, and he sounded different from when he had helped me find the book. As I tried to pinpoint why, I realized I couldn't remember exactly when I had seen him last. I remembered him giving me orders to find the Beast of the Woods. I remembered traveling alone to the Woods and being unable to get into them, but memories of my travels through the Forest were hazy and void of details. I remembered that Valdra had met the general and me here on the Southern

Continent after we escaped the shipwreck, but I couldn't recall any actual images.

"What happened?" I asked. "I...I'm having a hard time—"

"You tried to enter the Woods. You almost died," he responded. "Ruth, the old lady from the Hills, saved you. She gave you the sword and shield and—"

"—and told me to find the rest of the armor because it would lead me to a gate," I finished as some memories seemed to peek out from behind a shadow in my mind.

Valdra nodded. "You were injured in the shipwreck. No one knew it was a head injury until you collapsed last night," he said, examining me closely.

"What?" I asked.

Valdra hesitated, then shook his head. "Nothing." He looked away. "The general wants you to find the armor and close the Gate before any more of the Great Beasts can come through," he explained plainly before running a hand through his shaggy black hair. "Do you remember that?" he asked with a sigh.

I frowned. The memory was there, but faint, though it seemed to clear a little as Valdra spoke. "Yeah. Where's the general?"

"He is coming," said Valdra as he walked off toward our horses. "We will be leaving shortly."

I nodded as I followed. I approached Jeb and stroked his nose, watching as soldiers tore down the tent I had just woken up in and stored the contents in carts. Jeb offered a low, nearly inaudible nicker that ended in a snort and nuzzled my chest, notably a little harder than usual. I frowned and gently redirected his nose before giving him a reassuring scratch at the base of his mane, not sure what had gotten into him.

As the others finished tearing down camp, I tacked up Jeb and settled into the saddle—the one my father had given me. Momentarily, I recalled my life before this mission. My wife Mary, my father, mother, and siblings, now all dead and gone.

The general arrived and informed everyone it was time to leave. With a weary heart, I moved out, joining the caravan destined for the Southern Mountains.

As we left the area, I was reminded that winter was in full swing, and the next war with the Great Beasts had begun. I remembered that when I had left to find the Gate, the land had been covered in falling leaves and the silence of entire villages and towns awaiting destruction. Now, the people's fears played out around them in the war-torn countryside.

Snow covered the land, coating it in a thick blanket of white that was regularly replenished. The scenery would have been magnificent, but the Great Beasts of the Southern Mountains had clearly reared their ugly heads again. Though it was too early in the war for beasts to frequently hunt during the day, their presence was readily apparent at every turn. As we traveled, the beautiful winter landscape was regularly interrupted by scenes of destruction—property looted by the beasts, abandoned by survivors, and eerily silent. The buildings left standing housed multiple families, as neighbors took in neighbors who had lost everything. Fires were scattered amidst these pockets of destruction, originally started in hopes the flames would keep the Great Beasts at bay. Much of what had been rebuilt into farms and small settlements over the past six years or so was now reduced to rubble and ash. Where farmers and settlers eked out a meager existence, the vicious beasts had taken livestock and people for food, tearing apart families. The crimson snow told a dark story of death. A story I knew all too well.

"It never ceases to amaze me," commented General Delaney as he urged his horse up next to Jeb.

Looking through the lightly falling snow, I continued my examination of the landscape around us. A few fires that had gotten out of control were now slowly being cooled by the frigid air and snow. Many populated areas were surrounded by tall walls, but not all had succeeded in keeping out the overpowering beasts. Unlike in wars between countries, the beasts had no limit. They would not stop when we surrendered. They would have their way like mindless mercenaries out for blood until, for some unknown reason, they would return to their homes in the Southern Mountains until their next urge drove them to attack.

"In one night, they tear away any hope that was built up during the times of peace," I concurred with a shake of my head.

"Hmm." The general nodded in agreement. "It would seem so."

We rode on in silence, keeping an eye on the trail behind us in case any beasts were out in search of a meal they could drag off to their caves in the mountains. The closer we got to our destination, the worse things looked, and the closer attention we all paid to the trails left behind by the bloodthirsty creatures. It was easy to tell where they were headed, as blood-stained snow and broken foliage marked the paths of beasts whose hunts had been successful. There were no dead bodies to be seen, though, for the beasts took their prey alive to be eaten later in the mountains. The very place we were headed.

The thoughts of the beasts caused my mind to wander to the Beast of the Woods. I recalled that I had once thought it was connected to the Great Beasts, but, for some reason, I currently had the feeling it was not. Maybe something had happened that I could not remember during my attempt to capture and kill it. Something that had changed my mind. Maybe that was why Valdra and the general didn't seem interested in the Beast of the Woods anymore. It seemed they were more interested in this gate the book had talked about. A gate, I recalled with ease, that needed to be destroyed to stop the Great Beasts and end these wars. I paused at the thought. Though that information seemed to come easily, I found myself unable to recall the exact moment I had heard about the need to destroy the Gate. Something about it felt wrong. My chest began to hurt, as if the armor didn't fit right. *When was I told of the need to destroy the Gate?*

"You seem distracted," said the general, interrupting my thoughts.

I nodded. "I was just wondering why the beasts attacked the Southern Country first," I lied, not wanting the general to know my thoughts, for fear of...something. Again, it felt like there was a memory there that I simply couldn't access.

The general was silent for a moment, considering the question. "I am not entirely sure. Some believe the beasts were an accident produced by an experiment gone wrong. The Southern Country was once known for its ingenuity and creativity. It was the place where inventors lived. Things were designed and built there. Then the beasts came and wreaked destruction. The Great Beasts' numbers only grew and spread from then on. These people have known nothing but loss ever since."

I nodded. "All things come to an end."

General Delaney offered a sad smile. "I know. I am sorry for your loss, my boy. I have seen how it has impacted you." He paused. "But thanks to that book you found with the old lady, we now know the beasts and darkness really came here through the Gate. Maybe you can finally finish what you started."

I considered the general's comment. "Maybe?" I asked with a raised eyebrow. "What do you mean?"

General Delaney gestured to the deteriorating landscape around us. "This. I have learned from personal experience, Benjamin, that things fall apart and decay. Time is no one's friend. It is the culprit that causes so much pain." The general looked around us as our horses plodded along on the half-frozen dirt trail. "Sometimes, I wonder if it would not be better to simply accept defeat rather than continue to try and find a solution. Close down the towns, hole up in a stone castle as the kings and many of their people have done so many times..." He trailed off.

"You sound as though you have thought about this before," I commented. "Why have you not done it?"

The general let out a hard breath. "The people," he said as he looked at me, his thin face creased with weariness. "They love this land. It is theirs, not mine. But to protect them...to build a safe place...they would have to change their ways to fit in behind walls." General Delaney frowned down at his hands. "They would have to follow someone else's rules. Something I was once familiar with..." His voice trailed off again. Then he turned back to me, breaking away from some memory of his past. "But sometimes, containing people is all one can do to keep them safe."

"You're afraid they would lose freedom," I commented.

The general nodded. "But as time goes by, I wonder if that is not the only solution left." He winced at the thought.

"There must be a different way. I know the people of this land," I said as I looked into the distance at the ruins of a house standing amidst still-burning embers. The snow around its base had melted away, making the scene a dire blemish in an otherwise white landscape. "These people are tough. They can survive," I said as I watched a man, possibly the owner of the home, kick snow over the flames.

General Delaney smiled. "I am sure they could," he said.

"It won't be an issue if we succeed," I reminded him, sitting up a little straighter in my saddle. "If we complete this mission, the Gate will be destroyed, and the dark beasts will no longer have access to this land." But as the words left my mouth, they felt wrong, and my chest began to hurt again, as if the armor were rubbing me wrong.

"Yes, but what if we fail? The fate of this land is in our hands," he said, sounding defeated.

I shook my head. "We will not fail. We can win the war against darkness and evil. We just have to find the last piece of armor."

"Hmm. Yes," the general agreed in a distant voice as he glanced once more over the landscape before focusing on the trail ahead of us.

We camped that night in a wooded area near the road. Beasts would be roaming wherever they pleased, but at least we had quick access to an easy escape route if necessary. We settled down for the night and ate dinner in silence. The general's soldiers cycled through a night watch, and we made it to morning in one piece.

It was not until the second night that we encountered a beast, soon after reaching a small settlement. Beasts were often attracted to more populated areas because they usually contained more food. However, there were also more people to fight them.

When we arrived, we began making our way around the outside of the small town's walls. There was clear evidence that at least three beasts were roaming the area and had broken down part of the wall. As we came to the opposite side of the little town, screams rang out from within as a beast found a meal.

My body tensed, along with Jeb, and I felt a pull to go to the people in danger. "We have to help them," I said as I spun Jeb toward the desperate cries. But the general grabbed Jeb's reins.

"Benjamin, we don't have time. Fighting three beasts here will decrease our numbers and lower our chances of making it through the Southern Mountains," he warned. "We need to keep going."

I shook my head. "We can't just leave them there. We have all fought beasts and won. We can help them!"

"Benjamin, if we don't make it across those mountains, there will be no one else to find the armor," said the general with a cautioning glare.

As the sounds of the senseless attack died down, the feeling that something was off returned. I wanted to go to them, to help. But I felt weak. My headache came back in full force, and I winced. I exhaled slowly and nodded, conceding to the general's point as I looked back toward the small town. Smoke rose from within the walls, and growls and cries of sorrow and anger seemed to rise with it. I let out a heavy sigh. The general was right. We needed to make it across those mountains. If we didn't, no one else would.

As our caravan turned onto a foliage-lined trail, a beast suddenly burst through the town's gate, tearing a new hole in the wooden boundary. Those of us still out in the open darted for the trees. Once concealed, we watched in silence, not wanting to move for fear we would draw attention to ourselves.

The Great Beasts always started out small, about the size of a large dog or wolf. But they grew as they fed on the land. This beast was already massive, nearly twice the size of Jeb, which explained how its pack had broken through the wall. If the beasts were already that large, we were running out of time, for no war before this had produced such large beasts this early on. Things were progressing much faster than we could have expected.

The massive brownish black beast held a person trapped in its jaws as the villagers pursued it, attacking with spears, flintlocks, and arrows in an attempt to free the beast's prisoner. But the beast was too big and fast. It darted off into the foliage not far from us and disappeared into the trees as the people cried for their lost friend.

The general let out a heavy sigh as the victim's screams faded. "Come. We need to keep moving," he encouraged us.

I frowned in the direction of the beast and kept Jeb at a standstill as the others began to move out, toward our destination. I winced as pain shot through my head. *This is not right. We are here to protect the people. We can't just leave them to fend for themselves. But if we fail our mission, these people will have died for nothing.*

General Delaney called back to me. "Benjamin. It is time to leave," he commanded, leaving no room for argument.

For some reason, I followed, and my headache eased as I did. But as I looked ahead to the others, I could not help but notice Valdra watching me. His flat expression appeared tired, and he still looked a little pale. But that wasn't all. There was something else—something in his hard eyes that didn't fit with what I normally expected from him. *Pity?* Valdra broke our locked gazes and moved on with the others as I followed.

My headache flared again, and I gripped my forehead, cringing in pain as I let Jeb steer on his own. Valdra appeared next to me and raised his eyebrows nearly imperceptibly, as if to silently ask if I was okay. Up close, I could see he was not just tired. I had seen that look before. I had seen it on my own face. He was depressed and regretful. But not just that. Before this had all started, I had worn that same look of hopelessness. *That is what it is. Hopelessness.*

"What's wrong?" I asked through gritted teeth. "You remind me of myself," I said, attempting a joke.

"Shhh," he said as a spark of fear ignited in his eyes, though his expression remained dejected. He glanced at the general. "Just keep going. We're almost there," he encouraged.

As we continued on our way, I left Valdra to his emotional pain and focused on dealing with my own, physical pain. But no matter how much I rubbed my temples, the headache would only subside temporarily. It would not leave me. Suddenly, my headache flared again, and I leaned forward in pain. As I did, I felt an odd sensation from the armor around me. A thought began to tug at the edge of my mind—a memory that would tell me what the armor used to feel like. But the memory just wouldn't come out where I could see it. So instead, I focused on trying to pinpoint what the armor felt like now. My headache flared again as I realized the armor felt dull, like it was covered by something. Like it needed to be cleaned. I absentmindedly rubbed my hand over my chest, trying again to remember exactly what it had felt like before I had apparently hit my head. But still, no clear memories came to mind. *It probably isn't the armor that feels odd,* I told myself. *It is probably just me.* My headache eased a bit. *I just need to get through this mission. Then I will be able to take my leave, like the general told me I could all those months ago.*

As we got farther into the Hills, I found my gaze wandering behind me, almost without my permission, to stare at the view of the Town and the Woods below us. I slouched in discouragement at the realization that, again, lack of clarity in memory kept me from understanding what was going on. I looked at the trees of the Woods, drawn to something within them. There was something in there. *The Beast?* Suddenly, I saw its eyes in my mind's eye. Green and piercing. My headache flared, overtaking the edges of a memory. A memory of someone I had met in those woods. Someone powerful.

"Benjamin, if you wait around in the open, you will become easy prey," called one of the general's men.

I nodded. "Coming," I grunted as I reluctantly tore my gaze from the distant woods, feeling unusually groggy.

I turned Jeb and joined the rest of the group as we followed the river until we reached the Southern Mountains. Having only stopped for a brief amount of sleep the night before, we camped for the night. We were about to enter one of the most dangerous places in the world, and we needed to be rested. We would set out at first light, heading for South Town on the other side of the dark, beast-infested mountains before us.

Darkness surrounded me. So thick I could not see. A vein of darkness was attempting to penetrate my chest, but it was stopped by the armor. I looked down to see the sword in one hand and the shield in the other, but they felt dull and heavy.

For some reason, unlike in previous dreams, I felt no fear of the darkness around me. Something had changed in me. I looked up in search of the Ice Dragon, but she was not there. Instead, before me in the distance was the door I had seen in my vision on the ship. The path I had seen in my vision in the Northern Country also stretched before me like a river, sparkling, showing me the way through the darkness that attempted to engulf me. As I stood there, I heard something. A distant sound I could not quite distinguish. Then it hit me. Someone was on the other side of the door, knocking. They wanted me to open it. I placed the shield on my back and approached the door, but when I arrived, I found, as before, that it had no handle.

Suddenly, the darkness around me took on a personality of its own. A dangerous, violent personality. The darkness lunged at me, moving like fog as it closed in from all sides, threatening to blot out the door before me. I grabbed the shield in self-defense, turning away from the door to face my enemy.

As I came to face the darkness, I saw that it had transformed into soldiers of darkness that seemed to fan out in all directions like reflections in a mirror. Each attacked me, aiming veins of shadow at my mind, one at a time. As I fought them off, my sword clanged against theirs with a hollow thud.

The dark soldiers moved so fast that I felt myself quickly growing weary. They morphed into the Great Beasts of the Southern Mountains as I stood my ground with the sword at the ready, the shield as my protection, and exhaustion in my bones.

Looking at the darkness around me, I could feel my confidence waver, for in response to my stand, the darkness transformed yet again into a new creature, one I had never seen before. My wavering confidence now vanished, for the being was so dark, so thick, it seemed to overshadow all else. It walked on two legs, its penetrating red eyes reminding me of the Creature, though its features were different. Something about it broke my heart, and I felt as though I had suffered a deep loss. Then, it lunged at me, mouth agape and fangs dripping ink-black saliva. I lifted the shield in defense as the sound of someone knocking came yet again from the other side of the door.

Chapter 6

MY EYES SNAPPED OPEN, and I gasped as I jerked upright, my hand reflexively grasping one of my pistols. As I looked around me, I saw there were no beasts in the camp. Realizing it was just a dream, I let out a sigh of relief and placed my pistol back in my belt. I lay back down and stared up at the sky as I caught my breath. Feeling myself calm as I looked at the stars, I let out another sigh and observed the magnificent view. The twinkling lights in the sky were like cracks in the darkness of night. They reminded me of someone. But again, I couldn't figure out who. I got the sense that whoever it was had meant a great deal to me once. But all I could remember was a compass. Not entirely an odd thing to think about when looking at stars, but still, I had the feeling there was something out there. Something I longed to remember.

Frustrated by my inability to remember, I let go of the illusive memory as the sun slowly began to outshine the stars, bringing the safety of daylight. Rubbing sleep from my eyes, I sat up, wondering what my dream meant. To my recollection, my dreams had always been related to each armor piece, but I had not added a new piece since the dragon attack on the Western Island. I did faintly recall having a dream on General Delaney's ship, though. I just couldn't recall the subject.

Suddenly, my headache flared, and my vision went blurry. Grasping my head with one hand, I stood up slowly, sucking in a deep breath to counteract the pain. As I moved, I felt weak, and my vision momentarily went dark as I was overtaken by a spell of nausea. I swayed to the side, catching myself on a nearby rock. As I did, I vaguely recalled a time on the ocean when I had been afraid that I was losing my mind. *Maybe I'm losing my mind now,* I thought. As I regained my vision and balance, I felt as though part of my mind was gone. *No, not gone,* I realized. *Stuck...in a thick, muddy shadow.*

Taking a few more deep breaths to recover from the throbbing pain in my head, I began packing up my things as the others gradually awoke and did the same. The general's soldiers were not friends—there was no talking or bonding. Everyone simply did their job and moved on. It was a far cry from the conversation and enjoyment of traveling with Ivan and Nadia. I smiled at the memory of Ivan's elaborate storytelling. His bushy mustache and wide eyes accentuating his animated personality. Nadia rolling her eyes at her brother's acute exaggeration of events. I missed them.

As I swung into Jeb's saddle, my thoughts turned from old friends now gone to pondering my current mental state. *The darkness the general warned me about is probably playing tricks on me,* I told myself. I took a deep breath and resolved to let it go for now. I needed to focus, for we were about to enter one of the most dangerous places on earth.

⚘

The general led the way as we set out in single file up the trail that led into the Southern Mountains. As it rose and fell with the rocky landscape, the temperature did the same, though it never seemed to rise above freezing. Evidence of beasts was everywhere, in the form of paw prints and frozen blood, and we were careful to do what we could to hide our presence. But it was nearly impossible to mask our scent.

It would take roughly three days to get through the pass, and already by the second night the temperatures dropped so low that we began to wonder if the cold was the threat we should be more worried about, for the beasts seemed content to stay away. In the afternoon on the third day, a blizzard moved in, covering the land in fresh snow. During the worst of the storm, we took shelter in a cave system in hopes that we could wait out the freezing winds. But we quickly discovered that we may have saved ourselves from one fate only to be consumed by another, for growls and rumbles echoed from deep within the mountain.

The caves were occupied by beasts.

We ate food we had brought with us, as fresh meat would likely draw in the beasts, and everyone remained on high alert, flinching at almost any sound from within the dark cavern. At one point, one of the general's men almost shot his own horse in fear that it was a beast.

In an attempt to calm us all during our nerve-racking stay in the mountains, General Delaney began a conversation. "I heard in an old story that dragons made these caves," he commented as we sat listening to the winds howl outside and warming ourselves around a small fire that we hoped would keep the nearby beasts at bay. "The people hunted them all, leaving these caves open for the beasts to occupy when they came to be."

Seemingly in response to the general's words, Valdra chewed his food a bit slower for a moment, then resumed, avoiding the general's gaze.

Not a very good story to distract from our current situation, I thought, shifting to sit more comfortably on a large rock.

Ignoring Valdra's odd behavior, I looked around the cavern, imagining a time when dragons roamed the land and possibly lived in this dark cave now lit by the small fire and the dim light from outside. The patterns in the rocks were unique. Looking at them, I could imagine a dragon burning a hole in the stones to build itself a home.

"Benjamin," said the general, pulling my attention back to him, "Valdra has informed me that you have been experiencing headaches and memory loss."

I glanced at Valdra, but he didn't look at me, so I turned my gaze to the general. "It's probably nothing. I will remember eventually," I responded, brushing off the general's concern with a wave of my hand.

General Delaney nodded. "Do you remember being injured?" he asked, cocking his head slightly to one side.

I glanced outside at the falling snow as I tried to remember details of the shipwreck, then shook my head. "I must admit that I don't. Do you?" I asked in curiosity.

The general gave a slight shake of his head. "You have not been the same since the shipwreck. We are not sure exactly what happened, but we think you hit your head when the ship fell apart," he explained. "I am sure you will remember things over time. The doctor we spoke to said you may suffer from memory loss and nightmares, maybe even hallucinations."

I nodded. *That explains the dream.*

The general leaned forward. "Benjamin, I appreciate you helping with this even in your state. As soon as we acquire the rest of the armor, we will use it to find the Gate. Do you remember?"

I nodded. "Destroy the Gate, and the beasts and some kind of evil darkness will stop entering our land." Then I had a thought. "But where do they come from? Where does the Gate lead to?" I asked. "I mean, I recall that there is a dark force on the other side that is trying to take over, but what is that place?"

The general frowned. "No one knows. Do you not remember discovering the book with the old lady in the Hills?" he asked.

My headache flared as a memory of the old lady from the mountains came to mind. "*The Story,*" I said with a nod. "I remember. It said that the door was allowing an ancient evil into our land." I recalled the information from a foggy memory and wondered if that was how I knew about the darkness on the other side of the door. I frowned. "You still believe all that stuff?" I asked skeptically.

The general smiled. "You know me. I will try anything to protect this land from those who wish to take it." The general laid out his bedroll and climbed in. "Plus, we found that armor, didn't we?"

I nodded as the general fell silent, and my mind began to wander again. My headache pounded as my vision grew blurry yet again, and I sucked in a deep breath, trying to calm the nausea that was overtaking me. I dropped my forehead into my hands and concentrated on deep breathing. As I did, I happened to glance at the sword secured in its scabbard at my waist. My mind attempted to replay a memory, but I could not see the images. All I could see was darkness. But then, the color green flashed through my mind. For some reason, I felt the need to look closer at the sword.

I sat up a little straighter and pulled the sword from its scabbard. To my surprise, as the sword exited its sheath, a rush filled my body, causing goosebumps that had nothing to do with the temperature to spread over my skin. For a moment, all the pain in my head was gone, and my muscles relaxed in its absence. Then my headache flared back up with a passion. I grabbed my head with one hand and leaned forward again as I took a deep breath, trying to get through the pain. As I focused on my breathing, I realized the sword was getting lighter and lighter, as if it were calling out to something in the distance, pulling me toward something. I looked in the direction it seemed to be pulling me and found myself faced with the blizzard framed by the cave's entrance. There was nothing out there but snow. I felt myself lean forward, almost against my will. I stood to get a better look, drawn forward by some deep need to find whatever the sword was pointing out to me. Then I saw something through the billowing snow. It took me a moment to figure out what it was—a dark hole in the rock across the path outside our cave and off to one side.

"What's in there?" I asked, looking to the general and Valdra as I gestured to the other cave.

Valdra's expression hardened, and for a moment I thought I saw worry in his eyes. "Nothing," he stated flatly.

The general shook his head. "Well, not nothing. As I mentioned before, these caves were once occupied by the dragons who lived here long ago. Now, there is only one dragon left. That is one of the entrances to the section of the caves still occupied by that dragon," he said, sounding tired.

I turned and looked at the dark opening in the distance. "Zath," I remembered as the name rang a bell in my mind, though I wasn't sure how I knew it.

The general was just getting comfortable but stopped and propped himself up on one elbow, a frown creasing his forehead. "Yes. How did you know?" he questioned.

I shook my head. "I think someone told me about him once," I explained, not entirely confident in my answer.

With a shrug, the general lay down as the rest of the group followed suit, except Valdra, who was on watch.

As the others went to bed, I struggled to recall the last time the sword had drawn me to something. I knew it had happened; I just couldn't remember what it had led me to. Suddenly, my headache flared again, and I felt weak. Letting my knees buckle, I dropped the sword as I sank down onto the large rock I had been sitting on. I reached up and grabbed my head with both hands as the pain seared through me once more. As I bent over in agony, something dripped onto my pant leg. I examined it closer, blinking against my temporarily blurred vision, and realized with surprise that it was blood. I reached up and touched my nose, then looked at my fingers. Blood. I had never had a nosebleed in my life that wasn't preceded by a blow to the face. This one was not bad, only a small drip that mostly quit when I wiped it away with my hand. But something was definitely wrong with me.

I glanced back at the others to see if anyone had noticed my condition. Valdra was on watch for beasts and didn't seem to be paying any attention to me. The rest of them were asleep; even the general was dozing off.

Turning my back to Valdra, I quietly searched my pockets for something to fully stop the bleeding. I found a green scarf in one pocket and pulled it out. I placed the scarf under my nose and held it there. After a moment, I pulled it away to check how much blood there was. Not much. Just a light pink drop. Finding a new section of the scarf, I lifted it back to my nose to make sure the bleeding had stopped completely. As I did, I took in a deep breath, relieved that the bleeding was not bad, but I paused as a faint smell drifted up from the scarf. Suddenly, my mind was gripped with dim, hazy memories, almost like a dream. Something was familiar about that smell. Not just familiar but important. I smelled the scarf again and one memory began to grow clear. A woman. Dark hair, smooth, unblemished tawny skin, and eyes as beautiful as sunflowers in the moonlight, with flecks of mysterious green. *What is her name?* The image of the woman reminded me of something else. Green, like the green I had seen when I felt the need to hold the sword. But not just the color green. Green eyes. *The Beast of the Woods!* I saw the Beast's green eyes clearly in my mind. However, they were not the eyes of a menacing creature but rather a friend and guide. I had been right before. The Beast of the Woods was not anything like the Great Beasts of the Southern Mountains. I now somehow knew for certain that it was on my side. Or more accurately, I was on its side.

My headache flared again, worse than before, and I grabbed my head as a groan slipped from deep in my chest. Desperate for release, I picked up the sword, hoping whatever had happened before would cause the pain to go away again, even if it was just for a moment.

As I wrapped my fingers around the black leather-covered hilt of the unsheathed sword, my body filled with the same sensation as before. One I somehow knew for certain I had experienced before this day. But instead of trying to weed out a memory I knew I could not find, I closed my eyes, enjoying a moment of painless peace.

When I opened my eyes, I found myself staring through the blizzard at the distant cave. It sat on the other side of the snowstorm outside, its presence drawing me in at the behest of the sword. Something within me had to go to it. As if in a trance, I stood. With sword in hand and shield at my back, I walked toward the cave entrance, the general and his soldiers fading from my awareness. Stepping out into the blizzard, I was met with a gust of freezing wind as snow blew all around me, so thick I could barely see where I was going. But I never took my eyes off the distant cave.

As I approached the opening, one step at a time, I thought I saw something standing in the cave's entrance. Something large. *A dragon!* But just as I realized what it was, it vanished. I tried to pick up the pace, but my head throbbed, and my body felt weak and tired. The closer I got to the cave, the more I began to drag my feet. As I passed through the entrance, I stumbled to one side, catching myself on the stone wall as I collapsed to one knee. Setting my jaw, I forced myself to stand, only to stop suddenly when my headache flared again. After taking a moment to recover, I slowly rose to full height.

Drawn forward by something the sword seemed to want and pulled backward by something that seemed to want me, I pressed on. With each step I took, it grew harder to walk and hold onto the sword, for it felt as though I were being pulled in opposite directions. But I was desperate to continue forward. I had to keep going. This process had happened before. I recalled the sword leading me to something in the past, but my headache flared, and the memory was overshadowed by confusion. Yet still, something within me told me to press on.

With no light to guide me as I descended deeper into the mountain, I followed the wall of the cave, keeping one hand on it at all times. I stumbled again, dropping to one knee and planting the sword's tip into the ground to keep myself from completely collapsing. *I can't do this. I can't take one more step,* I thought. I gripped the sword's cross guard with both hands and rested my forehead on my wrist, crumpling to both knees. I had no idea where I was. I wanted to move forward, but my legs felt weak, and my body felt heavy. Still, I was drawn to go back and drawn to go forward as if my body and my soul were at war within me.

Alone, surrounded by darkness, and too weak to go on, all I could hear was my hard breathing echoing off the stone walls around me.

As I knelt there with my eyes closed, leaning on the sword, I gradually became aware of the feeling that someone was standing next to me. But I was too weary to open my eyes, exhaustion seeming to grow with every second. Then I felt someone touch my hands, gently removing them from the sword. I opened my eyes, fear momentarily coursing through my veins as I wondered if this person was an enemy. My headache flared and I snapped my eyes shut before I could determine who was with me. Then I felt the sword being placed in its scabbard. Relief washed over me as I realized that the mysterious person didn't seem to want me dead.

Whoever it was wrapped an arm around the back of my rib cage, looping my arm over his shoulders, and stood. I tried to open my eyes, but my headache intensified again as I noticed a faint glow lighting the cave, though I couldn't tell where it came from. I squinted, and my vision went blurry as I felt the unknown man lift me to my feet.

I stumbled along, not fully aware of what was happening, as the stranger guided me through the darkness. Rumbles of beasts echoed off the walls, and at one point I thought I saw dark soldiers hiding in the shadows around us. But for some reason, they did not attack.

Finally, the tunnel opened up into a massive cavern filled with piles of something I couldn't make out through my blurred vision. The mysterious man gently lowered me to my knees before one of the piles. He left a reassuring hand on my shoulder, and my vision cleared just enough for me to identify what was in front of me, though my headache seemed to grow ever worse. Focusing intently, I found myself faced with nothing but a pile of junk. However, amidst the junk, a plain wooden box drew my attention. The man gently placed my left hand on the hilt of the sword sheathed at my side. With my other hand, I reached for the box, pushing through the pain of my headache, which was now making my eyes water.

As my hand came in contact with the box's lid, memories of the other pieces of armor suddenly flowed through my mind, and I felt the pieces I was wearing relax around me. The belt, the breastplate, the shoes, and the shield all felt suddenly so present. My headache flared and I gritted my teeth as I opened the box and peered inside, my blurry vision seeming to clear a little more, just enough to see the object within the box. It was almost as if this man were somehow helping me see.

Resting in the old box, shining like new silver, was a helmet of armor. Mysterious words that resembled those on the sword were etched into its rim, identifying it as part of the armor I was collecting. As I studied the helmet, I thought I saw fresh blood trickling down from its pinnacle. In confusion, and thinking I might just be seeing things, I reached out and touched the blood. As my fingers made contact with it, everything around me changed.

The sensation of my headache changed in an instant. It was as if I existed between my pain and my freedom from that pain. The pain in my head was present but felt strangely behind me, while the total absence of that pain seemed to be before me but not yet within my grasp. The darkness around me fell away as a new silence filled the air. A calm silence. I felt the presence of someone familiar, and I looked up to see, through vision only blurred at the edges, the Ice Dragon. Her white, ice-covered scales shimmered, her blue-green eyes reminding me of the Beast of the Woods. *Adournath!* I remembered. *That's his real name!*

I took a deep breath, somehow knowing she was there to give me this final piece of armor. But she did nothing. She simply watched. Confused, I looked down at the helmet. As I did, the mysterious man next to me touched my forehead, and I felt as though a dark fog began to lift from my mind. Then a memory became clear—crystal clear. A memory of when I had accepted the breastplate. When I first encountered the breastplate of armor, I had not been sure I wanted it. But I learned later on that it was a gift I needed to accept in order to complete my mission. And I was glad I had.

That must be what I need to do. I need to accept this gift, I realized.

Just as I decided to accept the gift but before I could take the helmet, the Ice Dragon stepped to the side. As she moved, she revealed the door from my dreams. The wooden door stood in the near distance like a beacon in the darkness.

As I stared at the door, more memories came back to me. Past visions of a dome of darkness, darkness I was always trapped in, and this very door standing in the distance at the end of a sparkling path, as if it were the only way out. The only way to freedom.

As had happened in those previous visions, the Ice Dragon faded away completely as I became fully aware of the dome of darkness around me. A boundary keeping me out of the Unseen Lands. But this time, the darkness looked thinner, almost transparent. Though the image was still hazy, I could more clearly see that there was a land beyond the darkness. It was a world I deeply desired to access.

Then the silence was broken. The sound of someone knocking on the door rang out, echoing around me, drawing my focus. The darkness seemed to respond, sending out swirls of black fog like ink in water. But for the first time, it felt as though none of that mattered. Nothing mattered but opening the door.

I set out to answer the knock.

Darkness grabbed at me as I approached the door, but unlike in previous visions, I did not hesitate even for a second. I reached for the door, feeling a desperate need to see who was on the other side. I recalled my vision on the ship before the dragon had destroyed it. Standing on the deck of General Delaney's ship, I had reached for the shield and seen a vision. A door. A door with no handle. A door I realized required faith to open. In faith I had reached out toward a handle I could not see, and I reached for that same handle now. The handle miraculously materialized. I wrapped my fingers around its smooth metal surface and twisted to the right. I pulled the door open.

As the door opened, light shone from the other side and pain suddenly seared from my head all the way through my body, my headache flaring more intensely than ever before. At the pain, I abruptly jerked back, pulling my hand from the helmet I had forgotten I was touching, and the vision around me vanished. As I lifted my hand to grip my throbbing head, I accidentally knocked the box from the pile of junk. As the box tipped over, the helmet fell from it, but the mysterious man snatched his hand out and caught the helmet before it hit the ground.

The man placed a reassuring hand on my shoulder, and my headache seemed to fade a little. He then reached up and offered the helmet to me with care. I stared at it for a moment, in a daze fraught with an odd sense of indecision. *Will it cause more pain?* I wondered. *Does it matter if it does? Some things are worth the pain one goes through to achieve them. But is the land on the other side of this darkness worth it? It is just a vision, isn't it? Is this even real?* In my moment of hesitation, I heard the voice of the woman from my memories the scarf had triggered. *"Have a little faith,"* she said gently, her smile dancing through my mind.

I reached for the helmet.

The moment my fingers touched the helmet, the vision fully returned. The door was before me, open and waiting. I lifted my arm to shield my eyes from the light that emanated from the other side. But once my eyes adjusted, I finally saw who had been knocking on the door. Standing on the other side of the doorway was the Prince of the Unseen Lands.

That's who I met in the Woods! I recalled joyfully as the memory suddenly became clear.

Beyond the wooden doorway, behind the Prince, stood a nearly transparent door, open, with blood streaked on its upper frame. The Prince held one hand outstretched toward me, and his other hand held the helmet. An encouraging smile lit his face. The woman's words came to me again. *"Have a little faith."*

A little faith is all I've got, I admitted to myself.

Another memory became clear then. In a previous vision, I recalled fearing that someone, maybe the Prince, would come through the door to kill me—to rid the world of my darkness, which went against the King's Original Power and everything he stood for. *I am unworthy of such a place, such freedom from the darkness I chose to be part of. Will I die if I enter that land?* Then another memory resurfaced, as if in response, one so distant I thought for a moment it would vanish before I could grasp it. But then it grew crystal clear. The day I met the Prince. I had entered the Woods to kill Adournath in hopes I could use his death to save Solace. Adournath had asked me why I was there. I had admitted I was there to kill him and told him someone always had to die. Adournath had responded with a sentence that had changed my life from that moment on. *"Someone already did."*

I recalled the story of the Prince's sacrifice. It was a story I now knew well. But for some reason, with every recollection of its details, I felt its meaning deepen. Hope filled my soul as I looked at the Prince before me now. *The Story* said he had already made a way—the transparent door behind him, the one that was already opened. I looked at the blood above the transparent door. The Prince had died to open that door. All I had to do was answer his call and enter. Pass through the door of faith, through the door that led to the life I now knew I truly wanted. The life I was made for.

Taking a deep breath, I reached out with a shaky, exhausted hand and grasped the outstretched hand of the Prince who had given his life to free his people from an evil we had abandoned him to follow. He led me through both doors, holding out the helmet as we passed through the second door. Some part of me had expected to die the moment I stepped through the transparent door controlled by the Prince. But the light around me felt surprisingly refreshing. Safe.

Maybe the Prince before me, and a little faith, will be enough to free me from darkness, I thought.

With relief in my bones, I accepted the helmet, placing it on my head. As I did so, I took a deep breath to hold back the pain that was still trying to overtake me. The moment the helmet of armor was in place, light blazed through my mind so bright I instinctively shut my eyes. As the light burned through me, I felt the presence of the Prince standing next to me, his hand gripping mine. Light and dark began to war within me, but then it felt as though the Prince were pulling the battle from me. He fought that battle for me, as if he were protecting me from the opposing powers warring over my mind. Their power was too much for me to handle alone.

In my mind, I saw light banish shadow, and I realized the source of my pain. *The Creature!* Memories of my conversation with the Creature came flooding back. The Creature had convinced me to let him rule over me, and I had given him the very shadow that allowed him to do so. But now I felt the Prince's power rush through me, the light of his father's Original Power consuming the darkness like fire licking up water.

As I felt myself set free from the Creature's hold, all the memories that had been covered with shadow were suddenly accessible again. The old lady with the book was Ruth, the Prince's betrothed. The ship had been wrecked by the dragon, and Lance had betrayed us. General Delaney was the Creature. The woman from my memories was Solace, my wife! It all came flooding back to me. My eyes snapped open, my vision now clear. But I no longer saw the doors or the Prince. I was face-to-face with the Ice Dragon once again.

The dragon reached forward and dipped a claw in the blood on the helmet. She then reached it toward me, her claw mysteriously passing through the helmet, which was now transparent, to touch my forehead between my eyes. "Be at peace, my friend, for you are a treasure deemed worthy by blood." As she spoke, *The Story* erupted around us. I saw the Prince's sacrifice, spreading blood over the land. But this vision showed a missing detail from that day. A detail that revealed just how much the King and the Prince loved their people.

As in past visions of *The Story*, the people attacked the Prince, who attempted to explain that he was there to help them. In their anger, they forced him to the border of the Woods. They believed he would die if they pushed him into the Woods, for they had forgotten who he was and refused to believe that he had any intention to help.

The Prince stood between the world of light and the world of darkness, harassed by angry people until he stood only inches from entering the Woods. The people had been corrupted by greed and anger and had filled the land with hatred and war. But the King and the Prince still loved them. As I watched in horror, waiting to see Ruth shove the Prince to his death as in past visions, I saw a new detail. Ruth did not just push the Prince into the Woods that day. Ruth, filled with rage, having believed the Creature's lie that her prince was the enemy, plunged a gleaming knife into the chest of her betrothed. The Prince remained silent. He did not resist. He accepted his fate. I could see the hurt and pain in his eyes. But what I didn't see was hatred.

Why is this new detail important? I wondered. There was so much I knew from reading *The Story* but so little I understood. Now, a new piece of that understanding seemed to fall into place as I realized what this meant. The blood on the helmet made sense. The Prince was an eternal being. But he had died. He had shed blood. He had not been forced to the edge—he had allowed himself to be taken there. I knew now why the blood was so important. A prince was typically seen as someone who ruled over others. Someone loftier and more important than his people. This prince had all the more reason to be so because he was an eternal being. But he had given up that status. He could have refused. He could have stopped his own death. But he didn't. He had given up everything, including his life, for those he ruled over. All so we could have a choice between darkness and light. *Why would someone do that for people as horrible as these?*

I looked to the faces of those around him. None of the people understood what he was doing there. None of them understood why he was silent and did not fight them. None of them realized he was taking their anger, their hate, their corruption and darkness—taking all their evil upon himself. Taking it so that he could do with it what the people could not. Darkness seemed to be sucked from Ruth and those around her, flowing through the knife and into the Prince. Ruth then shoved the Prince into the Woods as he held on to the darkness he had gathered from the people. The light of Original Power burned away the darkness of Corrupted Power, and the Prince fell dead within the Woods, blood pooling beneath him as the land around him went dark. But *The Story* didn't end there, for the King used Original Power to bring the Prince back, creating a gate that stood as a way home.

I was one of those people, I thought, dread falling over me. A memory of Solace came to mind. I had told her my darkness would keep me from entering the Unseen Lands. Thinking I would forever be trapped in darkness, I had been determined to save this world for those after me. Suddenly, the Ice Dragon's words came to mind. *"You are a treasure deemed worthy by blood."* My dread was replaced by an odd sense of calm. I was fighting a battle already won. The Prince had given everything to overcome the power of darkness. *Even mine.* While the Creature lived in shadow and the King in light, the Prince stood between the two, as he had between the doors in my vision, offering a way from darkness into light. A way to freedom.

As I felt the weight of all I had seen and realized the depth of the power in *The Story,* I accepted the armor in full. I let go of my fear that I was lost to darkness forever and took hold of the hope found in *The Story.*

As if in response to my acceptance, the armor I wore became visible once more, erupting with light, and a surge of power flowed through me. My calm turned to a peace beyond anything I had ever known. The feeling was so intense, so refreshing, I collapsed to my knees once again as the power filled the armor and created a protective barrier around me. Never before had it felt so alive. Never before had I felt so free.

But amidst the power, something subtle about the armor felt disjointed, as if it were still not fully connected. Something was missing. *There is still one final piece.*

Chapter 7

The vision fell away, and I found myself on my knees in the dark cave. I took in a deep, refreshing breath and let it out. My headache was completely gone. My mind was clear. *And I can see? In this dark cave?* I thought in wonder. I stood and looked around. Though I was still in the depths of the cavern, something was providing light. At first it seemed to be coming from everywhere, but then it grew smaller until I could tell its source was below me. I glanced down to find the shoes of armor on my feet, shining with the light of Original Power. The light illuminated the rest of me just enough to see that all the armor was visible again, though it appeared as a transparent silver. An inadvertent smile spread across my face, and I let out a soft chuckle. Relief washed over me as I ran a hand through my hair, faintly aware that the helmet I now wore allowed for that motion. Everything was back to normal—better than normal, actually. The last time I had seen the armor outside a vision was on the Western Island. Now, I could see it once more and feel it close to me, like a protective blanket. Though I could tell it still missed something, it was stronger than ever. And somehow, I knew it wasn't going away.

As I let out a sigh, remnants of the Creature's presence tugged at the edge of my mind like a dissipating black fog. I could feel him trying to claw his way back in. It was as if he had been able to see into my thoughts but had only glimpsed the information he desperately sought. But he no longer had access to me. Not like he did before.

"Everything is about to change," said a voice from behind me.

I spun around in surprise, drawing the sword in a smooth, familiar motion and holding it at the ready. After everything that had happened, I was on high alert. But I hoped it was the man who had helped me get here and not a soldier of darkness, or worse.

As I came to face the source of the voice, I saw before me a man with unmemorable features and dark hair, dressed in simple work clothes. He had no weapons, though he seemed unworried about standing face to face with an armed soldier in a dark cave. He seemed strangely familiar to me.

"Who...Who are you?" I asked, unsure if he too was an enemy. He appeared to be on my side, but I had been wrong before.

The man smiled warmly. "I am the carpenter," he said simply.

Memories of the captain using the passphrase "I am a friend of the carpenter" to gain access to different places throughout our journey sprang to my mind. I slowly lowered the sword. "You helped me get here."

The man nodded. "Everyone needs help now and then," he said with a sparkle in his eye that reminded me of Ruth.

I studied him. I could not put my finger on what seemed familiar about this man who had apparently played a role in my journey. "You look familiar," I said, deciding to voice my confusion. For some reason, I felt like we had spoken before, but I couldn't place where or when.

The man chuckled. "No need to worry about that right now," he said. Then his smile faded, and his expression turned grave. "The Creature saw part of your vision. He will use it to try to find the Gate and destroy it. But he cannot find it without you, for he cannot wield the armor. He needs you to do that for him. He will use what he saw in your mind to guide his soldiers in their search for the Gate, but he will keep coming after you until he has what he needs," the man explained as he began to look glance around the cave as if looking for something. "You must heed my father's words and use the key to open the Gate," he commanded.

The mysterious man continued to glance around, appearing to search the empty air before him. At this point in my journey, his strange actions did not surprise me, and my lack of surprise made me smile and shrug. My life could never go back to how it was before, nor did I want it to.

Finally, the man stopped with his hands flat out in front of him as if they were resting on a wall. A small flame of white fire suddenly appeared under his hands and burned away the seemingly empty space before him like paper, revealing a door made of stone.

"Follow the road I place you on," said the carpenter. "It is called the Smugglers' Road. Do as I have instructed, and you will find what you need. You must hurry, though. The armor will protect you," he said as he opened the door and motioned for me to go through. As I did, I stepped onto a snow-covered path among what I assumed were the Southern Mountains. *The Smugglers' Road, like the one in the note from Ruth's cloak?* I wondered. I turned toward him to ask about the road, but he spoke first. "Things are about to change," he warned again as he locked eyes with me. "Darkness will seem to take hold. But you must remember, Ben, have faith," he commanded. Then the door closed before him, and both he and the door disappeared.

I stared at the space where the door and the man who called himself the carpenter had vanished. *What just happened? Who was that man? And why didn't those dark soldiers in the cave attack us?* I filtered through everything I knew and everything I had learned about reality as a whole and those who wielded Original Power. There was so much more going on than I could see. To my knowledge, only soldiers of light, the King, and the Prince could wield Original Power. *That must be it—he must be a soldier of light.* But that would not explain why Captain Bates and his contacts had built a code around him, using his name to get in and possibly out of places. *Maybe he is a general or something,* I guessed.

Leaving the thought behind, I examined my surroundings. Behind me rose a rocky precipice, the cloudy night sky above. In front of me was a very faint deer path that led through some thick trees and underbrush packed tightly amidst the rocky terrain. Directly across from me, on the other side of the path, was a massive blanket of quilt moss growing up the cliff face. Normally, I would have paid the moss no mind. It grew all over the mountains. But something odd caught my eye. A set of fresh deer tracks veered off the path and seemed to end suddenly, disappearing into the mossy wall. This deer path was almost certainly not the Smugglers' Road, unless it had been overgrown for decades. But this new trail of tracks made me curious. With no other path in sight, I approached the moss and pulled out a small knife I kept in my sleeve.

I stuck my knife into the thick moss and, surprisingly, was not met with the clang of metal on stone as I had expected. It seemed there was nothing but air behind it. Cutting a slit in the greenery, I pulled the moss back like a curtain and stepped into a short tunnel just big enough for a horse and rider. Within a few horse lengths, it spilled out onto a new, much broader path that stretched beyond my view to my left and right. *This must be the Smugglers' Road,* I thought.

The Smugglers' Road appeared to be more of a tunnel than an open road, though much larger than the one I had just come through. This tunnel was surprisingly spacious, containing a hidden oasis between its curved rocky walls. The rounded walls, which arched out and up from the ground, were separated at the top by a massive crack that continued down the road as far as I could see, giving light to the plants that grew below. Much like the other dragon caves I had seen, the walls showed signs of the rock having been scorched by heat. It was as if a dragon had melted a tunnel into the mountain, but over time the mountain had shifted, causing the crack to form in the tunnel's ceiling and allowing the stone to become overgrown with life.

The road down the center of the tunnel looked like it had once been a dried-up riverbed. Moonlit snow fell through the crack in the ceiling, paving the riverbed in white. The road led straight through patches of green grass, trees, and bushes that were partially in shadow at its edge. There was no evidence that anyone had used the road recently, for the strip of snow was untouched, save by a few small wild animals and possibly a horse, though those tracks were mostly covered in fresh snow. I wondered if this road had any other significance beyond a smuggling route, and I wished Ruth were here to explain it to me. But for now, I needed to get going.

I wasn't entirely sure where I was in relation to where I had been, but I decided to simply start walking toward what I believed was the south, headed for the fourth corner of the earth and the small village of South Town. I walked for a few minutes but stopped short when I rounded a nearby bend in the path and found Jeb. Tacked up and covered in a light dusting of fresh snow, he stood grazing on some grass he had uncovered at the edge of the path.

"How did you get here?" I wondered out loud as I greeted him. He nuzzled me joyfully. "Did you run off when you noticed I was gone from the cave?" I asked as I looked back the way I had come to make sure no one had followed him. "Doesn't matter how, I guess. But the general and Valdra will be looking for me. We'd best be on our way," I said as I swung onto Jeb's back. "Let's go."

Jeb immediately set out in the direction I pointed him. Since we were on unfamiliar ground, I kept him at an easy walk despite the fact that I knew we were likely being pursued. I had no idea how far we were from the cave I had started in, but I also didn't know what to expect around each bend in the road.

As we moved along, I was surprised to find that the crack in the ceiling went on for miles, casting a narrow path of moonlight like a ribbon through the otherwise night-dark landscape. With the moonlight shining down on us, darkness loomed on either side in the areas the moon and starlight could not reach. Shadows seemed to be etched into the space around us, their jagged edges cast by the rocks and plants.

I glanced at the shadows on either side of us as we moved, re-membering the dark soldiers I thought I had glimpsed in the other cave. The Creature's explanation of how he and his soldiers lived in the shadows flooded my mind, causing the hairs on the back of my neck to rise. The soldiers of darkness in the previous cave had stayed at bay while the man who called himself the carpenter had led the way through the darkness to the piece of armor that would free my mind. But now, walking through the moon's light, I felt exposed to them. They could see me, but I could not see them. I drew the sword in hopes it would reveal them so I could at least see how many there were. But it didn't work. Though their eyes and outlines briefly became clearer, they still somehow disappeared into the darkened edges of the path. As I returned the sword to its sheath, I let out a shaky breath. Every fiber of my being wanted to retreat into shadow, but I stayed in the light.

In an attempt to distract myself, I pondered the events that had led to me finding the helmet of armor. *Who was that man in the cave?* I wondered again. Suddenly, a memory sprang to mind. *No. It can't be,* I thought. *That's impossible...or is it?* The only person who might know was Captain Bates.

My thoughts of the carpenter reminded me that he had instruct-ed me to hurry. Having encountered no surprises on the road so far, I cued Jeb to pick up his pace until we were sprinting down the trail of snow. Despite my urge to conceal myself for tactical reasons, we kept to the middle, avoiding the darkness on either side and sticking to the narrow path of light before us.

After traveling at varying speeds for nearly an hour, I began to see things in the shadows. It started when something moved in the darkness to my left. As we continued our journey, I saw more and more movements. *Soldiers of darkness!* I thought in horror. *But I am not holding the sword,* I thought with confusion. I had hoped they would not show up, but now they were here, and I could see them even without the sword in my hand. *"The armor will protect you."* The carpenter's words echoed in my mind, and I calmed a bit. But as Jeb and I continued on, the crack in the ceiling began to narrow, blocking out more and more light. The path of moonlight and snow grew thinner and thinner as the darkness closed in around us.

Starting as a small prick and growing from there, fear began to build up inside of me as the dark soldiers grew closer. *The Creature and other soldiers of darkness walked in dark shadows amidst the moonlight. Are these soldiers different from the others?* I wondered. *Can they only walk in shadow?*

As the path of light ended, I abruptly pulled Jeb to a halt. He pranced in place, and I struggled to hold him back as he fought to continue forward. I stared at the darkness before us. If I went ahead, there would be no light guiding my path. If I was right about these soldiers, then there would be no light to stop them from attacking, and there might be too many for me to handle alone. Caught between the fear of what I saw and the knowledge that what I saw was not what should guide me, I hesitated. In that moment of hesitation, I heard something I had prayed to never hear again.

A deep rumble seemed to come from all around me and grew into a screech. *Zath.* With nothing left to lose, I leaned forward and cued Jeb into a sprint. He leapt from a standstill and hit the ground running, straight into the darkness before us. But to my surprise, I could see, for the shoes of armor glowed with the light of Original Power and lit the way, as they had in the cave.

Oh, how quickly I forget, I thought with a grin.

Jeb galloped as fast as he could without losing his footing in the dim environment as dark soldiers seemed to fade back into the darkness around us. Relief filled me but faltered at the sound of Zath as he grew closer and closer. He clawed at the rock, attempting to get through the crack we had left behind, but he couldn't fit. Instead, he simply thrust his head through and opened his mouth. The path behind us lit with fire as the dragon let loose his orange flames.

With no light to feed them here, plants did not grow in this section of the tunnel, giving Jeb room to jump to one side, off the riverbed, dodging the fire as I held the shield at an awkward angle to keep us both safe.

Jeb picked up his speed as we darted through the darkness with Zath's rumbling growls confirming he was on our tail. But just as abruptly as it had ended, the crack in the tunnel's ceiling returned, leaving a moonlit path before us. We burst from the darkness as Jeb broke into a sprint once again, running so fast I had to focus to stay on his back.

The joy of having the path clear and bright again was short-lived. Zath suddenly slammed into the rock above, launching another stream of flames down at us. Jeb darted again to one side to avoid the flames as the resilient stone held up under Zath's blows. Seeing that his strategy was not going to work, Zath changed tactics. For a moment, I thought he had left, but just as Jeb and I returned to the lighted path, Zath let loose a new stream of fire. Directly ahead of us. The flames rushed down through the crack, funneled by the two rock walls on either side. Instinctively, I reached for the shield. But seeing the fire, Jeb planted his front feet and skidded to a halt, throwing me over his head. Having trained with Jeb for years, I had learned how he braked and many times had practiced performing an emergency tuck and roll at the last minute, and in midair. Though it wasn't graceful, I managed to tuck enough to keep the wind from getting knocked out of me when I hit the ground. With barely any time to think, I rolled out of the fall, bringing the shield up in front of me to protect both myself and Jeb from the incoming flames.

The fire hit the shield like a wave of water, and I leaned in, my shoes of armor gouging grooves in the dirt and snow below me as the force of the fire pushed me back a few feet. I growled in my effort to hold back the flames. Just when I thought I would fail, I felt the armor assist me. The shoes gripped the ground, the belt and breastplate reinforced my strength, the helmet seemed to fill my body with power I did not understand, and I found myself leaning farther into the attack until Zath finally relented.

As the fire let up, I fell to my knees, the force I was leaning into having suddenly vanished. Breathing hard to catch my breath, I stood and looked at the sky. Zath stood over the crack in the rocks, staring down at me with anger burning in his eyes. Seeing he could not beat me with fire, Zath pulled away from the crack. For a moment, I again thought he was leaving. Instead, he transformed. To my shock, his body became surrounded by black fog as his wings vanished and he morphed into something smaller, allowing him to fit between the rock walls. As the black fog descended onto the path before me, it cleared, revealing the face of Zath's human form.

Valdra!

I stared in shock at the man before me. I had known Valdra for a long time. But even after I had learned he worked for the

Creature, I never would have guessed he could be the human form of a dragon.

"Are you surprised?" asked Valdra with a mocking smile, holding his hands out to the sides.

I remained silent. Earlier, he had looked so tired and almost sad. Now, I struggled to find that same hopelessness I had seen in his expression. *Is he hiding it for the sake of intimidation? Or did I just imagine his tiredness and depressed mood due to the Creature's hold on my mind?*

"You were foolish to come here, my old comrade, for your friend in that cave did not tell you everything about this place," he taunted.

"What do you mean?" I asked, taking a step back to create more space between us and give myself time to react if he attacked.

"This place is called the Smugglers' Road, but it also bears a different name—an ancient name. The Valley of Zath!" he announced with a menacing grin.

"It does not matter what this place is called," I growled. "I will not let you stop me from accomplishing my mission!"

Valdra raised his eyebrows. "I seem to have already done that," he said sarcastically. "Face it, Ben. You've been beaten. Your comrades are all lost, you are alone, and your armor is not fully connected," he continued, raising his voice slightly in pride. "So, even if you somehow did make it past me, you'd have nothing to show for it. If the armor is not united, you cannot open the Gate!"

"I trust that the man in the cave had a reason for sending me this way. He said the armor will protect me. I believe him!" I said defiantly, my theory of who he was springing to mind. If my theory was right, the man in the cave definitely knew what he was talking about.

Valdra frowned. "Then you should know, I cannot let you leave here alive. The people of this land are and will remain under the Creature's control!" he growled.

But for a moment, I thought I saw something in his eyes. *I was right before, on the trail and in the caves!* I recalled Valdra's mood on our travels. *He seemed hopeless, even worried.* But before I could fully understand his demeanor and the look in his eyes, Valdra transformed before me once again. His body grew into the scaly, ink-black form of Zath, and his immense frame pushed up against the rock ceiling. The force of his abrupt transformation caused the ground beneath me to crack, and it rumbled and shifted below me as I struggled to find my footing.

Zath crashed through the rock above us, chunks of dirt, snow, and stone falling around me as his wings fanned out and he rose into the night sky. Moonlight poured into the space around me, banishing to distant corners the few soldiers of darkness still lurking in the shadows. Having taken to the sky once again, Zath took advantage of the large hole he had created in the ceiling of the stony tunnel and launched a stream of fire from almost directly above me. I lifted the shield and held the fire at bay. The flames' impact caused me to slide back only a couple of inches in the half-frozen dirt before the shoes of armor gripped the ground, stopping my backward progression and aiding in my balance and stability. Zath dove and transformed, again, into Valdra. As soon as he landed on the ground before me, he drew a sword and charged.

I drew the sword to defend against Valdra's attack, and his blade clashed against mine. A bright light flashed in my mind's eye, and all the visions I'd had over the past few months cycled through my head. The belt, the breastplate, the shoes, the shield, and the helmet. Then I felt it. The sword suddenly grew weightless, though it held up to Valdra's attack. Still blocking Valdra's sword, I looked at mine to find that light was beaming from within its blade, making the letters on its shimmering surface shine. I knew a vision was coming. But this time, the sword didn't draw me anywhere. The world around me simply changed.

As the space around me transformed into a vision, I found myself looking at the all too familiar dome of darkness. Its surface swirled like fog, bending high overhead and flowing down to the ground around me. Then, in the distance, I saw the wooden door from my previous visions. The door was open, as I had left it in the vision in the cave, and I eagerly set out toward the comforting sight. As I drew near, I saw that there was not just one door. The transparent door stood open on the other side, much closer than it had been before. But it wasn't just the second door that grabbed my attention. I stopped at the wooden door's boundary and stared. Barely contained by the transparent door's frame was a mesmerizing sight. Light so thick it seemed to move like water. I hesitated, unsure what to do. Then I recalled entering the door with the Prince. He had led me through before and granted me the helmet. But now I was here alone. The door was open, waiting. It was almost as if I were being tested. As if I had been granted, by the Prince, the freedom to enter there. But now the question was being posed, would I still enter when I could not see the Prince?

Standing there as I was, I could see nothing but light on the other side of the door. A place free of darkness and totally unknown to me. Like an ocean, the light lay before me, inviting me in. Feeling the weight of the choice I now faced, I reached out and touched the light. It sent a shock through my body that was almost painful. I remembered the Prince's actions. Inviting me in, leading me through the doors. He had opened one, and I had answered his knock on the other. Now I was given the choice. They were both open. There was nothing left to do but go through.

I crossed the boundary into the light, and I found myself at the base of a path. This path led up to a magnificent castle. Like a mountain, its highest peak was pointed, carved out of rock and stone, and covered in living gardens. In the distance, on the path, I thought I saw the Prince. He appeared to be beckoning me to follow him, and I did. I ascended the path, which led up and around the castle, until I arrived at a marble courtyard that seemed to be sculpted from the cliff itself. Rather than finding the Prince, I came upon a fountain with a stone at its top in the courtyard's center.

Before I could go any farther, the Ice Dragon appeared in front of me. In her paws, she held a sword. When I approached her, the castle vanished from the vision, leaving only the dragon and me.

The Ice Dragon spoke. "Draw the sword you were given," she instructed in a gentle but commanding voice.

I drew the sword. The dragon held her sword out so the blade was next to mine. The two were identical, though hers was transparent and emanating light, as if it were the spiritual representation of the sword. The sword's spirit. She placed the spirit of the sword on top of my sword and said, "Be strengthened, my friend, for he is yours and you are his. A treasure claimed by light."

As the sword's spirit filled my sword, it erupted with light. Veins of light branched from the blade, down the hilt and up my arms, spilling into the armor I wore. The pieces of armor shone bright all around me, and I noticed that something about them felt different. More solid. More tangible. But only the belt gleamed as bright as the sword. The belt and the sword seemed to have a special connection that now caused the armor to unite. The armor seemed to fit to my body until it was all one piece that fit so well that it was as if it were part of me. The armor was complete.

As I accepted the sword, the vision of the dragon faded as her words rang in my head. *"Be strengthened, my friend, for he is yours and you are his. A treasure claimed by light."* The words reminded me of the sentence on the sword that Trixie had translated. *"When truth be known has strengthened thee, the Lion's sword will set you free." We were right!* I realized. Otto and the others had developed the theory that the armor must be found and united to open the Gate. This vision seemed to confirm that assumption. *Now that the armor is united, I can use the sword to open the Gate and make the unseen seen!*

But as that realization settled reassuringly in my mind, to my surprise, the vision continued, and I found myself looking at a familiar image. I was back in the dome of darkness, the glittering path before me, the door at its end. The vision lingered there, the path sparkling like a river in moonlight. Then, it vanished. The vision was over.

Suddenly in reality again, I was faced with Valdra's attack. It appeared that time had passed, for we were now farther down the Smugglers' Road in a part of the tunnel that Zath had not damaged. I had no idea how I had been fighting while immersed in the vision, but that was exactly what seemed to have happened. Distracted by that thought, I was caught off guard as Valdra pulled away and swung his sword for another strike. I blocked his blow, realizing that the armor felt different. Acted different. The shield jumped to my grip. The sword came to my aid, as if the armor knew my very thoughts. The armor around me felt united. But not just that—I could feel it was not just on me, but it was beginning to connect with me in a way that it never had before. Power flowed through its parts, flowing through me as well. I could feel it coursing through my veins with each swing of the sword and block of the shield. Yet, somehow, it felt as though we, the armor and I, were still not yet fully connected.

Finding an opening in Valdra's attack, I struck him with the sword, slicing his shoulder. In pain, Valdra screeched like a dragon and transformed into Zath, destroying another section of the tunnel and flying high into the air. As he ascended, he spit orange flames at me, each of which I stopped with the shield. As I repositioned to block his attacks, the shield happened to catch the moonlight just right. The light bounced off the shield's silver surface and struck Zath in the side. He screeched and retaliated with more fire. Distracted by the sudden reflection, I barely managed to block Zath's fire, and I was instantly swept off balance by his massive paw as he took a swing at me. I somehow managed to roll to one side, narrowly avoiding his tail as it crashed into the tunnel wall only inches above my head, showering me with dirt, snow, and small stones.

As Zath came around to face me again, something caught my eye—around his neck hung Trixie's stone medallion. It was so small against his massive frame but still easily identifiable by the S-shaped symbol on each side. But as Zath began to circle around to my side, I realized for the first time that there were not one but two S-shaped symbols on each side. I had missed them before because the second S shapes could only be fully seen from certain angles. A familiar image. *Where have I seen that before?* Trixie had found the medallion on her travels when she came across the Channel Treasure, a stone we thought had something to do with the Gate. Then it came to me. *We were right!* I thought. *We had to have been. All three artifacts must be connected somehow, for the only other place I have seen that double S shape was on the Prince's pendant, when I first saw him in the Woods. If he was wearing the symbol and he made the Gate, then the two must be connected. Zath must have taken Trixie's medallion when he killed everyone in the shipwreck! But why would he take it and not hand it over to the Creature?*

As Zath continued moving, a strange sensation came over the armor, drawing my attention away from the dragon to the armor around me. It was as if it became stronger or more solid in the medallion's presence. This was different from before, when the sword had led me to other armor pieces. Rather than the sword leading me to a missing piece, it was as if the armor as a whole sought this medallion. *Maybe the sword is not the final piece?* I wondered as I spotted Jeb, who was running past me. Whatever he was running from caused him to put in a burst of speed down the trail.

Alerted by Jeb's behavior, I spun around just in time to see Zath attack me again. Having been distracted by the medallion, I wasn't able to respond in time to block, and Zath landed a blow that sent me flying. I hit the ground with a thud, sliding a few feet in the muddy snow as I felt the air rush out of my lungs. The ground shook as I rolled over onto my side, desperately gasping and trying to recover in time to brace for the next blow. The armor had protected me, but my distracted mind seemed to have impacted its effectiveness.

As I looked up, Zath was in full attack, but he momentarily slowed, then let out a growl before turning back into Valdra and attacking me with a sword. With no time to decipher his odd behavior, I lifted the sword, blocking Valdra's attack as I finally sucked in a deep breath. Lying on the ground as I was, I sent the heel of my boot into Valdra's stomach as he raised his sword above his head. Valdra doubled over and I struck out again, this time aiming for his face while I blocked his sword hand. The strike hit Valdra square in the nose, and he pulled back long enough for me to get up. I scrambled to my feet, and Valdra swung a punch that glanced off my cheek as my body seemed to react without my instruction, dodging almost out of his reach.

I turned and sprinted in the direction Jeb had run, passing through another section of the undamaged tunnel before finally bursting through a loose patch of quilt moss into a snow-covered clearing about twenty feet in diameter overlooking South Town. Panting and willing my muscles to keep fighting, I let out a harsh sigh of frustration as Valdra raced out of the tunnel behind me and leapt into the air, turning into Zath once again.

Weary from the fight, my reaction time was slow, and Zath struck me with a paw, sending me flying into a nearby rock. The armor protected me, but I struggled to my feet in exhaustion as Zath rose into the air above me. As I came up into an unsteady stance, I found myself looking out over South Town. What I saw sent a surge of joy through my body. In the midst of the town was Eyethanoff with a small group of soldiers of light fighting against soldiers of darkness. Eyethanoff and his army stood out among the shadowy soldiers they fought, an image of hope I hadn't realized that I longed to see. I was not alone.

Turning to face the approaching Zath with renewed confidence, I yelled, "You have lost! Eyethanoff is beating back the Creature's armies as we speak. This land will not be yours for long."

"You are wrong!" snarled Zath. "Those soldiers came for you! They will not fail. The Lion's Sword soldiers are too few! They will die here, and all that you have done, all that you have lost, will be for nothing!" he growled in anger. "The people of this land cannot understand what is happening around them, and they will never understand! They will stay trapped under the Creature's control!"

Instead of attacking me, Zath turned on the small town, descending beyond the rocks and trees toward the battle taking place in the streets below. A battle that the people of this town could only partially see and whose outcome they may never fully grasp.

Though they had already been fighting the pillaging beasts, the townspeople ran for cover at the sight of the massive dragon. I had to stop Zath. As I ran after him, not knowing how I could possibly catch him, I saw him land on the ground just outside the town's shredded main gate, ready to blast Eyethanoff and the others with fire and wind from his wings. But he suddenly stopped short.

"No!" I heard a familiar voice yell.

Captain Bates! From my position behind Zath, I could not see the captain, but there was no mistaking his voice. I ran through the bushes, trying to get around the dragon as I scrambled through snow and mud to a vantage point that would allow me to see what was happening.

Captain Bates and the crew of the *Lyonsword* were fighting by Eyethanoff's side, though it was clear they had no idea Eyethanoff and the other soldiers of light were among them. They were fighting the physical enemy, General Delaney's Martecytes and two Great Beasts. But now the captain cried out and ran for Zath. Scrambling down the steep trail that led into the town, I finally made it far enough around Zath's large frame that I was able to see what had stopped him in his tracks. Or rather, who.

There, standing before Zath, was little Yuuki. She stood her ground with a resolute posture I had never seen in such a young child. Her small hands were clenched into fists at her sides, and her feet were braced apart in a protective stance at the entrance to the town.

"I will not let you harm the people any longer," she said to Zath in a surprisingly calm and commanding tone.

As the captain fought past a beast to reach Yuuki, Zath stared down at her little frame. "Get out of my way!" he demanded.

"No," stated Yuuki evenly, lifting her chin.

"So be it," said Zath with a snarl.

Zath launched a stream of fire directly at Yuuki as the captain and I both raced forward to reach her before she met her fiery fate. But what happened next left us both gaping in surprise.

Like a wave turning to ice, Yuuki transformed. Her body grew into that of a gorgeous animal, covered in shimmering icy scales, with eyes of beautiful turquoise, like the ocean on a clear day. Ice-laden wings expanded from her shoulders to nearly the same width as Zath's, and she let loose a stream of ice from her throat that held back Zath's fire.

The Ice Dragon! I realized with shock as I skidded to a halt on the snowy trail.

As Zath let up on his flames, the Ice Dragon ceased her icy defense and yelled in a stern voice, "You will not harm them any longer!" She stood her ground before the larger dragon, her wings a protective shield blocking the path to those behind her. She curled her long scaly tail to one side as she poised her body to take a blow. But her fierce stance was contrasted by the sorrow in her eyes.

Zath snarled, but he was clearly struggling at the sight of her majesty. He paced to and fro, as if he wanted to attack but part of him was holding him back. With a shake of his head, Zath attacked. Ice and fire met in a burst of steam. The bright white, shimmery scales of the Ice Dragon posed a stark contrast to the darkness that surrounded her, just like the soldiers of light who fought in the small town behind her.

As the dragons battled, I thought I noticed something strange about Zath's coal-black scales. They seemed to not be part of him but rather on him, as if they were enclosing the bright orange scales beneath. Trapping them. For a brief moment, I thought I saw the dark scales grow smaller, as if the trap were faltering, exposing the orange beneath them. But it must have been my imagination, for they remained in place as I ran to join the Ice Dragon, Captain Bates, and a small group of Lion's Sword soldiers who had come to her aid. Through the town's main gateway, I could see the crew of the *Lyonsword* ship and the remaining soldiers of light beginning to overpower the armies of darkness.

With their forces now outmatched, the dark soldiers and beasts finally retreated, Zath following close behind as they all fled to the safety of the Southern Mountains.

Chapter 8

With Zath and the armies of darkness in retreat, Eyethanoff and his soldiers followed them all the way into the mountains to make sure they left completely. In excitement over our victory, I turned and embraced Captain Bates in a hug as Christopher, Dan, Casey, and Catherine appeared through the gateway and gathered around us. I greeted them each in turn with hugs and forearm grasps as we rejoiced at our reunion. We had thought we would never see each other again. It was good to be back together.

As I finished greeting Dan, I turned to the Ice Dragon, the others doing the same. She gazed down at us with a gentle smile. For a moment, I felt as if I were about to go into shock, but then the feeling faded. Apparently, all the crazy things I had seen of late had made me immune to the surprising revelation that someone I knew was actually a dragon. *But Yuuki?* I shook my head and chuckled to myself.

"You have been with me this whole time," I said in disbelief. "How could I not have seen it?"

"You think I would not protect the one chosen to wear that armor?" the Ice Dragon asked in a kind voice. "And I chose my human form exactly for that purpose, for no one would suspect it," she said, a playful grin curling the edge of her scaly lips.

"So, are you still Yuuki?" I asked.

She dipped her head in confirmation. "Those to whom I do not wish to reveal my true identity only know me as Yuuki. But it is time you knew who I truly am. My name is Eyerkishta. I am a Treasure Keeper to the King."

"She was the one who moved the ship to get us to the Western Island, Ben," said Captain Bates.

I turned to the captain. "Did she also save you from Zath after you left the island? How are you all alive? Lance—"

The captain nodded. "I know," he said with a frown of anger. "He betrayed us." Everyone grew quiet, and the captain's frown was soon reflected on the others' faces as well. "I had suspected for a while that there was a traitor among us. I was hoping the second pirate attack would cause them to slip up and show themselves. But it didn't seem to work. I had no idea it was Lance until we were too far out to sea to help you."

"What happened?" I asked.

"Lance told us that you and the others were trapped and needed us to come to a different part of the island and pick you up. But by the time we realized he was lying..." The captain trailed off, his tone sorrowful. His eyes met mine, and I saw the pain of loss. "The dragon attacked...Yuuki—I mean Eyerkishta—tried to help, but her connection to the King's power was limited at the time." He shook his head. "She couldn't hold her dragon form long enough to make much of a difference. Eric...Eric took a small boat out to try to rescue you and the others, but he was overtaken by Zath's fire," said the captain. "Those who survived swam back to land. I don't think Lance ever found out I realized he was a traitor. I was careful to keep it from him."

I let out a sigh and placed a hand on the captain's shoulder. "I am truly sorry," I said as I recognized I was not the only one to have lost someone.

"We came back to look for you after things cleared up, but we couldn't find you," said Dan. "Then that dragon drove us off before we could attempt another search."

"We thought you were dead. So, we figured we should finish the mission as best we could," added Casey. "We delivered the final copies of *The Story* to the contact here in South Town," he explained. "And we recently heard confirmation that the book has been successfully printed in the other three corners of the earth. Many people have the book now and know the story it contains! Some have even offered to fight if the need arises."

I allowed a small sigh of relief. "I am glad to hear the mission has been completed."

The captain clapped a hand on my shoulder. "When duty calls, we come," he said with a smile, though it was still laced with sadness. "But what did happen to you?" he asked. "We searched that area all night until the dragon chased us off."

I shook my head. "You were not far off in assuming I was dead, for I almost was. The others...they didn't make it. The general and I ended up floating on a piece of debris, but one of his ships rescued us, and he brought me back to the Southern Continent to find the last armor piece...It turns out Solace was right, though. He was not to be trusted." I looked to everyone. "The general is the Creature...I assume he made sure you were unable to rescue me. He might have even been controlling Zath."

"What?" exclaimed the captain with genuine surprise in his eyes. "General Delaney is the Creature?"

I nodded. "He took over my mind somehow...and..." I looked up at Eyerkishta, and she tilted her head to meet my gaze. "Zath turned out to be Valdra, and..." Suddenly, I realized something odd about the helmet's location. "...and the last piece of armor I had to find was in one of his caves," I said as I wondered why it was there. "Did you put it there?" I asked.

Eyerkishta's eyebrows rose in surprise. "No. I hid it in some woods south of this town. He must have..." She stopped. "Feyerndur," she whispered as she looked off in the direction the Fire Dragon had gone.

"Who is Feyerndur?" asked Christopher with a frown.

"Zath," I explained, remembering the Creature's story.

"No, Feyerndur," corrected Christopher.

I shook my head. "Feyerndur is Zath—his true form, before he was corrupted."

"But he is also a person?" asked Dan with a raised eyebrow.

Eyerkishta nodded. "Feyerndur is...my mate. We...The King appointed us as leaders of the Treasure Keepers. But when the Creature was cast out of the castle, long before Ruth betrayed the Prince, humans started attacking us and stealing the treasures we were tasked with protecting. So, the King gave us human forms. It gave us the ability to hide while still protecting his treasures, including his people. But our human forms are weaker, susceptible to the Creature's lies. Feyerndur was corrupted by the Creature, though I am not sure when exactly, or how," she explained with teary eyes. "*Zath* is an Eeffraylick word for 'death.'" She took a deep breath and transformed back into Yuuki. Swaying wearily, she looked at me, her young human face etched with sadness. "I thought he was lost forever," she said, a small glimmer of hope in her eyes.

"Thought?" I asked.

"The helmet," she continued. "The armor pieces have power together, but in addition to that, they each have a power of their own. The helmet was created to protect one's mind, for without it, the Creature can infect you with shadow and turn you into a Martecyte, or something much worse. Dragons cannot be turned into Martecytes, but their human forms can be, to a certain extent. When that happens, it traps the dragon within a prison of darkness." A tear slipped from her eye. "Feyerndur must be in there somewhere, trying to get out. He knows the helmet could free him, but it is hard for someone to use the helmet on its own."

"You mean without the other armor?" I clarified.

Yuuki nodded, then glanced around. "Let's get out of the street. There is an inn here that will be a good place to talk." Yuuki led the way into South Town to a building partway down the main street. As we walked, I noticed people starting to come out of their hiding places, and I wondered if any of them had seen her transform.

We entered the warm inn and were greeted with an eruption of cheers and happy townsfolk shaking our hands and thanking us for ridding their town of the beasts. We humored them politely, then found a secluded corner to talk.

The barman approached us with a smiled as he wiped his hands on his apron. "I know your kind. Not much for public thanks. But I must say, words cannot express our gratitude. No one has successfully prevented the beasts from taking prey here for years. And when that dragon showed up, we were sure it was the end."

"You're welcome," I said. "I am glad we could help. But, um..." I glanced around the room briefly, but he responded before I could finish.

"Not to worry." He winked. "Anything for you and your crew. This corner is quiet, and I'll get you all some ale."

I smiled. "Thank you. We really appreciate it."

Once the barman had delivered our drinks and the passing thanks had died down, Yuuki leaned in. "The helmet can only be used when all the other armor is in place. Feyerndur once had his own armor, as did I. His must have gone dormant when he was corrupted. Mine has been dormant since shortly before I stopped walking in my dragon form. The helmet would only be able to provide him temporary relief if he does not have the other protective pieces," she explained.

"He had something else with him, when we were fighting," I said. "Something that caught my eye." I recalled seeing the medallion and how strongly I had felt I needed to get it from him.

"What?" asked Dan.

"Trixie's medallion. He had it around his neck. I know it was the same one because I spotted a symbol on it...I have only ever seen that symbol on Trixie's medallion and briefly on the door in one of my first visions," I explained. "I think I need it."

Yuuki shook her head in confusion. "When I first got my armor, it came with a medallion that was made specially for me. But that armor, the armor Ruth gave you, has never had a medallion. I had never seen Trixie's medallion until she showed it to us. I don't know why Feyerndur—or Zath—would have taken it from her. Even if it were connected to the armor somehow, he wouldn't be able to use it. Each medallion is made for one specific individual, and only that individual can use it."

"Maybe it is his medallion?" suggested Casey.

Yuuki shook her head. "His medallion didn't look like that." Her nose contorted in a frown of thought. "I don't think so, at least. I am sorry, Ben. I am having trouble remembering what Feyerndur's medallion looked like. The longer I am under this lie, the less I remember about life before."

"Did the armor call to it?" asked the captain.

I considered the question. "Kind of...It felt different. Before, with the other pieces, it felt like the sword was calling out to something it wanted, like a missing piece of the armor. But the armor feels complete now. This was more like the armor as a whole was attracted to the medallion. I am not sure if it is a piece of the armor or not." I recalled the moment I had seen the medallion on Zath. Then I remembered the mysterious man in the cave, and I was lost in thought for a moment. "There is something else, too," I said. "I had help getting the helmet," I explained, glancing at Yuuki. "Help from someone familiar..." I recalled my earlier theory, but it had to be impossible. I looked to Captain Bates. "Captain, where did you hire the *Lyonsword*'s carpenter?"

Captain Bates gave me an odd look. "I...Well, I actually hired him shortly before I met you, while we were docked at the secret port there. Why?"

I rubbed my chin. "How did you hear of him?"

The captain's brow furrowed. "Through Ruth."

I shook my head. *It can't be. It's not possible...*

"Captain, when I was on your ship, I had a conversation with your carpenter. He said some things to me that were...well, they were exactly what I needed to hear, as though he knew what I would be dealing with once we got on land."

"Well, he knew what our mission was," said the captain.

"Yes, but...but this was different." I ran my fingers through my hair. "I think I might have met him again, in the cave where I found the helmet...Could it be that he is a soldier of the Lion's Sword?"

The captain raised his eyebrows. "Well, I guess it could be possible. But then how would I have been able to see him?"

"That's a good question..." *So maybe not a soldier of light.* The ship carpenter's words sprang to mind. *"But remember, seek truth, always. It is worth more than you realize. For it is not you but truth that will set you free."* The words reminded me of my ongoing battle against the Creature. It was *The Story*—the truth contained in *The Story*—that had helped me through the darkest moments. Not only that, but it was the truth of *The Story* that had erupted when the helmet was placed on my head...the helmet that had fully freed me from the Creature's clutches. *Was it the helmet that freed me? Or did the man who led me to it play a role?*

"The man who helped me get the helmet called himself the carpenter," I mentioned, looking to the captain for his response.

"Interesting...'I am a friend of the carpenter' is a code among those loyal to the King that was developed years ago and passed to me by Ruth. She said it was a reference to someone from *The Story*...Who could it be?" he pondered out loud.

I replayed in my mind what the ship's carpenter had said to me. *"It is not you but truth that will set you free."* What came after that? I thought there was something else he had said, something important. Then I remembered. *"Just have faith, my friend."* The code said "a friend of the carpenter." And the carpenter on the ship had called me his friend. I had to be right—he and the man from the cave were one and the same person. Not a soldier of light but rather this mysterious person from *The Story* whom the code referred to.

Then the words of the carpenter from the cave came to mind, and with a jolt, I realized who it was. *"Heed my father's words."* There was only one person I knew from *The Story* who could possibly show up at just the right moment to join the crew of the same ship I was boarding. There was only one person who could appear in a cave when I needed him most and send me through an invisible door to the exact place I was supposed to be. There was only one person from *The Story* whose father had spoken relevant words that I would know and that I needed to heed. There was only one person the code could be referencing.

The captain's eyes suddenly shot open wide in a rare expression of astonishment, and I knew he had come to the same conclusion.

"The Prince!" we both stated in unison.

"He's here," I said.

"But how is that possible?" asked the captain with a thoughtful frown.

I shook my head in uncertainty as another question presented itself. *I saw him in the Woods. Why did I not recognize him on the ship or in the cave?* I wondered. There was still so much I didn't understand, but I was certain of one thing.

"I was wrong," I said simply, realizing again that I had been completely off in the way I was thinking about reality.

"Wrong about what?" asked Dan.

"This whole time, I have been assuming that the Prince was trapped in the Unseen Lands, unable to make himself seen outside the Woods or visions. I thought it was my job, my mission, to free him—to free the unseen. But if the Prince is here, then…" I shook my head and smiled. "He is not trapped. We are!" I laughed at my own blindness as I recalled the vision of the dome of darkness. "I was wrong. I somehow got it in my head that making the unseen seen meant that I was to free it from some cage that keeps it hidden. A cage the Creature made to trap the Prince and the King. But that is not it at all. We are the ones who are trapped! We are the ones who need freedom from this darkness the Creature has covered us with. And we can only gain that freedom by letting Original Power back into our land!" I explained with excitement. This changed everything.

Catherine had been quiet until now. "Wait, if this is just about revealing the truth, then what is the Gate for?"

The captain responded. "Remember, *The Story* says the people tried to get back into Eeffrayldour and corrupted it in the process, so the Prince created a gate that would give people access to the Kingdom," he explained.

"Okay, so where are we?" asked Catherine. "Did we go back into the Unseen Lands or are we in the Land Beyond? And why would we need to get into the Kingdom? Isn't that just another name for Eeffrayldour?"

"All of these different names are so confusing," pointed out Dan.

I shrugged. "I don't fully understand it either. All I know is that the Prince seems be asking me—us—to open the Gate and free this land, not Eeffrayldour. We need to find Ruth—she can help us get some answers."

"Did the Prince say anything to you?" questioned Yuuki, changing the subject.

"He told me to take the Smugglers' Road and that I would find what I need. I thought it was the sword...but now I am not so sure, as I have had the sword all along. I just hadn't been granted the sword's power. When that happened, I received the spirit of the sword, while I was fighting Zath, but still the armor called out to the medallion." I looked to the others. "I think he meant that I would find the medallion."

"Then we must get it back," said Yuuki with a look of determination.

Just then, Eyethanoff entered the inn and quickly approached me. "We need to regroup," he said. "Some of the soldiers of darkness stopped in the mountains. Others seemed to head farther north, maybe to get ready in case we make it through. Zath was with them, but we lost track of him. We are not safe here. Tell the others to follow you," he commanded, reminding me that my companions could only see Martecytes and beasts but not the soldiers of light and darkness.

I nodded and turned back to them. "Follow me. Eyethanoff wants to regroup before the Creature and his armies come after us again." My thoughts briefly settled on the strange fact that, much like with the dark soldiers on the Smugglers' Road, I could see Eyethanoff even though I wasn't holding the sword. I flexed my hand, wondering what had changed. I didn't have time to dwell on that now, though.

With that, we thanked the barman, who kindly refused to take money for our drinks, and headed out into the snowy, moonlit landscape.

We rode through the trees, headed south—to where, Eyethanoff didn't tell me. I knew the land ahead of us spread out in a massive expanse of unexplored forests, deserts, bogs, and, eventually, the southernmost tip of the Southern Country—an ice-covered land only a few sailors and explorers had survived to tell tales of. Captain Bates, being one of them, had told me about some of the things he had encountered. Based on those stories, I hoped Eyethanoff wouldn't take us too far south. We had enough on our hands as it was.

As we followed Eyethanoff, Captain Bates urged his horse up next to me. "Do you see what I see?" he asked.

I looked at him. "What do you mean?"

He gestured toward Eyethanoff. "There is something there. I can't tell what it is. It's like...a...a ghost," he whispered, glancing warily in Eyethanoff's direction.

I looked at the captain. *Could he be seeing Eyethanoff?*

Before I could offer an explanation, he said, "Maybe it is just my imagination."

Yuuki smiled. "Maybe..." she suggested cryptically.

We rode in silence for the rest of the trip until we came out into a clearing only a few miles south of South Town. As we entered the clearing, Jeb slowed when I inadvertently pulled back on his reins in surprise. Before me was a military camp. But not one of the southern king's camps. This was a Lion's Sword encampment. White tents, with blue and silver flags that bore the symbol from the shield on them, were laid out in neat rows. *That must be the symbol of the Lion's Sword!* Men and woman dressed in white, silver, and blue military attire sharpened and cleaned weapons as horses roamed about, free of restraints, grazing and enjoying themselves.

As I halted Jeb, Dan and Casey both jerked their horses to a stop as well.

"What is that?" demanded Casey, his eyes slightly widened with fear.

"I see it too," said Captain Bates.

"You can see that?" I asked, confused. *How can they see without the sword?* I wondered.

"I don't know what I'm seeing, but it's freaking me out," said Dan.

Yuuki chuckled.

"What?" asked Dan.

Yuuki smiled. "You will see."

Eyethanoff turned to me. "Tell them it is safe and not to worry. Yuuki is often right."

I passed on the message, and we all continued following Eyethanoff into the camp.

"Where are we?" I asked Eyethanoff as I let my gaze scan the camp. The others, apart from Yuuki, glanced around nervously.

"My encampment," explained Eyethanoff.

Casey looked at me with a concerned expression. "Who are you talking to?"

"Eyethanoff," I explained. "He just led us into his military camp."

Casey raised his eyebrows and looked around at the others. "So, we are not seeing ghosts?" he asked.

"You can see people?" I queried.

He shook his head. "Not really. It's like...occasionally there is an outline of one. Then it's gone," he said with a shiver.

I turned to Eyethanoff. "How can I see you and everyone else when I'm not holding the sword? And how can they see you?" I asked.

"You can only see this place because the belt and the sword are now fully connected. They reveal the truth to you, giving you the ability to see the unseen whether you hold the sword or not," he explained. "You will begin to see more and more as the King reveals things to you through his armor."

"And the others?" I asked.

"Honestly, I am not certain," he said as he led us to the center of the camp. He looked up at the sky. "But it could be a sign that things are about to change."

The Prince's words in the cave came to mind. *"Everything is about to change."*

As we reached the center of camp, I heard the others gasp. They all pulled their horses to a stop, and Eyethanoff cued his horse to approach the captain. "Can you see more?" he asked, halting before the captain and the others.

Captain Bates nodded. "Yes, I can see...a camp...and you, but only as though you are a ghost...Actually, all of it is...ghostly. What are you?" he asked.

"As Ben might have mentioned, I am Eyethanoff, a soldier of the Lion's Sword. You need not fear me, or my soldiers, as we were all assigned to help you on this mission and protect you." He gestured to a group of his soldiers, who smiled. "These are the brave men and woman who have been tasked with your safety during this time."

Dan and Casey stared in awe, but Captain Bates smiled and nodded to them. "Thank you for your service. I am glad to have you with us."

"It is our pleasure," said a male soldier in front.

Eyethanoff turned to me. "I have a scout who is monitoring the activities of the Creature's armies. She will send a messenger with news of their whereabouts. If it is safe, we will stay here for the night. But for now, give your horses a break."

"How long have you been here?" I asked as the others began to dismount and untack their horses, doing their best not to run into any of the partially visible soldiers and equipment in the camp.

"These soldiers have been stationed here since you arrived back on the Southern Continent. Usually, it is just me watching your back, along with their guardians," he said, gesturing to the *Lyonsword* crew who were mingling with their soldiers of light. "But I saw evidence that the time for you to complete your mission was approaching. I have a few other camps set up near what you call the Town," explained Eyethanoff as we dismounted our horses as well.

With a nod, I began to remove Jeb's tack as Yuuki wandered off to speak with the soldiers in the camp. One soldier came up to me and offered to clean Jeb's tack, and I gladly handed it over. After the soldier left, Eyethanoff spoke.

"Sheelarah, I must speak with Benjamin. Take his companion, and his friends, and show them around," he said in a kind voice.

For a moment, I had no idea who he was speaking to, but then I saw Eyethanoff's gray horse offer him a regal bow before tugging on Jeb's mane and leading him and the other horses away. The spectacle had regained the others' attention, and we all stared at them in shock until I heard Eyethanoff chuckle.

"Your horse doesn't speak to you much, does he?" he asked with a grin.

I continued staring after the horses, trying to think of a response, but it was Dan who spoke first. "Should he?"

Eyethanoff laughed. "Horses are creatures of few words, usually more interested in listening than speaking. But some do respond."

I swallowed and let out a nervous chuckle. "Is that normal or an Eeffrayldourian thing?" I asked.

Eyethanoff gave me a questioning look. "I am afraid I do not understand."

"I mean..." I cleared my throat. "Animals don't speak," I explained with a one-shouldered shrug.

Eyethanoff looked around. "Many animals speak," he said with a perplexed frown.

Yuuki, who had been speaking with a group of soldiers nearby, interrupted her conversation and looked at Eyethanoff. "This land is so full of darkness that many have lost their ability to hear, as well as see," she said, then returned to her conversation.

Eyethanoff's expression relaxed, and he nodded. "Ah, I am sorry. I am not used to seeing things from your perspective. I forget that the Lie has closed off much of what really goes on around you. Perhaps you simply cannot understand your horse?" he suggested. "Some animals prefer not to use words."

I nodded with raised eyebrows. "Perhaps," I agreed, still a bit shocked.

Just then, a large white owl swooped down out of nowhere and landed on top of a nearby tent. Eyethanoff held out a leather-wrapped forearm, and the owl left its perch, landing on Eyethanoff's arm.

"What did you find?" he said, apparently speaking to the bird.

The owl eyed me closely. "Who is this?" it asked in a deep voice. Something about its tone made me think it actually did know who I was and was just picking on me. Eyethanoff glared at the owl, who fluffed its feathers irritably and adopted a slightly less pretentious tone. "Ah. Benjamin Arlin, I presume."

"Did that ghost owl just speak?" Catherine whispered to Dan.

"Of course I spoke!" the owl snapped. "What kind of self-respecting owl would do otherwise with humans?" he asked haughtily. He seemed to narrow his eyes at her. "You must be with this Benjamin Arlin fellow," he mumbled irritably. "And I am not a ghost."

Eyethanoff cleared his throat and glared at the owl. "Shasha, get to the point, please," he commanded.

A nearby soldier who had been identified as Hannaff, Solace's guardian, leaned over to me, holding back an amused smile, and mumbled, "Shasha doesn't like mercenaries or pirates and wasn't happy that you were chosen for this mission. Don't mind him, though. He will come around."

I nodded distractedly, focused on this talking owl but appreciative of the explanation.

Shasha fluffed his feathers and stood up a little taller in what I assumed was an owl's version of a frustrated salute. "The shadow armies have settled in the mountains. It appears they will be there for the remainder of the night. The Creature is with them. He seems content to leave us be for now."

"I have all the armor. Why doesn't he come take it like he planned?" I asked.

Eyethanoff shook his head. "He planned to keep your mind trapped just long enough to find out what visions you were having. But you are more of a threat to him now than you ever have been. He will play it smart and take his time. For now, we are safe here." He turned to Shasha. "Keep a close eye on them and report back to me if anything changes."

With a nod, the owl took off, disappearing into the night on silent wings.

Eyethanoff smiled and turned to all of us. "I know what you see is hard to accept. But I would believe Yuuki if I were you. Things will become clear over time, I'm sure. For now, please make yourselves comfortable." He gestured to a soldier of light with shoulder-length brown hair wearing a set of silver Lion's Sword armor. "This is my second in command, Mythair—he will show you your tent for the night." He turned to me. "There is much to talk about. We will eat first. Then we can discuss the questions I see burning in your eyes," he finished with a smile.

Mythair led us to a large tent across the center of camp. The camp consisted of three spacious tents angled out from a central fire pit, with lines of smaller tents stretching between their ends, forming a triangle in the middle. According to Mythair, one of the larger tents was the war tent, one was a mess tent, and the other was the gathering tent, where soldiers assembled to hear their unit's teacher tell stories of the King and the Prince. It was in the gathering tent that we were given places to sleep and told where water was stored so we could wash up for dinner.

"Please keep in mind that many come in and out of this tent on a regular basis," said Mythair. "You may hear stories and group studies, as many soldiers like to share insights about *The Story* and other old texts about the King. They are required to bed down at sundown, though, unless they are on watch. Tonight, the owls are on watch, so the rest of us will sleep."

"Thank you, Mythair," I said with a polite bow that he returned before leaving us to wash up.

"This place is creepy," commented Catherine with a frown.

"I think it's fascinating!" said Dan.

"You sound like Otto," Casey joked.

We all laughed at the memory of Otto, but the laughter died down just as quickly as it had come. We finished washing up and getting settled in, then joined the soldiers for dinner, eager to get our minds off what we had lost.

Chapter 9

WITH THE OWLS APPARENTLY on watch, the soldiers in camp made sure to eat a good meal and take the opportunity to relax and recover from their most recent battle. As we ate, we began to get to know the unit. There were thirty soldiers in the camp, almost a third of whom were those assigned to protect our group, including Solace and the others now gone. Two of the remaining soldiers were trackers, apparently trained in the art of tracking soldiers of darkness. There was also one physician and one cook, and the rest were foot soldiers or cavalry from various countries within Eeffrayldour.

As the meal wound down, we sat around the fire, and the soldiers exchanged stories of places far beyond the lands I knew—stories of the unseen lands. The comradery was high. Everyone laughed and joked with each other like siblings, enjoying the opportunity to tell tales of their adventures to people who had never heard them before. It reminded me of how much I missed Ivan and Nadia. Nadia's soldier of light seemed to catch my mood shift and offered me a sympathetic smile.

After I finished eating, Eyethanoff waved me over to the war tent. Happy to leave behind thoughts of those I had lost, I immediately excused myself from the group and joined Eyethanoff before following him to the map table within the tent.

"I have overheard many discussions between you and your friends during this journey, about *The Story* and your mission. But you were not ready to hear answers until now," he stated as I glanced over the maps.

"Why do you think I wasn't ready before?" I asked, genuinely curious.

Eyethanoff chuckled. "When did you stop doubting this is all real?"

I opened my mouth to answer, then paused. "Well, to be honest, the thought still comes up." I laughed at myself. "I see your point."

Eyethanoff clapped a hand on my shoulder. "It takes time to see clearly, Benjamin. I have lived outside of the Lie my whole life, yet I still struggle with doubt as well."

I frowned. "Really? Aren't you in the Kingdom, a place of freedom from all this?"

Eyethanoff shook his head. "That is the first thing I wish to clear up. I didn't realize how confusing this would be for you, in reference to the three kingdoms. It is important you understand. So, I thought it would be helpful for you to see my maps." He gestured to a large map in the center of the table. "This is Eeffrayldour as I see it," he said.

The map showed a land shaped like an hourglass within a circle of large and small islands. The only part I recognized was a very small portion in the middle. According to this map, the lands I knew as unexplored regions contained all kinds of countries and villages. Each place was labeled with a name I didn't recognize, including the area that appeared to contain the Town. The names of all the places I was familiar with were impersonal and dull. The Town. The Hills. The Crescent Hill. The Forest. The Woods. The Southern Mountains. However, on this map, each of those places had its own unique name. Durthair, the Vardourian Hills, Creal Hill, the Bawtha Forest, the Ath Woods, and the Beldour Mountains. Boundary lines separated various countries and territories, one of which appeared to encompass everything from just south of the Beldour Mountains to just north of the Northern Mountains, called the Fridour Mountains, and was referred to on the map as Alussiathair.

Eyethanoff continued. "Remember, *The Story* says that the Kingdom became unseen when the King created a boundary to protect the people from his own power. So, the Kingdom has been unseen for longer than the Lie existed. The Lie was set over Eeffrayldour, not the Kingdom. We both live in Eeffrayldour, the Forest Kingdom."

"That is why I could see you while holding the sword?" I asked.

Eyethanoff nodded. "The sword gives you the ability to see the world as it really is, or at least parts of it. Not everyone was trapped by the Lie. The Creature's powers are limited. While he has influence over everyone, he was only able to gain complete control over those who feared him deeply enough to serve him directly. They were leaders of this land. Leaders who did not believe the Prince when he came to tell them of his gate—of what he would become. They had forgotten that which is unseen and refused to believe what they did not understand...They refused to believe the simplicity of what the Prince did."

"And what exactly is the unseen?" I asked.

"According to ancient texts, there are three kingdoms. There is the Land Beyond, known as Hargoth, which was ruled by the Creature; the Forest Kingdom; and the Kingdom, which is ruled by the King, Ather, and his son, Sathair. The Land Beyond and the Kingdom are both referred to as the unseen kingdoms. They were separated from Eeffrayldour by the King. They were once seen by our ancestors, but now they cannot be seen and cannot be accessed by the seen. To enter them, we must become something different."

"You mean...die?" I clarified.

Eyethanoff considered the simplification. "Essentially, yes."

I raised an eyebrow. "So, like entering the afterlife?"

Eyethanoff nodded again. "One could say that. The unseen kingdoms are, in a way, outside of this world. Places we are only able to access in death, though some have gone there without dying. But those kingdoms have always existed in connection to this world. Our ancestors saw them when they lived in Tha Athoir, the Father's Land."

I didn't recall seeing that name on the map. "You mean the Kingdom?"

Eyethanoff nodded. "Yes, in Eeffrayldour, we call it Athoir. By the time Ruth wrote *The Story* down, the Lie had changed what she could remember, so she just called it the Kingdom."

I rubbed my forehead. "Okay. I have seen...things. Things I can't explain. Things that have led me to believe that you are telling the truth and all of this exists. But if there are people who do not believe in all of this, they must have a reason. How do we know for sure that this is all real?" I asked. "It seems a little farfetched. Borderline fairy tales and mythology."

Eyethanoff pursed his lips. "Many do call it a fairy tale or mythology. But I tell you, fairy tales and mythology are created by people who wish to explain away their pain with something they can control and understand. This, though," he said, pointing to the center of the map. "This is reality. What is true is not always within our realm of understanding. The Creature uses that which seems impossible to produce shadows of doubt within people's minds. And he uses that doubt to convince us that the unseen is not real. If it is not real, then we have nothing to look forward to—no hope that there is something more than the pain, fear, and conflict, which he uses to gain control. But the King and the Creature, and their kingdoms, are very real, whether people believe it or not. I know because I have fought the Creature's soldiers and I have seen what he can do to those who deny the reality of the unseen," he warned.

I let out a breath. He was right. I had seen it too. This fight was not just imagined. It was real, and we were in the thick of it. "So, the Creature has convinced us to abandon truth under the guise that it is unbelievable..." I said, shaking my head at the idea.

Eyethanoff nodded. "Our ancestors made a mistake by following him. Now, we are suffering the consequences of the corruption they ushered in to the land."

I ran a hand through my hair, glancing over the maps. "Speaking of following, I've been wanting to ask you—where have you been all this time? I tried to contact you several times during our journey, and you didn't answer."

Eyethanoff smiled slightly. "I have been around. Before you began your mission, the Prince came to me in a dream and told me to watch over you and help you until you are free of the Lie. It is my job to fight off those loyal to the Creature as they come for you. But I could not always do that by your side. Some days I had to be elsewhere. Other days I was simply too caught up in battle to come to you when you called. Now that you have all the armor pieces, you will be able to see me and much more...though I am still not entirely sure how the others are gaining their sight..."

"So, I was right. All those times you left abruptly or didn't show up when I called, you were still there, just busy?" I clarified.

Eyethanoff smiled again. "Though we of the Lion's Sword are powerful because of the King's power, we are not the King, nor do we aspire to be. I cannot be in more than one place at a time," he said by way of an answer. His expression turned serious. "That is why you need to be on guard. Even with me by your side, and now others of the Lion's Sword to help, we need to be careful, for the Creature will be coming after you. I saw him reach into your mind before you were freed from his grasp. If he has learned where to look for the Gate, he will place a guard there. And if he finds the Gate, he will corrupt it with shadow, possibly destroying it for good."

I nodded in understanding and looked back to the large map. "The names of places on this map...they are different," I pointed out. "Why is that?"

Eyethanoff nodded. "Mm, that is part of the Creature's lie. He has twisted every aspect of life under the Lie to keep people trapped in dull compliance. He erased even simple truths, starting with the real names of these places, which he replaced with depressing names that inspired lack of interest and complacency." Eyethanoff gazed at the map thoughtfully.

"What?" I asked.

He shook his head. "The Lie has changed over time. The descendants of those who were originally trapped have gradually moved to different locations, but the majority of them settled in your hometown. The strongest, darkest area of the Lie is focused over there now." Eyethanoff pointed to the middle of the map. "The country of Alussiathair, which contains Durthair, where you are from."

"What do you mean the Lie is focused there?" I asked.

"I am not entirely sure, actually. When the Lie was first set in place, it was extensive but spread thin, and people still remembered certain things. But it worsened over time. I was taught that the Creature formed it to prevent people from finding the Gate, intending to make people forget who the Prince was and what he had done to overcome the Creature's power, which would explain why the Lie was so widespread." Eyethanoff rubbed his chin in thought. "But, even though the Lie still exists everywhere, its darkness has gradually become more focused as the people trapped under it have moved into Alussiathair. That area is so corrupted now that most of those outside the Lie will not enter. This is why I have limited resources to help you. Alussiathair was once where Lion's Sword soldiers were trained. But over time, everyone left as the Creature's power over that land grew, and the school was abandoned..." Eyethanoff frowned. "It is as if the Creature is looking for something in Alussiathair."

"He is looking for the Gate," I said. "Right?"

Eyethanoff nodded. "That was my belief for a long time. Still is..."

"But...?" I asked.

Eyethanoff crossed his arms and shrugged. "I am not sure. I could be wrong—at this point, it is really just a gut feeling—but I think there might be something else going on here."

I considered the possibility that the Creature could have a different target. "Either way, he still needs to find the Gate, or he won't be able to keep anyone trapped under the Lie."

Eyethanoff raised an eyebrow. "Correct, and time is running out."

"So, this gate…What exactly does it do?" I asked. "I mean, *The Story* says that the Prince made the Gate to free us from darkness and that he guards the Gate."

"That is true. The Prince is the guardian of the Gate. One could say that, in a sense, he is the Gate. No one gets through the unseen gate without him guiding them."

I recalled my vision in the cave. There had been a wooden door and a transparent door, one I had to open and one the Prince had opened for me. *Could they have something to do with the Gate?* "Like when I received the helmet," I mumbled to myself.

"Yes. Exactly," Eyethanoff responded.

"Okay. But if darkness and evil still remain, even outside of the Lie, then what is the point? If the Prince is, or guards, the Gate, and it is open, so to speak, then why do I have to open another gate?"

Eyethanoff considered my questions for a moment. "Because you need to," he said with a smile.

I narrowed my eyes. "What?" I asked, confused.

Eyethanoff chuckled. "Well, first you must remember there are the two gates, the seen and unseen. They both have a real-world and personal significance. In the real world, they play a part in setting mankind free from the Lie. On a personal level, the unseen gate represents what the Prince can control and you can't—the way back to the Kingdom. The seen gate represents the part of the process that requires your participation—the choice you must make between light and dark. You see, all things work in harmony, Benjamin. The same is true for the Gate. What you see here under the Lie, or anywhere else, for that matter, is related to what happens in the unseen. This connection is a result of something called Eeeye," he explained.

"Eeeye?" I asked, my brow furrowing at the strange word.

Eyethanoff nodded. "You saw its symbol on Trixie's medallion. I bear that symbol on my armor's medallion as well," he said, pulling his blue cloak to one side and revealing his breastplate. At its center, sunken into the armor, was a medallion with the same symbol. "To many viewers, only one shape is visible, but to those who know the truth, both are visible from certain angles," said Eyethanoff with a smile of admiration.

"Is Trixie's medallion part of the armor?" I clarified.

Eyethanoff raised his eyebrows. "I must confess, I do not know for sure. There are many medallions, and not all of them were made only for armor, but they were all made for specific individuals." He shrugged. "If the medallion Trixie found does have anything to do with your armor, it would make sense, as the medallions help those who wear armor develop a stronger connection with the King and, thus, Original Power. But I don't know of any medallion having a connection with the seen gate."

I let out a breath, my hands settling on my hips. "Okay. Maybe Ruth knows." I shook my head, wondering how we were going to find her and if she was even alive. Moving on, I nodded toward Eyethanoff's medallion. "So, you were saying about Eeeye?" I prompted.

"Oh, yes. *Eeeye* is an Eeffraylick word that refers to how certain things are connected. People under the Lie have lost their understanding of the word, but Ruth penned something that I think might help," he said. "When Ruth was helping her first disciple, the second Night Rider, understand how things work, she wrote what is known as the Rule of Eeeye," he continued. "It says, 'For every step seen, there is a step unseen. For every point of success realized, there is an unseen sacrifice made. For what is seen is intricately tied to what is unseen.'"

"So, you are saying that what we see here is tied to what exists in places we cannot see...like when we accomplish something with help that we don't know took place?" I clarified as I pondered how much work the King might have put in to making me successful on this mission thus far.

Eyethanoff nodded. "Yes."

"Okay, so the Gate I need to open just...exists...because the Prince exists?" I asked, my brow furrowing at the thought that it could be that simple.

Eyethanoff smiled. "Yes."

My frown deepened. "But why?"

Eyethanoff considered my question, his smile broadening almost imperceptibly. "In ancient Eeffraylick, the most accurate translation of the word *Eeeye* would be 'the life of two lives.' It is a depiction of a relationship...a true relationship. In a relationship between people in Eeffrayldour, the word *Eeeye* is often used to express a love for someone that is so deep it is hard to explain and cannot be broken. A relationship that cannot be broken by anything made, anything evil, any distance, or any mistake. It is not that it permits mistakes or condones them, but it...endures. Not because it feels it must, but because the clutter of the world pales in comparison to that kind of love. It is...real, true love. Not necessarily the kind where you fall in love, but the kind of love that you would die to preserve."

I nodded in understanding. I was familiar with that feeling.

Eyethanoff continued to the next phase of his explanation. "This kind of love produces the most selfless acts as a seen expression of something unseen. But, as with any true relationship, it is not just a momentary thing. It is also ongoing. It is both a process and a moment at the same time. It is a form of love that takes two individual lives and so deeply intertwines them that they become one, taking on a new life of their own...It is..." Eyethanoff paused, considering the best way to explain his point. "...a story. Two people who are truly dedicated to each other are one life made of two lives, sometimes even before those two lives encounter each other. Those two lives make up one story. A story of their own. A life of two lives."

"Okay."

"Together, two people—or two things—create a unique relationship that works in a cycle of seen and unseen. To make that life of two lives, there is always something seen and something unseen, and the two are intricately intertwined. There are those involved and the connection between them, actions of love and the emotions that produce them, and so on," he said, studying me to see if I was following his logic.

I nodded. "Okay, I think I follow you."

Apparently satisfied, Eyethanoff continued. "Now think of it in terms of the Prince and his people. Eeeye, a true relationship, exists between the Lion of Eeffrayldour and the souls of Eeffrayldour who are loyal to him. When the people betrayed the King and the Prince, an unseen need arose within their souls. Because of the Prince's love for his people, he died, a seen act of love, to overcome the evil that plagued them. That relationship is ongoing, though. Remember, it is the life of two lives. So, when the Lie was put in place, those trapped under it then had a new unseen need—the need for freedom. The Prince saw that those under the Lie needed a physical way out, something that could be seen. So, he produced a seen solution, the Gate you are now seeking. To protect it, though, he made it seen only to those who wear your armor," Eyethanoff finished, watching for my response, as if trying to discern if I needed more information.

I frowned. "So, what you are saying is that the Gate I am seeking is there simply because we need it?" I asked.

Eyethanoff smiled. "Mm, you've almost got it. That is good enough for now."

"But why not just end all evil?" I asked, confused. "How does the Creature have any power if the Prince has given us an out, not to mention the fact that *The Story* says he will come back. Why doesn't he come back now?"

Eyethanoff's brow furrowed. "Be careful what you wish for, Benjamin. According to *The Story*, if he came back now, we would all end up in the Land Beyond, forever," he warned. "Purging a deeply corrupted land of that which has corrupted it will not be a pretty sight. I don't know that we should wish it to happen any sooner than is already planned."

I nodded, remembering that part of *The Story*. "I had never thought of it that way." I let out a sigh.

Eyethanoff placed a reassuring hand on my shoulder. "We are easily distracted by the things we don't understand. We forget we were not made to understand all things," he said.

Just then, Captain Bates and the others entered the tent.

"There you are," said the captain. "Jeb has been getting antsy, so we came looking for you. He won't listen to any of us."

"What is he doing?" I asked, confused.

"He stole my sword belt," complained Catherine.

Before I could tell her he was probably just bored, Dan spoke up.

"What are you two looking a—" he started but suddenly broke off. "Woah!" he said as he saw the map on the table. "Is this where we are?" he asked, leaning over the edge of the table to examine the map more closely. "All these places have different names," he noticed.

I nodded. "That is a map of Eeffrayldour as those outside the Lie see it. Eyethanoff was just explaining some things to me."

Dan nodded, eyes wide, as he and the others bent over the map to examine the real names of each location.

"Durthair..." Casey mumbled. "I like that name much better than 'the Town.'"

"Yeah, I always thought that name was so boring," said Dan.

"Look at this!" exclaimed Christopher. "Even the seas have different names! The Arth Sea, the Waydern Sea...Wow, Captain Bates, you are from the Fridathian Sea! Or somewhere around there..."

"Look, the Channel is called the Lor Channel," said Dan. "What is Lor? Is that a person?"

"That reminds me, did you ask Eyethanoff about the stone?" asked Captain Bates.

"Oh, I forgot." I turned to Eyethanoff. "We found an old journal that seemed to indicate that someone was updating Ruth on the state of the Channel construction way back when it was first built. We thought they were looking for the stone that was removed from the Channel. Do you know what that stone might have to do with the Gate?" I asked.

Eyethanoff shook his head. "There are many stones with special properties given them by the Prince, but I am afraid I do not know of a stone having any connection to the seen gate."

"Are you sure? Otto thought it might be some kind of conductor of the King's power."

Eyethanoff shook his head again. "The Lor Channel was dug when two kings were at war, and it was never proven that the removal of that stone caused the land bridges to collapse. It could have just been from all the digging. However, there are a lot of things I don't know. The Prince has many artifacts that he has created over the years. Maybe it was one of those?" he suggested.

"Hmm...Maybe we were wrong about the stone, then." I rubbed my chin in thought. "Either way, if I am going to succeed, I need more information about this armor I have. You said that medallions help those who wear armor by connecting them to the King and his power...How does that work? Or even better, how does the armor work?"

"Lion's Sword armor is unique," said Eyethanoff, "but I must say your armor was originally made for Ruth and under unusual circumstances, so I am not sure if it is the same as the armor I wear.

However, I can tell you what I know about standard Lion's Sword armor."

"That will work for now. I will verify the rest with Ruth when—if—we find her."

Eyethanoff gestured to some cushions in the corner of the tent, and we all sat down to listen to his explanation. "The armor we wear is said to have been made by the Prince himself, though no one knows how exactly. Each new soldier gains their own set, starting out as something that only the wearer can see and eventually becoming visible to others and fitting the individual in a way that is unique to them and their needs," he explained. "After it becomes visible, it can be removed, but only in a physical sense. The unseen version...behaves differently. This armor protects us from many things, including the Creature and his soldiers. But each piece has a special purpose. The belt shows us the truth and helps us discern what is truth and what is lie. The breastplate guards our hearts from the Creature's corruption. The shoes give us stability and sure footing on any terrain. The shield protects us from the eyes and weapons of the enemy, and the helmet guards our minds from the Creature's tricks."

"So, Otto was right! The shield does hide us from soldiers of darkness?" I asked.

Eyethanoff nodded. "It can make you unseen to dark soldiers and those deeply impacted by the Creature. Until you learn to use it properly, though, you may become exposed at the wrong moment. It works in unusual ways."

"How so?" I asked.

"The shield is dependent on light and faith. The one who wields it must take refuge in light to be shielded from the enemy. We all bear the impulse to hide in darkness. It makes us feel safe because we ourselves can't see into the dark. But the unseen is not bound by what we can or can't see and understand. And because the shield also requires faith to work, it is somewhat dependent on our willingness to use it in the way it was designed."

"So, it can falter if we don't use it correctly?" I asked.

"More accurately, you can falter in a way that impacts your ability to use it properly. That is why I didn't explain it to you when you first asked. Using the shield to hide from the enemy takes experience, not explanation. Based on what I know about you, you in particular need to experience things for yourself. You will learn in time how to use it," he explained.

"Aren't there other armor pieces too?" asked the captain. "What about the sword?"

"Yes, after the helmet comes the sword, which is the only piece said to have been made by the King, for it is said to contain his words. Then, though the armor you wear now doesn't seem to have one," Eyethanoff said, looking to me, "a medallion unites the armor as one object that is deeply connected to the King's power. There are other tools you will discover once the armor is fully united."

"So maybe that is why my armor seemed to call out to the medallion. Maybe it does belong to this armor," I said hopefully.

Eyethanoff nodded. "It would make sense, for you cannot progress through the Lion's Sword training levels without a medallion. Then again, it is Ruth's armor. Maybe you don't have a medallion yet simply because you will receive your own armor after you complete your first trial, which could be opening the Gate."

"Levels?" asked Dan.

"Trial?" I echoed.

Eyethanoff smiled. "The armor has much more to offer than you can see right now. But the wearer must learn important lessons before they can understand how to use the armor the way it was designed. To begin, they must first encounter each piece of armor and choose to accept it, as Ben has been doing. Many must go through a personal trial before they learn to put on the armor in full and complete the first level of training. After that, the levels are less linear. The term 'levels' was chosen simply because it was easier to quantify the concept that way, but it does not always follow the same pattern for everyone. Put differently, these levels are more like stages of understanding. While the one wearing the armor might have knowledge about its abilities, as that person grows closer to the King, they develop more understanding of what he has provided in the armor. Understanding is deeper than knowledge and thus provides a deeper connection. Along the way, there are trials that teach the wearer about each part of the armor and how to use it to the best of their ability." He turned to me. "You are just at the beginning, Ben. There is a lot to learn. But you will know when you have reached the end of the first level, for that is when the voice of the King, sometimes also referred to as the voice of Original Power, presents itself, like a second conscience. It is different for everyone and comes at different times, often when we least expect it, but you will know."

"What level are you?" asked Casey.

"Level five," said Eyethanoff.

Casey grinned.

"How many levels are there?" asked Dan, wide-eyed.

Captain Bates chuckled and shook his head at Dan and Casey's excitement.

"Eight," responded Eyethanoff.

"How long did it take you to get there?" I asked, ignoring Dan and Casey's excitement.

"Not many progress beyond level six. I acquired level five when I was sixty-three," he said.

Casey's jaw dropped open. "What? How is that possible? You don't look any older than Ben!"

Eyethanoff smiled. "My people are human, but we...well, put simply, we live a long time."

"Why is level six where people often falter?" asked the captain while Dan and Casey mumbled to each other, speculating about how old Eyethanoff could be now.

"The armor's effectiveness depends entirely on one's connection to the King, something the Creature actively tries to disrupt. The Creature has a hold on this world—a very strong one. His corruption and chaos impact everyone. His influence over this world makes it very challenging to surpass each level, especially five and six," he explained.

Catherine crossed her arms and raised an eyebrow. "How does he have that much influence if most people don't even believe he is real?"

Eyethanoff's expression turned grave. "The Creature is a master of illusion. He does not need people to believe he is real in order to influence them or even take control of them. He simply needs fear and doubt, things that weaken our connection to the King, to produce enough shadows within us that he can take hold. Even the best of us fall prey to his dealings." Eyethanoff locked eyes with Catherine. "Never forget, darkness is a cruel protector."

"Okay...So, how exactly do the Creature's powers work?" inquired Catherine.

Eyethanoff considered the question. "In training, they explain it with an example," he said as he stood up and grabbed a lantern and a nearby empty clay pot with ornate holes in it, dumping out the collection of water costrels it held. "Whereas the King and his power are light, the Creature and his power are darkness," Eyethanoff began as he returned and sat down with us. He placed the lantern under the clay pot, lighting its interior and casting a beautiful design on the inside of the tent around us. "There are two ways to produce darkness," he said, gesturing to the light inside the pot. "The source of light leaves..." He took the lantern out of the clay pot, leaving the interior dark. Then he put the lantern back under the pot. "Or the source of light dies," he said as he blew out the lantern flame through a hole in the clay pot, leaving the inside of the pot dark again. Eyethanoff turned to us. "Darkness cannot necessarily be created, for it is simply the absence of light. When the Creature chose to betray the King, he rejected the light of Original Power, and he became darkness. But because he had such a deep tie to Original Power, his darkness corrupted the Original Power within him, giving him a twisted power of his own."

"He had the King's power?" I asked. "Why did the King give it to him?"

"Everyone has been touched by the King's power in some way. The Creature once had quite a bit, as do many eternal beings from the Kingdom. But when he corrupted that power through selfishness, he was left with nothing but the power of shadows and evil," he explained.

"So, he is just a shadow of a man?" asked Dan, holding back a smile.

Casey burst out laughing at his best friend's joke, but Eyethanoff frowned. "I would advise you to take his darkness quite seriously, for it resulted in Corrupted Power, which is extremely dangerous," he warned.

Casey and Dan cleared their throats, forcing themselves to become serious again.

"What can he do with that power?" I asked.

"He can build strongholds in our minds and drive us to follow him. He has many skills that are born out of the control we give him in our moments of fear and doubt. He has six main skills that these shadows within us give him. The first skill is called a Stronghold. He uses the shadows of fear and doubt to gain influence over how our thoughts are formed. This can allow him to control how we recall events and how we feel about others. This is the most common tool he uses, and it can be used on anyone, even a Lion's Sword soldier. The second skill is called a Shadow Lie. This is when the Stronghold becomes so strong that the Creature can impact how we remember things and see the world around us. He can make us believe things we would not otherwise believe and forget things we would not otherwise forget. This is also a common tool he uses. His third skill utilizes the second one. If someone gives in to the Creature's influences, he can take over their mind, in a sense, and trap them in what is known as a Shadow Prison. It is at this stage that the individual can become a Martecyte if they stay trapped there for too long. A Martecyte is someone who is so filled with darkness that they are part of the Creature's horde. Like an infection, his darkness and influence spread through them and slowly take from them, eating away at their life and giving him strength. If they are killed at this stage, they simply die, and their death provides enough shadow for a dark soldier to live in, as all dark soldiers must have a shadow of some kind to sustain them. If a Martecyte is not redeemed in this phase, and is not killed, then they will eventually fall to a Shadow Death. This occurs when they fully give themselves to the Creature, and there is no coming back from it. Shadow Death is how someone becomes a soldier of darkness. These soldiers have short lives, as the pain and suffering the Creature uses to keep them under his hold drains them of life. It is these dark soldiers who give the Creature enough power to perform his last two skills, Shapeshifting, his ability to change form, and Shadow Shifting, which is his ability to move certain shadows to protect himself and his dark soldiers."

I recalled my memory loss after my encounter with the Creature at the prison. *That must have been a Shadow Lie or a Shadow Prison.* I swallowed hard. "He has to have weaknesses. What are they?"

Eyethanoff nodded. "His main weakness is that he depends on those he preys upon to gain his power. Each individual must give in. He cannot force anyone under his control. He can only badger them until they give in—they must make the decision. Those who have taken refuge in light are protected. Though they are still susceptible to many of his tricks, they cannot be so corrupted that they become a soldier of darkness."

"So, he stays away from light?" I asked.

Eyethanoff grimaced. "He does, but again, you must understand that you are dealing with things unseen. Not all light that you see is the light you should take refuge in, and not all shadows you see hold the Creature and his soldiers. The light you must take refuge in is the light of Original Power."

"But how do I do that?" I asked.

Eyethanoff smiled. "Faith."

My shoulders sagged.

Eyethanoff put a hand on my shoulder. "Benjamin, belief is a powerful thing. It does not make anything real. It simply gives you access to what is already there."

I straightened again and nodded. "I'm sorry. I just keep expecting something..." I paused, searching for the right word.

"Seen?" suggested Eyethanoff with a grin.

I glared at him. "Yes, I suppose."

He gripped my shoulder. "It is time to let go, Ben."

I nodded. I was trying.

"It seems the Creature has a lot of power," pointed out the captain, bringing us all back to the discussion at hand. "So why did Ruth give up this armor if it would protect her?" he asked.

"The Creature originally formed the Lie to prevent people from remembering the Gate," Eyethanoff said. "He has been spending all his time trying to snuff out that memory from all those under the Lie and destroy the Gate. He stripped the land of its names, erasing the land's history along with them, for in Eeffrayldourian culture, names hold an important significance. He convinced people Adournath was a beast, like his dark beasts of the Beldour Mountains. But Adournath is an Eeffraylick name that means 'beacon of truth.'" Eyethanoff shook his head at the thought of that deception. "Once the Creature had removed the truth that threatened him, he convinced the people under his lie that this land was..." Eyethanoff shrugged. "...hopeless. Then he moved on to ensuring that he could maintain his control. At one point, he discovered that the armor the Prince gave Ruth was the key to finding the Gate, but he couldn't use it himself as it does not work for those who wield darkness. So he went after Ruth in an attempt to corrupt her once again. She had not found the Gate herself, so she decided to hide the armor. She gave it to Eyerkishta, who hid the armor to protect it from the Creature."

"So now he wants it from me?" I clarified.

Eyethanoff nodded. "That is probably the case, though I am not certain he knows what it does in reference to the Gate. I believe he wishes to control you so he can weed his way into your mind to find out what secrets the armor holds."

"Eyethanoff!" a voice suddenly called from outside the tent.

"Excuse me," Eyethanoff said, standing. "I should see what that is about."

I followed him from the tent as the others engaged in conversation with a soldier who came in to check the map. Outside, in the early morning light, a soldier was waiting to speak with Eyethanoff. She had braided white hair with a streak of light blue in it that matched her uniform. "Eyethanoff, the Creature is looking for Ben. He has left the Beldour Mountains sooner than we expected and is on his way here. They are traveling along the central path," she reported in a clipped, formal tone. "Zath is not with them, though. Shasha believes our earlier report was incorrect—Zath does not seem to have left the mountains with the soldiers who headed back to Durthair. There is a good chance he is still up there now."

Eyethanoff nodded. "Thank you, Ahrdah," he said. "Go, tell the others we will be leaving shortly."

Ahrdah offered a respectful bow, then turned and began giving orders to the other soldiers in the camp.

"We need to move now," said Eyethanoff, turning back to me, his tone urgent.

"If Zath is still in the Southern—I mean Beldour—Mountains, he is probably in his caves. We need to find him and retrieve the medallion, but once we get it back, we have nowhere to go. I don't know where the Gate is," I reminded him.

"It doesn't matter. You can't be here when the Creature arrives. Though we won the last battle, he will be bringing more soldiers and beasts this time, and you do not yet fully understand the bond the armor makes available to you. We will retrieve the medallion first, but we need to move fast and be careful. I know a route that will lead us around the path the Creature is taking. If we can get to the mountains before he realizes we are gone, we should be able to make it through without being caught." He began moving away, headed toward the mess tent. "Get ready. We will be leaving for the dragon caves as soon as camp is packed up. You need to retrieve that medallion."

With a curt nod, I headed back into the war tent and explained the situation to the others. "Eyethanoff says we need to leave immediately. The Creature is on his way."

The captain nodded. "Where are we headed?" he asked, his tone telling me he was committed no matter my answer.

I glanced toward the Beldour Mountains. "The dragon caves."

Chapter 10

We packed up camp faster than I could have imagined possible and headed out while the sun was still below the treetops. About twenty of Eyethanoff's thirty-person troop took the camp supplies and traveled a different route in hopes that some of the Creature's soldiers would follow them. They planned to meet us in Durthair, so we would be without them for the rest of our travels. But hopefully they would be able to keep most of the soldiers of darkness off our tail. The rest of us headed back to the Smugglers' Road. With the Creature and his soldiers coming out of the mountains along the central path to find us and us going into the mountains to find Zath, we stuck to less traveled roads, and everyone remained as silent as possible. Eyethanoff took the lead, and I decided to see if Yuuki knew anything that could help us.

"Do you know how to get to Zath's cave?" I asked her as we headed out of camp.

Sitting in front of me in Jeb's saddle, Yuuki nodded. "There are many ways in. But many of them are occupied by beasts. The fastest way there is through a door."

"A door?" asked the captain.

"You mean an invisible door that can be opened with Original Power?" I asked, recalling the Prince opening such a door in the cave.

"You know of them?" Yuuki asked, craning her neck to look at me in surprise.

I shook my head. "Not until just recently. The Prince opened one."

She nodded. "The doors are a common form of transportation among those in the Lion's Sword, but they have their limitations. Much like roads, they are only attached to specific destinations. But there is one that can take you to Zath's cave."

"Then that's where we need to go," I said to Eyethanoff.

Eyethanoff nodded and let me take the lead as Yuuki pointed us in the right direction. We snuck around South Town, which Eyethanoff's map had called Ffairnour, and reached the base of the Beldour Mountains as the people of Ffairnour began to start their day. We headed up a narrow trail, then off the beaten path to the place where I had previously emerged from the Smugglers' Road, passing through the hanging quilt moss. I waved everyone past me, checking to make sure we were not spotted before riding in behind them as we ascended once again into the beast-infested Beldour Mountains.

"This road has many cave entrances. Which is the right one?" I asked Yuuki as we stopped outside a small cave.

Yuuki smiled up at me from her place in Jeb's saddle. "I am still weak from the amount of darkness under this lie. I can only show you the general location. But the door moves. You must find it with the sword."

I nodded and drew the sword, careful not to hit Yuuki on the head with the hilt. With a deep breath, I cued Jeb forward and led the group down the Smugglers' Road toward the dragon caves. As we traveled down the apparently infamous road, sunlight shone through the crack above us, leading the way. We continued past the patches Zath had destroyed and beyond the stone face I had stepped through when the Prince opened the door, heading deeper into the snow-covered mountain range.

"This is near where the Prince sent me through a door. Could we use that door?" I said.

Yuuki and Eyethanoff both shook their heads, but Yuuki was the one to answer. "The Prince makes his own doors sometimes. I don't remember there being one here. Even if it were here, I doubt we would find Zath on the other side. The main cavern is much farther. I don't remember exactly where the door to it is. It's around here somewhere," she said as she examined a few sections of rock. "Unless I'm wrong about where he is probably hiding…The door kind of moves depending on which cave is occupied at the moment."

The day turned into night with still no sign of the Creature or his soldiers—comforting evidence that the rest of Eyethanoff's soldiers had successfully led them astray. On the second day, our trek through the mountains turned stormy. Ice covered everything as a blizzard blew in once we reached the highest point of the Smugglers' Road. But Yuuki was able to lead us to a cave that was unoccupied by beasts.

As we traveled, the sword did not seem to respond to anything the way it had in the past when I was near other armor pieces, and by the third day, I began to worry that we would not find the door.

As the third night fell, I became distracted by the shadows around us. For a moment, I thought I saw a dark soldier watching us, stirring feelings of fear and uncertainty within me. But when I looked closer, there was nothing there. *It must just be my imagination,* I thought.

When we were almost to the other side of the mountains, I glanced down at Yuuki. "Nothing has happened yet," I said. "Are you sure we haven't passed the door?"

She smiled up at me. "What power you have is of the unseen. To access it, you must trust the unseen king," she explained reassuringly. "Have faith, Ben."

With a sigh and a nod, I continued.

We all remained silent as we traveled. Thoughts of being discovered by Zath or stalked by beasts floated in the back of my mind. With this many people, both Zath and the beasts were bound to smell our presence at some point.

Suddenly, the sword went light in my hands. I stopped, dismounted Jeb, and followed the sword to a nearby rock face. I glanced at Yuuki with a skeptical expression. The Prince had opened a door in seemingly empty space. But I was not the Prince.

"There must be another way," I suggested.

Yuuki shook her head. "There is a door here," she assured me. "The doors can only be opened by those who naturally wield Original Power or who have been granted the ability to do so by the King. Those whom the King has endowed with his armor he has given the ability to move mountains. If the sword responds as if there is a door here, there is a door."

I looked at the rock before me. *The King's power.* I recalled what the Prince had done with his hands in the cave when he opened the door. Sheathing the sword, I rolled my shoulders and took in a deep breath, letting go of my doubt as I exhaled. With nothing but a little faith in the King and some determination, I reached my hands out before me. As my palms came in contact with the ice-cold stone, the armor seemed to call out to something. Somehow, I knew it was calling to the medallion. *I guess we are bonding,* I thought with a smile. At that moment, the armor faltered, and the feelings vanished.

"What happened?" I asked Yuuki. "I could feel the power, but then it just...left."

Yuuki smiled. "The *King's* power," was all she said.

I looked at the rock wall and recalled my battle with the soldiers of darkness on the Western Island. I had survived because I put my faith in the King and his power to overcome what I could not. *The King's power,* I repeated to myself. As I released all thought of my own determination and will, I could gradually feel the armor call out again. But it felt as though something was between me and the medallion. It felt like rock in my mind, but it was somehow different. *The door.*

"Now what?" I asked.

"Open the door," she said, as if it were a simple task.

I glared at her. "Don't get smart with me now, Yu—Eyerkishta," I corrected myself.

She giggled. "I'm sorry. Just...focus. And either name is fine with me. I treasure them both," she added with a smile.

I nodded and turned back to face the rock and did my best to concentrate. Not entirely sure how to use something I could not access, I hesitated for a moment. But then my mind moved to thoughts of the King's power. I felt something. The armor stirred at the moment I least expected. Then, light shone from within the sword, and the belt lit up as if in response. The glowing belt and the glowing sword seemed to connect, and the light spread through the armor, then down my arms. It entered my hands, filling them with an almost painful sensation that startled me so much that I flinched, pulling away from the door.

Yuuki chuckled as she climbed off Jeb's saddle and approached me, scrambling up onto a rock so she could reach my hands. "Original Power has a unique feeling, doesn't it?" she said as she gently placed my hands back where they had been. "It feels oddly like fire. To those who are not of the right mindset, it can be quite painful," she explained. "But you are a treasure claimed by light, Benjamin. This power does not belong to you. Power belongs to the King. It flows through you—claims you," she said gently. "I will help you," she reassured.

Yuuki placed her hands on the stone next to mine. She closed her eyes, and I did the same, doing my best to surrender control and let Original Power begin to flow. This time, the light seemed to come from both my belt and from Yuuki. Power flowed from within them, uniting as it made contact with the stone wall, where it burned the rock away like paper. As the stone burned away, it revealed a door made of a much darker stone with a symbol of two dragons wrapped nose to tail around a tree and a stone.

"What is that?" I asked.

"The dragons' crest," responded Yuuki with a distant smile as she examined it, reaching out to run an affectionate hand over its rocky face. "This door leads to what was once one of our homes."

"Inside the mountain?" I asked.

Yuuki dropped her hand and nodded. "Not just inside. The heart of the mountain," she elaborated. "A place even beasts will not roam."

I nodded and wet my lips. Not seeing a handle, I touched the crest at the center of the door. Running my hand around its edge, I saw that the stone of the crest was separate from the rest of the door. I pressed on the crest, and the door opened, scraping against the ground as a gust of cold, earthy air washed over us from within the mountain. On the other side of the door was a massive cavern of rock with a ceiling so high it would have dwarfed even Zath.

"The Creature has probably discovered that the other group of soldiers was just a distraction by now," warned Eyethanoff from behind me, reminding me that time was limited.

Yuuki nodded. "We will stay out here and keep him and his soldiers at bay," she reassured me. "These caves have many entrances and exits. Do not get lost. Be careful."

"I will," I said as I swung into Jeb's saddle and Eyethanoff handed me a torch.

I glanced at the open door and the cavern within. With one last confident nod to the others, I turned Jeb to face the entrance and cued him forward, the lit torch in hand. As soon as we were through the door, it closed behind us and vanished.

As the door vanished, I found myself quite happy that I was holding a torch. The sword had, in the past, lit up at times, as had the shoes. But I had no idea how they worked or how to get them to light up now. And the cave was darker than any place I had been before. The small flames cast dancing shadows on the cavern walls, bringing to life the stone formations around us. The moving shadows sent chills down my spine, and I rested a hand on Jeb's warm, soft shoulder. I was glad to have him with me. But, as we began to walk, I quickly discovered that the noise of his hooves echoed through the cave. *Not great for sneaking up on a dragon.* Thankfully, patches of the cave floor were covered in dirt as well as rock, so we kept to the softer ground, avoiding the rock as best we could.

The ceiling above us was full of long cylindrical pillars that hung down to a point. Many similar pillars reached up from the ground, and I could hear water dripping from deep in the cave. As I glanced over the flickering shadows around me, I became aware that there were no dark soldiers here. It seemed odd to me that they would not use this place as a base of operations, considering the shadows that filled every corner. *Maybe they, too, fear the dragon that lives here,* I thought.

I became more convinced of the idea when I noticed marks on the cave walls that could only have been left by the fire of a dragon. But there was more than burned rocks. As we traveled deeper into the cave, the walls came alive with depictions of dragons—stories of times long past etched into the stone. I saw drawings that reminded me of Eyerkishta's story of her mate, Feyerndur. Details that told of dragons and their families who once lived in a wonderous land, side by side with the humans they had been tasked with protecting.

Jeb and I moved on, keeping a steady pace as I steered him through the stretches of soft dirt that dulled the sound of his hooves. When a rock fell without warning, bouncing off something in the dark distance, Jeb tensed beneath me.

"I know," I whispered as I allowed him to stop. I stroked his neck. "This place is stressing me out too," I said as I glanced around before letting my gaze return to the darkness ahead of us.

Having recovered, Jeb began to pick his way forward again. We gingerly moved through the darkness until I saw another source of light. It was dim and came from the other side of a large rocky ridge. To avoid giving away our location, I snuffed out the torch but attached it to Jeb's saddle to save it for later, just in case.

As we neared the light, Jeb's ears pricked forward, and he offered a low nicker of nervousness. "Shhh," I said, cueing him to remain silent as I scratched his favorite spot at the base of his mane. He took a deep breath as I asked him to stop, and I let him settle for a minute. I needed him confident if we were going to get out of here alive.

I observed my surroundings as I waited for Jeb to relax. For some reason, there were no drawings here. The cave was pretty bare. Just rocks, dirt, and water dripping from unseen places. The air was musty and damp, smelling of earth and a lingering hint of smoke. *Zath must be close.* Jeb finally let out a hard breath and relaxed beneath me. Giving him another scratch, I waited another few seconds before cueing him to move forward. He set out with no hesitation, and we continued up the rocky ridge.

Just before reaching the crest of rock, I dismounted Jeb and told him to stay. Careful to avoid causing an avalanche of dirt and loose rocks, I crawled the rest of the way up the ridge on my belly. As I peered over the edge, I saw the source of light—a massive golden chandelier hanging from the cavern's ceiling—and what it was illuminating.

Below me was an expansive, flat open space cleared of rocks all the way to the walls, which were pocketed with various entrances to the cave. Shiny objects were strewn all over the ground and embedded in the rock walls and the ceiling of stone. At one end of the cave, to my right, was a chair and a bed that looked like they would fit a human. The rest of the space was open enough to easily accommodate the massive body of a dragon.

In the center of the cavern, Zath paced back and forth, mumbling to himself. But he looked different than he had before. I pulled back from the edge of the ridge and closed my eyes. *What is happening down there?* The dragon I saw here seemed completely different from the one that had attacked on the island and on the Smugglers' Road. *Could Yuuki be right about Feyerndur being in there somewhere?* I wondered. *Could it be that Zath is not losing his mind, but rather that Feyerndur is still in there, trying to escape the darkness that has imprisoned him?* I shook my head, not convinced that was the case.

I peeked over the ridge again to examine the dragon. His black exterior, rough like lava rock, seemed to have changed, the scales shrinking to reveal the lava orange scales of Feyerndur beneath. The ground trembled with his pacing, and smoke occasionally puffed from his nostrils as he grumbled under his breath. His face contorted in anger and pain as his self-talk continued, growing louder. As I observed him, I realized he seemed to be struggling between his two selves, switching from the deep but pleading tone of a tired Feyerndur to the angry, thunderous roar of Zath. As each version of himself spoke, his scales seemed to change to match. The ink-black scales seemed to shrink as Feyerndur argued his case, then grew again as Zath retorted.

"Stop it!" pleaded Feyerndur.

"You do not get to tell me what to do," replied Zath in his harsh, gruff voice.

"This is not right!" said Feyerndur desperately. "Let it go!" he pleaded as he paced and shook his head. "Let go," he added under his breath, pulling at the black scales on his head with a clawed front paw as if he were in pain.

"No!" roared Zath, his dark scales expanding suddenly, choking out the bright orange ones of Feyerndur.

Whatever was going on, if I was going to get anything out of him, I had to get him to turn into Valdra. Valdra had seemed more stable, and he knew me. I might have a fighting chance if I could talk to him, for I knew I could not win an argument with the dragon in his current mental state.

Based on the size of the bed and chair, Zath at least occasionally spent some of his time here in his human form. If I could find a way to get him into his human form and restrain him, I could figure out what to do from there.

Then again, maybe he happened to leave the medallion in one of his piles of treasure, I thought. I peered over the ridge again and began scanning the cavern below me in search of the medallion. The closer I looked, the more I realized that not all the treasures had any clear value. Mixed in with gold and silver were random objects and trinkets that appeared worthless. I wondered if Zath was hoarding things simply because it was in his nature to protect treasures and he had no other options as his true charges were lost and out of his reach.

Unfortunately, the medallion was nowhere to be seen. I scrutinized Zath's neck to see if he was wearing it, but his slightly curved jaw horns, wings, and incessant pacing made it hard to get a good view. I didn't see it. Instead, I returned to scanning the cave for anything that could help me. Directly across the cavern from my current position, in the heaps of junk and treasure, I spotted a rope that was attached to another chandelier. It was similar to the chandelier that hung from the ceiling, but this one was much smaller and broken. No matter—it was not the chandelier I was interested in but rather the rope tied to it.

I studied the cavern carefully until I had plotted a concealed route leading to the rope. Then I scrambled backward down the ridge and headed for Jeb, who was waiting nervously right where I had left him.

Maneuvering Jeb around the rocks as quietly as I could, I led him to flat dirt ground where he could remain while I went after the rope. Thankfully, Zath was apparently distracted enough that he didn't notice whatever small sounds we were making. Hopefully it stayed that way. And hopefully he didn't smell me coming.

Telling Jeb to stay put, I snuck around the edge of the cavern, keeping out of Zath's sight, until I reached the pile of junk where the chandelier and its rope were located. Now that I was closer, I could see that this was going to be harder than I had thought. In order to get to the rope, I would have to go around a pile of junk and climb up and between two large boulders protruding from the wall. Then I would have to climb down a small slope into another pile of junk and treasure. And I had to do it all without being seen, heard, or smelled.

I took a moment to examine the climbing challenge before me. It looked like, as long as I stayed close to the wall, I would be mostly in the shadows. Since there did not seem to be any dark soldiers here, sticking to the shadows seemed to be in my best interest. But still, to avoid being seen, I would need to make sure Zath's back was to me. Hopefully his present state would keep him occupied and distracted.

With this plan in mind, I began the climb. The rocks were slippery in places due to water dripping on them, probably through a small unseen crack in the ceiling high above me. But thankfully there were various large hand and footholds that I could take advantage of. I climbed up the first big boulder and slithered feetfirst in between the two rocks to get down the other side. Twisting onto my belly, I slipped between the rocks protruding from the wall as quietly as I could. I slid out on the other side and placed my boot on a rock to steady myself. But the rock was not as big as I thought, and my foot slipped. I slid down the smooth slope on my stomach and landed with a faint crunch on a pile of junk.

Suddenly, the noisy argument between Feyerndur and Zath stopped. I froze. Unable to see him over the junk heaped around me, and with no place to go, I had no choice but to lay still and stay quiet.

The ground gently shook as Zath ambled closer and closer, until the smell of smoke wafted through the air above my head. I forcibly calmed myself. So far, Zath seemed to have missed the presence of both Jeb and me. He hadn't shown any signs of having seen or smelled either of us. But there was no way he couldn't smell me now. Not this close.

I heard him grumble in Feyerndur's voice, "Don't change. Don't change. Go back. Go back."

Finally, the sound of his footsteps fell silent and he seemed to stand still for a moment, as if he were deciding what to do. Then his argument with himself resumed, and he retreated in the direction he had come.

I let out a silent breath and reached for the rope. The chandelier that it was tied to was broken in pieces, and I had to pull on it very slowly to keep it from making more noise. Finally, the chandelier was close enough, and I untied the rope, coiled it up, hooked it over my shoulder, and began the precarious climb back through the rocks. Now all I needed was for Zath to turn into Valdra.

As I returned to Jeb, it dawned on me that I had no idea when or why Zath might turn into Valdra. But I didn't have much choice. I needed him to turn, as his human form would be easier to contain. The problem was that the only thing I could think of that might possibly cause him to change was me. He had fought and spoken to me in his human form many times, but I had only seen him transform from Zath to Valdra out of frustration because the shield had protected me from his fire. *I really hope I don't have to start a fight to get him to change forms,* I thought. It would be a deadly challenge in these caves.

I led Jeb along the base of the ridge to a section of the cave that provided a clear view of the dragon but allowed us to remain concealed behind some rock formations protruding from the ground. Then I settled down to wait for what felt like hours. Zath's argument with Feyerndur continued, eventually fading to occasional grumbles as he began meticulously organizing one section of the treasures. Zath's rough black exterior was like a fluctuating cage that Feyerndur desperately wanted to escape. His longing for freedom just barely kept him visible beneath the darkness.

Eventually, with a shake of my head, I decided that maybe a fight was what it would take. I drew the sword in hopes that its power might help me win such a fight, and I was reminded of the sentence on its blade. I ran my hand over the words and wondered if I had all the pieces of the armor. Trixie had thought that the sentence said, *"When truth be known has strengthened thee, the Lion's Sword will set you free."* I recalled the Ice Dragon telling me to be strengthened as she granted me the spirit of the sword. *Maybe I do have all the pieces.* I glanced in Zath's direction and wondered if I really needed the medallion or if I was just making things up at this point to avoid facing the Creature again. But something in me told me I wasn't making anything up. I had to get that medallion. But as I listened to the arguing dragon, doubt seemed to come out of nowhere, and I suddenly wasn't so sure I could find the medallion. Then I had a thought. *What if I could get Feyerndur to help me?* I immediately shook my head at the idea as, based on what I had witnessed so far, Feyerndur seemed too far gone. He had been lost to darkness for so long that I had little hope he could return to his former self.

I watched Zath fight within himself and found myself feeling sorry for him. While his corruption did not make what he did okay, it did bring something to mind. *I am just as messed up as he is; we both are filled with darkness.* I had killed innocent people in the name of what I now knew was evil. *Maybe we are not all that different. Maybe the only difference between Valdra and me is that I found the right path and he is still shrouded in darkness.*

Zath slowly calmed down until finally his demeanor turned dark and broody rather than argumentative as Feyerndur seemed to recede within him. The cracks in his dark scales grew smaller, concealing the orange beneath. For whatever reason, probably exhaustion, Feyerndur gave in to the fight, and the darkness took over. *I know the feeling,* I thought.

Zath settled in the center of the cavern, brooding. He grew completely quiet, and his eyes seemed to stare at nothing, a part of him locked away. Taken hostage. Finally, he began to transform. His wings vanished and he shrank in a cloud of black fog. But as Valdra emerged, he listed to one side, catching himself on a nearby pile of junk. The fight was wearing him out. Valdra wearily walked to his chair, slumped into its seat as the last evidence of scales faded from his skin, and rubbed his temple with two fingers as if in pain. "Just a little longer," he mumbled to himself. "Just a little longer."

What does he mean by that? I wondered. *Just a little longer till what?* I watched Valdra for a moment, then studied the cave, trying to figure out how to approach his position. Not wanting to give away my presence, I moved slowly around the rocky ridge and worked my way closer until I came out behind Valdra. With him tired from his ever-fluctuating internal fight, now was my chance.

I placed each footstep as deliberately and precisely as I could, coming up behind his chair. The chair had a high back that I could not see through, but I heard Valdra let out a sigh on the other side, giving me a reference point for where his head was. I sprang. With the sword still in my hand, I lurched over the back of the chair and struck him on the temple with the sword's hilt, knocking him out cold. Valdra's body went limp, and, sheathing the sword, I immediately got to work.

Using the rope I had found, I tied Valdra's hands in front of him where I could see them and secured him to the chair. Then I stepped back and examined him. I had worked with Valdra for years. We had once been friends and fought side-by-side in multiple wars. But I had changed. The night I had seen Adournath in the Woods—the Ath Woods—had changed me and started me on the path that led us here. Valdra was the man, or dragon, who had played a part in setting the world as it was—who had left me in hopelessness by killing my family and friends. On top of that, he had pretended as if it hadn't happened. I took a deep breath as anger rose within me. Time to get started.

Chapter 11

I CALLED JEB UP from where he had been waiting and grabbed my costrel from the saddlebags. I took a sip, then splashed Valdra in the face. Valdra snapped awake, gasping and sputtering at the cold water. He glared at me, his black, shaggy hair dripping. But the anger in his eyes was far outweighed by exhaustion. The look caught me off guard, causing my anger to fade. But just for a moment. I found myself wondering if that was his play—make me see he was as tired and depressed as I had been when this all started and maybe convince me to go easy on him out of pity.

"Why are you here?" he snapped, seemingly unconcerned about his restraints.

"Why do you think?" I snapped back. "Where is the medallion?" I demanded.

Valdra slumped in his chair as his eyelids drooped in a disinterested expression. "Why should I tell you?" he asked, his tone annoyed.

I frowned. "Because you know as well as I do that everyone will talk if they are..." I searched for the right terminology. "...properly motivated," I said with a smile.

Valdra's expression remained passive. "I know you," he said. "You won't do anything I can't handle."

"Do you really know me?" I asked. "Things have changed. It is no longer my job to please your precious leader," I sneered. "Everything you once saw me do to the enemies of General Delaney I will now gladly do to him and his people."

Valdra's expression wavered slightly at the realization that my loyalty to the general had kept me under control, and that loyalty was gone. It was a bit of a gamble on my part because I was loyal to someone who might not want me to do things the way I used to do them. But Valdra didn't need to know just how much I had changed. I smiled again, a little wider this time, and Valdra's jaw clenched in defiance, his flicker of fear passing faster than I had hoped. His top lip twitched almost into a sneer, but then he looked away and grumbled, "Do whatever it is you came here to do."

Valdra's demeanor triggered memories of how morally compromised I had been before this mission started. I hesitated, trying to decide how I should handle this situation. But I didn't have time to waste. I needed that medallion.

"Where is the medallion?" I demanded as I set the thought aside.

Valdra tensed. "You won't find it," he growled.

I examined Valdra's expression. He was sweating, his jaw set in a manner that suggested he was fighting some kind of silent battle. Feyerndur was growing stronger. Something told me Valdra, or Zath, would not be able to conceal his presence much longer. *"Just a little longer,"* he had told himself. I pondered again what he could mean by that. *What is he waiting for?*

"What are you keeping it for?" I asked. "It is useless without the armor."

Valdra's eyes darted away for a moment before returning to mine, but he remained silent.

Valdra's reaction triggered an epiphany. "You don't know why you took it, do you?" I asked with a grin. There was a chance that Valdra was not entirely in control. There was a chance that Feyerndur was not as far gone as I had thought.

"Keep out of this!" Valdra snarled as a battle waged in his eyes.

I had struck a nerve.

"Keep out of what?" I asked. "Where is the medallion and why do you have it?" I demanded again. "Did your better half take it?" I asked, referring to Feyerndur. I watched Valdra's face for the slightest confirmation that I could be right.

Valdra attempted an irritated frown, but his body tensed again, and the corners of his eyes wrinkled as if he were in pain. I was nearing the truth. *Maybe it wasn't Valdra or Zath saying "Just a little longer." Maybe it was Feyerndur.* I looked at Valdra and decided to rephrase my question to see how he would react. "Feyerndur took it, didn't he?"

In response, Valdra suddenly lurched forward, throwing his weight against the ropes that restrained him, as if he couldn't contain what was inside him any longer and anger was his last resort. "You came here to kill me, didn't you?" he yelled. "Well, do it! I helped the Creature make those beasts. I helped him kill your family. I am to blame, so take your revenge!"

But I could see a deep pain in his eyes—one I understood. He was simply trying to rile me up. Something about my question had set him on edge, and I had a pretty good guess as to why. The part of him still tied to the Creature was fighting to keep Feyerndur trapped. If I killed him now, then Feyerndur would never taste freedom, and the medallion might be lost forever.

"No," I said plainly. "I will not kill you. But I will drag the location of that medallion out of you if I takes me all night!" I snapped.

Valdra had apparently had enough. Zath seemed to erupt from within him, snapping the ropes I had so foolishly thought could hold him. "If you will not kill me," he growled, "then I will kill you!"

I bolted for the other side of the cavern but wasn't fast enough to escape. He struck out with a paw, and I felt the impact, then saw the cave wall sail by as I flew through the air like a sack of potatoes. The armor held up, but I hit the ground hard. Lying flat on my back, a thought popped into my head as if the impact had dislodged it from the back of my mind. The sword had called out to the medallion when I was looking for the door. Maybe it would do it again. I placed a hand on the sword's hilt and was instantly rewarded. The armor and the sword felt suddenly different, as if they were calling to something. Something nearby. *It is here!*

I scrambled to my feet as Zath let loose a stream of fire. Grabbing the shield, I managed to get it into position just in time. The flames came so fast, though, that I didn't have time to brace myself. Their force collided with the shield, knocking me off my feet and sending me rolling as the fire let up. I awkwardly scrambled behind a huge rock just in time to avoid being burned to a crisp by Zath's next blast. It seemed like a miracle that I made it to cover fast enough. *Feyerndur must be doing all he can to keep Zath under control, or I surely would have been killed by now.* But whatever he was doing, it was barely enough to stop Zath's fire each time it almost overwhelmed me.

As the fire let up again, I peeked out from my hiding place and searched the cave for the medallion, feeling the call of the sword to what might be the final piece of the armor. But the medallion was nowhere in sight. *If it is in one of those piles of dragon treasure, I am doomed.*

Zath stalked toward my hiding place, and I knew I couldn't stay where I was. I took a risk and darted out from behind the rock, headed for Jeb, sticking to the shadows outside of Zath's vision. But something got his attention. Just as I got to Jeb, Zath swung around to face me. I grabbed Jeb's mane and cued him to bolt as I swung into his saddle, ducking under Zath's swinging paw as he made another attempt to wipe me out of existence. Barely outrunning Zath's attack and his next burst of fire, Jeb and I turned down a tunnel, exiting the main cavern and plunging into darkness.

Jeb's speed faltered in the low light, but the shoes of armor gradually lit up, giving him just enough illumination to keep his footing and take each stride, propelling us forward. As we ran down the unfamiliar tunnel, Yuuki's warning to not get lost in the caves rang in my head, and I suddenly realized Zath was not following us.

I pulled Jeb to a stop, keeping him in place as he pranced nervously beneath me. Silence fell, broken only by the sound of Jeb's hard breathing. I looked around, but I could not see into the darkness.

Tense and unsure, I cued Jeb to walk on. He took one step forward, and rock erupted just a few feet before us. Zath came slithering out of the stone onto the path ahead. Startled by the dragon's sudden appearance, I scrambled to get a grip on Jeb's mane as he reared, but I was too late. Jeb's neck struck me in the shoulder as I tried to move my head out of the way. The force of the impact threw me backward so fast his reins slipped through my fingers before I could tighten my grip, and I fell, hitting the ground hard as the wind was knocked out of my lungs.

I gasped for air, unable to tell Jeb to run. He hesitated, wanting to stay near me. Zath ignored Jeb and stalked toward me, his black scales, resembling lava rock, making him blend into the dark, stony terrain.

"You think you can come into my home and take what is rightfully mine?" yelled Zath from the near total darkness as he came to stand over me. His voice was like thunder, deep and penetrating. His breath was hot on my face, accented by the smell of smoke now burning my eyes.

"That medallion is not yours." I coughed, still trying to catch my breath. "It was the Ice Dragon's charge," I said, not knowing if that was true but hoping the mention of Feyerndur's mate would rattle Zath.

Zath's dark eyes were black with red surrounding the narrow pupil, but at my mention of Eyerkishta, the orange of Feyerndur's eyes broke through. The color of the irises fluctuated back and forth as though an internal struggle had been triggered. *He is in there and he can hear me.*

Zath shook his head as if trying to clear Feyerndur's presence from his thoughts, then leaned forward, his nostrils within inches of me. "You cannot manipulate me," he growled. His front paw clawed at the ground and his jaw set hard. Feyerndur was barely keeping Zath under control.

As if it would help him gain the upper hand, Zath raised his head high and let loose a ground-shaking roar that threatened to bring the mountain down around us. Dirt and stones crumbled from the tunnel's ceiling as he snarled, "You cannot have him, and you cannot have the medallion!"

Zath's roar had left my ears ringing, and I could barely make out his words. But I knew at some point, Zath would regain enough control to kill me. I had to move. I struggled to my feet and drew the sword in defense, standing only inches from Zath's massive jaws.

"Then why are you trying so hard to hide Feyerndur from me?" I asked, hoping to drag this conversation out just long enough for me to get my bearings and find a way out of this tunnel. Then I saw it. Standing this close, the shoes of armor just barely provided enough light for me to catch a glimpse of it. A mysterious chain hung around Zath's neck. It was hard to tell if the metal links were solid or made of the fog that swirled around them. The chain looked tight, digging into Zath's black scales so deep it touched the surface of Feyerndur's scales below. A length of chain extended from his neck into the darkness behind him. I hadn't seen the chain before, but knowing what I knew now, that didn't mean it hadn't been there. *Or perhaps the chain is new,* I thought. *Maybe I can make a deal.*

Angry at my question, Zath opened his mouth to spit flames that would be too powerful for me to withstand at this proximity.

"I can free you," I announced quickly.

Zath closed his mouth and examined me. His tension seemed to ebb and flow as if he were deciding whether my statement was meant for him or Feyerndur.

"You are trapped here in this mountain, aren't you? Did the Creature do this to you after you failed to kill me on the Smugglers' Road?" I asked.

Zath narrowed his eyes and tilted his head to send a searing stare directly at me. Then his lips curled as he chuckled. "Do not think you understand. This chain locks me nowhere," he said with a growl as his eyes grew even darker than before. Then his chuckle faded, and his expression turned serious again.

Taking slow steps backward as he spoke, I tried to put some distance between us without triggering an attack. Zath growled, and I instinctively lifted the shield in defense. But no fire came. Only more growling. I lowered the shield just enough to see Zath over the top. Feyerndur's orange scales flared as the black scales shrunk more than ever before and his eyes shone orange. "It's here," Feyerndur managed to get out before the dark scales overtook him once again.

Zath shook his head in an attempt to get rid of Feyerndur. "You know nothing!" he snarled at me, his anger giving him an edge over his other self.

But I was not listening to Zath, for at Feyerndur's words, the medallion was revealed. It was right where it had been before, attached to the chain around his neck. I must have been right. It was Feyerndur who had taken the medallion. *Maybe that is why I didn't see it,* I thought. *It is connected to Feyerndur, not Zath.*

Suddenly, Zath charged, and everything slowed for just a moment as I felt the sword call out to the medallion. The medallion momentarily shone brighter, light coming from within and threatening to break apart its stony surface before it faded. Then all returned to normal as I reacted, dodging Zath by rolling forward underneath him. As I scrambled out from behind him, my mind raced to come up with a way to take the medallion from around the neck of the corrupted dragon. *I have to get him out of the caves.* With that thought in mind, I ran.

Not knowing entirely where I was headed, I ran around Zath, ducking behind the shield and diving behind stones with each swing of his paw and launch of fire. As I sprinted down another tunnel, having completely lost my bearings, the sound of Jeb's distant nicker drew me to the right, down a larger tunnel. He must have headed down a different route while I was struggling with Zath. I took a deep breath as I put in a burst of speed, trusting that the shoes of armor would keep me from stumbling in the dark. I banked around a corner to the left, then right, doing my best to follow Jeb's calls, and spotted the welcome sight of daylight ahead.

Zath, barely hindered by the sharp turns, pursued me through the tunnels. As we came to the exit, Zath launched himself at me, and I dove for the snow-covered ground outside. Rolling to a crouch, just out of Zath's reach, I quickly scanned for Jeb, but he was nowhere to be seen. I still appeared to be within the Southern Mountains but in a lightly forested area surrounded by rockier terrain. The early morning sun was just beginning to spill through the mountain peaks to my right. I pushed myself to my feet, preparing for Zath's inevitable attack. I wasn't entirely sure where I was, but I needed that medallion, so I stood my ground with the sword and shield before me.

Zath came at me head-on, and I rolled underneath his blast of fire. He swung a paw, striking me in the shoulder and launching me to the side. I hit the ground, sliding into a rock. The armor held up, but this time it felt different. It guarded me from the blow enough for me to keep my breath, as if it had anticipated the impact. I was growing tired, though.

I tried to pick myself up, but I could not get my fatigued muscles to move fast enough. Instead, I managed to roll onto my stomach in time to see Zath headed my way. The image of him barreling down on me sent enough of a jolt through my body that I managed to twist out of his way, rolling over a couple times before scrambling behind a tree just as Zath snapped it in half with a paw, barely missing my head. Still crouched behind what was left of the tree, I turned to face him. I sucked in a deep breath and held the shield over me to defend against Zath's hot, fiery breath, which I knew would come next. The fire hit hard, shoving me backward and gouging a path through the snow and mud. As the fire let up, I stood to face Zath again, the mountain behind him framing his massive size. All alone, I felt my fear bristle, causing the hairs to rise on the back of my neck. I was facing impossible odds. But I had to get that medallion.

I raised the sword. "I will not stop until I have the medallion!" I yelled, trying to boost my confidence with my brash words. But it didn't work. Though I had armor with great power, I was just a man, and each blow reminded me of that reality. I didn't stand a chance.

Zath swung a paw at me but barely missed as I ran underneath him again, toward his belly. It seemed that the saftest place to fight a dragon was much closer than one might think, assuming you were agile. Zath immediately backpedaled, trying to step on me, but I managed to dodge his massive, clawed feet. With no way to get to his head, I stabbed the sword into his foreleg between two black scales, hoping I could use it to get a leg up.

Zath growled in anger as my sword pricked his thick, nearly impenetrable skin. The sword, though filled with the King's power, didn't penetrate deep enough to stay in place and hold my weight. So, I abandoned the idea, sheathed the sword, and grabbed one of Zath's big black scales with my hands. The scales were rough and only protruded enough for me to get a questionable grip, but it was the only option I had. I climbed up his leg as he lifted his paw and tried to shake me off.

I grasped his scales tightly, but my fingers were cold, and I slipped. As I fell through the air, Zath's bared teeth registering in the corner of my eye, I groped for one of the horns protruding from his jaw. Managing to wrap both arms around the horn, I held on tight as Zath snapped at empty air, my grip keeping me out of reach as he turned his head. Seizing the opportunity, I let go with one arm and let Zath's momentum swing me toward his shoulder, where I planted a foot on a scale like I was climbing a rock wall and pushed up hard while letting go of his horn completely. Briefly suspended in midair, I reached for the chain around Zath's neck, hoping it was solid enough for me to grab. Thankfully, its foggy appearance was deceptive. I gripped it tightly and held on as Zath swung his head from side to side.

Hanging from one hand, I reached for the medallion but pulled my hand back as Zath tried to scratch me off with one of his hind paws. His claw struck armor, scraping across the shield at my back with a piercing metallic screech, and I curled up as tight as I could, managing to get my body of out harm's way behind the shield. Switching to a new tactic, Zath spread his wings, taking to the air. My eyes widened in fear as I watched the ground vanish beneath us, and I abandoned the medallion. I desperately clung to Zath with one hand still gripping the chain and the other grasping a scale on his shoulder.

As we sailed toward the heavens, I took a moment to get my bearings and make sure I didn't fall. Then I began to pull on the chain, still hanging on to Zath's scaly shoulder with my other hand and digging in with my feet. It took a moment to get the chain to move, but after a good couple tugs, it slid between the dark scales, and I rotated it around Zath's neck to get to the medallion. Just as the medallion came within my reach, Zath shook himself in midflight like a wet dog. Between the cold air turning my fingers to ice, Zath's shaking, and the wind bombarding me, I finally lost my grip again. This time, there was nothing else to grab but the medallion. I snatched my hand out in an attempt to take hold of the stony object, but I missed, and only my finger came in contact with its rough surface.

As my finger touched the medallion's edge, the world around me suddenly transformed, and I was immersed in a vision.

Silence fell, and I found myself standing on solid ground. Gradually, I became aware of the sounds of nature. Some sounds were familiar, like the gentle whispering of a stream and the chirping of birds. Other sounds were new—elaborate trills and grunts of creatures I had never heard before—and I realized where I was. I was standing in Eeffrayldour. At least, that was my first thought, but then I wasn't sure. I remembered Eyethanoff's explanation of the Kingdom versus Eeffrayldour, and I realized I couldn't be certain which place this was.

For a moment, I thought I was alone. Then I saw the Prince—the Carpenter. He stood on a nearby hill and waved to me.

"Come up here," he called.

I walked up the hill and stood beside him. Together we looked out at the scene before us. The land was amazing. The stone castle built into a mountain, which I had seen in the vision of the sword, overlooked a wonderous dreamlike landscape. The details were hazy, yet somehow, I felt drawn to this place, as if I were meant to be here.

Whether this was really one of the Unseen Lands or just the way I imagined they would be, I didn't know. But I did know one thing. It was calming. An air of peace came over me that so contrasted the rush of battle that it took me a moment to calm my mind and let go of the need to be on guard. I found myself tripped up, though, by the thought that I would have to leave this place at the end of this vision. I did not want to leave. Eyethanoff's explanation of the difference between living under the Lie and outside of it had seemed muddled and confusing. But if living outside the Lie was anything like this, I wanted to live there. Compared to this place, living under the Creature's lie felt like living in a suffocating cloud of smoke. I wished I could stay here. Wished this wasn't just a vision.

The thought of returning to live under the Lie reminded me of all my failures. The killings, the lies, and even the manipulations I had tried to use with Zath. He was in pain, suffering under the Creature's oppression, and I had simply pushed his pain aside to focus on my own objective. I had put myself first, just as I had with Solace. I remembered Eyethanoff's explanation that even he struggled with doubt and the Creature's influence outside the Lie. If I was fighting for freedom from the Creature's lie, but his oppression still existed in a different form outside of it, what was the point? I could still fail. I would still fail. And both under the Lie and outside of it, others depended on me to succeed. To protect them from these evil unseen forces.

"What is wrong, my friend?" asked the Prince.

The Prince's voice shattered my depressing thoughts. I had almost forgotten he was there. I let my gaze fall from the view before me to the ground at my feet as I pondered the question.

"Eyethanoff explained that the Creature's oppression still exists outside the Lie. That it impacts everyone. In a way, it sounds worse than the wars with the beasts. In other ways, it sounds better. But…" I looked at the Prince. "I fear failure. I thought that I was supposed to free you so you could come rid us all of this pain and suffering. But it turns out that you are freeing us so we can free others from pain and suffering. I don't know that I have it in me to succeed at that mission. What if I don't get the medallion? What if I lose the armor?" I shook my head.

"You will not lose it," he said reassuringly, "for it was mine to give, and it is only mine to take. And I will not take from you what I gave with my life."

I looked at the Prince for a moment. "But why?" I asked. "Why give your life for me? For the people who chose darkness over this?" I said, gesturing to everything around us. "Over you! And who still do, even outside the Lie."

"Because I love my people, Benjamin. And you are one of my people."

Something Ruth told me once echoed in my mind. *"Thankfully for us, true love is not bound by what we deserve."* But for some reason, I still had trouble believing it. "If you love us so much, why did you leave us in the dark, alone? Why didn't you show your face until now?" I asked, genuinely trying to understand. "Why does pain and suffering exist anywhere?"

"I did not leave you," the Prince explained gently.

"I don't understand," I said with a frown.

The Prince smiled. "Some things cannot be understood when we look at them from the wrong perspective."

"What do you mean?" I asked.

The Prince reached into his sky-blue cloak and pulled out the medallion I had last seen hanging from Zath's neck. Before I could voice my surprise that he had it, he answered me. "This symbol on the medallion, the symbol of Eeeye, appears different depending on how you look at it. But that doesn't mean what you cannot see is not really there. It doesn't mean you have to understand why part of it is only visible from some angles. Sometimes, you simply have to look at it differently." He raised his eyebrows. "And sometimes, you don't have to know all the answers to understand what matters most. What this symbol stands for."

"Eyethanoff tried to explain it to me," I said with a nod. "I didn't fully understand."

The Prince smiled again. "Some things are hard to explain because they were made for action, not words, and built on the unseen, which cannot be fully grasped by that which is seen. That is why faith is so important."

"What is the medallion for?" I asked.

"You know already, for it is something you used even before you had the armor. But to fully understand it, you must first understand the armor."

"Will you teach me?" I asked.

The Prince's smile softened and responded with an explanation. "The armor was created to protect you from the Creature and the Lie he put in place. You need all its protection to stand and face him and his deceptions. The belt is where it begins, for your foundation must be truth—the truth of who I and my father are. The truth of Original Power. Everything else will lead you astray. The breastplate is next because your heart must be protected, and to be so, its true state must be revealed—what it contains and what it is missing. The truth of your heart, of who you really are, leads you to seek that missing link. What you miss is light, my friend. But the shoes will take you to it. They will show you the way, the only way, and on the way, you will stand on firm ground no matter the terrain. To fully stand firm, you must have faith in the unseen, for unbelief is the only barrier between the way and where it leads. If you have faith, no battle can move you, for what can be seen can be moved, but what cannot be seen is written on your heart, now protected by armor, and is not dependent on this changing world. For once you stand in truth and walk by faith, you will be free to battle darkness no matter the odds, not because of your strength but because of the strength given to you. A strength that will not fail even when you tire. And when you are free to fight, the sword will come to your aid, for my father's words give this armor its power and, in turn, give you the power to stand and fight the battle before you. But the armor is all connected, for truth not only provides a firm foundation, but its power is a weapon unmatched.

"And the medallion?" I asked.

"Truth is only powerful when its source is unshakable. And so, we return to the foundation. A foundation of truth must be reinforced by someone outside of you, for a foundation is only as strong as the one who created it." The Prince looked at the medallion. "It is the medallion that reconnects that power to the one who gave it in the first place, completing the circle." He ran his finger around the circular edge of the medallion, then looked at me. "This medallion offers you a deeper connection to a power not your own, the power found in Eeeye. A connection stronger than anything the Creature can touch."

I nodded. "Eyethanoff told me about Eeeye. A connection between the seen and unseen."

The Prince half shrugged. "That is an easy way to explain it to those who cannot see. But in Tha Athoir, where all is seen, Eeeye has nothing to do with sight. Eeeye is about a connection. A true relationship. An unbreakable covenant. The kind written on the heart."

I raised my eyebrows. "Eyethanoff told me a bit about that. But where is the power in a simple connection, or relationship, as you call it?"

"The power is in who you share that relationship with," he explained. "But you must dedicate yourself to that relationship, wholeheartedly, in your thoughts, your words, and your deeds. In the unseen core of your heart is a void waiting to be filled with the power that once dwelled there, for only in the depths of that relationship will we become united."

"So how does it work?" I asked.

The Prince gave me a soft smile. "As I said, some things were made for action. But there is power in the simple act of asking from a place of faith, for if you ask, my father will answer."

"But I live in darkness, a place where his power cannot go. How is this possible?" I asked.

The Prince gave me a pondering look as though deciding whether to answer. "I have paid the debt you owe to darkness," he said simply, then paused, watching me.

"What must I do?" I asked with conviction.

The Prince smiled. "Follow your compass, and—"

Suddenly, something collided with me, and I felt myself being pulled from the vision. I tried to hold on to it, desperate to know the rest of the Prince's words. But there was nothing I could do, and the vision vanished.

Having been abruptly torn from multiple visions before, I accepted my circumstances and focused on my new surroundings. I found myself in the grasp of Zath's massive paw. He must have caught me in midair, pulling me from the vision, which had apparently all taken place in a matter of seconds.

"You cannot escape that easily," he growled, unfazed by my failed attempt to steal the medallion. I saw his eyes shift from red and black to orange and what looked like yellow, then back. Feyerndur was in there. "Give me the helmet!" he roared, and for a moment I couldn't tell if it was Zath or Feyerndur speaking. Torn between his light side and dark side, Zath was angry and desperate to get the helmet. "Give it to me now!" he roared.

"No." I grunted as his grip on me tightened, and I struggled to keep him from crushing me.

My desire to escape from his grasp quickly vanished when Zath lifted me higher into the air, then took a nosedive straight for solid ground. I clamped my eyes shut, fully expecting to be smashed into the ground below, but then Zath suddenly jerked to the side and let go of me. Falling the last few feet to the ground, I barely managed to avoid a headfirst impact. I awkwardly rolled to the side, coming to a stop on my back in a pile of snow.

With a groan, I forced myself to roll over and look for whatever had knocked me loose from Zath's grip. Before me, Eyerkishta clashed with Zath, their arms locked in battle, their jaws open wide, their tails balancing them as they stood on their hind legs. Despite Eyerkishta's slightly smaller size, she was holding her own. Clawing at Zath, she swung her massive white tail through the air, smashing it into the side of his head. I scrambled out of the way just as Captain Bates appeared at my side and helped me stand.

"Did you get it?" he asked.

I shook my head. "No, but I had a vision," I said, out of breath as I stumbled to my feet. "We definitely need to get that medallion."

"Maybe she can get it?" he suggested, gesturing to the battling dragons.

"Good idea," I said with relief at the idea that I would not have to continue this fight alone. "It is around his neck. I don't know if she can hear us, but we can try to call out to her," I explained, exhaustion expelling any other ideas that might have been more effective.

Before the captain could respond, Eyethanoff's soldier Ahrdah burst through the trees. "We have to go! The Creature has broken through Eyethanoff's defense, and we are outmatched. We are out of time!" she announced as five more soldiers spilled through the trees behind her.

Whether it was the presence of the Lion's Sword soldiers that chased Zath away or the presence of the Creature quickly approaching that made Feyerndur retreat, I didn't know. But suddenly, the Fire Dragon pulled away from the fight, lifting into the air.

"This is not over!" he growled before flying off toward Durthair.

Chapter 12

"Why did he just leave?" asked Dan as he came up next to me and the captain, Christopher and the rest of the group following close behind.

"It must be Feyerndur. It's like Yuuki said, he is in there and fighting to survive. He has been trying to keep Zath from killing me during this whole fight," I explained.

"We have to leave now!" Eyethanoff called as he rode through the trees behind Ahrdah, pushing branches out of his way. "We will go to Ruth's home near the entrance to the Smugglers' Road."

I raised my eyebrows. "Ruth's home is at the entrance? You mean her tree home?"

Eyethanoff's only answer was a quick nod before he began delivering orders to his soldiers. I wondered if there was a reason Ruth's home was near the entrance. I would have to ask him sometime.

With the medallion out of reach, I had no reason to remain in these caves, and I could not catch Zath in the air. With no other option, I swung into Jeb's saddle as Eyerkishta transformed back into Yuuki, exhausted from the battle, and I pulled her up in front of me.

Eyethanoff took off, urging his horse into a sprint, and we all followed. He led us through a blanket of quilted moss, over a deer path, and through another blanket of moss that hid a small tunnel. The tunnel spilled out onto what looked like the Smugglers' Road, possibly just closer to the end I hadn't traveled on. As we returned to the road, I took up the rear, making sure everyone was present and accounted for. I glanced behind us to check that no one was coming from the other direction, and my stomach dropped at what I saw. Three Great Beasts were charging down the road at top speed, headed straight for us. Their already large size reminded me that this war was different from those before it.

"Faster! Beasts are coming!" I called to Eyethanoff.

We ran down the trail with Eyethanoff in the lead and me at our flank as the beasts pressed closer with each stride. As the first beast reached Jeb and me, I pulled out a pistol with my left hand and fired a shot, but it missed, the beast lunging to one side just as I squeezed the trigger. I rotated the revolving barrel and fired a second shot that went right between the animal's eyes. The massive beast collapsed to the ground in mid stride, and its comrades left it behind, continuing their pursuit at full speed.

Another beast appeared from the shadows off to one side to take the dead one's place, and I reached around Yuuki for the sword with my right hand. My pistol had none of the King's power, but maybe the power in the sword would offer an advantage against these dark beasts. Before I got my hand past my waist, the sword seemed to jump to my palm of its own accord, reacting to my need. Its response caught me off guard, and I almost dropped it, but I managed to get a grip and slashed at the second beast as it came dangerously close to Jeb's flank. The beast was so close that Jeb nearly kicked it in the face, but it was able to dodge my awkward strike with the sword. I tried a pistol shot again. The bullet hit its target, and the beast crumbled.

We rounded a bend in the path, and I looked ahead to see the end of the trail before us. A figure waited on a horse where the road gave way to forest, and I was stunned when I recognized the familiar face. Ruth. She took off into the foliage, waving us to follow her, and we did, never breaking stride.

I holstered my empty pistol, keeping the sword in my hand, wrapped my arm around Yuuki to grab the reins, and focused on balancing in my seat to allow Jeb to run freely. Jumping over bushes and weaving around rocks, we continued following Ruth as she slowed slightly but kept moving through the now forested terrain.

After running at full speed for what felt like forever, we finally lost the last two beasts. Ruth brought her horse to a stop at a large, intertwined section of underbrush near a rocky ridge that rose to about the height of a horse. She dismounted and approached the underbrush, then reached through the thick foliage and grabbed a large branch. Pulling it back, she revealed a crevice that sloped gently into the rocky ground below, just wide enough for a horse and long enough that it looked like at least most of us and our horses could fit without spilling out through the bushes at the other end. I wasn't sure how this space would shelter us from beasts that could smell and hear just as well as any other predator, but I didn't see any better options.

"One at a time," whispered Ruth as she waved us forward. "We will be safe in here for now, and the Lion's Sword soldiers will hide in the light. We must be quiet, though. There may be dark soldiers close behind. They often send out beasts first to track down their targets."

"Where have you been?" I asked Ruth suspiciously, remembering how the Creature had taken on her form in his prison.

Ruth looked at me and smiled as we all dismounted our horses. "Don't worry, the Creature is cunning, but I am who I appear to be," she said with a smile. "Now go, they are near," she warned.

While the soldiers of light found their own hiding places, the rest of us entered the large crevice on foot, horses and all, lining up in single file with Ruth and me entering last. Ruth pulled the expertly woven foliage back over the opening and turned to face us, a finger held to her lips.

We stood in silence and listened to the sounds of the approaching beasts. One sniffed at the foliage, its hot breath creating a plume of fog in the cold morning air. But rather than bursting through the covering, the beast simply grunted, then walked off. Soon, the rest of its companions followed suit, and the sounds of their footsteps slowly receded into the distance. We all remained stock-still, holding our horses' noses to make sure they made no noise. Two dark soldiers followed the beasts, but only Solace seemed to sense their presence, as she winced and glanced at me with a concerned expression. I copied Ruth's gesture and held a finger up to my mouth. The dark soldiers passed without hesitation.

After a few tense moments, Ruth peered cautiously through the foliage, then turned back to us. "The way is clear."

She lifted the natural covering and led us out of the fissure, signaling us to remain quiet. In silence, we mounted our horses and followed Ruth through the trees to her home. The large tree brought back memories of meeting Ruth for the first time, bringing a smile to my face. I had not been happy to be here then. Now, it was a welcome sight.

So far, it seemed this person who looked like Ruth was, in fact, Ruth. But I wasn't sure how to tell for certain. "Where have you been?" I asked again as we stopped outside her tree and dismounted. Eyethanoff and his soldiers reappeared out of nowhere as though they had stepped out of the light beams shining through the trees.

Ruth smiled. "We each have our role to play," she responded, avoiding the question with a smile and a glint in her eye.

I frowned. Ruth's cryptic response and that look in her eye very nearly convinced me it was her, but still, I was hesitant. "Why should I believe you are who you appear to be?" I questioned.

Ruth looked at me. "I cannot convince you. Belief is a decision only you can make. But..." She opened her hand and began to reach forward. "May I?" she asked.

I raised my eyebrows. "May you what?" I asked.

"The belt," she said. "May I touch it?"

I frowned. "Umm...sure."

Ruth reached out to my side where a belt would sit, her fingers making contact with the belt of armor that I had thought only I could see. I looked up to ask her how she could see the belt and was met with an astonishing sight. Ruth was transformed. Her face was no longer wrinkled. It was young and smooth. The face of the woman from *The Story*.

"But...How...? You..." I stuttered. I had known she was the woman from *The Story*, but this took that mystery to even deeper levels. All my questions about her age and how she was still alive, which I had long pushed aside, suddenly came crashing through my head.

Ruth removed her hand from the belt and stepped back, her appearance returning to normal.

"What is happening?" asked a very confused Dan.

"You saw that?" I asked, glancing around at the others. Everyone looked just as astonished as Dan. Everyone except Yuuki, who was smiling at Ruth without a hint of surprise, as though she had known all along.

Dan and the others all nodded.

I turned to Ruth. "How? And how is that supposed to convince me you are who you say you are?"

She cocked her head to one side and shrugged. "Like I said, that is up to you. But whatever you choose, I am who I say I am."

"How?" I repeated in disbelief.

"That armor was once mine," she responded. "You think I don't know how it works?" she asked with a smile. "That belt reveals the truth. The truth is that I was an eternal being."

"Wait, you were an eternal being?" I asked. "Why wasn't that in *The Story*? You wrote it."

Ruth nodded. "I did. I left that detail out. I just...I didn't think it was important at the time. And things changed. I was an eternal being, but only until I betrayed the Prince. After I betrayed him, I never thought I would marry him, let alone be once again bestowed that privilege of long life. But the King granted me eternal life, saying it was a reward for choosing to return to his son, though we are not officially married yet. But the Lie damages one's body. When I gave up the armor to protect it from the Creature, my appearance began to age under the Lie. But I will be restored when the Gate is opened," she added, "for it is the King's power that sustains the armor, and me, and it will be his power that will return me to my true form, as it will this land."

"Long life?" asked Casey. "How long? Based on when this story supposedly took place, you are like eight thousand years old."

Ruth chuckled. "Well, I have been alive since Eeffrayldour was founded. No one really knows how much time has passed since then. Some say this land is as old as time itself. Others say it is older," she said with a sparkle in her eye. "In light of that, eight hundred years is not that long."

Just then, a small creature peeked out from behind Ruth. The little animal was about the size of a rabbit. It had big eyes, long ears that dragged on the ground, a bushy tail like a squirrel's, a tiny set of velvety antlers, and faint patchy markings on its gray and white body.

"What is that?" I asked.

Ruth looked down. "Oh, this is my friend, Neyelah. She is an isp. They are a type of Eeffrayldourian rodent, but with a special ability," she said as she gestured to the trees around us. "They can hide in plain sight."

I looked at Ruth's tree and the plants around it and noticed for the first time that the little creatures were everywhere. Some had their large ears fanned out in various shapes, allowing them to blend in with their surroundings. Others seemed to mostly use the colors and dappled, striped, and freckled patterns of their fur coats as camouflage against the backdrop of the sky or amongst the shadows and light within the foliage.

"As you can see, they are adept at remaining hidden from on-lookers," Ruth explained. "Some even live in the plants covering the crevice where we hid. More than most other creatures, isps have a unique connection to Original Power. As a result, the beasts are repelled by them, and the armies of darkness avoid them as much as possible. We are safe here in their company." Ruth looked down again at the one sitting near her foot. "Neyelah is called a Neyem isp—*Neyem* is the ancient Eeffraylick word for 'moon.' You can tell what kind she is because when her ears are expanded, they touch at the top of her head and under her chin, forming a dappled circle that makes her look just like the moon," said Ruth with a smile as Neyelah stood up on her hind legs and examined me for a moment before sniffing my hand, her tiny nose twitching up and down.

"How have I not seen them until now?" I asked curiously as I squatted down and scratched Neyelah behind one of her big, floppy ears.

"They are closely tied to the unseen kingdom, often serving as messengers of change. In my experience, they have a close tie to the King himself." Ruth waved for us to follow her. "Come, I will explain inside."

We quickly untacked our horses and left them to graze before Ruth led us into her house. "When you came to get the book from me, I knew the King had picked you as the final Night Rider. My mission changed that day," she said as we all settled around her table, some sitting on her bed and some on the floor. "The Creature couldn't break me, so he let me go in hopes that I would lead him to the other copies of the book I had printed. I went into hiding but contacted the broker between Captain Bates and I," she said, looking to the captain. "I knew you would be working with Ben from that point on, and I wanted to explain that to the broker to ensure he would trust you, as he is wary of new people. Then Ben showed up again. Things were moving along faster than I thought they would, so I gave you the sword and shield," she explained, gesturing to me. "Ever since then, I have been gathering those loyal to the King." She paused and looked at Neyelah, who was digging through a basket of fruit on the table. "*The Story* has power. I don't mean Original Power," she said, locking eyes with me. "Its power is simply in the truth it contains."

The Prince's words from my vision with the medallion came to mind. *"Truth not only provides a firm foundation, but its power is a weapon unmatched."*

"That truth sets people's minds at ease," said Ruth, stroking Neyelah. "And a mind at ease is not easily infiltrated by darkness. The more people find that truth, the less control the Creature has," she said, turning to me. "He is getting weaker. Neyelah and her kind can be seen because the Creature's lie is beginning to falter."

"So, the time is near," said Yuuki.

Ruth smiled at Yuuki and wrapped an affectionate arm around her. "Yes."

"If the time is near, I am going to need some answers," I said. "Like, for example, why is there a skeleton in a cave in the Western Sea with a journal that makes references to Eeffrayldour? And what does the Channel Treasure his journal seemed to talk about have to do with the Lie? And, as I have already asked twice, where have you been?"

Ruth's smile vanished and her eyebrows raised in recognition as she released Yuuki. Then her brow furrowed in a worried expression. "I will tell you what I know," she said simply. "When the Prince sacrificed himself to overcome the power of darkness, the

Creature panicked. He had been in control of me for so long. I was his ticket to destroying all of Eeffrayldour. But the sacrifice showed me what I had done. I went back to the Prince, leaving the Creature at risk of losing the power he had gained through me. To gain control over the people, he set the Lie in place and corrupted a dragon known as Feyerndur. He used the dragon to fill the people with fear, helping him to maintain the Lie. Life as I knew it changed. The Prince and all the peoples and creatures I had known faded from view as the Creature's shadow overtook the land. The Creature became obsessed with making his lie permanent and began looking for the Channel Treasure in hopes that it had some power that could help him. He spread the lie that the dig was the result of a war between two kings, which he orchestrated to cover up the discovery of the treasure. The land bridges crumbled, the Lie became stronger, and I began to forget many details of life before the Lie was in place. It was around that time that the Great Beasts arose to replace the dragon, and life as you know it began." Ruth sighed. "That skeleton you saw must have been the spy I sent to monitor the state of the Channel dig and whether or not the Creature had found what he was looking for. That spy's name was John. John Dur. He was a great man."

"So, Otto could still be right?" I asked. "The Channel Treasure could be some kind of conductor of Original Power? That would explain why the land bridges collapsed when it was removed."

Ruth shrugged. "Honestly, I don't know. All I remember is that the Channel Treasure was once believed to be a stone that sat atop the fountain at the castle the Prince and I were to live in once we were married. But it disappeared shortly before I became corrupted. Nothing seemed to change when it vanished. I assumed that if the Creature was looking for it, then it must have some kind of power, but I'm not certain. John was supposed to find out, but I never heard from him."

"His journal had a few poems that seemed to be a kind of code. Is that how you communicated with him?" I asked.

Ruth nodded. "Yes, what did they say?"

"I don't remember them word for word, but one said something about how the dirt sighed. Mean anything?"

Ruth nodded again. "It means the land was in pain. Maybe he thought the land suffered from the stone's removal. But that doesn't mean Otto was right. The land was there before the stone." She shrugged. "I just didn't want the stone to fall into the Creature's hands, in case it did have unique powers. The Prince has made many powerful tools for his people to use when they need them. But if the Creature has the stone, then he hasn't used it." She looked at me. "And he would have. I know him. If he could, he would have used it already to find the Gate and destroy it. Since he is still looking for the Gate, the stone is either useless, or it was only useful for some other purpose that I don't know about."

I let out a sigh and moved on to a different question. "Okay...and Adournath...He chose me as the last Night Rider, didn't he? But the Prince told me Solace was too."

"Adournath! That's his name! Yes. Years before I met you, Adournath reminded me that the Prince had prophesied that the Chosen and Guardians would unite. When that happened, it would be time to open the Gate. Adournath pointed you and Solace out to me and said the King had plans for you both, and when you were ready, I was to give you the two pieces of the armor

I still had. You were only a young boy at the time, and your father was the current Night Rider's best friend."

"So, Solace was right." I leaned back in my chair.

"About what?" asked Casey.

"When we first met, she thought I was the Night Rider because of my father's horse. It was a gift from a friend of his," I explained.

Ruth nodded. "Gray Harled. He was the last Night Rider before you and Solace. He was killed before you and your father went to the Great Volcano to lure the Great Beast to its death. General Delaney had commanded you and your father to go on that mission, though you did not know that at the time. Your father didn't want you to go because he had a feeling it would end badly. He went to Gray for help. But Valdra found out and killed Gray before forcing your father, with a promise of your safety, to complete the mission the general had given him and you. You were both intended to die that day."

"Why didn't I?" I asked.

Ruth sucked in a deep breath. "I can only assume the Creature found out how big a part you really play in this and hoped to use you to control the armor, as he has been trying to do."

I let out a sigh. "So now it is my job to find the Gate and destroy the Creature's lie," I concluded.

Ruth nodded. "But not alone, Benjamin."

"I know," I said. "I just...I am missing something. I don't know where the Gate is located."

"The Prince and the King came up with a plan to destroy the Lie," said Ruth. "But the Creature has a place in all shadows. So, the King has kept details compartmentalized. I only know what my role is. The rest we must discover together," she explained.

"Okay, what do you know?" I asked.

"I know we have all we need to take the next step," she said.

"What about the medallion?" I asked. "Do I need it to find the Gate?"

"What medallion?" asked Ruth, her brow wrinkling in confusion.

Chapter 13

I RAISED MY EYEBROWS in surprise. "You don't know about the medallion?"

Ruth shrugged. "The Prince has made medallions before, but I don't know of any that is connected to his plan. May I see it?"

I shook my head. "Zath has it. I have to get it back. When I touched it, I had a vision. The Prince began to give me an instruction, but I was interrupted, and the vision ended before he could finish speaking. I must get the medallion back to get the rest of the message," I explained.

Ruth nodded thoughtfully. "I am afraid I don't know anything about a medallion, at least not in connection to the Gate. Armor usually comes with one, but the armor I was given never had one. The Prince and the King are safeguarding their plan so that the Creature doesn't find out where the Gate is located. It doesn't surprise me that we don't know," she said. "But I know there must be someone who can give you the rest of the information. You just need find who has the final pieces of this plan."

"Right now, I would settle for the rest of that message..." I said more to myself than to anyone else.

"What was the part that you heard?" asked the captain.

I tried to recall the Prince's words. "Follow your compass, and..." I shrugged.

Casey raised his eyebrows. "Do you have a compass?"

"I don't think I have ever seen you use a compass," commented Dan.

"Maybe you will find one soon?" asked Christopher. "I mean, the Prince sent us out to take *The Story* to the four corners of the earth probably knowing it would lead us to the armor...Maybe this is a similar situation?"

The others continued suggesting ideas, but I tuned them out as Catherine's words sparked a memory. A memory of the first night I had spent with Solace under the stars in the Forest. That night, she had earned a nickname that stuck. "I called her my compass," I mumbled.

"What?" asked Casey.

I shook my head. "That doesn't make any sense." *She is gone. How could I follow her?*

"You are going to have to do better than that. We can't read your mind," said Dan.

I took a deep breath and let it out slowly, trying to understand. "Solace," I said.

Catherine's eyebrow raised. "That's right, you used to call her your compass," she stated with a nod.

"But she...she is gone," I said in confusion and grief.

Ruth looked at me. "What happened?"

"Zath," I explained as I tried to hide my pain at thinking about Solace.

Ruth gave me an apologetic look. "I am sorry, Ben," she responded sympathetically. "Perhaps there is a different compass he was talking about. Think on it today. We will be safe here, at least until Neyelah and her family leave," she reassured. "The isps will probably move on tonight, so we will have until then to recuperate and prepare for what lies ahead."

"That sounds like a good plan. I think we could all use another break before heading back into Durthair," I replied, pushing all thoughts of Solace and a compass aside. "You still haven't explained what you have been doing this whole time, though. We were looking for you."

Ruth sat up straighter in her chair. "I have spent my life preparing for this moment by showing others the truth—sharing *The Story* with them. When the Lie was set in place, the Lion's Sword was decimated. Many soldiers trapped under the Lie died or were corrupted." Ruth's expression tightened at the memories. "As I fought to keep this story alive, I discovered that part of my mission was to gather those loyal to the King and Prince in hopes that one day, when the Gate is opened and the Lie broken, they will follow you and help replenish the Lion's Sword's numbers. Now, you need those people. I have been reconnecting with believers. If all goes right, they will do their part in this fight. Some might even help return the Lion's Sword to its former strength."

I frowned. "You mean to help fight against the Creature if I find the Gate?"

Ruth smiled. "That, and more. Your friends—they saw what the belt did to my image." She turned to the group. "Can you see Eyethanoff and his soldiers?" she asked.

"Well, we can...but they look a bit like what I would imagine a ghost looks like," explained Dan.

"We began to see around the time we entered Eyethanoff's encampment," pointed out Captain Bates.

Ruth looked out the window. "Then they have arrived," she said with a smile. She turned back to me. "The rest of those who believe have come from around the four corners of the earth. They got my messages. The more believers are focused here, near the heart of the darkness, the more Original Power is focused here, for where believers are, there is the Lion and his power."

"You mean as more people believe and gather here, the more things will become visible?" I asked.

Ruth tilted her head from side to side. "Because the Gate has not allowed Original Power in yet, things will only become visible to a certain extent. But every little bit helps. Their belief weakens the Creature's hold, for light must illuminate the heart of darkness for the whole to be set free."

I took a deep breath. "We have no choice then. We must complete this mission now or all those people will likely be killed, and the opportunity will have been missed."

Ruth nodded. "For now, rest. You have been through a lot. We will remain here until the isps move on. They will leave when the Creature is getting close."

With that, we dispersed, each tending to our horses and making sure everything was in order in case we needed to make a hasty escape. Ruth made us breakfast, and then we spent the rest of the morning eating, chatting, and planning. It was nice to have a break among friends, but as I cleaned and reloaded my pistols, I found my mind constantly wandering to Solace and the Prince's message. I thought about it from every angle, and I could only come up with one answer. Solace was my compass.

I was reluctant to accept that answer, though, and it continued to haunt me as night fell around us. We all gathered in Ruth's house to look over which routes would be safe to use once we got back on the road in search of Zath. But while the others talked, my mind remained fixed on one question. *How can Solace be my compass if she is gone?*

We settled for the afternoon, safe under the protection of the small isps, and prepared for the coming journey and battle. I cleaned and polished the sword, and Eyethanoff and his soldiers tended to their weapons as well. But I was distracted by this issue of Solace being my compass. She was one half of the Night Rider, but now she could not help me. But maybe there was something in her memory that would guide me in the right direction. The more I thought about it, the more I became frustrated with my inability to solve this issue. So, taking advantage of the lull in our dangerous mission and wanting to get the issue off my mind, I asked Eyethanoff to teach me how to use the armor. But it wasn't as easy as I anticipated.

"To wield the armor, you must let go of control so power not yours can be granted you," said Eyethanoff.

"What does that mean?" I asked, holding the sword in both hands. I had assumed Eyethanoff would want to spar, but he seemed more interested in explaining things.

Eyethanoff shook his head. "I forget, you learn best by trial and error," he said with a grin.

With no warning, Eyethanoff's sword jumped to his hand. He swung it in a clean arc horizontal to the ground, aimed at my head. I ducked and spun, barely dodging the attack, but as I came out of the spin, two star-shaped knives came flying past my face, so close I felt the wind on the end of my nose.

"What was that?" I demanded, rubbing my nose as I recovered from the close call.

Eyethanoff chuckled, not a single white hair on his head out of place after his little display of skill. He had clearly mastered the armor, as well as a certain grace that I lacked.

Now I remember why I don't carry a sword, I grumbled to myself.

"Where did those come from?" I asked, seeing no sign of the star-shaped knives anywhere on his person.

"The armor released them to my hand, at my request," he explained.

"How?" I asked. "I mean how did you get it to do that?"

Eyethanoff grinned. He thrust out his hand, palm up, and bits of blue light like small bolts of lightning sprang from a circle at the center of his breastplate toward his hand. A star appeared in his palm. "I simply requested it to be done."

I looked down at my own hand and tried to replicate the motion Eyethanoff had made. Nothing happened.

Eyethanoff smiled. "And now we return to my original statement. Do you recall what it was?" he asked.

"Um...something about letting go of control to gain power."

Eyethanoff's chin wrinkled in a thoughtful expression. "Not quite." His sword returned to its place at his side. "I said that to wield the armor, you must let go of control so power not yours can be granted you."

I recalled Yuuki telling me at the door that the power belonged to the King. "Okay, so the power is not mine—it is the King's power. But if I am to use it, what good is letting go of control? I must have control to get it to do things, like when I need the sword to come to my hand. You have control over your armor," I pointed out.

Eyethanoff shook his head. "No, I have a connection to it, born of a connection with the one to whom the power belongs."

I raised my eyebrows and let my eyelids droop. "How am I supposed to develop a connection with a king I have never met and probably can't? You said it yourself back at camp. He is not seen—not by anyone. He is of a different world."

Eyethanoff smiled again. "Good question."

"And the answer is...?" I asked.

"Before the Lie was set in place, Lion's Sword soldiers used to train at a beautiful castle called Mair Pala. It is trapped under this lie, unseen by those under the Lie and unusable to those outside it. But it once was filled with stories of the Prince and his mighty warriors—legends of old. One of my favorites was one my father told me. It is the story of a young criminal who hid his dark past in shadows whose cruelty he didn't fully understand. The darkness overshadowed his whole life until the very shadows he hid within became his worst enemy. His wrongdoings were exposed, shedding light on his darkest deeds. But where light illuminated his dark secrets, he found a new protection. A protection unseen but free of darkness. He began to see the freedom that truth offered—a protection from those who took refuge in darkness—and he began to take refuge in light. Though light's protection exposes our darkest places, it also lights within us a power stronger than any shadow.

It was in this story where I learned a saying common among the Lion's Sword. 'Darkness is a cruel protector. Light's protection exposes all. Choose wisely.'"

"What exactly does that mean?" I asked.

Eyethanoff took a deep breath as if thinking, then he said, "Taking refuge in the Creature's darkness can cost you your life but give you the illusion of control and a place to hide your deepest secrets. Taking refuge in the King's light can cost you your control and secrets but give you a unique kind of freedom. What are you willing to give up and to whom?"

I frowned. "Not to belittle your favorite legend, but how does that help me?" I asked.

Eyethanoff chuckled. "Sometimes, we must lose what is seen before there can be room within us for that which is unseen. We hold fast to our secrets—to the things we wish to control. To the things we must give up to truly understand, to truly see, what the King has to offer. You seek a connection to a king you cannot see and the world tells you is not real? Seek light, Benjamin. You will find what you are looking for."

"What light?" I asked, eager to understand. "I can see a lot of light. Is there an unseen light?"

"The better question is, 'Whose light?'" he corrected me. "You are not dealing with light like the sun. When you put on the helmet, you were claimed by light—the light of Original Power. A light that now lives inside you but yearns to be awakened by the one who wields it. A light that is more powerful than you realize, if you would simply allow it to do its job within you. A light that belongs to you just as much as you belong to it." He gestured to the armor I wore. "That armor is a responsibility, a commitment—one you must take on every day, for we are weak and constantly at risk of falling prey to darkness. That is why we were given the armor. But the armor, and the one who made it, are not of this world and thus not bound by it." He took a step closer and placed a hand on my shoulder. "You want power, Ben? Then remember this: all you can do is make one choice, every day," he said. "Darkness or light. There is nothing else."

I frowned. "What did you mean in that story by taking refuge in light? One cannot hide in a place where all can see you," I pointed out.

Eyethanoff nodded. "Taking refuge and hiding are two different things. Refuge is where we go when we are in need of protection, while hiding is what we do when we are afraid of judgement. Those who are loyal to darkness are protected by lies and secrecy. They go to darkness for refuge and find nothing but fear of condemnation, for taking refuge there comes at a cost. They must give up themselves in exchange for their safety from others. But light...light is different. Light values those who put themselves at risk to remain loyal to it. Yes, it exposes the truth, even painful truth, and no, you cannot hide from others when you stand within it. But the light that now exists does not demand payment, only loyalty, for the one who sheds that light upon us already paid our debt to darkness. You must choose wisely, Benjamin, for who you choose to take refuge in will determine the course of your life."

Yuuki showed up just then with a message that dinner was on the table. I was grateful for the interruption, because Eyethanoff's riddles and stories were giving me a headache.

We headed to Ruth's tree and sat down at her table to eat. While the others were planning our next move, my mind wandered to what Eyethanoff had said. *"Seek light, Benjamin. You will find what you are looking for."* I looked down at my hand and recalled Eyethanoff using the armor. His armor had produced blue light when it gave him the star-shaped knives. Light made by Original Power, a power that belonged to the King. I recalled how it felt to open the door, the feeling of Original Power. It had come from somewhere outside of me and yet...within me. I closed my eyes and tried to find the light of the King. Nothing.

I opened my eyes with a sigh. As I did, my gaze fell on a wall at the back of the room. My thoughts distracted, I almost missed the sound of a voice. A sound that seemed to come from the direction of the wall. I froze, listening. It came again. Though almost inaudible, as if it were muffled, it was definitely a voice and it was definitely coming from the wall. For a moment, I pondered my sanity, but I quickly abandoned the idea as I had already been down that path and continued to find evidence that I was, in fact, sane. That theory had run its course a long time ago.

Leaving the others at the table, I stood and approached the wall. But there was nothing there. With a frown of contemplation, I turned to go back to my seat but stopped short when I felt the armor stir, and I placed my hand on the hilt of the sword. It too seemed to be responding to something. The sensation reminded me of how the armor had seemed to call out when I found the door at the dragon caves, though it didn't feel quite the same. At that moment, I heard the sound of someone knocking on a door. I turned to face the sound, but still all I saw was the wall.

I glanced at the others. They were not paying any attention to me, so I began to investigate the wall. Curiosity got the best of me, and I reached out and touched it. The moment my fingers touched the wood, I heard a voice. "Ben?" the voice said. It sounded familiar.

"Solace!" I said, suddenly recognizing the voice.

"What did you say?" asked the captain from behind me.

"I said 'Solace.' I...I heard her voice," I explained in confusion as I gestured to the wall before me.

Ruth came up next to me with a suddenly very intent expression, the others crowding behind her. "Tell me what happened," she said in a serious tone.

"This place on the wall—it caught my attention for a reason I can't really explain, and then I heard a voice. I came over to see if I was just hearing things, and the armor and the sword seemed to respond to it. Not like they were calling out to it, but..."

"Like they had encountered something of the same power," suggested Ruth.

I nodded. "Yes. It felt kind of like when the sword led me to the door at the dragon caves. How did you know?"

Ruth smiled and ran an affectionate hand down a nearby wall of her tree. "The Prince used to love this tree. We would pass it on our walks through the land. On the last walk we went on before I...betrayed him, he told me it would make a good home. When I moved in later, I wondered if there was something special here that he hadn't told me about. The armor never called out to anything here when I wore it, but I always suspected there had to be something special about this place."

"I heard Solace's voice," I explained again.

"Then follow your compass, Benjamin," said Ruth with a smile and that twinkle in her eye.

"Follow it where?" I asked.

Ruth glanced down at Yuuki, then back up to me. "I don't know," she said with a shrug. "I think that is for you to discover."

"Maybe you are right. Maybe it is a door," suggested Yuuki hopefully.

I nodded. "If it is, why didn't you ever find it before?" I asked Ruth.

She shrugged again. "There are things that I don't know and things the Lie has made me forget. But this seems like something meant for you to find," she repeated with an encouraging smile.

Yuuki nodded. "But you must be careful when opening a door, for each door leads to another door, and they both open at the same time. And if darkness is too close, the doors will not work."

"Then how did the Prince get through the door he opened with the dark armies so close?" I asked.

"Darkness can get quite close before a door will no longer work, and the Prince made the doors," responded Yuuki. "They will do his bidding no matter what, for he is guaranteed to be able to keep the darkness out of his kingdom. But if you do it, as you did at the cave, and one of the doors is trapped shut by darkness, you could get stuck in the Field of Doors."

"So, you let me go through a door when you weren't certain I wouldn't get trapped?" I asked, half teasing.

Yuuki rolled her eyes but chuckled. "The Creature was far behind us then...I didn't think it would be a problem, and it wasn't," she explained with a smile.

I nodded. "Okay, well, what now? Is there a way to tell if there is darkness on the other side?"

Yuuki nodded but said, "Not from here, though. And the Creature can place guards over doors, keeping them closed indefinitely."

"How would he find out if we were using a door?" I asked.

"Spies," said Ruth warningly. "Some doors move around, such as the dragon's door. The doors that move are connected to those who own them. But even those doors have limited places they can show up. Most doors are at fixed locations. If spies see us use a door, they will know where it is located and will then keep tabs on it. And even if no one sees us, using the doors causes a ripple effect in the Lie that can help spies find out where we are."

I let out a hard breath and considered our predicament. The Prince had told me to follow my compass. But I would be at risk of getting trapped in an unknown place. I frowned. If the Prince wanted me to go, then that is what I needed to do.

"I think I should go," I announced.

"Ben, what if you get stuck there?" asked Dan.

I shook my head. "I have gone through doors before, and it turned out fine. Plus, I trust the Prince will provide a way out," I explained. "He wouldn't send me in there just to leave me trapped."

"I was actually referring to the fact that you couldn't open the last door on your own," he pointed out.

I frowned. "Maybe Yuuki can come with me," I suggested, turning to her.

She shook her head. "I need to stay out here and help fight off the Creature. If you encounter Zath, my presence might rile him up in a way you do not want."

"Then how am I supposed to go through the doors if I can't open them on my own?" I asked.

Yuuki frowned in thought. "I cannot remember in full, but I recall there being a way...A way to have help..." She shook her head and let out a frustrated breath. "I am afraid I have been too long under this lie to remember. But my gut tells me there is a way out."

"Your gut?" I asked. "If your gut gets me trapped in there, then you all are on your own without the armor."

"You just said the Prince wouldn't lead you there without a way out," she pointed out. "If you and the captain are right in your assumption that the Prince came to your aid in the caves, maybe he will come to your aid in the Field of Doors."

I nodded and turned to Ruth. "It's settled, then. I will enter here and see what it is that the Prince wants me to find."

With the others watching, I turned toward the wall, reached out my hands, and rested them on it. Yuuki did the same. It took a moment for the Original Power to flow in the right direction, as I was still developing a connection with the armor. But when I finally got it, I knew immediately, for it was as if the armor could read my very thoughts. At the moment of connection, I let the power of the King flow through the armor and down my arms into my hands. The veins of light spread to my palms, where they came in contact with the Lie, burning it away like paper to reveal a door that was made of the very tree in which we stood. Yuuki let her hands drop. With one last glance over my shoulder at the others, I placed my hand on the door's center and pushed."

The door swung open. On the other side of the threshold, I could see nothing but light. I glanced at Ruth, and she nodded.

"May the King's power be with you," she said with an encouraging smile.

I gave a curt nod, then turned back to the door and stepped across the boundary. As I did, the door closed behind me. Immediately, a shadow fell over it. I winced and tried to open it again, but it would not budge. I frowned at the door for a moment, then turned to see if there was another door that was open.

I immediately knew whatever door this one was connected to did not open, for before me was a white field that stretched out in every direction, seeming to never end. There were grass and flowers everywhere, but each was pure white. A few trees and a couple boulders speckled the landscape, also white. The only color came from a pale blue, cloudless sky and the shadow that mysteriously sat over the door I had just passed through. Scattered around me in the distance were a few other doors, all of them closed. I was stuck.

The Field of Doors, as Yuuki had called it. Only five doors were within my view, two of them closer than the others. The three in the distance were barely visible on the horizon.

I suddenly noticed that, though there was no sun here to cast shadows, certain doors seemed darker, as though a shadow lay just on the other side. I turned back to examine the door from Ruth's tree. The shadow made its white surface appear grey, and it had a depiction of a large tree that stood out in the midst of a forested background. I studied the carvings closely and thought I saw something hidden in the art, but I was suddenly interrupted by the sound of a voice.

"Ben?"

Chapter 14

THE FAMILIAR VOICE CAME from behind me, and I spun around in search of its source, afraid I was hearing things. To my shock—and immense relief—standing before me was Solace.

I could not believe my eyes as I reached out and touched her shoulder, desperate for something tangible to tell me she was real. My heart began to pound in my chest, and I felt my breathing quicken before I forced myself to get it under control. "You're alive!" I whispered as I moved my hand to her check, her soft skin registering on my palm.

Solace smiled, a small tear glistening in the corner of her eye. "I am? You're alive!" she said as she wiped the tear away.

As if something unseen drove us together, we immediately embraced, and I never wanted to let go. Solace encircled me with her arms, the two of us fitting together like pieces of a puzzle.

When I finally released my hold enough for her to move, Solace stood on her toes and planted a passionate kiss on my lips, which I returned with no hesitation.

"What happened to you?" she whispered as she hugged me again.

"General Delaney happened," I explained in a low tone.

Solace looked up at me. "I was right?"

I nodded. "Yes, and thanks to you, I was hesitant enough to make it out of there...for a little while..." My voice trailed off as I recalled what had happened at General Delaney's mansion. I shivered.

"So, you were listening," she teased.

I rolled my eyes. "I listen more than you think...Speaking of you, what happened to you? Is everyone else here?" I asked, looking around at the strange scenery. "The twins and Otto? And Trixie?"

Solace shook her head. "I haven't seen them. At least...not in person."

I looked down at her again. "What do you mean?"

Solace frowned. "Well, we were on the ship while the dragon was attacking. Then it went after you. I thought for sure you had died when that fire enveloped you. The ship broke apart and I thought we were all going to die, but then..." Solace shrugged, as if unsure how to explain what had happened. "A door in the water opened up, and I was..." She hesitated, searching for the right words. "In a vision, I guess. I thought it was real until it was gone."

"What do you mean?" I asked again, sitting down on a nearby rock.

"Well, a lot of it was confusing, and I don't remember all the details. There was a lot of darkness and destruction. But for part of it, I was back home...I remembered everything that had happened, but you all were only there for a moment...like a memory that then faded, and it was like you were never there at all. I was trying to do this whole mission myself...and I thought I could at first. But then, I realized how much I needed you all." She shook her head at the memory. "I realized I was being selfish..." She looked at me. "The vision vanished after I realized something else...I realized that this whole time, I have been trying to be the one who makes you understand. I thought I knew everything about *The Story*. Even when we kept turning up more and more questions, I thought I could just have faith the King would pull through and everything would work because I had faith in him. But in that vision, as it played out, I realized that I believed I was the only one who knew what needed to be done. I tried to tell you, and when you didn't listen to me or understand what I was saying, I got angry. I kept it to myself, but that night when you told me about the Beast, I just…"

"I was selfish too, Solace," I said, bending my knees slightly so my eyes were level with hers. Then I straightened as she held my gaze. "I forgot that you were not just one of the group but actually one half of the Night Rider. I thought that because I was the one with the armor, I was the one who had to do all the hard work. But you—you are my compass, Solace. You are part of this because I would be lost without you. And somehow, the King knew that." I chuckled. "He knew I would be useless to him without you. Even when you were gone, it was your memory and your words that pointed me in the right direction when nothing else could." I shook my head. "I was wrong again. The Prince did keep his word. I should have trusted the Prince when I thought you were lost. I should have known to trust him even if I couldn't see how he was working things out around me."

"What do you mean?" she prompted.

I stroked her cheek. "When I met the Prince in the Woods the night he saved you from death, he told me you would become a mighty warrior…but I thought you were gone for good this time and that he hadn't kept his promise."

Solace's eyebrows raised. "He said that to you?"

I nodded. "Why?"

"I saw him, Ben," she said. "He was here."

I stood up. "The Prince was here?" I asked, pointing at the ground.

"Well, he was...kind of...At the end of my vision, he showed up. He told me that when my time came, 'you who can see' would lead the blind in battle. I wasn't really sure what he was talking about, but he left before I could ask. Then I was here," she said, gesturing to the landscape around us.

I smiled. "He meant you," I said. "I just know it."

"Do you think so?" she asked.

"I know so," I said before kissing her again.

"How?" she asked.

"Because you led me when I was blind. I am confident you can do it for others," I explained.

Solace smiled. Then her smile faded, and she pointed toward the horizon behind me. "Ben, is that a person?"

I spun around to see what she was pointing at.

"There is another one," she said, still pointing in the same direction.

"They are people...They...Wait. That's Otto and Trixie!" I said.

"And Nadia!" announced Solace, gesturing in a different direction as we ran to meet them.

As the five of us converged, Ivan appeared in the distance, coming from another direction.

"You are all here?" I asked with excitement as we embraced. "How is this possible?"

"How are you possible?" asked Nadia, mirroring my excitement.

"We saw you get engulfed in fire!" declared Otto with wide eyes.

"We all thought you were a goner," said Trixie.

"The shield. It protected me," I explained. "Though barely, because at the time I didn't have the rest of the armor."

"You found the rest of the armor?" asked Ivan.

I nodded. "Yes, I have all of it now!" I announced. "How did you all get here?" I asked. "Did you come through a mysterious door in the water, like Solace?"

Nadia raised her eyebrows in surprise. "Yes. Well, I did. I don't know about Otto and Ivan and Trixie. I didn't see them."

Otto nodded. "Yes, I did as well," he said, his posture a little tense.

"Did you see a vision?" asked Solace.

They both nodded. "And the Prince!" chimed in Otto.

"I saw a vision too," said Trixie. "When it was over, I just started looking around. That is how Otto and I found each other," she explained.

I turned to Ivan. "What about you?"

Ivan shrugged. "I saw something. Not sure what it meant though," he said halfheartedly.

"What's wrong with you?" asked Nadia, trying to cheer him up.

"Nothing," said Ivan, throwing an arm around Nadia. "It's good to see you, sis." He smiled, but it was tense. As he glanced around the white field, I could tell something was bothering him.

"It's good to see you too." Nadia hugged him back. "But you seem—"

Ivan interrupted before she could finish. "I'm fine. I just want to get out of here and move on with the mission. Where are we?"

Seeing Ivan's reluctance to talk about whatever he had seen, I decided not to press the issue.

"Ivan is right, we need to get out of here. Then we can discuss what happened," I said, looking around as Ivan was doing. "This is apparently the Field of Doors, according to Yuuki."

"How would Yuuki know anything about this?" asked Otto.

"Umm..." I wasn't sure she wanted me to tell them who she really was. She had been keeping her true identity from all of us until recently, and she probably had her reasons. But they were all her friends here, and the dark soldiers had probably already told the Creature what her human form looked like. "Yuuki is...Well, I guess there is no other way to say this. Yuuki is a dragon. Her dragon name is Eyerkishta."

Otto gasped audibly as Nadia and Solace's jaws dropped and Trixie raised an eyebrow.

"What?" asked Ivan, voicing everyone else's thoughts.

I nodded. "Yuuki is the name she uses for her human form, when she doesn't want people to know that she is a dragon. Her real name is Eyerkishta. She is the Ice Dragon," I finished, looking to Solace.

Solace's eyes widened a fraction of an inch. "From your visions?"

I nodded. "One and the same. Apparently, she has been keeping an eye on us this whole time."

"And she told you about this place?" asked Nadia.

"Yes. Well, I heard Solace's voice through one of these doors, which are controlled by Original Power...With Yuuki's help, I went through the door and then a shadow covered it, which means that there is evil close by, so the door won't open, and the destination door, if there was one, didn't open, so...I am not sure how to get out of here," I admitted.

"Nice going, Benny," said Nadia with a smirk.

"Hey, if I hadn't come in here, you all would be trapped for who knows how long," I exclaimed.

"So now we can be trapped together?" asked Solace, teasing.

I rolled my eyes. "Ivan, help me out here."

Ivan frowned. "One of these doors has got to open and lead somewhere."

"There are no handles," observed Otto.

Ivan strode to the nearest door and tried pushing it open from both sides. It didn't move.

"Maybe we have to say something?" suggested Otto.

We all looked at him. "Like what?" I asked.

He shrugged. "I don't know!" he said defensively. "I was just making a suggestion."

"Now what?" asked Nadia, throwing her hands up in the air.

I thought for a moment. We were stuck in an unfamiliar, probably Eeffrayldourian, location that we had no idea how to escape. I shrugged. "I don't know. Yuuki said this is a space between doors," I explained as I looked around at the white landscape.

Solace considered that. "You mean doors like the one the Prince brought us through?" she clarified.

I shrugged. "I assume so. Did it open out of nowhere?"

Ivan nodded, but Otto spoke up in his factual tone that I had come to miss dearly. "That is impossible. We probably just couldn't see it until it opened. Its location is likely connected to the unseen world."

I laughed. "I missed you, Otto," I said with a grin as I threw an arm over his shoulder in a loose hug. Otto gave an awkward smile, then straightened his slightly tattered shirt when I let go. As I released him, I couldn't help but observe a tinge of worry creasing his eyes. I had noticed that both he and Ivan seemed a bit downtrodden, Ivan more so than Otto. Ivan almost appeared slightly frustrated.

"So maybe only the Prince can open a door," proposed Nadia, interrupting my silent observations.

"Well, Ben did say he came through one to get here. Did you open that door?" asked Solace.

I nodded. "With a little help from Yuuki. I am still learning how to open doors and can't do it on my own."

Ivan glared at me. "You mean you got yourself in here without a way out?"

I frowned. "Well, what was I supposed to do? Leave you in here?"

"You could have brought Yuuki!" he snapped.

"What is wrong with you, Ivan?" I demanded.

Nadia stepped between us. "Just quit bickering. We need to get out of here, and fighting about how we got in won't help."

"There are dark soldiers trying to kill us all," I said. "Yuuki stayed out there to protect us while we are in here. Plus, she is still weak under the Lie. I am not even sure she could open another door."

"Okay, what do you know about how the doors work?" asked Trixie, joining Nadia between Ivan and me.

I shook my head. "Not much. But I do know that if darkness is too close to the door, it will not open."

"Well, how are we supposed to tell?" asked Otto.

"Have faith, my friends," said a jovial voice from somewhere behind us.

We all spun around in search of who had spoken. Standing near a white tree was a beautiful white rabbit. He was about the size of a dog, stood on his hind legs like a human, wore thin copper wire-rimmed glasses, and had a collection of rolled up papers under one arm and a satchel over his shoulder.

"Who are you?" I asked as I examined the visitor.

The large rabbit smiled. "My name is Reginald," he said with a courteous bow.

"Reginald?" asked Nadia with a raised eyebrow.

Reginald nodded. "My given ancient Eeffraylick name is long and hard to pronounce. So, humans from your land just call me Reginald or Reggie," he explained.

"Okay," I said slowly. "My name is Benjamin Arlin," I added politely, then gestured toward the others. "This is my wife, Solace, and our friends, Nadia and Ivan Kuzmich and Otto and Trixie Bilden. We need to know how this place works," I informed him, subtly aware that enough crazy things had happened over the past few months that a talking rabbit seemed almost commonplace. "Can I open one of these doors with only a limited understanding of Original Power?"

Reggie cocked his head to one side. "I am not sure I understand the question," he stated as his nose twitched, causing his whiskers to bounce.

"Do you live here?" I asked.

Reggie shook his head. "Oh no, this is the Field of Doors. No one lives here, exactly. I am just passing through on my way to see General Dii," he said matter-of-factly.

"Who is that?" asked Solace.

Reggie gave us a confused expression and leaned forward. "You are all new here, aren't you?" he asked.

I nodded. "I am afraid this is our first time here. Are there other humans who pass through this field?" I asked.

Reggie nodded. "Oh yes, of course. Anyone who is part of the Lion's Sword has special access to this place for easy travel," he said with joy. "Well, it is easy once you get used to it. For those, such as yourselves, who do not travel through here often, it can be...a bit confusing," he added, before pushing his glasses up the bridge of his nose.

"Why are you meeting with this general?" inquired Nadia.

"Well, there is a war that is about to happen, and I am a cartographer and navigator, you see, so the general has requested my presence during planning. This is the fastest way from my home," he explained. Then Reggie leaned forward so far that he had to place one front paw on the ground for support. His nose twitched as he sniffed at me, and he asked, "Are you the one who found the Prince's missing medallion?"

Surprised, I hesitated a moment before answering. "Yes...How did you know?"

"Delightful!" cheered Reggie as he hopped forward once on his hind legs, then stood up straight again. "The Prince mentioned that someone under the Lie had found his missing medallion. How did you come by it? Rumor is that once it is found, the time will be near," Reggie said with excitement. "I assume that is why the battle plans are being drawn," he added, more to himself.

"I actually found it initially in a cave while I was looking for the Channel Treasure," said Trixie. Then she turned to me with an apologetic wince. "But that dragon took it when he attacked us."

I nodded. "I know. I tried to get it back," I said, frowning at the memory of my failed attempt.

"Sorry," said Trixie.

I shook my head. "Don't worry. We will get it back."

Reggie cocked his head to the side again and said, "A dragon took it?"

I nodded. "I think he was trying to free himself from the Creature's influence, and I guess he needs the medallion and the helmet to do so," I said.

Reggie rubbed his chin. "Oh yes, each set of armor has its own medallion." He waved a paw to one side. "Well, except the set given to Ruth all those years ago, or at least that is what the story books say," explained Reggie. "He must have been trying to reactivate his own armor. But I am afraid he can't do it that way. At least not on his own. He must start with the belt. Everyone knows that."

"How was the medallion lost?" asked Nadia.

Reggie shrugged. "No one knows. It went missing around the time other artifacts made by the Prince disappeared, during the time the Creature was setting the Lie in place. Before that, nothing had gone missing since the stone from Mair Pala was taken." He shook his head in disapproval.

"The stone from Mair Pala?" I asked.

Reggie nodded. "Yes, according to history books, it once sat at the top of the castle's fountain."

I raised my eyebrows. "Mair Pala is the castle Ruth and the Prince were going to live in?"

Reggie nodded again. "Yes," he repeated as he slid his glasses up his nose. "That was its original purpose. Though after Ruth's fall to the Creature, it was eventually used as the main training site for the Lion's Sword soldiers," said Reggie, sounding a little sad. He let out a brief sigh. "Anyways, the stone went missing shortly before Ruth was corrupted, taken by a dragon. But after Ruth's corruption, we all lost interest in the stone. It was just a rock. Plus, it was apparently found later. I guess it ended up in the Lor Channel." He scratched his head. "Though I can't imagine why."

"What is the Lor Channel?" asked Nadia.

"It is the real name of the Channel," I said. "I will tell you about it later."

"Wait. So, if the stone and the medallion went missing at different times, then does that mean they weren't placed in the cave at the same time?" asked Trixie.

Reggie shook his head. "Probably not. According to the history books, the stone was taken by a fire dragon named Feyerndur long before the medallion went missing. I heard the Creature found the stone and moved it, maybe more than once." He seemed to think about that for a moment, as though that detail reminded him of something. His attention suddenly came back to us, and he shook his head. "As I said before, the reason why the Fire Dragon took the stone is not known to me, or historians. Maybe the Prince told him to." He shrugged again. "Whatever the reason, it had nothing to do with the medallion, at least not that I know of."

"Are you sure it was Feyerndur and not Zath who moved the stone?" I asked.

Reggie raised his eyebrows. "I believe Zath was not yet in the picture when the stone was moved the first time."

The others looked at me questioningly. "Who is Feyerndur?" asked Nadia.

"The dragon that attacked us, the one that has the medallion...except, that is Zath, Feyerndur's evil form. He was corrupted and helped the Creature steal the stone and set the Lie in place." I turned to Reggie. "Or at least that is what I thought. But you are saying that he took the stone before he was corrupted."

Reggie nodded. "I believe so, yes. He was not corrupted at that stage. Or at least, if the artistic depictions of that incident are accurate, he didn't look it."

Nadia rubbed her chin. "So the stone was not originally taken by the Creature..." she said, thinking out loud.

Reggie frowned. "No...Not directly, I mean. I am a bit hazy as to what has happened to it since. But I must admit, I am not sure what the Creature would want with that stone," he said with a shrug.

"It is a special stone, is it not?" asked Otto. "A tool of the King?"

Reggie raised an eyebrow. "The stone was made by the Prince long before my time. I have never heard of it doing anything special, though it is not my job to know these things. It just sat on the fountain at Mair Pala for hundreds of years, if not more. It was part of the fountain that produced the underground streams that run from the castle courtyard out into the land. Though some of those have dried up now..."

"Then why did Feyerndur take the stone?" I asked, my question not really addressed to anyone in particular.

Reggie shrugged. "Again, I don't know. I assume you would have to ask him, though I hear he is going through a rough patch right now, struggling within himself," said Reggie with a melancholy expression. "The Creature doesn't let the weary rest," he said with a sigh.

"Great. Now we have to go ask a crazy dragon for help," commented Ivan.

I shook my head. "No. Feyerndur is still in there. He wants out from under Zath's control, too. I think we can save him." I turned to Solace. "Ruth said that each person knows only as much as they need to know, and all I have to do is find the one who has the final piece to this puzzle. I think it is Feyerndur."

Solace nodded. "I also assume you are going to explain when you found Ruth?" she asked with a smile.

I grinned. "Oh, yeah. Ruth is back."

"How are we supposed to turn a corrupted dragon?" demanded the irritable Ivan, changing the subject back to the mission at hand.

Reggie chuckled. "It is simple, really," he said. "Trust the King. I know from personal experience that he knows what he is doing. He knows the Creature better than anyone else. Despite the Creature's feelings on the subject, the King most certainly has the upper hand," he said with a smile.

Suddenly, Reggie flinched. "Oh my, the meeting. I am going to miss the meeting," he said with concern. "I knew it was a good idea to leave ahead of time today. Especially when Harold canceled brunch," he mumbled to himself. "That was most unusual," he added, gazing off into the distance, seemingly lost in thought. After a moment, he abruptly looked at us, as if something had suddenly pulled him back to the present. "Oh. I am afraid I must depart. Good luck. Just find the white stag, and it will lead you to the right place. Once you learn where each door leads, it will become much easier to navigate this place," he called as he began hopping away. He disappeared over a small hill, his white fur blending into his surroundings and making it impossible to keep track of him in the distance.

"Great! We have to find a white stag in a place that is completely and totally white," announced Ivan with sagging shoulders.

Ignoring Ivan's unusually negative mood, I turned to the others. "Well, we better get to it. Reggie said they are preparing for battle, and the Prince told me I need to hurry. I have a feeling we are under a time crunch," I said. "Everyone fan out. We need to find that stag."

The field around us was surprisingly quiet. There were no animals anywhere. It reminded me of the Field in the Forest—bare, no life except for plants. But this place didn't feel odd. It didn't feel menacing. It felt calm and peaceful. Trees and bushes were scattered here and there, but they were just as white as everything else. It would be hard to find a white stag in this place. As we spread out, we looked behind the doors and behind the bushes and trees. Ivan even climbed on top of a door and looked around. But there was no white stag.

As I inspected the doors, I did notice something interesting. Upon each was a depiction of a location carved into the white wood, the front view on one side of the door and the back view on the other. None of the places looked familiar to me, though.

Eventually, we all found ourselves back by the door I had entered through, though I wasn't sure how we had all ended up there.

"Now what?" asked Ivan, throwing his hands in the air.

I shrugged. "No one found anything?" I prompted.

They all shook their heads.

I looked around one last time before my gaze fell on the door I had traveled through to get here. I examined the depiction carved into the wood. It resembled Ruth's tree, but the land around it looked different. Healthier. Surrounding the tree was a much wider variety of foliage than there was now. But in addition to that, there were images of animals carved into the wood. Not separate from the image of the tree and its surroundings but within it, as if the animals were part of the scenery. I ran my fingers over the carving. An owl sat in a tree. *No, wait, that is Neyelah, or one of her kind,* I realized. But then I saw something else. In the background of the image, nearly invisible amidst the trees, was a white stag.

"What did you find?" asked Solace as she came up next to me, examining the image.

"A white stag," I said as I pointed to the creature in the picture.

She frowned. "But that is the door you came out of," she stated in confusion.

"Yeah. And even if I could open these doors on my own, I can't open this one because it is shrouded in darkness," I mumbled, pondering the dilemma. Then Reggie's first words came to mind. *"Have a little faith."* I reached up and ran my fingers over the stag, wondering what it really meant to have faith in a way that would make an ancient power bend to my will whenever I wanted. At that thought, a jolt went through the armor, as though it were warning me against something. Something I couldn't quite pinpoint.

"Um. Ben," I heard Nadia say as she approached and touched my shoulder to get my attention.

I looked up and followed her gaze. In the near distance, standing before a door, was a white stag. It stood still, watching us.

"Where did it come from?" I whispered in surprise.

Nadia shrugged. "I don't know. It just...was there."

Then, with no warning, the door behind the stag opened, and the stag stepped through.

After a moment of hesitation, we all suddenly bolted for the door, not sure how long it would stay open. We darted over bushes and around trees until we reached it. I skidded to a halt and waved each person through, making sure we had everyone. Then I followed, and the door closed behind me.

As I surveyed our new surroundings, I found that we were standing on a moonlit road amidst high rocky ledges. The stag was nowhere to be seen.

"Where are we?" asked Solace, rubbing her shoulders in the cold air.

I continued looking around for a moment, wondering the same thing. As I got my bearings, I finally recognized it. "The Smugglers' Road," I said and immediately began walking north toward Ruth's tree.

Solace followed. "The one from the note?"

I nodded. "This way. Ruth's tree is not too far. We will see if everyone is still there."

As we headed down the snow-covered path, keeping a careful eye out for any signs of the enemy lurking in the shadows, I explained everything the others had missed in their absence. The armor, what each part did, how the Creature's powers worked, the dragons, the real names of all the places we knew, and all that had happened to Captain Bates and his crew. When we came upon the place where

I had entered Zath's cave, I told them about what had happened in the caves and about the vision I'd had with the medallion. Eventually, after I'd finished explaining all the important details they had missed, I spotted the end of the Smugglers' Road up ahead.

As we approached the place where the road ended in wooded terrain, I slowed everyone down and we veered off to the side, crouching behind a line of bushes to observe the area until I was sure the way was clear. Seeing no threats, I checked with Solace to see if she felt any dark soldiers nearby. She gave me a shrug, and I glanced around to see if I could see anything out of place. It looked clear to me, so I led us on, moving quietly and slowly with the others following suit.

We picked our way to the edge of the tree line. Once we were just inside the woods, I stopped, my fist snapping up into the air to tell the others to halt as well. They waited behind me as I listened. Happy to have my comrades back, I signaled to Nadia and Ivan to fan out so we weren't all clumped together and easy to spot. Ruth had said this place would probably be safe until Neyelah and her kin left, but I had no way of knowing if they were still there to shield us. I needed to know the location's status before we all proceeded to Ruth's house.

As we started moving again, I suddenly felt as though something were behind me, and I spun around with my pistol drawn, causing the others to do the same. But we all stopped short when we saw Captain Bates with a finger over his lips. He leaned in and said, "Neyelah left, and the Creature sent people to scope out this place. We are hiding until they leave. Follow me."

I nodded and signaled for the others to fall in behind me as we followed the captain to the small crevice that was covered in bushes—the one we had taken refuge in before. The captain moved aside the natural-looking cover over the crevice and waved us through to where Ruth and the others were waiting. Eyethanoff and his soldiers were nowhere in sight, but I assumed they were hiding nearby.

"Look what Benjamin found," whispered the captain joyfully as he joined us in the cramped hiding place. With all the people and horses lined up as they were, we filled the passage all the way to the vine-covered end. "I was so shocked to see them with Ben, I almost called out to them!"

Ruth smiled and we all embraced as well as we could in the crowded space, happy to see each other alive and well.

"How is this possible?" asked Catherine with tears of joy in her eyes. "Is Eric with you?"

Sadness filled Nadia's eyes as she shook her head. "I am sorry, Catherine. He didn't make it. The dragon got to him before the Prince opened the door to the Field of Doors."

Catherine's tears of joy vanished as anger overtook her. "What?"

"Shhhh!" we all whispered as Captain Bates clapped a hand over Catherine's mouth.

She struggled free of him, glaring at us all with fire in her eyes. "Your precious Prince couldn't have shown up just a few seconds sooner?" she snapped in a harsh whisper.

"Catherine—" I started, but she interrupted me with a look of hatred.

"Don't 'Catherine' me!" she snapped again, barely keeping her voice under control. "You got back what you lost!"

Not sure what to say, I simply looked to Solace for help. She was better at these things.

Solace stepped forward. "Eric gave his life to save us all," she said in a surprisingly stern tone. "Do not let him die in vain by giving away our hiding spot." A little more gently, she added, "We need to finish this mission. It is what Eric would have wanted."

Catherine's glare softened, but her jaw remained set and she spun in silence, crossing her arms and refusing to look at anyone.

Chapter 15

With a heavy sigh, I glanced at Solace. She shook her head, telling me to leave Catherine to her grief. There was nothing we could do to give her back what she had lost. All we could do was hope that Eric's sacrifice was worth it. With a heavy heart, I sat down next to Dan, noticing for the first time that he was injured.

"What happened?" I asked, still speaking in a low voice as I gestured to his bandaged leg.

"Daybreak came and Neyelah and most of her kin left," explained Christopher. "A beast showed up and found us. We fought it and killed it, but not before Dan took a claw to the thigh and the beast called for aid. We ran before more showed up. Ruth said this place is secure, as we saw a couple isps in this crevice when we entered," he added, glancing around. "But the beasts and Martecytes, and probably dark soldiers, are out there looking for us, and with only a couple isps here, we can't be sure they won't find us."

"So why don't we just leave?" I asked. "Wait, where is Jeb?"

"The beast caught us off guard while we were finishing packing for the next leg of the trip. We had all we needed, but Jeb wouldn't move for any of us, so we had to leave him in the paddock behind my tree," explained Ruth.

I rubbed the back of my neck. I was not going to leave without him.

Solace looked at Yuuki. "So, Ben tells me you are...not what you seem, Eyerkishta," she said with a smile.

Yuuki grinned. "I missed you," she said, hugging her as Solace knelt down in the cramped space.

"I figured it would be okay to tell them," I explained.

Yuuki nodded. "I am glad they know. I have missed hearing my name spoken by those I love," she said, her eyes tearing up for a moment before she regained her composure. "What happened while you were in the Field of Doors?" she asked.

"We met a rabbit named Reginald," said Otto. He had somehow ended up right in front of Betsy, who stood with the rest of the horses, Captain Bates, and his crew. With a scrunched nose, Otto wiped away her slobber from the side of his face and fixed the hair she had licked into sticking straight up. But it wasn't lost on me that he actually reached out and stroked her neck with a lopsided smile.

"Reggie!" Yuuki exclaimed softly with a smile. "I miss him," she added with a far-off look.

I chuckled, half at Otto and half at my memory of Reggie. "He is quite the character," I said of Reggie, "and he told us some things that didn't make any sense."

"Like what?" asked the captain as he handed Solace the reins to her white horse while Nadia and Ivan made their way to their own dappled gray steeds and the packs that had been stowed with them. Dan and Casey handed over the two horses' reins to the twins. Before we had reached land, we had all agreed that if anything happened to us, the horses and Betsy, excluding Jeb, since he wouldn't move for anyone but me, should be used by whoever needed them. But Otto, Solace, and the twins were clearly glad to have their companions back, along with their winter clothes.

"Well, he said something that led us to believe that Feyerndur might be the one who knows the final details of the King's plan. Reggie also said that the stone, which he claims was taken by Feyerndur before he joined the Creature, is just a stone from the fountain at Mair Pala," I said with a shrug. "There are some gaps in the timeline, but it seems that Feyerndur took the stone before he was corrupted, and then it ended up in the Lor Channel, where the Creature found it and took it. However, Reggie didn't seem to think it was a special stone."

Ruth rubbed her chin and frowned. "Like I said before, I don't remember much about the stone. It could have had some power, but if it did, it seems odd that the Creature hasn't used it yet."

"Can you think of a reason Feyerndur would take it?" said Solace.

Ruth shook her head. "I was not present when that happened. I just remember one day waking up and it was no longer on the fountain. I asked the Prince where it was, and he simply said he needed it for something. It seemed like he knew what he was doing, so I put it out of my mind," she explained.

"So, the stone has no value..." I said. "And we still don't know why Feyerndur took it," I mumbled to myself.

Ruth shrugged. "I suppose you will have to ask him. As I have spent time under this lie, my recollection of events has become hazy. I am afraid I am no longer able to remember all the details of that time."

I turned to Yuuki. "What about you?" I asked.

Yuuki thought for a moment, then shook her head. "I remember some things, but the Lie has muddled so much. What I do remember is that sometime around the Prince's sacrifice, Feyerndur just...left. I didn't know why. He said he would be back, but that was the last time I saw him," she explained, her eyebrows wrinkling in sorrow.

I placed a comforting hand on her shoulder. "Well, I need the medallion, and I have a feeling we will only get it if we can help him rid himself of Zath," I said.

"Then I guess we better find him," said Solace.

The captain turned to me. "Do you have any idea how you might be able to turn him back?"

I nodded. "I think I do."

"How?" asked Yuuki.

"The Ath Woods," I said as I began to gather my things.

"The Ath Woods?" asked Solace with raised eyebrows.

I nodded. "Reggie said that the medallion and the helmet wouldn't work to turn Feyerndur. I think I know what will, and it was something I was given by Adournath."

"The belt," said Yuuki with a nod. "All armor begins with the belt. But Feyerndur has his own armor. He already went through the process to gain his."

"Then he just needs to be reminded of the truth." I recalled something the Prince had said about the armor all being linked in a circle beginning and ending with the belt. "*Truth not only provides a firm foundation, but its power is a weapon unmatched,*" he had said. "He just needs to be reminded of the truth," I finished.

"Then let's go," said Solace. "There are currently no beasts or soldiers sniffing around our hiding place. If we leave now, they will never know we were here. Or we can wait until they leave the area entirely, but, based on their behavior, it looked like they were going to post guards at Ruth's tree."

I nodded. "I will go and get Jeb while you all get a head start. Do not wait for me. Solace will lead you, and I will make sure to catch up before you get too far."

"How are you going to get in without being seen?" asked the captain. "If they spot any of us, we will never make it out of here alive."

"Eyethanoff explained that the shield does actually hide me," I said. "I can use it."

Eyethanoff entered the crevice from the lower end just then and whispered, "Yes, but I also said that you don't know how to use it yet. You could expose your position at exactly the wrong time and get caught. Not to mention the fact that you definitely don't know how to cover both you and Jeb with it."

"I think if I focus, I can make it work," I said confidently as I noticed Solace, the twins, and Trixie and Otto all staring at Eyethanoff, wide-eyed.

Eyethanoff gave me a wary look. "Don't allow yourself to become overconfident, Ben. The Creature is not out of tricks yet, and he still needs access to your mind to find out where the Gate is located. Do not give the enemy any holds within you. Arrogance and overconfidence can produce shadows just as much as fear can."

I nodded. "I will be careful."

Solace, standing behind Ruth, pointed to Eyethanoff and opened her mouth, but Ruth, not noticing, spoke first. "Make sure you are, Ben. If you are captured now, this time may pass, and I am not sure it will ever come again," she warned, putting a hand on my shoulder.

I nodded. "I understand." Then I gestured to Solace and the others, drawing Ruth's attention to their astonishment. "Solace, this is Eyethanoff," I explained.

Her eyes widened even further, an expression mirrored by Otto and the twins.

"Who?" asked Trixie.

I smiled. "Um, he is…a guardian of sorts. Someone who has been helping me, even when I didn't know it. You each have your own guardian as well."

Eyethanoff smiled, as did Ruth. "I hate to interrupt introductions, but I must go off on my own, to gather those who have responded to my messages," Ruth said. "Be safe. All of you. I will meet you at the Ath Woods."

"You're right, we all need to get going. We will finish introductions later," I said.

With that, we all filed out, single file, from the crevice into the night. Ruth took her donkey and rode west while everyone else prepared to head north back to the mountains. Eyethanoff took a moment to quietly introduce Solace and the others to the soldiers assigned to protect them during this mission. They were excited to find out they too had soldiers looking out for them and gladly struck up conversations, though it took them some time to get used to speaking with their ghostly companions.

Since Solace and the others were back, there was now a shortage of horses, so everyone would have to take turns as needed. However, Eyethanoff gave his horse to Dan, so he wouldn't have to walk on his injured leg. Though Dan was hesitant to swing into the saddle of a horse he could only see as a ghost, Eyethanoff assured him it would work as well as any other horse. Once they were all settled, they moved out as quietly as they could, with Solace in the lead.

With the others on their way out, I headed to Ruth's tree, where I took refuge in the foliage a short distance away and examined the situation. I counted four soldiers of darkness, two guarding Ruth's tree in the back and two in the front. I didn't see any beasts or other soldiers. Jeb was in the back paddock, grazing. It looked like the guards had tethered him to a stake in the ground, and he was munching on grass in a circle around it. I frowned. I hated it when people tethered horses. Thankfully, Jeb was trained to stay calm if he got stuck, so he would be okay. But images of horses with broken legs and swollen sprains from spooking and getting caught in the ropes flashed through my mind.

Shaking the images from my head, I grabbed the shield and held it in front of me. I would have to get close enough to untie him. I took a deep breath and moved out.

I walked in a slightly crouched posture through the foliage, keeping the shield between me and the soldier of darkness sitting near Jeb. I managed to get within a few feet of Jeb before he lifted his head and looked at me.

I tensed. The guard stood and looked in the direction Jeb was looking. I shook my head at Jeb and gave him an auditory cue to turn away, one of two tricks I had taught him years ago when I had been playing a prank on my brother. I had convinced my brother that Jeb was broken when I had subtly cued him to refuse to look at my brother and to only walk backward. To get the walking backward trick to work at the time, Jeb couldn't be looking at me, so I had taught him an auditory cue that sounded like a bird. It wasn't a real bird call, but it was close enough that no one would notice it. Thankfully, Jeb understood my cue now, though we hadn't done it in years.

At the sound of my cue, Jeb backed up a few feet, keeping his gaze focused away from me. I stood stock-still, waiting for the guard to relax. But when he did, he still didn't look away from my direction. With a frustrated sigh, I realized I would have to take him out without alerting the other guard who was keeping an eye on the area beyond the paddock.

With the shield, this will be easy, I thought. I approached the guard, grabbed a knife from my boot, and wrapped both arms around him. With my shield hand, I covered his mouth, the shield strapped to my arm most likely causing him to disappear from any other guards' view. With my other hand, I plunged the knife through his heart. He never saw me coming. I grinned. *I have no idea why Eyethanoff was so worried.*

I turned to get Jeb, and the smile fell from my face when I saw the other guard staring at me. Both of us were frozen by shock for a moment, and then we burst into motion. The guard opened his mouth to call to the others, but I threw my knife. Its handle made contact with his head, just enough to knock him off kilter and momentarily halt his yell. By the time he recovered, I was on him. I dropped the shield and clamped a hand over his mouth as I wrapped my other arm around his throat.

He reached up toward me, and I almost didn't see the blade coming out of his sleeve as his hand moved. I ducked my head to one side, but the blade slid across my temple, opening a shallow cut. As I struggled to keep him silent and protect myself from his knife, blood dripped down my head into my ear. The urge to wipe it away was nearly overwhelming, but I ignored it and hung on, grabbing his wrist and twisting it—and the knife—away from my body as he finally came down to his knees.

The guard finally began to weaken as he struggled without air. By the time he went limp, my ear was full of blood and my arms were shaking. As the guard collapsed, I sank to my knees. I grabbed my knife off the ground and sliced deep into his neck to make sure he was dead.

Stumbling to my feet, I grabbed the shield and placed it at my back. I had to get out of here before the other guards noticed me. I cut Jeb loose and retrieved his tack from where it hung over the paddock fence, which was covered in vines and concealed from the outside by trees. Then I saddled Jeb, swung onto his back, and cued him into a quiet jog away from Ruth's tree, dabbing at my bloody wound with a sleeve.

Since Jeb was rested, it didn't take us long to catch up with the others. They had made it to a deer path at the base of a valley, headed toward Durthair. I wove my way through the group, headed for Solace, passing conversations as people got to know their soldiers of light.

"How do things look so far?" I asked Solace when I arrived at the front of the traveling group.

Solace's eyebrows raised. "Are you okay? What happened?"

"I'm fine. The bleeding has stopped," I said, gently touching the cut on my head.

Solace eyed the wound for a moment as she spoke. "So far, so good. We seem to be able to see things a little better, but not well. Eyethanoff and his soldiers are still only partially visible, so I have been keeping alert for any hint of darkness. I haven't sensed any dark soldiers nearby since we left Ruth's tree. Otto thinks it is going to start snowing soon, though, which will not make travel any easier."

I glanced up at the cloudy sky. "Are we going to make it with the supplies and horses we have?" I asked.

Solace nodded. "The horses are well rested, so they should be good, especially since we will have to go at walking speed for most of the trip. Yuuki explained that she can't remain in dragon form for too long because she isn't strong enough yet. But she said she is getting stronger, probably due to the cracks in the Lie. Maybe she can carry some of us later."

"Okay," I said. "She needs to stick to the ground, though. I don't want them knowing what direction we are coming from or when we arrive."

"So, what is your plan for freeing Feyerndur?" asked Nadia as she joined us at the front of the group on foot, Yuuki following close behind.

"In the Ath Woods, Adournath gave me the belt and showed me the truth—*The Story* as it really happened. I have a feeling the belt helped me see that story, as did the sword," I said simply.

Yuuki nodded. "I gave the belt to Adournath for safekeeping, as that was the only place it would be protected from the Creature. It was granted to you when you first entered the Ath Woods, starting you on this journey," she confirmed. "Both the belt and the sword work together to reveal the truth of the unseen."

"Exactly. But I don't know if it will work the same for Feyerndur, but he needs his armor back, and I think that starts with seeing the truth."

Yuuki nodded again. "It always does. I hope you are right, Ben. No one ever lost their armor until the Lie was in place," she explained.

Eyethanoff, who had been walking alongside us, spoke up. "He hasn't lost his armor." With Dan still astride his horse, Eyethanoff guided them around a rock in the trail. "Do you not recall that armor cannot be lost once the helmet is in place?"

Yuuki's eyes lit up. "Oh, you are right! I forgot." She shook her head. "I can't wait to be free of this lie," she said, rubbing her temples.

"So, if he didn't lose his armor, then what happened?" asked Nadia, looking at Eyethanoff.

"I was not there, so I can't say for sure. However, the armor will go dormant if it is not accessed for a long time. Like Eyerkishta's armor. She has not lost it. But when the Lie was set in place, she began to use it less and less, as she was in hiding. Over time, it went dormant. She will get it back as she begins to strengthen her connection to Original Power again."

"So, then, maybe he needs more than the truth," suggested Trixie as she and Otto approached from the back of the group, where they had been in conversation with Eyethanoff's soldiers.

I shook my head. "I don't think so..."

"Why not?" asked Solace.

"Reggie mentioned something about Feyerndur struggling within himself. When I found him in the cave, I saw him arguing with himself, as if good and evil were fighting within him. But, as

Yuuki suggested, that might be why he originally took the helmet. He just wants to be free of the dark hold on him. I think the truth is enough..." I explained, remembering the Prince's words. *"Your foundation must be truth—the truth of who I and my father are...Everything else will lead you astray."* "And the truth is that the world does not work the way it appears to work, not under this lie. He is free. He just needs to remember."

"How does knowing the truth help?" asked Nadia.

"Eeeye," I responded.

When I didn't hear a response, I looked around the group. Solace, Ivan, Nadia, Otto, and Trixie all looked completely confused. Eyethanoff, on the other hand, was smiling.

"What is Eeeye?" asked Otto, his nose scrunching in a frown.

"Eeeye is an Eeffraylick word," I began. "There is no word in our language with the same meaning. But the closest translation, according to Eyethanoff, is 'the life of two lives,'" I explained.

"What does that mean?" asked a confused Ivan.

"It is still hard for me to explain," I continued as I rubbed my chin, trying to remember how Eyethanoff had put it. "It is a connection...A relationship. Something unseen that produces something seen," I said, explaining it as best as I could in my own words, based on what Eyethanoff had told me. But as I spoke, I felt as though I were on the cusp of truly understanding the word. "It is...real, true love," I mumbled as I tried to pinpoint what I was on the verge of realizing. Then a phrase the Prince had said in my vision rang in my mind. *"A true relationship...The kind written on the heart."* Out loud, I said, "Not the kind where you fall in love, but the kind of love that you would die to preserve," quoting Eyethanoff more to myself than the others. Then I had a sudden thought, and I felt a deep realization come to fruition. "The kind of love that was shown in one moment in history. The moment a prince gave his life to create, for a people who had betrayed him, an opportunity to begin a new life..." I looked to Eyethanoff to find him smiling. "A new story—a story of the Lion and his people together again, despite the darkness we forged within our hearts. A story that is so deeply part of us that we can barely fathom its existence, but we can see what it produces—what it produced: a prince willing to die for those he loved and willing to stand between two powers at war to give us a way back home."

Eyethanoff nodded. "You are beginning to understand," he confirmed.

Everyone in the group seemed to have dropped their own conversations to listen now, and Dan piped up with a question. "So how does that help us free the dragon?"

"He needs to know he can't fight this battle alone. He will lose. The Creature would have us believe that we can fight our battles alone. But that is a lie. A lie that Feyerndur believed, and it cost him. He needs to remember that the battle he is fighting was already won." I recalled what Eyethanoff had said in our discussion of light and remembered for the first time that the Prince had said it too. "His debt to darkness was already paid." I looked to Eyethanoff. "What does that mean? What debt did we owe?"

Eyethanoff considered the question for a moment. "When you were on the ocean, you had dreams—dreams of the things you did when you fought for the Creature."

I nodded. "That is correct."

"What did those dreams do to you?" he asked. "How did they make you feel?"

I let out a sigh. "Guilty. Ashamed."

Eyethanoff steered his horse around a stump. "When we take refuge in darkness, we do things that cost us part of ourselves. When we give those parts of ourselves to the Creature, it is like he owns us. That is why the Prince had to overcome the power of evil within us all those years ago. We owed a debt to the one we had sold ourselves to, and only someone who had not fallen prey to that same darkness had enough light to pay for our freedom. He paid the debt that would have destroyed us for good."

I took in a deep breath as that sank in. A moment of silent thought fell over the group. Then Yuuki spoke.

"The dark armies followed Feyerndur," she said. "If he is to be reminded of the truth—that his debt was paid—then he will need our help."

I nodded. "I had Nadia and Ivan to watch my back while I was in the Ath Woods. Now, he will have us."

"We need to know what we are walking into, Ben," said Nadia.

"I agree." I turned to Yuuki. "I wanted to keep you out of the sky, but can you fly?"

Yuuki shook her head. "I don't think I am strong enough yet. But there are other ways to scout ahead, especially at night. I had better get going. I will get the information you need." With that, she ran off into the foliage around us, still in her human form. For a moment, I almost chased after her, old habits kicking in. But I found myself realizing I trusted that she knew what she was doing.

I turned to the others. "The rest of us need to be on the lookout for anyone who could give away our position," I commanded. "Surprise must be on our side if we expect to succeed."

Eyethanoff spoke up. "The time is near. The Creature's armies will gather to help the Creature maintain control. My armies are here to help."

"Thank you. We couldn't do this without you," I responded, placing a grateful hand on his shoulder.

Eyethanoff smiled. "It is our honor."

I released his shoulder, then turned back to the others. "I don't know all that will happen," I said as I looked at each face in the group, "but I know this: we have the Prince on our side. He is here with us, even if we can't see him or his power. The Prince has done his job to perfection. It is our turn to do ours."

Chapter 16

WE TRAVELED AS FAST as we could the rest of that night and all the next day before setting up camp at the base of the Hills—apparently named the Vardourian Hills—around sundown. Yuuki returned shortly after dark, having obtained the news that Feyerndur had made it to Durthair and was patrolling the area along with six beasts.

"Six beasts!" exclaimed Otto, his voice cracking slightly.

Ivan smashed a fist into his palm. "Let's put them in the ground," he growled.

"Is anything in town left standing?" I asked, ignoring the two dramatically different responses.

"Much of it is lost," replied Yuuki sadly.

"Missy!" said Nadia, realizing her friend was in danger.

"Who's Missy?" asked Christopher.

"She's a friend of the family who helps manage our inn," said Ivan.

"We need to focus," I said in as reassuring of a tone as I could muster. "I know this is hard, but we need to focus on the task at hand. If we do not, she may perish even if she survives this first attack."

Nadia sighed. She knew I was right. But I could see on her face that she was worried for her friend.

That night we all did our best to sleep, but we were now close enough to Durthair that the land around us was being patrolled by beasts, and we could hear the echoes of their calls in the distance. Creatures of darkness sounded in the distance, echoed by the screams of those they were terrorizing. With the Creature focused on his obsessive hunt for me and the Gate, his armies were no longer interested in protecting people to keep them on his side. Soon, we would either succeed in opening the Gate, or the Creature would succeed in destroying it forever and his chaos would reign in this land until the end of time.

At first light the next morning, we rose, packed, and got on our way. In springtime, I would estimate that we only had about a day left of travel, but this land was now infested with beasts, and the terrain was mostly frozen. There was no guarantee that we would make it that soon. We picked our way through the icy landscape, careful not to give our position away. The only way we would be able to get to Feyerndur was if the armies of darkness didn't see us coming. We had to stay hidden.

"Why can't we just use the doors?" groaned Ivan.

"Because we can't afford to get stuck somewhere if darkness overshadows a door we are using," I explained.

"Plus, we need to get there unannounced. If Ben uses a door, they will know where we are," Yuuki reminded us. "Each time we open a door, the Creature can feel a tear in the Lie, and he will know where to look. Even with Neyelah and her kin around, they could feel you open the door and know the general location to search. We are better off walking."

"Why didn't Ruth tell me when I went through before?" I demanded. "That is probably why those soldiers showed up after I left."

Yuuki frowned. "Probably because you might not have gone through the door. You still allow the circumstances to dictate how much you trust in Original Power," she reprimanded.

My shoulders sagged. She was right.

Ivan let out a sigh. "Well, it's not like we aren't expecting to fight them," he said, more to himself than to us.

"As much as I love your brash approach to things, now is not the time for people to see us coming," I pointed out.

"Why?" asked Ivan. "We are probably going to die anyways," he said gloomily.

"I would gladly give my life for the King," said Nadia, walking a bit taller. "A prince who will die for his people is a prince who deserves people who will fight for him to the last breath."

Otto glanced nervously at Nadia. She smiled. "It's okay, Otto. We will make it."

Otto's brow furrowed in an almost sorrowful expression. "You know...Nadia...I, um..."

Nadia looked at him expectantly.

"If my calculations are correct...I may have to leave when my part in this mission is over..." He swallowed hard at Nadia's disappointed frown. "But I just wanted to tell you—"

"Never mind, Otto," she snapped. "We have a mission to complete."

Otto glanced at his mother with a hurt expression. Trixie offered a comforting smile, though, based on the tension in her shoulders, it appeared that she, too, was worried about the mission ahead. Otto sighed but didn't press the matter.

We walked and rode in silence, each of us immersed in our own thoughts. Otto's attempt at telling Nadia about his feelings for her had put me in a melancholy mood, which the others seemed to share. It was clear that things would be different for all of us once we completed this mission. Finally, the silence was broken by Ivan.

"What is the point of this?" he asked pensively, a note of tension in his voice. "We have given up everything for this mission, and now we are on our way to fight a dragon? And probably die without getting to see the results we are fighting for? How is that worth the trade?"

I cued Jeb to a halt, bringing the whole group to a stop, and looked at him. "What happened in the Field of Doors, Ivan? Something has been bothering you since then, and I think we all need to know what it is."

"I agree," said Nadia, grabbing Ivan's arm. "If something has you worried, we definitely need to know about it."

Ivan frowned and slipped out of Nadia's grasp. "I came on this journey to get treasure," he said, dodging my question. "Then I decided to help Ben with this mission. Now we are off to fight a dragon, who could kill us all, with a bunch of people who still only look like ghosts, by the way. How do we know we haven't all lost our minds? Ben almost did, out on the ocean," he said, gesturing to me.

Catherine nodded. "He has a point, you know," she said, glaring at me.

My brow furrowed. "I don't know what to tell you, Ivan."

He shook his head. "I just..."

Solace's eyes narrowed. "The Prince showed you something in the Field of Doors, didn't he?"

Ivan gave Solace a wary look.

"Ivan?" said Nadia. "What did you see?"

Ivan turned away for a moment, scratching his moustache. Then he turned back. "I saw nothing but darkness, Ben," he said, finally making eye contact with me for the first time in days. "I saw death and destruction. I saw pain and suffering that I couldn't escape." His eyes remained locked on mine. "I saw greed for control end this mission in failure. We might not make it out of this alive...and I don't think we can succeed."

Silence fell over the group for a moment. I glanced around at the others. "What did the rest of you see?" I asked.

Nadia spoke up first. "I saw loss...and pain," she said. "But there was hope. I learned to trust the Prince in that trial, in my vision. I think we can do this with his help."

I looked to Trixie and Otto. "And you?"

They both swallowed and looked at one another. Trixie spoke. "I remember that the vision was clear, but since then, it has been like recalling a dream. I think Nadia is right—there was hope. I think everything will turn out alright. I remember seeing the Prince," she explained as Otto nodded in agreement.

I let out a sigh. "Why didn't you all tell me sooner?" I asked.

"From what I remember," said Nadia, "it was like the Prince was giving me a message. I don't recall the exact details, so I wasn't sure it was important. But now that I know others had visions..." She shrugged. "I guess it is. I still don't remember the details in full, but I know that I will remember when I need to."

The others nodded, except Ivan.

"I am not so sure," he said.

Otto fiddled nervously with Betsy's reins as he spoke up. "Is this worth dying for? The beasts serve the Creature, and he is just using them to try to keep us in line. There is a good chance they will stop attacking if we just let the Creature win," he pointed out. "What is the point of dying if we are not around to see the result of our work?"

Nadia answered calmly, "Some things are just that important..."

"Important enough to die for so that someone else can live a self-centered, cushy life because of your sacrifice?" Otto responded, his tone more worried than annoyed.

"Not to sound rude or anything," said Ivan, "but weren't you a spoiled rich merchant's son before you met Ben?"

Surprisingly, Otto nodded, apparently unoffended. "Yes, I was. And that is my point. I know what happens to people whose world has been saved by those who did not live long enough to show them what could have been lost. I grew up in a place where others always fought my wars. I simply reaped the benefits of their struggles."

"If you know that world so well, Otto, then tell me this," said the captain gently. "Would you have listened to them if they had survived and told you to use wisely the life you'd been given?"

Otto thought for a moment, then his shoulders slouched. "No," he admitted.

The captain nodded. "There are many things in life that are worth fighting for," said Captain Bates, looking at each of us in turn. "But there are few things that are worth dying for. No matter what people in the future might do with what we give them through our sacrifice, that sacrifice is still worth giving if for no other reason than to provide them with the opportunity to make the right choice—a better choice than those before them."

"I have never looked at it like that before," Otto admitted as his expression took on a hint of something like patriotism. It was a new look for him, but one he wore surprisingly well. Still, I could see he was scared as he stroked Betsy's neck. He had been through a lot, and he did not want to die. None of us did.

I looked at Ivan. "Ivan, we need you on this mission." I looked at each person gathered around me. "We need all of us." I placed a firm hand on Ivan's shoulder. "What do you say?"

Ivan took in a deep breath and looked at me. He seemed to consider the question, then said, "I don't know about this prince and power stuff...but I will come for you."

I nodded and we shook hands. I turned to the others. "From this point on, we are committed. We will not stop until this is over. I will do all I can to protect you, but if anyone does not want to fight, you should leave now. I will not hold it against you."

No one moved.

"Let's move out, then," I finished.

With that, we continued on. Though I wouldn't say the group seemed particularly confident, we each pulled our own weight, our goal clearly in mind. Each of us remained silent in our focus, though Nadia and I noticed Otto mumbling to Betsy at one point. It lifted our spirits, and we shared a smile at seeing them getting along.

Traveling quickly when we could and slowly when necessary to avoid drawing attention to ourselves, we followed a route not often used by humans. But with still a day's worth of travel left, a blizzard blew in, forcing us to set up camp rather than continue into town.

During the night, we huddled together for warmth and kept watch for beasts.

The next day, we set out early under a cloudy sky, and those who had not slept at night dozed on their horses, surrounded by those who were more alert. After nearly half a day of travel, Solace rode up next to me and grabbed my arm. I snapped up a fist to signal the others to stop. "What is it?" I whispered.

"Something dark," she said as she scanned the area. "Beasts, I think."

We all stood quiet and motionless as we listened. A breeze rustled the leaves, turning the foliage around us into a nerve-wracking orchestra of sounds.

"We need to keep going," I whispered as I motioned everyone to start moving again. "We are almost there."

"If we get caught now, we will never be able to surprise them," Solace commented. "We are hopelessly outnumbered, Ben. I can feel it. We need to play this safe," she warned.

I thought for a moment and realized Solace was right. We needed to approach this situation a little differently. I gave the signal to fan out, and we stayed loosely bunched into two main groups, my group and Solace's group. We split up but stayed within eyesight of each other as we trekked as silently as we could through the winter landscape.

After about an hour, a twig snapped somewhere ahead of us. We all froze. I listened for a moment, then signaled to the others to stay put while I dismounted to check it out on foot. As I crept forward through the foliage, I could tell that the Creature had sent his beasts to find us. Their massive paw prints were scattered across the snow and mud around me, and they were fresh.

I turned and headed back to the others. "At least one beast," I reported. "It is just ahead of us, but they usually travel in pairs or small groups, which means there are probably more nearby."

Solace nodded. "I think we need to get to higher ground."

I glanced around the area. For the past five miles or so, we had been traveling in a valley, using the higher ground on either side to shield us from weather and the enemy while Eyethanoff and his soldiers walked along the ridge above us, keeping an eye out. A half-frozen river flowed past us, and we were surrounded by bare trees and thick, ice-covered bushes, the air filled with the scents of old plants and ice. The beast whose tracks I had found was likely in the valley ahead of us, but there was no way to tell how many more we might encounter.

My frozen breath hung in the air for a moment as I thought, reviewing possible outcomes of each action that rushed through my mind. "The top of the hill above this valley is more open," I said, looking to Solace.

She nodded. "Yes, but if we get attacked here, we could easily be pushed into the river."

I nodded. "Okay, let's move."

We pulled closer together and formed three lines, one led by me, one led by the captain, and one led by Solace. Eyethanoff and the rest of his small group of soldiers fanned out around us, creating a distant circle. The soldiers of light seemed to fade into the landscape as they blended in with sunbeams streaming through the bare branches above us.

We moved on cautiously, headed for the nearest high ground. When we reached the top of the small hill, we stopped to survey the land around us, remaining as hidden as we possibly could. I signaled to Eyethanoff silently, requesting information on what he had found. He came up next to me to deliver an answer, then returned to his soldiers.

"We are surrounded by beasts," I told the others, relaying Eyethanoff's message. "The good news is that Eyethanoff believes they don't know we are here. We need to stay quiet and go slow. Everyone, get off your horses and keep them calm."

We headed out on foot with our mounts in tow. We decided the best formation would be in a loose group, keeping a few yards between each person. If the beasts caught wind of us, we would need everyone's help to fight even just one of them, but we didn't want to cluster too close together, or it would be easier for them to kill us all in one attack.

Eyethanoff signaled to me that the beasts were getting closer as we drew near Durthair, approaching from the east. The sound of a twig snapping caused us all to freeze yet again. But this time, it was not from the enemy. I turned slowly to find Ivan standing with one foot in the air and a pained expression on his face. We all waited in silence, listening, hoping that the noise would go unnoticed. But then I heard it. The sound of heavy breathing.

A puff of breath frozen by the cold air formed behind Ivan as a massive beast appeared in the brown bushes at his back, at least twice the size of a horse. This beast was slightly different from those I had fought before. It had a thicker coat—a winter coat—and its body resembled a bull's, complete with horns, though it had fangs. The beast let out a challenging huff as Ivan swallowed hard and turned slowly to face the terrifying animal. At his proximity, a quick movement would be futile. Beasts were fast, and this one's mouth was mere inches from Ivan's head.

For a moment, we all stood frozen. Even the beast held its ground. But then it lifted its head and began to call to its pack. The sound started as a low rumble. Then, suddenly, an arrow pierced the animal's throat, silencing it. Almost out of reflex, Ivan swung his sword in an upward arc, slicing through the beast's neck, and it dropped to the ground, dead.

Eyethanoff appeared next to me with a new arrow ready in his bow. "I think the Creature's armies may still be unaware of our location, but any beast within a half a mile would have felt that rumble. More beasts will be here soon," he announced.

As if Eyethanoff's words had cued it, another beast burst from the bushes.

"This way!" I yelled as I waved the others forward.

Solace, Ivan, Nadia, Christopher, and the captain took up positions alongside me as Casey swung one of Dan's arms over his shoulder and Catherine took the other. Yuuki led them to cover behind a thick tree, where they lowered Dan to the ground. They left Yuuki there to keep an eye on him while they returned to their captain's side, ready for a fight. We had to take this beast down before it alerted more.

Ivan was the first to attack, as usual. He lunged toward the creature's massive body with his sword held high and an animal-like growl in his throat. The beast rose on its hind legs, swinging a paw toward its incoming attacker. But Ivan knew how beasts fought. At the last moment, he dropped to his knees and slid across frozen leaves, slashing at the underside of the beast's leg.

The captain joined Nadia and I as we attacked the beast from the sides and Ivan swung for its belly. With the three of us distracting the creature, Ivan drove his sword into its stomach. Black blood spilled from its guts, covering Ivan and splashing Nadia and I as the beast pawed at the injury. Nadia, black blood half covering her face, went in for the killing blow, driving a knife through the eye socket and into its brain.

Just as she pulled her knife from the dead animal's head, the rest of the pack arrived.

Chapter 17

THE BEASTS CHARGED TOWARD us, smashing through the ice encased underbrush, their hot breath puffing from their nostrils into the cold air around them.

"We can't let them overwhelm us," warned Eyethanoff. "We need to split them up and keep them quiet so they don't alert the armies of darkness. Aim for the center of their necks just below the jaw. It will prevent them from making loud calls. If you hit them off to one side, they may bleed out eventually, but they will still be able to call. Make sure you hit dead center. We can kill them after."

With a nod to Eyethanoff, I signaled to the others to spread out into groups of about five, each focusing on one beast. I left my pistols in my belt, as they would make too much noise. Swords and arrows would have to do.

There were four beasts in this pack. Not a lot, but their massive size and thick skin would make killing them a challenge. Nadia and Eyethanoff fired their first arrows in unison, striking two of the beasts though the throat in exactly the right place before reloading and firing at the other two. Though it wasn't enough to take them down, it was enough to keep them quiet and make them bleed.

Ivan and Solace attacked the first newly silenced beast as Nadia fired a second arrow at a beast she had missed. She hit her mark the second time, but not before a low rumble escaped the animal's throat.

Solace took a lesson from Ivan and slid toward the nearest beast, under its belly. But the huge animal was faster than she expected. It sidestepped her, swinging a paw around backward in an attempt to flatten her. Solace barely dodged the attack, crying out when the beast's claw scraped across her back as she spun. The wound looked shallow but painful, and she winced as she faced the beast again.

While Ivan, Christopher, Casey, Catherine, and Solace fought their beast, Nadia and I went after another, along with the captain, Trixie, and Otto. Lion's Sword soldiers formed the other two groups, attacking the remaining beasts.

The highly trained soldiers of light took out their beast first. But just as things seemed to be going in our favor, the sound of more beasts charging in to back up their companions rumbled through the trees around us, and three more burst onto the battleground. Eyethanoff and Nadia immediately reacted, firing arrows that hit their marks and silenced the beasts but did not penetrate deep enough to kill them. With this many beasts to fight, we were pushed closer and closer to our destination and nearer their allies in Durthair, who might hear their calls.

"We can't let them get to Durthair!" I called to Solace and Eyethanoff. A cry of pain rang out behind me, and I spun just in time to see Otto's soldier of light crushed under the paw of a beast. I ran to his aid, but it was too late. The beast spun on me, and I dodged it at the last moment, coming up on the other side. The battlefield was before me. Ivan was bleeding from a wound on his leg, Solace from the wound on her back. Two more of Eyethanoff's soldiers were down. *This isn't working. We can't afford to lose anyone else.*

Before I could come up with a plan, the beast turned on me again and Nadia came to my aid. Just as we managed to finally kill it, Otto and Trixie appeared at the edge of the trees nearby.

"Ben!" called Trixie. "Otto and I have a plan!"

"Do it!" I said as I dodged the paw of a beast riddled with arrows in its neck and shoulder, only to be knocked off my feet by another.

Otto and Trixie disappeared into the brush and trees, and I stood on unsteady legs as Eyethanoff and his soldiers dispatched another beast and came for the one attacking me.

Suddenly, Otto yanked me into a bush where he was hiding and handed me a grass-like plant with thin, white leaves. "Here. Get them to eat this!" he ordered.

"Are you insane? I am not going to shove this in a beast's mouth, Otto. What is it?" I asked, grabbing Otto and pulling him out of harm's way as a beast fell, dead, onto the bush we had been occupying.

"Remember the monsters in the Valley?" he asked. "The ones we fed those plants that made them tired?"

I nodded, beginning to understand his plan. "This will make them easier to kill?"

He grinned. "Even better. Trust me. Just don't eat it yourself," he warned before rushing off to give some more of the plant to the others.

I glanced at the plant in my hands and shook my head. *There's no way I can get this in the mouth of a beast,* I thought. Then I spotted a bow and arrow on the ground next to Otto's dead soldier of light. I looked to Nadia as she fired another arrow at a beast, then dodged its attack, and I had an idea. Trusting that Otto and Trixie knew what they were doing, I headed for the bow and arrow. But as I stepped from the foliage, I spotted a beast headed straight for me, leaving me only an instant to move from its path.

I dove to one side and grabbed the bow and arrow from next to the crushed body of the Lion's Sword soldier as the beast's momentum carried it by me and it slammed its paws into the ground to turn for another charge. I rammed the tip of the arrow through a handful of the leaves from Otto, rolled to my back, and nocked the arrow. Moving as fast as I could, I barely got the shot off as the beast opened its mouth wide in mid charge and let out a roar like a bear. The arrow hit the beast square in the back of the tongue, and it skidded to a halt, pawing at its mouth. When it couldn't get the arrow out, it turned on me with wild rage. The beast reared into the air on its hind legs, then dropped to resume its charge. I ran.

I tossed aside the bow and unsheathed my sword as I tried to gain some distance from the beast. Then I spun to face the creature and spotted Nadia and Ivan racing up behind it to help me, but suddenly, the beast slid to a stop, inches from the tip of my outstretched sword. It stood there for a moment, blinking, before shaking its head and jerking from side to side as if looking for an invisible attacker. It began lashing out at empty air and opened its mouth to sound its displeasure, but only a faint hiss came out as it began foaming at the mouth. The beast collapsed to the ground, groggily swinging at nothing, then let out a heavy breath and went still.

"What was that?" asked Ivan with wide eyes.

"Otto found a plant," I said with a shrug.

Ivan let out a laugh that could only come from someone who had been sure they were going to die but now saw they might have a chance at living. "Of course he did, that little wizard!"

I reached out to Nadia and handed her some of the leaves. "Here, attach these to your arrows and fire right into their mouths. Ivan and I will be the bait while you take the shots."

With the new strategy for taking them down, Nadia and Eyethanoff made good use of their archery skills. The beasts fell, one by one. But just before we could drug the final beast, it took off toward Durthair at a sprint.

"I got it!" I said, whistling for Jeb as I grabbed a bow and arrow from Nadia. Jeb burst through the bushes, and I ran to catch up, swinging into the saddle. As I passed Otto, he handed me another blade of the white grass. Leaving the battlefield behind, I chased after the beast, which opened its mouth in an unsuccessful attempt to call out for help.

The beast accelerated to full speed, barely seeming to notice the arrow still protruding from its neck as it gradually pulled further ahead. If it kept up its pace, it would surely get close enough to Durthair that simply the sound of it crashing through the underbrush would alert the others. I couldn't let that happen.

Jeb darted through bushes and trees, his breath a passing fog in the cold air as he carried me through the frozen landscape. Thankfully, the beast left behind similar clouds of breath as well, making it easier to track. I also caught the occasional glimpse of small smears of blood on leaves and branches being torn from the bushes as the beast charged ahead of us.

As Jeb rounded a corner, he very nearly lost his footing on a patch of ice. I shifted in the saddle to help him balance, and he managed to stay upright while sliding across the slick ground. As soon as he regained his footing, we continued our pursuit. But the beast was still faster. *We aren't going to make it!*

Suddenly, a loud crunch sounded up ahead, and I cued Jeb to slow. As we broke through some bushes, I realized we might still be moving too fast, as I could see a drop-off ahead where ice had given way. Just in time, Jeb slid to a halt at the edge of the cliff, barely keeping us from meeting the same fate as the beast we had been chasing. We were so close to the edge that I could see the beast's motionless body on the sharp rocks below.

Breathing hard, Jeb and I stood there for a moment, making sure the beast was actually dead. Just to be certain, I put some of the plant on the end of the arrow and fired it into the beast's back. I had no idea if it would do anything, but the beast's lack of movement when the arrow hit convinced me it was dead. Satisfied, I cued Jeb to turn back the way we had come.

When we arrived back at the battle scene, all the beasts were down, but so was the one Lion's Sword soldier. I dismounted Jeb and looked to Solace to make sure she was okay. Her expression told me she was in pain from the wound across her back, but she was otherwise alright. I took her hand in mine and turned to Eyethanoff as we gathered around the dead soldier. I placed my other hand on Eyethanoff's shoulder as he knelt over his fallen comrade.

"I am so sorry," was all I could say.

Eyethanoff simply nodded, then closed the dead soldier's eyes. He took in a deep breath and stood. "Solace, Ivan, Hannaff, and Ash are injured," he said, gesturing to two of his soldiers. "My physician, Leigheas, can help them, but we need to get moving again soon."

I nodded. "Thank you." I glanced at Otto, who was staring at the fallen soldier assigned to guard him with a look of worry on his face. He had only known the soldier for a short time, but he was clearly affected by his death.

While Leigheas tended to the wounded, I gathered the others around.

"Where did you find those plants?" I asked Otto, drawing his attention to me.

"They grow all over the place," he responded matter-of-factly, as if I should know that.

"Well, thanks for the idea," I replied, ignoring Otto's tone. "Who knew it was easier to get a beast to eat something than to die."

Everyone let out a chuckle and then a collective deep sigh of relief.

Otto turned toward me and smiled. "You're welcome."

Suddenly, Otto's eyes widened, and he leapt for Nadia. Eyethanoff drew his bow and arrow, and I drew my sword, reacting to Otto's behavior. Turning, we were met with a barrage of four arrows flying toward us in an arc above the brush. Everyone took cover. I shoved Solace behind a boulder, leaving myself exposed to the attack. But Ivan yanked me behind a tree as an ink-black arrow trailing black fog pierced his shoulder.

Peering around the edge of the tree, I spotted two soldiers of darkness reloading two arrows each for another attack. But Eyethanoff and his soldiers were already retaliating, killing one soldier of darkness before the other began to flee. They quickly pursued him, as we could not allow him to return to Durthair with news of our whereabouts.

Ivan and I scanned the surrounding area in search of any more enemy soldiers but thankfully found none.

"Otto!" Nadia's scream drew our attention.

Otto's impact with Nadia had knocked them both to the ground, saving her life. But the arrow that had been heading for Nadia was now protruding from deep within Otto's chest.

Lying on the ground, Otto had a frozen look of shock on his face, his mind probably trying to grasp what had just happened. He let out a gurgling cough, grabbing at the arrow as Nadia desperately inspected the wound for evidence that he could survive. But it was too deep. The moment the arrow had struck him, it had immediately begun to leach some kind of ink-like poison into his chest and clothes. Blackness was seeping into Otto's clothes as dark veins crawled up his neck. His skin was growing pale, and dark circles appeared under his eyes.

Seeing the life begin to drain from his eyes, Nadia grabbed Otto in her arms. "No, no, no!" she cried, as if confusion and desperation had rid her mind of anything else to say. "Otto..." she began, but she couldn't continue. Tears began to stream down her face as she desperately held on to the only person she had ever been in love with. Trixie and Ivan dropped to their knees next to Otto. Trixie pulled Otto's shirt open so they could get a closer look at the wound, but Leigheas stopped them as the wound was exposed.

"That is shadow poison," said Leigheas softly, "and the arrow has pierced too deep. The infection is spreading fast—there is nothing we can do," he explained as the black ink-like poison consumed Otto's chest.

Otto attempted to gasp for air as he grabbed Trixie's hand. She tried to force a reassuring smile. "It's okay," she said as Ivan stood and took a few steps away, his jaw clenched in shock and anger. His shoulders tensed under his black fur cloak, and he ran a hand over his head.

Trixie swallowed hard, then took Nadia's hand and placed it in Otto's. With what little strength he had left, he gripped her hand in his and gazed up at her. "I love you, Nadia," he choked out, tears filling his eyes. "I...I am sorry it took me until now to say it. I..." Otto attempted to gasp again. "I didn't want...t...to hear you say you didn't love me b...back."

Fresh tears spilled over as Nadia responded. "I love you too, Otto. I will always love you."

"Really?" he whispered, looking slightly surprised. "I did not predict that," he added before coughing again. This time, blood trickled from his mouth.

Nadia forced a smile. "Really."

Otto's expression filled with joy, and he whispered, "The captain was right. There are a lot of things w...worth living for. But only one thing worth dying for." Otto's voice weakened. "The P...Prince said it well in my vision. The only thing worth dying for is..." He coughed.

"Is what?" asked Nadia with a trembling voice.

"You." The word barely escaped his mouth before Otto went limp in Nadia's arms as she placed a kiss on his pale lips.

"Otto, no!" she sobbed. "Please don't leave me!" she begged. But he was gone.

Forcing myself to hold back tears of my own, I knelt next to Nadia and Trixie. "We have to keep going," I said, blinking hard. I could mourn later. "The enemy kno—"

"I am not leaving him!" snapped Nadia as she clutched his lifeless body in her arms.

I had never seen her like this before. Nadia had never been the type to fall in love. But she had fallen in love with Otto after knowing him for only a few weeks. Now he was gone. It was a nightmare I knew all too well. The feeling of holding your loved one in your arms as their life slipped from their body pierced one deep inside, leaving a scar that would slowly heal over but never fade from memory.

I looked to Trixie. She was staring blankly at her fallen son, tears streaming down her face. I placed a hand on her shoulder, and she tore her gaze from her son to look back at me. She opened and closed her mouth as though struggling to form words. Then she looked back at Otto's body and whispered, "How could this happen? We were apart for so long, and now—"

Her last words were cut off as she fought to hold back sobs. But I knew what she was going to say. She and Otto must have thought they would have more time now that they were together again.

I stood as Eyethanoff and his soldiers returned just then, their bows loaded and ready to defend against any more dark soldiers. He sent me a look that said we needed to get moving. I had to think of something to say. Something that would get Nadia to move. I squatted down and placed a gentle hand on her back. "Nadia. Otto gave his life to protect you and to give us a chance to accomplish what we came here to do. Do not let that go to waste," I pleaded.

"We need to fight. As he did. We need to make sure he didn't die in vain. We need you."

Eyethanoff laid a hand on my shoulder, "Ben, we have taken out the two who saw us, but more dark soldiers will be on their way," he warned tactfully. "If they find us here, we might all perish."

I pushed myself to my feet and quietly backed away as Nadia gripped Otto in her arms, shaking with silent tears. Trixie remained on her knees next to her son's body. Though she seemed to have already prepared herself for this moment, she struggled to stand as soft sobs threatened to overflow again. But ultimately, they both knew I was right. There was no time to do anything but leave him where he fell. Ivan, his jaw still set and anger boiling in his eyes, gently took Nadia in his arms and pulled her away from Otto as she reluctantly let him go. Christopher wrapped a dark cloak and a comforting arm around Trixie's shoulders, offering his support as they began to move on.

Eyethanoff led the way as we all followed, leaving Otto's body behind on the frozen ground.

The rest of our travels were completed in silence. The anticipation of nearing the end of our mission, and hopefully success, was harshly contrasted by the searing pain of loss. Even the landscape around us seemed more dull and dreary than before as we moved in silence, doing our best to keep up the pace despite our sorrow. Though Otto had started out as a nuisance, he had come to be an integral part of this group. Someone who meant something to all of us, even if we perhaps hadn't fully realized it until he was gone.

This loss cut deep. It forced me to realize who we were fighting. Our enemy did not always seem to be one of flesh and blood. But he was real. And if we didn't succeed, we all would meet the same fate as Otto, or worse.

When we finally approached Durthair around sunset, we slowed our pace. With our minds now haunted by loss, we needed to be careful that we didn't make any more mistakes. Before we came within sight of Durthair, Eyethanoff disappeared into the trees, looking for the rest of his troop, who had split up with us at the mountains. They had said they would meet us here. When Eyethanoff finally reappeared in the distance, he silently waved us over. Solace took the lead as we joined Eyethanoff and followed him deeper into the foliage. I kept an eye on our flank as we traveled up a ridge on the west side of the Crescent Hill, which I remembered was called Creal Hill, where there was a good view of Durthair. Staying low and out of sight along the ridge were the soldiers of light, waiting and keeping an eye on the streets below.

Mythair approached on foot, joining Eyethanoff and I among the trees.

"How did it go through the pass?" asked Eyethanoff.

"The Creature caught on to us about halfway, but we hoped you had made it far enough ahead by then," said Mythair. "We managed to make it here only an hour ago, in time to see the beasts attacking, though it looked like they had already come through once or twice. We were able to help a few people out, but we didn't want to give away our position, as we are currently outnumbered."

"By how much?" asked Christopher as he and the captain joined us.

"We have counted about fifty soldiers of darkness and Marte-cytes, not including a few beasts and Zath." He gestured to the ridge above us. "Come take a look for yourself."

We joined the line of soldiers, fanning out to one side of them, and surveyed Durthair below. What we saw laid out before us only mirrored our emotions. Destruction. Illuminated by moonlight breaking through the clouds, Durthair's streets were spotted with bodies. No living townspeople were anywhere in sight, for they surely knew they would have a better chance of surviving if they remained hidden. Blood seemed more prevalent than mud as melted snow created small crimson streams along the roads. Most of the buildings were charred and collapsing, and some fires still burned in the late evening light. The scene posed a dismal contrast to the white winter landscape around it.

On Creal Hill to our right sat General Delaney's mansion. The only untouched building in sight. Its magnificent architecture had once been promoted as an image of hope. But now I knew the reality of what it stood for. Darkness and corruption. I shook my head as I recalled the work I used to do for the Creature. But that time was in the past. *It is time for his lie to end.*

From our vantage point, we could see just over the few buildings in Durthair that were still standing to the trees on the other side that made up the Woods and the Forest beyond—the Ath Woods and the Bawtha Forest. Within Durthair, the beasts that had caused so much destruction still roamed the streets, along with the Creature's soldiers. Some looked as though they were watching for someone—probably us. Others were picking through the rub-ble, possibly looking for any survivors the Creature could recruit to his armies. Then I spotted him. Zath. He was speaking with some

Martecytes and dark soldiers closer to the Ath Woods, and even from here, I could tell he was unsettled. Angry.

Casey leaned over to Christopher and whispered, "Why are those shadows moving down there?"

Christopher glanced over the town below, and his eyes widened. They both looked at Eyethanoff.

"Soldiers of darkness," he said. "You can see them?"

Casey looked back at Durthair. "No. Well, maybe. Now that you told me what they are, I can see their resemblance to people." He shivered at the sight.

I considered the situation. Eyethanoff was right in camp. Things were about to change. It seemed we had reached the pinnacle of this mission. We had to succeed. If we failed, the Creature would find the Gate and destroy it, keeping us all trapped under this lie and ruling for who knew how long with his ravenous beasts at his side. "We need to get Zath to enter the Ath Woods," I said aloud.

"To do that, we should take cover in them and draw him in," said Solace. "Will we be safe there?" she asked, looking to Eyethanoff.

Eyethanoff nodded. "To the best of my knowledge, dark soldiers cannot enter the Ath Woods. But to be honest, things are changing, and Original Power is coming back into the land. So, anything is possible at the moment."

"Good point." I frowned in thought as I studied the scene before us. Durthair was filled with debris. "If you all wait in the woods, I could go out and lure him in. That way, if I can do it alone, we won't risk losing anyone. But if I need backup, you will be close by and ready."

Solace nodded and passed the plan down the line until it reached the soldier of light at the other end. I saw him survey the area before us, thinking through the idea. Then he looked back to us and nodded.

With Eyethanoff in the lead again, we headed west around the edge of town, staying hidden behind Creal Hill until we passed the west side of Durthair and into the Bawtha Forest. From there we headed east until we entered the Ath Woods.

Once within the circle of trees, we continued to the clearing in the center and stopped near the large stone where I had met Adournath before. There was no sign of him now, though.

I turned to the others. "Is everyone ready?" I asked, glancing at each of the injured in turn to ensure they were alright.

Ivan set his jaw. "We're good," he said. But I could tell he was in pain, and I suddenly remembered the arrow that had hit him.

"No, you're not good," I said. "That arrow that grazed your shoulder was the same kind that killed Otto."

Leigheas stepped forward. "Let me check—"

"I'm fine," growled Ivan. Suddenly, it was as if the anger he had been holding back since Otto's death came rushing out. "We are wasting time! We are wasting everything!" He turned to me. "This mission is doomed to fail, and if you had just listened to me when I told you that the first time, Otto would still be alive!"

I swallowed hard as the others grew quiet and seemed to pull away from where Ivan and I stood face-to-face. "You don't know that, Ivan."

"Really?" he snarled. "And you do? You think you have this all under control, but people are dying now, Ben! Dying! All so you can find some missing artifacts that no one even knew about until a few months ago!"

"Ivan, you know the Gate is more tha—"

"All I know," he said, jabbing himself in the chest, "is that the man my sister loved, Trixie's son, is dead, and we are too few and too worn out to make anything of it. He died for nothing, and we will too if you don't abandon this mission right now."

I glared at him. I knew he was angry, and he had a right to be. But he was taking this too far. "You can leave if you want to, Ivan," I said, not wanting to drag this argument out any longer. "But if you stay, you better have my back, because I'm here to do a job, and people are counting on us even if they don't know what for."

Leigheas gestured to Ivan's arm. "Whatever you choose, please let me at least look at that wound. If you were struck by what is called a shadow arrow, you could die. Or worse," he said.

"And what could you do to stop the poison?" Ivan snapped.

Leigheas frowned. "If I can get it in time, I could save you," he said.

Ivan relented, glowering at me. "Fine."

Leigheas checked the wound, exposing ink-black flesh around the cut on Ivan's arm.

"How does it look?" I asked.

Leigheas shook his head. "We might have caught it soon enough. But I am not sure. I will treat it."

I nodded and looked at Ivan as Leigheas made him sit down and got to work. "I get why you are angry. But you know as well as I do that we need all the help we can get. You included. The King has given us everything we need so far, and he will get us through the rest of this."

Ivan glared off into the distance. "As I said before, you I will fight for. I will stay for now, but when this over, I'm done with this king of yours."

Nadia's eyes widened in shock as a jolt shot through my chest that had nothing to do with the armor. The idea that Ivan was angry at the King hit me harder than I would have expected. I took a deep breath and shot Nadia a look that told her to stay calm. We couldn't deal with this now. We would talk when this was over. But that thought didn't sit well as I realized we might not all make it out of this alive.

Turning away from Ivan, I glanced around the woods we stood in, trying to put his statement out of my mind. "Adournath is not here," I observed aloud, wondering where he could be.

"Of course not," mumbled Ivan.

"What do you seek?" A soft but deep voice seemed to come from everywhere, floating on a breeze that rustled the branches. I recognized the voice. It was Adournath.

Ivan shook his head but didn't look up to see where the voice came from.

I searched the foliage around us but couldn't find the magnificent animal. "We have come to free Feyerndur," I said.

Suddenly, Adournath was there, high in the branches of a tree. "You came to the right place," he said, his voice now clearly coming from his location.

"Can leading him here really free him?" asked Solace.

Adournath turned his piercing green eyes on her. "If freedom is what he seeks, then freedom he shall have. He needs but ask."

"Can he enter here?" asked Eyethanoff. "He is corrupted by darkness, and darkness cannot cross the boundary."

"All are corrupted," said Adournath. "All but one."

"Who?" I asked.

"You know who. Only he who has overcome darkness can pave the way to light."

"But the Prince is not here," I said, confused. "All I have is the armor."

"The Prince has done his part. Now it is time you did yours," he said, reminding me of the Prince's words spoken in my vision when I touched the medallion. *I have paid the debt you owe to darkness.*

I looked to Solace. "He's right. I am just as stained by darkness as Feyerndur and the Prince let me enter these woods. We just need to get him here. If the Prince made it possible for me to enter, then he will make a way for Feyerndur."

Solace nodded. "Then go. We stand ready to defend you."

I looked at the others. I could see the sorrow of loss in their eyes. Their jaws were set, their movements tense, their gazes set forward. They were each putting aside their pain to complete the task at hand.

Turning back to Solace and holding her gaze, I nodded. I was counting on her to make the right call if I needed their help, for she was the only one other than me who could reliably sense where the dark soldiers were. And I trusted her judgment. "Stay hidden until I get him to enter here," I instructed.

Solace gave a curt nod.

I turned to head out, but Eyethanoff stopped me. "Stick to the light, Ben, no matter how much you want to hide in the dark," he warned, holding my gaze.

I nodded, recalling what he had told Catherine. *Darkness is a cruel protector.*

Exiting the safety of the Ath Woods, I stepped from the trees onto the road, memories of the day this all started flashing through my mind as I spotted the signpost at the edge of Durthair. I had been so unaware of what was really going on back then. Now we were here at these woods again, but everything was different.

I crossed the road with my sword in one hand and the shield in the other. I had tried twice to use this shield to keep others from seeing me, but now I knew something I had not known back then. The shield would hide me. I just had to have faith and take refuge in light.

I observed the streets and buildings ahead of me, noting the shadows and beams of moonlight. I shook my head. If I stood in those moonbeams, I would be exposed. But Eyethanoff had explained that there was some form of protection in being exposed. I just didn't understand it yet. I had to make a choice, though. I stepped out, into the light. Nothing happened. No soldiers of darkness rushed to attack me. I took three steps and immediately pulled back into a nearby shadow when I saw a soldier of darkness coming around a bend in the road. Realizing my mistake, I scrambled for a beam of moonlight. The soldier rounded the corner and stopped. He searched the area, his gaze falling on my location. I forced myself to settle in the reassuring memory of using the shield to get Jeb. I let go of control and put my faith in the unseen. The soldier moved on. I sighed and nodded to myself. It was odd to have faith and not be certain at the same time.

Careful to stick to moonbeams, I fought the urge to take refuge in darkness as I made my way to the edge of town. I wove through the streets, in and out of ruined, burned houses, careful to avoid stepping in or on anything that would announce my presence. A few times, I inadvertently pulled back into a shadow to conceal myself but promptly remembered that I was more exposed there than I was in the light.

Finally, I came within earshot of the group of dark soldiers I had seen speaking with Zath, though the dragon had now moved off to pillage a building with two beasts.

"The general says he thinks something might be wrong," said one of the dark soldiers.

A second one nodded. "I know. He is not sure what, but he told me that something was off. The actions of the humans have been odd—not what he predicted. It is as if they don't even care about the stone."

I shook my head. *Why would it matter to them if we care about the stone?* I wondered. Then I had another thought. *If they find out we are after the medallion, they will take it from Zath, and then I will never get my hands on it.* I had to act fast and quietly. I glanced at the shield and reminded myself of what Eyethanoff had told me in the church when I had first wanted to use it. *"Have faith,"* he had said. I smiled. It really was that simple. Recalling the shield's wavering ability to conceal me when I doubted it, I gripped the shield, this time trusting that it would do its job.

I headed down the street toward Zath. If I could get his attention in a subtle way, he might just follow me into the woods without a fight. I continued weaving between the shells of demolished buildings until I came to one adjacent to where Zath was sniffing through rubble, looking for treasures. Stopping to gather myself, I took a deep breath and had a sudden thought. *Maybe I can get his attention with the helmet.* If I showed myself just for a moment, maybe Feyerndur would see it and try to come after it.

I hesitated for another moment but knew I had to commit. With the shield before me, I stepped out onto the road right in front of Zath. Positioning myself so I was certain he would see me, I moved the shield away, then back, before darting behind another building. I felt exposed the whole time. But from Zath's vantage point, he would have only seen me for a split-second right in the middle of the road—hopefully enough time for Feyerndur to see the helmet.

However, as I moved the shield back into place, just before I dove for cover, I glimpsed Zath's eyes turn bright orange. Surprised, I stole a glance around the edge of the wall, careful to keep the shield in front of me, and saw Zath's eyes return to red.

"You think I cannot see you like these blind men around me?" he asked in a mocking tone as I moved farther behind the building. "The prisoner within me has shown me your location. He has shown me what you truly are," he growled. "A sinner and a failure! You reek of darkness."

I squeezed my eyes shut in a silent self-reprimand. *I must have faltered, and the shield did not hide me.* But then Zath's words sank in, and I realized Feyerndur must be able to see the whole armor, including the shield, even when I was using it to hide. *He is not a soldier of darkness, simply trapped by darkness. Zath knows where I am now.* I opened my eyes to see if anyone had heard Zath speak to me. My stomach flipped when I saw four dark soldiers in the shadows across the street, staring in my direction with cruel smiles as they drew their weapons.

"Come now," started Zath as he stalked toward the building I was concealed behind. "Stand and face me," he challenged.

With his attention now on me, I darted to a nearby pile of rubble, still hidden behind the shield. Zath reached my previous hiding spot and hesitated. I saw his eyes flicker orange as he looked around before he locked onto my location again. I ran to another building, and Zath pursued with Martecytes and dark soldiers in tow, following his lead.

"Will you scurry about like a rat in a kitchen?" bellowed an angry Zath. "Show yourself and fight me! You wish to get the m—what you want?" Zath stumbled over his words, as if Feyerndur didn't want him to reveal to the others what I was after. "Come get it!" growled Zath.

Chapter 18

WITH ONLY A COUPLE broken-down buildings and the main road between me and the Ath Woods, I knew I had to keep moving and not let Zath rope me into a conflict. He was so close, and the woods were right there. All I had to do was get him to enter, and Adournath would do the rest, or so I hoped.

Shoving aside the thought that this might not work, I darted to the next building, Zath and the others still in tow. But as I rounded a corner, I lost my footing. I skidded on mud, causing a small splash, but caught myself on a rain barrel. Hoping I hadn't just given away my exact location, I steadied myself, then let go of the barrel. But as I did, something darted behind me through a nearby shadow. A dark soldier must have heard my scuffle. The rain barrel was still wobbling from my momentary contact, and the movement of the dark soldier finished the job. Before I could grab it again, the barrel toppled over and crashed into a pile of rubble, drawing the attention of all the enemy soldiers in sight. Immediately, they turned to face me. After only a split second of hesitation, they charged my position, Zath close behind them.

With my cover blown, I darted for the safety of the Ath Woods, hoping Zath would follow and enter after me. There was no guarantee it would work, but I had to try. As I sprinted for the trees,

I glanced over my shoulder to see if Zath was following. He was. But something else caught my attention. Behind him, surrounding General Delany's mansion and Creal Hill, dark figures occupied the shadows. Soldiers laden with dark armor, ready to fight. And they were all looking at me. Then I heard a scream.

"Ben!" cried Solace from the trees ahead of me. "Look out!"

I turned back to see what Solace was yelling about, and a Martecyte seemed to appear out of nowhere. He swung his sword at me, slicing through the air high to low, and I instinctively raised the shield and ducked. The dark blade bounced off the shield, which was filled with the light of Original Power. Darkness collided with light, causing a flash to blaze from the shield. As if in response, everyone sprang into motion, and battle erupted all around me.

Yuuki and the others charged from the woods, coming to my aid. Soldiers of darkness took to the sky on the backs of strange winged beasts like massive bats, which I had never seen before. Yuuki transformed, her proximity to Adournath seeming to give her enough strength to fly. Eyerkishta clashed in battle with the soldiers in the sky as Eyethanoff and his ground forces entered Durthair to hold back the soldiers on foot. Those who only saw the dark soldiers as shadows faced the Martecytes and beasts as they fought alongside their evil comrades.

With my plan to do this quietly now thoroughly abandoned, I would have to lure Zath to the woods a different way. I dispatched the Martecyte who had attacked me and turned to Zath. "You want a fight?" I taunted. "Your precious master has lost! Give me what I came for or I will take it by force!" I demanded.

Zath chuckled. "My, you are a cocky fellow," he mocked in his deep, rumbling voice. "If a fight is what it will take, so be it."

With that, Zath let loose a stream of fire. But I had fought him enough to know that would be his first approach. I easily blocked Zath's flames with the shield, the shoes keeping me steady, before I turned and ran for the woods, hoping he would follow. But I quickly skidded to a halt when three more Martecytes appeared, blocking my path. Hesitating for a moment to gauge my chances against them, I committed and charged. Clashing swords with the closest Martecyte, I blocked his swing, then spun to keep track of Zath. His mouth was agape, aimed at me. But he stopped, stomping the ground as if angry. He didn't seem angry with Feyerndur, though. I spun back around to see what he was looking at and saw three soldiers of darkness join the Martecytes. Zath must have been ordered not to harm the Creature's armies.

With an overwhelming force between me and the woods, I ran back the way I had come, headed toward Durthair, where my comrades were engaged in battle on my behalf. I dodged Zath's massive paw and slid between his front legs before coming up and sprinting past his tail, ducking as it swung over my head. Feyerndur would have to wait.

The Martecytes followed, pursuing me into the town as I joined in the raging fight. The armies of darkness had probably been instructed to distract me from my goal, and I had no choice but to defend myself. I clashed in battle with Solace and the others by my side. As I fought, I noted that Zath had come after me, but Eyerkishta intercepted him while I took out a dark soldier that rushed me from behind.

As the battle raged on, I eventually found myself facing the south side of Durthair and Creal Hill. That is when I saw him. I froze. Standing in the midst of the burning destruction—the remnants of my hometown—was the Creature. He stood on a carpet of black fog and liquid shadow, his dark cloak flapping in the wind as snow and ash fell around him. He stood still, watching me. The battle around me faded to white noise as he smiled an evil smile. Then, suddenly, he charged.

As the Creature sped toward me, he stretched his arms out to his sides, his fingers wide. At the Creature's gesture, shadows began to move. A jolt of fear coursed through my veins as I recalled the night I had first seen his true form. The night I let fear take over and the Creature had overpowered me. The memory turned my stomach sour, and as my fear grew, so did the shadows under the Creature's control. They morphed to liquid, carrying with them all that they touched—rubble and fallen weapons, as well as the bodies of his own dead soldiers, their lives ended from doing his bidding. The liquid shadows brought to the Creature that which belonged to darkness. Veins of darkness shot out from within the Creature, stabbing into the objects and fallen soldiers. The darkness seemed to pull them all apart, shattering them into deadly shards that dripped with black, ink-like liquid and trailed black fog, reminding me of the dark arrow that had killed Otto. When he had what he needed, the Creature thrust his hands forward, sending the sharp fragments of rock and metal and bone straight for me. Leashes of darkness connected them to his outstretched hands, arms, and back like strings on a puppet.

The shards flew through the air, piercing through everything in their path, including the Creature's own soldiers. Fully expecting the shield to defend me against the attack, I held it over my head to block the blows and hide me from the Creature's sight. But before the poisoned shards hit their mark, the Creature shifted his hands, and the dark leashes parted, spreading the shards around me so they came at me from behind. I slashed at them with the sword and blocked them with the shield, knocking most of them aside. I felt panic taking hold as my faith in the armor began to falter. It seemed to offer no protection from the Creature. Distracted by confusion, I failed to dodge his last few shards, and they ripped through my shirt, slicing small gashes in my left shoulder, their black liquid shadow searing into my skin. Though the pain was sharp, I could feel the armor sending Original Power to the wounds and fighting against the shadow poison.

I grunted in pain but forced myself to turn toward the Creature with the sword at the ready. As I came to face him, the Creature lunged forward and was upon me before I could react. He reached out a hand and wrapped his long, strong fingers around my throat, then slammed me into what was left of a chimney.

"You think you can beat me?" he snarled in a low voice, his face only inches from mine. "You have no idea what you are doing."

"I know more than you think," I croaked as I let go of the sword and shield. To my surprise, the sword returned on its own to its sheath and the shield to its place on my back. I gripped the Creature's hand at my neck and struggled for air.

"Not enough to save you," he sneered as the pressure on my throat tightened even while I fought to escape.

Suddenly, the Creature released me and spun around, his veins of darkness and the shards of debris rushing together to form a shield before him. As my feet hit the ground, I collapsed to one knee and gasped for air, the sound of arrows striking the Creature's shield faintly registering in my ears. My head pounded as my chest heaved, and I blinked away the pressure that had built up behind my eyes. Finally catching my breath, I looked up to see what had caused the Creature to let go.

Solace stood before the Creature, a sword in one hand and a shield in the other. I had no idea where she had found them. Behind her stood Nadia with a drawn and loaded bow, Ivan with two swords, and Trixie with a sword and a pistol. Each was flanked by their soldier of light, some armed with bows and arrows and others with swords and shields.

The Creature smiled at Solace. "Hello, my dear. Come to save your man?" he scoffed.

Solace smiled. "Yes, actually," she responded conversationally.

I smiled to myself at her comment and stood unsteadily, catching my breath. "Thanks," I rasped to Solace through my sore throat, some of my confidence returning at the sight of her.

The Creature rolled his eyes. "You two are in over your heads. You think that your ragged group and a few of the Lion's Sword soldiers can defeat me, but you are wrong," he snapped. "I will squash your rebellion and take back what is mine!"

I stood up a little straighter, trying to hold my smile without wincing at the pain I felt throughout my body. "You might think this world is yours, but it won't always be shrouded in your lie. I think you know it is not just us fighting you," I commented.

"Really?" challenged the Creature. "Where is your oh-so-faithful prince?" he mocked.

I took another deep breath and summoned the sword to my hand. "He will come back one day, perhaps not in my time. But until I die, I will stand and fight."

Solace lifted her sword. "As will we," she said, the others at the ready behind her.

The Creature smiled. "So be it. You will all die!"

With that, the Creature lurched toward Solace. She blocked his blow as I came up behind him, but he was too fast, and his shield of shards and veins of darkness came to his defense, blocking my attack without him even turning to face me. The Creature sent a wave of black fog at Solace, knocking her off her feet. Before she could even try to get up, we were all forced to dive to the ground for cover as the Creature's veins of darkness shot out, releasing their shards of debris, launching them in all directions. Everyone managed to get out of the way. Everyone except Ivan, who was struck by something that sent him flying backward and slammed him into an exposed brick chimney. He slumped to the ground, unconscious or dead. I couldn't tell.

The Creature stopped and spun, looking at Ivan's limp body. A vein of darkness shot out and caressed the wound on Ivan's shoulder. Then, suddenly, the Creature snatched up Ivan and ran for Creal Hill and his mansion.

As quickly as we could, we leapt to our feet and pursued him up the hill. From behind us, the Creature's armies charged, and from ahead, his beasts came to his aid, blocking the way and preparing to attack us as we approached.

In the midst of our pursuit, I suddenly remembered Feyerndur. Even if I saved Ivan now, if Feyerndur was not freed, this would all be for nothing. Without breaking stride, I turned to search for Zath and was stunned when I spotted him. The battle waged on between us and around us, yet Zath stood motionless at the edge of the Ath Woods, locked in a trance. Frozen between two worlds. One decision lay before him that could change the course of life as we knew it. There was something familiar in his posture—the way he stood staring at the woods. I had done the same thing once. I searched the tree line and saw them. Adournath's green eyes staring back at Zath, drawing him in to see the truth that he so desperately needed. *Maybe I won't have to fight Zath for the medallion after all,* I thought.

I had no idea what had led him to meet Adournath at the woods' edge, but I did know that Feyerndur now had to make the choice on his own. Right now, all I could do was buy him time and help Ivan. But before I turned back up the hill, I spotted Trixie. She stood at the bottom of the hill near the main road that led to the mansion. She was partially concealed in the trees at the edge of the road, her dark cloak billowing in the light breeze as she stared up at the mansion with a distant look in her eye. For a moment, I thought I saw her expression tense with anger as she glared at the building, probably thinking of the Creature's ultimate role in her son's death. But there was something else in her distant gaze that I couldn't identify. I shook my head. *I can't focus on this now.* There was nothing I could say to fix what had happened, and I had a job to do. I turned back toward the mansion. I needed to focus on keeping the Creature and his men distracted long enough for Feyerndur to make his choice—hopefully, the right choice.

With that thought in mind, I pursued the Creature up the remainder of the hill, sword in hand and shield at my back, his dark soldiers close behind. But Solace sensed them and turned to defend me. Though they were becoming more and more visible, they still floated in and out of the darkness like ghosts. But she could feel them. For a moment, I gazed back in awe at her display of faith in the mysterious king she so dearly loved as she struck out and fought an army she could not fully see. She exhibited the faith and strength of a mighty warrior, even though she had no divine armor to protect her.

Ahead, two beasts had attacked Nadia, and I ran to her aid, two Lion's Sword soldiers joining me. As we reached her side, she cried out after the Creature, "Ivan!"

I pressed on, following the Creature toward his mansion as Nadia and the others drew the beasts away.

When I arrived at the steps to the Creature's mansion, I slowed. *This could be a trap.* I hesitated for a heartbeat. *I'll have to risk it. I need to find Ivan and buy Feyerndur time.* I pressed on. The sounds of battle faded from my awareness as I climbed the stone stairs one at a time, scanning the area with the sword held at the ready and the shield at my back, waiting for a signal to defend me.

I knew this place well, but the Creature had probably not told me everything there was to know about this grand building he called home. He had survived for centuries without the public finding out who he was. He had to have some hidden tricks. I needed to be on guard.

I took my time ascending the stone staircase and approaching the front door. The door was still cracked open when I arrived, and the distant sounds of the Creature moving down the halls faded as I entered the dim, still interior. I closed the door behind me, its hinges creaking in the silence. I stood, apparently alone, in the grand entryway, surveying it for any sign of where the Creature had gone. I moved past the winding, double-sided main staircase and down a hall that led deeper into the house, careful to keep my footsteps quiet.

"She lied to you, Ben." The Creature's voice came so suddenly that I jumped. It seemed to echo off the wood-paneled walls, making it hard to tell where it was coming from.

"Really?" I asked, letting out a slow breath as I recovered from the jolt of surprise. "And, pray tell, who would 'she' be?" I prompted as I searched for him.

"You know who. That old woman you are so fond of." The Creature's voice floated to me in a tone of disappointment.

"How so?" I asked, hoping to keep him busy as I checked down a corridor. *Nothing.*

"Why do you think the Prince hasn't told you everything?" the Creature asked.

"I don't need to know everything," I said as I peered around a doorway into a hall that led to the kitchen. The house was eerily empty. No servants, no guards, no one.

"Is that what the old hag has told you?" asked the Creature with a chuckle. "She is lying to you, Benjamin."

"You still haven't told me how," I said as I stepped into another room, staying close to the walls. This mansion had secret hallways, I knew. I had used them many times to bring General Delaney sensitive information during wars with humans and beasts. *That must be where he is,* I thought.

"She has told you to give up everything, even your life and the lives of your friends, to fight for a king that you have never truly seen," he explained, his tone concerned. "A king too cowardly to show his face...or a king she simply made up..."

"I have seen his son," I responded as I searched for an entrance to the hidden passages. "That is good enough for me."

"Really? Then where is he now?" asked the Creature. "Why has he left you here to fight all his battles?"

I rounded another corner but jumped when something moved behind me. I spun toward the sound and saw a small statue teetering from side to side on its pedestal as if someone had bumped it. A small remnant of black fog still hung in the air around its base.

"You don't have an answer, do you?" taunted the Creature as I approached the statue and tightened my grip on the sword's hilt. "But I do. He isn't real, Benjamin. Think about it."

I reached the statue and rounded its edge, only to find a blank wall. But when I looked closer, I saw a seam in the wallpaper. *He is in the passages! I was right,* I thought.

"There is nothing to think about," I said as I ran my hand along the seam, looking for the trigger that I knew would open the passageway.

"Really?" responded the Creature. "The first time you saw any signs of something called Original Power was in the Woods. That so-called beast of the Woods supposedly showed you the truth. But my soldier was there watching over you, making sure you were not corrupted. What you saw was an illusion. The Beast of the Woods was a first attempt of mine to create an army. I banished it to the Woods to keep people safe. But that old woman found it and uses it to gain long life and power of her own," he explained.

Against my better judgment, I found myself contemplating the Creature's recounting of events. I recalled that night in the Woods, as the Creature still called it. All the stories I had heard growing up said the Beast of the Woods was an evil creature. It wasn't until I had met Ruth that I had started to see it as an ally.

"You must be thinking, 'But Ruth, that poor old lady, said I could trust it,'" the Creature mocked. "That old woman plays tricks—ones that you will soon regret falling for," he said in a gentler tone.

As if in reaction to the Creature's words, the belt about my waist momentarily glowed. *"Have hope, my friend..."* The Ice Dragon's words echoed in my mind. *"...for the truth is a treasure worth knowing."* I shook off the feeling of doubt as my hand landed on something under the wallpaper that gave way to pressure, and a door popped outward. I pulled it open, and, still holding the sword in one hand, I drew a pistol as I stared past stone walls down the dimly lit staircase that descended beyond.

"Come on, Benjamin," prodded the Creature. "Think about it all. It started with that old woman. Ever since then, you have been seeing things that you cannot explain."

"I can explain them," I retorted. "The things I have seen are from the real world. It is I who live in darkness," I said as I slowly descended the stairs, one step at a time.

"Do you really believe that, Benjamin?" I heard the Creature say. "I know you have doubts. My soldier who is charged with watching over you heard you voice those doubts only a couple months ago."

I recalled the conversation I'd had with Solace. I had wondered if I had imagined the whole thing with the Prince and our mission. I had wondered if I was losing my mind. The shield at my back glowed faintly. *"Have faith, my friend..."* The Ice Dragon's voice returned. *"...for the unseen is a treasure worth believing."* I shook my head. "Then how do you explain Solace sensing the same things I saw with the help of the sword?" I asked. "Not everything is seen."

The Creature's quiet chuckle briefly filled the dim staircase. "She only began to feel unseen things after you reconnected with Ruth," he pointed out. "Don't you see, Benjamin? The old lady has been messing with your head!" he warned, his voice now steady but concerned.

"Then why have you hidden your true form from me all these years?" I asked as I reached the end of the staircase, where it emptied into a small, dimly lit room. The helmet stirred for a moment, but the feeling faded when I became distracted by what I saw. Sitting at a table against the far wall was General Delaney. Ivan was nowhere to be seen.

"What are you talking about, Ben?" General Delaney asked, his brow furrowing slightly.

I frowned at him. "You are the Creature," I stated. "Your true form is that dark being."

General Delaney gave me a confused expression, then began to nod. "Okay," he said in a sympathetic tone. "Benjamin, I think that woman has gotten into your head," he said with worry. "She is twisting your mind."

I glared at General Delaney. "What are you doing?" I snapped suspiciously. *I knew this was a trap.* "Where is Ivan?" I demanded.

"Now, Benjamin, calm down, and we will figure this out," the general said as he poured me a cup of tea.

"What are you doing?" I repeated as he stood and offered it to me with a troubled look on his face.

"Benjamin, I am just offering you some tea. Come, drink. Please."

"You lured me in here!" I snapped as I lifted my sword defensively in a two-handed grip. "I just came from outside. There is a war going on!" I growled.

General Delaney studied me carefully, deep concern creasing his eyes. "Benjamin, I descended those stairs by your side. You do not remember?" he asked with a troubled frown, gesturing behind me.

I threw a glance over my shoulder at the stairs I had just descended. *What does he mean? What is happening?*

I shook my head. "You are lying," I snarled. "You led me in here to trap me," I stated. But for some reason, his explanation felt plausible. *Am I losing my mind?* I asked myself in alarm, wondering if he could be telling the truth. "But what about this?" I said, holding out the sword. "Explain this sword and its power! It is real. I got it from Ruth."

General Delaney gave me an odd expression. "What do you mean, Ben? There is nothing there," he replied sympathetically.

I let go of the sword, and it returned to its scabbard but then vanished along with the armor I wore. Panic coursed through me, and I struggled to retrieve the shield. I felt something in the armor, but I was too focused on my fear and desire to prove the general wrong. The shield did not appear in my hand. "What have you done to me?" I asked as my body went rigid with horror.

"Ben. I think you need to sit down," suggested General Delaney as he approached and tried to lead me to a chair.

"No!" I snapped, yanking my arm from his grip. "There is a battle outside!"

"Ben. I believe you. But please, sit and eat something," he pleaded, worry creasing his brow.

"No. You are lying!" I snapped again as my gaze searched him for any evidence that he was lying. But I found none. "You were the Creature. You took Ivan! I came in here to save him from you!" I yelled. "I can prove it!"

I turned and ran up the stairs, out the hidden door, and through the mansion to the main entrance. I pulled open the double front door and stepped outside.

Durthair was still and calm, no signs of war in sight. Not a single body lay dead in the moonlit streets. Everything was in its place. No one I knew was anywhere to be seen. *What is happening?* I thought in terror as my heart pounded in my chest and my hands began to tremble.

I spun when I heard General Delaney come up behind me. "You are lying," I managed to repeat as I backed away from him down the stairs, pointing an accusatory finger at him. "I know you are lying!" But as I spoke, I felt my confidence evaporate.

"What are you talking about, Benjamin?" asked General Delaney.

"You were lying on the Western Island, and you are lying now!" I yelled, desperate to convince myself it was true.

"Benjamin, I tell you, I have not traveled to the Western Island since the last war," he said with a confused look. "Benjamin...I don't know what that woman did to you. But you need to calm down," he said, attempting to soothe me.

"Where is Valdra?" I demanded.

"He is not here. He left on another mission after you went to retrieve the book from the old woman," explained the general. "Benjamin, I need you to tell me what happened so I can help you," he said as he took a couple tentative steps in my direction.

Panic rose within me even more potent than before. *It can't be! Did Ruth do something to me that day when I retrieved her? That smile she had on her lips that whole time—was it because she was manipulating me? Is that why she knew so much?* So many questions had only been answered by her and Eeffrayldourian creatures and a story contained in a book. All of which were now gone.

I took a few steps back. "No. It can't be. I was there!" I said, attempting to convince myself that the general's claims were not true.

General Delaney nodded. "Okay. Benjamin, why don't you show me where you were," he said calmly. But then he suddenly glanced past me, and I spun around just in time to see two of his guards coming up behind me.

"See, I knew you were lying! This is a trap!" I yelled.

"Ben, this is no trap. They are not here to harm you," he said, making a calming motion with his hands, palms down. "They are going to take you back inside, where I can get a doctor to come free you from whatever that old woman has done to you," he reassured me.

I shook my head. "No. It doesn't make sense. Why would she do this?" I said, thinking aloud.

"Ben. I should have told you this before I had Valdra send you after that book. That book has unknown powers. She has used it for centuries to lure people into a life they think is their purpose. When they get in deep enough, they are so convinced her spell is real that they give her everything, even their lives, allowing her to stay alive for centuries on end," he explained.

I frowned. "No...It...it can't be true!" I said desperately. I thought through everything Ruth had said to me. She had taught me to give up everything. My security. My home. My life. *What have I done?* I thought in despair.

General Delaney waved his men forward, and they led me into the mansion. I glanced over my shoulder in search of anything that would show me what was real and what was a lie. But all I saw was evidence that I had been tricked by an old woman with a book about hope.

Chapter 19

MORNING LIGHT SHONE THROUGH the window of the room General Delaney's men had brought me to. I sat on the edge of the bed in a daze as the general's physician left, having finished checking me over. Two maids entered and began to get me ready for a bath. I came out of my haze of confusion long enough to shoo them away before they got too far, and I finished the process myself. I never liked others doing simple tasks for me.

More than once during the bath, I found my mind going completely blank, as if I were too shocked to think straight. The events of the night swirled through my head. I could remember everything. But there was no comfort in those memories. *Surely, if everything I remember had actually happened and the Creature had simply taken my mind again, I would not be able to remember so freely.* Standing half dressed in front of a mirror, I recalled the scene I had encountered when I exited General Delaney's mansion. Everything had been as it should be. No war. No destruction. Just a town waiting for war, as I had left it when I traveled to retrieve the book.

A knock sounded on the bedroom door.

"Enter," I called, turning away from the mirror and putting on my shirt.

A maid walked in. "General Delaney wishes to speak with you in his study."

I nodded. "Tell him I will be there shortly."

With a curtsy, the maid left, closing the door behind her.

Turning to a nearby dressing screen, I reached for the sword and was promptly reminded it wasn't there. It had disappeared when I was talking to General Delaney. I let out a sigh and grabbed the twin pistols hanging from the screen, securing the strap over my shoulder and making sure both guns were secure and loaded. Then, I made my way downstairs and entered General Delaney's study, where I found him at his desk.

"How are you feeling now that you are cleaned up?" he asked with a smile as I came to stand before him.

I frowned and tried to pull my mind out of its stupor. "I need sleep," was all I could get out. The events of last night were still racing through my thoughts. *How could I have been so deeply convinced?* I wondered. I only vaguely heard General Delaney's response.

"Benjamin. Are you listening?" he asked when I didn't reply.

"Sorry, what did you say?"

"I said sleep will come later. For now, enjoy a vacation. There is a celebration tomorrow night. You must join me!" he said with a smile. When I didn't respond, he stood and approached me before resting a slender hand on my shoulder. "You have been tired for a long time," he said in a saddened tone. "I am sorry I did not see it sooner, my boy."

I took a deep breath and nodded.

"You may stay here until you are feeling better," said the general as he returned to his desk.

"Thank you," I said simply. I cleared my throat. I wanted some explanation as to what was going on here. "General, if I may..." I started.

General Delaney looked up at me and smiled. "Of course. What's on your mind?"

"Last night—"

"Don't think anything of it, Benjamin. We will catch that woman and make sure she cannot do this to anyone else," he reassured.

I nodded, unsure what exactly I had been planning to ask other than whether it was all true. With a respectful dip of my head, I turned and left the room. I couldn't believe I had let myself be so convinced that it was all real. The last year of my life was a lie. One created by an old woman with a book who wanted nothing but eternal life.

I spent the rest of that day at the general's mansion. General Delaney kept me up all night for a debriefing on what had happened when I found the woman in the mountains. I told him I had brought her back here and then was sent to kill the Beast of the Woods. As a result of that apparently incorrect response, the general had me checked out once more by his physician. It would seem I had brought the woman back with the book, but the general claimed he had not sent me to kill the Beast, as he had done that before and it hadn't worked.

After finding nothing physically wrong with me, the physician advised that I shouldn't be left alone and should stay at the mansion until further notice just to be safe. So, I spent the second day wandering around the general's home, checking out his book collections and artifacts, a soldier or maid always within sight of me. A headache slowly moved in, and I eventually made my way to the kitchen for a remedy from the cook. Before I had gone to retrieve the book from Ruth, I had wanted a break. *Maybe now is the time to take it,* I thought. *Unless this is the general's idea of a break, being trapped in his mansion under medial watch.* I frowned and made a mental note to discuss that with him the next time I saw him.

Having taken the remedy for my headache, I went in search of a quiet place to relax, other than my room, since it seemed like every time I went up there I got interrupted. The general's library seemed the best option. Plus it held the largest private collection of books I had ever seen. It was a single-level rectangular room with floor-to-ceiling shelves filled with books. Some were books I had never even heard of, but others I recalled reading while waiting for him to call me into his office after past missions.

I grabbed a book off a shelf and began reading as my headache began to fade, but my mind wandered to Solace. All my memories of the past year were apparently false, including the journey through the Bawtha Forest, if that was even what it was called, the *Lyonsword* and its crew, my relationship with Solace—everything.

I reached up and rubbed my shoulder, where my memories told me I had been wounded by the Creature just before Solace had come to my rescue. I could almost still feel the pain when I touched the area. But I knew it was not real. I had already checked my shoulder and saw no wound.

After sitting down and reading for a little while, I began to doze. I was so tired from the night of debriefing and the doctor examining me. I could feel my body calling for sleep.

"Sir Arlin," said a gentle voice before I could drift off completely.

I started, and my eyes sprang open to find a maid standing in front of me.

"I am so sorry to startle you," she said politely. "But I wanted to let you know that you might find a better resting place in a less populated area."

"No, thank you," I responded gruffly, noting that the room was only occupied by maids. "I am fine here."

The young woman gave me an uncertain look, as if she wasn't sure what to do now that I'd declined to move.

"Um...I am sorry, sir, but I do need to clean this area," she explained.

I frowned. "Look, I don't mean to be rude. But I am exhausted, and I would like to just sit here and relax!" I snapped.

The young woman's eyebrows creased into a nervous furrow at my tone. Then, finally, she offered a polite curtsy and left.

I closed my eyes again and felt sleep begin to take hold.

"Excuse me, sir." Another voice prevented me from falling asleep yet again.

I took a deep breath. "Really? You really want to clean in here that bad, right now?" I asked in frustration as I opened my eyes.

A man stood over me, dressed in the uniform of someone who ran the house. He looked a bit confused. "I apologize, sir, but I was simply sent here to let you know that your presence has been requested in the banquet hall."

I frowned. "Why?"

"Well...because the celebration has started, and the general thought you would be hungry. After all, you have not eaten since you returned with the old woman," he explained.

I let out a sigh. "Fine," I said and stood.

I left the obnoxious staff to their duties and headed to General Delaney's banquet hall, where most of his men were gathered, though I had no idea what they were celebrating. *Maybe the return of the book,* I thought. I looked for Valdra but could not find him. So, I grabbed some food and found a quiet place to eat.

The food was extravagant, as always, and General Delaney didn't skimp on the entertainment for the night either. An eclectic band made up of various instruments, some I had never seen before, played in one corner, and the grand dance floor was full of guests twirling and stepping in time to a fast-paced, playful tune, their faces lit with smiles and laughter.

Curious about this celebration, I approached a familiar face—a man who worked for Valdra. "What are we celebrating?" I asked.

"The general didn't tell you?" he responded with wide eyes as he refilled his drink.

I shook my head. "We were focused on the debrief," I explained.

"The general seems to have found a new way to keep the Great Beasts at bay! It will hopefully delay the next war, or even stop it completely."

"How?" I asked.

The man grinned. "Never mind that! You've got all night here. Have some fun! Tell me, the word is that old lady tricked you into thinking you had been on a yearlong journey! Is that true?" he asked a little too expressively. Apparently, his drink was stronger than its pinkish hue suggested.

I frowned. "Keep it down," I warned.

He leaned in a little closer. "What happened in this illusion?" he asked, drawing out the last word to make it sound spooky.

I rolled my eyes. "Nothing important. None of it actually happened, anyways."

Intrigued by this new solution to the beast problem, I left the drunken soldier before he could ask any more prodding questions and searched for the general to inquire about his plan.

After weaving through the crowd gathered around the dance floor, I found the general in his usual spot during such parities, seated near the back of the room on an ornate golden chair, his own little version of a throne. It was much smaller than a real throne, but it got the point across.

"Ah, Benjamin! How are you feeling?" he asked, standing and coming down to my level as I approached.

"I would feel much better if I could get some sleep," I complained.

"Oh, well, I will make sure my staff readies your room for the night. For now, let's celebrate!" he said as he led me toward a table of food that stretched down one wall.

"What is this new beast solution I have been hearing about?" I asked as we reached the table.

General Delaney wrapped his long, slender fingers around a slice of fruit, bit into it, chewed, and swallowed as he considered my question. Something about the motion felt like a deliberate delay. Before I could prompt a faster answer, though, there was a small rumble in the ground. I froze. But as I looked around the room, no one else seemed to have felt it.

"What was that?" I asked.

General Delaney smiled. "That is the solution to our beast problem," he said with a grin.

"What is it?" I asked. "The solution, I mean."

"I have put together a team, who, at this very moment, are digging an underground tunnel to get into the Southern Mountains. A natural philosopher friend of mine is working on a gas that we will then send through the tunnels to kill the beasts all in one fell swoop!" he said.

I nodded. "Well, good. Then we can be done with this," I said. But I suddenly realized that I had nothing to return to without beasts to fight. I let out a sigh. "I think I am going to turn in for the night," I mumbled.

"No! Benjamin, you must stay and celebrate!" said the general with a grin and a pat on my back. "Come, come, there are many guests here tonight. Find a dance partner and have some fun!"

The general shoved me toward the crowd, then got distracted as one of his staff members drew him aside. "Things are progressing as planned," I heard the man explain. "The clouds look as though they will bring rain. But that might give us an edge over one of the issues we may end up facing," he finished with a suspicious glance in my direction.

As I turned and headed into the crowd, I heard the general respond, "Good. Keep me posted."

I wandered to the edge of the room and found a chair in a quiet corner out of the way. If the general expected me to be at this party, maybe I could at least sneak in a nap. Hopefully, the noise of the party would wash away the memories of the past year of my life, a lie that now plagued my mind.

I sat down and closed my eyes. Finally, I felt sleep pull me in. Memories faded to nothing, and exhaustion took over as the sounds of the party faded around me.

Darkness tugged at the edge of my mind as if something were trying to get in. It emanated a feeling of frustration, but then it was overcome by a voice. *"Just because you can see something doesn't mean you have all the information."* Solace's words echoed in my hazy dream. Images of her smile, her lips, her eyes, flickered by before they were interrupted by the bright green eyes of the Beast. Adournath.

"Benjamin, sleeping at a party?" said a voice.

I jolted awake to find one of my old comrades, a man named Henry, standing before me with a grin on his face.

Why is everyone so happy to see me? I thought in annoyance, wishing they would all just leave me alone to sleep. I let out a hard breath. "Can I not get a single wink of sleep around here?" I asked in irritation.

Henry chuckled. "You were never one for a party, were you?"

I shook my head. "Especially not tonight."

"Yes, I heard what happened. That old lady can be dangerous. I had a friend who went totally insane from trying to get that book from her."

"Was it me?" I asked sarcastically.

He laughed. "What are you talking about? You look great!" he said as he slapped me on the back.

"Well, I feel like I got hit by a boulder," I muttered as I ran a hand over my face, trying to get myself to wake up. As my hand passed over my face, I spotted movement across the room. Someone in a dark cloak that seemed familiar passed through the back of the party and disappeared through a door to the halls that led to the upper rooms. *Where have I seen that cloak before?* My attention snapped back to Henry as he let out another hearty laugh.

"I bet!" he said. "I heard she convinced you a whole year had passed!" He leaned in a little closer. "And there is a rumor that she was using you to find a priceless artifact."

I raised my eyebrows. *That one is new.* "Who told you that?" I asked.

Henry shrugged. "I think Valdra mentioned it. He was the one who led you back here, you know. He said the old lady was probably looking for some mythical gate." He laughed again.

I rubbed my head. "He's not wrong," I mumbled.

Henry grew serious. "It's true, then? How could convincing you of all those things help her find some artifact that is probably not even real?" he asked, bewildered.

I shrugged. "I don't know. Maybe she thought I would find it for her."

"How?" he asked.

I recalled the visions of the Gate. "I remember seeing the Gate...in dreams...It was—"

Suddenly, the ground rumbled again. But this time, it was accompanied by a strangely familiar scent. "Do you smell that?" I asked.

"Smell what?" asked Henry.

"Smoke," I responded as I stood up and looked around the room.

Henry shook his head. "It must just be some of the equipment they are using. I heard that they got this new natural philosopher to build some crazy machine that can help them dig faster. It might still take months to get it done. But at least it will go faster than a bunch of us doing it by hand," he added with a chuckle. "Anyway, you were abou—"

"Yes, but aren't you worried about the beasts hearing it?" I interrupted, not wanting to discuss what the old lady had done to me.

Henry appeared caught off guard by the question. "Well...I'm sure it will be fine. The general knows what he is doing."

I nodded. "Yes, he does," I said as I tried to place that familiar smell. "What exactly is this machine?" I asked.

"It is like a cart. But it is pulled by a...special animal," Henry explained with a mischievous look in his eyes.

"What animal?" I prompted.

Henry looked around the room, then leaned in and whispered, "A dragon."

I stared at him. "What?" I asked as hope flared within me. *That is why it smells familiar. It is the smoke of a dragon's fire!*

"Yes, some of the general's soldiers found this massive blue dragon in the Northern Mountains. They arrived with it while you were retrieving the book," Henry explained with excitement.

"Blue dragon?" I asked, disappointed. The only bluish dragon I knew of was Eyerkishta. However, though she had blue undertones, I would hardly describe her as a blue dragon. She was mostly icy white. Then I shook my head. *She is just a false memory. She is not real. But still...*

"Yes. They have it down there pushing the machine. The thing isn't all that happy, but we have it under control," explained Henry, pulling me from my thoughts.

I nodded. "I'm sure you do," I said as hope faded again. I had to stop thinking about what Ruth had done to me.

"So, the false memories," said Henry, raising his eyebrows. "Come on, we all want to know what happened," he encouraged.

If I wanted to stop thinking about what happened, I would have to get away from this party. "Not now, Henry. I'll see you around," I said, then walked away before he could stop me.

I shook the memories of dragons from my mind and exited the dining hall. I desperately needed sleep, and everyone around here seemed to think that I could survive without any.

I headed to the door that led to the hall—the same door the stranger in the dark cloak had slipped through. I nodded to people as I passed them, doing my best to be polite. Leaving the party behind, I stepped into the hallway, which was lined with artifacts the general had collected over the years, and made my way toward the nearby stairway.

I passed a guard who was in charge of protecting the artifacts and glanced over the collection as I walked by. Most of the valuable objects the general acquired were sold to help rebuild the Town after wars. But these were different. A sword. A jewel of some kind. Three old books. A stone. A golden necklace. And a painting of a pillar of light. I recognized them, as I had retrieved all of them, except the sword and the stone. The sight of the items filled my mind with memories of men I had killed to get them. Thankfully, my blood-stained memories were quickly overtaken by a realization. The general usually put these artifacts on display at parties, so it was odd that they were out here, away from view. But what he chose to do with his possessions was none of my business.

Footsteps sounded from somewhere behind me, around a corner, then abruptly stopped. "What are you doing, you peasant?" someone demanded.

"I am so sorry, sir," said a strangely familiar female voice. "I am a new stable keeper, and I got lost."

"The stables are that way! You shouldn't be anywhere near these artifacts!"

"I'm so sorry. It won't happen again," said the woman.

"It better not!"

Footsteps sounded again, headed in my direction. Not wanting to be roped into another conversation, I headed for the stairs that led to the upper rooms. After only a few strides, I was outpaced by a well-dressed man mumbling to himself about bad hiring practices. Thankfully, he didn't acknowledge me as he passed, and I felt myself relax as I reached the base of the spiral staircase.

As I climbed the steps, I glanced back down the artifact hall, my view partially obstructed a pillar. For a split second, I thought I saw a small hand reaching out toward the stone I had passed. I didn't want to get involved, though, so I kept walking. No one had hired me to protect artifacts.

Passing a second guard snoozing at the top of the stairs, I made my way down a couple corridors until I found my room. I entered and closed the door, blocking out the remaining sounds of the party as the ground rumbled again. I shook my head at the general's plan. There was no way they would make it all the way into the

Southern Mountains' cave system without the beasts hearing them and attacking long before the gas killed them all. *I definitely need sleep, because their plan will fail and then they will come calling on me to fix it,* I told myself.

I stripped down to my pants and sat on the bed. I rubbed my hands over my face and looked up at the night sky through my window. It was dark out, but I could see the full moon through the branches of a tree. It looked so small tonight. Just like I felt. Small, and back where I started. Yet, for the first time since I had learned what Ruth had done to me, I didn't feel as hopeless, though I didn't know why. But I did feel tired. I let myself fall backward into the pillows and sheets and closed my eyes. Finally, sleep hit me, hard and fast, and I let it pull me under.

Darkness pushed in but seemed to be held back by something. Something green. Then it became clear. Green eyes stared at me through the foliage of the Ath Woods. Adournath watched me, his catlike form perched on a thick tree branch. Those eyes drew me in, just as they had in past dreams. But this time, I was different. Unlike in past dreams, I followed with no hesitation. I entered the woods to find that they looked different. It was as if I had walked into a different land. A beautiful land. A land vaguely familiar. A man stood in the center, though I couldn't fully make out his appearance.

"Each piece of the plan is almost in place, Father. We are on schedule," said the man to someone I could not see.

"The time has come, my son," responded a deep voice.

"But what about him?" asked the man. "The others are tiring and losing hope. They need him."

"Our enemy has trapped him," replied the voice. "But he is there for a reason. He is part of a story he is only just beginning to see. He will not be held down for long, for he knows the truth, and the truth will set him free."

With that, Adournath pulled me from the Ath Woods and placed me outside.

"Remember what you have seen. But trust what you have not," he warned, holding my gaze.

Then everything vanished.

I snapped awake with a jolt, bolting upright. I was panting and beginning to sweat, which seemed odd, as the dream hadn't felt like a nightmare. But for some reason, I had desperately needed to be free of it. Seeing that I was just in my room at the general's mansion, I heaved a sigh and let myself fall back into the pillows. I stared at the ceiling for a moment, pondering the dream. I forced myself to imagine what had happened in the illusion that Ruth had pulled me into—to remember the dreams I'd had during that time. I found the memories quickly and clearly. *That must be it*, I thought. *It is just a memory of Ruth's lie.* But some part of me still wanted to believe it had not been a lie.

I sat up in bed and rubbed my eyes. I was still tired, but now my mind was reeling. The ground shook again, but this time the rumble was louder. I glanced out the window past a tree toward town. For a moment, I thought I glimpsed something, and I walked to the window to see what it was. Something had flown through the sky. But it was gone. *I didn't get enough sleep. My mind is playing tricks on me.* I rubbed my eyes again. *I am losing it,* I thought as I got dressed.

Once I was decent, I made my way downstairs to the dining hall, where breakfast was being served. While I ate, I thought over last night's news that the general had found a way to rid the world of beasts. If that was true, then I could take a real break once they were gone. I might even be able to retire altogether and start a farm like my family had once run between wars. By the time I had finished my meal, I decided that the general needed my help on his new project, so I returned to his office.

"What do you need today, Benjamin?" he asked in a tone that said he was very busy.

"I am ready to start working again," I explained. "I can help with this tunnel project."

General Delaney shook his head. "No. You still need time." He came around the front of his desk and handed some papers to one of his men. "I will let you know when we need your help," he said with a distracted smile. "Now if you will excuse me, I need to get back to work." He headed toward the door.

I watched him walk away, wondering what was really happening in the tunnel. It wasn't like the general to miss such an obvious problem as being heard by the beasts while trying to sneak up on them, and to not accept my help with the matter. He had grown to value my input on many topics over the years. But now, it seemed as though he didn't trust me anymore. *Do you blame him? You have gone insane,* I thought to myself. *I wouldn't even want my advice right now.*

The general suddenly stopped at the door and turned back to me. "Oh, Henry was looking for you. He said there was a conversation he wanted to finish. Something about a dream you had once. It sounded very interesting. I myself would like to know more about it...What was it about again?"

I raised my eyebrows in surprise. "Why would you be interested in a dream about a gate?" I asked.

The general's eyes grew hard. "A gate, you say..." He smiled. "I guess I'm just curious about what happened to you." He glanced through the door to the hall as if thinking, then looked back at me. "Do you remember the details?"

I opened my mouth to tell him about the dream, but just then the ground rumbled again.

The general frowned. "Don't worry about that. My soldiers will deal with it. Go on."

Just then one of his soldiers entered. "I'm so sorry, sir, but there is a problem...um...outside," he said, glancing at me warily.

The general glared at him. "Handle it," he ordered.

The soldier gave him a tense smile. "Um, I think you'd better come help. The dragon we have down with the machine is—"

"Yes, fine. I'm coming." The general looked at me again. "Talk to Henry," he said, pointing at me. Then he paused. "And Benjamin, I think you need to speak with someone about your memories...and dreams. I think it best that you discuss what you remember with my physician. Work it out." He pursed his lips. "I do need your help. But..." He didn't finish.

I knew what he was hinting at. He too thought I had lost my mind. As much as I didn't want to talk to anyone about it, I knew he wouldn't let me return to work until I did. I could always fake that the memories were gone. "I'll talk with him," I replied.

The general smiled and nodded, then left.

I spent the rest of the day reading and chatting with anyone I ran into about the tunnel project. But the more I spoke to people about it, the more determined I became that I needed to see it for myself. They had an opportunity to use a dragon against the beasts, but if they didn't think this through, that dragon could become their worst nightmare. I needed to make sure they were doing things right. I was also eager for any excuse to avoid talking to the physician.

By the time I made the decision to insert myself into the project without permission, night was falling again. I exited the mansion in search of someone who could point me to the tunnel project site. When I didn't find anyone immediately, I glanced up to the cloudy sky to see if there was enough smoke from the dragon to lead me in the right direction. The sky looked exactly as it had the night before. No smoke, and not a single star peeking through between the thick clouds.

Suddenly, I stopped. The conversation between the general and his assistant at the party played in my mind. *"The clouds look as though they will bring rain. That might give us an edge over one of the issues we may end up facing,"* the man had said. Green warning eyes from my dream glowed faintly in my mind as I pondered the conversation. The man was right. It had been cloudy last night. *So, if it was cloudy, why had I seen a full moon out my window?* Then Solace's warning voice came to me once again. *"Just because you can see something doesn't mean you have all the information."*

My pulse suddenly quickened, and I started breathing faster as another memory emerged. A memory I had forgotten until this very moment. I glanced around to make sure no one was watching, then took off around the side of the mansion to the tree outside my bedroom window. I looked up into its branches, searching for the smallest, most adorable sign of hope I would ever see in my life.

In the haze of the evening, I almost missed it. But its curiosity drew its attention to the man staring up at it. *Neyelah!* The little Eeffrayldourian rodent Ruth had introduced me to, whose ears resembled the moon. Isps—that was what Neyelah's kind were called. They were tied so closely to Original Power that they had been one of the first things to become visible when the Creature's lie began to crack. But not only that—Ruth had said they were messengers, often appearing mysteriously when someone was in need of the King's help or when something miraculous was about to happen.

I was so filled with joy at seeing her adorable little face that I struggled to stay calm. Especially after I felt the armor around me just barely stir. Never in my life had I been so happy to know that I had been lied to—not by Ruth, but by the Creature. It was all another of the Creature's illusions. The smoke and the rumblings must have been from the battle. The dream last night had not just been a dream. The Beast of the Woods—Adournath—had drawn me to the truth yet again. All my memories were real! I just couldn't see that with my eyes. *But why? And why can I see Neyelah in this new charade I find myself engulfed in?*

I looked back up into the tree and whispered to Neyelah to come down. But when the ground shook again, she extended her ears into the round moon shape and went stock still. I shook my head. "Please come down, Neyelah. You are the only thing from Eeffrayldour that I can see right now, and I need your help," I pleaded. But she simply adjusted her position to face the stables, then froze once again, refusing to budge.

Noting Neyelah's very precise movements, I pointed to the stables and looked back up at her, silently asking if she wanted me to go there. She hunkered down without changing the direction she was facing, as if to say, "Yes, for goodness' sake, go over there." Hoping I was reading the situation right, I snuck around a well and made my way toward the stables. As I ducked inside, I overheard two men speaking as they patrolled the horse stalls.

"The general says we have to make sure Ben doesn't leave the compound. The illusion only works if he is here. The number of people who believe in *The Story* is weakening the Lie, and this new layer of the Lie will not hold if he leaves," the first man was saying.

I guess that confirms my theory, I thought to myself.

"What about the other one?" came the second voice.

Just then, I heard a familiar nicker. *Jeb!* Briefly wondering if Neyelah had somehow brought Jeb here, I crouched down behind a stall door and hoped that Jeb would stay quiet. But I had no such luck. He nickered again, and I could just imagine his ears pricking so far forward that they looked like they were going to snap off as he tossed his nose in playful excitement to see me.

"That's Ben's horse," said one of the men. "I didn't even know it was here."

"Shut up…There must be something over there," said the other man.

The sound of footsteps grew louder as the men cautiously approached my location. I reached toward my waist to grab the sword, but it wasn't there. I felt the armor stir around me, though, and wished I could get it to work. I went still. I couldn't use my pistols—they would be too loud. If I made a sound, everyone would know where I was. As silently as I could, I took in a breath and braced myself for combat. *Two against one. That isn't exactly fair...but I can make it work.*

The footfalls sounded closer and closer until the guards were right outside the stall I was hiding in. As one man leaned over the stall door, I sprang forward. I swung my right fist across his temple, knocking him out cold with one blow. With the first man down, I leaned out over the stall door and managed to get a hand over the second man's mouth just in time to stop him from yelling an alarm.

Releasing his mouth, I quickly pulled him close into a neck hold sure to cut off his air supply. In one move, I bent my knees and leaned back, dragging him over the stall door and onto the floor on top of me. As the man grabbed at my face, I tightened my grip, rolled over, and pinned him to the ground. With my grip still firmly in place, I whispered in his ear, "Don't say a word or I will end your life right here."

Chapter 20

THE GUARD MANAGED A nod, agreeing to remain silent, as he began to grasp at my arms, attempting to breathe. In a swift motion, I released his neck, grabbed both of his arms, pinned them behind his back, and tied his wrists with baling string. With his hands now secured, I dragged my prisoner to the corner of the stall and shoved him onto a stool. I pulled one of my pistols from its holster and looked him in the eye. "I will use this pistol if I need to. If you try to yell for help or make one peep other than to answer a question, you will never speak again. Am I understood?"

He nodded.

Leaving him there for a moment, I retrieved the unconscious guard from where he had fallen and tied him up as well.

Turning back to the man on the stool, I asked, "Why am I here?"

"For the party," he responded sarcastically.

With no warning, I swung a punch, aiming a tad low so as to break his jaw instead of knocking him out. I immediately stuffed a nearby burlap bag in his mouth to dampen the moaning. Then I pulled it out. "Why am I here?" I asked again in a firm tone.

The guard's response was slurred, as he was forced to speak without moving his mouth much. "Because you are their leader.

Though an army will still fight when their leader is gone, hope will dwindle when he does not return."

I shook my head. "I am not their only leader," I parried. I leaned forward, placing my hands on my thighs but making sure to keep a safe distance in case he tried something. "You are lying," I stated flatly.

The man did his best to chuckle, but I remained silent.

"Okay, fine. Tell me where the Creature took Ivan," I demanded.

He simply smiled slightly through his probably partially numb jaw, though I could see he was in pain.

I could tell by the look in his eyes that he was not going to tell me the truth unless things got bloody—and loud. Then I realized something. This whole charade seemed to be orchestrated for me personally. It was all as though the Creature was trying to keep me here for a specific reason. This soldier must know why. But he wasn't about to tell me, at least not willingly.

My mind began to wander. I thought about why the Creature would want me up here. *He is probably trying to get in my head and find the Gate,* I speculated as I recalled him and Henry prodding for the details of a dream about the Gate. Then another idea came to mind. *I think Feyerndur has the final piece to this puzzle. Maybe the Creature doesn't want him to go into the Woods—the Ath Woods—for fear that I might find out what he knows.* I recalled the last time I had seen Zath. Poised on the edge of those woods, he'd been so close to the truth that would set him free. If we were to have any hope of finding the Gate before the Creature did, I needed to get to Zath. I needed to recover that medallion and learn what Feyerndur knew about the Gate and the stone.

Seeing that I was wasting my time with this interrogation, I delivered a knockout blow to the guard in the stool. I checked on the other unconscious guard still lying on the floor before stepping over him and heading out to retrieve Jeb and his tack. I saddled Jeb, swung onto his back, and headed for the door. As I exited the stables, Neyelah saw me, darted down the tree, and scampered up a hay bale before leaping onto Jeb's saddle and stuffing herself into one of my saddlebags.

"Oh, now you come down," I commented, rolling my eyes.

Jeb carried Neyelah and me past the mansion just as some of the Creature's soldiers emerged from the main entrance.

"Hey!" one yelled.

"Stop him!" added another as two more came around from the back of the building.

So much for a quiet escape, I thought.

There was no use in trying to hide any longer. But if I was to complete the mission set before me, I needed to break free of this new lie. *How, though?*

Almost as if someone had handed me the response, Adournath's eyes flashed bright green through my mind, reminding me of *The Story* and the truth it contained. It played in my thoughts as I pondered my problem, looking for a way out. Memories of old battles with my past darkness seemed to jump to my attention as though the enemy were grasping at straws to keep me filled with fear and under his control. I remembered that desire to hide in darkness and let my failures overtake me. But then I recalled the pieces of the armor I had received throughout this journey and the things I had learned about my darkness—all of it culminating with the helmet and the sword. A reassuring thought overwhelmed the darkness. *I already faced my past with the Prince by my side, and the Prince won. The armor now protects me.*

But there was something about this armor that I didn't yet fully grasp. I recalled the moments when it had felt as though the armor offered no protection—moments when I was lost to fear—and I wondered what I had been doing wrong. *The Story* and all the lessons I had learned up until this moment seemed to produce a feeling within me that I knew the answer. It was as if it were on the tip of my tongue. Then a detail in *The Story* stood out to me. *It was the King who brought the Prince to life. The King is in control.*

Eyethanoff's reminder to let go of control sprang to mind, and the armor stirred as though confirming I was on the right track. I smiled as I accepted a truth I had been so close to accepting multiple times throughout this journey but I hadn't quite gasped until this moment. This was never about what I could do. It was about a relationship. *"The power is in who you share that relationship with,"* the Prince had told me. I realized that all this time I had been trying to do everything on my own. I was trying to control the armor—to master it and make it work when and how I wanted it to. But now I realized that it was not my armor. It was the King's. And like Yuuki said, *"Power belongs to the King."* That simple truth was the key to it all. It just hadn't sunk in deep enough for me to fully see. Until now. Using the armor wasn't about me bending power to my will. That was not the faith so many had told me to have. Faith was trusting that the power had already been granted to me and letting it flow at the will of the one who wielded it—the King. This was about what the King could do. This was about letting him fight for me. *"All you can do is make one choice, every day. Darkness or light. There is nothing else."* All I had to do was choose.

I choose light.

That commitment seemed to release a floodgate within me, and a memory came to mind. A dream. A man speaking to someone I could not see. *"He is part of a story he is only just beginning to see."* Suddenly I felt a rush of emotion as a final piece of understanding fell into place deep within my soul.

It was as though my mind turned upside down—or maybe it was finally right side up—and I realized why this idea of letting go of control to use the armor had been so hard to understand. I had thought this mission, this whole journey, was about me letting the King into my world so I could free it from darkness. I thought it was about me doing something for him—me allowing him into my story. But that was all wrong. This was about the King inviting me into his story. Into *The Story*. A story that was being told long before I was born and would continue until the King had accomplished his mission. This wasn't about me. I recalled the words Eyerkishta had spoken when she gave me the helmet and sword. *"Be strengthened, my friend, for you are his and he is yours. A treasure claimed by light."* This was about us. The very things I had been fighting to gain had already been granted to me. The King was just trying to get me to see it—teaching me to accept his protection rather than try to protect myself with the things he gave me. *But light's protection exposes all*, I remembered. *"Whose light?"* Eyethanoff's correction jumped to mind along with the answer. *The King's light.* Now I realized I didn't care that light exposed all. It had already exposed my darkest fears, and still I wanted it. I needed it. I needed to choose the King. *As he has chosen me.*

Like a floodgate broken by this realization, at last, I began to see the unseen. To really understand it.

I choose the King.

With faith banishing fear, doubt, confusion, lack of under-standing, lack of ability—everything that had been holding me back, I let go.

Jeb skidded to a stop at the edge of the property as unseen power from an unseen source suddenly burst through me like fire. Its presence hurt, but the feeling was like no other. For a moment, it felt as though it would overtake me, but then I had the sudden sense that I was not alone. The feeling was so strong that I looked around to see if the Prince was there. I saw no one. But I could feel his presence. A presence that felt like freedom. Freedom I had never tasted until that moment. Freedom that was not of this world.

As the power filled me with clarity and relief, arresting any traces of darkness within me, I realized what that freedom really was—what its presence, here and now, with the Lie still in place, meant. Even if I didn't find the physical gate, even if I didn't make it in time and end the Lie, the King had already granted me freedom from darkness and made a way for others to do the same. This mission to find the seen gate and open it suddenly seemed amazing to me. The King had orchestrated a way out of both lies—the lie within our souls, that we were trapped by our own darkness no matter what, and the lie within our world, that what we could see was all there would ever be. It had taken me three days in a trick of the enemy, three days in darkness, to finally see. The truth of *The Story* was not just what was seen in its pages but the unseen truth that freedom exists wherever the Prince dwells. Eyethanoff was right. *"Sometimes, we must lose what is seen before there can be room within us for that which is unseen,"* he had said. And it was true. In the midst of this trial, I had found the space to realize what freedom really was: with or without the life I thought I wanted, with or without the people I thought I needed, with or without the Lie in place, I needed to be part of the King's story.

I am part of the King's story. I have been claimed by light. I am a soldier of the Lion's Sword.

The King's power now flowing freely through me began to fill the armor, which appeared around me once more. But it was no longer transparent. As it filled with the light of Original Power, it seemed to solidify into silver armor with a subtle design of vines and leaves at its edges, along with the Eeffraylick writing I had seen on it before. The thick brown leather belt lit up around my waist and changed color to match its silver buckle and the armor it held together, shining brightly, fed by an unseen source. Original Power flowed through the belt into the breastplate, the shoes, the shield, the helmet, and, finally, the sword as it flew from its scabbard into my hand. I held its hilt in a tight grip, feeling it fully connect with the armor around me. The armor was united. And this time it felt different. It felt free. I didn't try to control the power. I understood now that it was a power wielded through me, not by me. A gift. A gift that was no match for my enemy. There was nothing left holding me back.

I sat in Jeb's saddle, Original Power coursing through the armor, its light spreading down my arms to my fingertips as if it were in my very blood. Remembering what the guards had said about the Lie only holding up if I stayed on the property, I returned the sword to its sheath, then looked at my hands as the light began to fade, though I could still feel it within me. With an idea in mind, I reached my hands out before me. Original Power came in contact with the dark lie around me, and the collision erupted with searing light. The powerful eruption burst out from the armor, colliding with the soldiers behind me who had managed to get their horses and pursue me. Only inches from attacking, they and their horses were thrown back as if struck by a massive wave. Before me, like a scroll rolling up, the Creature's illusion vanished.

Breaking free from this new lie, I found myself on top of Creal Hill, staring down at the battle that raged on below. From where I was, I could see Durthair, the Ath Woods, and some of the Bawtha Forest beyond. Dark soldiers were materializing from the shadows and spilling into Durthair from either side of Creal Hill, coming to relieve their comrades. But light was coming as well. Ruth and those she had gathered poured from the Bawtha Forest around the Ath Woods. She had brought many who believed *The Story*, and they were joining in the fight, battling against the things they could see. Though they had never seen the Prince, they believed in him.

Her mission to rebuild the Lion's Sword just might work.

As I surveyed the battle below, now reinforced by Ruth and those she had gone to retrieve, I realized the days that had passed while I was in the Creature's mansion had just been part of the illusion, for Zath still stood poised at the edge of the Ath Woods. I was about to run to him, but then a memory struck me. The dream I'd had of the man and the voice. Free of the Creature's lie, I recalled why the man had looked familiar. *It was the Prince! The voice must have been the King. What else was it that he said?* I tried to remember. Then the words jumped out at me. *"He is there for a reason."*

Suddenly, Jeb nickered a warning, and I looked behind me in time to see three Martecytes swiftly approaching. I called the sword and shield to my hands, blocking a blow and stabbing the first Martecyte in the heart. I sent the shield to my back, drew a pistol, and fired it at the second Martecyte, dropping him in mid stride before he got within range of my sword. The third reached me, but I blocked his sword with mine, then fired a round into his chest from such close quarters that black powder burned his already black jacket.

With my flank clear of any immediate threat, I turned back and looked out over the scene below, my eyes darting across the land-scape. *Why am I here? What do I need to see?* I silently asked the King. Durthair stretched out before me, awash in battle. The Ath Woods lay at the edge of the fight. Beyond was the Bawtha Forest, the Field somewhere within its vastness and the Great Volcano on the far side.

Then I saw it. Or, more accurately, I realized what I was looking at, for the battle that was raging on before me had moved, just then, into place. If I had been anywhere else or even here at any other moment, I would have missed it. The dark soldiers had taken to the clear night sky on their flying beasts as they battled with Eyerkishta. In their progress, they briefly moved over the Ath Woods. A dome of dark soldiers momentarily hung above the circular patch of woods, and memories of my visions flashed before my mind's eye. A dome of darkness, and a path that led to a door. When I'd had visions of the path, it had reminded me of something. *What was it?* I tried to remember as Jeb shifted nervously beneath me, telling me a threat was near. Then it came to me. *A river! Like the three rivers that run from the Ath Woods through the Bawtha Forest. A river leading to a door...But perhaps it's not a door,* I realized. *Perhaps the Gate was disguised as a door in my visions so if the Creature were able to see into my mind, he could not see its true form. The visions were a secret map to the Gate's location!* There were three rivers leading from the woods. I just had to figure out which one was the right path.

Silently thanking the unseen king, I cued Jeb forward as more Martecytes rushed up from behind, poised to attack.

Jeb sprinted down the face of Creal Hill, and Neyelah suddenly jumped out of the saddlebags and disappeared into the foliage. Jeb and I continued on through Durthair, headed straight for Zath at the edge of the woods, dodging Martecyte attackers as we went. I now knew how to find the Gate. But still, the armor called out to the medallion, and I knew I needed it.

Before I could make it to the main road that led past the woods, two dark soldiers appeared in my path, most likely sent to prevent me from reaching Zath. As I engaged them in battle, Solace appeared to help me.

"Where have you been?" she asked as she braced herself to fight at my side. "I thought he'd killed you!" She raised her voice over the sounds of battle as Ruth rode up on her donkey with a sword in her hand. "And where did you get that armor? Is that the King's armor?"

"He didn't," I said. "And yes. We will discuss the armor later." I adjusted the uncomfortable breastplate, realizing for the first time that it rubbed a little in places. "Right now, we need to focus on the mission. I think the Creature was keeping me from getting the medallion and trying to get in my thoughts again to find the Gate's location," I explained, recalling the moments the Creature had tried to get into my head. Then I remembered something else—the soldiers of darkness who had been discussing the stone. They had noticed we no longer seemed interested in finding it. "I think he knows the medallion is what we are after, not the stone."

"That explains why they are going after Zath now," said Nadia as she joined us, pointing to some Martecytes headed for the massive dragon.

"But it was more than that. The King wanted me up there. I needed to see something." I killed a soldier of darkness and then drew Solace close. "I know how to find the Gate," I whispered, pulling away again. "But the sword still calls out to the medallion. I need to get Zath into the woods. At least in there, Adournath will help us," I called over the noise of the battle.

"Many people joined me and are now fighting by our sides. We will guard the woods. You get him in there and get the medallion!" ordered Ruth.

Before I could react, Solace grabbed me and planted a kiss on my lips. She pulled away. "Be careful."

I nodded and headed toward Zath yet again, but Nadia pulled me to a stop. "Where is Ivan?"

"We will find him, Nadia. But this will all be in vain if I do not complete this mission."

Worry creased her brow, but she nodded, letting go of my arm and turning back to the fight.

Nadia stood back-to-back with Solace, and together they fought off the soldiers of darkness, seeming to see them more clearly. I cued Jeb to head for the Ath Woods, but we were stopped short once again by a beast and more enemy soldiers. They attacked, firing arrows and charging full speed ahead with swords, pushing Jeb and I back toward Solace and Nadia. Nadia blocked a blow, but an arrow pieced her shoulder. Dan was still on his feet not far away but struggling to keep his balance on his bad leg as he wrestled a soldier to the ground. The captain and the rest of his crew were scattered throughout the battlefield, challenging the enemy with all they had. Eyerkishta fought hard, her ice stopping beasts, some of which were nearly three times the size of a horse, but she was no longer flying.

We were wearing out. Getting sloppy. If I didn't open the Gate soon, we would lose this battle.

Suddenly, a cry of pain sounded from behind me, and I turned to see Catherine stabbed in the back with a Martecyte's blade. Her wide-eyed expression seared into my mind as I was suddenly aware of the bodies of fallen Lion's Sword soldiers and three of Ruth's recruits. Around them, our army was fighting against an enemy that still outnumbered them despite Ruth's reinforcements. Two injured Lion's Sword soldiers battled on their feet alongside the rest of their unit and some of the new, less trained volunteers. Christopher was bleeding from a shoulder wound, and Casey and the captain looked determined but worn, locked in a battle with a beast and unable to help their fallen friend.

Stuck in my own battle, I could not go to Catherine, but Dan struggled to her side. She collapsed into his arms, gripping the blade protruding from her chest. It had gone clear through her. There was nothing he could do for her now. Dan looked up and locked eyes with me. His expression said it all. She was gone. Time was running out.

I shook the image from my head and turned back toward Zath, but he was gone. Instead, sitting at the edge of the Ath Woods, just inside the trees, I saw Adournath. His green eyes flashed at me, drawing me toward him.

This time, it didn't take a trance to pull me in. I steered Jeb toward the tree line, dodging arrows and slashing Martecytes as we raced ahead. Arriving at the woods' edge, I dismounted Jeb as Adournath vanished into the trees, and I followed. Pushing through the thick foliage, I came to the center of the woods, where Adournath sat on the large rock, the sounds of the raging battle dampened by the dense vegetation. Before Adournath stood Zath, locked in a battle with himself.

Adournath looked at me. "He needs your help," he explained.

"My help?" I asked. "How?"

"He has seen the truth, for he can see the vision of *The Story* just as you did. But he needs protection from darkness, for Feyerndur must be cleansed of his prison. Use the medallion," instructed Adournath.

Nodding, I turned toward Zath, and the sounds of battle faded away completely as I watched him. He struggled within himself, Feyerndur longing to be free of the dark prison that trapped him. I knew the feeling of being trapped in darkness. I had felt it before I found the helmet. I'd had help then. Now he needed mine.

With determination—and compassion for his plight—I approached Zath slowly so as not to startle him. He was distracted by his internal fight, facing away from me and clawing at the ground, probably in a desperate attempt to keep Feyerndur from the truth. His darker side was unwilling to look at the vision Adournath had revealed to him, but his lighter side fought to come face-to-face with the Prince he so dearly loved.

As I approached the torn and tormented dragon before me, I saw the medallion hanging from his neck. It would be hard to get to without Zath noticing me, but I had to do something. I had no choice, for with this dragon lay the answers I sought. Sheathing my sword, I approached Zath slowly from behind, careful not to alert him to my presence. I managed to get into a blind spot and make my way up near his shoulder. From there, I could see the medallion dangling above me, well out of reach. Locked in his self-struggle, Zath tossed his head, and I barely managed to get out of his way when his head dipped down to my level. As one of his horns came within my reach, I decided this was my chance. I grabbed the horn and held on as he tossed his head upward. The movement gave me the momentum I needed to let go and drop to his neck. I landed firmly on his rough scales and scrambled down near his shoulders to the chain. I quickly rotated the chain around Zath's neck, bringing the medallion up within reach. Then, with nothing left to do, I reached out and grabbed it.

As my fingers closed around the medallion, the King's power connected with it immediately, and its stone face broke apart. Light erupted from within, covering all I could see. Then the light faded, and I found myself in the medallion's vision.

All was calm and quiet. The Prince was standing before me, on the same hilltop from my previous vision.

The Prince smiled as I ascended the grassy slope. "We were interrupted last time," he commented. "I am so glad to see you again."

I nodded and let out a sigh, dropping to my knees in exhaustion when I reached him. "Yes. I need to know. What was it that you were going to tell me?"

The Prince smiled as he sat down on the ground, inviting me to sit next to him. "You have done well, my friend. You have persevered in the face of adversity at a time when others would have chosen the easy path of ignorance or complacency."

I took a deep breath and let it out. "I only did what I was called to do."

The Prince smiled. "And for that, my father and I are grateful."

The Prince had the medallion in his hands, and he looked down at it, then to me. "You followed your compass, though you did not know all the information. You were faithful, and now you will have the knowledge to finish what you started," he explained. "Take this medallion, for the light within you will be magnified by what the medallion can do. Free my father's Treasure Keeper, for with him lies the final key to opening the Gate." The Prince held out the medallion to me, and I accepted it. A peace I did not understand fell over me as it was placed in my hands. I'd had brief glimpses of this peace before, but this seemed different. Deeper.

"I will," I responded with a respectful bow of my head.

The Prince placed a reassuring hand on my shoulder and spoke once more. "You are free, my friend," I heard him say as he and the vision disappeared, "for darkness has no hold on thee."

I suddenly found myself sitting on top of Zath once more with the medallion in my hands. Its stone image had fallen away, and I now saw that it was made of beautiful, gleaming silver to match the armor I wore. Not only that, but the armor around me felt snug, as though it now fit me perfectly. I felt excitement at the armor's change, but I forced myself to focus on the task at hand.

I looked down at the dragon, and the Prince's words echoed in my mind. *"Free my father's Treasure Keeper, for with him lies the final key to opening the Gate."*

With very little information on how this medallion worked, I held what the Prince had told me in my mind and grasped the medallion in my hands. The symbol on its surface shimmered back and forth between the two identical images that stood for Eeeye. True relationship. *"For every step seen, there is a step unseen,"* Eyethanoff had said. *The King and I,* I thought as I realized the parallel. *I am seen, but I have never seen him.* Not entirely sure what to do, I recalled the piece of Eyethanoff's armor that held his medallion. His breastplate—that which protected the heart.

I scrambled down off of Zath and ran to his chest. I had no idea if this would work, but I let Original Power flow through me as I placed the medallion on the chest of weakening dragon. Veins of light traveled from the belt up my arm to the medallion. As Original Power made contact with it, the medallion erupted with light. The light shone out in all directions, so bright that I had to shield my eyes, but when it faded, I was astonished to see a similar light erupt from within Zath. It started out small, like a tiny seed within his darkness, and grew brighter as the light found its way out between the dark scales. Zath fought it, but I could see Feyerndur within, letting it pass over him like water. The cracks in the ink-black scales that covered his body began to widen, and I scrambled out of the way as Zath let out a cry of pain. But the cry contained an echo of another sound. The sound of someone so close to freedom that though he fought through pain, he could not contain his excitement.

The light that filled the medallion began to spread, pushing back the ink-black scales. In their place grew golden armor. A belt of armor appeared around his waist—a belt fit for a dragon. It was soon followed by a breastplate over his chest, where the light had originated. Each armor piece formed to fit his smooth, bright orange scales as if they had always been a part of him. The rough black scales receded ever faster until, finally, a thin layer of almost delicate golden armor washed over the dragon's horns, head, and down the center of his nose, shielding his mind. At that moment, the light erupted again, and Zath let out one last screech of pain, dripping with anger and defeat as the last remaining scales of darkness fell from his eyes. Feyerndur was free. He collapsed in a heap on the grass as silence fell around us.

I stood still, staring in shock at the magnificent dragon before me. With the armor fully in place, he now bore a protective covering down his neck, over his back and tail, and shielding his wings, shoulders, and chest. The golden armor fully coated his horns and claws, but the edge of each orange scale was left visible. He almost beamed with light, and his armor seemed to shimmer of its own accord.

A sound suddenly came from behind me, breaking the silence, and I instinctively spun while raising the sword in defense, but no one was there.

"They need you," said Adournath.

I gave the dragon one last glance, but the sounds of death and destruction beyond the boundary of the woods had returned, growing louder, and I ran to help my friends.

As I exited the Ath Woods, I was immediately confronted by a soldier of darkness who came at me with his sword raised. I blocked his attack and pushed him back. He stumbled, then recovered and attacked again. I dodged the blow as a cry of pain came from behind me, and I spun to see Casey cut down by a Martecyte. Whether he was alive still or not, I did not know. I was still not fully engaged in this fight, my mind with Feyerndur. *Focus!* I told myself.

Finally regaining my composure, I dispatched the soldier of darkness, only to be attacked by an evil beast. Eyethanoff and another Lion's Sword soldier came to my aid, and together we fought the horse-sized creature. As I struggled to hold up against the beast, I could see and hear my allies tiring around me. Worn and weary, and almost all of us wounded in some form, we battled on bloody ground. The conflict was raging all around, and there seemed to be no end in sight. *Feyerndur, where are you?* I silently asked.

Just then, a sound came from the woods behind me. It started low and rumbled through the air until it pierced even the sounds of combat around us as the ground beneath our feet began to tremble. The fighting faltered as the low sound shook the trees. Everyone turned toward the Ath Woods. The roar stopped. Silence fell over the battlefield. For the dark armies, that roar undoubtedly instilled fear that their greatest ally had turned against them. For our weary warriors, it represented hope that our friend was now free.

Suddenly, Feyerndur burst from the woods to the sky with another roar that seemed to slam into my chest. His wings wide, his brilliant scales, bright orange as the sun, shimmered with beauty and renewed strength, posing a shocking contrast to the dark and damaged land around us. His black prison of darkness was gone, replaced by the magnificent golden armor that seemed to contour to his every scale, making his orange scales appear even brighter, and his eyes held a light I had never seen in them before.

He was free.

Chapter 21

A FRESH SURGE OF Original Power seemed to course through me, as though Feyerndur's liberation from his dark prison had given the power a stronger hold in the face of the Lie. The armies of darkness froze. Their great dragon had been turned. Their master's prized possession had been freed from his evil grasp. But the look in their eyes was more than fear. It was confirmation that they knew what Feyerndur could do to end their reign.

Landing in front of the Ath Woods, his stance wide and commanding, Feyerndur opened his massive jaws and sent forth a blazing flood of fire. Immediately, Eyerkishta, bolstered anew by the strength of Original Power, poured out a stream of ice that guided Feyerndur's destructive fire, aiming it into the armies of darkness, preserving the innocent and those who fought for the King. As she did so, a sheath of armor appeared, covering her from head to tail, like Feyerndur's covered him, but hers seemed to be made of pure ice. I noticed as well that both sets of armor were etched with elegant, subtle designs, with a Lion's Sword symbol on each shoulder. Their renewed connection seemed to impact them both, a display of the living image of Eeeye. Two lives in action as one, a seen expression of an unseen connection.

The armies of darkness were no match for the dragons' united might, and they fled, retreating toward the Beldour Mountains and their haven of darkness. Eyethanoff and five of his soldiers pursued them to keep an eye on their whereabouts, disappearing into moonbeams to remain hidden. I knew this fight was not over. They would be back.

With the enemy temporarily in retreat, Eyerkishta approached her beloved with tears in her eyes at the sight of him free of his dark bonds. Snow began to fall softly and silently as Solace and the others gathered around me, some admiring my armor, which was now visible to everyone. The captain helped along an injured but alive Casey, and Nadia embraced a dirty but joyful Missy. I grinned, glad to see they had been reunited.

Together we all watched as Eyerkishta and Feyerndur lay down, nose-to-nose, and closed their eyes. Their breathing gradually changed until they matched in perfect synchronicity. Then Feyerndur opened his beautiful, fire-colored eyes, which sparkled like orange topaz gems. The corner of his mouth curled into a soft, lopsided smile, and a single tear rolled down his face.

"How I have longed to see you through my own eyes," he said in a gentle tone.

Eyerkishta smiled as well, through her tears. "How I longed to see those eyes," she responded. They stood and pressed their foreheads together in a moment of tender connection.

Then a thoughtful frown fell over Eyerkishta's scaled face. "How is it that this armor was returned to you?" she asked.

To my surprise, Feyerndur looked to me. He handed me the medallion I had placed on his chest, and I noticed for the first time that there was a new one in its place. "This medallion and the armor you wear are unique, for it is the only set that can be worn by anyone." He turned to Eyerkishta. "When Ben gave me his medallion, though I only had it for a short while, it restored the armor I once had before the Lie."

"Feyerndur, you must tell us all you know," I said. "The enemy will return soon. Why did you take the stone from the fountain at Mair Pala if it is worthless? And how do I open the Gate? I have the sword and the medallion, and thanks to my visit to Creal Hill, I now know how to find the Gate. But the Prince said the key to opening the Gate lies with you."

Feyerndur nodded in understanding at my confusion. "The King had a plan, and I had a role to play. The Prince told me that if I would accept it, he had a mission for me under this lie, but that it would seem to cost me everything."

"What happened?" asked Eyerkishta with anticipation.

"The Prince explained that for a short while, after he weakened the Creature's hold on the people, the Creature would cover this land in a lie in an attempt to gain more control," started Feyerndur. "He said that the Creature had been searching for a way to rule over Eeffrayldour for centuries and was getting close to enacting a devious plan. The Prince told me not to worry, because his father was still at work. He said that, when the time was right, I was to take the stone from Mair Pala's fountain and place it at the heart of the land, which later became the Lor Channel. Then I was to watch over it, along with my other charges.

"One day, the Prince told me the time had come. So, I took the stone and hid it. Not long after that, Ruth was corrupted, the world collapsed into conflict, and wars began to break out throughout Eeffrayldour. Then the Prince sacrificed himself, and

I began to lose hope, but still I watched over the stone. I didn't know what else to do.

"Then, the Prince came back to life, and I knew his father's plan must still be in play. That is when the Gate was created, and the Creature immediately sought to either destroy or control it. He always sought to gain full control over people and use them for his own greedy desires. The Creature set the Lie in place in an attempt to keep people from accessing the Gate, and shortly after he established the Lie, he came to me in search of the stone. He believed it would give him power to prevent the Prince from ending this lie. Sadly, when he arrived, I made a mistake. I was not ready for him, and I found myself in my human form. He took advantage of my weakness in that form and imprisoned me in shadow." Feyerndur shook his head at his own failure. "The Creature got me to tell him where the stone was, and then he dug the Lor Channel in search of the stone, and he took it from the place where I had concealed it. That was when the land bridges collapsed. Seeing that the stone seemed to have power over the land, the Creature tried to use it, but it wouldn't do anything for him. So, he relocated the stone to a cave where he kept protected treasures he had stolen." Feyerndur looked at me. "But then Trixie found it and put it back in the Lor Channel. When the Creature found out, realizing that his hiding place was compromised, he sent soldiers to retrieve the stone. They found it and took it to his mansion for safekeeping. It sits there now." Feyerndur shrugged. "I am afraid I still don't know exactly why the Prince wanted me to move the stone," he admitted. "The Creature's soldiers said that the Creature had tried many times to corrupt it, but it simply did nothing. Originally, I think he kept it and other things he stole as trophies of some sort. He seemed to love that he had it even though it had no power he could use. But recently he started using the stone as a distraction, hoping to keep you focused on it rather than the Gate, but his plan didn't work."

"What about the medallion?" I asked as Ruth joined us with her recruited army, who approached the dragons hesitantly. Among the recruits, I spotted Mrs. Alves, along with some other familiar faces from the Village. Resisting the urge to run to them in greeting, I smiled and nodded to them instead before turning back to Feyerndur. There would be time for proper greetings later. Right now, there was something I needed to know. "How did the medallion get to be in the cave with the stone in the first place?" I asked.

Feyerndur shook his head thoughtfully. "I saw it in that cave once, long ago. It was with the other artifacts the Creature stole after he corrupted Ruth. I assume he stole it alongside them. I didn't recognize it at the time. Back then I was so...small." He frowned as though he couldn't think of a better way to explain it. "Maybe I didn't recognize it because I was so trapped within Zath. I have recently discovered that many of the Prince's artifacts look different to those in darkness." He sighed. "When I saw it on Trixie, Zath took it because he thought he could return it to the Creature in hopes it would please him. But when Zath touched it, there was something about it that stirred me. It almost felt as though it renewed me in some way, and I knew I had to prevent Zath from giving it back to the Creature. So, I convinced Zath to take it to my cave in the Beldour Mountains. By the time you got there, I had realized what it was and put it on in hopes that it worked like my old armor medallion and would free me from Zath's control. I have had it on ever since. I tried to keep it hidden from view, but the Creature noticed it just before he attacked you in town. I think he realized it was important to your mission because he became angry with me. But he stormed off to attack you and told his men not to let you near me," he finished.

Ruth frowned. "Wait, go back to the stone. Why did the Prince have you move it and watch over the stone and not the Gate? We know the Gate is important, but the stone doesn't seem to have any real value," she pondered.

"As I said, I do not fully understand it myself. But the Prince may have wanted to protect something not more valuable than the Gate but rather something more vulnerable. I recall him acting as though the Gate was well protected," said Feyerndur. "And it's possible that the stone could have some power—we just don't know what it is yet."

"Do you know how to open the Gate?" I asked eagerly, shifting the subject a little.

Feyerndur gave me a half nod, half shrug. "I am not sure of the details of the key, but the Prince said that when the time was right, someone called the Night Rider would know what to do. All I was to do was relay this message from the Prince: 'Unite what has been given. Heed my father's words. Speak, and it will be granted to you.'"

"The Night Rider...That's Solace and me," I said, glancing at Solace. "But I don't know what that message means," I said in confusion.

"Word is that the King made sure that no one being, save himself, knew where all the parts were to open the Gate. But now the Prince has given you everything you need," Feyerndur reassured me. "The Creature is beginning to put the pieces together, though.

He now knows that the medallion plays a part in this story. We must find the Gate and open it before he can stop us and send someone to destroy that gate for good."

Just then, Eyethanoff appeared with a warning. "The armies of darkness are on their way back. They didn't even make it to the mountains, and they are bringing more soldiers. The owls say it is all the soldiers the Creature has under this lie. We must find the Gate now!"

Feyerndur turned to me. "You must go to the Gate, Ben. Open it and defend it. Eyerkishta and I will defend the skies," he finished.

I nodded. "I need a door," I said with a look of determination.

As if in response, Jeb nickered, and Eyethanoff glanced at him, nodded, then turned back to me. "Get on your horse. He will take you where you need to go. Take Solace and Nadia. The rest of us will stay here and do what we can to keep them off your tail," he said as twenty or so soldiers of light approached on horseback.

Captain Bates and his crew all nodded in agreement. "We will fight with Eyethanoff," said the captain. "Go."

Solace, Nadia, and I all mounted our horses. "To the woods," I told them. "That is where we need to start. The King revealed to me that the Gate is at the end of a river. I think it is one of those that begin in the Ath Woods."

Entering the unique circle of trees, we approached the stone at its center. Adournath was nowhere to be seen.

"There are three rivers that flow into these woods. Which one do we follow?" asked Nadia.

Solace cocked her head to one side as she examined the rock. "Ben, there is something on this stone."

I looked at it. "I don't see anything."

Solace smiled. "It's a compass." She dismounted her horse and approached so she could study it more closely. "Adournath sat on this rock, right?" she asked me.

"Yes. At least that seemed to be his favored spot when I was in here before."

Solace ran her hands over the surface of the stone. "There are four paw prints. They sit at exactly north, south, east, and west," she said, pointing in each of the directions.

I nodded. "Is there anything that will tell us which river to follow?" I asked.

Solace shook her head. "N—" She broke off. "Wait." Solace leaned forward, looking at something from a different angle. She smiled. "There is a small symbol on the north paw. Two S shapes."

"That's it!" I said. "The river between the Ath Woods and the Great Volcano must be the correct one." I briefly noted that Solace could apparently see the entire symbol of Eeeye, and I smiled. She had believed long before I had, but for some reason, this reminder that she knew the truth and believed brought joy to my soul. "Let's go!"

Solace mounted her horse again, and we took off at a gallop in the direction of the river, though it was Jeb who seemed to lead the way. Recalling Eyethanoff's odd response to Jeb's nicker and our discussion about talking horses, I let Jeb decide where we were headed. *Maybe he does know where we need to go.* Jeb raced north into the Bawtha Forest and along the river toward the distant volcano with the others in tow. As we ran, I noticed the sky. The stars shone brightly overhead, but when I looked closely, I saw that some of the stars were connected by thin lines, as if the darkness around us were beginning to crack. The Creature's lie was failing.

He would be desperate to destroy the Gate. We were nearly out of time.

As we made our way through the forest, Jeb suddenly came to a stop and listened, his ears twitching and his gaze shifting around the area before us. Confused by Jeb's abrupt halt, I was about to take control and urge him forward when an isp appeared in a tree nearby. It ran down the trunk and headed away from our path along the river just a few yards, drawing Jeb to follow it.

"Jeb, we need to stay with the—"

Then I saw it. A magnificent white stag. It stood at the base of a distant tree that the isp had ascended into. The stag watched the isp as it darted up the tree, then turned in our direction. Spotting us, it sprag into action. It dashed gracefully through the brush as Jeb followed of his own accord. The stag led us back to the bank of the river and right into the water. As it reached the center of the river, a door materialized out of nowhere, opening just in time for the stag to lead us all through. Emerging on the other side, we found ourselves in the Field.

The stag continued its journey, and we followed. But as we ran, I realized the Field looked different now. Golden stags grazed in the grasses, and they joined in on the run to shield us from the golden ghosts, which came after us. I also noticed that, unlike the last time we were in the Field, the moon and stars shone bright in the sky. However, when I looked closer, I realized that the stars actually were, in fact, cracks in the Lie, and in some areas, it seemed as though the lines now connecting them had thickened.

The stag led us through another door, and we came out on the far side of the Valley, where the river reappeared from the land. The stag ran through the water until a third door opened, but this time the stag veered off at the last moment, leaving the rest of us to go through on our own. We skidded to a halt on the other side of the door, and I glanced back in time to see it close behind us and vanish, revealing some distance away the section of river that widened and coursed around the small island we had traveled to all those months ago. I turned back around to face what was in front of us and was met with a daunting sight.

Before us stood the Great Volcano. Between us and the volcano was a barren landscape of cooled lava rock. Occasional streams of lava flowed through the cracks, making the landscape glow. Unlike the first two doors, this one had put us quite a distance from the river, which now flowed red. In this mysterious place, the water and lava seemed to combine into a dangerous substance that looked like lava but moved like boiling water.

This landscape was where my father had died. The place where I lost the last of what had been important to me. I could feel the memories well up within me, but for the first time, the pain was not overwhelming.

Solace came up next to me. "Is it here? The Gate?"

I nodded. "Somewhere," I reassured her. "It has to be, or the stag wouldn't have stopped here," I responded as I searched the landscape for any sign of the Gate.

"How are we supposed to find it without the stag? There is nothing here," asked Nadia, wincing as she gently cupped an injury on her shoulder.

"I am not sure," I replied as I looked around, consciously letting the Original Power now flowing through the armor guide my vision, knowing my eyes were not reliable. But before I could locate the Gate, an eerie sound came from behind me, stopping me in my tracks.

Slowly, we all turned in search of the source of this strange sound. What I saw sent chills down my spine.

Coming toward us, like a tiger stalking its prey, was a great, foggy, black beast. It looked like the one my father had died defeating, but it had grown to a massive size and was covered in lava and lava rock, as if sending it to its death in the volcano had simply made it stronger. It was not flesh and blood anymore. It had a shape and face, but its body morphed as it moved.

"What is that?" asked Solace breathlessly.

"The Great Beast," was all I could get out as I drew the sword and shield.

Suddenly, I felt a hand on my shoulder, and I flinched. It was Solace. "Ben?"

I swallowed. "The Great Beast…The one that killed my father…It…" I couldn't finish the sentence.

Solace gripped my shoulder tighter. "Ben. Do not let what you see stop you. We are not dealing with flesh and blood but shadows created by fear. Is it possible that this beast looks so much like the one that killed your father because the Creature knows it will cause you to pause?"

"We need to move," said Nadia, backing up her horse as the massive creature before us stalked closer.

I looked at the beast. Eyethanoff had explained that the Creature was a master illusionist. Maybe Solace was right. He had been preying on my mind this whole time, trying to find what would convince me to give him full control. Could it be that this was simply another ploy to break me?

With a deep breath, I nodded to Solace. "What do I do?" I asked. I couldn't let go of the image of my dying father, bloodied and broken as his life slipped through my fingers.

Solace gently gripped my sword arm. "Have faith."

I took another deep breath and sheathed the sword and put the shield in its place on my back. I took Solace's hand and closed my eyes. She gripped my hand tighter, and I felt the armor around me. I let go of control. Original Power seemed to remain still for a moment, as if asking if I really wanted to release control. And I did. Suddenly, it flowed free, as it had on Creal Hill. I opened my eyes, and the beast was gone.

Solace smiled. She opened her mouth to say something, but it wasn't her voice I heard.

"You have no power here."

My heart sank, and I saw Nadia's expression melt into shock. We turned again to look behind us. There, framed by the bubbling volcano, stood Ivan.

Chapter 22

Pale and bruised, even bloody in places, Ivan stood among ash and burning embers floating through the hot air, the lava-encrusted volcano behind him. He glared at us, his eyes filled with hatred, as though the Creature himself were looking out through him.

"No," I whispered.

Darkness swirled around him, creating a protective shield that I knew was powered by my own grief.

"Ben." Nadia's voice cracked, breaking my heart.

I shook my head. "I didn't know that is what they would do to him, Nadia."

"We can't kill him," she pleaded.

I looked at her. "We will not!" I said as I dismounted Jeb. "Back me up," I said, but I could feel that my confidence had left me. I had no idea what my next move would be.

Suddenly, Ivan charged. The fog around him split into three other figures, which attacked the others, but Ivan came for me.

Unprepared, I reached for the sword, but it jumped to my hand, surprising me so that I almost dropped it. Securing the sword in a tight grip, I held it at the ready and stood my ground, but I had no intention of using it on Ivan. The heat emanating from the volcano made me sweat as I realized that this was the one thing I didn't know how to handle. The fog was a clear enemy, but Ivan...Ivan was my friend. Fear gripped me as I realized that the Creature had found a hold on me.

Mid charge, Ivan drew a sword and slashed at me in a diagonal arc. He was a formidable opponent, and I was at a disadvantage. Not only was he a friend, but he was a better swordsman than I.

I dodged the attack, only to find him coming in for another strike with a look of pure hatred. My mind reeled as I tried to think of what I could do to keep him from killing me. *I can't kill him, and I if I can't kill him, I can't beat him. I need to turn him back,* I told myself. *I need to free him from the Creature's control.*

With a growl of anger, Ivan pulled back and spoke. But there was something in his voice that made me wonder if he was reciting the Creature's words.

"You can save me," he said. "If you turn back now, no further harm will come to me," he stated as he paced back and forth before me, remnants of black fog flowing around him.

I gripped the sword, trying to remind myself of the power the armor contained. "Ivan, please. Don't do this. It's me, Ben!" I pleaded. "Don't make me fight you."

Ivan's hatred burst from within him. "You left me!" he yelled. "You left me to die!"

"I...I didn't know. I—"

"You don't know what I am!" he snarled. "Your friend is gone."

"Then tell me," I said, trying to keep the conversation going until I could think of a way to save him. "What are you?"

"I am fear!" Ivan lunged at me, moving so fast I barely had time to react. The shield jumped to my hand just as Ivan's sword came down, striking the metal surface with a force I had never felt from him before, knocking me to the ground.

"You have no power here," growled Ivan. "You have nothing. Nothing but a trinket made by a man lost in hopeless love for those who betrayed him."

I pulled myself to my feet. "Ivan, I can help you. Please. We can overcome the enemy together."

Ivan circled around me, leaving a trail of ink-black fog in his wake. As I moved to remain face-to-face with him, I saw something that drew my attention. The boiling red river flowed past behind Ivan before it disappeared into the volcano, reminding me how we had gotten here and what we were looking for. But as we moved, I realized for the first time that the river was not made of lava. It only looked as though it was because the lava from the volcano reflected off the water's surface as it flowed over black rock.

Remembering why I was here, I felt myself being torn between my two duties. My duty to my friend and my duty to the Prince and the King.

I felt the belt stir around my waist. I was here to open the Gate and end the Lie.

Keeping Ivan in front of me, I looked at the river behind him as I recalled what the stag had done. Three times it had stepped into the water, and then a door had been revealed. The doors that had led us here had all been found in the river, just like the visions had hinted. *Follow the river from the Ath Woods to the Gate,* I thought to myself as an idea began to formulate in my mind. *Can I survive stepping into water that is probably boiling hot?* I wondered. I decided to act on my hunch.

"Ivan, the Creature is just using you to stop me from completing my mission," I explained. "Please, do not let him use you like this," I added as I stepped to my right toward the river until I was standing at its edge. "Please, Ivan. Don't make me choose between you and the freedom of the people trapped under this lie. People that include ones we care about. Think of Nadia, Ivan!"

Internally, I braced myself as I placed a foot in the water. But to my surprise, the water was not hot. It was mysteriously cool, even refreshing. I suddenly remembered Yuuki pointing out that Original Power felt a lot like fire, though it wouldn't burn you. *Maybe that is what this river is—a river of Original Power.* It felt like nothing I had ever experienced before.

I continued stepping tentatively through the water, keeping Ivan's attention on my words as I moved. "The unseen king knows what he is doing, Ivan. He has a plan. He made this land, and he is trying to protect it from us—from the people who abandoned him! He is trying to protect those who are loyal to him, Ivan. Please, just let me help you," I pleaded.

As I reached the center of the river, in the corner of my eye, a gate suddenly became visible in the distance. It was white, round, and framed by the volcano behind it, which made it look as though it were rimmed in orange fire. It fit perfectly into the riverbed, its base concealed by water that now appeared calm and blue. The King and the Prince really had set everything up perfectly. I dared not look directly at the Gate, or Ivan might see it as well. I wasn't certain whether it was visible without the armor, but I didn't want to risk it. I continued moving across the river, hoping I could use it as a barrier between Ivan and me. But as I moved toward the riverbank, the Gate vanished from sight and the water turned red and boiling again. *Maybe I just need to keep Ivan away from the center of the river.*

Soon, we stood on either side of the water, staring at each other, swords held at the ready. Waiting. *But for what?*

Ivan laughed. "You think your precious unseen king is trying to help us? You are right, he made this land. But he made me too."

I froze. I looked into Ivan's eyes and realized I couldn't tell if he was talking about himself or the Creature.

"What do you mean?" I asked.

Ivan chuckled. "You did not know?" he asked. "Your king has been lying to you."

As his words echoed in my ears, I found myself entertaining doubts. Through the armor and my experiences meeting creatures and humans from the unseen land, I had witnessed the power of the King of Eeffrayldour. But if he had made the very evil that was hurting us, who was I really fighting for? Just then, a vision of Adournath floated through my memory, and the belt stirred. Then the breastplate of armor stirred as I heard Eyerkishta's words in my mind. *"Be on guard, my friend, for your heart is a treasure worth protecting.*

The fog that surrounded Ivan expanded as my thoughts filled with doubt. *It is just another trick—a lie to trap me and create a shadow the Creature can occupy.*

"No!" I yelled as my grip tightened on the hilt of the sword. "I will not believe your lies!" I stated with confidence as I felt Original Power respond to my grasp. For a moment, I felt a soft breeze flow by, its cool touch a refreshing contrast to the heat and darkness around me, and I heard the Prince's voice floating to me on the wind. *"You are not alone."*

"Ah, but lies they are not," said Ivan, "for your precious king made the Creature the highest in his house, save himself. He gave him power and taught him wisdom. Then he cast me out when I no longer served his purposes!" Ivan said, the Creature now speaking directly through him. "Your precious king does not love you!" he warned. "He wants you to complete his kingdom. He needs you to take back what he thinks belongs to him. He will cast you out as soon as you fail him, for you are of the Land Beyond, and to be cast out is what you deserve!" he bellowed.

I shook my head as the armor stirred around me, starting with the belt and moving through the breastplate and shoes. *"Be ready, my friend, for* The Story *is a treasure worth following."* I recalled the vision with the shoes. When I had first encountered them, I wasn't sure of their purpose, but I had later learned that they offered stability—a foundation built on the truth of what had been done to overcome darkness. In that vision, I had recited the truth of *The Story*, which had given me the confidence to walk past a dark soldier I later found out was the Creature.

I began reviewing *The Story* in my mind, gaining strength from its truth. The story about a prince who, despite what I deserved, had sacrificed everything to give me a choice. *How did Ruth put it? "Thankfully for us, true love is not bound by what we deserve."*

I smiled. "I am no longer of the Land Beyond. I am a soldier of the Lion's Sword!" I stated with confidence. If this was going to come to a battle, and it seemed that was the only option, I needed to keep Ivan from reaching the middle of the river.

I lunged into the water and managed to pass the center point just as Ivan entered the far side. Trying not to kill him, I instead focused on attempting to wear him out and keep him from moving farther into the river. I thrust my sword toward his shoulder, but the fog came to his aid, blinding me momentarily before it pulled away, revealing Ivan poised to attack. I barely blocked his blade in time, trying to keep my footing in the water.

"You have no power here!" he yelled again. "Just like last time. You will lose what little you have. Are you willing to let them die?" he demanded, gesturing to the others.

I glanced at Solace and Nadia, who were struggling to defeat the fog that had morphed into beasts that were not of flesh and blood. I turned back to Ivan. I couldn't let him get in my head. "They know the risk."

Ivan's pale lips curled into a cruel smile. "Are you willing to kill me?"

My growing confidence from recalling *The Story* faltered.

"You want to complete your mission? You must go through me first," he taunted.

I had to find some way to get through this. I had to let him go. With a growl of anger fueled by sorrow, I charged. I slashed at Ivan's shield of fog, this way and that, searing more and more of it away. But Ivan just laughed as I stumbled through the water. The black fog that burned away was simply replaced by more.

I took a step backward to put some space between us, careful not to get too close to the middle of the river. The sword didn't seem to be doing much, so I switched to the shield. It had stopped Ivan. Maybe it could weaken whatever power he had gained from the Creature.

Changing tactics, I taunted, "Fine. You are right. I did leave you in that mansion! I left you because you were deadweight, and I didn't have time to find you. I must complete this mission, no matter the cost." Something about that last phrase resonated in me, turning my gut as I realized what I would have to do.

Ivan returned the taunt. "You? Beat me alone? I am more powerful than anything you could imagine!"

With that, we erupted in battle. Swords clashed as we sloshed through the water at the edge of the river and up onto land, and I parried his blows until I saw an opening. As his blade came down, I pulled the shield over myself and dropped to one knee, trusting the shield would hold.

Ivan hit hard, and a loud clang sounded as darkness collided with light. Ivan snarled in anger and charged again. Again, the shield held him at bay. But as I stood, lowering the shield, I saw the opposite of what I had hoped for. The fog around Ivan grew. It expanded to three times his size, as did the foggy beasts attacking the others. Ivan let out a yell that the creatures of fog echoed—a call that could be heard for miles.

"No," I said in dismay, for he had not only grown to a size I could not face alone, but he and the beasts had alerted the Creature and his armies to our location—and the location of the Gate.

"We cannot fight these creatures with these swords," called Nadia in desperation as she ran up behind me, the foggy beasts circling at a distance as if waiting for something. She looked at Ivan and seemed to become frozen in place, holding back tears.

I reached out to touch her shoulder, but then I saw something in Ivan's eyes. Recognition. For a moment, he stood staring at his sister. They had been close since childhood. They shared a bond only shared by twins. Something about it had gotten his attention.

"*We* cannot fight the darkness," I said as I realized what Ivan and Nadia had. A unique relationship. Seen, but connected by something unseen. The Ice Dragon's words came to mind as the armor stirred around me, ending in the shield gripped in my hand. *"Have faith, my friend, for the unseen is a treasure worth believing in."*

"What are we going to do?" asked Solace as she joined us.

My thoughts began to form another revelation, and I felt uncertainty come over me as I wondered if I was on the right track or just grasping at straws. But then I felt the stirring in the shield move to the helmet, and I recalled the dragon's words. *"You are a treasure claimed by light."*

"Faith in unseen light," I whispered as my realization came to a head, and I understood that I was doing this all wrong, again. Ivan's transformation had thrown me into a state of fear that had made me forget what I had learned on Creal Hill. Faith. *"All you can do is make one choice, every day. Darkness or light. There is nothing else."* There was a connection I was not taking advantage of. A connection more impactful than just me and the armor. An unseen connection. *But how do I access it?*

Just then, Ivan shook his head, breaking his focus on Nadia. He drew the foggy beasts to himself, uniting them into a thick cloud. I held the shield up, hoping it would protect us all. The fog was held back by the shield, but it grew stronger and stronger, swirling like a whirlwind that threatened to take us into the sky. The wind was so strong that I felt the medallion move around my neck, and it floated up into my field of vision. Then I realized, *I am not using all the armor!*

The Prince's words seemed to echo in my mind as my last vision of him played out in my memory. *"You are free, my friend, for darkness has no hold on thee."*

I looked around at the dark whirlwind that threatened to overwhelm me. I had been fighting with the goal of victory. But I had forgotten what I had learned. Victory was already won. *The darkness has no hold on me.*

I closed my eyes and recalled that I had already chosen light, back on Creal Hill when I had finally understood what it meant to let the King be in control. A memory from my dream in the mansion came to mind. *"Remember what you have seen. But trust what you have not."* For a moment I didn't know what it meant, but then it came to me. I needed to remember the things the King had shown me—the dreams, the visions, the soldiers of light, the armor. Because in every trial, there would be the temptation to forget. But I also needed to trust what I could not see. Trust the King. Always. Because no matter what I could see, he would fight for me. *This is about us,* I reminded myself as I remembered what the Prince told me about the medallion. *"This medallion offers you a deeper connection to a power not your own, the power found in Eeeye. A connection stronger than anything the Creature can touch."*

I choose light. I choose the King.

With renewed vigor, I placed the shield at my back and the sword in its scabbard. They had jumped to my hands before, and I trusted they would again. I took hold of the medallion and looked at it. To free Feyerndur, I had placed it at his chest, and it had united his armor. I placed the medallion at my chest and let go.

Metal touched metal, and light burst from within the medallion. It fused with the armor, and small flashes of lightning shot out from its circular edge in all directions. Then, suddenly, the light vanished, and everything seemed to slow. The darkness around me was still there, like a bubble I could not escape. But then I saw something within the dark cloud. A man. Not just any man. The Prince.

"You are not alone," he comforted. "You never have been."

Filled with relief at the Prince's presence, I called out to him. "Help us, for this being is too strong."

The Prince smiled. "The battle you see is not yours to fight, for that is why the Night Rider is three."

"Three? What do you mean?" I asked, for I only knew of Solace and me.

But as my confusion took over, the darkness around me grew until the intimidating fog was all I could see. The Prince vanished. I ran after him, needing to know what he meant. But then I stopped when suddenly he was before me. He held out his hands to either side, me on his right and Solace on his left. Power flowed through him, and he moved his hands above and below the medallion. It split in two, forming two medallions. On one side of each was a single S shape. On the other side was the unique pair, the one always visible and the other only visible from certain angles. He placed one before Solace, and armor grew from it, covering her as mine covered me.

The Night Rider is three! Solace, the Prince, and me.

Then the Prince vanished.

"The battle you see is not yours to fight." I turned and looked down the river to the place I knew the Gate stood. It was there. I could not see it through the darkness, but it was there. I turned back and looked at Solace. The armor stirred between us, as though it were connected. I could feel her as though she were part of me. We locked eyes, and she nodded.

Trust the King. He has provided what I need. This battle was hers to fight. Mine was to open the Gate.

Chapter 23

I TURNED TO FACE Ivan and his darkness with renewed vigor. But this time, though it broke my heart, I looked beyond what I could see toward the goal I was striving for. I moved to the edge of the river, ignoring the darkness around me as Ivan screamed through his foggy storm in an attempt to draw me back to him. But no matter how much it hurt me, I couldn't respond. That battle was not mine to fight. It was Solace's.

Letting go of what I had thought I must face, I opened myself to the power not my own, knowing the unseen could protect me. Immediately, I felt the presence of Original Power. With a deep breath, absorbing the strength it gave me, I entered the river with Original Power as my companion.

As I reached the middle of the river, the Gate appeared in the distance, a dim glow of hope shining through the cloud of darkness still whirling around me, the water at its base calm and blue. I surged through the knee-deep water toward the only way to freedom from this lie as it disappeared once again in the fog.

The ground beneath me rumbled as the distant armies approached, coming for us. I could imagine the dragons defending us as best they could, holding back the oncoming army from the sky. But I left that battle behind me, focused my mind on what was before me, and pressed on. I pushed through the dark fog the Creature had tried to trap me in—darkness so thick I could barely see. I knew he was trying to fill me with fear that would give him a place in my mind. I knew he was trying to fill me with sorrow that would break me. But I would not give in this time. I kept my eyes on the place I knew the Gate was located and pressed on in faith that it was actually there.

With every step I took, the Gate gradually became visible through the storm like a beckoning guide. The darkness began to fade as Ivan's cry of anger grew distant. I took another step and saw the Gate in full, shining like a beacon in the dead of night.

I continued forward and finally exited the cloud. My body cried out for rest, but I was quickly reminded that there was no time to spare. The scene around me was dire. Above the desolate and scarred land, the volcano rumbled and spit lava, threatening to erupt at any moment. The heat was unbearable, but the river I trudged through felt cool and refreshing, giving my body just enough relief to keep moving forward. So, I pressed on toward the Gate, its bright white glow posing a stark contrast to the dark landscape around it.

Arriving at the Gate, just as the first hint of dawn began to lighten the sky, I collapsed to my knees, the cool blue water splashing up around my waist. I braced my hands wide apart on the Gate's surface and let my forehead rest on the white wood. I could feel carvings under my hands as I caught my breath.

Finally, I was here.

Then I heard—felt—something. In my mind it sounded like a knock, but in the armor it felt like a calling that reverberated through my chest. Lifting my gaze to the Gate, I felt the sensation grow stronger, as if someone were waiting on the other side, waiting to release power into this land that so desperately needed it. Taking a deep breath, I ignored my aching body and forced myself to my feet. *I am not finished yet.*

Standing before the Gate, I was faced with what looked like a shimmering red seal at its center, almost like the wax seal of a letter. The seal was round and indented with the symbol of Eeeye—two identical S-shaped letters that were taller than they were wide, one clearly visible and one only visible from certain angles. The letters had little curls at the top and bottom and lines to accent and connect them.

I examined the seal before me, recalling all the information I had on how to open the Gate. The sentence on the sword. *"When truth be known has strengthened thee, the Lion's sword will set you free."* The medallion that bore the symbol of Eeeye. And the message from the Prince that Feyerndur had given me. *"Unite what has been given. Heed my father's words. Speak, and it will be granted to you."*

All the pieces were here. Now I just had to figure out how they fit together. I grabbed the sword and analyzed the sentence. I recalled my theory that the sword might act as a key of sorts to open the Gate, but I saw no lock or opening where a sword would fit. I ran my fingers over the symbol at the seal's center and realized that it matched the medallion. I grabbed the medallion and detached it from the armor, feeling the armor loosen. I hesitated for a moment as fear that I was no longer protected threatened to distract me. *Solace will protect me,* I reassured myself. That is her job given to her by the King just as this job was given to me. That is why the Prince united us as the Night Rider. We were meant to do this together.

Knowing I was guarded by someone well equipped to do the job, I placed the medallion in the red seal on the Gate. It fit perfectly, and after a moment, a slight click sounded from the medallion. But still, the Gate did not open. I recited the sword's sentence in my head to make sure I wasn't missing something. *"When truth be known has strengthened thee, the Lion's sword will set you free."* I shook my head. I knew the sword had something to do with opening the Gate because the sentence literally said so. But there was no place on the Gate for the sword. *What am I missing?* Like the writing on the sword, Eyerkishta's message when I received the sword had mentioned being strengthened. *"Be strengthened, my friend, for he is yours and you are his. A treasure claimed by light."*

"There has to be something here..." I muttered to myself.

I reached up and ran my fingers over the seal again, then decided to check the sides. As my fingers reached the side of the seal, I felt something. There was a flat opening that went through the seal, through the medallion. It had not been there before I pushed the medallion into place. The first part of Feyerndur's message came to mind. *"Unite what has been given."* I had been given the sword and the medallion. *That must be it!* I tried to push the sword into the opening from top to bottom, but it wouldn't go in. So, I tried bottom to top. It worked. The sword slid into the slot, blade tip pointing up. As it locked into position, a deep thud rippled through the ground around the Gate, sloshing the water of the river.

With the two pieces in place, I grabbed the hilt of the sword and pulled. But it would not budge. I frowned and tried again. Still nothing. I tried pushing. Nothing. I let go and stood back, wondering, again, what I was missing. *There is more,* I thought as I recalled the rest of the message Feyerndur had given me. *Stop getting ahead of yourself and pay attention,* I chastised myself. I recited the message one more time. *"Unite what has been given. Heed my father's words. Speak, and it will be granted to you."*

"'Heed my father's words,'" I said out loud. "What words?"

I looked at the Gate, the seal, and the pieces that made up the key until my gaze fell on the part of the sword's sentence that was still visible.

"'When truth be known has strengthened thee, the Lion's sword will set you free.'" I repeated the whole sentence with a perplexed frown. "I did that," I mumbled to myself. "I used the sword."

I examined the beautiful script a little closer. As I searched my memory of the words for some clue as to what I was missing, I recalled listening to Trixie translate them. She had said something about the challenge of translating ancient Eeffraylick. She had mentioned she had a hard time with possessives for some reason, but I couldn't remember why. Something about there being a possibility that the sentence was saying something else. *But that can't be it because the sentence is right, the sword is part of the key,* I thought in confusion.

I looked at the medallion and the symbol of Eeeye on its face. As I did so, I happened to shift so the second symbol appeared. Suddenly an idea sparked to life as I remembered the unique connection to the King the medallion offered me.

"Because there is an intricate connection between what is seen and what is unseen," I said out loud as I began to realize what I was missing.

I recalled the rest of the conversation with Trixie the day she had translated the sword. She had explained that the sentence said "the

Lion's sword," referring to the sword, but that she could be wrong. It could say the "the Lion's word." *That is it! The sentence has more than one meaning! One seen and one unseen. The sword is seen. But spoken words are not seen—they are heard!*

"Speak, and it shall be granted to you," I said with a smile as it dawned on me that the true meaning of the word "Eeeye" resonated with what I was doing here—opening a connection between this place and the King, a connection stronger than anything the Creature could touch.

"Eeeye," I whispered.

At the sound of the word, the lock shifted once to the left. I grabbed the hilt of the sword and pushed it counterclockwise. This time, it moved easily. The seal began to rotate quickly, but then a deep rumbling shook the ground off in the distance from the direction of Durthair. The seal suddenly became difficult to rotate, as though a great pressure had built up behind the Gate, eager to get out.

I tightened my grip and put all my strength into turning the unique key all the way around, a scraping sound now emanating from the lock. As soon as the hilt of the sword was pointing up and the blade down, the lock released, and the Gate burst open. I was nearly knocked down, as if a deluge of water had been released from the other side. But it was not water that came through.

It was light.

Light shot from the Gate, and I ducked as I realized it was streaming toward Durthair, as if it were attracted to something in that direction. But I didn't have time to figure out what. I closed my eyes against the blinding brightness and felt it pass over me like silky water.

Silence. I opened my eyes. The land around me was pure white. Grass, trees, rocks, sky—all were doused in a light that made them almost glow.

Before me stood a ring of twelve doors, the closest ones facing away from me. I could not see into the center of the circle. I looked around, trying to figure out if I was in a vision or if this was real. The gently rolling hills surrounding the ring of doors were bare, save for a few plants, rocks, and trees. It looked like the Field of Doors, though the only doors I saw were the ring of twelve.

Suddenly, an isp appeared next to me, seemingly out of nowhere. Its grayish fur had a green tint to it, making it the only source of color I could see. I squatted down, and it moved a little closer as I reached out to pet it.

"Where am I?" I asked, not expecting it to answer.

The isp rubbed affectionately against my hand as I stroked it, its velvety antlers briefly catching on my sleeve. Suddenly, it darted off, passing between two doors.

"Hey, wait!" I called out, chasing after it.

I squeezed through the ring of doors and stopped in my tracks.

Before me was a large white tree, taller than everything else I could see. I looked around, wondering how I hadn't seen it before. I didn't find any answers, so I turned back to face it. Amidst the white leaves on its branches were delicate, ink-black flowers. Around the base of the tree, petals and leaves had fallen, leaving a ring of black and white around the magnificent tree's broad trunk.

"What is this place?" I wondered out loud.

I turned and looked at the doors. Each had a carving on its face, each of a different person. They all looked like royalty. Six queens and six kings. King, queen, king, queen, all the way around. Each person held a sword in their hands. The only thing that made some stand out were the shadows that had fallen over five of them.

All the figures were gazing at the tree, so I did the same. I approached it to get a better look and found that there were carvings on its trunk as well. I walked around the tree, examining the designs. Three carvings of three doors, with three different carvings within them. A crown, a flame, and a circle. I had seen those images somewhere before.

I drew the sword and unwrapped the leather-bound hilt. There they were. The only other place I had seen these three images was on the Prince's pendant, but they had been combined into one.

I frowned, wishing I knew what they meant. Wishing I knew why I was here.

The tree's branches rustled, and I looked up. A black and white isp was looking down at me. It cocked its head to one side, then bared its teeth and jumped. I blocked my face with the shield.

"Ben!" I heard Solace's voice call out to me.

I moved the shield and looked around. I stood in the middle of a dry riverbed, sunlight just beginning to spill over the horizon. Before me was the Gate, which was no longer emitting light. It was still open, and I could see through it. Then I realized, all around me, the land...It had changed. The once barren black ground was now partially covered in snow and bursting with surprising color—patches of white dotted the bright green grass, and green pine trees and mysterious trees with purple and pink leaves I had never seen before surrounded us in the near distance. Plants that bloomed with unusual winter flowers of various colors grew throughout the landscape. Where the volcano once stood was a castle, carved from the top of the mountain itself. It was overgrown and unkempt, but its magnificent stony structure was a sight to behold. Circling down from the castle wall to the base of the mountain was a sprawling village. The Lie was broken. I stood in Eeffrayldour.

"We did it, Ben!" Solace appeared next to me, nearly toppling me over as she wrapped her arms around me in excitement. Still stunned, I looked around, spotting a few soldiers of darkness fleeing into the trees.

"What happened?" I asked, embracing her.

"What happened?" she said, pulling away gently and gripping my face in her hands. "The dark soldiers arrived on their flying creatures, but we held off the enemy while you opened the Gate! Didn't you see? The light poured out, and the Creature ran! He ran, Ben! And his soldiers followed. The sky cracked apart and peeled back, and the volcano turned into a castle." She spun around, gesturing to the landscape around us. "Look at it, Ben! I never expected it to look like this! The illusion is gone, the Lie has been broken, the Creature is on the run, and this place is magnificent!"

Just as she finished speaking, a strange sound came from the direction of Durthair, and we turned to see what it was. My eyes widened briefly at the sight, and Solace grabbed my hand, taking off toward the edge of the riverbed with a laugh of excitement. Water was rushing toward us, filling the riverbed once again, flowing from Durthair toward the castle.

I outran Solace and stepped up onto the bank, grabbing her in my arms and pulling her out of the way of the rushing water just as a group of Lion's Sword soldiers erupted in a cheer. I glanced around, spotting Eyethanoff, the dragons, Captain Bates, and the remaining crew of the *Lyonsword* nearby, along with a few of the volunteer soldiers. "What was that? And how did everyone get here so fast from Durthair?" I asked.

Solace smiled and stepped back as I released her, taking my hand in hers again. "The doors, of course!" she said, answering my second question.

I grinned, about to laugh, but then I remembered. "Ivan!"

Solace turned, and her smile fell. "When you opened the Gate, he ran too, with the other soldiers..."

I looked at Nadia.

Her lips were pinned in a thin line, and she held back tears. "Ivan is still out there, Ben."

I grabbed her shoulders. "I know. We will find him," I reassured, looking her in the eye.

Solace nodded. "We will find him, and we will free him, as we did with Feyerndur." She looked at Eyethanoff. "That is possible, right?"

He dipped his head in confirmation. "He is in the first stages of corruption. It is still possible. But if he gets much worse, we may lose him forever."

Nadia winced.

"What about the Creature?" I asked. "Do we need to go after him and make sure he doesn't come back?"

Eyethanoff shook his head. "The Creature took a big blow to his strength when so much Original Power was let into this place so quickly. He will need time to recover. He will seek out others he can manipulate to regain power. And we will help them. But for now, we need to recover as well. We have many wounded. We took heavy casualties. Those who came with Ruth have asked to join the Lion's Sword, though." He smiled brightly. "The King's army will be rebuilt, and we will be ready for the Creature when he returns."

"Where is Ruth?" I asked, realizing she wasn't with us.

Everyone glanced around. "I don't know," Eyethanoff said. "She was here a few moments ago."

"Hey, who is that?" asked Solace, pointing to a rider coming through the trees from the direction of Durthair. The figure was wearing a familiar dark cloak with the hood pulled up and was coming toward us at a trot.

"That looks like Betsy! But who is riding her?" asked Nadia.

I had seen that cloak somewhere. *Where was it? The mansion! That is the cloak that mysterious person was wearing!* I pulled my sword. Seeing my reaction, everyone else grabbed their weapons as well.

"Who is it, Ben?" asked Solace.

"I don't know. But I saw them at the Creature's mansion."

Solace narrowed her eyes at the approaching rider. "I don't sense any dark soldiers." She glanced at Eyethanoff and his soldiers of light. "Then again, I can see everything clearly now, so I don't know if that all works the same still."

"I can see Eyethanoff clearly as well now," pointed out Nadia. "I think we would all be able to tell if there were dark soldiers about."

Still on guard, we all watched as the rider approached and brought Betsy to a stop.

"Who are you?" I called. "Show yourself!"

The rider reached up and pulled back the hood.

"Trixie!" I breathed, relaxing and lowering my sword as everyone else did the same. "Where have you been?" I asked.

Trixie gave me an uncharacteristically soft smile. "I...I had to do something for Otto," she said.

I recalled Trixie standing outside the mansion, a look of anger on her face. I frowned. "It was you in the mansion," I said.

Trixie nodded.

"What were you doing there?" I asked.

Trixie dismounted Betsy. "My vision. When we were in the Field of Doors, I had a vision of good things. Of everything working out." She let out a sigh. "But when Otto died...I was confused and angry. I didn't understand why the King had allowed that to happen. I must confess, I did not enter that mansion with the right intentions. I managed to get in without being seen, but then I noticed something." Trixie looked at me. "I saw you. You were wandering around speaking to some of the Creature's soldiers who had gathered and seemed to be putting on some sort of party. It was a little strange. I think you were in some sort of illusion, though I know not how the Creature formed it." She shook her head. "When I saw you, I remembered something Otto said in the Field of Doors when we first found each other. He told me about his vision. He said he knew how it would all end but that his part was nearly complete. I didn't understand at the time, but just before he died, he whispered to me, 'I was right about the stone. You must set it right.'"

Trixie looked at Nadia, holding back tears as she recalled her son's death. "I didn't know what he meant at the time, but then I remembered that he thought the stone was a conductor for Original Power. When I was in the mansion, I suddenly realized what he had been telling me to do. I had to put the stone in a certain place in order for it to conduct Original Power again." She looked at me. "There had been one part of my vision that hadn't made sense until that moment, and I knew it was my job to move the stone. So I did. I took the stone from the Creature's hall of artifacts, but I wasn't sure where to put it. I struggled to remember everything from my vision, but when Feyerndur was freed, all the details came flooding back and I knew. I snuck through the mansion and managed to get there in time. When I put the stone in place, the whole hill shook, and I ran for the door. By the time I got outside, there was a massive blaze of light headed straight for me, and everyone was running for cover. If Betsy hadn't shown up, I would not have gotten out of there in time."

"Where did you put the stone?" I asked.

"In the Creature's study. In his chair." She frowned. "His throne. The heart of darkness," she whispered.

I raised my eyebrows, realizing what this meant. I shook my head in awe. "The King and the Prince had every detail planned from the start," I said. They had set this all up long ago. The Creature's favorite place, his self-glorifying throne, had been exactly where light was most needed. And now light had won and darkness had fled.

"They always have a plan, Ben," said Eyethanoff.

I clapped a hand on his shoulder and grinned. "I know that now."

We turned and looked around the battlefield. We had won this fight, but darkness had left its mark. Though the land had been transformed, the bodies of the fallen were everywhere, some friends, some enemies. I took a deep breath. This land was free, but it had come at a cost. Freedom always cost something. I felt a melancholy smile cross my face. The Prince had paid that price first, only asking us to follow in his footsteps. And now I understood. We were not alone on that path. The Prince had not left us to fight his battles alone. He was here, helping us fight ours.

I turned to Trixie. "You did well—and so did Otto." I looked back to Eyethanoff. "Thank you for your sacrifice. We would have been trapped under the Creature's lie for good if you had not been here."

He smiled. "Again, I must deflect your praise to my king."

I returned his smile. "I understand." And I did. For the first time, I fully understood.

I glanced around at the others who had helped us. Captain Bates and his crew were worn and weary, and the volunteer soldiers were in even worse shape. They had given much and lost friends and family to help those around them who needed freedom just as much as they did. I clasped a firm hand on the captain's shoulder, nodded to him, and smiled. He smiled back and wrapped me in a hug. We released each other and thanked a few of the recruits standing nearby, all of us taking a moment to let what had just happened sink in.

"Now what?" asked Solace, her tone suggesting she already knew the answer.

Eyethanoff let out a heavy sigh. "We must get the slain to Mair Pala. They will be buried there." He offered a hopeful smile. "It is a place Lion's Sword soldiers have not been for centuries," he said as he turned to look at the castle towering above us. "It is magnificent," he whispered.

I looked at the castle as well. "You have never seen it?" I asked.

Eyethanoff shook his head. "This area of Eeffrayldour was shrouded in darkness under the Lie. No one was allowed to enter. For centuries, our ancestors used this as the home of the Lion's Sword." He looked at me with joy in his eyes as he gripped my shoulder in his strong hand. "Now we will again. Our numbers will grow, and we will be strong once more," he said.

I nodded and clasped my hand over his. "I can't wait to see it."

He took a deep breath and smiled. Without another word, he turned and began gathering his fallen soldiers.

Chapter 24

Solace, Nadia, Trixie, the captain and his crew, and I joined Eyethanoff and the others and began to move the dead. We laid them in white sheets brought by the Lion Sword soldiers, and large eagles came and took them away, flying off toward the castle, Eyethanoff and his soldiers following on horseback. Leigheas and Missy remained behind to tend to Dan, Casey, and the other injured soldiers.

When we had overseen that the burial places were prepared correctly and the eagles had delivered the bodies to the correct places, I took a moment to survey the land. There was so much I had not been able to see. This place, though it was the same land I had always lived in, was completely different. It felt different. The life that spread across Alussiathair, the people who appeared from all around to lend a helping hand in the burial, the animals—the presence of Original Power sat deep within it all. It seemed to course through it like blood through veins, touching all corners, reaching out to the dark fringes of the world, seeking to light that which was overshadowed. But still, this place was not what I had imagined. With the power that flowed through it, there was an undercurrent of groanings. Something about this place was still not...finished. I looked out at the trees that surrounded us and wondered what was really out there. What did my home really look like? And what was beyond the places I had visited?

In the midst of my musings, Eyethanoff returned. "Someone wishes to speak with all of you," he said. "Follow me."

As Eyethanoff turned and began walking toward Mair Pala, we all followed—Solace, Nadia, Trixie, the captain and his crew, and Eyerkishta and Feyerndur, now in their human forms.

The sun shone bright over the land, and I found myself continuing my study of the area. Though its main features seemed the same, things I had not seen before were now visible. Animals I had never known existed began to tentatively reemerge into their home that had once been overshadowed in evil. They seemed to come out of all corners, small and large, of all kinds—kinds that had only existed in stories.

Eyethanoff led us back to the Gate, which now stood at the entrance to a road that led up to Mair Pala. I had not noticed the road before and glanced at Eyethanoff. He smiled but didn't say anything.

As we passed through the Gate, for a split second I thought I saw a white tree. But I must have just imagined it. Eyethanoff led us up the road, which was made of stone and inlaid with flecks of colorful glass. The road led up the base of the mountain, winding through the village before turning into a stone bridge that extended across a rocky ravine. Solace pointed to the trees that stood on either side of the entrance to the bridge. Within their branches were isps of all kinds, their adorable little faces tucked under their hind feet like fawns, sound asleep, waiting for nightfall.

As we stepped onto the bridge, I peered over one of the shoulder-high walls to the moss-covered cliffs dotted with ice below and saw what looked like an expertly hewn canal that extended into the village. We progressed over the bridge, and I realized that the walls on either side and those that made up the castle were not just walls but a village in and of themselves. Tiny homes filled with cobwebs and old disintegrating decorations were built into the stone, evidence of what this castle had once been.

Eyethanoff noticed us all examining the little homes and finally offered an explanation. "This castle was originally built as the dwelling place of the Prince and his bride," he said. "But when the land and people fell, it became a sanctuary for those who were still loyal to the King. Eventually it earned its name, Mair Pala, which means 'Living Palace' in Eeffraylick. No one really knows how it got its name, though some say it is because its walls were homes for the smallest peoples and societies. Others have a different story. The castle seemed to change at various times, sometimes with the seasons, while other times the changes seemed to have nothing to do with the weather. Some even believe it reflects the souls of those who live within it, exposing their true nature."

"Wow," breathed Trixie as she examined the small empty homes. "What kind of people are so small?" she asked.

Eyethanoff chuckled. "Many actually. You will likely meet them soon. They have been waiting for centuries to have their homes back."

We stepped off the bridge and entered through the castle gate. Before us was an open area with three roads, one leading to a stone courtyard and the others leading off to the sides through unoccupied buildings and stables that made up this lower section of the castle. As we continued up the middle road and crossed the courtyard, a path split in two, leading up and around a small, withered garden before meeting again on the other side and passing through a pointed stone archway in a long stone wall.

Beyond the archway was another courtyard, a garden courtyard, that spread out in a large circle. On its far side was a three-story building with two-story buildings angling out from each side. Occupying the skyline behind them were various pointed towers, rounded stone walls, and A-frame roofs over long abbey-like buildings that formed what looked like three more levels above. Each level, section, and building was masterfully hewn from the mountain itself and intricately nestled together with streets leading between them. The castle must have been stunning in its prime, for even now it seemed to command all our attention as we approached.

Throughout the garden courtyard, silver gravel pathways led through outlines of gardens long dead. The remnants of the plants that had once grown there left behind traces of their former beauty, as if someone had drawn over everything with brown ink. The plants in the centers of the gardens seemed to have been tall and magnificent, whereas the plants closer to the paths that wove through them were smaller. Bordering the paths were the tiniest plants, spread out in a magnificent design of intricate curls and flower shapes.

"These gardens were once tended by some of the people who lived in the walls—a race known as the Lahlgan," explained Eyethanoff. "They are master gardeners. Once they discover this place is free, they will have it back to its former glory in no time," he said proudly.

In the center of the courtyard stood a fountain. It was overgrown with decayed plants and partially covered in snow, but its beautiful design was visible underneath. The stone was filthy, but I could imagine that it was once so polished that it must have shone brightly in the sunlight. It was made of stone that matched the castle, with vines carved into it, making it almost look alive. Simple yet stunning.

"That will be repaired by the stone workers," said Eyethanoff when he saw Nadia brush away some of the dirt and dead plants from the fountain's surface.

She nodded but didn't say anything. I could tell she was preoccupied with worry for Ivan.

Solace took Nadia's hand in her own as we entered the middle building of the castle, on the other side of the garden courtyard. We stepped through two massive doors, bordered in intricate designs depicting *The Story*. I noticed shimmering flecks within the designs, as though they had been inlaid with silver or gold long ago. Once inside, we were met by Mythair and the other soldiers who had been tasked with guarding us. As Eyethanoff led us all through the high-ceilinged halls, he explained that this palace had once beamed with even more beauty and soon would again.

Eyethanoff ushered us into the throne room. I found myself briefly marveling at its size, but my attention was quickly drawn straight ahead. Standing by the old, intricately carved brown wooden thrones, with her back to us, was Ruth. Her rags were gone, as was the gray of her hair. She wore a green dress fit for a queen, with a design of raised velvet flowers and vines in a darker shade of green. Golden flecks were sewn into the hems, which glistened as she moved. Her hair, which was now a youthful brownish red, flowed long past her shoulders, the sides twisted back and woven into a single braid. She was the Prince's bride from *The Story*.

Ruth ran her hand over the two old, decaying wooden thrones that sat side by side. She stood in silence, clearly remembering life with her Prince. "This place was once my home," she said, a slight quiver in her voice. She paused, then turned to face us. "But my time is near."

Ruth descended the steps to the throne room floor and approached. Solace, Nadia, Trixie, and I stood with the captain and his crew, alongside Eyethanoff, his soldiers, Yuuki, and Valdra. We were ragged and tired, filled with loss, but our hope renewed.

"I have called you all here because it is time. You have all displayed great faithfulness in the face of darkness. And now he has asked me to give you your true missions," Ruth said.

"If you don't mind my asking, who is 'he'?" asked Dan. Casey nodded as if to second the question.

Ruth smiled. "The Prince, of course." Her eyes sparkled with joy. "You have all done well," she began. "Tasks were given to each of you, and rather than crumbling at the sight of the unfathomable, you rose to the occasion and stood with that which is unseen, even when you didn't fully understand. In your faithfulness, you dedicated yourselves to be soldiers of the Lion's Sword. And now, it is time. Time for you to embark on new missions." A moment of silence fell as Ruth looked over us. Then her gaze landed on Captain Bates. "Captain Nathaniel Bates, you have followed what you knew to be right, even when others around you did not. You took the ship that was given to your ancestors and used it wisely. You and your crew will become the leaders of the

Lion's Sword Sailors. You will protect the sea from the enemy and take care of the creatures and everything that lives there."

The captain and each of the *Lyonsword*'s crew bowed, and the captain said, "It would be our honor to serve my Lion." I could see that they were pleased with their assignment. But it was not just that. Something about the assignment was special to them. As though it was what they had always wanted. What they had longed for. As though they were now serving where they had always been meant to serve.

Ruth smiled. "Go. You will find your ship where you left it. Guard the seas wisely, my friend," she ordered.

"I will," replied the captain and turned to leave. He and his crew gave us nods as they passed, headed for their ship and the seas they so dearly loved. They did their best to keep their excitement under control until they exited the throne room, for Ruth was a princess and spoke with the Prince's full authority.

But as they neared the door, Ruth called out to them. "Joy in one's purpose is not something to hide, my friends," she said in an encouraging tone.

The *Lyonsword*'s crew all broke out in grins, and a few even whooped and hollered as they exited the room. Captain Bates and Christopher turned to face Ruth, and, with joy on their faces, they respectfully saluted her, then left.

With a smile, Ruth's gaze lingered on the captain and his crew until the doors closed behind them. Then, she turned to Trixie. "Beatrix Bilden. Mother of Otto Bilden and wife to Arthur Bilden. You played a part in this story before you even knew it, and you have lost much." Her expression turned sorrowful. "My prince and I are grateful for your sacrifice."

Trixie bowed respectfully. "Thank you, my princess," she responded politely.

"What is it that you wish in return for your services?" asked Ruth.

Trixie looked up in surprise. "Um...I...I don't know," she said. Then she appeared to think of something and said with a smile, "I wish to know and understand. I wish to learn of your kingdom and how I can be of help to those who live here, and to serve you and the Prince. It is what Otto would have wanted," she added, keeping her chin high and holding back her tears.

Ruth placed her hands on Trixie's shoulders. "A noble desire. I put you and your husband, Sir Arther Bilden, in charge of the Lion's Sword healers, as the Prince knows he is a believer as you are."

Trixie's expression filled with delighted surprise. "It would be my—our—honor," she said with a bow.

Ruth and Trixie embraced, then stepped back from one another. "I have been informed that you have already sent for your husband. Does he know of your son's fate?" Ruth asked.

Trixie swallowed. "I did not want to inform him by letter. I—" She stopped.

Ruth took her hand. "I understand. When he arrives, please take all the time you need."

Trixie inclined her head. "Thank you."

Releasing Trixie's hand, Ruth nodded, offering a smile. "Go in peace. The Prince knows your pain, and he will comfort you if you wish."

Trixie smiled, bowed, then left the room.

As the door closed again behind her, Ruth turned to Eyethanoff and the soldiers who had been tasked with guarding us. "My prince picked you to protect the ones whom his father chose to find the Gate. You and your soldiers have served well," she commended.

Eyethanoff bowed. "Thank you, my princess," he replied with reverence.

"You will join the ranks of the Lion's Sword generals, and you may pick the men and women who will work alongside you to protect this land from those who follow the Creature," she said with a proud smile.

"It would be an honor," replied Eyethanoff with a smile and a bow.

"Go. Assemble what you need," commanded Ruth.

With that, Eyethanoff and his soldiers left the throne room, nodding to us as they passed.

Ruth turned to Valdra and Yuuki, who now stood before her in their human forms.

"Eyerkishta, my friend," she began. "You persevered and did so with kindness in your heart, despite the loss you were faced with. You have done well." They bowed to each other. Then Ruth turned to Valdra. "Feyerndur, it warms my heart to see you free at last. The task given to you was hard, and though you faltered for a short while, in the end, you fulfilled your mission. My prince and I are glad to have you among our ranks again," she said with a reassuring smile. Valdra's expression was a mix of shame and joy, and Ruth cocked her head to one side, holding his gaze. "At no point was your value diminished. The Prince never leaves those who are his."

Valdra's eyebrows twitched, and his jaw clenched. For a moment, he looked as though he would cry. But he simply nodded and remained silent.

Ruth stepped back so she could look at them both. "I restore you to your original positions as Treasure Keepers and leaders of the race of dragons. Now that the Lie has been broken, you will be able to transform into your dragon forms whenever you need to. The world may still be at odds with dragons, but you will always be treasured members of the Lion's Sword." Ruth smiled a deep, joyful smile. The kind of smile someone might use when something extraordinary is about to happen and only that person knows what it truly entails. "The Prince has informed me that the time has come for the dragons to return."

Yuuki and Valdra beamed with joy. Yuuki even squeezed her eyes shut as Original Power flowed down Ruth's arms, from armor I hadn't realized was part of her dress, into her hands. As she laid hands on them, they were transformed into their dragon forms. Their scales shimmered with a brightness I had never seen, and they were each covered in armor, unique to their shape and personality. Their massive bodies somehow fit within the room, and they both grinned at Ruth.

"Thank you, my princess," said Feyerndur. "I cannot fully express my joy, it is so great," he responded humbly.

"Thank you," echoed Eyerkishta.

Ruth smiled. "Go in peace," she commanded.

As the dragons left, Ruth turned to Nadia. She gripped Nadia's shoulders and looked into her eyes. "You have lost the most," she said, her brow furrowing in sorrow. "But despite that pain, you pressed on. You defended the weak. You rose to the challenge and stood strong."

Tears welled up in Nadia's eyes. "I only did my duty."

Ruth smiled. "And did it well, for your heart is strong. Soon you will receive your own set of armor and join the ranks of the Lion's Sword."

Ruth embraced Nadia, and Nadia hugged her back, gripping her tightly for a moment before she recovered and stood straight as Ruth released her.

Ruth turned to Solace and me. "You have both done well. One day soon, you will participate in an official ceremony to receive the broaches and blue garments of your Lion's Sword uniforms. It will be the first ceremony held at Mair Pala in centuries." She smiled at the thought. Then her gaze turned more solemn. "In the meantime, the Prince has asked me to commend you with words of his gratitude. And mine. You were chosen as the final Night Rider, to protect those less fortunate, to spread the truth of the unseen, to do your part to finish the mission I was given by my prince, and to free this land from the Creature's lie. You have completed this mission, and my prince and I thank you."

We dipped our heads in respect.

Ruth stepped back and addressed all three of us together. "You have completed the tasks set before you under the Lie, and my prince and I are most grateful to you all. For now, this lie will no longer hold Alussiathair captive. This land will be used for good once again." She looked between us. "But one of you is missing," she said. "You must find your friend, your brother. You must find him, and, in doing so, you will find much more." She paused, looking us each in the eye. "Do you commit to serve the Lion of Eeffrayldour?" she asked.

We each nodded in unison and answered, "We do."

"Then go, for you have work to do in this land," she said. Then she looked to Solace and Nadia. "I must speak with Benjamin."

With a bow to Ruth, Nadia offered me a nod, and Solace squeezed my hand before turning and leaving the throne room.

As soon as the doors shut behind them, Ruth turned to me. She watched me for a moment, as if deciding something. Then she took a deep breath. "Benjamin, when I was trapped under the Lie, as were the land and all who lived in it, I forgot many things. But my mind is clear once again, and there is something else you must know."

"What is it?" I asked.

Ruth locked eyes with me. "The land in which you now live, this land known as Eeffrayldour, is not the end. The stone you were referring to before, the one Trixie moved, is called the Land Stone. It once fed this land with Original Power, and the Prince told Feyerndur to move it in preparation for its role in battling the Creature's lie. What Trixie did attracted the Original Power held behind the Gate. Once you opened it, that power broke the Creature's hold, filling with light the very place the Creature lived and destroying his illusion. It even returned the rivers to flow in their original directions, from the Ath Woods through the Bawtha Forest. The Land Stone will soon be returned to its place on the fountain as a signal to many that it is safe to return here once again. This is all just the beginning for you," she said. "Prepare your mind for action, my friend, for you are part of a much bigger story." She placed a hand on my shoulder. "Your part, the Arlin chapter, has just begun. Whether it is you or your descendants, the Lion of Eeffrayldour will call on you again."

"When?" I asked as she released my shoulder. My mind swirled with images of the ring of doors, the white tree, and isps.

Ruth smiled. "At exactly the right time."

Before Ruth could say another word, something seemed to get her attention. Something I could not see.

Returning her gaze to me, she smiled. "Go to your friends. Enjoy the celebration of this lie's destruction and the new Lion's Sword soldiers. You will know your calling when you hear it."

With a bow, I turned and headed to the doors, wondering what lay ahead. As I left, a new door began to appear near where Ruth stood, but I did not have time to see who stepped through it before the throne room doors closed behind me.

By the evening, the Land Stone had been returned, and the village and castle had begun to fill with those who had longed to live there once again. Though more would be on their way, those from nearby lands had traveled to the palace when they had seen the dark lie peel back and vanish. As the sun set, what little snow remained in the castle was cleared away, and everyone present at Mair Pala threw a grand party in celebration of what we had accomplished. The castle lit up with the lights carried by visitors and came to life even as the day came to a close. The castle was a magnificent sight as the sun set and the moon rose high above. The night wildlife came out—winter fireflies, fairies, rabbits, birds, and other animals I had never seen before. Some glowed in the moonlight, and all joined the people to celebrate the triumphant return of Mair Pala and the destruction of the Creature's lie.

Neyelah and her family filled the trees, along with night butterflies that glowed in the light of the moon and seemed unbothered by the cold winter air. Little insects flitted about in a dance that I could only marvel at. Night birds filled the sky in bubbles that moved like water, their beautiful songs filling the air.

Having spent the afternoon wandering the halls of Mair Pala, exploring the long-uninhabited village around the castle, and meeting the growing number of peoples and species we had never seen before, Solace and I now returned through the castle gate, where we were greeted with the most delightful smells and sounds one could possibly imagine. Music from musicians both small and tall, playing in the stone courtyard, floated through the cool evening breeze. People danced and mingled with one another. Some congratulated us on receiving our armor, expressing their desire to do the same one day.

We entered the garden courtyard, and I immediately spotted a Lion's Sword soldier telling a story to a group of onlookers eating and drinking, Missy among them, and my heart ached for Ivan. Mrs. Alves and the others from the Village mingled among the crowd. Trixie was sitting at a table with a group of tiny gardeners who were showing her how to prune a small tree exactly right, so it was healthy and not hurt. The captain and his crew were spread out amongst the crowd. They had traveled on the wings of the Driilar, massive white flying creatures that resembled a lion, eagle, and dragon, to check on their ship in the western port, then returned for the evening celebration. Feyerndur had built firepits for those who wished to stay warm and cozy, while Eyerkishta had built a beautiful ice-skating pond for further entertainment.

As we approached the center of the celebration, I noticed Eyethanoff standing near the fountain, speaking with one of his soldiers. When their conversation ended, he waved to the soldier, who turned and rejoined the party. Then Eyethanoff approached us with a look of joyful anticipation. "I saw Reggie during battle clean up, and we discussed how he met you all. Just a moment ago, he came by and told me he and the horses and Betsy did something that they wish you to see."

"What?" I asked.

"Get Nadia and Trixie, and I will show you," he said with a smile.

After we retrieved them, Eyethanoff led us to a field at the back of the castle. It was encircled by a wall, and within it was evidence of a once beautiful garden.

"This was the garden of memories," said Eyethanoff. "It is a place where we remember those we have lost. Those fallen in battle. In Eeffrayldour, we believe that death is not the end, for those loyal to the King become one with the unseen," he said. "They enter an unseen paradise."

"The Kingdom?" I asked.

Eyethanoff nodded. He led us past Lion's Sword soldiers who were clearing away snow and cleaning off stones, some of which were engraved with names, while others had sayings in a language I guessed was likely Eeffraylick. We followed Eyethanoff through the garden, passing many memorials to soldiers long gone, but never forgotten. But then Eyethanoff stopped at the top of a small hill overlooking the moonlit battlefield below. He gestured to a smooth, medium-sized stone as a small, green, glowing butterfly landed on its surface, illuminating the words inscribed at its center. *"So those who follow will have the opportunity to choose."*

Nadia sat in front of the stone and ran her fingers over the name engraved beneath the words. "Otto Bilden."

"Otto was quite taken with a similar statement made by Captain Bates." A gentle voice came from behind us. We all spun around to see Betsy approaching.

"Hello, Betsy," said Eyethanoff, smiling.

My mouth fell open, but Betsy didn't seem to notice as she continued. "Otto told me something before he died. He said he had seen a vision of this place." She looked out over the land from our vantage point. "He said that the Prince told him he had a job to do, and it wasn't what he expected." She looked at us. "He was to come home when his job was complete."

"Home?" breathed Nadia.

Betsy dipped her head. "Yes. Home. A place beyond even here. Where the King himself dwells." Betsy seemed to smile. "He loved you, you know. But he knew he would have to say goodbye. He didn't know how, but he told me that if it came to it, he would die in service of the Prince, for the Prince had once died for him—for all of us. He would fulfill whatever job had been prepared for him, even if it cost him his life." Betsy looked down at the stone. "I asked him why. I believe in the Prince just as much as he does, but I was curious. Otto told me it was as the captain had implied—so those who follow after us will have the opportunity to choose a life of light or a life of darkness. The most important choice anyone can make." She seemed to smile again. "I couldn't fit all of that on one stone. But I think I captured his sentiment."

Nadia looked at Betsy. "Thank you, Betsy."

"It was my pleasure to serve such a man as Otto Bilden," she replied.

Trixie sat down next to Nadia and wrapped an arm around her shoulders.

"I will always love him," said Nadia, leaning on Trixie's shoulder.

Trixie smiled. "And he will always love you."

"Yes," said Betsy. "He particularly loved your voice. Said it nearly made him rethink his 'strong belief that one's heart cannot involuntarily leave one's chest through their mouth.' Not sure what he meant exactly, but those were his words."

None of us could hold in the laughter that brought, and the mood lightened as Trixie began telling us stories of a young Otto and his experiments in their greenhouse. We remained there for what must have been an hour, laughing and reminiscing about our short time with Otto and the adventures that had brought us to this moment. The journey had been a long one. A hard one. But in the midst of the loss, there was a distinct lack of loneliness, as though, despite the pain, we knew deep down that this was not the end.

As the stars grew brighter, Betsy silently slipped away, and Solace, Eyethanoff, and I decided to give Trixie and Nadia some time alone. The idea of returning to the celebration still seemed odd, though. Otto was gone, and Ivan was missing. But there was a calm within me. A peace I didn't fully understand. Somehow, I knew that one was safe and there was hope for the other.

"We will find him," said Solace, wrapping an arm around my waist as we left the grave behind.

I smiled, trying to cover up the sorrow she must have seen in my eyes. "Yes, we will," I said before kissing her hand.

"The armor looks good on you both, by the way," commented Eyethanoff as we walked. "Will you wear it for the remainder of the party?"

I smiled. "To be honest, I am not used to wearing armor."

"Me neither," said Solace.

"What happens if I take it off?" I asked.

Eyethanoff smiled. "Well, that depends on which part you take off. But I think you should wear it for the party."

Solace frowned. "Wait, you are just going to skip over the part about taking it off?"

Eyethanoff chuckled. "Wear it tonight. I can tell you more about it later."

Back at the party, Solace and I drifted through the festivities, getting to know people here and there and enjoying the food and dancing. We eventually made our way to the upper levels of the castle, where we had a view of the party below and the land around us. Eeffrayldour's beauty stretched out far and wide. As we watched the people gathered for the celebration, the music floated up to where we stood.

Surrounded by all the beauty, I still felt preoccupied by Ruth's words. Wanting to distract myself from the confusion of the mysterious mission Ruth had promised, I turned to Solace. At the sight of her moonlit face, my tension faded, and her profile drew me in. "You look beautiful tonight."

Solace looked up at me, a twinkle in her beautiful brown eyes, which could have been from her soul or the moon—I couldn't tell. "Really?" she asked with a jovial grin.

"Really," I assured her. "You looked beautiful in battle, and you look beautiful now," I said, tucking a loose hair behind her ear. "You are always beautiful," I whispered as I looked deep into her eyes.

Solace blushed. "You are a romantic."

"At least I am not a hopeless one," I joked.

Solace laughed out loud, then leaned her forehead on my chest as her laughter faded to a soft chuckle and then a sigh, her warm breath rippling the front of my shirt. As the music wafted through the cool night air, I began to sway back and forth. Taking Solace's hands in mine, I asked, "May I have this dance?"

Solace smiled. "I wouldn't wish it any other way."

Her smile was contagious, and I felt myself smile along with her as I moved with the music, letting it take hold of us.

"Ben," said Solace after a few moments. "Do you think the Creature will come back soon?" she asked, sounding worried. "Do you think he will ever be strong enough to make another lie that large?"

I considered her question for a moment. "I don't know," I responded, again thinking of the white tree and the isps. Ruth had said the isps were messengers from the King. I had noticed there was a whole group of them here tonight. *Maybe they are just here to celebrate,* I speculated. "I do know that the King knows what he is doing," I said, repeating what Solace had once told me. This time, I whole-heartedly believed it. "And we need to trust him, even if we don't fully understand."

Solace playfully smacked my arm. "Those are my words!" she teased.

I chuckled. "Really? I thought they were the words of a wise woman who taught me to love the life I have rather than waste it longing for what I lost."

I felt Solace watching me for a moment. "Do you?" she asked.

"Do I what?" I responded, looking down into her eyes.

"Do you love the life you have?"

I looked deeper into her eyes, searching for that beautiful twinkle of hope she'd had since the day I met her. "Yes," I replied with confidence as I found it. "Every minute of it."

With a smile, Solace rested her head on my chest again, and we stood at the balustrade of the castle, looking out over the grounds and the celebration taking place below.

As we stood there, something caught my eye.

"Is that Ruth?" I asked.

"Where?" asked Solace, standing straight again.

I pointed to a section of gardens a short distance from the party. "There."

Solace leaned forward and looked where I was pointing. "I do believe it is," she said with a smile. "And who is that with her?"

In a quiet corner of the decayed gardens, standing among the moonbeams shining through the foliage around them, Ruth was embraced in the tender arms of her beloved.

"The Prince," I said. For a moment, I felt an overwhelming urge to go to him, to ask him all my questions, to learn from him. The Prince—a being not bound by time nor corrupted by darkness. But Solace grabbed my arm. I looked at her. "What?"

She smiled. "You want to go speak with him," she observed. "But he is not here for you. Not yet," she said with a nod toward the couple.

I looked at them. They began dancing. They started out slow, gently swaying from side to side as they gradually turned together. But soon the Prince spun Ruth, and her distant laugh floated up to us as their graceful movements flowed like the night birds in the air around them. Then the Prince pulled her in again. He held Ruth close and looked her in the eyes. His lips moved with words only meant for her ears, and she smiled. They shared a gentle kiss, then their dancing resumed, and Ruth rested her head on her prince's chest.

Two lives that had been separated by darkness, reunited by the truest form of love. Two lives moving as one in a relationship seen, yet unseen. A relationship many in this land would call Eeeye. A life of two lives. A story of true love, renewed by light.

Their dance came to an end as a door appeared in the garden. The Prince opened the door and held his hand out to Ruth. She took it. With not even a glance behind her to the land that had been her home for so long, she followed him through, and the door vanished.

Will we ever see them again? I wondered. I felt Solace in my arms and hugged her tighter as Ruth's words came to me. *"Prepare your mind for action, my friend, for you are part of a much bigger story. Your part, the Arlin chapter, is just beginning. Whether it is you or your descendants, the Lion of Eeffrayldour will call on you again."*

I pondered that statement as I wondered if the Prince would be the one to deliver a new mission. A mission to find all those like me, perhaps. Those who needed *The Story* more than they realized. Those who needed the truth. *That is the job of the Night Rider, isn't it?*

As Solace and I swayed to the music, Ruth's words swirled in my mind, sparking questions. *When will the Lion call? And for what, exactly?* I recalled the mysterious tree in my vision again. *I opened the Gate and completed my original mission, but then I was shown the vision of the tree. Why?*

As if in response to my question, the armor around me stirred, and a voice—not my own, but somehow within me—seemed to respond, *"Now that is a good question."*

Benjamin Arlin and friends will return.

About the Author

Ondrea Keigh grew up in the forested Pacific Northwest, in Washington State, before moving to live near the sandy beaches of Florida. She loves to write and will do so at any time and in nearly any place. Her first published story was a short story titled *The Night Rider Adventures: Episode 1 – The Night Rider*, and she has many more stories on the way! Ondrea graduated from Liberty University with a degree in psychology and also holds a certification in dog training. Before becoming an author, she worked as an animal trainer, and when she is not working on a new story, she can still occasionally be found training puppies!

ONDREAKEIGH.COM

ISLE OF WINN
THE SEA OF DREAD
Wolstone
TRUNE
Dramin
Torrance Village
Lake Dramin
ROSENFEL
THE IMPERIAL FORES
Dukestown
Mintar
NAZLIN
PIRAN
THE WASTES
Plum Village

SARAKAN
Ila
THE FROZEN LANDS
Kilnic
KOSEL
Audier
Koselvue
THE SARAKAN RIVER
SARAKAN OCEAN
Getchian
OBAN
Peaksmouth
RAKAN RANGE
Kurstia

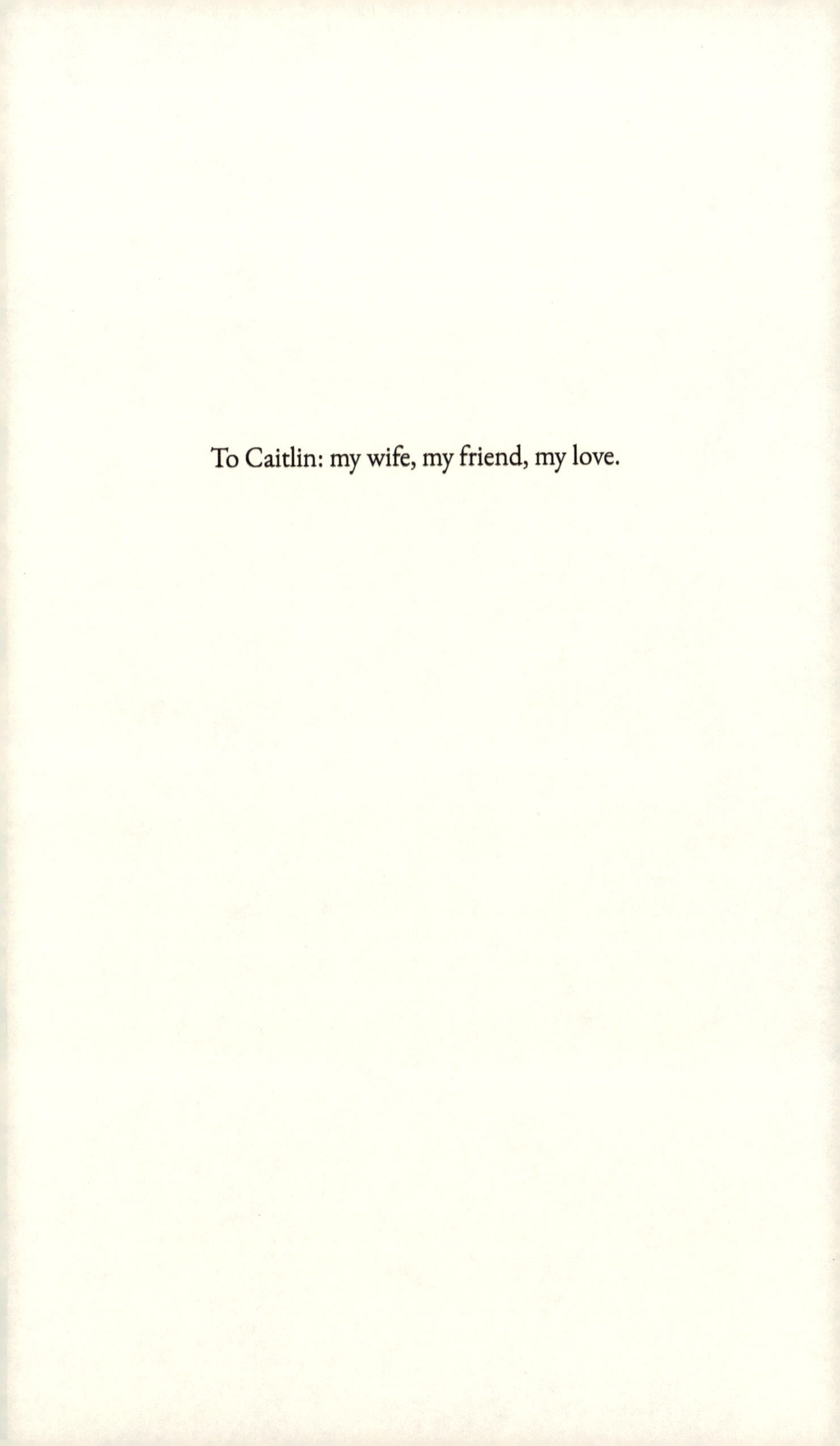

To Caitlin: my wife, my friend, my love.

Part One
The Mission

The turmoil of war compares not to affection,

Indeed, in both you oft find yourself betrayed,

But war follows rules, an affair of honor,

Affection is chaos, sheer emotion conveyed.

Such matters are tedious, I cannot deny,

That often with companions, 'tis best just to lie.

--Cordyn Tallen

ONE

Nothing worse than an empty wine bottle.

Gen sat at a round wooden table outside Ned's café in Mintar, glaring at the smudged fingerprints on the glass in front of her, the forlorn bottle beside it.

Winterplum trees lined the boulevard, towering over the ramshackle storefronts of Dockside. Their sweet pink fruit glistened in the light of two morning suns while the imposing trunks cast shadowy stripes across her table.

If a noble ever spent more than a few minutes in Dockside, Gen reckoned they'd see the beauty.

Ned was her oldest friend. He was at least thirty years her senior, but he'd been there for her since she was fifteen. Ned's once slender frame now showed the beginnings of a potbelly, and his head had barely any hair left. The dirty gray of his beard had transformed into a stark snow-white. He wore a finely starched white shirt and well-pressed black trousers, projecting an air of meticulousness.

No one here knew he was a mage. He was simply Ned, the unassuming owner of the finest café in Dockside.

"Madam," Ned said, the soul of formality. "More wine?"

"I shouldn't," Gen said. "King's business and all that." She glared at Ned. "And what have I said about calling me madam? I'm not a noble."

He bowed. "Of course, madam. However, when you're my guest, you are indeed a lady."

Gen rolled her eyes and took the last sip of wine.

Kirth take the king's business.

"To what do I owe the pleasure of your company today, Gen?"

"Met the king today. And Master Gillus."

"And now your life is complete?"

"Hardly. Cordyn and I received a new mission. Traveling to Kosel to deliver a message. Something about sending ninety thousand winterplums, whatever that means."

"Ah, yes. Cordyn," Ned said. He pursed his lips in a sour expression.

"Cordyn and I make an excellent team," Gen said. "He attends to detail and makes the plans, and I provide the protection."

Cordyn communicated with the nobility, usually, which made today's events even more troubling; never before had she been summoned to any sort of official meeting.

"The joys of royal service." Ned brought forth a pristine white towel and wiped the smudges from Gen's wine glass. "Seeing the world and traveling into war-torn regions."

"Hmph, I'd be fine just staying in Piran."

"Did you tell the king that?" He placed the glass back next to the wine bottle.

"Gods, no. I'd prefer to keep my head." Without thinking, Gen reached to confirm her neck was still there. "But the worst part was Gillus. He's a miserable crow of a man."

"As any self-respecting high mage should be." Ned folded his arms across his chest and pinched his mouth shut.

Gen cursed herself for bringing up mages. Ned would be in a sour mood for hours now.

"Excuse me, madam," Ned said, standing. He swept past her and into the café.

Kirth take Gillus and the mission.

Kosel, Piran's closest ally, was under siege from Oban, a country Gen knew little of other than how they enjoyed invading neighboring nations. Foreign wars weren't Gen's concern, though she liked working as an envoy, other than dealing with the nobles. They were a confusing lot, with their bowing and frilly language, and back-stabbing. Gen didn't trust them. She'd scarcely been able to contain her shaking at the palace, and her neck was still raw with tension.

Of course, Cordyn had been at ease among the royals and mages, twirling his curly locks and making pithy comments as if he were at a garden party. He looked the part, too, in his waistcoat, burgundy frock coat, and dark purple mage captain's hat he always wore.

Gen couldn't have felt more out of place, though she donned a cobalt double-breasted overcoat and black linen trousers. The ensemble had cost a fortnight's wages, and while she did not exude the elegance of a gentlewoman, she certainly looked the part of a palace bureaucrat. An exceedingly tall palace bureaucrat with straight black hair cropped close above her ears and a nose that was slightly too big for her otherwise delicate features. No one would accuse her of being pretty. Pretty faces were for people like Cordyn, with their tailored wardrobes and impeccably coiffed hair.

After leaving the palace, she'd strolled by the docks and fish market, never forgetting the monstrous white palace looming over the wooden shacks. The markets of Dockside stirred with activity. Crowds of merchants, soldiers, and harlots traversed the teeming boulevard, the screams of a fishwife intermingling with a nearby lute. The music reached a crescendo amid a carriage clattering the cobblestones.

Piranese army troops marched down the thoroughfare, a sea of indigo and yellow brushing past customers and merchants. They headed toward the quieter stalls in the northern part of the market, where a few bakers and confectioners hawked their wares. Several stray dogs roamed nearby, hopeful some baked goods would find their way to them. The looming war startled many of the merchants away, but Gen's favorite bakery was still there. She'd snagged some rolls, which now sat in her lap.

Ned's was a block off the water, far enough from the fish markets to avoid the smell of fish and unwashed sailors. The café catered to some of Dockside's wealthiest lodgers, and Gen would often slip in through the back to visit Ned. Today, however, she'd strode to the front entrance and asked Ned for one of the prime tables on the front terrace and ordered the finest bottle of wine they had.

The wine did little to calm her nerves. She fidgeted restlessly, watching the residents of Dockside go about their daily business, wishing she could flee.

Her hands trembled as she lifted the bottle, attempting one last pour. Only a few drops fell. With glazed eyes, she stared at the nearby stables, watching a stable boy saddle two horses.

Her pulse drummed a frantic rhythm, each beat echoing in her ears like distant thunder. She ground her teeth, eyes darting from side to side. If she never had to go before the king again—or see Gillus—she'd be perfectly content.

Where was Cordyn? He'd gone to 'settle affairs' before their journey, but the horses would be packed and ready soon and Gen couldn't get out of Mintar fast enough.

The king wouldn't care if she had one more glass. Yes, she had a mission, but Cordyn was off gods knew where, and she couldn't very well leave Mintar without him.

Godsdamn him. Wine makes me a terrible friend.

Gen eyed the wine.

"I trust you are sober enough for this conversation?" Master Gillus, the high mage of Piran, peered down on her through narrowed, bespectacled eyes. Sickly thin with bulbous sunken eyes and a thin mustache, Gillus had all the grace of a newly commissioned soldier in full plate armor.

Kirth take him, all spindly legs and elbows; he still appeared out of nowhere. If I'd had any wine left, it would be down my front now.

Gen blew a ragged breath and rose. One did not sit in the presence of the high mage until he'd taken a seat and given you permission to do so. Gillus took her chair, his green and purple silk robe billowing up as he sat.

"Sit, Gen," Gillus said, as if she were a dog. He pointed to the chair across from him. "I wanted to talk to you before you start your journey. We've had some news come to our attention that is vital for you to know."

"Of course, Your Grace," Gen said, complying. "Though Cordyn is more of the remember the plans and strategize person. I'm there to hit things with my sword."

"You sell yourself short, Gen. You are indeed skilled with weaponry, but I feel your mind is keener than you let on."

I'm better with a sword.

"Of course, Your Grace," she said.

"Mr. Tallen, however, is the subject of our news, I'm afraid." Ned appeared at Gillus's side, pouring amber liquid from a decanter into a tall glass. Gillus took a long sip. "Excellent choice," he told Ned. He turned to Gen as if Ned was no longer there. "What I'm about to tell you must stay between us. You are earnest and kind and I respect that. It does not serve our present needs, however."

"Yes, Your Grace. I shall stop being kind."

Gillus waved her comment off. "Aspersions have been cast upon Mr. Tallen's loyalty. High-ranking members of the nobility and our military have expressed concerns about the amount of funds Mr. Tallen seems to have at his disposal. His wages are not so different from your own. He does not come from a family blessed with great wealth, and yet he seems to have money to spend—more money than someone of his station should have."

Gen gaped at Gillus, leaning one hand against the table to steady herself. "Cordyn would never. He loves Piran," she insisted.

"I've no doubt he does," Gillus said, adjusting his spectacles and peering at Gen. "But the evidence is damning. The man has an absurd amount of funds for a mere envoy."

Annoyance rose up in her. She squeezed her hands into fists. Envoys deserved more crowns per trip. She wanted to suggest that Master Gillus give her a raise, but the retort died on her lips.

"I do not say this to suggest that he, or you for that matter, does not deserve greater pay." Gillus tossed Gen a heavy pouch stuffed with coins. "I have pulled together this small bonus for you, as I know you will need funds on your journey. However, Mr. Tallen spent more money on clothing this year than any of our nobility, excluding His Majesty the King."

"Is it treasonous to spend too much on clothing?" Gen asked.

"No, but where is he getting the money? My colleagues have suggested that he may be taking bribes or spying for our enemies."

"I can assure you that Cordyn—"

"I know, Gen," Gillus interrupted. "I believe he is an honorable man, and a loyal subject of the king." He sneered, showing he thought exactly the opposite. "However, questions have been asked, and it is my duty to look into them." He paused, taking another drink. "Your mission does not matter."

"What?" Gen gasped. She felt the café spinning around her. Her heart thumped even faster. She rubbed at her temples, hoping to push the thoughts away. Gods, her coat itched. She scratched where the collar pressed against her neck, wanting to tear the coat off and fling it into the street.

"It's a sham. An elaborate ruse, if you will."

"What about the Kosellans?" Gen asked. "The war?"

"I've already sent messengers to Kosel. The news will reach them before you even leave Piran."

"But why send us?" She fought the urge to put her head in her hands. It was all too much.

"I ask that you watch over Mr. Tallen on your journey and report back on any suspicious behaviors. Monitor his every move."

Gen breathed in deeply. Then exhaled. Another inhale. Her heart eased its rapid hammering. She couldn't afford to lose her position over this. She had to push her emotions away.

"Of course, sir," Gen said. Gillus watched her. *Shit.* "I mean, of course, Your Grace." A slight nod from Gillus. "I promise to report back anything and everything to you."

But I sincerely hope you're wrong.

Cordyn wouldn't betray Piran. He was a libertine and a scoundrel, but he was also a loyal friend. Whereas Gillus was just a prick.

"Splendid. Pass back any information through my agents if you encounter them along your way. Mr. Tallen knows their locations, but it would be best for you to know as well. If you travel through Dramin, look for my man Arsene at the Daft Bugger. If you go the Nazlin route, you'll come across my man Lorons near Peaksmouth at the Buckhorn Tavern. They'll assist you with your needs and will provide information on my other agents, assuming the mission isn't over by then." Gillus finished his drink and stood. "And if Mr. Tallen does betray us, be prepared to do what you must." His eyes flicked to the ground beneath the table, where Gen's greatsword, Maralda, lay. "We behead traitors here, Gen."

"Yes, Your Grace," Gen said, though she wanted desperately to refuse.

No, Your Grace. Go to Kirth, Your Grace.

After Gillus left, Gen sunk deeper into despair. She now had to choose between friendship and betraying Cordyn for the sake of the nation.

Gen cursed the Swordsman. What kind of god would put such a conundrum upon a faithful servant? Gen had worked for the crown for several years now, protecting messengers traveling on the king's business, and had done an excellent job, thank you very much. Delivering messages to country nobles and fending off underfed bandits was easy. You rode horses and killed those who tried to kill you. Sometimes, you made a friend and shared a bottle. Those missions never required secret meetings with the high mage to discuss betraying the trust of your friends.

Shuddering, she glanced at the Winter Palace. The west side of the ivory stone walls dominated the horizon beyond the docks, towering over the other buildings, great bay windows sparkling in the two suns. If you opened the west windows of the palace, you'd get a strong stench of spoiled fish, she reckoned. Yet, the two rooms she had been in were filled with fragrances of lilac and rosemary.

Perhaps to hide the stench of dead fish Gillus.

Her stomach rumbled. With all the events of the morning, she'd forgotten to eat breakfast. Thank the Swordsman for the sweet rolls. The brown paper wrapping around the rolls crinkled as she placed them on the table. Four sweet rolls: two for her, one for Cordyn—he would be hungry this morning, and she wanted to start the trip with a small gift for him—and one for her canine friends. She often went to the market and shared with one of the more adventurous dogs, the ones that would walk right up to her and nuzzle her with affection.

A gentleman in a feathered hat stepped into the café, and Ned greeted the man cheerfully. Much too cheerful, considering Gen's depressing lack of wine.

She raised her hand and motioned toward her glass. Ned acknowledged her request, laughing at something the feathered hat man said.

A few moments later, Ned presented her with a fresh bottle, this one with a silver and yellow label, proclaiming it to be a sweet winterplum wine, with a hint of cinnamon.

All hail Piran, land of winterplums and betrayal.

A newer vintage but would still quench her thirst. If only something would quench the gnawing feeling in her stomach, which was now spreading into her chest and shoulders. She quaffed half the bottle at once.

Perhaps one more bottle won't be enough.

Next door, the stable boy brought out saddled and packed down horses. The larger horse, a dappled gray, carried almost everything Gen owned: a change of clothes, some salted meats and dried fruit, and three bottles of winterplum wine.

Everything but Maralda, of course. Gen went nowhere without her sword. Placing Maralda on the table, most of the weapon jutting off the side, Gen stroked the steel and marveled at the craftsmanship. A leather-bound hilt connected to an ornately jeweled crossguard, intricate carvings running down both sides of the blade in a language Gen didn't recognize. Even Ned didn't know the meaning of the carvings, but he'd told her everything he knew about the sword when he'd gifted it to her on her eighteenth birthday, when she'd left home to seek her fortune in Mintar.

Mage-forged in the icy depths of the Sea of Dread, unbreakable, and able to penetrate chain mail. A warrior's weapon.

Of course, Ned gave it to a farm girl. Not that it hadn't come in handy.

"Madam," Ned asked behind her, his voice wrought with concern. "Is something amiss?"

"Hm?" she asked.

"Your weapon," he said. "We generally prefer our guests not behead their wine." His eyes flicked toward the nobleman, who was fixed on Gen.

"My apologies," Gen said loudly enough for the nobleman to hear. "I was just admiring the blade." She placed Maralda at her feet, then raised her wine to the man and saluted. The man turned away.

A small black dog with curly fur and long ears trotted over from the alley behind the stables. He nuzzled his wet nose into her pockets, eager for her attention and a taste of her sweet roll. She tore off a piece and tossed it to him. He began with a cautious nibble but soon devoured it with a ravenous swallow.

"If you would please not feed the dogs," Ned scolded from the café. "They're intolerable beggars."

"Sorry," she called. "Don't listen to him," she told the dog. "I know you'd never leave me waiting for hours." She took out Cordyn's sweet roll. "Shh, don't tell Ned."

"Ned already knows," Ned said from behind her. He sat down at the table across from her. "What did that oaf Gillus have to say?"

Gen's cheeks bloomed red from the wine and embarrassment from getting caught. "I've got another mission. A secret one."

"Ah." Ned furrowed his brow. "Moving up in the world or closer to a hangman's noose?"

"Maybe both." Gen took a swig of wine. "Kirth's bloody bollocks."

"What's bothering you, friend?"

"It's Cordyn."

Ned rolled his eyes. "It's always Cordyn. Gods, that man is a lout."

"Cordyn's a good friend. He's always been supportive and kind."

Ned harrumphed.

"And that makes what I have to do all the worse. Gillus asked me to spy on Cordyn."

"Why?"

"Unexplained funds. Cordyn spends more on clothes in a month than he makes in a year as a royal envoy."

"Like I said, a wastrel."

"Perhaps, but he's a *friend*." Gen gave Ned a warning glance and took another swig. "And now I might have to betray him."

Ned put a hand on her wrist. "You'll do what's right. You always do."

"Oh, we're traveling through Rosenfel." Gen gave him an inquiring glance. "Any message you'd like to deliver to all your friends and family there?"

"No." A vein on Ned's temple twitched. "Best to leave them thinking I'm dead." His eyes shot back into the café, then back at Gen. "If you're going to Rosenfel, I've got something for you. Come with me."

Ned led her back into the café and up into the apartment above, where Ned sometimes stayed when he didn't feel like walking back to his house—a pleasant stone cottage near the markets.

Ned dug through a rucksack and pulled out a flask, handing it to Gen.

"Rosenfel's dangerous, Gen. If you ever get badly wounded, drink this. It won't cure you, but it'll help you stay alive long enough to get help."

"Thanks, Ned," Gen said, "but I don't think I'll need it."

"Take it just in case. To ease the mind of an old man."

"Fine, but just remember that I'm pretty good with my sword." Gen took the flask and put it in her breast pocket.

"And I was pretty good with my, ahem, skills, and yet you found me dying in a field."

"Fair point. What exactly is it?"

"Energy-infused water, with a hint of lime. My own personal recipe." He smiled. "I'd sell it at the café if I could do so without people realizing I'm a mage."

"What does the lime do?"

"Makes it taste better." Ned sat down at his desk. "I've got letters to write, so I'll take my leave. Stay alive, won't you?"

"I'll do my best." Gen gave Ned a quick hug of thanks and hurried down the steps. She still had half a bottle left, and nothing to do but wait.

As she stepped onto the terrace, she heard a scream—a man's scream, but not a manly one. She turned to see a man, naked except for his undershorts and a leather satchel, running through Dockside.

"Must be another thief," she told her canine friend, who sniffed at her and implored her to share another piece of sweet roll. "He'll get what he deserves, I'm sure. Thieves usually do."

The thief ran in her direction, his eyes wide. Gen planted her feet firmly, anticipation surging through her veins as she prepared to trip him. He shouted a frantic warning, then rummaged through his satchel, producing a large purple ship captain's hat with a swift, desperate motion.

Gen's feet were glued to the floor, her mouth slightly agape as the realization hit her, rendering her motionless.

"Gen!" the unclothed man yelled. "Gen! We need to get the hell out of here!" Cordyn Tallen sprinted toward her, breathless and frantic. He skidded to a halt, his arms flailing as he pointed urgently to the stables. Without a word, he dashed off again, this time to their horses.

"What did you do?" Gen asked, trying to catch up with Cordyn. She was in good shape, but she valued brute force over speed, and so sprinting was not something she practiced often.

"Those men and I had a disagreement," Cordyn said, wheezing.

"Yes, I can see their swords," Gen replied, lagging behind him. "They seem furious."

"You just can't reason with some people," Cordyn yelled back, worry contorting his handsome face. He placed the hat atop his head, allowing curly brown ringlets to escape and fall past his ears.

They mounted their horses, spurring them toward the city gates. The horses galloped down the road, sending beggars and fishwives sprawling for the safety of the sidewalks. One beggar crashed into a fruit stand, knocking winterplums and melons out into the road.

They weaved through the winding streets of Dockside, past the palace, and through a wealthier neighborhood full of shrubberies and marble balustrades. Finally, they reached the city gates.

Cordyn slowed his horse to a trot and patted its mane. "Well, those bastards will just have to live with the disappointment. Cordyn Tallen is victorious again!"

He turned to Gen with a jaunty smile just as a crossbow bolt flew, striking the left thigh of her horse. Gen waited for the horse's inevitable descent to the ground, and the pain that would follow. But it did not come. Despite its injury, the horse continued to run with surprising vigor, almost as if it was in perfect health.

However, her bag of provisions clattered to the ground. She heard a cacophony of sharp cracks. Turning, she watched as all their food, and more importantly, her wine, lay splayed on the ground, lost forever. They could not turn back to retrieve it, as their pursuers, no more than a hundred yards away, were already preparing their crossbows for another attack.

Gen realized she'd left the remaining sweet rolls at the café on the table. The dog would eat well today, but Gen certainly wouldn't.

"Godsdamn," she muttered.

They rode on for an hour, leaving Mintar behind them, until they came to a pond, where they dismounted to give their horses a rest, and for Cordyn to put some clothes on.

"This would be the perfect time for a meal," Gen said, sitting by the water's edge. "If only our food wasn't scattered along the ground outside Mintar."

"I'm sure the birds are having an excellent meal," Cordyn said, pulling a linen shirt over his shoulders. "Piranese sparrows are known for their excellent taste, you know. I'd trust the wine knowledge of a sparrow over half the nobles in Piran."

Gen kicked an especially tall piece of grass that reached her shins. "I'm glad you find this so amusing. We have no food."

"Yes, that is lamentable. Alas."

"Why were those men chasing you?"

Cordyn's smirk turned into a nervous grimace. "I may have made a slight error in judgment."

"I'm shocked," Gen scoffed.

"Yes, yes. Well, I was packing for our journey, and I realized I did not have suitable attire. Swordsman knows I couldn't embark without a pair of gentleman's trousers." He regaled her with his most charming smile.

"Yes," Gen said, not returning the smile. "You would have been summarily executed for dressing like the rest of us envoys."

"I'm so glad you understand how vital it was."

Gen cracked her knuckles. "Get to the point." She reached into the pond and splashed some water on her face.

"I went to my clothier to purchase a new pair of trousers, and a waistcoat to accompany it. While I was waiting for the clothier to make alterations, I slaked my thirst at a nearby establishment of mirth."

"Which one?" Gen asked. She was certain she already knew the answer.

"I hardly remember the name."

"The Dancing Lady, I would guess?" Gen asked.

Cordyn coughed. Was it a cough to hide his embarrassment, or had he picked up a cold from one of his conquests?

"Perhaps," he conceded. "That may have been the name of the establishment."

"And by mirth, you mean, as the name implies, dancing ladies. The kind wearing only corsets and underskirts."

"Erm, possibly."

Gen picked up a rock and threw it at him, losing her temper. "So, you caused us to lose all our food and flee our home in a rush, all because you couldn't go one day without women?"

"How was I to know that the lovely lady I asked to join me at my table was not one of the dancing girls at all, but the betrothed of Duke Kuran? She seemed quite content to be in my company and did not reveal that she was promised to a peer of the realm. I hardly think I am guilty in this matter."

"You hardly think," Gen replied.

"Perhaps," Cordyn admitted, tipping his hat to Gen.

"I can't believe you chose Duke Kuran. Not only is he richer than we can ever hope to be, but he doesn't exactly let people cross him."

"Yes, I know. I've seen the society pages in the paper. He often has his own affairs, if my sources are to be believed."

"I don't care if he's seduced half the nation. He's not the type of man I want as an enemy."

"Well, I suppose he's my enemy now, but he doesn't have to be yours."

"He's the enemy of my friend, therefore, he's my enemy too."

Cordyn's eyes scrunched and his nose wrinkled, as if he was holding back tears. "That," he took a moment, inhaling sharply, "that means a lot to me, Gen. I hope you know that."

Cordyn sneezed, mucus exploding from his nostrils and showering the grass. It was too much to hope that he would burst into tears and declare her his best and only friend, Gen decided.

"I love my friends," Gen said. "But don't get complacent. I'm still pissed at you. Kuran won't just forget about this. Why couldn't you have seduced a cobbler's wife? Or better yet, no one's wife?"

"The heart wants what the heart wants, dear Gen. I am but a man."

Gen grunted. Throwing Cordyn in the water sounded wonderful. Alas, that wouldn't bring back her wine.

"Anyway, to business," Cordyn said. "We should avoid as much of Rosenfel as possible. Journey through Nazlin, around the Imperial Forest, and through the mountains."

"We have no food." Gen said. "How can we travel?"

"There are inns, taverns, farms along the way. We shall purchase provisions, never fear."

"No," she said. "We go to Dramin and get provisions. Master Gillus said we could meet his man Arsene there. Once we have food, we can travel wherever you damn well like."

And I have to report to Gillus's man about any suspicious activities on your part.

Cordyn ran a hand through his hair. "How are you with accents?"

"I can get by," Gen said. She tried to learn the Rosenfellian language in her youth, but never moved beyond learning basic greetings and how to ask for a drink.

"Excellent," Cordyn said, affecting the near perfect voice of an educated Rosenfellian. "I would love to hear your Rosenfellian accent. It is one I had quite a difficult time learning, by Hurod." Hurod was the God of Commerce, which reigned supreme in the crowded, prosperous cities of Rosenfel.

"Yes, we all know you're good with accents. Makes me wonder why you didn't choose the stage."

"Actors don't get paid as well as envoys, dear Gen." Cordyn twirled his fingers. "Now, your turn. Let us hear your glorious accent."

"Hello, my good sir," Gen attempted in a faltering Rosenfellian accent. "By, Hurr—" she coughed, the guttural Rosenfellian accent irritating her throat. "By Hurod."

Cordyn laughed. "Oh dear, I suppose we should take the southern route and avoid the cities. I think I had better do the talking, too. May I present to you Master Forthwynn, a professor of Obanni Literature at Dramin University?" Cordyn executed a complicated bow, spinning both arms and kneeling on one knee. "And you can be my faithful bodyguard and servant, Imogen. Imo, whenever I want to annoy you, but never Gen."

"How kind. Do you know anything about Obanni literature?"

"Kirth, no," Cordyn said "However, they are quite a dull, somber people. I suppose it is rather grim."

She rolled her eyes at him. "You'd find anything that wasn't scandalous to be grim."

"Perhaps, but you can't say that scandal isn't exciting."

"I don't need the excitement." She gave the pond one last lingering glance. It would be a peaceful camping spot, but they had several more hours of travel ahead of them today, and at least five days more to Dramin.

"You're wrong there," Cordyn said, winking. "I know you're not the romantic sort, but excitement is something everyone needs. A sword battle, the hero arriving in the nick of time to save the day—"

"The two envoys *actually* doing their job and making the king happy, so they can keep those jobs."

"We need to work on what you find exciting," he said.

"So, they can use that money to buy more wine," she suggested.

Cordyn tipped his hat to her. "Now you're on the right track. Just remember the message in case something happens to me. Ninety thousand winterplums and a bountiful harvest in the future."

"But what does the message even mean?"

"The winterplums are troops, dear Gen. We'll be telling the Kosellan army how many troops Piran will send to help stop the Obanni invasion."

"Oh, and here I was excited about the idea of more winterplums meaning more wine."

"When did Gillus tell you about Arsene?" Cordyn asked, mounting his horse. "You weren't in the room when he gave me his list of contacts."

Shit.

"I, well—" It was no use lying. "I saw him at Ned's."

Cordyn frowned. "Gillus needed a drink that badly?"

"I don't know," Gen said, intently studying her horse. If she looked at Cordyn, she'd give everything away. "He had some recommendations for the best kind of wine."

But mostly, he told me all the ways you may have betrayed Piran.

Cordyn smirked. "So mysterious you are, dear Gen. Very well, keep your secrets. How very like me you're becoming. You are no longer the student, and I, no longer the master."

"I was never your student, Cordyn," Gen said. "You'd make a terrible professor." She climbed onto her horse, wincing at the tightness in her thighs from the morning's ride.

"You are a most singular young lady," Cordyn said in his best stuffy old professor voice. "I find you most intolerable, by Hurod." His face became solemn.

She felt a pang of guilt upon seeing his expression, so rarely serious.

Stay strong. You can't say anything.

"Are you really not going to tell me what you and Gillus discussed?" Cordyn asked.

"Master Gillus suggested that I be ready at any time to take control of the mission," she said, fabricating the truth a bit. "He's afraid your drinking and whoring might lead to difficulties or even your untimely death."

Cordyn's posture stiffened. "My passions are fierce, Gen, but they've never kept me from serving my king."

For the first time, Gen's certainty shattered—could this all be a lie?

TWO

GEN WOKE WITH A start. Her heart thudded like a shipwright's hammer against a wooden hull, her neck tingling.

She opened her eyes, shivering, as she pulled her thin blanket tighter against her body. Light streamed through the tent entrances, illuminating her cramped quarters. The tent was merely a woolen blanket draped on metal stakes; it kept the rain out but not the cold. She eyed her bed: a haphazard pile of leaves hastily gathered the night before when Cordyn took over on watch.

Shit.

Cordyn was gone. He should've been sitting outside the tent entrance, keeping watch, but the entrance lay open.

Swordsman's tears, Cordyn couldn't survive on his own out here.

Gen threw off the thin blanket she'd slept under and got to her feet, brushing leaves off her trousers and gambeson. Her sword harness lay on the ground. She unsheathed Maralda, leaving the harness on the grass. Whatever she found in the forest, she wouldn't need to sheath her blade.

Once she exited the tent, she scanned the clearing. Their horses were still there, hitched to a nearby oak. A good sign. The horses munched on grass, pausing to whinny at Gen as she passed by.

Scowling, she peered into the surrounding trees, stepping into the forest at various points to check for evidence. The forest teemed with life: rabbits fleeing hawks, songbirds chirping their morning dirges, the oaks and pines standing tall and firm, giving shade to the clearing where she and Cordyn had set up camp the night before. Drops of frozen drizzle congregated on her bare arms, an intricate pattern of goosebumps interspersed with the droplets of water.

Yet, there was no sign of Cordyn. No footprints, no paths cut through the branches. He just vanished.

"Cordyn!" She called. A bird trilled a song of warning, and trees rustled in the distance. "Cordyn?" Pushing branches aside, she moved through the forest toward the sound, weaving her way to another clearing, this one much smaller than where they camped; barely big enough to fit a tent and fire.

She saw movement out of the corner of her eye, and relief washed over her.

"Kirth, Cordyn—"

Across the clearing stood a spider the size of a small pony, its eyes bulging and sparse woolen hair bristling in the cold light of two suns.

The spider hissed, its maw ragged and bloody, the surrounding ground littered with corpses. It advanced, baring a red-tipped fang.

What a pleasant Kirthed day. Gen readied Maralda. The sun was out and the icy rain soothed her skin. She and Maralda were making new friends, even if those friends wanted to eat her.

"I'm going to call you Francois," she told the spider. "It is so nice to meet you."

Francois lunged, its fangs darting toward Gen's leg.

"If we could work this out, maybe we could travel together."

The beast inched closer, moving past a clump of stubby brown trees with no response.

"Even the trees are dead here," she said. "I'm assuming you ate Cordyn. But I won't be next." She took a step back, planting her feet and preparing to strike. At least, that was the plan. Instead, her foot caught on a stray limb—a forearm? She plummeted to the ground, dropping Maralda. Gen's face crushed into the spongy, festering mess that had once been a man's ribcage.

She retched violently.

She extracted her head from the decaying abdomen and took a breath, the glacial air clearing her senses.

Well, now I'll never have to wonder what the inside of a corpse smells like.

Before she could stand or find Maralda, her leg erupted in pain as Francois sunk his fangs into her.

Gods. She'd been bitten before, but never this bad. She'd killed, but never pressed her face into the dead body's ribcage.

A day of firsts, but the unpleasant kind.

Blocking out the pain, she rolled away from Francois, kicking out at him. Her foot made solid contact, knocking the spider back. She stood and scanned the ground for Maralda, but her heart sank at the sight of the sword's silver glint.

Francois stood over Maralda as if knowing to keep the blade from Gen.

"If you give me my sword, I promise to only kill you a little," she said through gritted teeth.

Francois stared.

Do spiders blink? She pushed the thought from her mind. It didn't matter. Blinking or not, the beast had her godsdamned sword.

And that was cause for death.

She could wait for Francois to advance and try to sprint around him to Maralda, or she could charge him and take back what was hers. An obvious choice. When someone takes your sword, the only recourse is to take it back. And then use the sword on them.

With a roar, she attacked: a kick to the beast's hind legs, a punch to the thorax, and a spin over the spider's body. Landing on her knees, she grabbed Maralda, leaped up, and drove the silver-tinted blade through the spider's head, splitting it in half.

She collapsed to the ground, fighting to catch her breath. Sweat dripped down her forehead and onto her cheek. Gen sighed, wiping the sweat away.

Lungs burning, she turned away from the spider, her eyes snapping to the forest of pines that dotted the snow-covered landscape. Gusts of wind careened into her, and she pulled her fur-lined gambeson tighter across her bare neck. She'd had a scarf in her rucksack, along with the wine.

Godsdamn, Cordyn.

She wiped Maralda's blade in the snow, removing bloody entrails and promised herself she'd properly clean the sword that evening. After declaring Maralda fit for sheathing, she looked back to the forest, detecting movement behind the tallest tree in sight.

"Thank ya fer that," a low voice spoke from behind her. She turned to find two men armed with swords and daggers. Short and emaciated, the men wore rags of what Gen thought had once been sailor's uniforms, based on the blue and white tartan print. They must not have visited a barber in years, their scraggly hair intermingling with matted beards. The combination made Gen think of a wild horse's mane, though these men weren't wild animals—at least, not yet. The taller man bared his teeth. A greeting or a threat—maybe both. Gen couldn't see his lips through the mane, but he and his companion both held swords, and they weren't in a hurry to put them away. "That godsdamn bastard ate three of us. Right unfriendly of him. Ya saved us, ye did."

"Happy to be of assistance." Gen patted Maralda, hoping the men would recognize the greatsword-wielding spider-slayer should not be trifled with. "Now if you'll excuse me, I have much further to travel today."

"We do appreciate ya. Makes what we've got to do all the harder, don't it?" They raised their swords and stepped forward.

Typical.

"You could walk away and not get hurt," she said, gesturing to Maralda. "I'm sure you see my sword is bigger than yours."

The taller man showed the yellow and black rot of his teeth. "Aye, that is a beautiful sword, and my companion here fancies yer armor. It'll look fantastic in his collection."

They were sorry excuses for bandits; they had rusty swords, likely dull too. No wonder they wanted hers.

Gen gave the men a steely glare. "You should walk away now, gentlemen."

"Gentlemen?" The men laughed. "Ain't no gentleman here, woman. To show our gratitude, we'd like to apologize in advance fer what we've got to do."

"Sadly, I can't accept your apology or give you my sword." Gen raised Maralda and moved into an attack stance. "Farewell, sirs."

She pivoted onto her left foot, spinning into the path of the men's blades. Maralda blocked them with ease, pushing the rusted blades away. She swung a heavy cut over her right shoulder, her blade coming down sharp against the taller man's blade, pushing him backward as he tried to parry.

He thrust toward Gen's shoulder. She spun, swinging Maralda from the left, this time knocking the man to the ground. A quick thrust into his throat, and a shower of blood across her face.

The remaining man threw his sword at her, and it clattered against her shoulder, falling harmlessly to the ground. He held a dagger at the ready, yet his hands trembled, and his eyes were wide.

"You can still run," Gen said.

"Go to Kirth," the man snarled. He raised the dagger and charged.

She sidestepped his charge, then grabbed him by the shoulder and head-butted him, the crack of his nose telling her she'd made excellent contact. He crumbled to the ground, dropping the dagger, hands cradling his shattered nose.

"You, sir, made a mistake."

"Please, ma'am, don't kill me." The man sobbed. "I'm sorry. I won't do it again, I swear."

"You made your choice." She raised Maralda. "Accept the consequences." Maralda came down, cutting off the screams.

Now I'm thirsty. Flushed from the exercise, she sat down on a patch of ground free of snow and glowered into the darkness beyond the tree line.

Cordyn emerged from the trees, brushing leaves from his ringlets. He wore a burgundy frock coat over his dark blue waistcoat and trousers, dark hair topped with mage-captain's hat, looking more suited to a Duchesses' parlor room than the unforgiving wilderness. He shivered, rubbing his arms together.

"What was all that noise?" he asked. "I came back to the tent, and you were gone."

"You could have been a bit more helpful, you know," Gen said.

"I could have," he agreed, "but at first, I was evacuating my bladder, and by the time I finished, you had the situation under control. I do so love watching you work." He walked over to the spider's mangled remains, stepping over a pool of congealing blood, giving Francois a cursory kick. "Those men never stood a chance. That spider, however, was massive. Much too big to be natural. The magically enlarged pet of a mage, I'd wager. Either abandoned or misplaced by his former master."

"Francois would have been an excellent pet," Gen said, stepping over a forearm and the remains of someone's intestines.

"Except for wanting to kill you. Francois, huh?"

"I get lonely," Gen said.

"You know you're always welcome to join me for my revels about town."

Gen grunted.

No, I won't be attending your tedious dinner parties, or talking to your many conquests.

"Let's get riding," she said. "It's just going to get colder."

"We're near Nazlin," Cordyn said, pointing to the frozen tufts of grass beneath their feet. "All it does is get colder." He gestured to a nearby tree, mangled and dead, with icicles hanging from the gray branches.

"Which is why I'd prefer to sleep in an inn tonight."

Nazlin was an icy wasteland sandwiched between eastern Piran and Rosenfel. With only a few villages and no strategic importance, the glacier-ridden slopes of Nazlin were often overlooked. There was no reason to go there, except to travel through to Rosenfel. They rode for a few hours, stopping when the landscape changed from grasslands to the barren dirt of Nazlin. Cordyn stretched his legs while Gen fed her horse a piece of hay. She looked around at the flat expanse: tufts of grass sprouted at random among the cracked, frozen dirt, and the trees barely reached Gen's shoulders. The only thing that grew large out here was despair.

The sky was lighter in Nazlin than Piran: the smaller of two suns never fully descended, the ethereal glow giving the horizon a near permanent sunset at night. The lights never went out. Nazlin never knew complete darkness. Not that it mattered. No one was there to enjoy the eternal daylight.

In her nearly thirty years, Gen never ventured into Nazlin, which she considered a blessing. Piran was cold too—finding a place on Sarakan's western side that wasn't an icy hellscape was nearly impossible—but at least Piran was *her* icy hellscape. Plus, Piran had some excellent cafés and pubs there, unlike Nazlin, which seemed devoid of them.

"I need a drink," Gen said.

"And yet you criticized me for enjoying my drink yesterday." Cordyn replied, leaning against his horse.

"You weren't drinking, you were seducing."

"I may have been enjoying the company of a young woman, but I was indeed drinking."

"You lost my wine."

"Hardly," Cordyn scoffed.

"You can deny it all you want," Gen said, "but we both know the truth."

After too much galloping through the snow, they arrived at a village. A sign stood along the road proclaiming their entrance into the borough of Dukestown. Quite the impressive name for a farm town in the wilds of Nazlin.

"I need a nap," Gen said. "Also, a hot meal and a warm bed."

"I'd settle for a tailor's shop and a crust of bread," Cordyn said. "I'm not sure either of us will find what we want here."

Dukestown, unfortunately, failed to live up to the name. Seven buildings: a stable, three houses, a general store, what looked like a blacksmith, and, thank the gods, an inn. Though at first glance, the inn was dark and uninhabited, with what looked like axe marks on the stained oak door, and a thatched roof that seemed on the verge of collapse; the middle of the roof sunk in, and a heavy rain might bring it down.

"Perhaps they'll have an excellent dust and spider stew. With a side of rotten wood toast." Cordyn opened the door and entered the inn.

Gen followed Cordyn into the neglected building, leaning down to avoid hitting her head in the entryway—Nazlins were a diminutive group. Cordyn, who was a head shorter than Gen, entered without ducking.

The inn was not unoccupied, and Gen made a quick prayer to the gods as she and Cordyn were directed to a shabby bench by an even shabbier old woman. Gen took solace in the aroma of stew wafting through the air, and her stomach rumbled. Yes, she would eat well tonight.

"Hello, ma'am," Gen said. "I am so glad to see you."

The woman looked at Gen and Cordyn like they were a pair of bugs. "What will ye be wantin', then?"

Gen smiled and tried her best to appear charming. "We've been traveling through the wastes all day. We wouldn't turn down a hot meal, or your company."

"No," the woman grunted, and turned away. Gen looked at Cordyn, the dream of a hot meal fading into the abyss.

Cordyn took a breath and displayed the beaming smile that so many Piranese women found themselves unable to resist.

"My dear woman," he said, "I'd love some of whatever stew it is that I'm smelling. Indeed, it smells of the heavens. I am a man of the world, and I have been to many a city. Yet, I have not, until this moment, smelled anything quite so wonderful."

"Ten silver pieces," the woman said.

Gen choked. Ten silver was half of her weekly pay and would buy several gallons of stew in Piran. "That is quite high for stew," she said. "Is that your usual price?"

"No," the woman said, ladling some golden broth into a mug. She pointed at Gen. "But yer overly cheerful and annoying." She looked at Cordyn. "And ye talk too much. You'll pay extra."

Gen had to stop herself from grabbing Maralda and greeting the woman with a strike to the head. Annoying? Gen spent much of her time alone and rarely socialized with others beyond a brief conversation here and there, but she found herself delightful.

"Now, now, my good woman," Cordyn said. "Perhaps we got off to an inauspicious beginning. I'm Cordyn, this is my colleague Gen, and though we're passing through on a much longer journey from Piran, we would gladly spend an hour or two assisting you with any tasks you need completed. Perhaps a door that needs repair," he pointed at the tattered entry way, "Or a pest causing you difficulty that we can exterminate. I am a friend and a trustworthy soul. Gen is the veritable soul of kindness. I know we'll grow to have a most pleasant rapport. Therefore, stew please!"

The woman spat onto the floor. "Ye Piranese bring death. We have enough of that here already. Pay yer ten silver pieces, eat yer damned stew, and to hell with ye."

Gen sighed and handed over the money. The price was exorbitant, but gods, she was starving. The woman handed her and Cordyn each a mug of stew. Gen took a large gulp, the stew soothing her body and soul—a near religious experience. Her body warmed and her worries faded. She almost forgot the woman hated her and wanted her gone. The broth was rich and meaty, perhaps lamb or goat, and the buttery potatoes melted in her mouth. Cordyn's contented sighs confirmed he found the stew excellent, too.

Gen's stew vanished faster than hoped, and she sat in sadness, mourning the loss of the stew. She contemplated paying for another mug, but she knew they couldn't afford to throw away all their resources on food.

After a few minutes of sitting in silence, Gen and Cordyn exchanged looks. The warmth of the fire soothed Gen's cold bones, and she wanted nothing but to stay in the fire's glow for a little while longer. The woman, however, appeared to be getting more impatient for them to leave as time went on, staring at them and motioning to the door with her broom. They stood and gathered their belongings.

"May the gods keep you safe, my good woman," Cordyn said as they left the inn. In response, the woman spat on the floor.

Francois had been nicer than that.

THREE

THEY CAMPED IN THE Nazlin wastes, huddled under blankets. Cordyn cursed the wind; it bit through his frock coat with ease, and he spent more of the night shivering than sleeping. Gen slept across the clearing, her snores echoing through the clatter of the wind. Gods knew how she could bear the cold, though she certainly came from heartier stock. The hours passed and Cordyn praised the gods when the suns began their ascent in the western sky.

Once Gen awoke, they continued on, passing through the rest of the Wastes and into the towering forests near the Rosenfel border. Cordyn's heart soared at the thought of trees taller than him. At least they'd block the wind.

Near the border, they reached a fork in the road. They could either head south through Nazlin into the forested regions of Rosenfel or travel north on the road toward the city of Dramin, the largest city on Sarakan.

Sat atop his horse, Cordyn stared down the southern path. It was damned pristine: towering pines and brisk air beckoned, promising the safety of an untraveled route. His stomach rumbled in response. Too untraveled to find the needed provisions.

"Fine, let's go to Dramin." Cordyn said. "If we must."

"Because of your error," Gen said.

"Yes, I admit it," he said in a contrite approach.

Because of Duke Kuran's damned fiancée's error.

"Thank the Swordsman for that." Gen spurred her horse forward.

"We'll get supplies and plan out the rest of the journey," Cordyn continued as if Gen had said nothing. "Make contact with Gillus's man there." Gen pressed forward, the distance between them increasing.

"Gen!" he yelled. She paused, turning back to look at him. "We need to be careful. If the Rosenfellians find out we're Piranese spies, we'll be hanged, and I rather like my neck." He tenderly massaged his throat, wincing in mock discomfort with each touch. He imagined the rawness of rope burn would be like sandpaper scraping against his skin. "So, considering the state of your accent, I'll do most of the talking."

"That's what I'm afraid of." She turned back and galloped noisily down the path.

The stubby Nazlin trees vanished and towering pines and yorn trees took their place, massive branches blocking some of the wind. The air was still brisk, but slightly less apt to kill you.

"I could get used to this," Gen said. "Warmer weather, pristine forests. Who wouldn't want to live here?"

"And thus, Rosenfel continues its rise to power."

Piran began as a Rosenfellian fishing colony, and even though it had grown to become the third most populous nation in Sarakan, Rosenfel was at least triple in size. From what Cordyn heard, Dramin had even prettier women.

As the suns descended in the late afternoon sky, casting a shadowy glow over the forests, they reached a mage compound. Black stone buildings towering over the trees, blue mage-glass alcoves shimmering in waning light of the suns. Mage-glass wouldn't break unless you lit it on fire; then it melted like ice.

A high wooden fence surrounded the compound, the only way through an entranceway along the road, where an old man sat cross-legged, chewing on a strand of hay. A tattered straw hat draped over his wrinkled face, his gray woolen tunic stained and torn.

"A good morning, by the Swordsman," Cordyn said with cheer. "We come seeking a bed and sustenance."

"Aye," the man grunted. "Head on in, then. Them mages'll take care of ya."

"Are you not a mage?" Gen asked.

The man guffawed. "Do I look like one, missy?"

"I don't know many mages," Gen admitted.

"What about your friend, then?" The man pointed to Cordyn. "I seen his hat."

"Alas, I am not a mage-captain," Cordyn said. "My father was. I just wear his hat."

Mages could control water, and with the rough seas surrounding Sarakan, any ship captain wanting to live through their maiden voyage had to be a mage, calming the waters with their incantations and creating currents to push the ship along. Cordyn's father, a hard, often unfeeling man, was rarely home. Always out on the seas, sailing between Piran and the Isle of Winn, never spending time with his son.

Damn him.

Though his father had made amends from beyond the grave.

"Pity." The man turned away, done with the conversation. He began chewing the hay with increased fervor.

"Shall we?" Cordyn asked Gen, gesturing to the compound.

"I wonder what they have inside?" Gen asked.

"Probably more giant spiders."

"That wouldn't be so bad."

"You may think so," Cordyn said, "But I choose not to meet my death via spider today."

"Do you think we're in danger? I've heard stories about mages."

"Most of those are just stories," he said. "They don't usually freeze their enemies to the point where one blow shatters the bodies into thousands of pink blood-ice chunks. Though it has happened." He grinned. "Most mages are quite harmless. Not afraid of old Master Gillus, are you?"

"No." Gen looked away, face flushing.

So, the old bastard does scare you. "I thought you were too strong to be afraid, dear Gen."

"Well, I'm not," she snapped. "I don't want to be an ice cube. I don't trust most of them. My friend Ned's told me stories."

"Well, Ned is a gossip who should stick with serving wine and leave the storytelling to experts like me. He's probably never even met a mage. Anyway, we need food."

"My father didn't trust mages either," Gen said. "That's why we lived in southern Piran. Driest area in the country. Father used to point at our wilting crops proudly and say, 'Drier the area, weaker the mage,' as if the lack of mage interference made our suffering lighter."

"Every time you tell me of your childhood, I become more grateful to my own father for choosing nautical endeavors instead of agriculture."

"My brother Huber wanted to a be a captain. Course, he wasn't a mage, so that was that."

"What did he end up doing?"

"Dying."

Sweet bloody Torr.

They passed by two squat stone cottages prior to reaching the compound proper, traveling over a rocky hill into a small grassy courtyard near the ornately carved wooden doors of the building.

It looked like a castle, with towers and turrets flanking each side, connected by a parapet where archers could rain down arrows from above. A great stone wall served as an unyielding shield, with no entryway except a drawbridge, which remained lowered. Four arched windows on the front wall of the keep sat open, like smiling mouths. An agile man could climb up the stone and enter through the windows.

Two walls and a drawbridge, yet they'd entered with ease.

"Their security leaves something to be desired," Cordyn said, striding to the wooden doors of the compound, and knocking.

"It ain't locked," a voice called from the windows above.

The door creaked as Gen opened it. A brightly lit hallway lay before them, lanterns hanging from the ceiling illuminating a red and white velvet rug. The air was thick with the sweet, tangy scent of berries. What kind, Cordyn didn't know.

"I'm thirsty," Gen said.

"Come up the stairs," the voice called.

"Up the stairs?" Gen asked. She bit her lip and shook her head.

Cordyn nodded. "Keep your weapons ready." Though it was no use. Against mages, their weapons would do little.

Upstairs, three men, all wearing black and gold flowing robes sat, dining. They were silly-looking, at a table set for at least thirty, sitting all in a clump at the head of the table. Cordyn's eyes strayed from the steaming plates of mutton and potatoes in front of the men to the hearth behind them, where a fire roared. He shivered.

A large, bearded man with a jolly smile and a protruding gut waved them over.

"Welcome, my friends," he called out in a booming voice. "Sit, *sit*. Have a drink. You're among friends. We're not Winn bastards."

"Indeed, we shall not kill you," the thin, balding man next to him added. He raised a goblet to Cordyn.

"Unless you give us a reason." The bearded man guffawed, winking.

"Thank you for your hospitality," Cordyn said, bowing. *And for your veiled threats.*

He moved over to the hearth and huddled around the fire, allowing the flames to soothe his rigid fingers. After a few moments above the fire, the feeling returned, blood flowing through his extremities once more. He walked over to the table and sat next to Gen, on the right of the three men. The third man, bald with a hawkish nose, scooped roasted mutton and potatoes onto plates, which he handed to them. Before Cordyn could put his plate down on the table, Gen started eating.

"I'm Jonas," the bearded man said. He patted his chest, then pointed to the thin man. "This is Menson."

Menson slapped the bald man on the back, harder than necessary. "And this oaf is Yole." Yole gave a slight wave but remained silent.

"You coming from Nazlin?" asked Jonas.

"Yes," Gen grunted in between shoveling chunks of potato into her mouth.

Cordyn took in a sharp breath.

Of course, let the swordswoman with a terrible Rosenfellian accent do the talking, not the experienced adventurer with acting training.

"Whatcha doin' there?" Menson asked.

"Business," Gen said.

"I was visiting a fellow scholar in Mintar," Cordyn explained, "and discussing the depiction of self in Piranese poetics."

"This is good fish," Jonas interrupted.

Not a poet, then?

"Swordsman take those dirty Piranese bastards," Menson said, wrinkling his nose.

"I heard a rumor that they eat fish raw." Jonas grabbed a piece of fish and shoved it in his mouth.

"Not only raw, but live," Cordyn said. "Often while in the nude."

"Cordyn," Gen said through gritted teeth.

"But the Piranese are civilized compared to the Winn. Those buggers are savages."

The Isle of Winn, to the north of Piran, was a mage stronghold. Rumor was that only mages lived on the Isle and outsiders were discouraged, if not prohibited. Many a sailor spread tales of non-mages being captured and executed for trespassing, though Cordyn's father had always dismissed those stories as poppycock. His father had worked closely with the Winn, delivering food to the islanders; the island's terrain was too rocky to grow many crops or support livestock.

"I heard they eat people," Jonas said.

"Naw, they just spirit away young mage women in those bloody creepy ships of theirs," Menson said. "And take 'em back to the Isle. For breeding stock, ya know."

"And then they also feed their non-mage children to the sea," Cordyn added.

"Or, to all those enhanced animals they have," Jonas said. "Tigers, wolves. I heard one of them rode around on a giant ostrich."

"I've heard it's covered in ice," Gen said.

Yole shivered. "Cold."

"It *is* godsdamned cold up there at the isle, I've heard," Jonas agreed. "Why they're so powerful. Gods know we can't ever relax, what with the war in Kosel and the Kirthed Winn."

"At least the Piranese aren't a threat." Menson laughed in derision. "Too busy fishing to fight."

Gen dropped her fork to the table. "I don't—"

"Do you have any news of the war?" Cordyn asked.

After chewing, Jonas responded. "From what I heard, Oban has taken Trunel and will have Kosel soon enough. We had a visitor from the Imperial Academy yesterday who said the Kosellans are cooped in their cities while the Obanni lay siege. It won't be long."

Damn, by the time they arrived in Kosel, the war might be over. It was imperative that they moved as quickly as possible.

"Thank you for your hospitality, gentlemen," Cordyn said, beginning to gather his effects. "I regret that we must continue our journey now."

"You've barely touched your food." Jonas gestured at Cordyn's plate.

"We could stay a while longer," Gen said. Her eyes fixed longingly at the bowl of potatoes in the center of the table.

"No," Cordyn snapped. He took a breath, pushing his anger deep into his stomach. "We must go." He followed Gen's gaze to the potatoes. "But perhaps we could bring some food along with us?"

They rode through frozen marshes, mud and grass flying as the horses galloped. Cordyn's face was soon covered in mud while Gen, damn her, remained spotless.

As they left the mage camp behind, the terrain dried. For the next few days, they camped in the forests and traveled the Dramin road, meeting farmers, soldiers, and the occasional nobleman's carriage, but avoiding highwaymen. Perhaps the soldiers scared the brigands off.

A week after leaving Mintar, they reached Dramin, the largest city in Sarakan, flanked by the Sea of Dread to the west and Lake Dramin to the east. Around twelve warships docked in the harbor, their rust-colored oak and black iron hulls gleaming. Hundreds of men scurried across the decks, preparing the ships for travel. Heading for Trunel, perhaps? Despite being officially neutral, Rosenfel seemed eager to claim Trunel, doubling their empire's size.

Swordsman take them all. For a neutral nation, Rosenfel spent too much time planning on conquering their neighbors.

Dramin's port made Mintar's look like a small country town. Scores of fishermen and laborers moved around the docks, shipwrights hammering away at the iron seams on the outer hulls of the warships. A group of children, dressed in dingy black rags, stood by the docks, calling out their wares, harassing anyone who didn't purchase from them. The air was heavy, as if it would rain at any moment. Yet, it remained dry. Cordyn started to sweat in the humidity of the port. He loosened his linen shirt and considered taking his waistcoat off.

No, he was a gentleman, not a dockside ruffian.

Wriggling his nose at the smell of fish, beer, and piss, he urged his horse through the teeming masses, with Gen by his side.

How would they ever find their contact in this throng of people? Mintar appeared big, with over fourteen thousand citizens now, but Dramin was home to over two hundred thousand. He'd been to Dramin twice before, but he'd never get used to the crowds.

"We should head to Old Town," he said. "That's where we'll find the inns. And presumably this Daft Bugger."

Ah, Old Town. Inns, taverns, and a plethora of houses of ill-repute, all packed into the quaint, winding cobblestone streets. A visit to some of the establishments they passed by was in order, but first, supplies.

Old Town reeked of sweat and burnt meat. Three and four-story buildings leaned over the road, giving the impression they'd soon give in to their weight and collapse. Hard-faced men and women looked out from the broken windows onto the glass strewn street below, calling out curses at any passersby who annoyed them. A harlot spat on the ground as Cordyn passed, his horse almost trampling the woman's foot.

"The locals might prefer it if we dismounted," he said.

They did so, then led the horses down the winding alleys. Cordyn asked a snaggle-toothed child of no more than ten for directions.

"Bloody Swordsman's Bollocks," the boy said. "The Bugger? Wot do you want with that festering piece of shit?"

"You are most charming," Cordyn said, "but impertinent. I'll give you a crown if you promise to speak no further except to give us directions."

The boy grimaced. "Keep going down the alleys. 'Bout another few hundred paces or so. Once it starts smelling terrible-like, you've arrived."

Cordyn flipped the boy a coin and continued on.

"It already smells terrible," Gen said, ducking to avoid a low hanging sign for an opium den.

Cordyn scrunched his nose. "In the immortal words of many a poet, things can always get worse."

After what seemed like at least a thousand paces, the odor of the streets became immeasurably worse. Cordyn retrieved a handkerchief and placed it over his nose. He offered one to Gen, but she waved it away, staring at the sight before them. She looked quite pale.

An overflowing chamber pot teeming with flies sat outside of a dilapidated tavern. Feral dogs munched at the contents of the pot. One relieved himself on the post of a hand-painted sign reading The Daft Bugger.

Cordyn gave the dogs a wary look, then squeezed past them, tying the horses to the post outside the inn.

"Take everything with you," he told Gen. "I doubt our horses will still be here when we exit."

They entered the tavern, walking into what appeared to be either a boxing match or a scuffle between two shirtless men. The other customers were all yelling and cheering. "I suppose we ought to order a drink and wait for the entertainment to end before looking for our man," Cordyn said. Walking past the fighters, they headed to the bar. Cordyn's boots squelched against something wet and sticky on the floor and the entire inn reeked of onions. Cordyn didn't dare inspect his shoe to see what he'd stepped in.

They ordered two large tankards of dark ale, sitting down to watch the fight, which seemed a mismatch. A hulking giant of a man, his chest rippling with muscles, was the superior fighter. He was bald, clean-shaven, and had the tattoos of a sailor or an infantryman. His opponent, who could barely stay on his feet amid the punches flying at him, was a smaller, mustachioed man who looked fit, but not as strong as the man who was attacking him.

"That was an excellent punch, sir," the mustachioed man said, his voice crisp and diction pristine.

In response, the behemoth punched the mustachioed man in the stomach. He gave a strangled gasp and fell to the floor in a heap. The crowd cheered for their champion, who went up to the bar to enjoy the free drinks his admirers would purchase for him.

Cordyn took a sip of ale, scrunching his face up. Bitter, stale, and tasting of vinegar. He wiped the sweat from his brow and motioned to the barkeep.

"Do you have food available, good sir?" Cordyn asked.

"A little," the barkeep said, wiping the counter with a dirty rag. "Not sure if gentlefolk like you would find it appetizing."

"I have quite the hankering for roast mutton," Cordyn raised his voice over the cheers. "Do you happen to have any on hand?" A silly thing to ask—gods knew he didn't want mutton, but Gillus said his man would reveal himself after they'd inquired about mutton.

"No mutton," the barkeep said. "There may be some pork in the back if you'd like me to look."

"No matter," Cordyn said. "I had my heart set on mutton."

"There's nothing like a leg of mutton, is there?" the mustachioed man asked, standing up and putting a tunic on over his bare chest. "I'm Arsene. Damned good to meet you. I assume you're Cordyn Tallen, and you must be his assistant, Gen."

"Good gods, man," Cordyn snapped in fluent Rosenfellian. "Not so loud."

Gods, the man was an utter dolt.

"I am hardly anyone's assistant," Gen scoffed in Piranese.

"Hush, both of you," Cordyn responded. "I am Master Forthwynn, professor of Obanni Literature at Dramin University, and this is my faithful bodyguard and servant, Imogen. She is strong and loyal, but rarely speaks, by Hurod!"

"Of course, of course," Arsene said. "My apologies, sir. I don't know what came over me. I mistook you for someone else. Too many blows to the head, you know." He pointed to his bruised face.

"Indeed, my good man. We have had the misfortune of brigands and blackguards stealing our supplies, and we have little time before we continue our journey to Oban, where I will be speaking at a conference. Tell me, do you know of anywhere nearby where we might refresh our supplies?"

Arsene looked over at the other end of the bar. There was still a crowd around the victorious boxer.

"Indeed, I know just the place," he said. "They may even have some mutton."

Cordyn grimaced. "I don't actually like mutton, you know. I'd accept goat, though."

"I'd kill for a goat right now," Gen said.

"You may get your wish," Arsene said. "Goats are plentiful in Rosenfel, as is violence."

Arsene was a bastard.

After only a short time in his presence, Gen wanted to knee him in the face.

Not only had he spent the entire six-block walk talking about himself, but now, as they stood outside a nondescript white wooden building that was likely a storehouse, he rummaged through his trouser pockets while staring balefully at the dark stone door.

"Oh dear," he said, "I seem to have forgotten my key." He looked at Gen. "Imogen, it would be ever so helpful if you could kick the door down for me."

"It's stone," Gen said.

"Don't be so negative," Cordyn said. "I'm sure even stone quakes at the thought of your boots."

Sighing, she kicked the door hard enough to break a wooden door, but not enough to injure herself. The door stood firm.

"Perhaps we should go get the key and then return," Cordyn suggested.

Arsene laughed. "Your poor leg, dear girl! I didn't think you'd actually kick a stone door. Don't worry. I believe I found my key." He then moved his hands in front of the door to begin an incantation, his fingers rotating a semi-circle, the signs too rapid for Gen to understand.

So, Arsene was a mage. It made sense that Master Gillus's associates would be mages. She had to update her opinion of Arsene. As a mage, he was not the weak, silly fop she thought he was initially. He was still a prat for making her kick the door like that, though.

How would you feel if someone took your mustache and ripped it off?

Arsene finished the incantation, and the door opened. "There we are," he said. "Please, after you. You are my guests, after all."

The warehouse was bare, apart from crates lining the walls, enough to supply a platoon. A staircase in the far west corner led to an alcove.

"My study." Arsene pointed to the alcove. "A bed and a desk, but perfect for those nights when I don't wish to walk to my lodgings."

"I wonder," Cordyn asked, "if I may use your desk? I have letters to write to the king about the situation in Kosel."

Or letters to write to your contacts, betraying us?

Gen watched Cordyn's face for signs he was lying, but he looked like the same Cordyn as always.

"Of course, sir," Arsene told Cordyn. "Consider my office yours for the duration of your visit." Gen rolled her eyes at Arsene's cloying subservience.

What a prick.

After Arsene procured parchment, a quill, and an inkwell, he led Cordyn up the stairs and into the small room at the back of the alcove.

Gen looked through the crates of supplies, stopping at different points along the way to dig through stashes of wool, dried corn, and some cheap-looking daggers. There were at least twelve crates of loose hay.

A horse would be quite happy here. But no wine.

Footsteps rang from the stairs, and Gen turned to see Arsene descending.

"Do you have any available rope?" Gen asked. "All I see is hay."

"Rope?" Arsene's eyes flitted from the backroom then to Gen. "Yes, rope. Loads of it." He stared as if waiting for something.

"Could we have some?"

"Just enough for Mr. Tallen to hang himself with." Arsene grinned, looking quite pleased with himself. "Master Gillus's letter arrived yesterday. I'm all caught up." His expression turned somber. "Have you witnessed any treasonous actions yet?"

"What? No," she whispered. "And this is not the place for that."

"It will have to be." Arsene glanced toward the warehouse entrance. "Could you help me carry in some of these bushels of hay?" he called out in a loud voice.

"Fine." She sighed. "Let's make this quick." She followed him outside and leaned against the doorframe. He sat on a makeshift wooden chair constructed from shipping crates, staring at her once more. His eyes bore into her, making her squirm.

You speak first, you oaf. You wanted to do this.

"Well?" he asked.

"Cordyn hasn't done anything unordinary." She shrugged, noticing a brown and white bird soaring, leaving the warehouse far behind. If only she could escape the same way. "Besides losing our wine."

"He hasn't spent any large sums of money?"

"We've been traveling through forests."

Arsene considered for a moment. "Gen, dear. I need you to take this seriously. You really are rather beautiful, and I'd love to make your acquaintance further, but Master Gillus has imparted all authority to me—"

Gen kicked the side of Arsene's chair, toppling him. "No," she spat out. "You won't speak to me like that."

"Kirthed damn!" Dust rose into the air where Arsene fell. He went onto his knees, brushing dirt from his trousers. "What was that for?"

Gen crossed her arms, scowling, nostrils flared.

"I'm just following orders," Arsene said with a petulant glare.

"Gillus ordered you to seduce me?" Her skin prickled as if bugs were crawling over her.

"No, just to ask about Tallen. See if he's overspending and try to find out where all his excess money's coming from."

"And that's what I'm doing." She kicked the chair again for emphasis. "So let me do my godsdamned job, or I'll cut your mustache off."

Arsene's hands rushed to his face.

"One more thing," she said. "That authority Gillus gave you? It's mine now."

FOUR

Hands raised in the *Vida,* Tobias Stinton muttered the incantations, swirling his hands in an intricate pattern. To the uninitiated, the *Vida* resembled a bird flailing in a storm, but to Tobias, it was art. The bowl of water in front of him crackled. The water slowly turned to ice. He sat in an oversized velvet chair in his library—a room that was barely larger than a closet, packed to the brim with leather-bound books, along with the one chair and a small wooden desk. Cramped, yes, but big enough for one person. The solitude was refreshing.

He heard the clattering of footsteps from the drawing room and sighed. So much for solitude.

"Surros, Aqui, Firrenna." The ice melted. *"Firenna, Rentos."* And began to boil. Tea sounded wonderful.

He rose, brushing strands of hair off his face. He wasn't handsome, that much he knew, but he had a striking face. Hawkish nose, firm lips usually pursed into a grimacing sneer, and sallow, ever angry eyes. Not a face you'd forget easily. Draping a dressing gown over his broad shoulders, he moved to the drawing room.

Tobias's godson and erstwhile assistant, Topper, sat on the sofa in the drawing room, grimy boots propped up on a white cushion that had cost twenty crowns.

"Feet," Tobias commanded, motioning to Topper's boots with a finger.

Topper moved his boots to the floor more languidly than Tobias would have preferred.

"Sorry, boss." Topper refused to call him Uncle, or simply just *Tobias*. "Got news, boss." Topper looked to the kitchen.

"What is it?" Tobias asked, sitting across from Topper on an oak chair with blue silk cushions.

"Important news. I worked hard for it."

"Get yourself some food, then."

Topper scurried into the kitchen, returning a few minutes later with a bowl of bean soup and bread. Tobias tossed him three crowns as an extra incentive to speak quickly.

"There was a Piranese toff in town. Mage-captain, or the like," Topper told him as he gorged himself on soup. "I know you're always asking questions about them, so I figured I'd watch them and let you know."

Tobias scowled at the boy's accent. Topper's parents had been prosperous merchants, and yet the boy refused to stop speaking as if he were an Old Town ruffian.

"And no doubt you thought the information would be worth a few crowns?"

Topper shrugged. "I was hungry, wasn't I?"

"What did he look like, this Piranese mage-captain?"

"Dressed all nice-like; waistcoat and shoes that look like they've never been muddied. Long black hair. Might've been wearing makeup, his skin was so clear."

Ah, a dandy. Intriguing. And yet, it might be too much to hope for.

"Not every well-dressed fop is a Piranese."

"He spoke a lot like you. Perfect accent. But his associate was Piranese through and through. Bigger than most everyone I know. With that Piranese whine. Like she'd got something stuck in her nose, innit?"

"How do you know this mage-captain isn't just traveling with a Piranese immigrant?" Tobias asked.

"They met up with Arsene Killens," Topper said. He bit viciously into a crust of bread, crumbs spraying about the table.

Tobias cursed under his breath. Arsene Killens was a known Piranese spy, though harmless enough to have no one attempt to arrest or kill him. Always useful to have a few known spies to feed misinformation to.

"Definitely Piranese, then," Tobias said. "Fine work, Topper. Do you know where they are now?"

"Killens's warehouse, the one near the fish market. They was headed there less than half an hour ago."

"Lead the way, Topper. With your accent, you'll fit in perfectly with the port's clientele."

"Dunno what ya mean, boss," Topper said, though his lips curled upward.

"Hmph. If our Piranese toff is indeed still there, I've got another ten crowns for you."

And, if by some stroke of luck it's who I hope it is, I'll buy you a Kirthed house.

When they arrived at the warehouse, they climbed up onto a nearby roof, waiting. Tobias sat on the wooden slats of the roof, stomach churning. He ground his teeth; his legs wouldn't stop fidgeting. With a deep breath, he closed his eyes to stop them twitching and attempted to push the anticipation and anxiety down.

Topper nudged him. Tobias looked down to see a man walk out, not only with a purple bicorne, but the distinctive Tallen features Tobias knew so well.

"Swordsman's blade," he whispered.

He'd never met Cordyn Tallen before, but knew his description by heart. The bicorne, of course the curly black, foppish hair, a nose that was too long, sallow cheeks, and clothes more expensive than most people's yearly salary.

And now the man stood below him, unaware of his impending death. Tobias planned to enjoy himself.

The deep-rooted feelings of rage had faded as he aged. Though, seeing that hat again, after sixteen years of waiting, planning, and hoping caused his heart to beat with the speed of a shorebird flapping its wings in the midst of a storm. Dizziness overcame him; he had to put out his arms to steady himself, attempting to avoid tumbling off the roof.

His moment had finally come.

"By Hurod," Tobias swore. He tossed Topper another twenty silver. "Here, you've earned it."

Tobias followed the younger Tallen and his companions—Killens and a tall woman—from the warehouse to a nearby inn, The Golden Crown, known to the locals as the Waste of Crowns because of the high prices for less than stellar rooms. The inn looked clean and inviting from the outside and was popular with travelers who did not know of the cheaper and more comfortable inns only a few streets away. After a night spent there, you could anticipate flea bites and lingering dampness.

The Golden Crown suited Tobias, though. Pickpockets and con men lurked, targeting unsuspecting travelers. Constables passed through occasionally but mostly kept away. An understanding existed between local crime gangs and the constables: minor crimes such as pick-pocketing and mugging caused the police to turn a blind eye. Though, serious crimes like murders or property destruction drew immediate and swift justice.

Tobias had a distinct advantage. He wasn't a criminal. Neither constables nor local crime gangs saw him as a threat. He wasn't an upstanding citizen either, so he didn't worry about his reputation when engaging in shady activities. Tobias was a shadow. Knowing many, but known by few. He preferred it that way. Friends got hurt or died; working alone was safer. Of course, there was Topper, but he was just a boy.

"Head back home," Tobias told Topper. "I'll be out late tonight."

In an alley near the inn, he found a beggar who was close to his size.

"How much for your coat, friend?" The beggar's coat had at one point been the property of a wealthier man, judging by the stitched gold monogram above the lapel, and the quality of the black wool. The coat was still in passable shape—not a heap of rags, but also not the coat of a well-to-do merchant or man about town. Tobias's own coat was not expensive, but it had been well cared for and looked far too elegant for his current needs.

"Wot d'you need me coat fer?" The beggar's stringy brown hair hung in clumps over his dirty brow, and when he opened his mouth, two missing front teeth and the distinct odor of rotten fish greeted Tobias.

He hadn't thought of a reason for needing the coat. He'd assumed the beggar would just take the coins without second thoughts. What kind of beggar asked questions?

"My wife," he said. "She has betrayed me, seeking the company of another man. I'm following him so I may find out his identity, challenge him to a duel, and hopefully kill the scoundrel."

The beggar laughed. "That's marriage fer ya. Me own wife died last year. I hated the woman more than I hate most things, but gods, if I don't miss her sometimes."

"So, how much for the coat?"

The beggar pondered, looking to the sky as if asking the gods for backing. "Twenty crowns."

An astronomical amount. Tobias's own coat hadn't cost more than ten crowns, and that was new.

"Swordman's bloody bollocks," he spat. "I'm not a fool."

"And I quite like my coat."

"Five crowns."

The beggar considered this. "Twelve."

"Eight."

The beggar turned to walk away. "May Torr keep you, sir."

"Fine, twelve." Tobias tossed a bulging purse of coins to the beggar, who caught it as if it was lighter than air. The beggar counted the coins, took off his coat, and then handed it to Tobias.

"Pleasure doin' business with ya, sir. If ya need trousers, underpants or me shirt, I'll gladly sell those fer another five crowns."

"That is a delightful offer I must refuse." Tobias shuddered at the idea. Wearing the man's coat was bad enough, but at least the coat had not been pressed up against too much of the man's skin. He took off his own coat and then realized he had nowhere to put it. He could not wear a coat and carry another without risking unwanted attention. Unfortunately, the only solution was to abandon his own coat.

"I seem to have an available coat," he told the beggar. "Perhaps you would like to buy it?"

The beggar made a show of inspecting the coat. "It looks decent, like. I'll give ya two crowns for it."

Tobias gritted his teeth in anger, but he accepted the man's offer. He made a note to ask Topper to fetch him a new coat. He put on the beggar's coat, bracing himself against the stench of sweat and vomit, and turned toward the inn.

He took a deep breath—a terrible idea given his attire—and stepped into the Golden Crown, certain revenge was near.

The whiskey in front of him had warmed. He'd been so focused on watching Tallen and planning his next move, he'd forgotten to drink, though drinking was a key element of his disguise. He sat in the inn's corner, coat lapel raised to cover his neck, doing his best to look haggard, intoxicated, and on the verge of passing out. Normally, if his drink warmed, he'd call upon the *Vida* to cool it. He was tempted to do so now, but it'd ruin his disguise. It would be silly to destroy the illusion that he was not a mage, especially after spending time and money on it.

Tallen and his companions sat near the fire, drinking wine and chatting too quietly for Tobias to hear. He supposed it didn't matter what they were saying. He was here for Tallen, not to interfere with their business.

He sipped whiskey, noticing a shadow looming over him. He saw a man standing before him. Tall, muscular, with short well-manicured hair, and clean skin. Rare for these parts. However, the man looked familiar, though Tobias couldn't place him.

"You've taken an interest in our purple-hatted friend," the man said. "I can't help but notice you've been watching him. And doing a piss-poor job of trying to hide it."

Upon hearing the man's voice, Tobias recognized him as the beggar from the alley, except he'd transformed in thirty minutes from a dirty wretch to a gentleman.

How did one make teeth appear and disappear?

"Where in Kirth is my damned coat?" Tobias asked.

"You recognize me? Good. Makes things easier." The man pulled out the chair across from Tobias and sat down. "What's your interest in Mr. Tallen?"

Tobias searched for words, but nothing came out for several seconds. How could the man know he was there for Tallen? Had he been betrayed? Gods, had something happened to Topper?

He sipped the whiskey to give him a moment to ease the anxieties pooling up inside him. After three deep breaths, he was ready to continue.

"I don't know what you mean, sir," he said. His voice trembled, but at least he could speak once more.

"No need to lie, sir," the man said. "We have common goals, I reckon. You and I both have business with our purple friend. My employers want him to suffer, and I suppose you have similar intentions? You don't seem to be looking at him as if he's a long-lost friend you're about to go embrace."

"If indeed I wished harm on that man, I would hope that he would suffer," Tobias said, gritting his teeth.

"Well, that's perfect, then." He clasped his hands together. "I have a business proposition for you."

"I'm listening." Not that he could do much else without risking the man ruining his plans.

"I could talk better if I had something to ease my dry throat."

Tobias pointed to the whiskey in front of him. "Be my guest."

The man frowned in mock distress. "Oh, but my palate is quite refined, sir. I dare not drink after another. Another glass of that fine whiskey would be much appreciated, though, and then my throat would be ready to discuss the situation."

Tobias scowled and handed the man a crown. "Go get your drink. I don't have time for this coyness."

"I'm but a blushing maiden, sir. It can't be helped." He scooped the coin out of Tobias's hand and stood up, walking to the bar. He and the innkeep spoke for a moment, and then the man returned, glass in hand.

The man calmly sipped at his whiskey. After a minute of silence, Tobias motioned to the man to begin.

"I've been hired to make your friend over there disappear," the man said. "Not kill him, or the like. My employers would prefer that he never return to Piran, and I am authorized to do whatever I see fit to make that happen. I'd considered having him arrested or pressing him onto a ship setting sail for distant lands. Then I see you, watching him like he's a bottle of wine and you're a very thirsty man. And I think to myself, what if you and I work together? You want Tallen, I want to move on to other, more lucrative jobs. You and I could make an arrangement."

Tobias erred on the side of caution. "If I wanted revenge on someone, I'd want more than just imprisonment or a long sea voyage for him."

"Ah, and that's the beauty of my plan. See, my employers, they want him out of the way, but they're not here in Dramin. If Tallen accidentally met a tragic end and my employers remained unaware, thinking him safely imprisoned, well, they'd never be the wiser. And you and I would both get what we want."

"I would never wish ill upon others."

The man snorted. "Of course, sir, you are the soul of charity and only wish the best for your fellow man."

"However," Tobias said, then paused, sipping his whiskey. "Say that, for the sake of argument, there was a man who I wanted ills to befall—"

"If that were the case, I'm sure you'd have an excellent reason, sir."

"Why should I do your job for you? Why should you get paid for something that I have done?"

"I'm a kind soul, sir." He placed his hands on his chest. "You wound me. I'd gladly do the job, honest-like, get my pay, and go on about my day, but I have a sentimental streak. My mother always said it would be my downfall—"

"Get to the point."

"I see you over here, gazing malevolently at our friend Tallen, and I couldn't live with myself if I took vengeance out of your hands. Especially after our little business deal in the alley. Felt bad about that, I did."

The man's faux innocence irked Tobias. What he wouldn't give to cut the bastard's tongue out.

"You don't seem to feel bad at all," Tobias said. "And you still haven't told me where my coat is."

"My apologies. The coat's in the alley, sir. You may not want it anymore. Quite dirty out there." He gave Tobias a roguish smile. "Don't worry, you can keep my coat."

It would be so easy to send ice shards through his throat right now and end this nonsense. Tobias squeezed his hands together. No, let the man prattle on all he wanted. Tallen was the goal.

"From how you look at Tallen," the man continued, "I can tell you're a man who has a reason to be here watching our mutual acquaintance. I'm just here for crowns, and those I can get anywhere."

"Well, begone, and get crowns elsewhere, then."

"Sir, I am but an honest businessman. I have a family."

"No doubt they are as conniving as you."

The man regarded Tobias for a moment. "All right, I'll give you half."

"Agreed." The man lifted his whiskey to toast Tobias, and Tobias returned the favor. The warm whiskey's rancid bitterness did nothing to ease his nervous stomach.

"Oh, one thing. My employers—our employers now—they want nothing to happen to the woman with Tallen. They were adamant she be kept safe." The man tossed him a small purse. "And now that we're partners, sir, we have a slight problem."

"Which is?"

"I may have sent in an anonymous report to the mage-wardens about Tallen. They'll be looking for him, and if they find him first, getting him back will be harder than scratching Kirth's balls with a prickled feather."

"I can deal with mage-wardens. That doesn't worry me."

The man hesitated. "I also hired some local toughs to rough them up a bit, then take Tallen to the docks for pressing."

"You've been quite busy."

"Working probabilities, sir. Either he gets arrested or pressed, and I get paid. I'm sorry if I've buggered things up, sir."

"No, I think affairs are perfectly in order. Go find your pressing gang and tell them to be ready."

"So you're going to let them press Tallen?"

Tobias drank the rest of the whiskey. "No, but I have a plan."

The Golden Crown wasn't the nicest inn Gen had ever seen. But they had a winterplum wine available, so she was content, even with the stained wooden pillars and the dirty floors. The sweet liquid soothed her throat, putting her at ease, as she and Cordyn sat by the fire in what the innkeep had called the "Great Hall," a small, shabby sitting area that smelled of sweat. The chairs they sat in must have been red at some point, but over time, they'd become threadbare and more of a pinkish brown.

She noticed a few other guests in the Great Hall, and Gen found herself watching them, wondering if they could tell that she and Cordyn were Piranese spies. She felt like she stood out among the other guests, who all seemed more worldly than her, speaking Rosenfellian in Obanni, Trunellic, or Kosellan accents, sitting and talking comfortably with their companions. Gen was anything but comfortable, though the wine helped a little.

They'd chosen supplies at Arsene's warehouse, and Arsene assured them that the supplies would be packed and ready for them the next morning. Cordyn suggested they find an inn to rest at, and Gen, for once, agreed with Cordyn. She was ready to find her bed and sleep, but Cordyn insisted they order wine—of course, he chose the most expensive bottle he could find—and sit in the Great Hall for an hour or two to get an idea of what the other guests were like. Arsene remained at the inn for dinner and was already on his third glass of wine. Cordyn conversed with Arsene while monitoring all the surrounding activity. Two merchants, dressed in heavy black overcoats, sat at the next table, arguing about the price of grain. A young, pretty woman sat in the lap of a grizzled, scarred old man, whose gray beard was long enough to brush against the table. The woman—a working girl, Gen assumed—laughed, either enjoying herself or the money she'd receive for spending the evening with her wretch of a companion.

"We'll sleep much easier if we know we aren't sleeping in the same inn as a gang of cutthroats," Cordyn said.

Gen agreed, and they ordered more wine, along with a beef roast that the innkeep had told them was famous throughout Sarakan. Gen still dreamed of the old woman's stew in Dukestown, and she had a hard time believing the inn's roast would be half as good.

The steaming roast came out a few minutes later, and Gen had to admit that the roast tasted decent. It was juicy and flavorful, with just the right amount of salt. Cordyn and Gen ate with fervor while Arsene picked at his own plate.

"Are either of you thieves by trade?" Arsene asked.

Gen shook her head. Thievery was not a skill she possessed. When she'd first moved to Mintar, she'd attempt to steal a winterplum off the ground near a market stall. The plum had fallen off a nearby display and may have been free for the taking at that point, but Gen, in trying to pick up the fallen plum, tripped, stumbled forward, and knocked over the entire display of fruit. After helping the incensed fruit vendor pick up all the plums, she'd failed to retrieve the original fallen plum and went home, embarrassed and empty-handed.

"I've been known to steal on occasion," Cordyn said, "though I tend to prefer stealing away into the night with a fair maiden."

Gen rolled her eyes at Cordyn, but Arsene looked quite impressed. "I envy you, Mr. Tallen," he said. "I wish I had your skill in such matters. It is difficult to meet new people, and I've grown quite lonely in Dramin." He twirled his mustache. "I wonder if you might teach me some of your methods?" He wagged his eyes at Gen. "Perhaps I could use them on your most appealing friend."

Gods, that sounds horrible.

Gen felt like the first lesson should be for Arsene to shave off his silly mustache, and to stay far away from her. She had no interest in men—or women, for that matter—and wished to be left alone. Punching Arsene in the throat sounded nice, too.

Cordyn frowned and looked thoughtful. "Unfortunately, my good man, I'm afraid that sort of thing is not something one can teach." He took a sip of wine and changed the subject. "But why do you ask if either of us are thieves?"

"The Imperial Academy is full of wondrous artifacts, jewels, and artwork. It would be quite profitable if one could discover a way to get inside and, ahem, relieve the Imperials of some of those possessions."

"Perhaps another time," Cordyn said. "While I would enjoy hearing more about these treasures, we are on business of great importance and can't afford to delay our business for any reason."

"Especially getting arrested for theft," Gen said, "going to prison, and being hanged. That would be an unnecessary delay."

"Speaking of unnecessary delays," Cordyn whispered to her. "Don't look right now, but when you have the opportunity, there is a group of men over there who don't look friendly."

"Do you think they're targeting us?" Gen asked.

"Currently, they're only targeting their tankards of ale, but men like that don't stay calm and gentle for long. I've seen a few of them give us long, lingering glances already, and I doubt it's just because they're jealous of Arsene's mustache. Go up to the innkeep and order another bottle of wine. On your way back, take a look at our new friends and tell me what you think."

Gen stood up and walked over to the bar, her shoulders stiffening with tension even as she tried to breathe and calm herself.

"Could we please have another bottle of the winterplum wine?" she asked the innkeep. He rummaged below the bar and retrieved a bottle, which Gen paid for in coin. She took the bottle and walked back toward Cordyn and Arsene, her eyes wandering to the men Cordyn had warned her about. There were seven of them. Muscular, armored, well-armed, all bearded, with the serious faces of professionals. Whether they were professional soldiers or professional bandits, Gen wasn't sure, but she intended never to find out. She sat back down next to Cordyn and said, "Our new friends over there are nothing to scoff at. It would be advisable not to draw their attention."

"Unfortunately," Cordyn said, his eyes looking beyond her, toward the men. "I believe it's too late for that."

Gen turned to see one of the men walking toward them with intent. Tall and muscular, he had a faded scar down the right side of his face that made his already cruel expression downright terrifying. A war wound?

"What did you do?" Gen muttered. "I leave for one minute and this happens?"

"I assure you, I have been minding my own business." Cordyn looked up at the approaching man. "Hello, my good man. How may I assist my fellow traveler?"

The man slowed his stride and pressed his teeth together in what might have been a smile.

"Just trying to be hospitable, ain't I?" His voice was gravelly, with a thick accent Gen didn't recognize. "I sees a friendly group of people like yerselves, and I thinks to meself, I should go introduce meself and invite them to tea."

"There is nothing better than a proper cup of tea," Cordyn said. "Or so my mother and my maiden aunt say. I prefer spirits, myself. Whiskey." He winked at the man. "But for those with a delicate constitution, tea is an admirable drink." As Cordyn spoke, Gen watched the man's face turn from a sneer, to confusion, and finally to anger, as he realized Cordyn's meaning.

"I thought we were trying to not draw their attention," Gen hissed.

"Yes, that was the idea. However, plans change. Give me a moment." He turned back to the man. "I would offer you a seat with us, but alas, we have none available. We will survey your wondrous Dramin baths tomorrow and will tour the Imperial Academy. I hope we will see you there and can further make your acquaintance."

"Now look here—" the man began.

"Of course, how silly of me," Cordyn cut in. "A man such as you, you wouldn't be going to the Academy. You are a man of action. A man who enjoys getting his hands dirty. We will, of course, see you at the ballet."

"Wot's that?" the man asked.

"You are so very droll. What's that, indeed?" Cordyn laughed as if he'd just heard a hilarious remark. Gen wasn't sure what Cordyn was doing, but the longer they avoided fighting their new acquaintances, the better. "You, my fine fellow, are a delight, and I cannot wait to see you in the morning. However, we must retire for the evening. I am, as always, your servant." Cordyn regaled the man with an elaborate bow.

The man sputtered but could not form words. He stood with his mouth open, watching as Gen, Cordyn, and Arsene stood up and exited the room, heading to their quarters on the second floor.

They had rented two adjoining rooms—one for Gen and one for Cordyn—but Arsene had overindulged on the wine, and Cordyn sent him into his room to get some sleep. Gen and Cordyn stood in the hallway. Gen watched the stairs in case any of the brigands followed them.

"How did you do that?" Gen asked. "You mocked that man and insulted his manhood over and over. I'm amazed we made it out of the room alive."

"Well, Gen, when you speak to an utter dolt like that, as long as you use a suitably advanced vocabulary, they will have absolutely no idea what you're speaking of, so you can say almost anything as long as your tone stays pleasant."

"What happens if they figure out later what you were saying?"

"You flee," he said with mock graveness.

"Often just wearing your underclothes and purple hat," Gen added.

"That is too often the case."

Tobias listened to the group of bandits argue among themselves after their leader made a fool of himself while talking to Tallen. The men had disappointed him. If they'd attacked, it would have given him the perfect opportunity to use the distraction and take Tallen for his own. Instead, they'd gotten confused—Tallen *did* have a way with words, he had to concede—and then Tallen had gone to bed, unmolested, while the damnable men sat around the fire, drinking and complaining about their evening.

"Wot the hells happened, Bort?" one of the men asked the leader.

"I don't bleedin' know. I went up to scare him, like, make him beg fer mercy. Then he said a lot of words and I's got confused."

"Are we's just movin' on to the next target, then?" a diminutive bandit asked.

"I reckon that bastard's too much work, I do," the leader said. "Maybe we's just go home."

Tobias had an idea. Not his best plan, but sufficient for the situation. He could still make use of these oafs, and Tallen would still pay. All Tobias needed was to re-stoke the men's anger. The more they wanted their newfound enemy dead, the easier it would be.

Tobias took off the fragrant coat and hung it on his chair. He checked his hair to make sure it did not appear too unruly. He stepped away from his table and walked over to the men.

"Good evening, gentlemen. My name is Tobias Stinton. I'd love to buy you all a drink and have a conversation." He saw several of the men's eyes light up at the mention of a drink.

"I will pay you handsomely to capture your new friends." He paused, favoring each man with a stern look. "However, if they die, I'll have no use for them, or you. Is that understood?"

Then once you've captured them, I'll rescue them. You, sirs, will be dead, but Tallen and his friend will be in my debt. All the easier to destroy him.

"I dunno," Bort said. "That bugger got me all mixed up. Might be easier to just go home." A few of the other men muttered their agreement. "Dunno what he was even talkin' about."

Tobias pulled up a chair and sat. "In that case, let me tell you all about ballet."

FIVE

Cordyn was not used to being alone in bed. His room was far too cold, and Arsene snored like two ships colliding at sea: a long, harsh grinding noise followed by a slight whine. After the tedious and less than successful travels of the day, Cordyn wanted companionship beyond that of an unconscious drunk. He had not seen many suitable options on display yet in Dramin, which was a disappointment. As the largest city in Sarakan, Dramin had beautiful women, of course, but where were they?

He had to be careful, though. Gen was annoyed already because of the Duke Kuran debacle, and he needed to make sure that any woman he bedded was not a vindictive nobleman's wife. She could be married, as long as her husband was a weakling or a nobody.

Every seduction was a risk, but he considered them a necessity. Gen was different. She didn't require physical affection. Cordyn had never seen her take an interest in anyone romantically, nor had he seen her express a desire to be physically intimate with anyone.

For Cordyn, that physicality was one of the few activities that gave him any semblance of contentment.

Cordyn knew the truth. People were not kind. They did not do things for strangers out of the goodness of their hearts. They were bastards and con men and tricksters and pieces of shit. The world was a miserable wasteland of disease, death, and betrayal, and if chasing a few moments of pleasure could give him some slight enjoyment in life, he would continue to do so. Gen always thought the best of people, but she was naïve. Friends were a myth, though Cordyn did have to admit that Gen was a trustworthy soul, and he had a tender spot for how she viewed the world. She was less of a bastard or a piece of shit than anyone else he knew.

He tried in cycles to sleep, to read, to write atrocious Obanni style poetry, and to think of a title for the memoirs he would one day write, but none of these activities eased his worry or the emptiness.

He was worried about Piran as well. Though his home country was by no means perfect, he loved Piran, faults and all. The current conflict in Trunel and Kosel was concerning. Oban was decimating Kosel in battle, and Kosel would surrender soon unless Piran sent troops in to assist. And if Cordyn didn't complete his mission, informing King Jok of the Piranese troops preparing to march to the battlegrounds to support Kosel, Jok might surrender.

And then Oban would focus their conquests on Piran, which did not have the military strength to repel invading armies. The only hope was for Jok to hold off surrendering until Piranese troops arrived in Trunel to keep the Obanni at bay. The worries filled his mind, and he knew it was no use. He would not sleep tonight.

Alcohol would have to do. He exchanged his nightshirt for a pair of simple wool pants and a linen shirt, as well as his hat. Before leaving, he remembered to hide a dagger in his boots, and he attached his sword to his belt. In Piran, he would have donned a waistcoat and jacket as well, even to go downstairs for a drink, but a Dramin inn at midnight did not deserve his full finery. Even armed, it was a risk to go downstairs alone, but gods, he needed a drink.

The main hall had emptied in the hours Cordyn had been upstairs. The innkeep sat behind the bar, smoking a pipe, watching two men—probably Obanni by the woolen coats they wore—who sat by the fire.

"What can I get you, sir?" the innkeep asked. "I've got a rare Trunellic whiskey that's quite delicious."

"That'll do," Cordyn said. "Must be rarer than usual these days, with the war. I've heard not much makes it in or out of Trunel anymore."

"I got it right before the Obanni sent their troops in, thank Hurod. I'd have hated to have lost the money I spent ordering it."

"Has the war been hard on you here in Dramin?"

The Innkeep grimaced. "It's not been damned helpful, that's for sure. We used to have a lot of Trunellic and Kosellan travelers; they'd always pay a bit extra for the softest beds and the finest liquor. The only visitors we've had lately are Obanni." The innkeep opened a glass decanter and poured an amber liquid into a glass. He slid the glass in front of Cordyn.

"Obanni in Rosenfel? Have there been a lot of them?"

"There's been quite a few men passing through. Thick accents, thick dark hair, and beards. None of my business, but it's different, what with the war going on. Never really know who's a traveler and who's a spy. None of 'em talk much. Too far away from the suns is my guess."

"The Obanni do not engage with strangers or in inane pleasantries," Cordyn said. "They are a misunderstood people. I study them, and thus, I appreciate them. Especially their writings. I'm a professor at Dramin University, you see." He took a sip of liquor, the rich caramel tang oozing down his throat. A pleasant warmness coursed through his body. "And my colleagues in the astronomical sciences college have stated that there is no evidence Oban is further from the suns. That's an old wives' tale."

"Scientists talk a lot, but their words ain't worth the shit my pigs eat."

"They're annoying blokes, indeed, but I defer to them on matters of celestial locations, just as they look to my opinions regarding literature."

"Obanni are fine, I suppose, if grim. Not like the Winn. Those blighters are downright scary."

"Aye," Cordyn said to the innkeep. "I avoid those buggers as well." He picked up the glass again, draining the rest of the whiskey. The innkeep poured him another glass. Cordyn cursed himself for forgetting to ask the price. Ah well, he would enjoy himself tonight, damn the consequences.

"I don't know if you noticed," Cordyn took another sip of whiskey, "But my companion and I had a pleasant chat earlier with a group of men, all very rough and well-armed. I wonder if that is the normal clientele?"

The innkeep seemed embarrassed by this. He looked away for a moment, cleaned a glass, and then poured himself a small glass of whiskey.

"Not normal, no. I've seen them before, but they haven't caused too much of an issue. In fact, men like that, they've always been scared to cause problems with the guests. You never know when the wardens might show up, and when the wardens show up, things don't go well for anyone who's doing something they don't approve of."

"Who are these wardens you speak of?"

"The local constabulary. Mages, all of 'em. They keep the peace, though they're not opposed to some violence. That's why it's odd that those delinquents were trying to cause problems with you, sir. Committing crimes in a heavily populated area, that's something that gets the mage-wardens involved. And the criminals rarely stay alive for long."

"Indeed, that is most odd." Cordyn wondered what possible reason the men could have had to risk angering these wardens. He and Gen were not so rich as to compel thieves to put themselves in mortal danger.

One of the Obanni men called for the innkeep to bring them more ale. Cordyn nodded to the innkeep and turned to survey the hall. In the far corner, near the entrance, a woman sat, tuning a lute. Her beauty struck Cordyn. He wobbled in his chair for a moment, and he knew the whiskey wasn't making him dizzy. Thick, curly red hair cascaded down the porcelain skin of the woman's neck, a delicate nose contrasting her lips, which were just too wide for her features to be considered a perfect specimen of beauty, but Cordyn appreciated this minor flaw. She wore a simple black frock, which accented the curves of her body. Many of his fellow men only appreciated beauty when the woman was slight and delicate, but Cordyn knew better. Short even for a woman, but with a solid frame, she could undoubtedly hold her own in a bar fight and would not be easily overpowered by a man. He sat back and gazed at her, waiting to find out if her voice was just as beautiful.

After only a few notes, Cordyn was entranced. She strummed the lute with a fury he had not seen before from a musician, and her sweet alto voice had a raw passion that only made him fall further under her power. She played a haunting ballad, a song to a lover lost at sea, and the wish the singer had to find her love again—even if it meant her drowning at sea in order to join her lover. When the woman played the lute, she bit her lip in concentration, a minor detail Cordyn appreciated. Maybe the night would not be such a waste after all. This woman would be excellent company.

When the song ended, Cordyn clapped heartily and stood. He walked toward the woman, and when he came within a few feet of her, he bowed, ever the gentleman. The woman's eyes caught his and flared. She then looked away, her focus on the lute.

"My lady," he said. "I wish to thank you for your song. It was most delightful."

The woman did not look up from the lute. "I did not play it for you," she said, her voice full of emotion. Cordyn had never met the woman before, or he would have assumed she hated him, perhaps for some indiscretion in the past. That had happened more than once.

"Of course." He bowed again. "However, I still found much enjoyment in it, and wished to make the acquaintance of one so talented." He gave her his best rakish smile, something that no woman in Piran could resist.

"You're not someone I would care to make the acquaintance of."

Cordyn found himself at a loss. This was not what usually occurred. Woman had declined his advances before, and that was fine. He was not a monster, and respected their wishes, but he'd never felt so inferior and unwanted. That the woman did not want to accompany to him to bed, he did not mind. But he was appalled to find that she did not find him suitable company to speak with at all.

"I confess, madam, that you have me at a disadvantage. I have never met you before, and yet you act as if you know me."

"I know your type."

What gave him away? He wasn't wearing his usual clothes, and he looked less the libertine tonight than usual.

"I assure you, madam, that I am an honorable man—"

The woman stared straight into his eyes. "Your hat betrays you."

Cordyn's hands went up to the purple bicorne. "My hat?"

"You wear the mark of a ship captain." The woman held her gaze. "A mage. I will not associate with your kind. Your kind took away almost everyone I cared for. They died at sea. Now, I do not care if you die. In fact, I wish it."

Cordyn's worries of inadequacy washed away. It was all a misunderstanding. He hadn't lost his touch. "There has been a mistake. I am not—"

"No, sir, I will not abide by your lies. Leave me. Each moment I look at you is another moment of pain. I would prefer to continue playing music." She turned her back to him.

Cordyn took off the hat and walked back toward the bar. He had worn the hat almost daily since his father gave it to him. It had been right before his father's last voyage to the Isle of Winn, the one he never returned from.

Coart Tallen was not a kind man nor a good father. He and Cordyn's mother had fought often, and Cordyn assumed his mother had been relieved when consumption took her. Cordyn had been nine when she died, and after that, he had not seen his father more than once or twice a year. The man was always on missions and never home to spend time with his son. Cordyn could not say he'd ever been mistreated by his father, though when his father was home, they spoke infrequently and always with affected formality. Before that final voyage, however, his father had embraced him and told him he was proud of the man he'd become. "You're a better Tallen than I'll ever be," his father had said. "Take my hat and try to forget the man I've been."

When Cordyn received news that his father's ship had gone down in a storm, he'd put the hat on, and vowed to wear it daily. It was a small way he could honor his family name and the baffling man that was his father.

He reached the bar and tossed three silver crowns to the innkeep. "Many thanks for the whiskey," he said. "I find myself tired."

The innkeep wished him a good night. Cordyn walked to the stairs, preoccupied by thoughts of the woman with the lute. The woman who hated him. He didn't notice the armed men surrounding him until he felt a dagger at his throat. He ascended from the depths of self pity to find himself only a few yards from the staircase, the seven brigands from earlier that evening surrounding him, all giving him their best intimidating snarls.

"Hello again, friend," the leader said.

"Good sirs," Cordyn said. "It is wonderful to see you once more. Might I buy you a drink?" A blade pressed into the skin at the base of his jaw. "I'm sure we can discuss this like gentlemen?"

"We's not gonna listen to you," the leader said. "Yer dead." He spat on the floor. "And I don't like no bleedin' ballet."

"Of course not, though you do have the grace of a swan." While the leader frowned in concentration, probably wondering what a swan was, Cordyn struck. He swung an elbow out into the man at his back and kicked the leader in the stomach. He'd been aiming for the man's bollocks, but he'd missed by several inches.

Cordyn ducked below a swinging dagger and made a run toward the stairs. If he could get upstairs to wake up Gen, perhaps they'd have a chance. He'd only made it a few steps before a brigand stepped in his path, sword raised. Cordyn ducked to the side and drew his own sword. He parried a few attacks, stepping to the right each time, maneuvering the man out of the way. As soon as he had an open pathway to the stairs again, he broke off and sprinted. He'd almost made it to the stairs when the lute came crashing down on his head, knocking him flat on his stomach. He heard the woman's determined voice from above.

"No, you won't escape. You deserve whatever suffering comes your way."

The woman walked away, leaving him prostrate and at the mercy of the men. She'd doomed him to a detestable fate. Cordyn watched the men's boots as they stomped toward him.

"Oh, bugger," he said. He waited for the men to drag him to his feet. He assumed he would not live through the night, but they'd do their best to extract every bit of coin he had before they killed him. His only hope now was that Gen would wake up in time to save him. The brigands crowded around him.

"Cease this immediately in the name of the Imperium," a powerful voice boomed. "Back away from that man." Cordyn's attackers dispersed. He rolled onto his side. Four uniformed men dressed in black tunics stood near the entrance of the inn. They carried no weapons, yet seemed in total control. These were the mage-wardens no doubt.

"Thank you, my good men," Cordyn said, standing up. "I am in your debt."

"Yes, you are," one of the mage-wardens said. Cordyn noticed that all four of the mages were moving their hands and chanting. Ice shot out toward the brigands, encasing them in a frozen cell. "Also, you're in our custody, sir." Shards of ice secured Cordyn's feet to the ground, and he found himself in a frozen cell of his own. The mage-wardens approached him calmly now, their tunics billowing as they walked. "You've been quite naughty, haven't you?"

SIX

IT TOOK GEN A few moments to identify the noise of swords clashing, a harsh clanking with intermittent screams. Once Gen gathered her wits about her, she knew she heard swords. Normally, this was one of her favorite sounds. She enjoyed the swish of the blade as it cut through the air, the clinging of metal on metal, and the ultimate goal—the crunch as the blade cut through bone and flesh.

How dare they start without me?

She remembered she was at a Dramin inn, on a secret mission, and had Cordyn to worry about. Cordyn. She grimaced, half sure he'd already found a way to get himself killed.

Gen got out of bed, throwing a cloak on over the simple tunic and trousers she'd slept in. She grabbed Maralda, smiling at the thought of combat, and opened the door, stepping into the hallway, Maralda at the ready.

The hallway was empty. Even though she'd heard footsteps right outside her room a few moments earlier, she stood in an empty corridor.

"Cordyn?" she called. "What did you do this time?"

After a few seconds of silence, she heard movement from the floor below.

"Imogen?" Cordyn's voice called. "You may want to get down here."

Godsdamn, she'd called him Cordyn instead of Master Forthwynn.

Gen took off running down the hallway, Maralda held high. She took the stairs at a sprint and entered the great hall of the inn. Four men, dressed in blue and red cloaks, stood near the innkeep, their eyes regarding Cordyn with suspicion. Cordyn stood near the staircase, his sword out but pointed toward the floor, a thin, hollow cone of ice encircling him. The seven brigands were also in the great hall, looking menacing, though all of their weapons were sheathed, and they were also encased in a wall of ice.

"What's going on?" Gen asked.

Cordyn opened his mouth to answer, but one of the cloaked men spoke first.

"Good evening. By the authority of the Imperial mage-wardens, we are investigating reports of an individual who has been terrorizing the countryside. A well-dressed man who is reported to have assaulted women and children near the Nazlin border. Apparently, he's traveling with a tall woman with a Piranese accent. We have been asking this gentleman here for information, but as of yet, we have received no answers. Please state your business and what you're doing in Dramin."

"As I previously stated," Cordyn said, "I am Master Forthwynn, professor of Obanni Literature at Dramin University, and this is my bodyguard, Imogen. We are planning an expedition into Oban so that I may continue my research of the works of the excellent

Obanni poet Gian Rennis, whom I have written about in several well-known academic journals."

"And I have previously stated," the mage-warden said. "I don't believe you."

"Obsidian waves, the corruption of the body," Cordyn recited in a learned voice.

"Lo I traverse these climes I find naught but death

And in death, I find where I must travel."

"Ah, Rennis has such a way with the language of emotions. You can, of course, connect his Death Verses to the masters of Obanni verse like Kirwin and Fohde because of their unique connection to the humanity of man's demise."

The mage-warden captain squinted at Cordyn but said nothing. He did not seem used to having potential suspects recite poetry to him.

"I heard swords," Gen said.

The mage-warden captain pointed at the brigands. "When we arrived, we found these men doing their best to relieve your employer of his life."

"He said rude things about me mother," the brigand leader said. "I's was very sad."

"We was challenging that bastard to a duel," one of the other brigands said.

"A duel is hardly seven versus one," Cordyn said.

"And you," the mage-warden captain said, "were defending yourself more adeptly than one would expect from a poetry professor."

Cordyn held his chin high. "When you travel through Oban as much as I do, you learn how to defend yourself. The roads up through the mountains are rife with bandits."

The mage-warden captain motioned for his associates to conference with him. They stepped over to the bar and spoke to each other in whispers. Gen took the opportunity to move closer to Cordyn.

"What happened?" Gen asked.

"I was sleeping and enjoying a wonderful dream. Lady Kuran made an appearance. I was riding a black stallion through the peaks of Oban—"

"Get to the point."

"Fine, I never slept. I came down to the bar to get a drink and failed to pay attention to my surroundings. Before I knew what was happening, there was a dagger at my throat and three swords pointed at my heart. As I had no plans of dying in this rat-infested inn, I grabbed my dagger from my boot and my sword from its scabbard."

"I didn't realize you had the skill to take on seven enemies at once."

"I don't. I managed to not die, but things were not going well. They cut me several times. I'd almost managed to get upstairs, when a most unkind musician hit me over the head with her lute."

"Another woman you scorned, eh?"

"Something like that. I was done for. Thankfully, at this moment, our new mage-warden friends arrived. They froze my feet to the floor, shot ice shards between me and the brigands, and ordered us to all cease violence in the name of the Imperium." His eyes scanned the layer of ice between him and Gen. "So, though I am shivering within this wall of never-melting ice, at least I don't have a dagger through the throat."

"Very nice of them," Gen said.

"They did also accuse me of hangable offenses and threaten to let me rot in prison until my inevitable demise, but at least they weren't actively trying to stab me."

"I don't think prison would have good food," Gen said.

"There are many reasons I would prefer to avoid prison, but the food is near the top of that list."

"We can't fight through four mage-wardens and seven brigands," Gen said. "I'm good with a sword, but not that good. I may be able to shatter your icy prison, but I'm not confident."

"I have a plan. Just nod along with me when I recite poetry and tell me I'm brilliant."

"That sounds like a trap."

"Indeed." Cordyn waved to the mage-wardens. "Excuse me, sirs, how much longer must we wait? I have many preparations to make before our departure this morning, and it will not do for our journey to be further postponed."

The mage-warden captain considered Cordyn for a moment. Gen reached down and placed a hand on Maralda. Even though she faced combat frequently, she'd always somewhat irrationally expected to die of old age in a comfortable house near the markets of Mintar, but now she would die in Rosenfel, in a dirty inn.

The mage-warden moved his hands in a semi-circle, muttering an incantation. Gen tensed, waiting for the shards of ice to pierce their bodies. She hoped the death was quick.

The ice around Cordyn vanished into nothingness. When Gen looked back over at the mage-warden, he'd lowered his hands and stared at them, almost sedated.

"You're free to go," the captain said. He seemed unsteady, so Gen stepped forward to take hold of his arm. "Best be leaving the city, though. Take a nice long vacation." The captain turned to the brigands. "And you lot, make yourselves scarce. If I see you around here again, I won't be so kind and gentle next time." The wall of ice around the brigands disappeared, and they retreated from the inn, showering the mage-wardens with thanks and promises to never return.

Cordyn took a step forward and saluted the mage-wardens, touching a finger to his temple and then bowing, which Gen assumed was a Rosenfellian tradition. She'd never seen it before.

"I appreciate everything you do for our city," Cordyn told the mage-wardens, who looked at him with confusion for a moment, before returning the salute.

"Have we met, sir?" the mage-warden asked.

"Apparently not," Cordyn said with a frown.

After the mage-wardens exited the inn, Gen and Cordyn walked back upstairs toward their rooms.

"Gods," Gen said, heart beating fast after the tension of a near death experience. "I assumed we were dead. Rosenfellian mages aren't known for their kindness."

"My poetry and I had everything under control," Cordyn said, smirking. Gen glared at him and he sighed. "Fine, I too thought we were dead." His expression turned serious. "That was most odd, Gen. The mage-wardens acted like they didn't know us, only moments after detaining me. Kirth, they were preparing to shoot shards through our skulls."

"Mages *are* mysterious," she said with a shrug.

"Hmm," Cordyn said. "There's something more at work here, I fear. But gods know what."

They went into Cordyn's room, where the still sleeping Arsene was snoring, his hair disheveled and his mustache hairs pushing up into his nostrils.

"You know, I forgot Arsene was here," Gen said.

"If we had died, he would have woken up very confused and alone." Cordyn walked over to the bed and shook Arsene, who grumbled but did not wake up. "And most likely with a terrible headache from all those bottles of wine."

"Wine never gives me a headache," Gen remarked. "Arsene needs more practice."

"What I wonder," Cordyn said, "is who accused me of attacking women and children by Nazlin. The only person we interacted with along the road was that old woman with the delicious stew and ghastly prices, and I don't think she's the type to be on speaking terms with Dramin's mage-wardens."

"Maybe it was one of Arsene's enemies?" Gen asked, glaring at the sleeping man.

"That's what I plan on asking, if the damned wastrel will ever wake up." Cordyn shook him again, more forcefully this time, then turned to Gen. "Gen, would you do the honors? Just pick him up and, well, shake him."

Gen did as she was asked, laughing as Arsene's arms flailed in the air. She imagined his mustache flying from side to side in the air as she flung him back and forth over her shoulder.

"What the damned Kirth?" Arsene bellowed.

Once Arsene seemed awake enough to answer questions, Cordyn put his hand on Gen's shoulder, and she stopped shaking.

"Arsene," Cordyn said. "Do you have enemies? People who, after seeing us with you, would seek to do us harm? We were just accosted by four mage-wardens."

Arsene groaned and held his head in his hands. Gen shook him once again for good measure, and he wailed.

"A traveler, by my description," Cordyn said, "was accused of assaulting women and children near Nazlin. We have met very few people on our travels and have no reason to suspect any of them of wrongdoing.

Arsene considered this for a moment. "Aye, I have enemies. One doesn't live in Dramin as a foreigner without angering a few of the locals. If you were seen with me, I suppose the Hillmen would want to have a few words with you."

"The Hillmen?" Gen asked.

"Criminals, underworld characters. They don't care for outsiders, and don't like anyone who isn't paying them for protection. They're mostly lowlifes and bandits."

"The men from last night did try to kill me as well this morning," Cordyn said. "Perhaps these Hillmen are an issue."

"You've had quite the exciting morning," Arsene remarked. "I've not nearly died like you, but I do have a headache straight from Kirth himself. We should get you back to the warehouse to get your supplies, and then you can get back to your journey. As much as the Hillmen are a danger, they have little power outside of Dramin."

"I'd very much like to get out of Dramin." Cordyn stood with his jaw clenched, no hint of the wry smile he so often had. He was worried. It seemed odd to Gen. Why would random criminals take such an interest in them? It didn't make sense that men would try to have them killed because they'd met with Arsene.

No, the men had to have a different reason for targeting Cordyn. Perhaps he'd sold information to them before and then betrayed them? Gen bit her lip in thought. Could she even trust Cordyn? Or would he get them both killed?

Gen noticed Cordyn staring at her. "Gen, if you're done daydreaming, we have supplies to fetch."

Gen grabbed her bags and met the others outside of their room. After moving downstairs, they paid the innkeep for their rooms, and stepped out into the cool air of a Dramin morning.

The walk back to Arsene's warehouse started out normal enough. They passed by the Imperial Academy, a towering collection of buildings that made the Piranese palaces look like mud-huts.

"So many treasures," Arsene said, a wistful look on his face. "One day, I'll see the inside of the Academy."

Cordyn put his arm on Arsene's shoulder and said, "I'm sure you will, my friend."

"Thank you," Arsene grinned at him. "Your words mean so much—"

His smile turned to panic as a crossbow bolt whistled through the foggy morning air and lodged itself in his skull with a squelch. Blood spurted from the cavity below Arsene's temple, and he gasped, opening and closing his mouth twice, as if to say something that would remain unspoken forever. Arsene collapsed to the ground, landing with a thud. The wooden shaft of the bolt lay crooked at the point of impact, and the goose feathers on the end of the shaft tickled Arsene's mustache, which now soaked up blood, the tips of the mustache curling downward under the weight of the blood.

Gen had Maralda in her hands in seconds and moved into a defensive stance. From a nearby alley, the seven brigands appeared, five swordsmen, the bowman who'd killed Arsene, and their leader, now armed with an oversized cleaver.

"Nice to see you again." The leader smirked and approached them, his minions fanning out behind him. They focused their attention on Cordyn, as if Gen was not even there. "I reckon we was in the middle of killin' you, wasn't we?"

In response, Gen charged.

The first brigand never had time to react, his head meeting Maralda and then leaving his body for eternity. Gen knelt, grabbing the dead man's sword and throwing it at another one of the men, the archer. She missed by over a foot, but she hadn't been worried about hitting him. All she needed was for him to take his eyes off her for a second to watch the sword fly by. Before he could turn back to her and ready himself for her attack, she thrust Maralda forward, piercing the man through the ribs, severing his internal organs. Blood spattered against her face, but she didn't have time to clean it off just yet.

She heard swords clanking behind her and assumed Cordyn was fighting off some of the men. She'd killed two, and she could still see three in front of her, including the leader, so Cordyn had two up against him. Hopefully, he'd be able to hold out for a bit, because she'd used up the advantage of her wild charge, and the men in front of her would not be as easy to take down.

They stayed back, waiting for her to attack, and then eased their way forward, one pace every few seconds. They knew they had time to their advantage. She couldn't outlast three men in a straight fight. She'd need to separate them. But surely the men wouldn't fall for any of her tricks, even though the men *were* stupid. They had watched two friends meet her blade, and they would be cautious.

The leader raised his cleaver.

"You've got skill," he said. "I's could use someone like you on me team. How's about yous help us kill the fop, and then we'll all get rich together?"

"I'm not in the business of selling out my friends," Gen said. "Even when they are fops."

"That hurts my feelings," Cordyn called, his voice tight. He sounded tired. Not much time left, Gen thought. She had to act now, or Cordyn would be dead, and soon after, when the men who killed him moved to her, she'd have five men to fight.

"Shut up and fight," Gen said, the perfect response for both Cordyn and the men, because Gen needed silence. The leader stood in the middle, with a man on either side of him, all of them watching her, fear in their eyes. How could she get the leader to step forward first, to remove himself from the cover of his men's swords? "I like your little knife," she said, indicating the man's cleaver.

"Big enough to kill you," the leader said with unconvincing bravado.

"You'd have to hit me first." Gen lunged toward the man to the leader's right, causing that man to take a step back. She moved back to her original spot, but the man stayed one step behind the leader. It was a start, at least.

"Cordyn, can you move toward me?" she asked.

"I don't know that I'd be much help," he called, his words punctuated by clattering steel.

"I just need your daggers," she called. "The throwing daggers."

"Headed your way," Cordyn said.

"You'll need more than daggers to deal with us," the leader said.

"Something like poisoned daggers?" Gen asked.

The leader's neck tensed. He turned to the men on either side of him. "Don't let 'em get the daggers out. Take the man down now. I'll handle the woman."

Both men turned to move toward Cordyn, and in this moment, Gen struck.

The men didn't know this, but Cordyn had only one dagger and no poison, and neither Gen nor Cordyn were especially handy with throwing daggers. Gen disliked the precision and gymnastics involved with daggers. It was much easier to overpower your opponent if you pummeled them with your greatsword.

Gen just needed the men to step out of their defensive formation, and as soon as they did, she sent Maralda into the side of the man to the leader's left, kicking out at the leader as she stepped past him. She misjudged the distance and lost her balance, and when she swung Maralda toward the leader, she hit only air.

The leader's cleaver struck her, pain searing through her shoulder.

She heard a crash from behind her. A man was down, and from the triumphant look in the leader's eye, it was Cordyn. Gen swung Maralda with ferocity, breaking the leader's guard. He stumbled and fell onto his back. Gen attacked again, knocking the cleaver to the ground. She lifted Maralda and brought the sword down into the leader's eye socket.

Her moment of triumph was short-lived. A wet pressure hit the back of her knee, and she fell to the ground, her body landing in a stream of water that had not been there moments before.

She saw a sword above her.

"Godsdamn," she said.

The sword descended.

The men were worse fighters than Tobias expected. Seven men, even if they were middling fighters, should have defeated two opponents with ease. And yet the tall, muscular woman had killed three, and seemed close to killing a fourth, the leader. Tallen lay on the ground, looking up at the two men above him who held him at sword-point. At least the men hadn't completely failed.

The woman called upon unexpected strength and forced the leader to the ground, then dispatched him with her sword.

The men had been so eager the night before, thinking of the promised three hundred silver crowns. Were the surviving men still so eager as their numbers dwindled?

Tobias's plan had fallen apart.

He sighed. Apparently, he'd have to do it all himself. He brought his hands together in the *Vida*. The intricate movements were comforting to him, something he could always rely on. He called to the water, feeling a pull in his stomach as he willed the floods up from the earth. He raised his hands an inch, pointing up in the *flumenta*, as the water pooled around his hands and waiting on his orders. He flicked his fingers forward and shot a stream into the woman's legs, knocking her to the ground. Her closest opponent, grateful for this surprising occurrence, raised his sword above the woman and began the downward motion that would end her life.

"*Issa,*" Tobias muttered, his voice calm. "*Issa Vida.*" The water around his fingers turned to ice and, with another almost imperceptible motion of his fingers, he sent the shards of ice into the neck of the man who was about to kill the woman. With another flick of his wrists, he sent two more shards into the skulls of the last two men, leaving only Tallen and his bodyguard still alive. Tobias stepped out of the shadows and walked forward toward them. Tallen looked at him but said nothing, while the woman seemed to search for her sword, which had fallen behind her. She reached out, found the sword, and picked it up.

"By Hurod," Tobias said, affecting a worried voice, "I thought you were done for. It looks like I arrived just in time." The woman found her sword and lifted it. "I'm Tobias." He pointed to the dead bodies. "We'd better get you out of here before any of their friends show up. Or worse yet, the wardens."

Gen had not expected to kill four men tonight. She'd also not expected Arsene to die. Both of those things seemed like the distant past now, as she, Cordyn, and their new traveling companion, Tobias, prepared to ride for the Dramin gates. Tobias had appeared out of nowhere as she and Cordyn were on the verge of defeat, and he had saved them, dispatching the three remaining men. Watching him make such quick work of the men made Gen glad she and Cordyn had escaped the four mage-wardens earlier. She'd never fought a mage, and hadn't been sure how powerful they were, but now she knew that, even against one mage, she and Cordyn may not have stood a chance.

Was Ned as powerful as this?

"You have excellent timing," Cordyn told Tobias, sounding more wary than thankful.

"I know," Tobias responded. He had a haughty air about him, his short cropped brown hair, tilted brows, and pugnacious nose giving the impression of a permanent disappointed frown.

"Thank you," Gen said. "We, I mean I," she trailed off. "I would have died."

"You're welcome for saving your life, but you can save the gratitude for later. You need to get the hell out of Dramin."

"Why, though?" Cordyn asked. "Are those dearly departed rascals really so popular that an army of their friends will pop out of the woodwork immediately, eager to get their revenge?"

"The Hillmen are not the danger," Tobias said. "They were merely an inconvenience." He looked Gen directly in the eye. Gen scrunched her shoulders together, somewhat like a small child receiving a lecture. "You underestimate mages. The mage-wardens at the inn were not as fooled as you thought, and you would not have made it out of the inn alive without my help." He looked at Cordyn. "I used my abilities to confuse the wardens. They did not believe you were harmless, a mere professor. Before I did that, they were preparing to attack." He nodded to Gen. "And though you are a fine swordswoman, you could not have defeated four mages."

Cordyn regarded Tobias with suspicion. "I did not see you at the inn. How could you have influenced the mage-wardens if you weren't even there?"

"I sat in the corner, pretending to be a drunk traveler sleeping off the evening's libations. However, I was watching you, and when the mage-wardens decided to take you in for questioning, I made sure they did not."

"I didn't know mages could do that," Gen said.

"It's not widely known," Tobias said, "or widely practiced. Many of the tutors at the Academy forbid it, finding it unethical. However, you can see how it has its uses."

"I thought mages could only control water and ice," Cordyn said. "And now you reveal secret mind-control abilities? Odd."

"We control anything with water in it. Blood, saliva, even your piss. I merely swirled the liquids in their brains for a moment, confusing them. Simple enough and mostly harmless."

"Yet unethical," Cordyn said.

Tobias put a finger to his temple. "However, the confusion only lasts so long. And once they regain their wits, they'll come for you."

Gen shuddered at the idea of mages being able to enter her mind and change her thoughts, perhaps even change her feelings. Ned had never mentioned such things—indeed, she could not imagine sweet old Ned committing such acts, though he'd always spoken with caution about dealing with other mages.

"But why did you choose to help us in the first place?" Cordyn asked. "Two unknown travelers."

"You were hardly unknown," Tobias said. "I knew Arsene well. He often entertained visitors such as yourselves."

Gen picked through the bandits' remains, taking a few silver crowns from a coin purse under the leader. She picked up the severed arm of one of the men Maralda had embraced.

"Anyone need an arm?" Gen asked Cordyn, who kneeled nearby, rifling through another corpse's coat pockets.

Cordyn huffed. "No body parts. We've talked about this."

"You never know when you might need a hand, literally." Gen guffawed at her joke. Cordyn and Tobias remained stone-faced.

"Our rucksacks are full," Cordyn said. "And that joke wasn't funny last time, either."

"At least let me bring a foot. I may be able to fit one or two. It would fit perfectly in your bag."

"Absolutely not. My spare clothes are in there."

Gen kicked the leader's gut. "You could have at least had more supplies on you." Stooping to the ground, she picked up his cleaver and showed it to Cordyn. "Rusted. Not even worth a crown."

"How tragic," Cordyn said. "Gen, while you continue your treasure hunt, I'll focus on the business at hand. Tobias, if you're Arsene's associate, would you be able to open his warehouse?"

"It has a magic lock on it," Gen added.

"Yes, easily," Tobias said. "Those locks are one of the first things you learn at the Academy. Arsene was a decent mage, but I am much more talented."

"You are indeed a talented mage," Cordyn said, silky with flattery.

"Well yes," Tobias said, lips curling into a wicked smile. "I watched you fight. It wouldn't do if neither of us had any talent."

SEVEN

THEY TRAVELED BY BACK-ROADS and alleyways, Tobias leading and stopping at each corner to check if the way forward was safe. He pulled water up from the sewers, using the brown sludge to peer around the corners. Gen was both impressed and disgusted. As far as she could tell, Tobias could see whatever was in view of the water. Yet another thing Gen had never known mages could do.

After Tobias verified a pathway was safe, the sewage seeped back into the ground, and Gen and Cordyn did their best to avoid the blotches of putrid wetness that stained the cobblestones. Gen was sure some droplets found their way to her shoes, and she wasn't sure if she now smelled like shit, or if it was just the surrounding air.

"I am one with the shit," Cordyn told her. "And the piss. You may call me Master Shit of Pissington now."

"I'll never think of sewers the same way again," Gen remarked.

"Did you often think of sewers before?" Tobias asked as he called forth more water to wash away their footprints from the alley they'd just left.

"No," Gen admitted.

"But now they will forever be imprinted on our minds," Cordyn added.

The walk to the warehouse took less than half an hour, but it was a tense experience for Gen. At each corner, when Tobias scanned the way ahead, she expected mage-wardens and Hillmen to descend upon them, swords or ice shards gleaming, eager to end her life.

The odor did nothing to make her feel better, either, putting her more on edge with every whiff.

Finally, they reached the warehouse street. Gen saw their destination, only a hundred yards away. She began to walk toward it, but Tobias put his hand on her shoulder to stop her.

"Wait," he said. He moved his fingers, drawing droplets of silver water to his fingertips. "There are three mage-wardens patrolling here. I need a moment to convince them to move their search elsewhere."

Gen sat in silence, watching Tobias's hands move faster and faster, until she could barely tell which fingers belonged to which hand. She waited for the mage-wardens to cry out, aware that someone was swirling the fluids in their skulls, and for the inevitable attack. A minute later, Tobias breathed deeply and his hands relaxed.

"It's safe now." He stepped out into the street. Gen and Cordyn followed, though Gen still half expected mage-wardens to attack them.

The street was empty. They walked across the road to the warehouse. Cordyn was watching Tobias closely, his brow furrowed in worry.

When they reached the door, Tobias muttered an incantation and moved his hands in the unlocking spell Arsene had used on the door the day before. Nothing happened. Tobias repeated the hand motions with a different incantation, but still, the door remained locked.

"No matter," Cordyn said. "It would have been nice to have food and clothing, but we can make do if you can't open the door."

Tobias did not respond and instead tried a third incantation. This time, Gen heard the lock click. The door opened, and Gen could see their boxes of provisions inside, ready to load onto a cart. Now, they just needed to find a cart.

"Not very secure," Cordyn said. "If any mage out there can open any magical lock."

"Oh no, you have to know the specific passphrase for each lock," Tobias said. "But as Arsene was a friend, I knew a few of the passphrases he preferred. It was just a matter of trying each to see which worked."

"How wise of you," Cordyn said.

Why was Cordyn acting so coldly toward their deliverer, who had so far been an immense help? Gen shook her head at him.

Cordyn. Shut up.

"Could you also whip up a cart?" Cordyn asked, ignoring Gen's look. "Perhaps an armed escort of twenty men? What untold feats will you perform next?"

Tobias nodded, seemingly unaware of Cordyn's sarcasm. "I cannot make a cart appear, but I know where we can purchase one. In fact, I sent a message to one of my assistants before we even began the journey here. The cart should be here soon."

"Thank you," Gen said. She needed to make sure that Tobias didn't think they were *both* ungrateful.

"As for twenty men, I can't supply that." Tobias picked up a small ledger and thumbed through the pages. "I will, however, travel with you out of Dramin."

Cordyn drew in a breath. "That's not—"

"No need to protest," Tobias said. "I assure you, I am as formidable as any nobleman's private army, more discreet, and I eat far less."

Gen began searching the crate for supplies. "We appreciate everything you have done for us today. You are truly a good man, helping two strangers like this."

"Ah, but you're not strangers," Tobias said, placing the ledger in his coat pocket. "Friends of Arsene are friends of mine, and I do not care for the way mage-wardens think they can terrorize the populace with impunity."

"You are quite the rebel," Cordyn said. He sat on a wooden crate, arms crossed. "What would your beloved Imperium say if they heard how you malign their law officers?"

Tobias shrugged. "I am no friend of the Imperium," he said. "If you stay in Rosenfel long enough, you will begin to notice that many of us are not as loyal to the Imperium as it may seem."

"Hopefully, I will not stay in Rosenfel long enough to notice that," Cordyn said.

"Will you be going back to Piran, then?"

"What do you mean?" Cordyn stood up, startled.

Tobias regarded him. "Piran. Your home."

"I don't know what you mean, sir," Cordyn said, his voice haughty. "I am Master Forthwynn, professor—"

"I know you're both from Piran," Tobias said. He ascended the stairs into Arsene's office and returned with two bottles of wine. "You forget, Arsene was my friend. I know what line of business he was in. Indeed, I will be seeing to his affairs in the short term, until his heirs can be located. So, I ask again, will you be traveling to Piran?"

"No," Gen said. Cordyn glared at her, as if she was betraying them to the enemy. "We're headed to Trunel."

Tobias's gaze darkened. "Trunel. Into the war, then. Good. I will accompany you to the Trunellic border. I have family near there, and it would do me good to visit them." He smiled, although it looked more like a grimace. Gen assumed he did not smile often. "And, of course, when traveling to visit my family, would I not bring two of my very best friends in the world along as my guests? My great-aunt Myrtha would have my head if I failed to bring along such a pleasant individual as yourself." He nodded to Gen and tipped his hat, then motioned to Cordyn. "And you are very demure and prudish, sir. My grandmother will adore you." He pointed Gen to the crates where Cordyn sat. "Sit, have a glass of wine. Relax while we wait for my associate. And for Kirth's sake, change your clothes." He stifled a yawn. "Now, if you'll excuse me, I need to rest for a few moments before we leave. My efforts this morning have taken their toll."

At this, Tobias walked across the warehouse and made a makeshift bed of hay and blankets, with his coat as a pillow.

"Prudish?" Cordyn hissed, kicking the ground. "I'll show him prudish when my *demure* boot crushes his godsdamn bollocks in."

A half hour later, a young boy who Tobias introduced as Topper arrived with three horses and a cart. Topper was thin and dark, with close-cropped black hair and a fresh, angry scar down the left side of his face and neck. Though he nodded at Gen and Cordyn, he did not speak. Tobias tossed Topper a rind of cheese and a small bag of coins, and they loaded the cart.

Tobias and Gen focused on the larger crates, and Topper assisted with securing the supplies into the cart. Cordyn, though he was always ready with a quip or a suggestion on how to load items, seemed to very rarely have any supplies in hand.

Typical. Cordyn was never one for manual labor or hard work. He always disappeared when the heavy lifting happened.

When they finished loading the supplies, Topper mounted the cart and took the reins of a black and white mare. Cordyn and Tobias had mid-sized gray mares, while Gen had a beautiful dappled brown stallion.

"I wonder, sir," Cordyn said to Tobias, "Why you would travel with us on horseback, and not in a carriage, which I know would be more comfortable for you. I know an important man, a mage such as yourself, especially in a city like Dramin, would usually only travel by carriage." Mages were known for their fine carriages, and most nobles felt riding on horseback had a connotation of poverty.

"Ah yes," Tobias said. "I do have a fine carriage. However, it would be much more difficult for me to protect you if I were in a carriage. And gods know you need the protection."

Gen had no interest in their petty squabbles, but great interest in her new horse.

"Hello, Francois," she told the horse. "I know we're going to be best friends. Also, you'll be much nicer than the last Francois."

They mounted the horses and rode toward Dramin's eastern gate, where they would connect to the road into Trunel and into the raging war.

At the gate, two mage-wardens and six infantrymen, all wearing the blue and gold of the Rosenfellian Imperial Army, inspected those wishing to enter or exit the city. Two merchants in long, black velvet robes stood next to their cart, stewing as the mage-wardens opened each crate and peered inside.

If Tobias had stashed any contraband in their supplies, their difficult morning would be getting worse.

The guards looked at them wearily. Gen assumed this was not a post for the best and brightest in the Rosenfellian military. Perhaps they would not look too closely at her, Cordyn, or Tobias.

"Where are you headed?" one of the mage-wardens asked in an uninterested voice.

"I am Baronet Stinfield," Tobias told him, straightening his posture and looking sufficiently regal. "My associates and I have been in town to acquire supplies for the people of my village, Sortown."

"Of course, Your Grace," the mage-warden said. "We wish you a pleasant journey." The guard stepped out of the road and opened the gate, allowing the horses through.

"I expected that to be more difficult," Gen said as they rode to the northeast.

The regal stone townhouses of the city gave way to smaller wooden structures, roofs caving in and second floors attempting to join the first floors. The abject poverty surprised Gen. Dramin, like any large city, would certainly have poorer residents, but she had not expected such a disparity between the wealthy and the less fortunate. Rosenfel had such a reputation of opulence that she had not considered that much of the populace would be poor.

"It would have been more difficult if we'd been entering the city with a full cart of supplies," Tobias said. "The guards aren't overly worried about what leaves the city, as long as no contraband enters the city. Especially if it's a nobleman leaving."

"Are you actually Baronet Stinfield?" Gen asked.

"No, Baronet Stinfield is a ninety-year-old man who hasn't left his estate in years. I met his son a few years ago, and he mentioned how sickly his father is. He lives in southern Rosenfel, on the other side of the forests. The chances of one of the guards knowing about a minor noble from across the nation are relatively small."

"You still took a chance with our lives," Cordyn said.

"And you wouldn't take a similar chance?" Tobias asked him. Cordyn said nothing in return, something that didn't happen often.

Cordyn had met his match, someone he couldn't control with his wits. Instead, Tobias had the control, and by Cordyn's glum expressions and lack of flowery speech, Gen could tell he did not enjoy this sudden change.

The wooden shacks gave way to a forested path, which at one point must have been paved with gravel, though now it was mostly gray, gravel-lined mud. They rode up into the mountains, the air growing colder, to where it was almost as frigid as Nazlin. Piney woods towered over them, and the freshness in the air made Gen feel better about their situation. Yes, they'd almost died, but gods, it was beautiful out here. She wanted to stop and bathe in a clear stream along the way, but Cordyn looked at her like she was insane.

"We have a mission. This is not a holiday."

As the suns descended into the haze of dusk, they stopped for the night in a small village, which had little else other than a few shacks and a tavern. No inn, but plenty of grass outside the tavern to set up camp. While Tobias went into the tavern to get mugs of ale for all of them, Cordyn pulled Gen aside.

"I don't like this," Cordyn whispered. "I have the impression he's hiding something from us. We need to be cautious." Tobias, even though he was inside the tavern, was only a dozen yards away from them, and the tavern door was hanging open.

"Shh," she whispered back, hoping Tobias hadn't heard Cordyn's words. "You're going to make him not want to continue assisting us."

Cordyn shrugged. "That wouldn't be the worst outcome."

"I haven't gotten the impression that he's hiding anything," Gen said. "He's been forthcoming about everything."

Cordyn shook his head. "There's just something wrong about him."

"I think he seems nice," she said. "It's wonderful to make some new friends. Someone to not kill in combat."

Cordyn smiled wearily at this. "I have a feeling that you'll meet more enemies than friends on our travels. I wouldn't expect to meet anyone you don't potentially have to run through with your sword."

Gen thought about that. "Oh, I'd still fight with my friends. Maralda needs to be included in any friendship."

"So, if I continue to travel with you, you'll stab me?"

Her knees faltered.

Swordsman's tears, I hope it doesn't come to that. Don't betray me, Cordyn. I don't want to have to kill you.

Pushing the worry away, Gen gave him a hearty slap to the shoulder "Don't worry, I know how to give someone a friendly slicing without killing them, usually. What are friends for if not for good-natured sparring?"

Cordyn rolled his eyes. "I know you're trying to cheer me up and put me at ease. And I know I'm usually the one who is doing what strikes my fancy, gods take the consequences. I'm serious, though. I feel that if we let our guard down around this man, he will find a way to take advantage of us."

"He could have already killed us if he wanted to," Gen pointed out.

"There's worse things a man can do than kill you," Cordyn said. "He may not kill us, but he could easily make it to where we have no way of completing our mission. All I'm asking is that you stay watchful."

Gen agreed and did her best to seem cheerful when Tobias came back out to them, mugs of ale in hand, which he distributed.

"The barkeep says there's a house around nine hours' ride from here to the northeast," Tobias said. "It's not an inn, but they welcome travelers. We'll stay there tomorrow evening." He lifted his mug of ale. "Drink up, sleep for a few hours, and then we're back on the road."

Cordyn hung back the next morning, chatting with Topper, most likely to get information on Tobias, though the boy only nodded and grunted. Gen had not heard him speak any actual words yet.

"The boy is very quiet," she said to Tobias.

"He used to be as talkative as you like," Tobias said, his eyes flashing with something akin to anger. "Running through the streets, playing with the other children, always quick with a joke."

He gave her a brief, tight smile. "He's my godson. His parents were my friends. They were killed just six months ago by a mutual acquaintance, someone they thought was a friend. The boy has taken it hard. I helped him get his revenge, but even the death of his enemies has done nothing to ease his grief. I fear the boy he once was is gone forever."

"That's horrible," Gen said. She wanted to ride back and hug Topper, to tell him she would do whatever she could to show the boy that there were good people in this world.

"You're a good man," she told Tobias.

He frowned at this. "No, I wouldn't say that, but I do take care of my friends."

"You helped us when you didn't have to."

"We are like all other people," Tobias said. "A mix of good and evil. We love, we kill, and, at some point, we die."

"Speaking of death, we met an enhanced spider on the way here," Gen said. "He was as big as a pony."

"Kirth." Tobias gripped his reins harder, jaw clenched. "Enhancement is unnatural. The mages who use it, on themselves, on creatures, they are beneath my disdain."

"I've never seen it in Piran," Gen said. She'd not meant to upset Tobias. "Are they common here?"

"Very," he said, voice barely above a whisper. "And they are a stain upon us all."

Wonderful, Gen. You've angered the man.

"You performed amazing feats back in Dramin," she said, hoping praise would change his mood. "Do you always get tired after using your abilities?"

"Yes, it's inevitable." His posture loosened, and he became more at ease. "There are different philosophies among us, but the one thing we all agree upon is, after a few minutes of using your abilities, you need a nap."

"That's not very long." She immediately cursed herself.

We're trying to not criticize the man, Gen.

He laughed, easing her fears. "No, it's not. That's why mages aren't the main military force in most nations. You can't very well nap on the battlefield."

"I've only known one mage before," Gen told him. She wasn't sure why she felt like she could trust him. Perhaps that Cordyn didn't trust him made Tobias seem all the more trustworthy in her eyes. Ned probably would've liked Tobias. "He helped me find my way."

"You can tell me about him if you'd like. We have another hour or so before we reach our destination, and I'm always happy to hear positive words about my brethren. We so often are thought of as powerful and heartless."

Before Gen could speak, she noticed the flames. The roadway ahead was blocked off, a raging fire eating away at the remains of an overturned caravan. The wooden wheels of the caravan had turned to ash, and the iron beams that would have propped up a canvas cover looked like the ribs of a fallen animal, picked clean by predators. Over the crackling hiss of the fire, Gen heard a woman scream.

Gen spurred her horse, racing toward the fire.

"Gen!" Cordyn yelled.

"Whoa, Francois," Gen said as she and the horse came within a few yards of the flames. On the other side of the fire, there was a young woman, her auburn hair and torn turquoise dress swirling in the mountain wind. She was barefoot and armed with a sword that was taller than her. She was solidly built, but the sword was at least half her weight. The young woman struggled to hold the sword up as nine armored men advanced on her, their uniforms displaying the red and black of the Obanni flag.

They were hundreds of miles from the border, in the middle of the strongest country in Sarakan. Oban could never hope to defeat

Rosenfel in a war, and they would be foolish to even attempt. So, what were the troops doing there?

She looked back to see Cordyn and Tobias were moving up to her position. Topper and the cart stayed back a hundred yards.

"There's a woman over there," Gen called to Cordyn and Tobias. "Obanni soldiers are moving in on her. Nine of them. There's no time for a plan." Gen dismounted and unsheathed Maralda. "I'm going to save her. Tobias, can you do something about this fire, please?" Cordyn opened his mouth to say something, but Gen cut him off. "Not now, Cordyn. You can express your disappointment after the Obanni are dead."

Tobias lifted his hands and droned the incantation. Within seconds, heavy rain descended, the droplets extinguishing the flames on contact. Gen didn't wait for the flames to die out completely before running through the smoke, Maralda at the ready. If she had a few burns on her legs afterward, that was fine. She would not let the Obanni soldiers take the young woman.

The first Obanni soldier died without ever knowing Gen was there, Maralda's blade piercing him through the small of the back where his breastplate ended and only chain mail remained. Maralda sliced through chain mail like it was linen, though full iron armor was a different story. Thankfully, most of the men were only wearing iron breastplates and helmets, their legs covered in a lighter leather armor that Maralda could easily pierce.

The other eight Obanni paused their attacks, gaping at their friend's corpse and the blood-splashed swordswoman charging at them, but they recovered their senses and dropped into defensive stances.

"My friends are on the other side of the smoke," Gen told the young woman. "Get to them. I'll take care of these bastards."

"My, my brother," the woman whimpered.

"If he's alive, I'll find him," Gen promised. "If not," she trailed off. "If not, then at least these men won't be alive, either."

"Cordyn," she yelled back through the smoke. "I'm sending someone to you. Protect her."

"Understood," Cordyn replied. Gen gestured for the young woman to move.

The young woman nodded, running through the smoke. Hopefully, the ground had cooled off enough to not burn the woman's bare feet. Gen turned back to the Obanni. They watched her, swords at the ready, their faces hidden behind black iron faceplates. Eight men were too many for her to take on by herself, but she had a plan.

"Tobias, I could use some help up here," Gen yelled.

Tobias said nothing, but the ice shards that flew past her into the necks of two of the Obanni soldiers told Gen that he had heard. The men were still alive—ice shards wouldn't pierce Obanni iron, but they were knocked off balance, which gave Gen the advantage she needed. She descended on the first man, crushing Maralda's blade against the man's face. He went down in a heap. Dead would have been preferred, but, at this point, unconscious opponents were better than nothing.

Gen kicked the unconscious man for good measure—it may have been unnecessary, but it was cathartic—and moved on to the next soldier. While she'd dispatched of her second soldier, Tobias had moved forward out of the smoke and had sent ice shards into the unarmored legs of several of the men, crippling them. Gen stepped forward and killed three men in quick succession, Maralda easily cutting into their chain mail covered waists. Defeating the four soldiers left? An easy training exercise. The men's eyes filled with fear, searching the trees, as if looking for a suitable path for their retreat.

"You know," she told them, smiling as if they were all friends having a conversation. "I had hoped our time together would be a little more fun. Couldn't you at least try to put up a fight?"

The men said nothing in return, so Gen continued. "It would be quite pitiful if I killed all nine of you and you failed to even wound me. At least try to hit me. Come on, make it interesting." Still no response from the men. "Okay, well, I suppose we should end this."

She raised Maralda and stepped forward.

Or at least tried to step forward. As soon as she moved, her entire body was gripped by coldness. Her muscles wouldn't move. She tried to break free of the icy grasp descending over her. She shivered and tried to breathe in and out. No breaking free, and no breathing. The shivering wouldn't stop. She couldn't move her neck, but she could just see a figure on her left, moving toward her.

"I'm happy to make things interesting," a cold, oily voice said in an accent Gen didn't recognize. "The two of you, mage and swordswoman, can defeat mere infantry troops. Bravo." She heard clapping. "However, it's only fair for our side to have a mage as well."

Tobias yelled incantations and ice flew past Gen.

"Oh, ice daggers," the mage said. "Very handy. Nothing I can't handle, though." More ice daggers flew past her, and the mage grunted. "Shit," he said. "You were lucky with that one. However, you won't breach my defenses again."

"I'm going to enjoy killing you," Tobias said.

"You *are* strong," the mage said. "However, I don't need to defeat you, only to distract you. You can't pursue me if you're, say, saving a friend, can you?" The mage laughed. "I still know a few tricks. I'll show you one. *Descarri!*" he screamed.

The coldness in Gen's stomach grew, the sharp pain pushing out from just above her waist, like crystals were forming inside her, pressing into her organs and skin, the cold so intense it burned worse than a fire.

She collapsed to the ground. How could pain this extreme exist? How was she still conscious? She heard a feral scream. It took her a few moments to realize she had made the sound. The ground seemed like a suitable place to die. And then the ice burst from her abdomen. She couldn't reach her stomach to feel the wound, and something—blood, her intestines? —seeped out and ran down her legs.

Her eyes were heavy, and her head swirled. She closed her eyes, likely for the last time.

Godsdamn, that's a lot of blood.

EIGHT

CORDYN WAS NOT IMPRESSED. Gen had rushed forward into yet another skirmish. Their mission was not going well at all, this mage fellow was a godsdamn prick, and, worst of all, his legs ached from hours on horseback. He'd thought things couldn't get worse.

Then, the young woman had emerged from the smoke and ran over to him.

Great bastard buggering gods.

It was her. The musician from the inn. She wasn't carrying her lute, but he remained vigilant. She'd not hit him over the head again.

Cordyn was still on his horse, so the damned woman just stood next to the horse, holding the bridle, waiting for Cordyn to do something. He supposed the only gentlemanly thing to do was dismount and introduce himself again. And face more of her scorn.

Reluctantly, he descended from the horse and stood next to the woman. He was not tall, something Gen, to Cordyn's chagrin, never stopped reminding him of, but he was still a head taller than this damnable woman.

"We meet again, madam," he said, bowing. "My name is Cordyn. You are safe with me. Though my own safety remains in question."

"They've got Ezra," the woman wailed, no sign of recognition on her face. Cordyn was unsure if Ezra was a dog, a person, or the name of her overturned wagon. Maybe Ezra was a forest creature the woman had just met. Gen was always naming things. Perhaps other women were the same.

"Oh, well, never fear. We'll do all that we can to bring Ezra back." He did not feel confident that they would ever find this Ezra, who was most likely already dead, and his lack of conviction showed.

He was not the emotional sort. Yes, he enjoyed the company of a woman, and he knew how to talk his way out of situations, but when faced with the woman's unfiltered despair, he could not think of what to say or how to act. He had tried to promise her things so that she'd stop crying, but his tone was hesitant and monotone, not at all his usually cheerful, charming self. Not at all believable. The woman just stared at him.

Unfortunately, she chose him as her protector and not Topper, who sat on the cart a hundred yards further back, seemingly unconcerned with any of the evening's events. The boy refused to talk to Cordyn. Godsdamn him too.

Cordyn was now playing nursemaid to a woman who hated him. The young woman would not stop crying. And Cordyn hated tears. They were so melodramatic and messy. He'd not packed a handkerchief, which was yet another reason the mission had gone to shit.

"Why don't we, erm, get you something to drink," Cordyn said. Drinks often helped people when they were emotional, did they not? He wouldn't say no to a drink if someone had been there to offer him one. Indeed, if Topper were a few years older, Cordyn would offer him a drink as well, even though the little bugger wouldn't talk to him. A drink would help calm all their nerves.

The woman continued to stare. Her eyes were large and brown, the pupils dilated in fear. Cordyn had to remind himself that, unlike him, the woman was not just facing a mildly inconvenient evening where progress had stopped because of a friend's utter inability to not save the weak, mend the broken, and smite the wicked. This woman had already watched all her friends and family die, according to her previous conversation, and now she'd been waylaid by soldiers, most likely losing all her worldly possessions. Cordyn shivered. The idea of losing his possessions was not especially pleasant.

"Like I said, my name is Cordyn." He spoke more gently this time, trying to keep boredom or annoyance out of his voice. "You may remember me from Dramin. I had the honor of greeting your lute with my skull."

A hint of recognition flashed in the woman's eyes, but none of the anger from before. She nodded but said nothing.

"The woman you met already is Gen. We're here to help. There's another man, Tobias, who you may have seen, but he's a prick. A mage, so you'll hate him too." He pointed. "The boy back there is Topper. He's a prick in-training. What's your name?"

The woman looked up and stopped sniveling for a moment. "Evalia," she whispered.

"Hello, Evalia." He fought the urge to bow or shake hands with her, as one would in polite company. "And who exactly is Ezra?"

"My brother." As soon as she finished the phrase, she put her head in her hands and began to sob even louder than before.

Godsdammit, Cordyn. You've only made it worse.

"There, there," he said, patting her on the back. He'd seen nursemaids do this with small children. Maybe it would work now as well? She put her head on his shoulder, muffling her crying, as she now no doubt rubbed all her tears and mucus and spittle onto his bespoke waistcoat. It had cost four hundred silver and was nigh impossible to clean without the proper materials. The nearest cleaner who Cordyn would trust with his clothing was most likely in Dramin, which wouldn't be safe to return to.

Ah well, he would just have to suffer the indignity of stains.

"What happened?" Cordyn asked. "Were you and your brother out here alone?"

Evalia took a deep breath and released his waistcoat from being her handkerchief. She took a step back. Cordyn looked at her again, paying attention this time. She was pretty, with wild, curly auburn hair and freckles that covered most of her diminutive nose and flushed cheeks. Underneath the freckles, her pale skin was almost pink, as if she had been out in the sun quite a bit lately after avoiding it for several years. She stood tall—or as tall as she could—and put on a brave face.

"Ezra and I, we're traders," she said. "Or at least we're trying to be. Our father died a few months ago. At sea." Her eyes flitted to Cordyn's hat. "And we've been working to learn the business and take over his routes. We weren't ready to go on the road, but the money was almost gone, and Ezra eats so much. I couldn't afford food. So, we packed up and went out on the road. I played in some inns along the way in exchange for dinner."

Cordyn breathed deep. Gods, she was frustrating.

I asked what happened, not tell me the story of your entire life, Evalia.

"And you met Obanni soldiers," Cordyn prompted.

"We only left home a week ago," Evalia said. "We went to Dramin to buy my lute and some new clothes for Ezra, and then we were heading north." She fought back tears. "We didn't even make it to the first stop."

"You'd just bought your lute and then you destroyed it on my head?"

Evalia blinked. "Your skull was quite soft. No harm was done to my lute." She sniffed. "However, it's broken now. The soldiers crushed it. They ambushed us on the road and took Ezra. They'd heard about us and were waiting to take him. Then they told me they were going to take me back to be one of their camp women, and I told them I'd rather die."

He patted her head, then forced himself to stop. She was not an adorable animal; she was a skull-crusher. "When you say they took Ezra, what do you mean? Where did they take him? What did they want with him?"

Evalia looked away for a moment, then back at Cordyn. She seemed nervous. "Father didn't like to tell anyone, but Ezra, he had skills. Mage skills."

A pit of tension formed in Cordyn's stomach. "Why would your father want to hide that? Mages are highly valued in Rosenfel. I feel it would have been a prudent financial move to tell the entire world and enjoy the extra funds."

"Mages are taken from their homes here," Evalia said. "For five years. It doesn't matter if you don't want to go. Anyone found keeping mage children from the Academy is imprisoned. And Ezra, he's a sweet boy, but so innocent. He thinks the world is a beautiful place, and he loved Father so much. They couldn't bear to be separated. The Academy would have destroyed Ezra."

Anger flashed through Cordyn. "You say you hate mages, yet your brother is a mage?"

"Father went to sea, to travel to the Isle of Winn. He thought they might provide a haven for us. His ship was sunk." She stared at his hat. "Sailors—mages—killed him."

"I'm not a captain," he bit out. "I just wear the godsdamned hat." Evalia closed her eyes in the face of his fury. He paused, calming himself. "My father was a mage captain. I'm just, well, Cordyn."

"Oh," she said, sounding embarrassed. "I'm sorry."

Gods, she looks like she's about to cry again.

"How did the Obanni soldiers find out about him?" he asked, hoping a question would keep her talking instead of sobbing.

"I don't know. I've never seen Obanni around here before." She brushed a strand of hair off her face. "Some people in the village knew about Ezra, and the local baronet knew, but everyone supported us, I thought. But somehow these soldiers knew. They tied him up, put him on a horse with one of their soldiers and headed north."

"I see," Cordyn said. He had a mission to complete, and saving children was not part of King Thorace's orders. He was saved from having to promise Evalia that he would help find Ezra by a scream of pain. A woman's scream.

Oh bollocks.

"Gen?" No answer. "Stay here," he ordered, unsheathing his dagger and sword. With a prayer to any and all the gods for Gen's safety, he charged through the remaining wisps of smoke.

When he reached Gen's body, he knew there was no hope. She lay in a heap on the scorched ground, an ever-expanding pool of blood around her. Gods, there was a lot of blood, and it kept seeping out of the gaping holes in Gen's stomach.

"Gen," Cordyn yelled. He sprinted the last few feet between them and kneeled down at her side. Were the Obanni soldiers still there? He was unsure. He thought to look around to check, but he couldn't take his eyes off Gen's wounds. He took her hand and squeezed it, then put his other hand under her head, so that she could look up toward him.

"Gen. It's okay. I've got you." Her blood stained his waistcoat and trousers, but he didn't care. He'd give up all his clothes and walk naked forever if she wouldn't die. "Keep breathing. I'll..." he paused, unsure of what to say. "I'll think of something."

He noticed movement to his left, and saw Tobias, also kneeling to inspect Gen. He assumed the Obanni soldiers had fled, or Tobias had killed the rest of them. "I don't need your help," Cordyn said. "Just leave us." If the gods cared at all, this would have happened to Tobias instead of Gen.

Tobias said nothing in response, but he didn't move away. "If you don't leave us," Cordyn's voice was steely and hopefully ominous, "I swear to the gods that I'll—" He noticed what Tobias was doing.

The mage was feverishly moving his hands, chanting, *"Surros aqui, surros aqui."* Gods, it's impossible.

Cordyn watched as Tobias pulled his hands to the sky, willing Gen's lost blood out of the ground. The blood swirled up in a thin stream as Tobias continued to chant. Cordyn noticed that his waistcoat was no longer wet—had Tobias pulled that blood out as well?—but the stains remained. After a moment, Tobias gently pointed his open palms at Gen, and the blood entered back through the wounds and into her body. Tobias kept his hands outstretched, to keep the blood from leaking back out, Cordyn assumed.

"I didn't know you could do that," he said.

"Blood is essentially water," Tobias responded. "I can't fix the wound, but I can ease the blood loss. Give her more time, at least. I can't bring back all of her blood, but hopefully enough."

"Thank you," Cordyn said. He took off his waistcoat and draped it around Gen's abdomen, hoping the wool of the waistcoat would work for a bandage of sorts. "Gen, you're going to get through this. I don't know how to stitch a wound, and I don't have supplies, but we'll figure something out." He looked at Tobias. "Any other skills you're hiding?"

"I know magic, not medicine."

"Yes, if you knew both, it'd be too good to be true."

"My mother taught me to stitch wounds," Evalia said from behind them.

Cordyn jumped. He had forgotten Evalia was there. She stared at Tobias, horrified. "You're a mage," she said accusingly.

"I am," Tobias said, bowing. "Tobias Stinton, at your service."

Yes, and you can hate him all you want, madam. I'll even buy you a new lute if you'll promise to use it on him.

"Hello." Evalia looked like she wanted to say something more, but thought better of it. She rummaged through the pockets of her dress. "I've never done one quite so big, and I'm not an expert, but I have needle and thread."

Evalia turned out to have a fair bit of skill with a needle. Cordyn applied pressure to the wound, Tobias continued his chants to keep blood from leaking out, and Evalia sewed up the ragged folds of Gen's stomach. When they were done, Tobias called forth water to wash off the stitches, while Cordyn continued to hold Gen.

"Where exactly did the Obanni soldiers go?" Cordyn asked.

"After the mage attacked Gen, they fled. If they were Obanni, they weren't very well equipped." Tobias pointed at the corpses. "Their armor, if you can call it that, was not uniform. One man had a breastplate and greaves, another just a chainmail shirt." He pointed to a particularly mangled corpse, a shattered shinbone sticking out with tendons hanging off it like a bloody flag. "That man didn't even wear Obanni colors. Just a common tunic and breaches."

"Their weapons do look worn," Cordyn said, glancing at a rusted spear on the ground.

"I don't know the Obanni well, but in Rosenfel, an infantry platoon wouldn't dare wear such piecemeal armor, nor would they allow soldiers to be out of uniform."

"Nor would they in Piran." Cordyn thought of Gen and whatever horror the mage had wrought upon her. "The mage was powerful, though."

Tobias sighed. "He took me off guard, and my defenses were down, but once I called forth my powers, he recognized a fight he would not win. It would have been a long, drawn-out engagement, but he would have fallen."

"Fallen. I like the sound of that. I suppose it's too much to hope they fall down a ravine and die."

"No, if anyone kills that mage," Tobias said, "it will be me."

"I look forward to that," Cordyn replied. Maybe Tobias wasn't all bad. Only mostly a prick. "I don't understand why, if the mage wanted to kill her, he didn't just slice her throat. Not that I'm complaining."

"He wanted to slow me down. If Gen were dead, I wouldn't have needed to leave off attacking him. But with her wounded, I had a choice between continuing to fight the mage or trying to save Gen."

"You made the right choice." Cordyn pressed his hand against Gen's.

Gods, it was cold.

"And thus, our enemy succeeded in slowing us down." Tobias stood, straightening his robes. "She's a good woman," he said, looking down at Gen.

Gen was breathing steadily, and Cordyn began to hope that she might survive the day, though a soft, clean bed would be more helpful for her than the packed dirt and gravel of the road. "We should get her somewhere safer."

"There's a village a few hours north of here," Evalia said. "Not my village, but I know a few of the locals. They'll be willing to help. We can put her on the cart. I'll sit with her."

"Why are you willing to do this for us?" Cordyn asked her. "Especially with your evident distaste for me. And mages." He noticed the determination on her face. Her eyes were still wet and her face blotchy from the sobbing, but now she was calmer than him, and certainly more composed.

"You're irrelevant." Evalia pointed to Gen. "She saved my life. The least I can do is attempt to return the favor." Her eyes darkened. "And we'll need her when we kill the bastards who took Ezra."

It took nearly half the day to reach the village. They had to stop multiple times to readjust Gen, and Evalia had to tighten the stitches twice. Cordyn hoped the village would have a healer, someone with the supplies to close the wound more permanently.

A church towered above the one-room buildings of the village, and Cordyn felt a sense of hope. He didn't always believe in the gods, but it couldn't hurt to pray. The gods might listen.

"This is the Holy Temple of Torr," Evalia said. "I know a few of the novices, and the Mother is a good woman. If anyone in the village has medical supplies, it will be them."

The gods were smiling down on them. Cordyn revised his previous thought. He most certainly believed in the gods today. Torr, the goddess of Home and Family, was known for healing the sick, and her worshippers had a reputation for being excellent cooks. A hot meal sounded wonderful.

Evalia knocked on the door of the temple, and an elderly woman opened the door.

"My child," she said to Evalia in a low, soothing voice. "It is good to see you again. We still pray for the soul of your father."

Evalia took the old woman's hand. "Thank you, Mother Tull. I appreciate all you do. I'm not here about my father, though. Obanni soldiers took Ezra today, and they would have taken me as well, but these—" she faltered. "These men rescued me." She indicated Tobias and Cordyn with her free hand. "However, their companion was wounded in the fight. We've tried to stitch the wound, but we're not healers. Would you care for her?"

The old woman hugged Evalia. "You have gone through many trials. We will pray for Ezra." She stepped back and bowed to Cordyn and Tobias. "Welcome, sirs. We will, of course, care for your companion. Please come in."

The interior of the temple was modestly decorated; golden curtains graced the tall windows and hundreds of candles lit the shrine around a statue of Torr, who was thought to be a young woman, blind, wearing a long dress that hung off her shoulders. Penitents who came to Torr for help often repeated the phrase "Torr, help me see," which Cordyn found ironic. Torr was supposed to assist those in need by giving them the intuition to know what to do in difficult situations.

Cordyn had a closer relationship with Alais, the god of love and lovers, and he usually took his prayers there, but he was willing to look to Torr for help now. Four novices carried Gen into a room to the back of the temple, behind a small marble fountain, while a priest and priestess of Torr brought a carafe of liquid and several pouches of herbs into the room. Cordyn wanted to be in the room with Gen while the healers worked, but they shut the door behind them, leaving him in the vestibule with Tobias, Evalia, and Mother Tull, who watched them closely.

"If she can be saved," Mother Tull said, "my children are the ones who can do it."

"She *must* be saved," Cordyn said.

"If that is what Torr wishes." Mother Tull looked to the statue of Torr and mouthed a silent prayer.

Cordyn wanted to say that Torr could choke on a crossbow bolt and die in agony if it meant Gen would survive, but, thankfully, Tobias spoke before Cordyn could utter the blasphemy that would get him kicked out of the temple.

"Thank you, Mother. We appreciate all you do for us, and all Torr does for us."

The old woman smiled at this. "You are most kind. Come, I will have my children prepare food and beds for you. You must be hungry and in need of rest."

She led them to a dark room filled with rough wooden tables and benches. The house of Torr did not care for decor, it seemed.

Cordyn preferred to eat his meals in front of pleasant views: a fresco, the wild beauty of a sunset, or indeed, with a wild Piranese beauty. There were several women of his acquaintance who would gladly share a meal with him whenever he asked. Instead, he sat on the hard bench, squirming. He'd grown accustomed to luxury and comfort, and these benches pressed on his spine. Tobias and Evalia sat across from him. Evalia had chosen to sit next to the actual mage instead of the man who'd valiantly comforted her during a most trying experience. Gods, she was infuriating.

They sat in relative silence, speaking only to ask someone to pass a dish or the pitcher of dark ale. Mother Tull served them a laborer's porridge; rich, meaty pieces of lamb, stewed carrots and parsnips, and a thick, spicy sauce that reminded Cordyn of cinnamon, honey, and Trunellic scorch peppers. They used crusts of hearty rye bread to soak up the sauce. It was a fine meal, and Cordyn decided he would ask Mother Tull for the recipe before leaving.

When dinner ended, Evalia broke the contented silence with her plans for finding Ezra. "We must travel north. There are only so many villages they could have taken him to. Obviously, we'll wait to see what happens with Gen."

She smiled at Cordyn with a touch of sadness. Maybe her anger softened? He nodded solemnly. Poor Gen.

"I know this must be difficult for you," Evalia added.

The situation *was* difficult for Cordyn, and not only because he didn't know if Gen would survive. The mission now hung on the weakest of threads, and that thread threatened to break entirely at every moment. Gen would most likely not be able to travel the rest of the way to Kosel. There wasn't time to wait for her to convalesce, assuming she survived. He would have to continue the journey alone.

"Yes, Gen will appreciate you staying here with her," he said. "I'm sure she will find things very lonely after I leave."

Evalia stared at him, her face cycling between confusion, anger, and disappointment. "You're leaving?"

"Well, yes." He shoveled more laborer's porridge into his mouth. "I have important business to attend to," he said, chewing as he spoke. "Business of an incredibly time-sensitive nature. I care deeply for Gen, and as much as I would like to stay here and nurse Gen back to health, I cannot afford to." He raised his mug of ale to his lips. "I assure you; I would make an excellent nurse."

"My brother was taken by the Obanni!" Evalia sprang back from the table and fixed a hateful glare on him. "You know this. Those same Obanni may have killed your companion. You say that you care deeply for her, and yet you abandon her. You abandon us."

Cordyn choked on the ale, taken aback by Evalia. "Madam, I sympathize with you about your brother. It is terrible what has happened to him. I hope you find him and that all will be well." He paused, coughing. The ale stung his throat. "However, I do not know you. I cannot abandon my mission to help every young woman in need of rescuing. I offer you my apologies and my best wishes for your future, but that is all I can offer you."

Cordyn stood, bowed to Tobias and Evalia, and left the room.

As he shut the door behind him, he heard Tobias say, "Don't worry. I will help you, Evalia. Also, I'll talk with that sanctimonious bastard. I have ways to convince him to help."

Cordyn kicked the door. "Godsdamn mages." He turned to see Mother Tull watching him. "The, uh, door was stuck and needed a bit of a shove to close all the way." He took a step away from her.

"I heard your conversation," Mother Tull said, her voice less serene than before.

"Of course, my good woman." He bowed awkwardly. "If you could show me to my bed, I would be obliged. I feel tired and would appreciate a rest."

"Evalia is a sweet soul." Mother Tull pointed to a set of stairs to the left of the dining hall entrance. "If you betray her, I will bring the wrath of the gods down on you."

"I hardly think—"

Mother Tull raised her right hand and motioned for him to stop. "Do not speak untruths in this holy temple. You do not deserve a bed here, but I will not cast you out. Your companion rests, but she will live. Evalia tells me that your companion saved her." She paused, then continued in a scornful voice. "It seems a shame that two such good, kind women should be forced to spend time with the likes of you."

"Mother—"

"May Torr walk with you, my child."

Cordyn watched her walk into the dining hall.

He'd been scolded again, told how worthless he was, and how he didn't deserve the love or respect of the people in his life. It was becoming a habit ever since he'd left Piran.

He bloody hated Rosenfel.

NINE

THE MATTRESS SHE WOKE on was firm but with some give, and if Gen's suspicions were correct, stuffed with goose down—a luxurious touch. It was more expensive than the beds she was used to, but a welcome change. Apparently, the Dark Beyond had better furniture than she had while living.

She was obviously dead. She couldn't remember what happened, but she was sure it involved more blood than a person could lose without dying. The only thing she could remember were pools of red swirling out of her body and soaking into the ground. The image was mesmerizing—a contrast of colors like something out of a painting. Sparkling blood, heartbroken friends nearby, the heroine dying bravely.

She opened her eyes. The room wasn't much bigger than a closet; when she got out of bed, she'd barely have room to maneuver, and with the low ceiling, she'd need to watch her head. The walls were white stone with no accents except for a shuttered window and a statue of a blindfolded woman. The woman's stone face, smooth and defined, showed a muscular jawline and a large hawkish nose—imposing rather than pretty. Someone you would not want to offend. Gen was confident she knew who the woman was, but the knowledge eluded her. Hopefully, she wasn't offending the woman by not knowing who she was. Her mind was foggy, and her feet were cold. Perhaps the woman was Kirth's wife? She'd never spent much time considering the death god or his family situation. Death always seemed far away. The Dark Beyond was Kirth's domain, which he ruled with ferocity, and those who had lived evilly in life suffered eternally when dead. She hoped Kirth was in a good mood.

Despite being dead, she was hungry. And gods, she was thirsty. Her tongue felt like sandpaper as she brushed it along the roof of her mouth, scratchy and dry as salted herring. Though her mouth was not as tasty.

How many days had she been dead? Was there water in the Dark Beyond, or wine? Her stomach ached, as if a rock sat just above her pelvis, digging into her skin. With every passing second, the rock sunk deeper, the pain increasing. Finding out what happened and where she was could wait. Right now, she just needed sustenance. She'd get out of bed, exit through the illuminated door, and see what sort of wines Kirth had available. Probably something ancient, rare, and strong. Maybe they'd have roast mutton. Mutton sounded good today, which was odd. She rarely sought out mutton, but after the talk of mutton at the Daft Bugger, she'd been craving it. She'd eat and drink and get to know her new companions here in the Dark Beyond.

There would be other sights, she was sure. All sorts of animals for her to pet, love, and name. After years of being too busy to have a pet, she was excited about the chance. There would be several Francois, but perhaps also a Pierre or two. She'd find a lovable old donkey and name it Cordyn. She'd eat sweet rolls, and the wine would flow endlessly. Perhaps some of her ancestors or her brother Huber would be there, waiting to meet her. It was going to be a glorious party. Death was wonderful.

She attempted to swing her legs over the side of the bed, but they refused to move. Despite being able to crane her neck enough to see the white cloth bandages covering her wounded torso, she couldn't move anything below her waist. Not even a toe.

Oh gods, was this her punishment in death? She must have angered the gods in some way. But how? She'd never been the best at praying to Kirth, and she'd failed to pray much at all the past few years.

I'm sorry, Kirth. I've been busy. I'll make it up to you. Please don't bind me to this bed forever.

Gen took a deep breath and tried to clear her mind, searching her muddled brain for memories, any recollections of misdeeds in her final moments. And came upon the slightest, hazy recollection of a mage. Yes, that was it. She fought the soldiers in piecemeal Obanni armor, then the mage arrived and made her feel so cold inside, to where she couldn't stop shivering. A searing pain in her stomach. And the blood. So much blood. Enough blood to fill up a case worth of wine bottles. She had to be dead—but then why did it hurt, unless Kirth was punishing her for her sins? She tried to remember the traditional prayers to Kirth, but she couldn't find that knowledge anywhere.

She'd have to make it up as she went.

O Kirth, good Kirth. No, he wasn't good. He was angry and foreboding and a punisher of the wicked. Even those he found favor in still had to sit before his judgment and atone for any slight wickedness.

O powerful Kirth. That was better. *I come before you to seek your forgiveness.* No, he didn't forgive. He judged.

I accept your judgment. Especially if it's positive. I lay myself at your feet and I acknowledge you as, well, as Kirth. Well, I don't have a future as a prayer-writer, that's for sure. Thank you, Kirth. I appreciate you, Kirth. Do you have any wine, Kirth? Maybe a spare meal or two, as well? How did one end a prayer? Certainly not the end, but what else could it be? *Thank you, Kirth, and I...look forward to your judgment.*

Apparently, you ended prayers with a lie. She winced at the thought of Kirth's judgment, ashamed of her poor excuse for a prayer. It was disheartening that, even in the Dark Beyond, she couldn't avoid sacrilege.

Pressing her neck against the bed, she tried to give herself leverage. Her neck twinged and warmth trickled into her feet. When she tried to rise from the bed again, her feet turned. Sitting up still seemed like an impossibility, but this movement in her feet was a positive sign. She took a deep breath, focused all her energy on her feet, and once more attempted to sit up.

And screamed.

The pain from her abdomen engulfed her entire body. There was no thinking, no fighting through this. She was pain, and pain was all. She continued screaming, cursing Kirth for this torture while praying to him to ease her suffering. Too immersed in pain to think of anything else, she didn't notice the door open, or a figure enter the room until she felt a hand on her arm. Her scream faded into a hoarse cough. She tried to breathe, but all she could think about was the pain. Breathing hurt, existing hurt, opening her eyes hurt.

"You're awake," a young woman's voice said.

"Gurrrrr," Gen said.

"The mother will be pleased to hear this. I am Initiate Brella. I'm so happy to see you awake. We had thought you'd passed the worst, but one can never be sure with wounds like yours."

Gen used all her energy to force one eye open. A young woman dressed in a simple black tunic stood next to the bed.

"I'll let your friends know as well. They've been so worried."

Gen wondered if Francois would be there. She imagined the massive horse walking into the small chamber and nuzzling her.

Instead of a horse, Cordyn walked into the room. Cordyn? What was he doing here? Either he'd died too, or she'd somehow survived.

Cordyn was more effusive with emotions than she'd ever seen him before. He hugged her, took her hand in his, and kissed the top of her head.

"I'm so glad to see you, friend." He put his hand on her shoulder. "I thought you would die. I'm so happy you didn't."

"Thank you, friend," she said. "How am I alive?"

"A miracle. I'll never say anything bad about mages ever again." He gave her his most serious expression. After a pause, he broke out into a grin. "Well, I can't promise that, but I'll say fewer negative things."

"A mage saved me?" She paused, thinking. "Tobias?"

Cordyn nodded. "He pulled all of your blood out of the ground and pushed it back into your body. I didn't know it was possible."

"I've seen it once before," Gen said. "When I was a girl." But telling anyone about Ned seemed dangerous. No one could know, or Ned might be hunted down. She needed to change the subject. "Tobias is a good man. He's saved us several times now. He must have been sent from the gods."

"I'm not ready to go that far," Cordyn said with a look of mock surprise. "I'll admit that he's helped us out some, but he's still an insufferable prick."

Gen laughed, which turned out to be a horrible idea. Her abdomen seared with pain again.

"Oh, gods. Don't make me laugh. I can't take it. It's too much."

Gen saw the concern in Cordyn's eyes as he scanned her wounded torso.

"Oh, Gen, if I had a silver crown for every time someone told me that, I'd be—"

"Just as annoying as ever." It was good to be alive, but her throat was dry. "I'm godsdamn thirsty," she said. "You wouldn't happen to have a bottle of wine on you?"

"Gods, it's a miracle. She's healed!" Cordyn winked at her.

"Water will be fine. And something to eat. I'd kill for some of that old Nazlin woman's stew."

"That was a simpler time." He looked up at the ceiling. "And yet somehow it was only a week ago."

"She was such a kind soul."

"So welcoming." Cordyn absentmindedly brushed his hand against the stubble growing on his face. Gen had never seen him with facial hair. He looked haggard: red-eyed, dark, puffy circles under his eyes, and the beginning of wrinkles on his forehead. When had he last slept?

"What have you been doing while I've been almost dying?" she asked.

"Mostly trying to avoid Stinton and Evalia. She's incorrectly decided that I'm a wastrel and a coward." He shook his head in annoyance.

"Evalia?"

"The young woman you saved," he said with a sigh.

That's what she'd been doing when the mage attacked. Saving a young woman from attacking soldiers. The young woman had a brother.

"What happened after, well, whatever happened to me?" She tried to lift her head to get a better look at the surrounding room, but her neck protested.

"Let me help you," Cordyn said. He took two of her pillows and put them behind her, then helped to prop her up. Her wounds tingled, but she managed to sit without further pain.

"The mage turned your insides to ice and pulled the shards out through your intestines." Cordyn sat on the end of the bed. "You lost consciousness, and then the Obanni mage and the soldiers fled. Then, like I said, Tobias saved you."

"And Evalia's brother?"

"The soldiers took him, I assume. We never saw him."

"We need to save him," Gen said. She was surprised by how forceful her voice sounded. She could barely remember Evalia's face, but she would not allow a young boy to be taken like this, especially after the bastards tried to kill her.

Cordyn ran his hands through his hair. "We have a mission, Gen."

"Kirth take the mission," she said through gritted teeth. "This is more important."

Cordyn stared at her in shock. "You would risk our entire nation, your home, to help save the younger brother of a woman you just met? A woman you don't even seem to remember?"

Gen paused to consider her words. "I've always appreciated Piran, Cordyn. I've had a good life there. The wine is excellent, and the sweet rolls as well. But these are people. Flesh and blood people who I know and like."

"You've spoken five words to Evalia and now you're bosom companions?" he asked with more aggression than she'd heard from him before.

"They've saved my life."

"And yet the king has always been there for us."

She scoffed and shook her head. Cordyn opened his mouth to interject, but she pressed forward. "The king isn't as supportive as you think. He might not be the man you think he is."

Cordyn stared at her, mouth slightly open. She'd never seen him look so lost for words. His eyes flitted from side to side and he ground his teeth. Finally, he spoke. "Godsdammit, Gen. You can't speak that way about the king, about Piran. That's treason."

"Well, King Thorace can hang me then." She met his eyes and refused to look away.

"Gen—"

"I've made my decision. You can either accept that and stay my friend, or you can restrain me and deliver me back to Piran in chains." Should she say something horrible? "Perhaps you could get a reward for me. Add it to your secret riches."

He leaned against the side of the bed. "What?"

"Gillus told me all about your finances." She watched the turmoil on his face and felt pity, but pushed it away. "Gods, even your precious king is convinced you're a spy."

"What?" he sputtered. He refused to meet her gaze. "I'm not a spy, Gen. But the money, it's something I can't talk about. If I could, you'd be the first person I'd tell."

"Forgive me if I struggle to believe you."

"Swordsman's tears." He threw his hands up in the air and raised his voice. "I've sworn an oath not to speak of it. I cannot go against my word as a gentleman."

"They wanted me to spy on you, you know."

"Gen—"

She scoffed. "I'm not a child. You're hiding things, which just makes me doubt you more."

"The Winn," Cordyn bit out. "My father worked for them."

"But they're savages."

"My father seemed to think otherwise. He died in their service, and they send me funds yearly, enough to fund my every desire. I've never asked for their money. It just arrives. And it'd be a shame to let it go to waste."

"You could just tell the king."

He shook his head. "Tell them what? That I received money from a mysterious, possibly hostile foreign power? They'd think I was a spy."

"And yet by not telling them..." she trailed off.

"All the more reason to complete my mission."

"The mission doesn't matter, Cordyn. They just wanted to see if you'd betray Piran."

Cordyn's resolve faltered briefly. Then he pursed his lips, resigned. "Gillus and His Majesty may doubt me, but I will uphold my honor."

"And I have no intention of continuing this sham of a mission." Gen turned away to hide the water forming in her eyes. "That may make me a traitor, but I don't care. Go, turn me in, do what you must. Prove your loyalty to the crown."

Cordyn's face softened. "Rest assured you have nothing to worry about, Gen. I am loyal to you. I could never turn you in. I accept that you have made a choice, one I don't agree with, but a choice all the same. I couldn't bear to see you in chains." He exhaled. "However, I will fulfill my mission. I swore an oath to the crown, and I will abide by that oath."

Gen tried to keep her eyes from watering. She had not cried since she was a little girl. There was no reason to start now. Cordyn's decision disappointed her, but it wasn't unexpected. "If you must go, you must go. I won't stop you."

"I had planned to come here to tell you I was moving forward with the mission without you, but that I would come back to retrieve you after I delivered the message." He stood.

"I'm not going back to Piran," she said. "At least not until I've found the boy."

"And how will you find the boy when you can't even lift yourself out of bed?"

"Shut up!" The force in her voice surprised Gen. "Just leave."

Cordyn bowed formally. "It seems now that you do not care if I return. Therefore, I will take my leave. I hope your wounds heal. I wish you every happiness in this world." Cordyn nodded his head, his expression steel. "Madam." He turned and left without looking back.

The tears fell, her cheeks drenched by the salty drops.

Gen woke from a dream. She'd been fighting King Thorace and a group of Piranese soldiers. The king called her a traitor, he'd sent his best mages after her, and they took Maralda. She watched as they melted Maralda into a puddle of silver, and she wanted to cry.

"You've been whimpering in your sleep," a woman's voice said from beside her. She opened her eyes to find Evalia sitting next to her.

"I don't whimper."

"Well, then you've been snoring in a very high-pitched, sad way." Evalia smiled.

It was good to see Evalia alive and smiling. Gen didn't know the woman at all, but she felt a kinship to her because of the battle they'd shared. Evalia wore a thin white frock, her auburn hair pulled up into a bun. Gen liked her freckles and the slight scar on her lips. She was a beautiful young woman, but these marks, unpopular by the day's beauty standards, made her unique. At this moment, however, Evalia's eyes were red and her cheeks blotchy, drying tears marring her cheekbones. Apparently, crying was going around today.

"Have you been talking to Cordyn too?"

Evalia wiped her eyes and sniffled. "I hate him."

"If I had a silver crown for every time I heard that—" Gen began, but then the phrase reminded her of Cordyn, so she stopped. "He's a good man, at heart. Perhaps too loyal to Piran. I suppose I'm not loyal enough."

"If I could have Ezra back, I'd gladly burn down all of Rosenfel. Wait, Piran?" Evalia asked.

Oh, gods. She was truly a terrible spy. "We're from Piran. We were on a mission. He's continuing, and I'm staying here and trying not to die."

"I've never been to Piran, but we had a book of maps at our house. My father would look at Trunel and Piran with Ezra." She paused for a moment. "Oh, Ezra."

"I'm going to do my best to help you. As soon as I can walk." She reached out her hand. "We haven't really had the chance to talk. I'm Gen."

Evalia took her hand and shook it. "Evalia. And I can't ever begin to thank you enough for saving my life."

Gen shook her head. "No thanks needed, really. It's what anyone would have done."

"Not Cordyn," Evalia said pointedly.

"He would have, he'd just have whined about it a lot while doing it."

"And I would have found him insufferable. Handsome, though. The horrible ones always are."

"You have no idea how often he's described that way."

"Tobias seems like a good man. For a mage, at least. He doesn't look as good as Cordyn, though." Evalia giggled. "If only we could put Tobias's personality in Cordyn's body. It'd be the perfect man."

"If that's the sort of thing you're into."

"Men or perfection?"

"I don't care about either."

"You've never wanted a husband?" Evalia asked. "To be married." She gave Gen a sheepish grimace. "I confess, at first, with how worried Cordyn was for you, I thought you and Cordyn were lovers."

Bile rose in Gen's throat. "Gods, no. There's nothing I want less." She hesitated. Could she trust Evalia? "I don't want romance or, gods forbid, a sexual relationship. With anyone."

Evalia scrunched her face. "But don't you find people attractive?"

Gen considered this. "Sometimes, but I want nothing beyond that."

"I want love and marriage." Evalia sighed. "I've never heard of a woman not wanting those things. It sounds freeing, not having to follow society's expectations." She took Gen's hand and squeezed it. "I respect you for your bravery."

Evalia's kind words eased some of the hurt Gen felt after the argument with Cordyn.

They spoke for a while longer, mostly about Evalia's history, her desire for love, and her hatred for that handsome rogue, Cordyn Tallen. Criticizing Cordyn helped push the pain to the back of Gen's mind.

They'd fallen into a companionable silence when the door opened and an older woman came in, followed by several robed men and women.

"Welcome to the temple of Torr," the old woman said, bowing. "I am Mother Tull, the chosen of Torr." Her followers bowed as well, and chanted, "Blessed is Torr."

Gen felt stupid. Of course, the woman in the statue was Torr. Not her chosen goddess, but one she respected. The Torrian temple in Mintar offered beds to the needy, and there were one or two times when she was just starting out in the city when she thought about asking for charity there. In the end, she found work and scraped up enough money to rent a room.

"Thank you, Mother. I thank you for your hospitality."

"You aided Evalia, beloved of Torr. You are an honored guest here, for as long as you wish to stay."

Worry crept into Gen's mind. How long would she have to stay? She'd planned to help Evalia find Ezra, but she wouldn't be much help if she couldn't get out of bed for the next several weeks or months.

"You are most kind. Mother, I wonder if you have an estimate as to how long it will take for my wounds to heal?"

The old woman seemed to think for a moment before answering. "You will not be fully healed for many weeks. However, you may be able to walk by this evening. Our healer has made a tonic for you to help you regain your strength." She motioned to one of her followers to step forward. Gen recognized Initiate Brella, who came forward, holding a small carafe of blue liquid.

"It tastes horrible," the young woman said. "I'm sorry."

Gen took the carafe and downed the liquid in one gulp. It reminded her of a mint-infused winterplum wine that had sat out in the sun for too long. Not as bad as she'd feared, but not something she wished to make a habit of drinking.

"Barkeep, another," Gen called out. A few of the Torrians laughed.

I'm not Cordyn, but I'm still amusing.

"You'll need to drink the tonic morning and evening for the next few days," Mother Tull said. "You should avoid strenuous exercise, but you'll find some of your strength returning. You will, however, need to ease yourself back into strenuous activity."

Gen could already feel the tonic working. Her legs tingled, then her knees, and finally the tonic worked its way into her stomach. The tingling felt almost pleasant, and some of the tightness and pain around her wounds eased.

She inhaled deeply, chest tightening as she braced herself for excruciating pain that she was sure would follow. As she stood, she awed at the simple act of rising to her feet. Sweet gods, she could stand. The joy was short-lived, however; within moments, dizziness and exhaustion threatened to envelop her. She felt the steadying presence of Evalia holding her left arm and Initiate Brella grasping her right. Determined not to fall, Gen paused, taking slow breaths to steady herself. She lifted her left foot and brought it forward, then did the same with her right. Each step was a victory, the ability to walk an exhilarating triumph.

"That tonic is a miracle." Her voice filled with wonder.

"No, it's magic," Initiate Brella corrected, her voice tinged with both respect and awe. "Our healer is a mage. But no ordinary mage. He uses magic-infused water from ancient springs to brew the tonic. His magic is so powerful, you should heal completely over time, except for a scar."

Gen didn't mind the prospect of another scar. She already bore several on her arms and shoulders, and one on her neck. They added character, each a testament to past adventures. Her favorite was the long, winding mark on her left arm, a vivid reminder of her first run-in with highwaymen. It was a cherished memory despite the pain it had caused.

She recalled that day vividly. She had been on her first mission for the crown, tasked with delivering a message from King Thorace to one of the southern Dukes. Along the road, four men accosted her. She hadn't had Maralda then, her trusted sword, and the poor excuse for a weapon she wielded did her little to no favors. She remembered the terror and the sharp sting of the dagger as it slashed her arm. She had pulled herself together, driven by sheer will. She managed to kill two of the attackers, wound another, and send the last man fleeing for his life. Every scar told a story, and this one, the deep, jagged line on her arm, was a testament to her bravery and resilience. It was a story she carried with pride, a constant reminder of her strength and the moments that had shaped her into who she was now.

She continued walking forward, each step giving her more confidence in her abilities. After a few minutes, she could walk without assistance.

"I may be overconfident," she said, "but I'm feeling pretty good."

"Wait until the tonic fades," Mother Tull said. "I have a feeling you won't feel confident anymore."

"Be that as it may, I appreciate your efforts." She put her hand on Evalia's shoulder. "Now where are we with finding your brother? It's time to make a plan."

TEN

FROM THE TEMPLE DOORWAY, Tobias watched Tallen pack his supplies. The cowardly cur was leaving, abandoning Gen, his supposed companion, without a care in the world. A real man would have stayed to care for his friend, perhaps even offering his help to Evalia, a sweet woman in need. A surprising rage ignited deep within him—not because of the wrongs the Tallen family had done to his own, but because of how Tallen treated Gen and Evalia.

Gen was a fine woman. She cared for others, tried to help whenever possible, and put her own life in danger—and almost lost it—to save a woman she'd never met. Tobias hoped he would've done the same under similar circumstances, but he wasn't certain he would have stepped in to assist if Gen hadn't already charged into battle.

Within hours of knowing her, he'd decided that, even without the agreement with the shadowy man at the Golden Crown to protect Gen, he would have done everything in his power to keep her safe. When the mage attacked and wounded Gen, saving her was the only option. However, it was best she didn't know about the revenge.

Stepping out from the doorway, he approached Tallen. "Are you preparing for your journey, then?"

Tallen scowled, throwing his rucksack onto his horse's back. "Yes. I am ready to be on my way, far from here."

"What of your companion?"

"She'll remain here to convalesce. Unfortunately, the nature of our business is urgent, and I fear I must depart immediately. I have every faith in the Temple of Torr to care for Gen."

"If you're leaving today, I'll accompany you some of the way."

"Sir, don't feel compelled to accompany me out of a sense of duty. I assure you I need no escort on my travels."

"Of course not, sir. I would not dream of suggesting such a thing, especially since you have had so much success already on your journey. I merely wish to check on my family's estate, which is a day's ride north of here. Instead of us both making our journeys alone, I thought we could share the first leg. There is strength in numbers, you know. And Obanni soldiers along the road."

Tobias was under no illusions that Tallen liked him. Their disdain for the other was mutual. However, he didn't think Tallen planned to kill him.

Tallen would pay now. Revenge would be glorious. Tobias would have been willing to postpone his revenge if Tallen had decided to help Ezra. He'd even considered that Tallen might be redeemable. He was mistaken—the man was a Tallen after all—and now Tallen was on his way to complete his blasted mission. The perfect time for an accident to befall him. In a way, this suited Tobias better. Gen would never know what had happened. She'd assume Tallen either completed his mission and decided not to return or that he met misfortune along the road.

And Evalia? Gods, that complicated things. Tobias had gravitated to Evalia quickly, enamored by her beauty, and he'd found himself thinking about her at the most inopportune times. The way her hair flowed in the wind when she rode a horse, the quiet determination on her face when she cursed Tallen and vowed to find her brother. He was smitten. Of course, she had given him no encouragement—she'd made it clear how she felt about mages. He would most likely let the infatuation run its course and wither. Love, romance, and women as a whole made him uncomfortable. Brooding over dusty tomes in his library was much easier, dreaming of all the ways he could destroy Tallen's miserable life.

"Of course, my good man," Tallen said. "I would be most pleased to share a bit of the journey with you. The pleasure of your company, and indeed your wit, will make our time together full of merriment and diversion."

They departed soon after. Tobias brought only a small satchel filled with dried meat, fruit, and crusts of bread. Tallen's horse, laden with several bags of supplies, looked tired already. They rode north at a leisurely pace, though it was likely as fast as the weighted-down horse could travel. There was no conversation beyond grunts and the occasional pointed finger, which suited Tobias just fine. He had no desire to interact with Tallen. They just needed to ride a bit further from the temple, where there was less chance of anyone witnessing Tallen's demise.

They came to a pond, its crisp, clear water shining in the noonday sun. The horses drank from the pond, and Tallen washed his face. Tobias stayed on his horse, surveying the scene for a few moments before deciding this place was as good as any for murder. Tallen sat at the pond's edge, eating a handful of nuts, completely exposed and unaware.

It was time. Tobias dismounted and waded into the shallow pond. Standing in the water gave him the slightest bit more power, and he wanted to feel all of it. He wanted to overpower Tallen and leave the man bloody and screaming, begging for mercy—mercy that would never be given. His hands curled into the *Vida*. The droplets pooled on his fingertips. All he had to do was recite the *Issa* and send ice shards into Tallen's hands and feet, crippling him. He raised his fingers to strike.

He couldn't do it.

The landscape around the pond was too open. He could cripple Tallen now with shards to the ankles, but Tallen needed to know why he had to die. Tobias needed time to explain all the particulars. If travelers happened by, they'd spot them.

Either all would be lost, or he'd have to murder innocent travelers to keep his secret. No one, not even a mage, could murder a man in public and escape judgment.

Tallen will die, but I won't kill innocents. I'm a man of honor, not a wastrel.

He'd have to wait a while longer for revenge.

They rode on for another half hour until they saw smoke in the distance. Not the smoke of a raging fire decimating a forest or town, but the more controlled smoke of a camp. They were at least half an hour from the closest village, so this was an odd place for a camp. He looked back to see Tallen watching him.

"Smoke," Tallen said.

"We should be careful," Tobias said.

"Agreed. I'd prefer not to die today."

I can't promise that.

Tallen unsheathed his dagger. "Be quiet. Follow my lead."

They led their horses into the forest, tying them to a sturdy tree a few yards in. No one would be able to see the horses from the road, but they were not so deep into the forest that they would be impossible to find again.

Moving through the forest was difficult. Tobias rarely spent time outside the city, and he was not adept at navigating between the trees and avoiding rocks. Within the first one hundred yards, he stepped on four branches, fell once, and made altogether too much noise.

Tallen, conversely, seemed at home in the forest. He weaved between tree limbs with an agility and lightness of foot that Tobias did not expect from such a preening fop. Tobias cursed under his breath and watched the ground beneath him. He vowed not to step on any more sticks. He would be silent. A ghost. He stepped forward and groaned when he heard another stick crack.

"You're a veritable woodsman," Tallen said. "Never before have I witnessed someone with your skill at seeking out and finding every last available stick in the entire forest."

"I prefer the city."

"That is obvious." Tallen frowned in mock worry. "Tell me, have you ever left the road before when traveling outside of the city?"

"I haven't had the need to." Tobias crossed his arms. He didn't need to explain himself. Not to a man such as this. "At least not on foot. I've gone on horseback."

Tallen cocked his head to the side. "Riding a horse across a pasture doesn't count as exploring the wilderness, you know."

"I know that, damn it." Tobias gritted his teeth.

Stay calm. You can't kill him yet.

"I struggle to see you, majestically astride your horse, galloping through the forest."

"I never said I did that." Tobias enunciated each word with venomous clarity.

"No, indeed, you did not." Tallen took out a dagger, cutting a clump of dark berries off a nearby log. "These are rot berries. The name makes them sound ghastly, but they're really quite delicious." He offered a handful to Tobias, who took the berries, popping three of them into his mouth.

What the hell, I am hungry.

The berries were sweet, with a slight sour kick at the end, and reminded him of a citrus fruit in berry form.

"Seems like they deserve a better name," Tobias said with his mouth full. "They're delicious."

"They only grow on rotting wood, hence the name." Tallen pointed toward a fallen tree which had crashed down into several of the other trees, creating a small rot berry patch.

"I may start a rotting wood farm, then," Tobias said. "I wouldn't mind a whole harvest of these."

"That would be an excellent idea. Assuming we leave the forest alive, that is." Tallen winked.

Gods, this man and his winks. Perhaps I'll send the shards through his eyes when I kill him.

Tobias pressed his lips together and inhaled, trying to avoid yelling and seeing red. He had to stay calm. It wouldn't do to send ice shards through Tallen's pompous face right now. Not with these unknown men so close at hand.

"I'd prefer that." Tobias clasped his hands together and spoke slowly, pushing the anger down.

"Yes, it is my ardent hope as well."

Tallen led the way through a copse of small trees resplendent with purple blooms. Tobias admired the flowers while also feeling an intense desire to wretch.

Tobias wrinkled his nose. "Gods, those smell horrible."

"The forest is full of many wonderful things," Tallen said in a nasally voice, holding his nostril closed with one hand. "The smell of the yorn tree is not one of them."

They hurried past the offending tree, and Tobias breathed easier after they'd put some distance between them and the blossoms. The smoke was closer now. Tobias could hear men's voices, though he couldn't tell any specifics as to their accents or what they said.

"You may want to stay here," Tallen said, his voice a whisper. "With your natural affinity for noise, it might not be safe for you to get too close to our new friends."

"I'm coming with you." Tobias didn't trust Tallen enough to let him go forward without him. He needed to see for himself. "I may be loud, as you say, but if it comes to a fight, we can both agree that I have the superior skills. Unless you have hidden talents you'd like to disclose."

"Oh, I have many hidden talents, but they don't relate to combat." Tallen gave a wry smile. "If only that Evalia woman wasn't so irritating. She *is* pretty."

Tobias did not respond. If he spoke, he would give away his feelings toward Evalia, and Tallen was the last person who needed to know about that.

He looked through the trees, wincing at the thought of listening to Tallen's complaints every time he made the slightest noise. "Fine. I'll wait here." He sat on a tree stump. "Try not to die."

Yet.

Tallen put his finger to his lips coyly. "Keep it down back here. Maybe you should refrain from moving at all." He turned and disappeared behind a billowing oak.

Tobias sat on a dry patch of ground by the oak, feeling the rough bark against his back. He didn't know how long he'd have to wait, and sitting alone in the forest made no sense. If he knew how to climb a tree, he would have found a perch in the oak.

He would kill Tallen today, no matter what they found at the camp. After they moved on from the camp and whatever awaited them there, he'd wait until they were due to part ways. Then, he'd reveal who he was, the monster Tallen's father had been, and how destroying the Tallen bloodline was the only solution. He'd tell Tallen he'd expected it to be difficult to kill him, but after meeting him and realizing what an ass he was, Tobias was actually excited. The world needed fewer people like Tallen. Killing him was a service to everyone. Finally, he'd avenge his mother and Master Renedian.

Wrapped up in his plans, he failed to notice Tallen returning until the man spoke.

"You are not going to enjoy what I have to tell you. Things have, to put it lightly, gone to shit."

"Well, who in Kirth's name is it, man?"

Tallen shushed him again with a finger to his lips. Tobias wanted to cut off those damned fingers. Maybe he would.

"Not so loud," Tallen said. "We've come upon old friends."

"Obanni? The men who took Ezra? Good, I'll rip their throats out."

"Those men, yes, but it's not good, because they brought three hundred of their closest friends with them."

"I don't understand." How could the Obanni have brought so many troops into the center of Rosenfel? It was one thing to skirt the border, but this was an act of war. "We're in Rosenfel."

"Indeed, we are. That's the troubling part. Oban and Rosenfel are not allies, as far as we know, and famously don't care for one another. And yet Obanni troops are openly camping along the road, three days' march from the border." Tallen paused, as if he was hesitant to mention something. "The even more troubling part is that they have captives. At least fifty of them. All children, from what I can tell."

"I need to see them." Tobias didn't know why he needed to, just that it was something that had to happen. He stomped around the tree, heading to the camp.

"What are you doing?" Tallen asked in a harsh whisper. "You're making so much noise, the Obanni will think an opposing army is descending on them."

"Maybe I am an opposing army."

"You have delusions of grandeur, at least."

Tobias didn't respond. He kept walking, ducking under a thorny branch and then came to a halt as the makeshift wooden walls of the camp came into view. Tallen had underestimated the number of troops. There had to be at least four hundred, most of whom wore the full dress red and black Obanni uniforms. However, at the north end of the camp, next to two massive ballistas, a group of men constructed a large complex of tents. Those men were dressed in the same piecemeal armor as the men who'd taken Ezra.

Kirth. Behind the tent, a group of children sat in the mud, dressed in dirty blue and red rags, their arms bound behind their backs, dirty pieces of cloth in all their mouths. Blue and red.

"Sweet godsdamn Kirth," Tobias whispered. "They're all mages."

"How do you know?" Tallen glanced skeptically at Tobias.

"Their rags," he bit out. "They're mage robes. Torn and dirtied, but mage robes all the same."

They sat in the trees for almost half an hour, watching the camp, before either of them spoke. Tallen finally broke the silence.

"You know, there's not much the two of us can do against this many men."

"I'd like to walk right in and kill them all," Tobias said, refusing to look away from the camp.

"And I'd like to spend three days in bed with an Obanni princess. I don't think either of us will get what we want. At least not today."

"How can you be such an ass?" Tobias had to fight off the urge to send shards into Tallen's smug mouth. "There are children imprisoned right over there, and you're making jokes."

Tallen pursed his lips. "It would be a good idea for you to move further away. Then, at least, you can reprimand me for my jokes without alerting the entire army."

"I can't abandon them," Tobias said. His jaw hurt from how tightly he clenched it, and he realized he was grinding his teeth. "You may have no honor, but you must understand that some of us do."

"You can't save any mages if you're captured. And I have my mission, after all."

"Yes, your godsdamn mission. It's all you care about."

Tallen glared at him. "Sir, I'll gladly let you thrash me and call me a wastrel once we have relocated to a safer distance. I will be moving away from the camp now. If you wish to stay here, then to Kirth with you."

Tallen turned and stalked through the forest. Tobias forced himself to follow, though it took all his strength to pull away from the camp. He told himself that he could leave this once because he would be back to save the mage children.

Once they made it back to the road, they traveled north for an hour until they arrived at a fork in the road, one way going north into Trunel and the other further to the west of Rosenfel.

"That's your path," Tobias said. "My journey north will have to wait. I must return to the temple and inform Evalia of Ezra's situation. And then make plans as to how I'm going to stop those bastards."

Tallen hesitated. "You may want to get some reinforcements before you go in."

"You mean you don't think I can defeat four hundred men on my own?" Tobias asked, feigning shock.

"You are powerful, but no one is *that* powerful." Tallen frowned. "Also, your anger blinds you. I always find it easier to plan when I can think clearly."

Tobias snorted. "You'll forgive me if I don't take advice from you regarding planning."

"Such is your prerogative, sir." Tallen nodded politely. "Thank you for the pleasure of your company."

"Goodbye. And good luck on your journey." *To Kirth*. Tobias planned to let Tallen travel a few hundred yards down the path, and then do what he must.

"You as well. You know, Stinton, I may not care for you as a person, and I despise your sanctimonious attitude—"

"Is there a compliment in this or just insults?"

"I'm getting there. You're a prick, and I'd love to punch you right in your wrinkled little nose. However, you've been helpful to us, and you saved Gen's life. Please watch over her. I'm most likely not coming back." He reached out his hand to shake Tobias's.

No, I don't suppose you are.

Tobias stared at Tallen's hand, making no move to shake it. "I will be a better friend to her than you could ever be."

"Yes, I believe that." He moved his hand away. "Farewell, sir." Pulling on his horse's reins, he set off down the path.

He wouldn't be traveling long.

But Tallen stopped only a hundred paces down the path. He sat on his horse in the middle of the road, not moving for several seconds. Then the insufferable man turned his head.

"Stinton!" His voice was raw with emotion. Fear? "You need to come here. Now."

"What is it? Did you have some last witty insult you forgot to leave with me?" Tobias asked.

"Gods," Tallen said. He put his head in his hands.

"Dammit, man, I tire of your so-called wit." Tobias spurred his horse forward, glaring down the path.

When he reached the other man, Tobias pulled his horse to an abrupt stop. His stomach churned, the sweetness of rot berries mingling with bile as he fought the urge to retch.

A tall rot berry bush grew from a fallen log, the pink of the berries intermingling with the bloody stains on the wood. Two bodies, a woman and a child, dried blood crusting over the holes in their foreheads. Shard-sized holes. The woman lay over the child.

"She must have tried to protect her son," Cordyn said.

"Mages did this," Tobias said. "But why?"

"We've already met one murderous mage along these paths," Tallen said. "We can assume he has friends."

"Kirth take them all." Tobias dismounted, kicking a rock off the path in anger. "If you'll help me gather the bodies and place them on my horse, I'll take them back to the temple."

Tallen paused, clearly conflicted by something. "Place one of the bodies on my horse."

Tobias stared at him. "Don't dishonor the dead," he spat.

"I don't plan to." Cordyn's face was more serious than Tobias had ever seen it. "I'm coming back to the temple." He spoke slowly, as if the words were difficult to form. "With you."

"What? Why?"

"We need to warn the others," Cordyn said, picking up the child's corpse. A boy of no more than ten. "And we have children to save."

"What about your mission?" Tobias lifted the woman's body onto his own horse.

"Kirth take my mission." Tallen placed the child's body on his horse and climbed into the saddle. "This is more important. An Obanni military camp in Rosenfel. Young mages taken captive. Some of them killed. I can't just leave and pretend none of it exists." He paused, his eyes thick with emotion. "I'm not a monster, Stinton."

No, at this moment you're not.

He supposed Tallen could live a little longer.

Part Two
The Scheme

If one should wish to become a mage
They first must become sanctimonious
Parading, arms raised, from here to there
As if they rule over the rest of us

If one should wish to travel with a mage
One should invest in a good deal of wine
For they'll moan and complain and ruin your days
Until for Kirth's peace in death you will pine

There certainly is nothing worse than a mage
They're buffoons, their wives must be unsatisfied
If I must spend one more day with their kind
Indeed it is more than I ever could abide.

--Cordyn Tallen

ELEVEN

As Gen climbed into bed for the evening, she marveled at how drastically she had improved. By the evening's end, she felt almost normal. She'd wanted to climb on a horse and go for a ride at dusk but decided against it after catching Mother Tull's disapproving glances. The mother warned that Gen might relapse and the pain could return, but with the tonic at hand, Gen felt invincible. She took the small flask of tonic Mother Tull had given her and drank. The tonic eased any lingering pain, and she wondered if it would help her sleep. It made her feel like she could sprint faster than a horse, carry more than an ox—maybe it even influenced her dreams. She hoped to make it through the night without severe pain, but wished for something more.

As she was finally drifting off to sleep, she heard a commotion outside—yelling, clattering hooves, and doors slamming. She rose from the bed, feeling only the slightest twinge in her abdomen as she stood. Taking no chances, she grabbed Maralda.

The noise could have been initiates of Torr engaging in drunken revelry, though she hadn't seen many signs that the Torrians were merrymakers. Whenever she saw them, they were either praising Torr, doing their tasks around the temple and surrounding farms, eating, or sleeping. However, even religious sorts needed a break from time to time.

Gen missed her wine. Ever since drinking the tonic, she hadn't felt hungry or thirsty much, if at all. Even though she missed the wine, she wasn't sure she could physically swallow any without retching.

The scene she found in the temple courtyard was the last thing she expected. Tobias stood next to his horse, looking grim and speaking with Mother Tull. Her voice was shrill. Gen knew whatever news Tobias brought would not be favorable.

Next to Tobias, looking far too calm as he consoled the distressed mother, was *Cordyn*. There was no way he could have completed the mission in less than a day—he wouldn't have even made it to Trunel. What had happened? For all his whoring and rakish ways, Cordyn had always prided himself on being a man of his word.

"Godsdamn," she whispered. But the worries could wait. Her friend was back, he hadn't abandoned them, and Gen wanted to hug him. She ran across the courtyard and threw her arms around him, picking him up in her exuberance.

"Gen, put me down." Cordyn's voice was full of good humor, so Gen didn't put him down.

"You came back!"

"Well, yes," he said, fighting for breath. "You could hardly hold me prisoner in your arms if I weren't here."

Gen released him. She felt the slightest twinge at the site of her wound, no pain.

Once his feet were back on solid ground, Cordyn hugged Gen back and said with a sincere tone she'd not heard often from him, "Gen, I'm pleased to see you."

"I thought you were off to complete our mission."

"I was an ass, shockingly enough."

"Yes, you were," she said.

"I feel bad enough about myself without you agreeing." His eyes stayed sad.

She hugged him again, hoping to squeeze the sadness out. "You're an ass, but I'm so happy to see you."

"There's something terrible afoot," Tobias said.

Gen released Cordyn, who looked at her with a grim expression.

"Compared to this, our sham of a mission isn't important in the least. The king will want to hear of this."

Gen's heart sank.

"We found the boy." Cordyn motioned to Evalia. "Your brother."

"Is he alive?" Evalia asked.

"Yes, as far as I know. What I should say is that we most likely found the boy. We found several boys, and some girls as well—"

"Cordyn," Gen broke in. "What are you talking about?"

"We found an Obanni military camp," Tobias said. "Four hundred soldiers, at least. They had captives. Children. Mage children."

"And one dead child," Cordyn added.

Gods, for an intelligent man, Cordyn can be an idiot sometimes.

"I'm sure it's not Ezra," Gen said in her most soothing voice.

Evalia shivered.

"No, it wasn't your brother," Cordyn said in a matter-of-fact way. "Never fear. We found his mother's body with him. Brought them back to be buried."

"His mother?" Evalia's fists tightened. "I'm going to kill them."

Cordyn averted his eyes and nervously adjusted his hat.

Gods, you can't help but make things worse.

Gen fought with the urge to smack Cordyn across the face. "What are they doing in Rosenfel?"

"An excellent question, one that we've been wondering ourselves," Cordyn said.

"I don't care why they're here," Evalia said. She stood straight, regal almost. "They could be here to overthrow the Imperium, and I wouldn't give it a second thought."

Tobais straightened his posture into a heroic pose. "We'll save him, Evalia. I won't rest until we do."

"Noble sentiments," Cordyn said, "though meaningless. Rest or no rest, we need a plan. A frontal attack, of course, won't work. There are four of us. Raising an army large enough to take on the Obanni forces will take more time than we have."

"We could recruit some of the Torrians," Tobias said.

"If we needed to pray the Obanni to death, perhaps." Cordyn said. "As it is, asking those with no combat experience to assault a military camp is a superb way to kill all our friends."

"Look, Tallen—" Tobias began.

"What about Topper?" Evalia asked.

Cordyn smirked. "Yes, the mute, scrawny twelve-year-old would be such a help to us in combat. He might kill one-fourth of a man."

"That's not what I meant," Evalia said, staring at Cordyn, her disdain for the man clear in the fire of her eyes.

"I sent him back to Dramin this morning," Tobias said. "There was little for him to do here, and he was feeling anxious for home."

"It seems our merry band of four and a quarter is down to merely four."

Evalia glared daggers. "Stop making jokes. There's nothing amusing about the situation. If you'd listen to me, maybe you'd find I have some helpful ideas."

Cordyn made no outward acknowledgment of Evalia's outburst. Gen wondered how he could be so good-humored. "You, madam, pardon my language, are not a damned soldier. Neither is the boy. And I can acknowledge my own shortcomings. I'm not so much better."

"I'm shocked you can admit to anything less than perfect about yourself." Evalia turned away from him, blowing out a breath.

"Yes, I have my wits, madam," Cordyn said, placing a hand on his chest, "but I am not a swordsman."

"I think you are more confident in your wits than you should be."

"Let's focus on the matter at hand," Gen said. She knew Cordyn and Evalia disliked one another, but listening to them argue was exhausting.

"What we have decided so far," Tobias said, "is that we cannot fight through four hundred Obanni, some of whom are mages. We can assume a frontal assault is out of the question. What is our plan, then?"

"I do indeed have a plan," Cordyn said. "We'll disguise ourselves, infiltrate the Obanni camp, befriend the soldiers there, and then free the mage children from under their noses. Simple really. However, we'll need some supplies."

Cordyn was either brilliant or insane. Gen rarely had confidence in his plans: full of secret identities, play-acting, and subterfuge, and not enough swords.

But this one had to be the worst yet.

"There's only four of us," Tobias said. "I still feel it would be better to recruit forces."

"And I still feel that we don't have several months to do so."

"What will we do once we infiltrate?" Gen asked. "Assuming we successfully make it into the camp, what's the plan, then?"

Cordyn shrugged. "I don't know yet. We'll need to see what kind of security they have, and the only way to do that is to find a way into the camp."

"I agree with Mr. Tallen," Evalia said, her voice shaking.

Cordyn bowed to her. "Thank you, madam."

"I still think you're a reprobate."

"As do I, madam. As do I." He took off his hat, scratching at the side of his head above the temple. "Now to business. In order to infiltrate the camp, there are some items we'll need to acquire."

He listed off the supplies he'd needed, a motley collection to say the least. No more than Gen had expected.

First, Cordyn needed a horse. Not the horse he already had, but a warhorse.

"My horse is not nearly large enough for our purposes. We'll require a warhorse; the strongest one you can find."

Tobias grumbled something about people making do with what they had, but Cordyn pressed on. "I will need a dark blue wool coat. It can be new or old, but it must be wool with no embellishments."

Gen inhaled. Gods, her neck and shoulders were wound tight as a dancing girl's corset. She focused on her breathing; some of the tension eased. In a village of one hundred souls, there had to be a plain, dark blue coat somewhere. It had to be easy enough to find.

"We'll need sacks of grain and a cart to carry the grain."

"We already have a cart," Tobias said.

"True. Then we just need the grain."

"The farmers aren't just going to give us their grain," Evalia said. "That's their livelihood."

"No, I assume we'll have to purchase it. No matter." Cordyn looked at Tobias. "You are a merchant of sorts, so you'll gather the grain."

"I'm sorry," Tobias said, scowling. "I didn't realize that we'd appointed you our captain. I will have nothing to do with this plan."

Growing tired of their constant bickering, Gen opted to express her annoyance.

"We know you don't like each other," she said. "That's fine. You can glare at each other all day and dream of the other's demise. Could we please focus on the task at hand?"

"Of course," Cordyn said. "I would be glad to. We also need charcoal. Only a small amount. A pound or so."

"How will charcoal help us?" Evalia asked. "I don't understand."

"Humor me, madam. I assure you; I have an excellent reason."

Evalia harrumphed. "I think you're just making up supplies."

"And finally," Cordyn said, ignoring her. "I'll need a whip."

"A whip?" Gen asked. "What for?"

"For whipping someone, naturally."

Cordyn's supply requests seemed random. What use would charcoal, grain, or a whip be? They couldn't attack soldiers with a whip, charcoal was useless for anything but artwork—and they wouldn't be painting portraits for the Obanni—and the cart of grain would slow their journey. However, Gen had spent enough time with Cordyn to know each seemingly random item would come together to form a vital element of his plan. Cordyn's plans were never simple, but she couldn't argue that they weren't successful, more often than not.

After they finished their conference, Gen had a moment alone with Cordyn.

He regarded her with an earnest expression and asked if she would go with Evalia to speak to Mother Tull. "Evalia knows the woman, so she'd be the best person to go. Alas, she despises me, so I should keep my distance." He wrinkled his nose. "The Mother has no love for me either."

"If you think it's necessary."

"I don't think Evalia would knowingly do anything to hurt our plans, but she's quite inexperienced. You and I know better when it comes to these matters." Cordyn lowered his voice and gave Gen a pained look. "There's something else I need you to do. One last supply I've just decided on."

"Torr keep you," Mother Tull said. "What can I do for you, my children?" Gen and Evalia sat in Mother Tull's chambers, a gray and austere room adorned with statues of Torr. A dark oak desk stood against one wall, accompanied by three wooden chairs without cushions. Gen assumed the mother would have nicer accommodations than her followers, but the bed looked ancient, covered by a threadbare blanket. Compared to this, Gen's own room was a haven of comfort.

"Mother," Evalia said. "We're planning a rescue for Ezra. We have a list of supplies and would appreciate any help you could give us."

"We Torrians have very little, except for what Torr bestows on us, but I will assist you however I can. However, I worry about you, my child. I will pray to Torr for your safety, but I fear four individuals cannot confront hundreds with any hope of success." Mother Tull had a resigned sadness to her voice, like she knew she wouldn't convince Evalia to abandon the plan, no matter what she said.

"Would any of your people be willing to help us?" Evalia asked. "Ezra and I would be grateful, and you've always been so good to us."

Mother Tull frowned. "We are not fighters, dear. We can give you supplies, but I cannot ask my people to put themselves in harm's way. It would be suicide."

"I understand, Mother." Evalia's voice went icy. Gen felt sure that Evalia did not understand at all. "You must do what you feel right."

The room endured a few moments of weighted silence before Gen, feeling the awkwardness in the air, broke the tension.

"The first item is a warhorse. Do you know where we could find one?"

Mother Tull shook her head. "I do not know of any in the village, but you might check with Baronet Trunbelch. He lives in the manor to the east of town. He's not a pleasant man, but if anyone in the area has battle-ready horses, it's him."

"Next, we'll need sacks of grain."

Mother Tull's frown deepened. "I cannot in good conscience give away our food."

"We can pay." Gen rummaged her pockets and pulled forth the coin purse Gillus had given her, lighter now after purchasing supplies—and wine—in Dramin.

The mother seemed unimpressed, and the frown remained. She pressed her lips together tightly. "Money will not feed us in the winter. The farmers in the village may have grain they'll sell to you."

"We also need charcoal, perhaps two blocks."

The mother's expression lightened. "That's something I can provide. I'll send word for one of my initiates to gather some blocks to bring you."

Gen nodded in thanks. "We require a whip. A cat-o'-nine-tails."

"Good Torr," Mother Tull said, gasping. "We have nothing of that sort here, or anywhere in the village."

"Do you know where we could find one? Perhaps with Baronet Trunbelch?"

"I doubt even he has an instrument of torture. He's a troublesome man, but not violent. We have whips here and there for the horses, but nothing so vicious as what you seek."

"We'll take a common whip, then," Evalia said. She rolled her eyes at Gen. "Mr. Tallen will just have to make do with that."

"I'll have my initiates find a few whips and have those and the charcoal sent your way."

"Oh, one last request," Gen said. "I'd almost forgotten. Do you have any shears?"

The only shears Mother Tull could find were the ones shepherds used on flocks, but Gen supposed they'd do well enough for whatever task Cordyn threw at them.

Gen's tension eased at the thought of her and Cordyn shearing sheep to prepare for a rescue mission. Maybe they would disguise themselves as shepherds, though she had no idea why the Obanni troops would allow a group of shepherds into their camp.

As she and Evalia walked back to the dining hall where Cordyn waited, Evalia hummed a lilting tune. Not Gen's usual style, but the haunting melody captivated her.

"What is that song?" she asked. "I've never heard it before. It's beautiful."

"My mother used to sing it to Ezra and me." Evalia brushed a strand of hair off her face. "Our neighbors would stop to listen to her sing. Always slow, mournful tunes." She smiled ruefully. "I became so tired of them that I'd find excuses to leave the house and avoid hearing them. After her death, it was all I wanted to listen to. I sing it to Ezra most evenings to calm him down. His emotions are—I'm not sure how to describe it—unfiltered."

"How so?"

"If he is angry, there is nothing in the world but that anger. If he's sad, all positive aspects of life disappear for him. He feels things more acutely than I ever could, but he has not yet learned how to push through emotions. They consume him. Perhaps they always will."

Those godsdamn Obanni bastards.

Gen winced at the thought of what hell Ezra was enduring as a captive. Each indignity must be tearing the boy apart. She did not mention these thoughts to Evalia. She assumed the woman already knew and Gen didn't want to cause her more distress.

"We'll find him," she said instead. She patted Evalia on the shoulder, a gesture that was intended to be reassuring but ended up condescending. "And when we do, Maralda and I will kill a lot of Obanni."

"Maralda?"

"My sword. Oh gods, I'm so sorry." She unsheathed Maralda and presented her to Evalia. "I can't believe I didn't introduce you. Evalia, this is Maralda. She's the best sword a woman could have."

"Nice to meet you," Evalia said. She reached out and mimed shaking hands with Maralda. "I'm sure we'll be fast friends."

When Gen told Cordyn about the outcome of the meeting, he took a quill, dipped it into an inkwell, and wrote something into a notebook Gen hadn't seen before.

"As I expected," Cordyn said. "I shall go into the village and make fast friends with the farmers. They will love me so much they'll give us all their supplies and thank us for taking them."

"You obviously don't know any of the farmers here," Evalia said.

Cordyn brushed a hand through his hair, and his face faltered. "No, but you do, madam, and some of them may know you. Would you perchance accompany me into the town?"

Not lifting her eyes to Cordyn, Evalia shrugged, but said nothing.

"It would be helpful if you could do so," Gen said.

Evalia still refused to look at Cordyn. "Of course, Gen. I would be happy to help you. I'll go to my quarters and change clothes." She exited the dining hall, never once glancing in Cordyn's direction.

"Oh gods," Cordyn said.

"Your trip to the village will be interesting. You may have met your match here, friend."

"I'm not sure if she's going to stick a dagger in my back, trample me with horses, or call me all sorts of names while stamping her foot. No matter which she chooses, it won't be pleasant."

It won't be pleasant for you. I think it's hilarious.

TWELVE

The village had seen better days. Houses on the verge of collapse from rotting wood, an abandoned, boarded up well in the village square, and more pigs than people, as far as Cordyn could tell.

"It's lovely," Cordyn said as he walked past a steaming pile of pig dung. "I may retire here when I'm through adventuring."

Evalia said nothing. She'd been silent on their walk from the temple into the village proper, looking at her feet and ignoring Cordyn, which was fantastic. He enjoyed the company of pretty women, yes, but only when they were pleasant companions. Evalia had the personality of a bad-tempered termite.

For all her faults, however, Evalia understood the villagers and might even know some of them. Cordyn, while he knew how to talk to people and convince them of things, wasn't sure how to connect to simple Rosenfellian villagers.

They passed by a general store—closed, of course. Next door to the store was a dressmaker's shop, which had a lamp burning in the window.

"Wait," Evalia said. She stood outside the general store, arms crossed, a troubled expression on her face. "I wanted to talk." She brushed a hand through her hair, pulling the curls behind her ears. "It's not been easy since Father died, and I took a lot of my anger out on you." She seemed hesitant, as if it hurt her to speak kindly to him.

"Don't be silly," Cordyn said.

Oh gods, more emotion.

He preferred the sullen lute-swinging Evalia over the talk-about-her-feelings version. "I enjoy nothing more than a thwack to the head by a beautiful woman, especially after a thorough emasculation." He smirked, crossing his arms to match her.

As she took a deep breath, her eyes narrowed. "I'm trying to apologize. I know you had your own affairs, and it means a lot that you have put them on hold to help find my brother."

"Of course. As I told Stinton, I'm not a monster." He shifted away from her.

"I did not imply you were a monster," she said, throwing her hands in the air. "I would say that to you outright."

Arms out in annoyance, he gave her a supercilious smirk. "And yet everything you say and the way you interact with me tells me you feel I am."

"I just want to apol—"

"I don't need any dresses." Cordyn pointed to the carved wooden sign which read: B. Abbott, Clothier for The Discerning Lady. "But perhaps the dressmaker can give us an idea of who in town would be best to talk to."

"I—" Evalia sputtered. She looked from Cordyn to the sign and back. "I suppose," she said.

"Are there enough "discerning ladies" in a village this small to support a dress shop?"

"There're hundreds of villages nearby, and the closest city is several hours away," Evalia said. "We have to buy clothing somewhere."

"And you are quite the discerning lady." Cordyn opened the dress shop door, holding it for Evalia. "Perhaps too much so. After you, madam."

They entered a sea of pinks, violets, and yellows. Fabric lay everywhere, covering much of the floor, a desk, and four chairs. Cordyn saw no completed dresses, though there were several works in progress hanging on the walls. Amid the chaos sat a woman around Cordyn's age with raven hair falling past her waist. She wore a simple green cotton dress, and yet Cordyn felt unable to move his eyes away from her. She was radiant, her skin pale as if she never left the dress shop to go out into the sun and had a look of extreme concentration on her rouge-free face.

"Good afternoon," Cordyn said.

Surprise rippled through the dressmaker's body. She dropped the patches of burgundy fabric she held. Her eyes met Cordyn's gaze.

"I'm so sorry, sir. I was lost in thought." She stood and curtsied. "I'm Beatrice. What can I do for you?" She moved about the shop, removing the piles of fabric from two of the chairs so Cordyn and Evalia could sit.

"No matter, my lady. You have quite a lovely shop." He bowed, ever the gentleman. "A lovely shop with a charming proprietor."

He heard Evalia let out a long breath.

"Thank you," Beatrice said, curtsying. "Would you like me to make a dress for your wife?"

His wife? Oh gods, she meant Evalia. He shuddered. He hoped he would never anger the gods to where he would be punished in that way.

"My *sister* and I are passing through the village and find our-selves in need of provisions. Sacks of grain, especially. We had hoped you would direct us to an honest local farmer who could assist us." The dressmaker's gaze dropped to the floor. "Of course, after seeing your lovely shop, I'm sure my sister would be honored to wear one of your dresses. Isn't that right, Evalia?"

"I do wear dresses. That much is true." She glared at Cordyn. "However, I am not your sister."

Beatrice stared at them in confusion.

"I meant sister of Torr," Cordyn said. "We're all brothers and sisters under Torr, are we not?"

"Praise Torr," Beatrice said, keeping her eyes fixed on Cordyn.

Evalia huffed. "I'm not—"

"She's not taken her vows yet, but Evalia here is considering becoming an Initiate of Torr." Cordyn gave Evalia an admiring look. "She's quite selfless and *rarely says a word.*"

"He's just trying to sleep with you," Evalia blurted out.

"Evalia," he snapped.

Godsdammit, woman.

Cordyn shrugged toward Beatrice, a contrite expression on his face. "I assure you, I'm trying to do much more than that."

Beatrice broke out into a wide grin. "Indeed," she said, twirling a lock of hair that fell down across her cheek.

"If you, dear lady, could help us with the grain, I shall surely return to order several dresses, and enjoy your excellent company." He winked and was rewarded with a giggle in return.

"Alain McDougal has the largest farm around. He's just up the hill. He should have grain for sale."

Cordyn bowed. "Thank you, Beatrice. I shall most assuredly return to thank you further for your help."

Evalia scowled. "You're a damned scoundrel," she whispered to Cordyn. Then, in a louder voice. "Mr. Tallen, we should get on with the task at hand. Thank you, Beatrice."

"Until we meet again, Beatrice." He winked again. He'd never relied overmuch on winking for his seductions in the past—usually it was just his favorite way to annoy Gen—but Beatrice seemed to enjoy it. "I will count the hours."

Beatrice's gaze wavered, as if she'd remembered something unpleasant, but then she winked back at Cordyn. "Mr. Tallen, please call on me if you require further assistance. I look forward to our meeting again."

As they walked toward the McDougal farm, Evalia scolded him. "I can't believe you. My brother might be dead, and you're flirting? We don't have time for this." Her face flushed, and she kicked a thin tree branch off the path.

"Not at the moment, no. However, once we complete our tasks, there may be some moments of leisure."

"She's married, you know." She pointed toward the dress shop. "To the mayor."

"That's not stopped me before."

In fact, it's often preferred.

This time, she kicked several rocks and a weed that sprung up through a crack in the path. "You have no honor."

He placed his palms on his chest in mock distress. "You wound me."

"I only wish I had a sword so that I could do so."

She stomped forward and spent the next few minutes walking twenty paces in front of him. When they passed an empty iron pigpen, she turned back around.

"I'm sorry. Let's try this again. I've let my emotions get the better of me." She took a breath. "I wanted to thank you. I shouldn't have hit you in the inn. Those men may have killed you, and your death would have been on my hands."

He scoffed. "Come now, I had those men right where I wanted them."

"You certainly seemed to have the upper hand. You run away from conflict quite well."

He regarded her with a withering glance. "Madam, you seem to struggle with apologies. Usually, one says 'I'm sorry, forgive me' without further insulting the person they wronged." His lips curled into a cruel smile. "And then one often shuts up about it so that they can get on with their day."

"You're impossible."

"You're worse."

"Sweet Torr's lips," she swore, stomping ahead of him.

The McDougal farm looked more prosperous than the rest of the village; stalks of corn glistened in the morning sun, a group of plump sheep grazed in a nearby pasture, and the farmhouse, a white and black cottage with a thatched roof, looked freshly painted.

A tanned man with a face wrinkled by weather and age stood in front of the house, clipping branches off a row of tomato bushes that were bursting with fruit. The tomatoes themselves were round and juicy-looking, and Cordyn wondered if the farmer would part with a few of them. He wanted to grab one and take a bite, but he resisted the urge. The farmer would be more willing to do business with them if Cordyn didn't steal the man's tomatoes.

"What?" the man asked.

Ah, such scintillating conversation.

"Beatrice told us you might have grain for sale," Evalia said.

"Forty crowns a sack."

I guess we'll haggle, then.

Cordyn had fifty crowns in his coin purse, and he needed two sacks of grain.

"Sir, I notice your crops look quite fine. You have admirable skill."

The farmer returned to clipping the tomato bushes.

"Your animals look hearty, as well."

The farmer peered at Cordyn, holding the clippers out of front of him, as if the clippers were a spear. "Yeah, I'm a damned excellent farmer. The emperor should give me a title. And his daughter's hand in marriage. It's still forty crowns a sack."

Evalia crossed her arms. "My father did business in this town. Rufus Whitefell. You may have known him?"

"Aye."

"He died last summer. My brother and I have struggled to survive after losing him."

McDougal looked at her with no pity in his eyes. "We've all faced hardships."

"You have weathered them well, then," Evalia said. "Your cows look healthy, plump, and full of milk. Your corn and tomatoes thrive. You either have excellent soil everywhere on your property or you have a mage who helps you distribute water."

"What's it to you?" McDougal's demeanor began to slip.

"My brother is a mage." Evalia's eyes bore into McDougal. "He's in trouble, and we need grain. Please. Beatrice in the village told us you were a kind man."

The farmer stayed silent for a moment. Cordyn could see the man's eyelids fluttering as he thought. "Twenty-five crowns a bag."

"Done," Evalia said. She gestured at Cordyn to step forward. "Pay the man."

"I would have haggled him down eventually," Cordyn said as they walked back to the village

"If you say so."

"I'm impressed. I didn't take you for the agricultural type."

"I'm not. I assure you, I did not know what I was saying. However, most of the successful farms around here have mages who help, so I made an educated guess." She gave him a wry smile. "Also, I've found that people will overlook your lack of knowledge if you're praising them enough."

Cordyn smiled back despite himself. Evalia was clever. Not as clever as him, but someone who could at least attempt to match wits with him. He may have written her off too soon.

"So, we just need a horse and a whip, then?"

"Yes, it seems I'll have to pay Baronet Trunbelch a visit. Do you know anything about him?"

She considered this for a moment. "I don't think I've heard the name before today. He can't be influential."

"I don't need him to be influential, just stupid and in possession of a horse. The whip, I can make do without. I must have the horse."

Stinton waited for them outside of the temple. He whittled a thick twig with his dagger, glaring at the stick as he skinned it. Cordyn hadn't realized Stinton had any skills beyond shooting ice and being annoying, but he marveled as the man worked. Cordyn was learning all about his companions today. Soon they would all be embracing and calling each other their bosom friends, no doubt.

"That stick will slay many Obanni," Cordyn said.

Stinton stopped whittling and looked up at Cordyn and Evalia. "Well?" he asked. "Can we get started?"

"Soon. I have one more trip to make. Stinton, my horse seemed tired this morning. I think he needs a rest. I'll need to borrow yours."

The journey to Baronet Trunbelch's manor took only a few minutes on horseback. Cordyn ventured alone. Gen had pleaded to accompany him, insisting she could provide protection and help persuade the Baronet, even if it meant using force. He refused, wanting her to rest and regain strength for the more difficult times ahead. Besides, he understood aristocrats. Violence seldom achieved the desired outcome. Instead, you had to manipulate the bastards into believing they *wanted* to help, either out of the goodness of their hearts or for their financial gain.

Cordyn rode into the courtyard's manor, clad in a tan frock coat of fine wool, complemented by a burgundy waistcoat and trousers. His low-cut, light brown leather shoes matched his coat perfectly. In this attire, he would fit seamlessly into the finest circles of the Rosenfellian court, so he had no concern about a provincial baronet denying him entry. He'd left his bicorne at the temple, aware it clashed with the aristocratic look. While ladies found the captain's hat rakish and mysterious, he doubted Baronet Trunbelch would share the same sentiment.

The manor itself was a study in contrasts. Majestic mahogany doors and pristine white shutters adorned a weathered stone frame. The courtyard was a muddy mess, overrun with pigs trampling the last few patches of grass. Several shovels leaned against the wide entrance doors. As he moved the shovels aside and rapped the door knocker, Cordyn noticed the crumbling stone near the entrance.

Perhaps Baronet Trunbelch needs masonry tools more than shovels.

"Who in godsdamn Kirth?" a man's booming voice yelled. "I'll kill you bastards." The man slurred his words.

This just got a lot easier or a hell of a lot harder. Hopefully, he stays an angry drunk.

With a cheerful drunk, you never knew when they were going to come out of their haze, realize the seriousness of the situation at hand, and become angry. Angry drunks were already ready to run you through with a rapier, so you just had to focus on appeasing them, appealing to their greed, and stroking their egos.

Cordyn straightened his back and lifted his jaw, hoping to give off an air of military training. He puffed out his chest and brought his heels together, hands at his side. He'd never been in the military, so had no inkling if he stood correctly or not, but the drunk Baronet Trunbelch, unless he was secretly an acting Rosenfellian general, would not be an expert on military matters.

The door swung open, and a short man, at least a head shorter than Cordyn, stood in front of him, a sneer of animosity flashing across his heavily bearded, flushed face.

"Who the hell are you?" the man asked. He wore a waistcoat that was at least a size too small, and his rotund belly peeked out through the bottom of the waistcoat; the bottom two buttons were undone, and the button just above those looked on the verge of popping off under the strain the man's stomach put on it.

Cordyn executed a brief yet deep bow, the Piranese military salute. He hoped the Rosenfellian version wasn't much different.

"Good evening, Your Grace," he said, his voice crisp with authority, a man used to giving orders. "I am Duke General Tobias Forthwynn, Imperial Forces. I come to you on a mission of great import. You, sir, may be the only hope Rosenfel has left."

Baronet Trunbelch opened his mouth and closed it three times in quick succession, looking to Cordyn like a bearded fish with a penchant for overindulging on wine.

"What?" the baronet finally managed to ask. "What do you mean, by Hurod?"

"I will gladly tell you, Your Grace. If we could adjourn to a sitting room? I have been riding these past few hours and would not turn down a fire, a glass of whiskey, and something to eat."

Baronet Trunbelch huffed. "Typical of the Imperial forces. Always after your food and drink, your lot is. Well, get inside. I don't have whiskey. You'll have to accept wine." Trunbelch led him to a dark room lit only by two tea candles and a fire. The room smelled of stale sweat and piss, the heat of the fire making it muggy.

Cordyn took out a handkerchief and wiped the perspiration from his brow.

The baronet pointed to a rickety chair and sat on an oversized chaise lounge upholstered in blood red velvet.

An ingenious idea for the alcoholic sort. When you've drunk yourself into a stupor, you won't have to worry about all those pesky stairs.

"Thank you, Your Grace." Cordyn accepted a glass and drank from it. And tried not to spit the wine into Trunbelch's face. It tasted cloyingly sweet, with a hint of the sticky syrup medics gave out for the sniffles. Worst of all, the wine had noticeable sediment in it, bitter chunks that turned rancid in Cordyn's mouth.

Not the dinner I'd hoped for.

"A fine vintage, sir."

"It's swill," Trunbelch said, "but swill gets you drunk the same as any other liquor."

"Words to live by, sir."

Trunbelch quaffed the rest of his glass and refilled it. "What do you want, man?"

"I am on a mission for the emperor himself, riding for the Obanni border to deal with matters of state. I must travel up into the mountains. Alas, my current horse lacks the strength to adequately travel through the peaks, and I fear the journey would kill him. You are the last man of means along these roads before the mountains begin. Do you have a more powerful horse available, sir, that I may use in the service of the Imperium?"

Although intoxicated, Trunbelch kept some of his wits about him. "Couldn't you travel back to the Imperial camps to the East?"

"Of course, that is an option." Cordyn did not know of these camps or how far a distance they were from the manor. "My mission must be completed without delay, per the emperor's orders. Traveling back to camp would add some hours—a day at least—to my journey, and I fear that would unravel the emperor's plans."

Cordyn stood and saluted. "You, sir, are the only hope of our nation."

Trunbelch considered this for a few moments, no doubt struggling to keep the information straight in his addled brain.

"You'll pay me for the horse?"

"I'll offer my horse as collateral and return your horse as soon as I'm able."

"No, damn it, you'll pay me," Trunbelch snapped, slamming his hand against the table. "Or you won't get the godsdamned beast."

This was what Cordyn had worried about. After spending most of his coin on grain, he did not have the available funds to purchase a donkey, let alone a war horse, and the damned man refused to trade. He would have to appeal to the Trunbelch's baser instincts.

"I shouldn't tell you this. I'm under strict orders from the emperor himself. To speak to unauthorized persons would be treason. I'd hang." He paused, pretending to struggle with betraying his emperor. "However, you deserve to know. The border, sir, is a wondrous place. Have you traveled there?"

"No. I have no use for mountains."

"Ah, but mountains conceal things. Shiny, *expensive* things." Cordyn paused for effect. "You may know of the Obanni raiders of old, who patrolled those peaks, waylaying travelers. The Imperium has long known that they hid their treasure somewhere in the caves, safe below layers of ice. Recently, we received word of Obanni dig sites springing up along the border, and caravans moving through the mountains back into Oban."

Trunbelch's eyes bulged at the realization. "They've found the treasure. Godsdamned Obanni bastards."

"They have." Cordyn nodded. "And they're taking all those riches—gold, gems, untold finery we can only imagine—back to Oban. Those riches belonged to Rosenfellian merchants once," he said with passion. "They belong to Rosenfel now."

"But how can one horse make the difference?"

"Again, I was to tell no one this, on pain of death." He placed a hand on Trunbelch's arm. "Do I have your word that what I'm about to divulge will never leave this room?"

Trunbelch clasped Cordyn's hand in his own. "I swear it on my honor, as baronet of these lands, and on the emperor's soul."

Cordyn squeezed Trunbelch's hand. "You are a man of honor. I can trust you." He released Trunbelch's hand and took a sip of the wine. He felt the slightest nausea this time. Perhaps the wine was growing on him. "We have troops at the ready. Imperial dig teams, oxen, carts, and mages poised to move the ice. The only thing we need is the exact location of the treasure. That's my mission. When I find the location, I'll send word to our people, and we'll descend. We'll destroy the Obanni, loot their caravans, and take back what's ours. That, sir, is why I need your horse." Cordyn stood at attention and saluted the baronet.

"By Hurod," Trunbelch said.

"You will, of course, be rewarded. A double share of the treasure, I should think. With that kind of money, a man could do anything. There are beautiful women who would marry a man with that kind of wealth."

Cordyn assumed Trunbelch was unmarried from the state of the manor, but this was a risk. None of the many married women of his acquaintance would have suffered a home in such disrepair.

Trunbelch rubbed his chin, blinking his beady eyes. He grabbed his wine and drained it in one gulp. "Take the horse. Gods, take whatever you need."

"I will leave my horse with you as collateral and will return with your beast when I can." He saluted once more. "One other thing. Do you, by any chance, have a whip? A cat-o'-nine-tails?"

Trunbelch shook his head. "Nothing like that. You're welcome to whatever whips I have out at the stables, though."

"The Imperium thanks you, sir."

Trunbelch led him out to the stables, an immaculately constructed wooden building in the most recent fashion, with stalls for several horses and shuttered windows built-in for any horse who may want to watch the world outside while resting.

"These are fine stables," Cordyn said.

"Horses, sir, are better than any man." Trunbelch indicated a fine stallion at least four hands taller than Stinton's horse, with a well-muscled loin and massive hooves. A horse fit for a general, or someone playing a general. "This is the finest horse this side of the Sarakan range." His eyes glinted with greed. "I hope you will remember my kindness when you return with the treasure."

"Yes, this beast will do perfectly. I am in your debt."

"And I yours. I will eagerly await your return."

Cordyn laughed. "Yes, I'm sure you will. We, Your Grace, will be rich."

THIRTEEN

GEN SAT PROPPED AGAINST the rough wooden exterior of the temple, drifting in and out of consciousness. Her trousers were covered in dirt, but she didn't care. The tonic had dulled almost all her pain, and the wound had closed. But godsdamn, the tonic was stronger than wine. Her head swirled, and she swayed when standing, like she was drunk. And perhaps she was.

Cordyn rode into the courtyard, sat astride an enormous black stallion like a conquering hero returning from battle. The massive horse dwarfed him, making him look almost like a child learning to ride. He gripped the reins, white-knuckled, face scrunched in concentration.

Conquering heroes can't be useless in battle.

"Nice horse," Gen remarked. "Did you find the whip?"

Cordyn shook his head. "There's a distinct lack of torture devices in these parts." He dismounted the horse, stumbling and landing in a dusty heap. He stood and brushed short black hairs and quite a lot of dirt off his coat. "I brought back four of the Baronet's whips. I'll put something together. If you could call everyone together to meet in the dining hall. We have much to discuss. Oh, and bring some rope, would you?"

"I'm sorry, Stinton, but I traded your horse." Cordyn gave Tobias an impertinent grin. "I'll need the warhorse once we get to the Obanni camp, but feel free to ride it for the time being."

Gen drummed her hand on the enormous rectangular oak table in the dining hall, sending silent prayers to the Swordsman that Cordyn would ease off Tobias. Tobias and Evalia sat together on one side, with Cordyn at the head of the table, whips in both of his hands.

Cordyn always did like a bit of drama.

Cordyn had used the shears to cut the tails of the whips, and now he was cutting pieces of rope, which he weaved together.

Tobias slammed his palm against the table, causing it to quake. Thankfully, Gen hadn't found any wine yet, or it would have spilled.

"That was a fine horse, damn you," Tobias said. "I'd had him for years."

"Unfortunately, Baronet Trunbelch is under the impression that he is holding your horse as collateral until I return from the Obanni border with his horse and thousands of crowns in stolen treasure."

Cordyn held the whip gingerly, as if holding a venomous snake, then twisted his wrist, flinging the whip forward—altogether too close to Tobias for Gen's liking—and the whip cracked. Tobias jerked away from the whip and he and his chair toppled to the ground.

"Gods, man!" Tobias's normally controlled voice transformed to a shriek. He lay on his back, tilting his head forward to glare at Cordyn.

"Cordyn," Gen said. "What the hell are you doing?"

"My apologies, Stinton." Cordyn stood, walked over to Tobias, and reached out a hand to help him up. "I did not expect it to come so close to you."

Tobias slapped Cordyn's hand away, grunting as he pulled himself up from the ground and sat back down at the table. He fixed an intense look of hatred on Cordyn.

Not the first time I've seen someone look at Cordyn that way.

"New rule," Gen said. "No whips at the table." She waited for Cordyn to nod his agreement. "Why exactly does Baronet Trunbelch think you're bringing back riches to him?"

Cordyn executed a formal bow before sitting back down at the table. "Didn't you know, Gen. I'm a general in the Rosenfellian army, and I'm hunting Obanni treasure?"

"Gods, you can't help but lie," Evalia said. "How do you expect us to trust you now?"

"You can choose whether or not to trust me, madam. I cannot change your opinion of me. I have more important matters on my mind, such as saving mage children from imprisonment."

"You are—"

"What is the plan, Cordyn?" Gen asked. "We've waited long enough."

"Fair enough. We might all have a drink while we discuss the plan."

"Cordyn," she said, warning him to not push his luck.

"I'm not being coy, dear Gen," he said. "I feel some libation might be necessary to help ease any worries."

She let out a frustrated sigh. "Fine. Tobias, will you get us a bottle from the cabinet in the kitchen?"

"Of course." Tobias exited into the kitchen and came back a moment later with two dark, unlabeled bottles and a tray of glasses. He sat and went about pouring the silky red liquid into the glasses, then passed them around the table.

Cordyn took a sip and began. "We will infiltrate the camp. Evalia will act as a medic, a kind woman along the road who graciously took pity on me and nursed me back to life. I know this will be hard for you, Evalia, but please, for the sake of the children, and your brother, try not to let your ill temper get the best of you. Gen and Tobias, you will act as Obanni soldiers. We'll need uniforms, and since I doubt the Obanni will loan us their uniforms, we'll have to go take them."

"Where do you plan to find these soldiers?" Gen asked.

"We know where the camp is. It makes sense for the Obanni to have patrols in the area. We'll go out tonight, find a place in the bushes to hide, distract the patrolling soldiers, kill the blighters, and behold, you are soldiers."

"I'm confused," Evalia said. "What will I be nursing you back to life from, exactly?"

"Ah, that's the next part of the plan. It'll have to wait for tomorrow, but it's why we need the whip."

Gen, Tobias, and Cordyn went out that evening toward the Obanni camp. Cordyn wore one of Tobias's black coats and took on the role of a merchant, driving a horse and cart while Gen and Tobias were on horseback. Cordyn brought an eyeglass with him, and kept putting it to his right eye, peering at Gen, and saying, "By

Hurod." She was ready to knock Cordyn off the cart and make him walk the rest of the way.

A few miles from the camp, they found fresh carriage tracks on the road, as well as several footprints.

"This will do," Cordyn said. "If the two of you will make yourselves scarce, I'll set about becoming a pitiful merchant in need of help from any kind soldiers who pass by." He turned to Gen. "The charcoal, if you please?"

After handing him the small block of charcoal, Gen found a low hanging tree limb on an oak thirty yards into the forest, and she sat, leaning against the solid trunk. Taking out a handkerchief she'd borrowed from Cordyn, she wiped Maralda's blade clean. Maralda had seen more action than normal the past few days, and she wanted to make sure the blade stayed sharp. Mage-forged blades were rust-resistant, but she still believed in proper care.

She'd just finished cleaning the blade and was preparing to put sword oil on it when she heard Cordyn wailing from the road. Overacting as usual.

"Help! Help, by Hurod!"

Gen left the comfort of her tree limb, got Maralda ready, and peered through the branches to the road.

Three Obanni soldiers stood beside Cordyn, who knelt on the road, moaning about his lost cargo and the evil highwaymen who stole it. The soldiers wore Obanni infantry uniforms, red and gold jackets over black pants, and all three carried standard issue Obanni swords. Nothing Gen couldn't handle on her own, and with Tobias there as well, it would be a massacre.

"Saviors! Deliverers!" Cordyn clasped his hands to his chest as he waxed poetic. He'd mussed his hair and painted bruises under his eyes with the charcoal, giving the impression of a man who'd been thrashed recently. "Good sirs, I pray thee help me. My horse has been stolen by highwaymen, along with all of my wares."

"Sorry to hear that, sir," one soldier said. "I wish we could do something, but we don't have time to help you."

"Please!" Cordyn begged. "I will reward you handsomely. I am a man of means."

The soldiers held a quick, muttered conversation. Then the one who had spoken before placed a hand on Cordyn's shoulder. "We'd be glad to help you, sir. Which way did the bastards go?"

"Hurod keep you! The scoundrels fled through there," Cordyn said, pointing into the forest, a few yards to the left of where Gen waited. "Oh, thank you, sirs. You are indeed sent by Hurod himself."

The soldiers strolled into the forest. Gen slid behind her tree and watched their approach. She knew they were only halfheartedly helping Cordyn; otherwise, they would have moved with more determination. Their languid pace worked fine for her, though. As the men passed, she jumped out from behind her tree and bellowed profanity at them. She wasn't sure what she was saying beyond a lot of "bleeding bastard godsdamn bloody bastards." Before the men could even unsheathe their weapons, two of them had ice shards protruding from their skulls, and the third looked down on Maralda, which sat hilt deep in his stomach.

"Their uniforms will be bloody," Cordyn said, entering the forest now that the combat had ended. "But blood washes away." He looked at the man who'd died by Gen's blade. "Did you have to stab him through the uniform, Gen? A nice decapitation would have been much easier. Now, Evalia will have to sew that one up."

Although Cordyn once more vanished as the work began, Gen and Tobias undressed the bodies and spread out the various articles of clothing. Until they'd undressed the men, Gen hadn't noticed how short all three of them were. She felt a pang of doubt.

"Before we pack the uniforms up, I want to check something." She took the jacket with the broadest shoulders and pulled it on over her head. "Swordsman's tears." The jacket stuck at her shoulders and wouldn't go down any further. "I suppose we could go out and find more troops," she said.

"We could," Cordyn said, reappearing from behind a tree, "but we'd still have to hope the troops were tall and broad enough for their uniforms to fit you. I think we'll have to change the plan. Evalia and Tobias will be our soldiers."

"Evalia is hardly the soldiering type," Tobias said.

"And you're not the planning type. Amuse yourself with your icicles while I think, would you?"

Gen had an idea. Not her best idea, but an idea. "You could bind me loosely and bring me in as a prisoner."

"No, they'd probably just execute you. We've no reason to assume the Obanni take prisoners. With your size and undeniable skill in combat, they'd surely see you as too much of a threat to trifle with. Anyway, it's far better for none of us to play the enemy. You'll just have to play the simpleton farmer who helped us, and whom we are forever indebted to."

"And what about you?" Gen picked up the uniforms and stuffed them into her rucksack.

"We'll get to that." Cordyn wouldn't look her in the eye, which worried her.

"I don't understand why you're being so mysterious about all of this." She handed the handkerchief back to Cordyn. So much for cleaning Maralda. And there would be more Obanni blood in the future, so cleaning the blade again now would be a waste of time.

"You won't like it, Gen."

"That's an assumption. I may find it lovely."

"When we get back to the temple, I'll need you to get the shears. And the whip."

"Let's begin with my hair," Cordyn said. He sat slumped in the corner of the dining hall, facing a small looking glass he'd retrieved from his bag. Gen stood over him, shears in hand, no idea what to do. Men went to barbers all the time; she knew. From what he'd told her, Cordyn saw his barber bi-weekly for a trim. She'd never seen him without hair reaching almost to his jawline; his hair was one of his most prized possessions. Often, when they sat around campfires on their travels, he would admire himself in his looking glass.

Today, however, he stared at the looking glass, hands clasped, his face devoid of expression.

Gen had never sheared a sheep—or a human—but Initiate Brella assured her the process was uncomplicated. The young woman brought them hot water when they returned from their encounter with the Obanni patrol, and she found a basin and jugs of water after Cordyn expressed his desire to be shorn. Gen inhaled, praying to Torr to guide her, and brought the sharp edge of the shears down on Cordyn's curls. Cascades of curls fluttered away to the ground, intermingling with the sawdust floor. After a few minutes, Cordyn's hair was barely visible, close-cropped to his skull. He looked older like this. Older, sad, and slightly haggard, wrinkles emerging on his forehead that his curls had covered before.

"You look different," Gen said.

"It's lamentable, but it had to be done. And I fear I must ask more of you, Gen. More onerous tasks. Things that will bring me pain."

"I wasn't aware anything could bring you greater pain than losing your hair."

"Yes, well, I would rather not do this, but I must. Gen, I need you to take my dagger." Eyes closed, he inhaled deeply, then placed his dagger in her hand. "Now, I need you to cut my face. Below my right eye, from my nose to my temple."

Frozen with shock, Gen gasped, "Cordyn, no!"

"It's what must—"

"What must be done, I know." She sighed. "I still don't understand why."

"I will be playing an Obanni officer who was ambushed along the road by spies." He gave the slightest of wan smiles. "Kosellan, no doubt. It's happening quite often around that camp these days, patrols going missing. The spies captured me and tortured me for information. They saw I was handsome, so they scarred my face, the worst fate they could devise." With one finger, he traced a path along his cheek, pressing hard enough to leave a trail of white behind. "Gen, cut my face."

Gen lifted the dagger and pressed it to Cordyn's face, near the bridge of his nose.

"This is not my usual kind of blade," she said.

"You did say I'd meet your blade at some point on our journey," he said with a mirthless chuckle.

"I meant a minor cut from a sparring exercise. Not me leaving permanent marks on your face."

"Perhaps the women will find the scar attractive in a dangerous way?"

They'll dislike the hair a lot more than the scar.

"I guess we'll find out."

She pushed the dagger's tip through his skin next to his nose. Blood welled at the point of impact. She dragged the blade across his face, the trail of blood following. When she reached his temple, he took a sharp breath and sucked his teeth.

"One more time across," he said. "And not so gentle this time. This needs to look like a slash across my face, not a delicate little cut."

Gen turned the dagger to its side and pressed the tip back into the skin near Cordyn's nose, just below the first cut. She dug the blade in again, and pulled it across his face once more, this time pressing it deeper and rotating the blade to increase the size of the wound. She felt Cordyn's hands gripping her sides. He inhaled sharply, but she did not stop. If she stopped, she wouldn't want to start again, and she knew he'd demand that she finish the job. Finally, the blade reached Cordyn's temple again. She pulled the dagger away from his face and looked at him. He was crying, his tears flowing into the blood on his cheek, the red droplets streaming down his face to his chin. Gen pulled him in for a hug, not caring if blood got on her shirt.

When Cordyn spoke, his voice was muffled by her shoulder. "Kirth, that hurt."

"Oh gods," Evalia said from the doorway. She stood with Tobias, both dressed in Obanni soldier's uniforms. Tobias looked almost natural, Gen thought, and his uniform fit well, albeit snug along the shoulders.

At least he could put it on.

Evalia's uniform engulfed her, the sleeves hanging off her arms, the trousers dragging on the floor.

"What are you doing?" Tobias asked.

"Getting into character." Cordyn blinked away a bloody tear and laughed at Evalia's appearance. Gen was surprised he could laugh after what had just happened.

"Madam," Cordyn said, "you'll need to find a seamstress before tomorrow, unless your goal is to play a small child playing at soldier."

"I know my way around a needle," Evalia said. "It will be done."

"Excellent. Tobias, could you hand Gen the whips?" Cordyn gestured to the dining table, where the roped-together whips sat. He had used the shears to cut the whip tails off, then bound them together, adding a woven rope to create a handle of sorts. His own version of a cat-o'-nine-tails: A cat o' five tails, he'd called it. The finished product looked more like a leather broom than a torture device, but Gen supposed it would do the job, assuming the rope held, and the tails didn't come loose.

Tobias retrieved the whips and handed them to Gen. She held the whips, praying again to Torr, to Kirth, to whatever gods would listen that Cordyn would not ask her to do what she knew he was going to ask.

Please, Torr, I'll dedicate my life to you.

"We'll need more rope," Cordyn said. "Tobias, if you'll bind my hands in front of me. And Gen, there's one last thing you must do."

The whip screamed through the air as Gen cracked it against the oak trunk, breaking off a large section of bark.

"Good," Cordyn said. "Your whip skills are satisfactory."

They stood in a small garden at the rear of the temple grounds, a menagerie of blooming pinks and yellows intermingling among flowering apple trees and finely manicured shrubs. Idyllic, peaceful, and soon to be dripping with blood.

Cordyn took off his shirt. "Now I'll need you to whip me. Three times should be enough and don't go easy on me. I need real wounds for any of this to be believable."

"Cordyn?" Gen asked. "What in Kirth are you talking about?" She'd known for several minutes now that he intended for her to whip him, but she didn't understand why.

"When I refused to betray my brethren, my captors tortured me." Hanging his shirt on a low-hanging branch, Cordyn turned his back to Gen. "I accepted the torture, but never broke. Thankfully, two Obanni soldiers heard rumors of an Obanni captive, and they stormed the dungeons, saving me."

"Isn't there an easier way?" she asked, searching the garden for something—anything—that could help her. She would not whip a friend. "Couldn't we just say you were starved?"

"No, that won't do." He shook his newly shorn head. "Anyone could claim starvation. It's impossible to prove and would lead to more questions than we'd want. We need the tangible evidence of torture, which is what you'll provide me with. I'd avoid this if I could."

"What if I won't do it?"

"Then I'll ask Tobias to do it. I have a feeling he'd enjoy it. Or fair Evalia. She also doesn't care for me. If you refuse, I'll find someone else, but rest assured, I intend to be flogged today."

Despair crept into Gen's voice. "I don't understand. A few days ago, you left, wanting nothing to do with any of this. And now I have to whip you?"

"I still want nothing to do with it. It's a mission with little hope of success." He craned his neck to face her and winked, an odd sight for one bound and soon to be flogged. "I suppose it may seem like I want the glory. Old Cordyn Tallen, showing up and taking charge, making the mission about him."

"The thought had crossed my mind."

"As well, it should. I've not always been in tune with the needs of others." Cordyn placed his hands in his trouser pockets. "I've been a bastard and a cad, Gen. And I need to make amends. To you, to Evalia, even to that intolerable prick, Stinton. One way I can do that is by bearing the brunt of the suffering that must happen."

"You don't have to play a tortured Obanni, you know." Gen squeezed the handle of the whip, willing it to break. The situation was hopeless, though. Once Cordyn had a plan, he didn't stop until he'd seen it to fruition. "We could change the plan."

"Or you could stop moaning and just whip me, for Kirth's sake," he snapped. "I've failed in my duty, I've failed in my mission, and I've failed in every other way.

"I can't."

"You must. If anyone is going to believe our plan, I need to be sufficiently injured. My imaginary captors would hardly just give me a quick tap with a whip and then leave me be."

"No, Cordyn. I can't." Gen's voice broke. "I've seen men whipped before. I could never do that to another person."

Tears welled up in her eyes; images of her father, bloody and broken, lying in a pasture, soldiers laughing as they tore into his flesh. And on the other side of the pasture, Ned, bleeding out from his own wounds—he'd been whipped and stabbed. Both had almost died that day, and Gen could do very little to help them. In the end, Ned had saved himself and Gen's father with his abilities, drawing the blood back into his body and brewing healing concoctions.

Cordyn furrowed his brow. "And yet you'll cut a man's head off without a second thought."

"That's combat, Cordyn. Whipping someone, it's torture. I won't do it." She crossed her arms firmly.

"You have to," Cordyn pleaded. "This isn't really torture. It's a favor for a friend. You're doing this for Evalia, for those kidnapped children." He paused dramatically. "For me."

"I watched my father almost die," she said. "Ned too. And I will not watch the same happen to you."

"Three lashes, no more. I shall not die. Please, Gen."

"Fine." Gen sighed. If it was what Cordyn wanted, it couldn't be torture. "I don't like this. But fine. Turn around." Gen raised the whip and snapped it forward, connecting with Cordyn's upper back, leaving a red welt. Cordyn took in a sharp breath.

"Stop whipping me like I'm your friend."

"You are."

"Pretend," Cordyn said, exasperated. "Imagine I'm an enemy combatant. Or a man who is mean to animals.

She swung the whip again, harder, and a second, large welt appeared. Blood trickled down Cordyn's back.

Cordyn closed his eyes, grimacing, tears running down his cheeks. "Gen" He whispered. "You're going to have to hit me again. Much, much harder."

"Cordyn, I think this plan is too complicated. I cut your hair and your face. I'm whipping you, for Kirth's sake."

"It needs to be complicated." He paused. "Now. Whip. Again."

Closing her eyes, Gen imagined Cordyn as the mage who attacked her on the road. That *bastard*. She swung the whip into the small of the mage's back, enjoying his screams of pain. How dare he? She swung again, and the whip made a squelching sound against the man's damaged back.

"Go to hell!" She hit him, blood splashing against her cheeks. Whipping wasn't that hard, actually. With a little practice, you got used to it.

"Gen," Cordyn said, his voice little more than a whimper.

Gen opened eyes. Cordyn lay in a heap on the dirt in front of her, face down and moaning. She dropped the whip to the ground and kicked it away. "I'm sorry. I didn't mean..."

Cordyn whimpered.

"Oh shit," she said. Cordyn's back was a mangled mess of torn skin and blood, several angry welts forming amid the carnage. "I ... I can't believe I did that. I'm sorry, Cordyn." She moved to his side, lifted him into a seated position, and hugged him. A terrible choice. He screamed in pain, and she realized she was pressing her leather cuffs into his open wounds.

"I'll get a cool cloth, and I'll see what Mother Tull has for treating wounds. She has ointments, I'm sure."

"No. We need to wait until the morning." He gritted his teeth. "It's no good if it looks like the wounds were treated too quickly after the torture. I will rest until then. I will have little trouble losing consciousness tonight." Gen untied the rope binding his hands together, and Cordyn brushed tears from his face. "I have one last favor to ask you, Gen."

"I'm not hurting you in any other way, Kirth take your plan."

"I don't need you to hurt me. Just carry me to my chambers. I'm not sure I can walk, and I'd prefer not to sleep in the dirt."

Although Cordyn refused her apologies, Gen still felt horrible about her actions. She carried him to his room and laid him on his stomach in the bed. She stood for a moment thinking of what she wanted to say, how she could explain her reprehensible actions, but by the time she'd decided on if she should begin with "I'm still sorry" or "I'm a horrible friend," Cordyn was snoring. Resisting the urge to cover him with a blanket—that would just cause him more pain—she left the room.

She wouldn't sleep that night, not after what she'd done. A walk through the temple grounds and into the village might help her clear her mind.

The three moons shone bright, and she could see well enough to not need a lantern as she strolled up the path by the stables and into the village proper. The village had an otherworldly sheen to it, pangs of moonlight reflecting off iron fences and signs, making the ground look spotted.

Two men stood near the abandoned well, across the square from Gen, engaged in intense conversation. Gen stepped into a nearby alley, not wanting the men to see her. They did not seem like they'd enjoy an interruption. She peeked around the corner to watch them.

The taller of the two men waved his arms about and spoke loudly. "I expected you back yesterday. Where have you been?"

"Sorry, boss." The shorter man—no, the boy, Gen decided—spoke with the squeak of a youth on the verge of adulthood whose voice dropped and cracked sporadically. "I got delayed. The guards was checkin' everything at the gates."

"Well, you're here now, at least. Things have taken a surprising turn. We have much to speak about." The man's posture was immaculate, and something about him seemed familiar, but his face was shrouded in shadows and his voice was muffled by the distance.

The boy bowed. "Yes, sir. What are we going to do about your target? Is he still—"

"Not here. Wait until we get to the inn."

They headed toward a long brick building—the inn, which Gen remembered had a painting of a rooster on the sign out front, but she couldn't recall the name. As the two figures entered the inn, Gen saw their faces. She stood next to the abandoned well, struggling to comprehend. The boy was Topper, who apparently knew how to speak. Gen's knees buckled as the man came into view.

Tobias.

FOURTEEN

If Cordyn hadn't been confined to his room and most likely unconscious, Gen would have gone straight to him with the news. Tobias, the man who'd saved her life and had been a selfless champion for Evalia, was a liar.

He'd told them Topper was homesick, but the boy had been on a secret task—something Tobias didn't want any of them to know about. And this man who Tobias called his target? It made no sense. The only man Tobias had spent any time with recently was Cordyn, but what would Tobias have against Cordyn? Yes, he was difficult from time to time and often deserved a pop to the nose, but Tobias barely knew him. People didn't put together complicated revenge schemes for a stranger they found annoying.

Cordyn had money. Enough to make himself a target. With his connection to Winn, powerful enemies as well—the kind who could hire a mage to travel with him all while waiting to—what? Kill him?

Tobias had been working with them and had even saved her life. He was their friend! First thing in the morning, she'd talk to Cordyn. He had a way of unraveling webs of confusion and making them seem simple.

She tried to sleep, but her mind raced with all the possibilities of Tobias's evil plans: assassination, torture, imprisonment. Who knew what he was capable of? Of course, she'd tortured Cordyn that evening, but he'd forced her to, and he would have found someone else to do it if she hadn't relented.

She rose from the bed almost as soon as she'd lain in it, put on her cloak, and went out into the night. The brisk air was pleasing against her skin, especially the slight mist coming down from the clouds looming over the mountains. The temperature dropped after the three moons replaced the suns, and Gen pulled her cloak tighter around her, trying to fight off shivers. During the day, the suns warmed the air to a tolerable level, but the nights were colder here than in Dramin. The mountains were only two days' travel, and Torrance, along with the entire valley beneath the mountains, received the full force of the frigid gusts swooping down the peaks.

Gen made her way through the village, stopping by the well to check for Tobias, but the area looked deserted. The only light in the entire village, as far as Gen could see, came from the inn.

I'm so stupid. I should have come here right after I saw Tobias.

Now that she'd given Tobias hours to plan whatever nefarious schemes he had in store for them, it made little sense to go into the inn. He had surely left long before now. She knew none of the villagers beyond recognizing a few faces, and the thought of making small talk with strangers made her queasy. What would she do? Investigate? Question the innkeep? Search the cellars for clues?

She could search the cellar for wine, at least. A drink appealed to her. A glass of wine, perhaps some mutton. Gods, why did she crave mutton so much? She walked across the town square and into the inn.

"They're upset, boss," Topper said after he'd sat down in a wooden chair across from the sturdy hickory chair where Tobias sat. "The Hillmen."

"I imagine they are." Tobias propped his boots on the table between him and Topper and regarded the boy.

He's getting older. Soon enough, he'll be a man.

"Did you have to kill them?" Topper brushed dirt off his tan linen shirt. A strand of blond hair hung down across his forehead.

"If I didn't, our friend Gen would have."

"I still don't understand. You hate Mr. Tallen. Fine, I don't care for him either. But why the secrecy and the lies? We could have just killed him in Dramin." Topper glanced toward the door leading out into the hall. "We could go kill him right now and go home."

"I have a long history with the Tallen family, Topper. I've wanted revenge for years." He brought his legs back down to the floor and sat up straight, looking Topper in the eye. "Simply killing Mr. Tallen would be rather anticlimactic, don't you think? I need him to suffer, to feel completely betrayed, to understand that I have complete power over him."

"Kirth, boss, that's dark." The boy gave him a worried frown.

"Well, yes. It's revenge."

"I dunno, boss. After my parents died, I didn't want to see the killers or talk to 'em." Topper rubbed his eyes. "I don't even know if I wanted the killers dead. I just wanted to forget they existed."

"And that's where we differ, my boy. I knew revenge was needed, and I got it for you. I'm an artist."

"I didn't ask you to!" Topper stood, hands in his trouser pockets, eyes fixed on Tobias.

"You didn't have to."

"I didn't want it." Topper's working-class accent all but disappeared as he looked earnestly at Tobias. "I never wanted that. Tobias," Topper stepped forward, placing a hand on Tobias own hand. Tobias felt a twinge of guilt as the boy used his name for the first time in years. "You're my godfather. I'm named after you. Both my parents loved you. I love you too. But I'm worried about you. You're not acting like the good man I know you are. Revenge isn't worth this."

Damn it.

Tobias averted his eyes, fighting the shame rising in his stomach. When had Topper grown so earnest and wise? He stood and hugged the boy. For a moment, they said nothing. Then Tobias stepped back and studied his godson's face. The beginnings of a blond mustache poked out above Topper's lip, and he'd grown several inches in the past few months. Gods, he'd turned thirteen five months earlier.

And I forgot his birthday altogether. I was so busy avenging his parents' death.

"You're becoming a man."

"Someone's got to take care of you."

"Hmm. You've grown impertinent, at least. And it appears you've been exaggerating your accent."

"Don't know whatcha mean, boss," Topper said in a thick Dramin drawl. "I's always talked like this, innit?"

Tobias shook his head at his mischievous godson. "Your parents would be proud." He tousled Topper's hair. "However, back to our current affairs. What are the bloody Hillmen doing?"

"They've ransacked your quarters, threatened members of the Imperial Academy to try to find your location, and they've sent squads of thugs to look for you."

"No matter." Tobias waved his hand dismissively. "They'll find nothing of importance, and other than you, no one knows where I am.

"Except for Mr. Tallen and Ms. Gen. And the pretty redhead. If I was a few years older…"

Tobias snorted. "Perhaps a decade older, Top."

"You said I was becoming a man."

"I'm sure the lady will be so impressed by the two strands of fuzz on your chin." Tobias sat back down in the chair, feeling the tension in his chest and neck loosen. "I suppose we'd better move on to Mr. Tallen, and what I plan to do with him. He's created quite a plan, too complicated by half and full of extravagance and arrogance. But he's allowed himself to be whipped within an inch of his life."

"Saves us some of the work."

"Indeed. Gen is a conundrum, though. She's a good woman, but too loyal to Tallen." Tobias pointed to the door. "Why don't you go down and order some dinner for us, and we can make our own plan? Tallen's ludicrous scheme will never work, and we'll need to have something ready to go."

"Are we still killin' him?"

"Probably."

"I don't like it," Topper said. "But you're the boss." He ambled to the door, but stopped before opening it. "Oh, I almost forgot. I've got a note for you, boss. Creepy bugger in a hood gave it to me. Didn't say nothin' else.'"

He walked back to Tobias and handed him a plain white envelope with Stinton written on it in a slanted, angry calligraphy.

Tobias opened it and read:

"Well, sir,

"When you signed on to be my business partner, I expected you to do your part. Why is Tallen still free? Kill the bloody oaf. Just keep the woman alive. I'll step in and do the work

for you, if need be, but that'd make me angry. And you wouldn't like me when I'm angry."

"I didn't like you when you were pleasant," Tobias murmured. The note was signed Your Thirsty Friend.

"What's that boss?" Topper asked.

"Kirth," Tobias said. "Things have taken a turn for the worse."

Topper grinned. "Don't worry, boss. I'll protect you."

"Thank you, Topper. I value your protection. Now, to business. I have some supplies I need you to procure."

"And that's when I realized King Jok of Kosel, wearing only a see-through sarong, was the bugger on the donkey, drunk as you like, singing ballads of lost love. Well, singing is a loose term. He was actually braying."

A chorus of guffaws greeted Gen's story. She basked in their laughter, the pats on the back, and, most importantly, the free drinks. She'd never met King Jok, but Cordyn had, and she found it easier than expected to repeat his stories as if they'd happened to her, changing the details when necessary. Most of Cordyn's stories involved a romantic conquest of sorts, and Gen refused to add any of that to the stories. While Cordyn may have seduced a young noblewoman of Kosel right before seeing the nearly naked king, Gen fought four thieves with her sword, teaching them a lesson: if you threaten a kind Piranese traveler, point daggers at her, and attempt to steal her coin, you'll meet her blade, and the last bits of your life will be pain. The men at the bar, in varying stages of inebriation, enjoyed the stories, at least. They bought her drinks and begged for more tales. She sipped on her sixth—or was it the seventh? —glass of winterplum wine. Not the best vintage, but drinkable, and for free, she'd drink swill.

"Yer the funniest woman I've ever met," a toothless man said. He stunk of whiskey and vomit, but he had a deep purse and had bought Gen three drinks. She considered him a dear friend.

"You're a gem as well, by Hurod." She slammed her palm on the bar top. "Innkeep, more wine!"

The dozen men around her cheered and slammed their own palms on the bar. The innkeep poured the wine, muttering curses all the while.

I seem to have made an enemy. I should check my next glass for spittle.

"Tell us another story," the toothless man said. The rest of her audience joined in with shouts of agreement.

"Well, I suppose I could tell you about the time I saved my weakling friend, Cordyn, from the jaws of death. And the jaws of a Trunellic lion. We were traveling through Trunel—"

A cloaked man descended the stairs and entered the bar. The man tried to hide his face, but she saw his upturned nose.

Tobias.

Assuming he'd not left and then returned, he'd been at the inn for at least three hours. They made eye contact for a moment, and then Tobias covered his face with a large scarf and stormed out of the inn. Gen saw no sign of Topper. The boy had either left earlier or was still upstairs.

"Glad to see the last of that bastard for the night," the toothless man said.

"Do you know him?"

"Know him?" The toothless man conferenced with his companions. "No, but he's been here every night this week, the nob. Using the rooms upstairs. It's godsdamned hard to get decent service when wealthy bastards show up and throw coin around."

"Do you know why he's been here?"

"Meeting a woman, I'd guess. Why else would a man rent a room at an inn he's not staying at?"

"Have you seen anyone with him?"

"I haven't." He turned to the other drunkards. "Boys, you seen anyone with the nob?"

"No," a short, tanned man said, his voice as dry as his desiccated skin. "He's kept to himself, that one. Ordered his coat cleaned by a servant boy but haven't heard him speak to no one else."

"Where's the servant boy?" Gen noticed the men beginning to grow restless from her questioning.

"Kirth if I know," the short man said. He picked at a tooth with a curled brown fingernail. "I's got too much at stake with my drinkin' to be lookin' for every servant who walks through."

"He's been with a woman, I tell you," the toothless man said. "Only likely reason for bein' up in those rooms."

"That must be it." She knew that wasn't the reason, but she saw no need to explain the situation to her intoxicated friends. "Anyway, damn him. Innkeep, where in Kirth's name is our wine?"

She'd go upstairs later to investigate, but what was the harm in one more glass?

Gen's head felt like it was cooking over an open flame while being pierced with ice shards. She opened her eyes—a mistake; the morning light assaulted her. She was back in her bed at the temple.

Shit.

She couldn't remember leaving the inn. The toothless man had bought their ninth bottle, this one a sweet rot berry wine. If her drunken taste buds were reliable, rot berry wine rivaled winterplum. She'd thumped Toothless on the back and sworn several vows of never-ending friendship. And then nothing.

So much for investigating the inn.

She squinted through the semi-open shutters at the sharp light of day.

Gods, it hurts. But Cordyn will be waiting.

Her gambeson sat by her bed. With great effort, she forced herself to rise and get dressed. Someone—probably Brella—had left a carafe of tonic. She swigged it, no longer minding the taste. It soothed her dry throat and eased the pain in her abdomen and the pounding in her head.

I need to keep this on hand after every long night of drinking.

Despite the tonic, she was still exhausted. *Swordsman's tears.* Ned had given her a concoction for energy. She dug into her coat pocket and retrieved the flask. Popping the lip off, she drank it in one gulp. As Ned had suggested, it tasted like limes.

Within seconds, her body tingled. Her heart thumped in her chest, but she felt alert. Calm. Powerful. She could run to Dramin and still not feel tired. It was going to be a good day.

After dressing, Gen left her chambers to find Cordyn already propped up on the cart, talking to Evalia, who led a horse through the courtyard. Evalia wore her Obanni soldier's uniform, which fit better after her alterations, but still made her look like a child playing dress up.

Cordyn winced as he turned his neck when he saw Gen. "You slept in," he said.

"Took me a while to fall asleep. I had a lot on my mind." Gen wished Evalia would go away so she could talk to Cordyn, but it felt rude to ask her to give them privacy.

Cordyn sniffed the air and scrunched his nose. "Yes, you had quite a lot of wine on your mind."

"Where's Tobias?" she asked, hoping to avoid any scolding.

"He had some last-minute business in town," Evalia said. "Sending letters to some business associates. He should be back soon."

Business associates named Topper. And no letters were involved.

She needed to change the subject. Otherwise, she'd feel compelled to tell Cordyn everything. Self-control had never been her strong suit.

"Cordyn, do you have any further schemes? Am I pelting you with rocks today?"

Cordyn's thin smile lasted only a moment. "No, I hope it will be a long time before you strike me again. The plan is set. We'll save the children, reunite Evalia and her brother, and then send a message to the king,"—he looked at Evalia—"to our, ahem, employers about what the Obanni are doing in Rosenfel."

"I told Evalia we work for Piran."

"Ah, well then. We'll send word to King Thorace, and when we do, we'll be loyal envoys again. In fact, we'll be hailed as heroes throughout Piran."

"That's assuming we succeed."

"Nonsense. We're fated to succeed. We have you on our side, don't we? The court poets will write songs about you."

"I doubt that. What would they say? *She was tall, she swung a sword?*"

"Hardly." Cordyn exhaled and bent his head forward, executing a wounded man's version of a courtly bow.

"A woman courageous, O mighty Gen,
Obanni, all slain by her righteous sword,
She stabbed the bastards, killed two hundred men,
The savior of Piran against the horde."

Gen applauded. "You have a way with words."

"I wonder sometimes if I should have chosen the safe life of a poet instead of that of an envoy."

"Less flogging, perhaps?"

"No, I would have offended too many nobles. I would be well-acquainted with thrashings." Cordyn fixed his eyes on Evalia. "The poets might write about you as well."

She failed to meet his eyes. "Oh, stop. I'm not important."

"The woman who saved her brother and brought down an empire. You'll be worthy of several epics, I'd wager."

Oh gods, Cordyn wants to get murdered.

"No, but thank you." Evalia's tone softened, and she smiled at Cordyn for the first time Gen had seen. "I appreciate laughing about it, though. No one will ever write poetry about me."

"I could write one now if you wish. You've already heard the masterpiece I penned for Gen a moment ago. I'd even promise to omit all mentions of your stubbornness. And your violent side."

"No, I don't believe you have the skill to capture me in verse."

"Alas. I could draw your portrait, but I have no art skills. A pity."

"Yes, you'll just have to find an artist lying about. If you'll excuse me, I must talk with Mother Tull before we leave." Evalia bowed and walked toward the temple.

"Most interesting," Cordyn said, scratching at his stubble. "Gen, how are you with a pen?"

"I prefer swords."

"You know what they say: the pen is mightier than the sword."

"Whoever said that hasn't had to fight Maralda and me." She patted Maralda's hilt. "Speaking of which, where in Kirth's gods-damned name is Tobias?"

"Quite sacrilegious of you." Cordyn interlaced his fingers over his chest. "I'm shocked and all a-quiver."

Gen patted her sheath again.

"Threatening to stab me again?" Cordyn asked. "I thought you didn't want to torture me any longer?"

"That was before you opened your mouth."

They laughed, but both stopped short, clutching at their respective wounds. Gen's abdomen only ached at this point, but

Cordyn, without the aid of the tonic and with fresh wounds, had to be in agony.

"We make quite the pair," he said. "Too wounded to laugh. I would have retired and bought a farm if I'd realized how strenuous this mission would be."

"I think you'd get bored as a farmer." She couldn't imagine Cordyn out in the fields, tilling soil in the noon suns or milking the cows and sheep.

"You wound me, Gen." He frowned in mock distress. "I find nothing more exotic than farm life."

"I was bored on the farm growing up. However, now that boredom doesn't sound so bad."

"Fresh milk and cheese, vegetables from my garden, no enemy mages seeking your death."

"Indeed." Gen steeled herself. She needed to tell Cordyn about the situation at hand, no matter how difficult it would be. "Listen, Cordyn, can we talk?"

"We'll have time to talk on the road," he said, peering toward the village. "I think that's Stinton." Placing his hands to his face, he called out. "Stinton! Hurry, man! We'll lose all our daylight." Gen turned to see Tobias walking from the village proper into the temple courtyard.

"I've concluded my business," Tobias said when he reached them. "We can leave at once."

Gen felt a sudden urge to strike Tobias and accuse him of, well, something. Treason, maybe?

"Gen, go find Evalia," Cordyn said.

Gen didn't have to leave the courtyard to find Evalia, who came out through the temple doors a moment later carrying a basket of breads, cheeses, and dried meats.

"Mother Tull packed some provisions for us."

"Excellent," Cordyn said. "One last thing before we leave. Tobias and Evalia, as Obanni soldiers, there are a few matters you should be aware of. First, the Obanni army is obsessed with swords."

"As they should be." Gen said.

"All of their officers have 'sword' in the title. Sword general, sword captain, sword lieutenant. It is dishonorable and offensive to not say sword before the title. You'd be court-martialed or worse."

Cordyn reached up to brush his hair out of his face, but found no hair. He held his hand against his scalp for a moment. Gen wondered if he regretted the shearing.

"The Obanni are a drab people. Humor will get you nowhere. Friendliness is a sure sign you're an impostor. Stay somber, stay silent." He looked at Tobias and Evalia. "Unless you're hiding talents, neither of you can do an Obanni accent. And Gen, your Rosenfellian accent is terrible, so talk in your normal voice."

"They'll know I'm Piranese."

"You seem like a born and bred Dukestown lass to me. Something about the Nazlin wastes grows the women tall as Trunellic hickories."

"Nothing more complimentary than tree comparisons."

"You're most welcome, my dear. Evalia, Tobias, I've written the orders you'll deliver to the camp leader. I'd assume he'll be a sword general or the like. Don't answer any questions he might have about the orders beyond stating that the sword brigadier sent you straight away, with orders to ride day and night. You know nothing about the contents of the correspondence. "

"And what are the contents?" Tobias asked.

"It's better you don't know."

"Dammit, man—"

"You need to look suitably surprised. You are not professionals on the stage, and I don't have time to teach you dramatic theory. Do not read the correspondence. Your shock at the news will seem genuine."

"We'll do as you say," Evalia said, no trace of her previous contempt for Cordyn. "Thank you, sir." Gen's eyes flitted between Cordyn and Evalia. They were watching each other.

What is going on?

"I have one last favor to ask, Gen," Cordyn said.

"No," she replied immediately. "Whatever it is, no."

Cordyn pulled his mage-captain's hat from the floor of the cart and tossed it to Gen.

"I told you I'd not make you torture me again. If you would take this to Mother Tull and ask her to watch over it. I'll retrieve it when we've completed our task."

Assuming we're still alive to return.

"I know where the mother is," Evalia said. "I'll take it to her."

Gen noticed how Cordyn's eyes followed Evalia all the way back to the temple.

When Evalia returned, they set off. Tobias rode on the stallion, as Cordyn was in no shape to ride a horse. From his grain sack seat, Cordyn explained that when they reached the camp, Tobias would need to tell the soldiers that he'd borrowed Cordyn's horse. "Tell them your own horse died in the fight against our assailants. It wouldn't do for an enlisted man such as yourself to ride an officer's horse, otherwise." Within minutes, Cordyn lay sprawled out on the cart, snoring, while Gen and the others rode from the village. Gen thought she'd have to wake Cordyn up so he could drive the cart, but the cart horses followed her own horse without assistance.

Gen moved her horse alongside Evalia's, and she peered at the other woman with none of her usual pleasantness. "Your anger toward Cordyn has lessened."

"Yes," Evalia said. "I may have been mistaken about him."

"How so?" Gen maneuvered Francois around a boulder, and the horse whinnied in protest at her use of the reins.

"What he did, the suffering, I didn't know a man would ever put himself through that. He may be insufferable, and I still don't like him, but he's the bravest man I've ever met."

"You *don't like him?*"

Evalia looked from side to side, as if searching for ways to escape the inquisition. "No. He's infuriating."

Not you too. It would be wonderful if at least one woman hated Cordyn, just for the novelty of it.

Now Evalia, her contempt softened, looked at Cordyn with a new admiration. Self-sacrifice was an effective seduction technique, it seemed, even if Gen was sure Cordyn had intended none of his plan for romantic reasons. He'd avoided Evalia when possible and rarely spoke to her.

Gen had a duty to warn Evalia. "He's a scoundrel when it comes to women. He may seem brave, but he's never been faithful to a lover."

"How sad." Evalia pulled the reins of her own horse, slowing it down as they crested a hill and began their descent. "But why are you telling me this?"

"I wanted you to know. In case you have developed feelings."

"Feelings?" Evalia dropped the reins, and her horse trotted with renewed fervor. "Oh, I have no feelings for him." Her voice turned cold. "It's insulting that you would suggest such a thing, really."

"I'm sorry," Gen said. "I was trying to help."

"I'll ask for your help if I need it." Evalia picked up the fallen reins, clenching her jaw in concentration. "I must ask Mr. Stinton something. If you'll excuse me." Without waiting for an answer, Evalia pushed forward, leaving Gen alone with Francois.

"Trouble with your new friend?" Cordyn asked.

Not alone, after all, godsdammit.

Gen held back, waiting for Cordyn's cart to reach her. He'd woken up at some point, but Gen didn't know how much of her conversation with Evalia he might have heard, and if he'd been offended by any of it.

"I need to talk to you," she said. She'd worry about if she'd offended him later.

"I cannot run away, so say whatever you like."

Gen kept her voice down as she said, "I saw Tobias last night."

"I did too. We had a meeting with him."

"No, I saw him later on in the evening, during the night."

"Gen? I'm shocked." He winked. "You and Tobias?"

Gen felt a wave of revulsion. "No. Gods, no. I don't want anyone like that, ever."

Cordyn lowered his eyes, repentant. "I'm sorry, Gen. It was a poor joke. Forgive me."

Gen did not respond. She didn't want to discuss that part of herself any further. Some things were just for her.

"I saw him in the village having a secret meeting." She paused for effect—Cordyn wasn't the only one who could be dramatic. "With Topper."

"The boy? I thought he'd gone back—"

"He did. He told Tobias he'd completed the task Tobias had given him, and he returned to the temple to report."

"There could be several reasons. Private business, mage affairs, Topper's his illegitimate child—"

"Or he's betrayed us."

"I doubt that. You weren't there when we saw the mage children. Tobias was so full of rage that he planned on attacking four hundred soldiers by himself. He's given no signs of sympathy toward the Obanni, and he's been helpful in our plans. Although I still think he's a prick, I see no signs he'll betray us. I think we can trust him to help."

"When you expressed your doubts about him," Gen snapped, "I pushed them aside. Now I agree with you, and you're doing the same thing."

"I've always been an enigma, Gen." He squinted toward Tobias, the dried blood on his cheek became more prominent and his cheek pushed out. "I understand your concern, and I'm sure the man has all the nefarious dealings a true prick would have, but I don't think he'll betray us."

"Fine, if you won't listen to me, I won't talk to you." Gen led Francois forward, leaving Cordyn alone with his sacks of grain.

She'd always been loyal to him, trusted in his plans, listened to his judgment, and when she came to him with knowledge of her own, he brushed her aside. Godsdamn him.

She unsheathed Maralda and swung at a tree limb, severing the limb in one blow. She wanted to hurl abuse at Cordyn, Tobias, anyone, and everyone. The whole godsdamned world could go to Kirth and suffer in the Dark Beyond. She cleaved another branch from a second tree.

"Gen, what the hell—" Cordyn began.

"Shut up." She galloped forward, leaving Tobias, Evalia, and Cordyn in her wake.

When she'd put a hundred yards of distance between herself and her companions, she felt her nose tremble. Her eyes watered, but she inhaled and willed herself to stay strong.

No crying, Gen. You'll kill some Obanni, and you'll feel better. Just keep it together.

A few minutes of slow inhaling and exhaling brought some sense of calm back to her, though she could not ignore the hollow sense in the pit of her stomach.

If Cordyn didn't believe her, then who the hell in their right mind would?

FIFTEEN

WHEN THEY WERE A few minutes from camp, Cordyn called everyone together for one last briefing. He felt confident in his own abilities and knew Gen would do her best in her role but had little faith in Tobias's acting talents and feared Evalia would lose all semblance of poise if she saw her brother or any of the other prisoners.

They huddled around the cart, and Cordyn did his best to sit up, even with his back radiating pain with every move. He gripped the side of the cart, pushing the pain away. It would not do for him to cry during the briefing. He had his reputation to uphold.

Let them say Cordyn Tallen had weakness for women, but never for emotions.

While Gen and Evalia dismounted and sat in the cart with Cordyn, Tobias stayed on horseback, surveying the surrounding forest.

Cordyn steeled his resolve with a sharp inhale. "In order to succeed, we must follow the plan in its entirety. There is no room for error or for improvisation. Gen, say little. They won't expect you to, and there's no need for you to put any strain on your cover."

Gen agreed, as he'd expected she would. Getting her on board with the plan would be the easy bit. They understood each other. Now, for Stinton, who loved nothing better than to argue with him.

The only thing Stinton understands is how to be sanctimonious.

Cordyn waved dismissively toward Stinton, hoping the man wouldn't try to wrestle control from him. There would be a time and a place for arguing over superiority—when they saved the boy.

"Stinton, say even less. If it were possible to convince the men you were mute, I'd suggest it, but as it is, you'll need to play the stoic soldier who only speaks when spoken to."

Tobias assented, but said nothing.

Well, thank the gods for that. Wonders will never cease.

Evalia clasped her hands together until they turned white. Cordyn reached out to take her hand, wanting to console her, but as he moved his hand toward her, he saw her lips tremble—with shock? Fear? Disgust?—and he stopped. His hand hung in the air, halfway between Evalia and him.

I look like a dog doing a trick. He brought his hand back to his side, vowing to never attempt such foolishness again. *No emotion, you imbecile. No bloody tears and no blasted empathy.* He pushed everything but the mission away.

"Evalia, I know this will be harder for you than for any of us. Your brother is here, and the uncertainty of the situation must be gnawing at your frayed nerves. However, this is important. The difference between success and escape or all of us hanged and gibbeted. Don't look at the prisoners." Evalia opened her mouth in protest. "Don't look for Ezra. I know that's the first thing you'll want to do, but we can't afford the Obanni getting suspicious about us snooping around. Pretend he's not there."

"But—"

"I'll look for him, and if he's there, I'll find him. What I need from you is to fit in with the rest of the soldiers. Eat with them, gamble with them. Hell, take a lover if you want to."

"Absolutely not," Evalia said. "I'd die before I took an Obanni lover."

"Seriously, Tallen," Tobias said, "you're impertinent."

"You could take a lover as well, Stinton. Gods know it might ease some of your tension." He noticed Stinton's face flush; the man huffed but said no intelligible words. *Good, I've embarrassed you.* He'd gathered Stinton had developed feelings for Evalia from Stinton's lingering glances and the way he followed her like Gen followed winterplum wine. He'd tired of Stinton stepping in like Evalia's protector and knight every time Cordyn spoke with her.

"Gods, Tallen, if it weren't for the boy—"

"I know. You'd whip me with your glove and demand satisfaction. How gentlemanly."

"Cordyn, the plan?" Gen asked. It was Cordyn's turn to blush. Godsdammit, he'd lost focus on his own plan, all to antagonize Stinton, and, if he had to admit it, to make Stinton look lesser in Evalia's eyes. Cordyn was a man, and she *was* godsdamned pretty, after all. And the way she'd haggled with the farmer and berated Cordyn, nostrils flaring as she argued...

No emotion.

Save the boy and then go back to Piran. If he never saw Stinton, Evalia, or all of Rosenfel ever again, all the better.

"My apologies, Gen. Evalia." He did not apologize to Stinton—one last bit of pettiness. "When we get to the camp, nod and agree with everything the soldiers say. I'll survey the scene and update the plan based on what I find."

"Won't the soldiers watch you too?"

"Not as much. First, I'm an officer. They'll want to avoid annoying or angering me, since I outrank them. Second, I'm wounded." He gestured to his wounds. "I'm not a threat to anyone in my current state, so my strolling about the camp won't seem as ominous. A man who's recovering from serious injury needs exercise, right?"

"I have my doubts about your ability to stroll at all," Gen said.

"I'll drag myself along the ground if I must, but I will do my duty. For Piran." He cuffed Gen on the shoulder. "And for you, Gen."

Well, perhaps just a bit of emotion.

He had no worries about his own performance. Some might call him arrogant or overconfident, but he knew his skills and trusted them. If something needed to be done, he'd be the one to do it, with Gen and her sword at his side to stab any unintended consequences.

Tobias was Cordyn's primary worry, and not because of Gen's newfound paranoia about Tobias's loyalties. The man was rigid. He would struggle to adapt to changing plans, and had no ability to deceive, which assured Cordyn that Tobias wasn't on the verge of betraying them. Cordyn had suspected him at first—altruism didn't exist, and he knew Tobias had to have an ulterior motive—but the man did not have the charisma to pull off a lie. Which made him a terrible candidate to play at being an Obanni soldier.

"Stinton, do I have your word as a gentleman to speak as little as possible?"

"As a gentleman, yes," Tobias said with a sour look. "Something you are not."

Cordyn tipped an imaginary hat. "I never claimed to be, though I come from noble stock. A long line of ship captains, as the lady was so kind to notice when we first met." He bowed to Evalia. Well, more of a slight flinch forward. Bowing after the whipping wasn't possible.

Tobias harrumphed and walked back to his horse.

"I shouldn't have hit you with the lute," Evalia said. "Even if I greatly enjoyed it."

"It's a story I'll always remember, dear lady. Indeed, if I ever have children, their favorite bedtime story will be the time I came within an inch of death after a beautiful woman brained me with a finely crafted musical instrument."

He assured himself he meant nothing by the comment. Deep down, he knew he was flirting with Evalia.

Godsdammit, Cordyn. Focus on the mission.

"And if everything else fails, these sacks of grain are soaked in oil. Light a match, toss it on the grain, and run."

"Quiet," Gen whispered. She stood up, unsheathed Maralda, and scanned the trees for movement.

"What do you see?" Cordyn asked, his voice a worried whisper.

"Something dark, flashing from tree to tree. I saw it twice, but I don't see it anymore." She shrugged. "I must have imagined it."

"Be on your guard. I wouldn't sheathe your sword just yet."

Gen jumped down out of the cart and stood between Cordyn and the tree line. She faced away, watching the trees. Cordyn saw no movement, but taking chances was reckless out in the forests.

Gen beckoned Stinton to move closer, and the four of them huddled closer together, Evalia and Cordyn in the cart, while Stinton and Gen flanked the northern corners of the cart and provided a layer of protection. They were near enough to the camp that the movement could have been Obanni scouts, but Cordyn thought scouts, upon seeing their own soldiers, would come out to greet them instead of hiding.

"It will be good to be back among our brethren," he said, his voice booming in a perfect Obanni accent. Evalia winced at how loudly he spoke, but he wanted any watchers to know they were Obanni. "I haven't had a decent Kurstian boar shoulder in weeks."

He didn't know what Kurstian boar shoulder tasted like, but he'd read it was an Obanni delicacy.

"I'm hungry too," Evalia said. "This journey has been taxing." Her Obanni accent sounded natural. *Impressive. If only she or I could do something about Gen.* Gen had practiced the Rosenfellian accent for hours the day before, but she still sounded like a Piranese farm girl.

"I could eat," Gen said. "I keep thinking about mutton."

"Ah, spoken like a Rosenfellian, dear girl. Wait until you try Obanni cuisine. You'll never desire mutton again."

A crossbow bolt whizzed past Gen, hitting Stinton on the arm. Stinton screamed—a hollow screech of pure anguish and pain—and fell sideways off the horse, collapsing in a heap among the leaves and twigs on the side of the path.

"What the hell?" Gen said. She had her sword out in seconds and charged toward where the bolt had appeared from the trees.

Thank the gods she'd not been on her horse.

Cordyn held a crossbow, sitting up in the cart and scanning the trees for enemies.

A group of men, dressed entirely in black, came out of the trees, wielding daggers, swords, and cleavers.

Oh gods, the Hillmen.

He'd hoped they'd left those bastards behind in Dramin.

He counted at least twenty men, more than they could have handled even before Stinton's injury, and now Stinton wouldn't be in any state to assist, assuming he was still alive.

I'll be no help, either, unless the buggers come up to me and beg to get shot in the face.

He'd shot a crossbow twice in his life, and no one gave out awards for missing the target by ten yards.

Evalia sat beside him, gripping a dagger, but she wouldn't be much help either. He'd have to talk his way out of trouble, as usual.

"Lovely to see you," a tall Hillman said, rubbing greasy hands through his graying beard. "You're the bastards who came into our territory and killed our friends. We're gonna kill you now."

"I appreciate your honesty," Cordyn said, "but there seems to be a misunderstanding. We are Obanni travelers who have never been to Dramin."

"No, Mr. Tallen, I know all about you. And I know that bastard as well." The man pointed at Tobias, who lay in a heap, clutching his arm while three Hillmen held him at sword-point. Good. It would complicate the plan if Stinton died this early on. "Master Stinton over there betrayed us. Betrayed me. I'd considered him a good friend, see? We shared a fine drink at the Golden Crown, and then he killed my friends. That's cause for death."

"You'll die," Stinton murmured. "I'll make sure of it."

"I'm not sure who this Tallen fellow is," Cordyn lied. "I'm Master Forthwynn of Dramin University. However, if it's Master Stinton you want, we'll turn him over. He means nothing to us. We hired him to guide us through these unfamiliar lands. I only ask that you let us travel unmolested to our destination."

The man stroked his beard again. A nervous habit? "Give me one reason why we should let you go."

"I have quite a large bank account, and I may find it in my heart to donate a sizable amount to a charitable organization of kind souls from Dramin."

The men exchanged looks. A mix of greed, ambition, and confusion, the usual expressions when his words worked their way into someone's mind. The men were off balance, unsure of how to proceed. The perfect time for Gen to strike. If only the odds were more favorable than this. If she attacked now, she'd kill a few men, but then they'd kill her.

Cordyn caught her eyes and shook his head.

"Why don't we all take a deep breath, stay calm, and keep our swords sheathed? What do you call yourselves?"

"The Hillmen. You've probably heard of us."

"The Hillsmen? No, never heard of you. Perhaps your fame doesn't reach past Dramin yet." Cordyn placed the crossbow on the floor of the cart and showed the men his hands. "But with my financial backing, you could be known across Rosenfel, even across Sarakan."

"I don't trust you."

"I don't trust you either. It's lovely how we can start a valuable business arrangement based on mutual distrust, your desire to kill this Stinton fellow, and my desire to remain living. Soon, you'll be wealthier, and I'll still be breathing. A lovely compromise."

The men spoke among themselves, and Cordyn used their momentary lapse in vigilance to gesture for Gen to step closer.

"Everything's going according to plan," he said.

"What's the plan?" Gen asked, whispering.

He paused. "Hope they agree."

"And if they don't?"

"Run." He clenched his jaw and took a deep breath.

"Tobias won't be running anytime soon," Gen pointed out.

"No." He released the breath. "We need to take out his captors first. Then, you throw him in the cart or on your horse. Then we'd run."

"That sounds like too much to hope for," Evalia said, crossing her arms.

"Evalia," Cordyn whispered. "I know what I'm doing. I'm exceedingly good at this. I expect the Hillmen will agree to my terms in a moment or two."

"Sir," the Hillmen spokesman said. "We've considered your offer, and we're happy to say that we're content with killing you as previously planned. May Kirth take your miserable souls."

"Now, Gen," Cordyn said.

She whipped her sword from the sheath, charging the men surrounding Tobias, cleaving torsos and arms from the bloody stumps that had once been two men. Cordyn winced as Gen took a crossbow bolt to the shoulder—a third wound in three days. She was slipping—but the archer only had a head for a moment longer. She grabbed Stinton, lifting him over her shoulder, and ran for her horse. Cordyn's cart raced by, and Gen heaved Stinton into the back and Stinton's body thumped as it hit the bags of grain.

Cordyn cursed. Gen's horse was twenty yards away with several Hillmen in her path. Not worth the risk.

"Gen, the warhorse!"

Lord Trunbelch's stallion, in the opposite direction of the Hillmen, ran free, riderless, since Stinton was in the cart wounded.

Gen looked toward him, and Cordyn held up a finger.

Wait a moment.

He lifted his crossbow, aimed at the Hillmen spokesman, and fired, missing by several yards. The distraction gave Gen a moment's head start, though. She feinted toward the Hillmen, then sprinted toward the stallion.

She didn't run fast enough. Before she'd made it even ten yards, three crossbow bolts hit her in the back. Cordyn drew in a sharp breath, but Gen didn't fall.

Thank the gods for reinforced armor.

None of the bolts pierced the armor, as far as Cordyn could tell, but Gen stumbled. A few seconds wasted while she got to her feet, and the Hillmen were closer. Too close. She'd never make it.

Stinton lay next to Cordyn in the cart, moaning and grasping at his wound.

"Stinton?" No response. "Stinton!" Cordyn slapped him across the face, and Stinton ascended from his reverie of pain. "Worry about your wounds later. We could use your help."

Stinton said nothing in return, but lifted his hand over the side of the cart. He chanted an incantation—Vidor, Issah, Vidor?—and ice shards flew from his fingertips toward the Hillmen, and unfortunately, toward Gen. A shard connected with her unarmored ankle. Gen's guttural howl rose above the noise of Hillmen yelling at one another.

Gods, that sounded inhuman.

One of Stinton's shards connected with the Hillmen leader's throat and he fell, gurgling, grasping at the wound, trying to push the blood back in. But he was no mage. And Cordyn doubted Stinton would be interested in saving this man's life. A few labored attempts at a swallow, and the leader stopped moving forever.

Cordyn stood in the cart. He wanted nothing more than to fall, grab at his wounded back, and focus on the pain radiating up through his entire body, but he forced himself to focus on Gen.

She'd have bruises from the crossbow bolts, but the shards had pierced her skin, and she was losing blood. There was no time to waste trying to stop the bleeding. Their only hope was to get to the Obanni camp.

Stinton's shards continued flying at random, which kept the Hillmen from advancing as quickly, but also slowed Gen down.

"Could you aim better?" Gen yelled, limping toward the stallion.

"Just get to the horse, Gen," Cordyn said. He loaded the crossbow, aiming as accurately as he could. *Thwack!* He killed a nearby tree branch.

"I'm trying to not take a shard to the face. Tell him to switch to water."

"Stinton?" Cordyn slapped him again. Stinton grunted but continued his icy barrage. "He's not responding. Just get to the horse."

"Fine, if I die, it's your fault."

Sending a prayer to Torr, Cordyn watched Gen sprint for the horse. A few shards connected with her armored torso, but none hit any exposed skin. The stallion looked at the charging woman as if she were an odd sight.

Don't run, horse. Wait for the nice lady.

Gen vaulted on to the stallion's back and spurred the horse forward. Now it was Cordyn's turn. He lunged into the driver's seat, pulled on the reins, and yelled, "Yah!"—the closest thing to a horse command he could think of. He'd never driven a cart before today.

His horse lurched forward and followed the stallion down the path toward the Obanni camp. Evalia lay flat on the floor of the cart—she lost her balance when the horse surged forward. Stinton wasn't moving beyond the slight rise of his chest as he breathed. A crossbow bolt thwacked against Cordyn's rucksack, but unlike the wine incident outside of Mintar, no supplies fell to the ground.

A stroke of luck Evalia fell to the cart floor. That bolt would have hit her.

They turned a corner on the path, and the Obanni camp came into view. Several guards stood outside, armed with pikes and shields, and one motioned for the onrushing group to halt.

"I am Sword General Rennick," Cordyn said in a crisp voice. "I'd appreciate it if you could inform your commanding officer of our arrival. We're fleeing Kosellan mercenaries."

"What do you mean?" a thin guard asked.

"You will address me as Your Eminence."

The guards exchanged looks. A sturdy guard with a pockmarked face smacked the thin guard across the stomach. "Show some respect." He saluted Cordyn. "What do you mean, Your Eminence, sir?"

Cordyn pointed to the Hillmen, who had turned the corner and came into view. "Kill those blighters, and then perhaps one of my companions will answer all your questions."

A guard took a goat's horn from his belt and blew. Upon hearing the discordant bleating of the horn, several Obanni soldiers emerged from the camp, armed with various weapons—pikes, swords, or crossbows, though one man carried an enormous wooden club.

"Kosellans," the thin guard said, pointing toward the Hillmen.

"Send them to Kirth," Cordyn said. "In the name of the Sword Brigadier, and for the glory of Oban."

A few of the soldiers looked up at Cordyn, their eyes drawn to his tattered clothes and wounds. He returned their stares until they looked away.

"Well, don't just stand there," the thin guard said. He spat on the ground and lifted his pike. "Listen to His Eminence and kill the bastards."

"You've been a busy man, Rennick," the sword general said, watching Cordyn as if he were an ant. High Sword General Koston, as he'd introduced himself, motioned for Cordyn to bow to him.

Cordyn did, hiding his wincing as much as possible. It would not do to show weakness in front of the sword general. He was at least fifty years of age, with close-cropped brown hair that flirted with turning gray and facial hair that already had. He twirled his bushy sideburns as he inspected Cordyn, a shrewd sneer on his face. "In fact, you may have been too busy. Meeting a knife and a whip in such a short time. Your captors must have disliked you."

Cordyn bowed deferentially. In his current role as Sword General Rennick, he was only one rank below Koston, but the man acted as if Cordyn was a newly promoted sword lieutenant. No matter. He thrived when underestimated.

"No more than they disliked anyone else from Oban. I would surely be dead if not for the heroics of Esmeralda here." He gestured to Gen, who stared demurely at her feet. He didn't have to give her such a frilly name, but why not enjoy himself a bit, especially with all the suffering he'd gone through?

"Esmerelda?" the sword general asked. "That's quite the name. A family name?"

"My father," Gen said. The sword general's brow furrowed in disbelief. Cordyn gave her a minuscule shake of the head. "My father's mother," Gen amended.

Thank the gods.

Cordyn patted Gen on the back, willing her to stick to the plan and say as little as possible.

"She's not one for words. I've only heard her speak once or twice a day, but in combat, she's like no other." He thumped her on the back again, hoping she'd realize his message: *shut up.* "She killed seven men. Swinging a greatsword like it weighed nothing. She's an asset to our cause." He stood at attention, saluting the sword general. Gods, it hurt to straighten his back.

"She's not Obanni, Rennick." The sword general flattened the sides of his mustache and twirled them until they jutted out in the front. He looked like he had small hairy horns on the sides of his mouth.

"No, Your Eminence, but she's expressed interest in fighting for us."

"Kill Piranese," Gen said. She tapped the hilt of her sword.

"Woman, you don't sound like a native Rosenfellian." Koston focused his full attention on Gen. Cordyn could do nothing to fix things now. If Gen couldn't talk her way out of this, their scheme had failed.

"Born in Nazlin," she said. "Got the hell out as soon as I could. Not before I realized I hated Piran. Treated us like animals. Bastards."

Koston stared at Gen, speaking in a low tone to one of his officers every few seconds. Cordyn started worrying. Would they decide to imprison or kill her? He'd assumed the Obanni would be desperate for soldiers and would take her on without reserve, but what if his decisions led to Gen's death? He'd never forgive himself.

"Sword lieutenant," Koston said to one of his officers, "When we finish, take the Nazlin woman to the mess tent. Give her food and clothes, but keep her under guard for now. After she eats, take her to train with your finest men."

Evalia and Stinton entered the command tent, flanked by two soldiers, standing at attention. Stinton's face was pale, his wounded arm wrapped in thick brown linen, but he seemed in control of his faculties once more. At least he wasn't spraying shards at random now. Stinton looked like a soldier, Evalia still like a boy playing soldier, though her salute was passable. Thankfully, none of the Obanni leaders seemed interested in them beyond the news they carried.

"We bring a letter," Stinton said. "From the high command." He held out the letter for an Obanni guard, who grabbed it, delivering it to the sword general.

"High Command promises to send us three thousand men. They fear a sizable Kosellan army has amassed along the Trunellic coast."

"By sea?"

"Sword Brigadier Tressan suggests the Kosellans have allied with the Winn."

Curses rang out from several Obanni officers. "The Winn?" a young man wearing a sword lieutenant's insignia asked. "But they don't like anyone."

"Apparently, they like us less than the Kosellans. We need to call a meeting of the squad commanders, as well as our visiting dignitaries. If the Winn are our enemy now, we must make new arrangements."

"Of course, Your Eminence." The sword lieutenant marched toward the western side of the camp, where Cordyn knew the mage children were held.

Koston eyed Cordyn with a flicker of annoyance. "Rennick, you'll be briefed on the meeting. For now, you'll be better suited retiring to the medical tent."

"I'd be honored to attend the meeting." However, as Cordyn finished the last word, he stumbled and collapsed to the ground. He'd felt sturdy enough on his feet, but now that he'd fallen, he didn't think he'd be able to rise on his own. "Perhaps the medical tent would be best, after all."

Two soldiers brought in a litter, lifted Cordyn into it, and hoisted him into the air.

"If I may be excused, Your Eminence?"

Koston nodded his affirmation, and the men carried Cordyn toward a black tent on the northern side of the camp.

"Sir, I must speak frankly," he heard Stinton say to Koston. "I refuse to be a part of this charade any longer."

"Wait," Cordyn said to the men carrying him. "Turn me around, please." They did so, and he saw Stinton, still limping and looking haggard, removing the jacket of his Obanni uniform, and calling upon the waters of the earth.

"I am not an Obanni soldier. I am a Rosenfellian mage, and I have come to you with vital intelligence regarding how to crush the Piranese."

SIXTEEN

WHAT THE DAMNED KIRTH?

Gen stood between three Obanni soldiers, watching as Tobias ruined their plan, betrayed them, and essentially sentenced them all to death.

Godsdammit, Cordyn. You should have listened to me. We could have slit the bastard's throat and dropped him in a creek somewhere. Told Evalia he'd gone home to deal with a family affair. Killing him would have been easy. Now, we're all going to die.

Tobias stepped forward but came to a quick halt as three Obanni soldiers lifted their pikes at him.

"I assure you I mean no harm to you or your men, sword general." He raised his hands. Gen hoped he would try to use his magic, so that the Obanni slit his miserable throat. *The bastard.*

The sword general considered Tobias with narrowed eyes, Koston's untamed beard billowing in the wind. "Why, sir, should I not cut you down where you stand? You have the temerity to stand before me and tell me you are an intruder here, perhaps the enemy."

Tobias smiled, the oddest possible reaction. Who the hell was he?

Cordyn smiled at threats, but Tobias had never shown this cavalier side of himself in the short time Gen had known him.

"Ah, but I am not your enemy, and I would be most displeased to die today. I've spent many weeks planning this; obtaining a uniform, meeting Obanni soldiers, convincing them I was one of their brethren." He gestured toward Cordyn and Evalia. "It would be a waste of my intelligence to kill me."

It makes no sense.

By the shocked look on Cordyn's face, it wasn't some elaborate part of the plan he and Tobias had secretly worked on.

"I knew there was something wrong with you," Gen said. She was on the verge of continuing, but stopped herself. An imbecile Nazlin farm girl wouldn't be so perceptive. She needed to sound simpler. "You're not strong. Soldiers strong."

"Quiet, woman," the soldier on her right said. "Don't interrupt his eminence."

"I—" She stopped as she felt a blade touch against her throat.

I interrupted Tobias, not the godsdamned Swords General.

Koston sniffed the air around him, as if he found it offensive. "You'll need to do more than tell me you mean me no harm."

"I have much to talk with you about, sir, but I would request we do so in private."

"You'll find such a meeting impossible if you're dead, Rosenfellian." Koston waved Tobias away, dismissing the men around him.

"I know of the deal you made, sword general. I'm here to help."

Koston's face lost some of its tranquility. Tobias hit upon a sore spot with the man. "Very well. We shall have a private audience. Rest assured that if you attempt anything I find even slightly rude, antagonistic, or annoying, I'll have your throat slit before you can call out for Kirth's judgment."

"I have no intention of being any of those."

"Sword Lieutenant, take him to the command tent. See to it he's given food and drink." He motioned toward Cordyn and Evalia. "I'll be there once I finish with our brethren. Sword Corporal, what excuses do you wish to make?" Koston asked Evalia.

Evalia straightened her back and stood with a poise that belied the seriousness of the situation. Gen knew she'd not be able to remain so calm in a similar situation.

"I have no excuses to make, Your Eminence. If you believe I deserve censure, I accept your judgment and will submit to any punishment."

Koston stared at her for a moment, eyes inscrutable. He ran a hand through his beard and pursed his lips. "Excellent, Sword Corporal. Find your way to the barracks and get a meal. We'll discuss a new assignment for you shortly."

"Of course, Your Eminence." Evalia bowed and took her leave.

Gods, food sounded good. First Tobias, then Evalia. When would they feed her?

"I'm still hungry," Gen said.

Koston glowered at her. "Impatient too, girl." He dismissed her guards with a wave of his hand. "Show her the barracks and then take her to the training ground. After a demonstration, give her food and drink."

Cordyn tried to catch her eye as she followed the guards away from the sword general, but she refused to look at him.

It's your godsdamned fault.

With only a few pushes and one halfhearted punch to her stomach, the guards led Gen toward one of the three barracks, which looked like several heavy linen tents tied together into one larger tent. At least a hundred bedrolls lay on the dirt and grass floor, packed in to where each soldier would have little privacy if all the troops slept at once. The snoring would be cacophonous.

"You'll sleep here," the guard said. He led her back out of the tent and pointed to an open area covered by a dark blue tarp. The grass around the mess tent struggled to emerge from the muddy ground, odd because the ground she'd just walked on from the barracks to the mess tent was dry, as if it hadn't rained in months.

"You'll eat there."

"Why is that one spot muddy?" Gen asked.

"What?"

"The mud." She pointed to the puddles surrounding the mess tent on all sides.

The guard shrugged, his shoulders tense. "I dunno."

"Oh, right," a second guard said, an even shorter guard than Evalia, and a woman. Gen had seen a few woman officers when they'd arrived, but no woman enlisted soldiers until now. "It's on account of the—"

"Shut your kirthed mouth," the first guard said. "We don't know who the hell this woman is."

"Esmerelda." Gen stuck her hand out. "Nice to meet you."

"Constine," the female guard said.

"None of your kirthed business," the male guard said. "Both of you shut up. That's an order. Gods, we're going to the sparring area, not making friends."

Gen and Constine shared a look; something akin to an understanding passed between them.

What a prick.

"I'll speak to my friends about you," Gen told the male guard. "They're officers, and when they're done with you, you'll be thanking them for giving you latrine duty."

"To Kirth with you, whore," he sneered. "You'll train there." Before Gen could strike the bastard, he slipped past the mess tent and into a clearing, where Obanni troops sparred with one another, using wooden swords to practice maneuvers.

An officer, a sword lieutenant if Gen remembered Obanni insignias correctly, turned to acknowledge her with a sulky frown.

"Ah, the Nazlin woman. You'll perform unarmed combat first." He pointed to a white painted circle on the grass where a brute of a man stood waiting. "If you harm any of the men, I am authorized to kill you. Understood?"

"Yes." She stepped into the circle and faced her opponent. He wore beige linen trousers cut off at the knee, his shirtless torso lined with muscles Gen didn't realize existed. He had a dark tan, a shaved head, and the beginnings of a black beard shrouding his face. As he pulled his arms up into an Obanni salute—both hands on the top of his head and a slight bow—Gen marveled at the black and red tattoos—swirling down the entirety of his deep amber arms; she'd not seen the design before, but she felt jealous she didn't have any similar markings. The man towered over her, at least a head taller. She didn't feel intimidated often, but this man looked strong enough to defeat her.

When he'd finished his salute, the man smiled at her, a wide grin that displayed surprisingly white teeth.

"Well, 'ello," he said in a thick accent she couldn't place. "I'm Cork. Don't got no other names anymore, but sometimes they call me the Big Bastard."

"Ge—" She paused, panicking. "Esmerelda. No other names either."

"Wonderful to meet ya. Says we gets to wrestling, then we can get drunk?"

"Loser buys the drinks."

She hadn't realized her jaw was clenched, but Cork's kind tone and confiding manner put her at ease. She took in a deep breath through her nose and blew it out, focusing on the task ahead. Her fingers tingled slightly, but she brushed that away. She'd fight to the best of her ability, of course, but she'd not attempt anything to seriously hurt this Cork fellow.

She raised her hands in front of her chest and bent her knees into a defensive stance, leaning onto her back foot for balance and mobility. Against a bigger opponent like Cork, she'd need to move faster to defeat him. If she let him get a hold of her, she'd struggle to break free from his grasp.

With a quickness his hulking frame and rippled muscles did not suggest, Cork lunged for her arms, grappling her and spinning her, twisting her body until her torso radiated pain. Gods, she'd forgotten about her wounds. Not the most recent shard punctures to her ankle—those still stung—but the cleaver to the shoulder and the icy desecration of her stomach. The tonic had done so much for the pain that she'd considered the wounds fully healed.

She'd been incorrect. "Shit, gods bastard shit."

Cork guffawed, a high-pitched titter more suited for a debutante or a child than a bruiser of a man.

"You's got quite a vocabulary, innit." With unsurprising force—he was a big bastard after all—he pushed Gen down, her stomach colliding with the ground and knocking all the air out of her lungs. Breathing—or at least attempting to—in shallow pain-filled spurts, she tried to roll onto her back, so she could at least see Cork, but he kept her pinned.

"D'ya yield?"

Gods, no. "Get kirthed."

"Okay." She felt Cork's knee press into her kidneys.

"Gods," she muttered, her voice an agonized whisper.

"Well, woman, do you yield?" the sword lieutenant asked.

"No." She grunted in exertion and used every bit of her strength to kick out at Cork, though none of her kicks hit.

I probably look like a farm animal.

She roared as she swung her torso, trying to throw Cork off; he still held her arms to her sides, and his grip only tightened the more she attempted to break free.

"You're strong," Cork said, sending his other knee into Gen's ribs. She lost what little breath she'd regained.

"I'm just getting started."

"Me too."

She threw an elbow at his face, hitting his clavicle instead, though he still reacted with a yelp. A solid hit, then. He released her arms. She spun away, then got to her knees and faced him.

"Let's try this again."

Cork grinned even wider, like a child receiving a gift. "That sounds excellent. Haven't had this much fun in months." He motioned to the ground in front of him. "Stand up. Ain't no fun if yer on the ground."

Gen stood and stared him down. They feinted at each other for a few moments, while hoots and laughter from the crown cheered them on.

"You're good at this," she said. "Better than most I've gone up against." She kicked at his knees, a speculative effort.

"So is you." He swiped a palm at her face, but she dodged, avoiding the worst of the blow, receiving only a slight scratch from his fingernails. "After I win, I think we's gonna be friends."

"I agree. We'll get drunker than we have any right to. After I win, of course." A quick grab for his shoulders, but her hands slipped off; the sweat on his naked upper body made it harder to hold on. Her wounds protested at her movements, sharp jabs like a dagger to the gut. She had little time left. In less than a minute, she expected she'd lose the required strength needed to defeat Cork. Time to do this.

She bent her knees, right foot forward, watching Cork's enormous frame moving toward her. Just as he reached where she waited, she rolled urgently to the side, out of his reach. He stumbled.

Thank the Swordsman—and Ned—for the energy-infused water. With a vitality she'd never had this late in a bout before, Gen popped up and pounced on his back and slammed him to the ground. Hand to the back of his head, elbow into the middle of his spine, knee to his pelvis.

"Yield," she said.

Cork said nothing. She pressed her knee further into his bollocks.

"I yield. Gods, I yield."

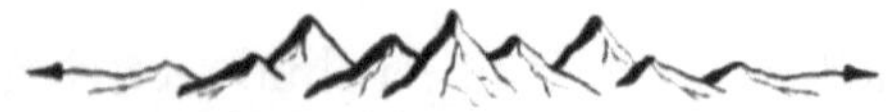

Ale sounded great, but the quartermaster rationed out something brown—like whiskey, but not quite—which tasted fine but did little to quench Gen's thirst. Splayed out on hay-filled mats, she and Cork propped their heads up against sacks of flour as they drank. Some flour had leaked from the sacks, creating a soggy mess of powder around Cork. Dressed in a loose white tunic now, Cork sat with his legs out in front of him, wiggling his bare toes as he drank.

"Thought I'd beat you," Cork said. "Was already plannin' out me victory drinks."

"You put up quite a fight. In the end, I was just thirstier than you."

They polished off their first glass, and Cork called for the quartermaster to bring the bottle. "We's got more to drink, so leave the bugger." His hands shook as he pointed to the half-full bottle of deep brown liquor.

"What exactly are we drinking?"

"Liquor!" he cheered.

"What type, I mean?"

"Gods if I know. Tastes decent, though, and gets ya drunk. Not like the liquor back home, though." His eyes glazed over as if he were somewhere else.

"Where is that? You have an accent I've not heard before."

"Trunel's home, but the accent...not acquainted with the Winn, then?" he asked. "A lot of you mainlanders aren't."

Cork was Winn? Gen knew little about the mysterious island and its mage inhabitants. According to an old sailor who frequented the taverns of Mintar, they hated all outsiders, performed water worshipping rituals, ate children, and had several other odd and gruesome customs. The old man was known for embellishing his stories for drinks, so Gen never gave him much attention. She wished she had paid him a little more mind just now.

"I've never met one." She paused, hoping she wouldn't offend him. "I didn't know you could leave the island."

"Aye, we don't leave often, but there's no rule about it." He shrugged. "'Course, once you leave, it's hard to get back."

"So, you're a mage?"

Cork downed his entire glass of not-whisky. "No. Sorry, that's mighty funny. I've got no talent fer that bollocks. I'm only half Winn, see. My mam was a mage, but my father came from the coast of Trunel. We moved back to Sarakan when I was a boy, but my mam taught me to speak, so I carry her accent."

"I don't really know how mages work," Gen admitted.

"Well, they stick their hands out and bloody ice—"

"I know that," she cut in. "I mean, why aren't you a mage if your mother was? Do both parents have to be mages?"

Cork scratched at his chin, looking up toward the two suns. "I don't rightly know. Mam never talked about that. I just assumed some people was born mages and some wasn't. There's lots of regular folk among the Winn. People think we's all mages, but there's all sorts."

"Are your markings—"

"Dreamshapes. That's what they're called."

"Are they a Winn thing?"

"You hear stories about how's they're supposed to make mages stronger, but usually only from drunks and troubadours. I just like the way they look. We's all got 'em up in the Winn."

She looked at the intricate layers of swirling shapes, almost like waves descending his arms. "They're beautiful."

"Well, get some." He made it sound like the easiest thing in the world.

"I'm not Winn."

But I'd happily pretend to be long enough to get those markings on my arms.

"Doesn't matter. We're not particular."

"That goes against everything I've ever heard about the Winn." She hesitated. "I've heard you hate all outsiders."

"We keep to ourselves, I s'pose, but we's got no special hatred for no one." He slapped the flour sack he sat again, and a plume of dust floated around him. "Well, I s'pose there are some right vicious psychopaths among us, but you can say that about everywhere."

Even Piran.

Memories from her childhood flooded back, trying to break the dam she'd built for them, but she couldn't face that right now. Not again, so soon after whipping Cordyn. Not with so much at stake: her life, the lives of her friends, and the safety of the captive children.

Yes, Cork is kind, but I'm using him for information, that's all.

"How did you come to join the Obanni?"

"Not too different from you, I'd assume. Befriended a man who turned out to be an Obanni while working a mercenary job. The sword general offered me double pay and unlimited drink. More lucrative than guarding whatever wealthy bastard needs protection on his journey to tup his mistress. More fun, too. You don't get to hit the clients when you're a guard, but as a soldier?" He paused. "The Obanni still think I talk funny."

"You do."

"So do you, friend." He took another gulp of liquor. "Where're you from? Can't be Rosenfel."

"Nazlin."

"Never been there."

"No reason to."

After Cork poured another glass for them both, Gen sipped the liquor, finding herself growing fonder of the smoky bitterness with each drink. She'd have to buy a bottle once this was all over.

She thought she could trust Cork: he seemed genuine, and with Cordyn wounded in a tent somewhere, she needed to talk to someone. She'd have to bring Cork into her confidence—not with everything, but enough to ask basic questions regarding the camp and the prisoners. He might even become a friend.

"Do you know why there's an Obanni camp in the middle of Rosenfel?"

He scratched his chin again.

He might need to grow a beard soon to hide the scratch marks. Perhaps I'm making him think too much.

"I don't know much about the politics, but I'd guess it's related to our deal with the mages."

"What mages?" *The children,* she almost said.

Godsdammit Gen, get a hold of yourself or slow down the drinking.

"There's a group of 'em who loiter around the big enclosure on the western side of camp. Haughty buggers, the lot. Don't speak to none of us, and act like we're lower than nothin'. Don't want us going inside their area neither."

"Do they let the children out of the enclosure?"

"What? Who said anything about children?"

"I—"

Shit. This is why you should never talk, Gen.

"I don't know. Are there any children in camp?"

"Gods no. This is the army, Esmeralda. We're soldiers."

"The mages aren't."

"The mages is adults, the lot of them," he insisted.

So Cork, and hopefully, the others in the Obanni camp, knew nothing of the child captives. Something she could use to her advantage.

Or something Cordyn could use. She needed to get this information to him as soon as possible. If only she could travel through the camp without attracting attention. However, Cordyn was off somewhere else, probably unconscious. She'd have to make the plans now.

Gods help us all.

"Are any of the mages psychopaths? Like what we just talked about?" She was hesitant to give more information, but it was necessary. "I was attacked on the road. By a mage with an evil voice. It sounded like oil. He ripped my stomach apart." She gestured to her torso. "I'd like to find him and cut his godsdamned head off, and I have a feeling he might be here."

"Sorry 'bout yer stomach, then." Cork gave her an apologetic smile. "I don't know none of the mages well enough to say nothin' one way or the other. They're all a bunch of bollocks-tuggers, far as I'm concerned."

"Cork, would you show me around the camp? I don't know where I'm going, but I'd like to see my friends." Gen yawned. "But perhaps a nap first."

"Sure, no harm in yous knowin' where you're walking. And I'm always happy to help a friend."

"I'm honored to have you as a friend, Cork." *I'm only using you a little.* "Call me Gen."

"Hi Gen." He greeted. "My name's still Cork." He treated her to one of his trademark grins. "We foreigners gotta stick together, don't we?"

"Yes, yes, we do."

SEVENTEEN

After the Obanni whisked Gen away for clothes, food, and to teach their troops a lesson, Cordyn waited for a debrief from a member of the Obanni command. No one showed. He sat on the frigid ground outside of the command tent, too far away to eavesdrop. Moving closer was out of the question. He could barely breathe without pain, let alone walk or crawl.

Evalia had already left for the troop barracks; she was probably napping after a delicious meal, dressed in a freshly pressed uniform.

No one brought him anything.

Typical. You get whipped for your country, and they won't even toss you a piece of bread or a blanket.

A short, yet broad soldier appeared, and Cordyn hoped he brought dinner. Instead, the man scooped him up—not gently—and carried him to the medic tent, laying him on a hay-filled mat. Cordyn lay sprawled on his stomach, trying to keep his head up to watch for movement in the soldier's barracks outside the tent, but fighting a losing battle with his neck. The wool lining of the mat itched his bare arms, a minor inconvenience compared to the pain—*and hunger, dammit*—overtaking him.

A sickly thin man with a receding hairline and bulbous eyes entered, introducing himself as Medic Thomos. His nose nearly reached down to his lips, and he reeked of bitter spirits, probably whiskey. Thomos leaned down to examine Cordyn's wounds, running a cold metal apparatus along the sores on Cordyn's back. Cordyn held his breath, both in expectation of pain and to avoid the man's odor.

"Hmm," Thomos said. Cordyn felt another frigid object pressed against the skin along his kidneys, this time accompanied by the prick of a needle.

"Gods," Cordyn said, gasping.

"I will need to test your blood," Thomos said. His monotone voice betrayed little of what he thought of his patient's condition. "To see if you have lost vitality. If your blood has soured, there is little I can do, I fear."

"Usually, people warn me before they stab me." Cordyn pressed his face into thin buckwheat pillow on his bed, wishing he could turn over to berate the godsdamned medic.

"Usually, my patients don't speak unless I ask them questions." Thomos then pressed the needle into Cordyn's back again.

"Shit bastard!" Cordyn wished he could be more eloquent, but moments like this called for visceral responses.

"Your blood has started to sour, but it can be fixed." Thomos placed a rancid rag in Cordyn's mouth, the soggy stench of saliva and sweat pushing him to the verge of vomiting. "This will hurt."

Cordyn moved his face away from the offending rag. "And what you've already done didn't?"

"No." Thomos pushed the rag back into his mouth. "Bite down."

Cordyn complied, somehow managing not to vomit as the repulsive liquid from the rag seeped into his mouth. He heard a cork pop, and a moment later his entire world became agony as liquid poured onto his back, ripping at his very soul. He heard screaming, failing to acknowledge it was his own. It was as if his body traveled across the room, and he was watching from afar. Although he could see the pillow in front of him, he didn't believe he was still lying on the bed. After the pain he'd felt, he had to be on the floor, or worse yet, in a torture chamber.

He attempted to speak, but nothing came out beyond gurgles. Breathing was hard for the first few minutes after the medic's assault, but when he could finally inhale again, the scent of alcohol stung his nose and eyes. The medic may still have been a drunk, but at least some of the alcoholic odor on the man must have come from his treatment methods, as barbarous as they were.

"Your blood should remain stable now," Thomos said. "I will need to apply more yorn liquor daily, but I believe you will survive, and stand a chance of healing back to an almost normal state."

Gods.

Yorn liquor was undrinkable, higher in alcohol than any other spirit Cordyn knew of, and its vile flavor made it a drink for only the most desperate of drinkers.

"You're going to do that every day? I think I might rather just die."

Thomos sniffed at him. "It will hurt, yes, but the pain will lessen each day. After a week, I could pour boiling yorn liquor on your naked back, and you would only grimace."

"He may have other things to grimace about," the sword general's crisp voice said from the entrance of the medic tent.

"Your Eminence." Cordyn could only see his blasted pillow still, but he imagined Thomos saluted Koston with all the deference due to a senior officer.

Have you come to pour alcohol on my back as well?

"Your Eminence, sir," he said aloud. "I am honored to have you visit me."

"I'm not here to visit you, Rennick. I want answers. Medic, turn him over."

"The wounds are on his back, Your Eminence—"

"I'm flattered that you care, Thomos," Cordyn said.

"Turn him over." Koston's voice took on a sharpness which suggested disagreement would lead to dire consequences.

"Of course, sir."

Thomos's bony hands gripped Cordyn's sides, and with a grunt, the medic flipped him over. He'd expected to descend into agony once more, but, while his wounds rubbing against the mattress hurt, it was manageable. The yorn liquor worked for all its downsides.

Koston stood before him, mustache twirled, looking down at him as if he were an exotic animal Koston had found wounded on the road. Draped in a cloak of pure white and wearing two rapiers—one on each side of his waist—Koston had the air of a man who did not expect to wait for the answers he desired.

"How did you come to be captured, Rennick?"

Cordyn had practiced an answer for this: he'd gone to a village to purchase supplies, where he'd been duped by a merchant who offered him food and weaponry, but instead betrayed him to Kosellan spies in the area. However, after watching the sword general in action, that story seemed simplistic and much too broad to convince a man as shrewd as Koston.

The best lies contain a bit of the truth.

"I'm embarrassed to say this, but I failed in my mission, Your Eminence." He lowered his eyes, attempting to look sufficiently ashamed. "I'd been tasked to deliver a message from the high command to our forces in Trunel, and the mission started off well enough, but I let the baseness of my passions get the better of me."

"How so?" Koston's lip curled into a frown.

"I met a woman, sir. At an inn in Dramin." He gave a lovelorn sigh. "A beautiful woman with a voice that made me question whether she was a goddess. As she sang, I wanted her and nothing else."

"What does this have to do with Kosellan spies?" Koston eyed him, no hint of emotion in his dark brown eyes.

"I'm getting there, Your Eminence. The woman, she took me back to her chambers, where we spent—" Cordyn broke off and covered his face with his hands, as if he were overcome with emotion. "We spent the most passionate and meaningful moments of my life together. After one night, I was ready to throw all my dignity as a sword general away and marry her, a foreign commoner." He rubbed his eyes, willing liquid to come out of them, though none came. Crying on demand was not one of his skills.

"I fail to see why this matters. Officers marry camp followers and whores often enough. You wouldn't be the first to fall prey to a woman's charms. You're a soldier. Pull yourself together and do away with the dramatics!" Koston pounded a fist against his thigh. "I have no patience for this. Tell me straight, how is this related to Kosellan spies?"

"She was a Kosellan spy! She betrayed me. I let myself fall prey to my baser emotions..." Cordyn looked down, the soul of contriteness. "I deserved the suffering I went through."

"Rennick," Koston started gravely, "You have delivered your message. You have gained helpful intelligence of the enemy and their tactics of luring away Obanni officers. I say you have served your punishment for this mistake, and yet..." Koston stroked his left sideburn in thought, pushing the white curls away from his face, giving him the untamed look of an explorer or scientist, not a strait-laced general.

This had been the part of the plan Cordyn worried about the most. If the sword general decided he had betrayed the nation to an unforgiveable extent, Cordyn would face execution, and while

Gen might still save Ezra somehow, he preferred a result where he still lived.

"I'd say that you've served your punishment," Koston said, twirling his sideburn, "but that depends on if you gave away any vital information while your captors tortured you."

Cordyn shook his head. "No, they wanted to know information I never had, though I would have never allowed a single secret to pass my lips. My erstwhile lover's associates bound my hands and threw me in the cellar of a farmhouse a few hours' ride north of Dramin. They starved me, kept water from me, and left me naked in those frigid underground conditions." He grimaced. "When I wouldn't talk, they resorted to further activities."

"A flogging."

"Several, actually, but first they decorated my face." Cordyn motioned to the crusted blood on his face. "As you can see, they were not artistic savants."

"How did you escape?"

"The woman, the one who betrayed me, must have had some small sympathy for me after the moments we shared, and she visited me in the cellars to apologize for what she'd had to do for the sake of her country. We shared a heartfelt moment, we kissed, and then she loosened my bonds. They were rubbing against my wrists and were on the verge of breaking skin. She told me it was one last kindness she could do for me."

Koston's eyes narrowed. "That was not wise of her."

"I overpowered her. She had a knife on her, and I managed to retrieve it and cut myself loose. Then I left the cellars and moved up into the farmhouse itself."

"And you left the woman imprisoned there?"

"No, Your Eminence." He paused for effect. "I stabbed her through the heart."

"Gods, man." Koston's face grew pale.

The hardened soldier has feelings. Something to remember.

"I had no other choice. I sneaked out of the farmhouse and had almost escaped the grounds when seven Kosellans surrounded me. With only a small knife, and wounded as I was, I had little hope of defeating such a force. That's when the Nazlin woman arrived with her sword and slaughtered my pursuers."

"Why did she help you?"

"I still don't know, sir. She doesn't say much, beyond that she hates the Piranese, and the Kosellans by extension. She retrieved my horse from the stables, then procured the horse and cart. We'd planned to pass into Trunel and meet our forces there, but then we met Sword Corporal Holz and the Rosenfellian mage, who I thought was Sword Lieutenant Brust until a few hours ago."

"You saw no signs he was not an Obanni soldier?"

"No, the man is a talented actor. I had no reason to suspect him."

"He fought against those bandits. What did you call them, the Hillsmen?"

"Yes, Your Eminence."

Close enough.

"Did he use his mage abilities?"

"No, he swung a sword like the rest of us. Had some skill with it too. The Imperial Academy must teach fencing."

Koston wrung his hands. "Very well. You'll receive no further punishment. Your wounds are enough."

"Thank you, your eminence." Cordyn bowed as low as he could.

"Now, let's get down to business," Koston said in a brisk manner. "You may have wondered why we're camped here in the middle of Rosenfel."

"That had crossed my mind."

"It's quite simple. Rosenfel and Oban came to an agreement. They help us take Kosel, and in return, we assist their invasion of Piran."

"Piran?" Cordyn asked, fighting to keep his voice as calm as possible.

"Yes," Koston said. "They invaded three days ago. Our last correspondence put the Rosenfellian troops just outside Mintar."

Bugger.

The room was growing smaller by the minute. Cordyn sat on the bed, cursing the sword general, the Obanni, and the Rosenfellians. Most of all, he cursed himself. His mission to Kosel was obsolete.

He rubbed crusted over liquid from his eyes, wondering what in Kirth's name he could do to fix the situation.

I can hardly flatter the sword general and the Rosenfellians into rescinding their invasion. Getting a message out would do nothing either.

He was in no shape to steal a horse and ride for Piran, that was certain. That left Gen as the only available option, but would she even be willing? No, she would want nothing of it until the mage children were safe.

And yet, in the back of his mind, he struggled to care about Piran. He was bed ridden in an enemy camp, days away, and, if Piran couldn't stave off the Rosenfellian invasion without him, then him rushing there would do little.

He pushed the thought away. Piran would have to wait. He'd abandoned one mission but found another, and countless young lives were in his hands.

Time to work.

"Medic Thomos," he said, "I wanted to thank you for all you've done for me." A bit of flattery never hurt. "You have been most helpful and truly an agent of Torr." He noticed Thomos's face redden. "Might I go for a walk, sir?"

"A walk?" Thomos squinted at him, his bulbous eyes sinking into the folds of his puffy cheeks. "In your condition?"

"I may be in pain, sir, but I'll be in worse shape if I'm not able to stretch my legs and get fresh air. I won't overexert myself."

"Five minutes at the most," Thomos said. "And use a cane." He handed Cordyn a whittled branch.

Cordyn agreed to Thomos's conditions and stepped out into the early evening air. The breeze woke him up a bit, and he hoped the invigorating feeling would keep him energized for his brief stroll. However, after less than a minute, he was heaving against a fence post, exhausted, and unsure if he could walk another step.

Overconfidence strikes again.

The mage children were in a tent complex within sight, but between the retching, back convulsions, and extreme exhaustion, Cordyn wasn't sure he could make it even halfway to the tents. The rescue would have to wait until after he had a nap.

Two robed men stood outside the tent complex, too far for Cordyn to see their features. Guards, most likely.

"I say," Cordyn called to the robed men. "I require your assistance."

"Indeed, you do, by Hurod." The man spoke with a precise air and had an odd accent. Not Rosenfellian or Obanni. Cordyn couldn't place it. "You Obanni haven't learned the meaning of leisure." The man looked down his hawkish nose at Cordyn, sallow eyes regarding him with suspicion. The man had a closely manicured black beard which contrasted his pale cheeks, his lips curled into a permanent sneer. A man who knew cruelty.

"I'm sorry?"

"You should rest. Have a glass of whiskey, entertain a young woman of your acquaintance. Instead, you attempt to do your duty when you are in no shape to do so."

"I always do my duty. I took an oath to the high sword general."

"Well, the sword general should provide better relaxation activities for you." The man walked forward, and through the strands of lantern light shining down on the man, Cordyn saw red and brown robes.

Mage robes.

Rosenfellian mages in an Obanni military camp. Not only Tobias, but who knew how many more? The situation grew more bizarre every minute.

"Surely you won't begrudge me the small pleasure of an evening stroll. One must convalesce somehow."

"Of course. You may stroll all you wish. As long as your strolls take you elsewhere."

"The sword general—"

"Will agree with us, you fool. I'll gladly summon him to dole out your punishment."

Bugger. He didn't need the sword general's scrutiny, especially so soon after avoiding further censure from the man.

"Forgive me for questioning you. I did not expect to find Rosenfellians in our camp. I arrived today. I hope we can move on from this with no residual enmity?"

The mage grunted an acknowledgment. "As long as you go back to your tent and leave us be."

"Ah, therein lies the issue. My turn about the camp started with high hopes, but I seem to have exhausted my strength. I wonder if you could assist me in getting back to my tent?"

The man scowled. "If we must." He stepped into the enclosure and spoke to someone inside. A damned nuisance—Cordyn could no longer hear what the man said.

Two men dressed in mage robes emerged from the tent.

"My associates will deliver you back to your bed," the condescending mage said. "See that we don't meet again."

Cordyn bowed. "Your servant, sir."

A broad-shouldered man with a receding hairline hoisted him onto his shoulder and carried him the fifty yards to the medic tent. When they arrived, he deposited Cordyn at the tent entrance and walked away without saying a word.

Cordyn pulled himself into a crouch and used all his strength to stand. Pausing for a moment to catch his breath, he glanced back to the mages who had disappeared into their enclosure.

How very singular.

A nap sounded excellent. A few hours of sleep and then he'd figure out how to get around the damned mages. He wished violent illness on them all—could he sneak yorn liquor into their wine? That would incapacitate them, but the chances of anyone failing to notice the sour taste and the stench of yorn liquor were low.

A nap and then I'll save the world.

He found Evalia, dressed in a new—and better-tailored—Obanni uniform, waiting for him in the medic tent. She wore her red hair up in a tight bun, and he noticed she had a small mole under her left ear, almost like a black diamond. Sitting by the bed, she read from a wrinkled parchment, her brow furrowed in concentration. He couldn't help but gaze at her face: scrunched, squinting, and, gods, as lovely as ever.

"Already getting love letters from your fellow soldiers?" He stumbled across the tent and collapsed onto the bed.

The beautiful woman will see me for the weakling I am. Something she's known for quite a while.

"I asked my superior officer if I could come visit you." Color rose into her cheeks, and she reached up to brush a stray hair away from her face.

"I'm glad they let you," he said in a soft voice. "The other company I've had so far has not been the kindest. I'll try not to bleed on you."

"I told her you and I had—"she hesitated—"become close while traveling together, and I wished to eat dinner with you."

"Lovers on the road." The pit of his stomach grew warmer. "An excellent trope." *And not a bad idea.*

"The sword lieutenant thought so, too. She thinks you're quite handsome underneath all the blood and scars. Perhaps even because of it."

"Oh? I may have to meet this fine officer." He faltered. There would be time later for mirth. Now, he needed information. "How are things in the camp? Where's Stinton?"

"I haven't seen Mr. Stinton since he revealed his true identity to the Obanni command. It's odd. He betrayed us, but, according to my sword lieutenant, he told the sword general personally that while he tricked me, I was an officer of the highest level, and I deserved commendation." She pointed to a gold pin on her uniform. "I've been promoted to sword lieutenant, second class."

"You've gone from enlisted to an officer in record time." He gave her an Obanni salute. "Salutations."

"Why would he protect me? Nor expose you and Gen's true identities?" She shook her head. "It makes no sense."

"Yes, gods know what the man is up to. I hope we'll have the chance to ask." He lifted the parchment, but avoided reading it. Gen was upset with him, no doubt. He should have listened to her.

"Have you seen Gen?"

Evalia placed her hands in her lap and scrunched her nose, thinking. Her freckles shone against the slight flush of her face, almost the same color as her hair.

She's godsdamned radiant, especially when she's not yelling or cursing my name. If I'm honest with myself, she's the most attractive woman I've met.

"Last I saw, she was wrestling against the strongest Obanni soldiers and showing off. She's making friends. Not surprising that they love her." She held up the wrinkled parchment. "She asked me to bring you a note. Oh, and I brought you food." She picked up a white cloth satchel from under her seat and put it on the bed. "It's not much. Bread, cheese, broth, and wine."

"That sounds like a feast to me currently. I see you've read Gen's letter?"

"She never said it was private, and I have as much a right to know as you."

"Of course." He unfolded the parchment and read the first line.

This pains me to say, but you should have listened to me.

"I made an error," he told Evalia. "Gen warned me about Stinton, but I brushed her off. It's my fault."

I've made a friend here. Cork. He's not Obanni either. With a little more time, I may be able to get him on our side. Give me until tomorrow before you go rushing in to save the day. I hope your back doesn't hurt too much. It'd be a shame to have to carry you as we flee the camp.

-Gen.

Gods. She would write everything in plain language. If this had been intercepted...

He looked at Evalia. "The situation has become more complicated. There are Rosenfellian mages here guarding the children. And that's not the worst part. Rosenfel has allied with Oban."

"What?" Evalia blinked rapidly. "No. We'd never."

"You have," he said, matter-of-fact in the face of his country's demise. "Rosenfel wants Piran, and Oban will help them in exchange for assistance in taking and holding Kosel and occupying Trunel."

"But the Imperium has always hated Piran." She looked pleadingly at him, as if she wanted him to admit he'd been lying.

"They're jealous of how attractive we all are."

She put her hand to her mouth, either to stop a laugh or cover a gasp. "Cordyn, stop that. Not at a time like this. It makes no sense why we'd help the Obanni imprison our own mage children."

"That's something we can ask later. Preferably while they're at sword-point."

They fell into silence for a few moments. There was little more to say beyond that they needed to make progress. Soon.

After a few moments, Evalia broke the silence. "You should eat." She tapped the satchel that sat on his lap.

He opened the satchel and took a bite of the bread, a thin crust that broke apart in his hands and softened in his mouth. "Our new friends may be derelicts and kidnappers, but they make a damned fine loaf of bread."

Underneath the cheese was a note—a crumpled piece of ripped parchment.

If you seek the children, meet me outside the tent complex at dawn.

He showed the note to Evalia.

"Cryptic of Gen," she said. "Though why she wrote two separate notes baffles me."

"That note can't be from Gen. The handwriting's different, much more legible." He crossed his arms and waited for Evalia to come to the same conclusion he had. There was only one person who could have sent the note.

"Well, then, who else knows that we're trying to save the children?"

"Either we've been less stealthy in our endeavors than we thought, or it comes from someone who's known the plan all along."

"Tobias." Evalia rubbed her hands together, as if they were cold.

"Yes."

"What will you do?"

He gave her a wan smile. "Oh, I'll go to the tent complex at dawn."

There's little else to do, beyond lying in bed wounded.

"What if it's a trap?" she asked, leaning closer to him.

"I'm certain it is. However, there's little else we can do, and if it isn't a trap, it may be our best chance."

"All right, we'll go."

"I think it would be best—"

"I'll not argue." She stood, left hand on her hip, right hand across her waist. Imperious, lovely, and on the verge of yelling.

Ah, angry again. That's more like it.

Cordyn brought his hands to his face, rubbing his temples, feeling the slightest bit of tension melt away. Evalia deserved to be part of the rescue. Her brother was among the prisoners, after all.

"We'll go together."

She exhaled, her posture loosening. No doubt she'd been gearing up for another argument.

"Thank you."

"Thank me when we succeed. For now, go find Gen and deliver a message. At dawn, we move."

After Evalia left to do her duties as a sword lieutenant and to pass a message to Gen, Cordyn lay on his stomach and slipped in and out of consciousness. He regained lucidity to hear rustling noises from above him.

Medic Thomos stood above him, yorn liquor in hand. "Time for tonight's bath, sir."

Oh, buggering bastard gods.

EIGHTEEN

AMID A SEA OF robes, Tobias scanned the tent complex for familiar faces. As soon as he arrived at the Obanni camp, he knew something was amiss. Odd. He saw a running stream traversing the length of the camp, yet it connected to nothing except divots in the ground. An easy way to provide drinking water for a large group of people, and something only a group of mages could create. One mage, whenever distracted, would lose grip on the water, causing the stream to disappear. The water lost no momentum, a sure sign several mages were working together to fuel the stream. Then, he saw the telltale red and brown robes of his brethren mages of Rosenfel.

He immediately knew Tallen's plan would fail, even if it had worked to get them into the camp.

And I'll be the reason it fails.

If any Rosenfellian mage had recognized him, and it came out he wasn't an Obanni soldier, Evalia and Gen would have faced unnecessary scrutiny. Better to have the Obanni command disappointed in Evalia's inability to spot an impostor than to believe she was an impostor herself.

He'd revealed himself, and the Obanni troops brought him here, to the tents where the imprisoned mage children sat under guard of twenty Rosenfellian mages. Tobias recognized two of the men as fellow untethered mages—those mages who did not live and serve at the Academy. He refused to enter the Academy unless under direct order from the Imperium, and even then, he resented being there.

He still waited for Sword General Koston, who'd suggested they have their private meeting with haste and had yet to show up.

I don't want to meet with you, anyway, Your bloody Eminence. In fact, you could fall into an icy river, and I wouldn't care at all.

Rosenfellian mages were selfish and corrupt, and he resented them: their money, their lavish chambers at the Academy, and their hardship-free lives.

Gods, if I could burn the Academy down, I would. For father.

Tobias's father owned a shipping company in Dramin, and Tobias grew up into a life of ease until he'd had to accept the Summons, which required him to move to the Academy and begin his training.

The Imperial Academy in Dramin loomed above the city, a beacon of knowledge and power. Or so the tutors there told their young charges. Tobias hadn't wanted to leave home to learn his trade with other young prospective mages, but arguing with his father changed nothing. He went to the Academy and never saw his father again.

He was nine years old.

Not so much a school as a boarding house where each young mage worked individually with a tutor, the Academy bustled with young mages learning the incantations, hand-signs, and best safety methods for their talents. Some of the young mages traveled with their tutors, only staying at the Academy when they weren't on a mission. Tobias's tutor, Master Renedian, was more an academic than a man of action, and he mostly stayed at the Academy, leaving Tobias comfortable, but bored by the peaceful life.

That all changed when Tobias turned fourteen, the age of manhood among Rosenfellian mages. He returned home, bidding goodbye to the tutor and a few other acquaintances—the mages at the Academy were not encouraged to interact socially; the point was to grow as mages, not make friends—only to find that his home was gone. He still remembered how it felt when the carriage brought him to his childhood home, a small yellow house near the Dramin harbor, a wonderful garden of winterplums in the front yard. His mother was born in Piran and grew the fruit as a way to remember her homeland. Tobias had never been to Piran, but he greatly enjoyed stealing the winterplums when his mother wasn't looking, and savoring the juicy, tart sweetness. Tobias descended from the carriage, eager to see his family, and more importantly, steal more winterplums, but he stopped short when he noticed the scene in front of him.

The yellow house was gone. The garden as well. In their place was a drab white building full of bustling, uniformed men. His family's home was now a supply depot for the Imperial Navy. Shocked, he walked into the depot and approached a clerk.

"Hello, where is my house?" he asked the clerk. The man looked down at him through bespectacled eyes.

"I am not your father, boy," he said. "I don't know where you live. You are on Imperial Navy property. State your business or depart." The clerk motioned to an armed guard nearby, who glared at Tobias.

"No," Tobias said, "This used to be my house. I lived here, on this land. Do you know what happened to my house? My family?"

The clerk's eyes turned suspicious. "Those who lived here were charged with treason and arrested. I don't know where they are now."

Tobias felt the world collapsing around him. His father had not been an especially kind man, but Tobias could not believe he'd been a traitor. He'd been so proud of his work as an imperial mage, traveling to mage camps along the border and assisting with the security of the nation.

Tobias left what had once been his home and wandered. He stopped at a forest green house across the street, the home of the McCalls, who'd had a girl a year older than him. He knocked on the white oak door, hoping someone was home, preferably someone who knew where his parents were.

Gregor McCall opened the door. He was a kindly man with a white beard to match the tufts of hair that sprouted wildly from his head. He wore a green and brown patterned waistcoat that did not fully cover his rotund belly.

"Tobias," McCall said. "What are you doing here?"

"My parents," Tobias said. "They're gone."

"A damned shame. They did not deserve it."

"But where are they?"

McCall motioned into the house. "Come in, boy, this is not a conversation for the streets." McCall led him through a dark hallway into his library, an imposing room filled from floor to ceiling with books. Tobias had to step over several piles to get to a chair. He took a deep breath, inhaling the familiar, calming scent of old books, the musty pages reminding him of better times at the Academy.

"There's no easy way to say this, Tobias," McCall said, his voice gentle. "Your father was taken to Stonegate."

"The imperial prison? But that's for murderers and criminals." Tobias was dizzy and he would have fallen had he been standing.

"Your father was accused of treason. I don't know for what or by whom. But he's in Stonegate now, and there's only one way out."

Tobias knew what that meant, but he didn't wish to speak aloud about his father dying. Stonegate gave prisoners two options: serve a life sentence or die. Those willing to perform manual labor may live for several years, while others would die within weeks.

"What of my mother?" Tobias asked, a sharp emptiness growing inside him, eating away at what little hope he had left.

"She's not in prison. I believe she was shipped back to Piran."

"Then that's where I'll go," Tobias said.

McCall lowered his eyes. "That would be dangerous, Tobias. You can stay here with us. We have the room, and your father was a friend."

"Thank you, sir, but there's nothing left for me here."

Tobias said his goodbyes and left the McCall house. He booked passage on a Piran bound carriage with what little pocket money he had left. He sat in the carriage, watching Dramin recede into the distance, and he vowed never to return until he had found his mother and restored his father's good name.

He traveled to Mintar, found an inexpensive room that didn't have too many cockroaches, and began searching for any signs of his mother. He spent his days haunting the Hall of Justice, bribing clerks for a chance to glance at old records. After three months, any hopes of finding her began to fade. She was nowhere to be found, and he discovered no leads.

Tobias knew no one and had no one to confide in, growing increasingly frustrated with this lack of progress. On the verge of giving up, he'd sent a letter to his tutor, Master Renedian, asking for advice. What strategies could Tobias use to improve the likelihood of finding his mother?

He did not receive a letter in response. No, when he'd gone to check on the post, Tobias found himself face to face with Master Renedian, who, upon receiving the letter, had ordered the Academy stable hands to ready a horse, and rode to Piran. Master Renedian had always seemed like a good man, but traveling to a different nation to help a former student was something one would have expected from one of the more adventurous tutors, not Renedian. The man spoke to his books as if they were old friends and left the Academy only to pick up pastries at a nearby bakery.

Within hours of his arrival, they were on horseback and traveling toward the south.

When they stopped to water their horses outside Mintar, Renedian called Tobias over to the sparkling pond where the horses drank. Renedian held a glass jar full of pond water in his thin, bony hands.

"I need something that belonged to your mother," Renedian said. "Doesn't matter what, just has to have been hers."

Tobias retrieved a locket his mother had given him before he'd left for the Academy and handed it to Renedian, who placed the locket into a jar of water. The water surged against the side of the jar, pushing toward the southwest.

"We'll find her if we follow the water," Renedian said, smiling grimly.

After following the water's direction for a few hours through the sparse valleys of southern Piran, Tobias and Renedian came to a thatch-roofed inn in a village of sheep farmers.

Tobias entered the inn, breathing in the aroma of roasted meats. A fire in the hearth crackled, warming the main hall. Tobias sat near the fire while Renedian ordered food and drinks. The warmth thawed Tobias's fingers, and his blood flowed again.

Things weren't so bad. At least it was warm.

Then Tobias felt a shiver run through him. Across the inn was his mother, but not the plump, gregarious woman he knew. She was thinner and sickly looking, working as a maid. Dressed in a simple white frock, she seemed a ghost of the woman she had been, her long curly hair cut into a short bob, wrinkles marring her once smooth skin.

Tobias strode to her and threw his arms around her. Despite her troubling appearance, his heart soared. He'd finally found her.

She, however, pushed him away, a terrified expression on her gaunt face.

"Tobias, you must leave here at once," she cried, panic clear in her voice.

"Mother, it's okay. I'm here. I'll take care of you." He tried to sound reassuring and calm as he spoke slowly.

"No!" His mother screamed. "You are in danger just by being here. If they find you, all will be lost. Go back to Rosenfel and never try to return." Tobias attempted to hug his mother again. She would be fine—they would be fine—his mother just needed a moment to find her wits.

"Mother, I have come here to help you. I don't care if I am in danger. I will protect you."

His mother either laughed or sobbed, Tobias couldn't tell which.

"There is nothing you can do to protect me," she said. "My fate has been sealed. You must listen carefully. When they come for you, and they will come for you, the less you know, the better. Go home. Do not look for me or for your father. I love you, my son, but you must never think of me again."

Tobias felt the tears well up in his eyes. His knees threatened to give out at any moment, and he felt weak, barely able to stand.

"Mother," he whimpered.

"For your safety, forget that I exist. Otherwise, you'll end up like your father, or worse." She pressed his hand and kissed him on the forehead. Tobias collapsed to the floor. He closed his eyes and tried to breathe, tried to keep from crying, but it was no use. The tears flowed freely. When he finally felt able to look up, his mother was gone.

Master Renedian placed a hand on his shoulder.

"We should do as she asks, son," Master Renedian said. "Though she may be sickly, she seems of sound mind, and we may be in danger. It's best that we head back for Rosenfel."

Tobias nodded, unable to find words. He wanted to protest, to insist that they stay so he could talk some sense into his mother, but he didn't have the strength to argue. He wished he'd been able to hug his mother one last time.

They left the inn, heading toward Nazlin and ultimately the Rosenfel border, but their troubles were not over. They were only a few miles from Nazlin when a group of armed men rode behind them, seemingly intent on stopping Tobias and Master Renedian from leaving Piran. A crossbow bolt flew past Tobias, and he breathed in sharply. He assumed the men were not common bandits, but rather the people his mother had warned him about.

The armed men soon overtook and surrounded them. They all wore armor and helmets except for their leader, a handsome middle-aged man who wore a large purple ship captain's bicorne. The man had to be a mage. Traversing the seas without mage powers was suicidal; the waves and storms too vicious for even the strongest ships men could make. The only way to navigate the rough waters successfully was to smooth them and command them to create currents that would safely and quickly send the ship to its destination.

"What did the woman tell you?" the leader asked them, his voice harsh and commanding.

"My moth—" Tobias began before Master Renedian interrupted.

"My sister told us that she did not wish to see us," Renedian lied. "It was quite emotionally affecting, as I have spent the last several years wishing for nothing but to see my beloved younger sibling again. I'm sure you will understand that I wish for privacy in this trying time, so that I may grieve the loss of one I loved."

Some of the armed men seemed sympathetic to what Master Renedian said, their posture softening, their hands leaving their sheathed weapons. The leader did not appear to share their sympathy, however, and drew his sword, a sailor's cutlass.

"You will not weasel your way out with your cunning words, traitor," he scoffed, looking from Master Renedian to Tobias. "If you tell me the truth, I won't kill you or the boy."

"May I have the honor of knowing whom I am addressing?" Master Renedian asked, still outwardly calm even as Tobias felt panic creeping in.

"Captain Coart Tallen," the man said. "By chance, I happened to be staying with my son at the inn where you met the woman. I was keeping an eye on her. Heard reports of spies and the like. Then you, two foreigners, show up and have a secret conversation. Like a good citizen, I reported this to the local garrison for the good of the nation. Your, ahem, sister will be imprisoned by now. She'll hang by next week. You'll do the same if you don't tell me what the woman told you."

"Captain Tallen," Master Renedian bowed. "With all respect and honor, I wish you to know that there is no kirthed way that I will ever betray my friends to you. You may arrest me or worse, I do not care. I will not allow you to hurt those I care about." Master Renedian raised his hands and began an incantation, drawing water from the swells beneath them, far underground, hurling blades of ice at the men. Tobias had never seen actual combat before, and he felt a sense of terrified wonder, until Master Renedian yelled to him, "Go, boy, ride for Rosenfel. Don't look back!"

Tobias spurred his horse, ducking out of the way of a swinging sword and riding as hard as he could. He heard the angry shouts of Captain Tallen urging his men to give chase. Tobias looked back, expecting to see several men close behind him. Instead, he saw men thrown from their horses by jets of water, and one man screaming as shards of ice impaled him. Tobias knew he would make it across the border safely, as long as there were no other men waiting for him along the way.

He looked back one last time and watched in horror as Captain Tallen's sword pierced Master Renedian and Renedian collapsed to the ground. Tobias screamed in anger, spurring his horse even faster.

The sound of footsteps broke Tobias out of his reminiscence.

"Who the hell are you?" A soft-jowled man stepped into the room, glaring at Tobias. "And what in Kirth's name are you doing here?"

Tobias shook his mother and Renedian from his mind and focused on the man wearing mage robes, with a belly that gave away the man's wealth, and a spindly mustache that hung down the sides of the man's pudgy face.

A punchable face.

"Tobias Stinton, Imperial Academy. I'm surprised to see you here."

The man scoffed. "Not as bleeding surprised as we are to see you. We'd not received news of any reinforcements."

"I'm not your new recruit. I'm on my own mission, involving the Obanni forces in Trunel."

"We have similar missions, then. We travel to Trunel as soon as we've gathered enough supplies."

"With the children?"

"What do you know about the children?"

"I'm not a dolt. I've seen their footprints, heard their cries. Felt their presence. Why do you have children here?"

"Our orders—"

"I did not ask for your orders, but about the children."

"They're our mission," a deep voice said from behind him. He turned to see a wizened man with strands of wispy white hair trying but failing to cover the crown of his head. He recognized the man. High Mage Wellise, the head of the Academy and all Rosenfellian mages. Next to him stood a younger man with a dark beard and a cruel expression. The man seemed familiar, but Tobias couldn't place him.

"Your Excellency." Tobias bent one knee and kissed the ground in front of Wellise, the traditional sign of respect.

Wellise stood tall, his hips clenched forward and back straight, his posture unnatural.

What sort of enhancements has he undergone?

Enhancements weren't common among the less wealthy mages, but the higher ups at the academy swore by the physical prowess or extended youth the enhancements could give. Wellise must have been nearly eighty, but he looked twenty-five years younger.

"Master Stinton," Wellise said, reaching out to help Tobias up from his prostrate position. "Good to see you again. Come in, we have much to talk about. Our mission may interest you, and we're always glad to add another man to our ranks." He gestured to the bearded man. "Do you know Marston?"

"I haven't had the pleasure," Tobias said, bowing to the man.

"Oh, but you have," Marston said, in an even more familiar voice. "Though you were quite busy at the time."

Gods, the mage from the road. The one who'd almost killed Gen.

"Perhaps," Tobias said, clenching his fists to stay calm. He could ill afford an outburst in front of Wellise. "I am often busy."

"Of course," Marston simpered. "I am delighted to formally make your acquaintance." He stared at Tobias, much like a wolf watching a lamb walking unattended through a pasture.

Wellise led them through an antechamber decorated in pale crimson statuettes of mages in various poses: a bald man reaching for the heavens, pulling rain from the sky; a robed young woman with shards on her fingertips; and a larger statue of a man creating a whirlpool between his hands, which he seemed ready to shoot into the path of a group of enemies to knock them off their feet, making the following *Vida* even more deadly. The man in this statue looked far too similar to Wellise for there to be any chance of coincidence.

They entered Wellise's chambers, an office the size of one of the sleeping chambers at the Torrian temple, and Wellise instructed him to sit in a red padded chair across from a sofa. Marston stood to the left of a velvet sofa where Wellise sat, clasping and unclasping his hands together. He repeated the motion several times before looking up at Tobias and beginning.

"We have taken on a vital mission for our country. The Obanni believe we are merely after Piran, and while Piran is a pretty prize, it pales compared to what we seek." He looked over his left shoulder, toward the tent flap leading into the middle of the complex. "The children we house here are not prisoners, but the children of loyal subjects who volunteered their services. We must do what we can to keep them from causing mayhem or running away." Wellise placed his hands on his lap. "You know how children are. You give them any freedom at all, and they come back battered and bruised, if they're lucky enough to come back at all."

"So, you've caged them to protect them?" Tobias asked. He immediately cursed himself for asking the question. No one questioned high mages.

Wellise, however, smiled indulgently. "Indeed. The issue at hand is twofold. First, we are vulnerable to attacks by sea. At any moment, the Winn could attack, and we would not have the strength to hold them off. Their mages are too powerful, their ships too fast and well-armed." He squeezed his fists together to the point his knuckles turned white.

A sore spot, then, High Mage?

"Normally, if we felt we could not defeat another nation," Wellise continued, "we'd do our damndest to be their ally, but the Winn want nothing to do with us. So, we can't defeat them in battle or be their ally. We're at a disadvantage, and the blighters won't give away even the slightest hint about their methods."

"We've decided the only possible recourse Rosenfel has is to make our own," Marston said, his lips curling in an evil grin.

"Our own what?" Tobias asked.

Wellise gave him a somber look. "Powerful mages who can stand up to the Winn. The kind of men and women who could fight one to one against the Winn without giving ground. And so, our plan was born. We commissioned a structure in Trunel, near to the coast, but not so near as to notify the Winn of our intentions, and we've been taking children there to continue our work on enhancing mage powers."

"This isn't the first group?" Tobias ground his heels into the floor and focused his weight on them.

I've got to stay seated. Lean back, dammit, and keep yourself still. If I get out of this chair, I'm going to rip Wellise's throat out.

"Gods, no," Wellise said, "though this is the first group with a high chance of success. The early experiments were misguided, something we must move on from. Our best scholars have developed a procedure that has been unsuccessful on the adult mages who were our initial subjects; however, I have been assured that the children will be more pliant to the stress on their magic. If they die, their parents will be at peace knowing their children died in service to Rosenfel."

I doubt that's what they're worried about right now.

"It seems a waste of young lives."

"It's only a waste if we don't succeed in our goals," Marston said.

Tobias kept his eyes on Wellise. "How do they plan to enhance their powers?"

"I believe the scholars use sensory deprivation," Wellise said, unconcerned. "Beyond that, I don't know. The specifics are beneath me. Marston knows more." He gestured to Marston. "He'll be taking charge of the experiments."

Gods, it is barbarous.

Almost as bad as what Tallen's father had done. Worse, if Tobias was honest with himself.

He had to do something, and quick. If the mage children made it to their final destination, there'd be no escape. He racked his brain for a plan, anything, but couldn't think of a single one. Damn Tallen, the bastard, for his quick wits and ability to plan things on the go.

There was little chance of freeing the children while they remained here in Rosenfel, safely encamped. However, if they were marching, it may be different.

Yes, not a bad idea.

"I'm happy to do whatever I can for the cause, sir. Whatever you need, I am here to assist."

And if Marston meets a horrible accident along the way, I'll be suitably heartbroken.

Wellise sniffed the air, as if he smelled something unpleasant. "I expected more difficulty convincing you, Stinton. You're known as a bit of a free spirit." He said the last two words as if they were an insult.

"You know me well, sir. I've argued with my brethren, I'll admit; I've been all too enamored by ideas of free will, forgetting that order must always come first. Without order, there is only chaos."

Marston cleared his throat. "And with chaos, all your precious free will goes to shit."

"Hmm," Tobias said. He took a breath, steeling himself for what was to come. "I realize now that we must secure ourselves against the Winn," he told Wellise, still ignoring Marston. "I don't like the idea of testing unproven methods on children, but I like the idea of a Winn occupation of Rosenfel even less. And so, I vow to not let my distaste affect my usefulness to the cause."

"More than anything, we must keep our true plans secret," Marston said. "If the Winn hear of what we're doing, their response will be quick."

"Godsdamned Winn," Wellise said. "They enhance all their animals, like those bloody wolf mounts of theirs, and they do Kirth knows what to themselves to become so powerful, but they'd treat us like monsters and declare war if they found us doing the same thing."

Wolf mounts? Tobias had never heard that story before. Yes, the Winn supposedly ate babies and drowned old women in their own blood, but now they also rode enhanced canines. "I assure you I will be the soul of secrecy," he said, bowing slightly to Wellise.

"Excellent." Wellise sniffed again, and Tobias decided it wasn't an affectation of displeasure.

"Are you ill, sir?"

"These damned yorn trees." He gave a petulant sniff. "They interfere with my breathing and make everything damned difficult. I've been confined to bed half the week."

"My sympathies, sir. That is most inconvenient."

Something to remember. Surely there would be yorn trees along the path of anywhere they traveled?

It would be terrible, Wellise, if you had an allergy attack just as the children and I make our escape.

"I know little of yorn. They are not in Dramin, if I'm not mistaken?"

"No, thank the gods. I'm safe there, though out here in the north, and especially in Trunel, they grow in abundance."

"And as they grow, so does your suffering."

"It's most lamentable."

"Indeed." *But rather fortuitous. Now to figure out what to do with that information.* "What can I do to assist you, Your Grace?"

Wellise considered this for a moment. "We always need volunteers on the watch. Some of the senior mages think it's beneath them."

"I'll take a watch," Tobias said. "The early morning shift will do."

And I can meet with my bosom friend Tallen.

It was imperative they save the children before they reached the Trunellic coast, but attempting to save them at the camp was too risky. They needed to make the Obanni move. And he had a plan.

Tallen isn't the only one who can make plans, though he, the bastard, won't enjoy this one.

After another sniff, Wellise stood, declaring he would walk to the eastern end of the camp, farther from the forest, to hopefully escape yorn pollen.

"Marston," Wellise said in between sniffles, "I'll leave you to answer any further questions Master Stinton might have." He grasped Tobias's hand in his own. "We're pleased to have you on our side, my boy."

Tobias willed himself to ignore the greasy nature of Wellise's hand.

Once Marston and Tobias were alone, Marston placed his hand casually on his hips. "So good to see you, Stinton. It was such an enjoyable meeting we had along the road. When you fought against the desires of the Imperium."

"What you did to my companion was unholy, and I will see you sent to Kirth to sit for judgment," Tobias said. There was no time for subtlety. "You will die."

"Perhaps, but not by you. I could expose your treachery to Wellise, of course, but what fun would that be? He would execute you or throw you in chains, and then I'd lose out on all my fun." He sat down where Wellise had been. "As it is, I look forward to matching wits with you and defeating you in the end."

"You bastard," Tobias said. Rage consumed him and he could think of nothing else to say.

Marston stood and bowed. "I'll send you your orders soon enough, my friend. Wellise might think he's in charge, but I hold the real power. Until next time, Stinton. I'm quite excited to see how this turns out." He swept out of the room, leaving Tobias alone with his thoughts. And bloody thoughts they were. He imagined shards impaling Marston, leaving the bastard mostly dead. Tobias would step forward with a dagger and cut his tongue out. Then he'd move to his fingers.

This changed things, but it simplified one aspect of the plan. He needed to deal with Tallen. Now. He could no longer afford to wait, not with Marston looming, waiting to derail Tobias's plans.

He moved into the common area, a thankfully empty spot in the back of the main tent. Two wooden chairs sat around a rough stone table.

Not luxury accommodations, but empty enough for my purposes.

He gathered a new piece of parchment and wrote. When he finished, he called for an Obanni messenger boy to deliver the parchment.

"Take this to the guards at the gate. Inform them that my servant boy will be arriving soon. When the boy arrives, have him sent to me. When you return with the boy, I will reward you handsomely."

The boy set off eagerly to fulfill the mission, and Tobias took out another piece of parchment.

He couldn't let the mage children suffer through this. The entire scheme was against everything he believed in. All of his ethics. He'd pushed his ethics aside to focus on Tallen and his revenge, but experimenting on mage children was unacceptable. These young mages may never see their families again, may never go home. In a way, they were all him.

The world doesn't need fifty of me. One is more than enough.

The children deserved a chance to have a better, happier life than he'd had.

He began to write. Hopefully, Tallen would remain as arrogant as ever, not realizing Tobias's true plan.

Thwack!

The axe flew past Gen's head and embedded itself into the wooden post behind her. From her standing position, she rolled to her left, crouching on one knee, searching for her own axe.

Shit.

She pulled on the axe, but it wouldn't budge from the holster she'd placed it in. She wasted precious seconds looking down at the holster, noticing a leather strap caught around the axe handle. Another axe flew past her, close to her shoulder. Too close.

The next one will hit me.

Where the hell was Cork?

Two men in dark leather jerkins hid in the forest just outside the camp, two men who wouldn't stop throwing godsdamned axes at her.

"I just want to talk," she called out. "Why don't we have a drink?"

"Get Kirthed," a high, nasally voice responded.

Gen pulled her axe free.

Thanks for the conversation. Gave me just enough time to pull my weapon free.

"Cork, if you'd like to join us, now would be the perfect time."

The big man stepped out from behind a large darkwood tree, his dreamshapes blending in with the twisted branches.

"Well, 'ello!" He was no more than a few yards from their assailants, and they had no axes left. "Lovely weather. Time to die." He closed the distance between them in mere seconds, bringing his axe down into the first man's sternum. Gen heard bones crunch. Before she could reach the men to join the fight, Cork took down the second man with an axe blade to the forehead.

She reached him and surveyed the carnage. "Gods, you didn't save any for me."

Cork's grin grew. "I enjoyed hidin' behind the tree. Don't get to hide much, being my size."

The man who had taken the axe to the forehead groaned and sat up. "That bleedin' hurt, Cork." Holding his head in his hands, he did not try to stand.

Cork shrugged, his shoulders moving up to the level of his ears. "Well, yeah. It's battle."

"It's godsdamned practice," the nasal-voiced man said, standing up and clutching at his wounded sternum. "I think you broke something."

"It's practice, yes," Gen said, "but if it were real, you'd be dead." She picked up one of the wooden hatchets and handed it to the seated man.

"You need more practice, I reckon," Cork added.

"Bloody gods," the nasal-voiced man said.

Several arrows flew in from the nearby trees, one of which took the nasal-voiced man through the throat. He gurgled, then collapsed.

Gen raced forward and grabbed the man on the ground, defenseless in his jerkin. Gen's leather armor would deflect some of the arrows, at least, but if the soldier was hit, there'd be little they could do.

I suppose I could let him die. But he's not the enemy right now, is he?

"Come on," Gen yelled. "We need to get back into camp." She didn't wait for a response, just dragged the man up and pushed him toward safety. "We need actual weapons, Cork."

"On it." Cork sprinted back into the camp, ducking through the makeshift wooden door attached to the tent flap. Gen positioned herself between the archers and the soldier and ran.

"Who's attacking?" Cork asked once they'd joined him inside the camp. He had Maralda in one hand and a war axe in the other.

"I don't know, but I wish they'd stop. Sword, please." She grasped Maralda.

Always nice to see a friend.

"It might be bandits," the soldier suggested, "Or Kosellans. We've heard rumor of them sneaking around."

Oh gods. Was she about to fight her allies? Were they even her allies anymore if they were shooting at her? Shit. Those were questions for scholars. She just swung a sword. And at a time like this, she couldn't stand by and let anyone, even allies, try to kill her.

Lifting Maralda, she nodded to Cork. "Ready for some exercise?"

He gripped his war axe and beamed at her. "Let's go kill these bastards."

"Argh!" Gen brought her blade down through the forearm of a pudgy bowman, his severed arm and the long bow it held toppling to the ground. The man stared in horror at the bloody stump, before he stopped staring altogether. A sword through the intestines will do that to you.

She stepped back and rewarded herself with a moment to look at the corpse. Black tunic, leather wool-lined boots, woolen black coat. Though Kosellan spies would hardly wear Kosellan uniforms as they marched through what was essentially enemy territory at this point, Gen knew these men couldn't be spies. They were Hillmen. Still obsessively meeting their death trying to get revenge for what had happened in Dramin.

A twig snapped behind her, and she turned to see Cork cleaving a man's head in two. Cork had excellent technique, and his footwork put even hers to shame. The best kind of person to have your back in a fight.

"They look like bandits," Cork said.

Gen scanned the trees for any further threats, but she neither saw nor heard anything suspicious. "They do, but I suppose spies would want to look like bandits." Cork didn't need to know about the Hillmen.

"Well, that's a job for a smarter man than I. Say we head back to our trusty waterhole and let someone else come out here to scout around the forest?"

"I have worked up a thirst."

Back at the mess tent, the quartermaster had found ale finally.

I'm sure the bastard didn't even look yesterday.

Gen and Cork sat at a wooden table together, eager to wet their throats after the exertion of the evening. They'd informed a sword lieutenant of the attackers and left the matter in their hands. The only duty they had now involved drinking until they could no longer stand.

"Hurry it up with the ale, Rufus," Cork bellowed.

"I'm going as fast as I bloody well can, ya bastard."

This is the life. Friends, companionship, drinking, fighting, and insulting. If only the Obanni weren't the enemy. I wish Cordyn was here.

However, before Rufus could make his way to their table with the ale, Evalia entered the mess tent from the direction of the officer's barracks, looking much too grim to be there to drink with them.

"What's going on?" Gen asked.

"The situation has—" she looked at Cork. "Changed."

"Cork, this is my friend, Evalia. Evalia, Cork." Cork waved, while Evalia stared at him. "Cork's a friend, too. I think he might be willing to help?"

"I enjoy being helpful. Help with what?" Cork asked, sounding less suspicious than Gen expected. He tossed the wooden hatchet from hand to hand, catching it by the handle each time.

"We may have a way to save the children. That, or we're walking into a trap." Evalia's eyes flitted from side to side, looking for anyone who might be watching them.

"Don't worry," Gen said. "Cork and I have been kicking the asses of so many other troops. They're giving us a wide berth. We're alone here."

"Cordyn received a letter, telling him to go to the mage complex at dawn."

"A letter from whom?"

"We don't know."

"You're right. That has to be a trap."

"Hate those buggers," Cork said.

"So do I," Evalia said. She relaxed her posture and uncrossed her arms. An excellent sign.

"Well, this will either be a fantastic decision, or it will all go to shit." Gen ran a hand through her hair. "Cork, it would be wonderful if you're not a secret bastard like everyone else I meet these days."

"I'll try my best," Cork said.

"They've captured children. Mage children. We've decided we're going to rescue them."

"Sweet bloody gods." Cork dropped the hatchet. "Children?"

"At least fifty of them. What do you say?"

Cork's expression was serious. He picked up the hatchet and flung it into the ceiling of the mess tent. Since the ceiling was only linen, the hatchet fell to the ground next to them, embedding in the dirt. Evalia only just managed to step out of the path of the falling weapon.

"Sorry Miss," Cork said to Evalia. "Children, huh?" he asked Gen. "The Obanni have been good to me, but I won't be party to abductin' children." He spat. "Shit, let's save 'em."

NINETEEN

An hour before the three moons would wane, and half an hour before Gen and Evalia were due to meet him, Cordyn went to the mage tent complex and peeked in the back entrance. He couldn't afford to wait for them. Going alone made more sense, even if it meant more risk for him.

If I die, perhaps a few women in Piran will cry for a fortnight before taking a new lover.

Although he hoped Gen would mourn him, he knew she'd be better off without him. She had the potential to make a life for herself, and there'd be less risk of dying if she didn't have to worry about him.

Evalia was right. It was a trap, the letter. He expected a quick capture, an audience with the Rosenfellian mages or the sword general, and a summary execution.

Ah well. I couldn't live forever. As long as Gen and Evalia escape with the children.

The confusion he felt about Evalia flummoxed him. A beautiful woman turning his head didn't surprise him, but he had always known each dalliance was merely that: a distraction to pass the time. He didn't love Evalia. Gods, he barely knew the woman, but there was something about her that made him feel, well, something that he couldn't put into words. He didn't like that. Feelings? No, thank you. Inability to find words? Even worse. When your life revolves around language, communication, and using those two things to get what you want, not knowing what to say is worse than death.

And so, death, it was.

Perhaps she'll go to my grave, dressed in the traditional grieving blues and gold of Rosenfel, the slightest tear running the length of her cheek as she thinks of the most infuriating—and infuriatingly handsome—man she'd ever met.

But now was not the time for daydreams. He had a trap to walk into. Get captured, spend hours leading the mages and soldiers through a maze of wits, and give Gen enough time to sneak the children out while the focus remained on him.

I've never been the self-sacrificing type, but there's no other way.

Darkness reigned inside the tent; if anyone was in this section of the tent, they were the nocturnal type, or they endured the dark while waiting for their quarry to arrive.

Here I am. Let's get this over with.

Even though he knew the outcome of the plan, he refused to embarrass himself by doing anything so stupid as lighting a torch or lamp to see by.

He opened the tent flap and entered the darkness.

The first thing he noticed was the smell. Not sweat and piss like expected in a prison, but fresh baked bread and—what was that smell?—blackberries? What the Kirth were the damned mages doing?

Hello, children, you are prisoners. Here are some homemade baked goods.

Pushing thoughts of pastries aside, he moved further into the complex. It was too empty, the darkness unceasing, no sounds beyond the wind and the tapping of rain on the tent roof above him. There were fifty children and gods knew how many adult mages in the complex. Silence this deep could only exist if there was a concerted effort to keep everyone quiet.

It was no use. He used a matchstick to light the glass lantern he had brought with him, just in case he needed it. The glow from the lantern illuminated the area a few yards around him, revealing dirty plates, half-empty glasses of wine, and someone's boot thrown haphazardly in the corner. It looked like everyone had evacuated in haste.

Something gurgled behind him and a spout of water careened onto his back, knocking him to his knees and leaving him soaked. He reached down to the ground to steady himself, but before he collided with the muddy surface, another blast slammed into him.

"Gods," he gasped.

A third attack came higher, crushing into the back of his skull. He fell, searching for some last bit of hope. But no, he'd failed. He heard a woman's voice in the distance.

"Tobias!" she yelled. "What are you doing?"

Cordyn saw Evalia's face in his mind, freckled and lovely, looking at him disapprovingly.

"Stop!" the woman shouted.

Something hard—and wet—slammed against him. He fell in a heap.

So this is how I die.

"I didn't know who it was," Tobias protested, attempting to avoid Evalia's glare. She knelt beside the unconscious Tallen, cradling his head in her arms while Tobias stood awkwardly beside her. "You weren't supposed to be here for another half hour. The other mages are still here. I was just about to put a bit of yorn tree in the high mage's room—he's allergic, you see—and then I'd set up a poison scare for the other mages. A rare Winn poison. They're dolts, the lot of them. But Tallen had to come early."

He hadn't known it was Tallen at first. And then, after he realized, Tallen was already on the ground, and one more blast of water wouldn't hurt him all that much. Knock the man out, perhaps. They'd have to postpone the plan a bit, but with Tallen doing whatever he damn well pleased, they weren't ready to make their rescue attempt yet. Better to bring everyone together to discuss the situation at hand.

"I went to Cordyn's chambers, and he was gone," Evalia said. "I worried something might have happened, so I came here just in time to watch you trying to kill him." She said the last part with such viciousness that Tobias winced.

"Well, if he'd have waited, he'd be awake right now." His brow furrowed. "You went to his chambers?"

"Yes," she said after a brief pause. "But you can keep your judgments to yourself. Nothing untoward occurred, and I'm offended you would even suggest such a thing,"

"I didn't—"

"At least you didn't kill him. Or perhaps you would have if I hadn't intervened."

"Madam," he spat out, the soul of formality. "If I wished to murder our friend Tallen, I could have done so at any point along our journey. It would be extreme stupidity for me to wait until now, when there are so many eyes watching."

"No one has accused you of intelligence."

"Godsdammit, woman—"

"Stop arguing and go fetch water," Evalia snapped. She placed a hand on Cordyn's head and began to lightly stroke his freshly shorn hair.

"Water? I'm a mage," Tobias said. He lifted his hands.

"Gods, no one wants your mage water." She stood and fixed an even fiercer glare on Tobias. "Help me lift him and let's get him back to the medic tent."

Tobias lifted Tallen onto his shoulder and carried him back to the medic tent, depositing him on the bed. He turned to Evalia, awaiting further instructions.

"Leave us," she ordered. "Go fetch Gen. She'll be heading toward the mage tent soon enough. If you'd intercept her and bring her here instead."

"As you wish," Tobias said. He left, grateful for an escape.

However, finding Gen would have to wait. Topper should have arrived by now, and the other mages would soon begin their training exercises. A few precious moments of freedom for him to speak to Topper and put his plan into motion.

When he returned to the mage tent, he was pleased to find Topper waiting for him in the foyer outside Wellise's chambers, holding a canvas bag, flanked by one of the younger mages.

"Ah, good, I see you've met my assistant," Tobias said to the mage.

The mage frowned at him. "He said he worked for you, but—"

"Yes, indeed, he does." Tobias began walking toward his own bedchamber, an enclosed space no bigger than a closet. "Come, Topper, we have much to discuss."

"But you can't bring him in without the high mage's approval."

Tobias laughed. "His excellency has already approved it. He told me I could have anything I needed if I joined you on your quest. Well, I need my assistant." He eyed Wellise's chambers. "If you don't believe me, I'm sure the high mage wouldn't mind you interrupting his nap."

The mage's eyes widened. "No, I'm sure it's fine. Have a good day, sir."

Tobias led Topper back to his chamber and indicated for the boy to sit. Tobias stood in the doorway, watching for any unwelcome visitors.

"Do you have the supplies?" Tobias asked.

"Nice to see you too, boss," Topper said. "I wouldn't mind some breakfast."

Tobias sighed. "I'll get you some food afterward. Supplies first."

Topper dug into his bag and brought out a small gold stamp. "It took hours to find this boss. Cost a hundred crowns too. Worked up a powerful hunger."

"Fine, I'll find you some food."

Topper bit his lip and shuffled his feet, as if deciding to speak or not. After a few moments, he did. "I need you to promise me something, boss." He looked down for a moment before meeting Tobias's gaze. "Please don't kill Mr. Tallen. I know you hate him, and you want revenge, but I don't like how it's changing you. Be the man I know you are, not a murderer."

"It's not for you to say what happens to Tallen." And yet, Tobias hadn't killed Tallen yet. He'd had opportunities, and could have done so, if he'd really wanted to. Every time, there was a new reason not to kill him.

"Please, boss," Topper pleaded. "For me. And my parents."

Tobias sighed. "Fine, I won't kill him. For now, at least."

Topper gave him a slight grin. "That's all I ask for, boss."

"We do, however, need Tallen to go somewhere. And I have a plan for that. In a moment, I'm going to send you out into the camp to find our friend Gen and ask her to meet us at the medic tent. It's high time we have a group discussion."

"I heard you met trouble from Kosellans outside camp?"

"Hmm, yes, they were certainly very Kosellan. Let's just say our lovely friend from Dramin who likes sending threatening notes—he's much too dead to bother us further."

Tobias retrieved a loaf of bread from his luggage and tossed it to Topper. "Eat quickly, my boy. We have much to talk about these next few minutes. Mr. Tallen will be leaving us."

Tobias sat in the cramped medic tent with Evalia, Gen, a groggy Tallen, Topper, and a big, tattooed axe-wielding brute who wouldn't stop smiling.

Well, who the devil are you?

"We need to talk," Tobias said.

"Explain to me again why we should listen to anything you have to say." Gen glowered at him, giving off an air of *leave now or I'll kill you,* but Tobias did not turn and flee.

"I understand you must be upset, but—"

"You understand nothing," Gen snarled.

"I saw some of my acquaintances from the Academy," he explained, his voice calm. "They would have recognized me, revealed I wasn't an Obanni soldier, and our plan would have failed."

"They still found out you weren't Obanni."

"Yes, but with revealing myself, I showed some level of honesty. It would have been worse if I'd tried to deceive Koston."

"You dare try to say you're honest, and yet you lied."

"How?" Tobias tried to remain stone-faced.

Gen gestured at Topper. "You said Topper went back to Dramin. But then I saw you meet with him in Torrance, and now he's here at the camp."

"It wasn't a lie. Topper returned to Dramin to resolve some of my business affairs. Then he returned."

"And why did that return need to be secret?"

"It wasn't. I felt no need to involve you in my business affairs when you had so many other things to worry about." He pointed to Cordyn. "Like Tallen's desire to get tortured."

"You and ya friends argue a lot," the tattooed brute said.

"Who in Kirth is this man?" Tobias asked.

"His name is Cork, and he's a friend," Gen said. "He's not Obanni."

"He's a mercenary working for the Obanni," Tobias said.

"I didn't know about the kids," Cork said. "I knew we's had a buncha mage pricks but didn't know they was capturin' kids."

"Cork is Winn," Gen said.

"I'd noticed his arms," Tobias said.

"You've met Winn before?" Evalia asked.

"No, but I've heard the stories." Tobias cocked his head toward Cork. "Don't let the Rosenfellian mages find out about your Winn ties." Tobias looked at Evalia. She sat quietly; jaw clenched. "They're taking the children to experiment on," he said. "They want to enhance them to fight the Winn. And there's little we can do to stop them once they've made it to their final destination. We need a plan."

Evalia's face twitched, and she squeezed her knee. Cordyn moaned something akin to words and sat up, unfocused, eyes blinking.

"Cork," Gen said, "What is the general feeling among the men toward the mages?"

Cork's forehead wrinkled as he pondered. Tobias imagined it must be hard for the big man to think so much, dolt that he seemed.

"The boys, far as I know, we didn't know what the Rosenfellian mages are doin. And trust me, my friends and I, we hate all of them bastards. Stuck up pricks, the lot of 'em." He turned to Tobias. "Beggin' yer pardon."

"Could you spread the news?" Evalia asked. "The more Obanni we have hating the mages, the better."

"Aye," Cork said.

"The Hillmen attacked again," Gen said.

"The Hillmen?" Tobias asked.

Kirth, those neer-do-wells won't stop. Something to use for my plans?

"We can use that to our advantage," Evalia said. "Put together a scouting party. Cork and Gen, myself, and some men you trust, Cork. We'll go out and—"

"And what?" Tobias asked. "Look for birds? Enjoy a campfire? That's not a plan, Evalia."

Evalia glared at him. "No, we'll take a cart with supplies and sneak a few children out each time. With enough trips."

Tobias fought to refrain from rolling his eyes. *Gods, I'm surrounded by idiots.* "I think that many supply trips would raise suspicions."

"Well, do you have a better idea?" Evalia asked.

Yes, I do.

"No. Make your preparations. I'll do whatever you ask."

Cordyn groaned from his bed. "Thank you for your input, Stinton."

"He speaks!" Tobias cried out in mock excitement.

"It's your fault he's like that," Evalia said. "If I hadn't shown up, who knows what might have happened?"

"I assure you, I have no intention of killing him. Or any of you." He made eye contact with each of them in turn. "Now that we've established my lack of murderous intent, let's move forward. Evalia, what would you like me to do?"

"Nothing yet. Cork, Gen, come with me. We'll go speak to Obanni command about a search party."

"Then I'll go back to my quarters and await your command," Tobias said.

He and Topper exited the medic tent, but did not go back to his quarters. "Topper, go get the carriage. I'll meet you at the appointed spot."

Topper slipped through a slit in the outer tent wall.

Tobias lurked behind a nearby tent, watching Gen, Evalia, and Cork leave the medic tent. Finally, only Tallen was left.

Time for a reckoning.

Tobias walked back into the medic tent. Tallen slept on the cot.

No matter, waking him up will be easy.

Tobias raised his hands into the *Vida* and shot a shard into the cot, right next to Tallen's head. Tallen jerked and sat up, eyes flitting wildly around the room. His jaw and neck muscles were tightly clenched. When he saw Tobias, he relaxed.

"Stinton? What the hell? You could have killed me."

"We must converse. Just us two," Tobias said. He twirled his fingers, readying for another attack. "I thought our friends would never leave. But now that they have, we can finally discuss the true plan." He stared straight into Cordyn's bloodshot eyes. "You'll be leaving us, my friend."

"I don't know what you want with me, Stinton, but don't hurt Gen or Evalia."

Tobias was amused to watch Tallen attempt gallantry. The man was a pitiful sight, lying on his side, barely able to move without assistance. Tobias walked to Tallen, lifted his foot, and pressed it down onto Tallen's raw back. Tallen screamed.

No, that will not do.

He called upon the *flumenta,* and streams of water darted into Tallen's mouth, cutting the scream off into a wet retch. Descending in a fit of choked coughing, Tallen whimpered in between each convulsion.

"I have no reason to betray them or hurt them," Tobias said. "They're decent people. You, Tallen, I'd happily betray. However, I'll have to be content with making you disappear for a while."

With Tallen otherwise occupied hacking his lungs up, Tobias gathered rope from the medical supplies and bound Tallen's hands behind his back. He was not gentle about it, tying the binds tight enough to cut off circulation, and in time, tear open skin. A palm to Tallen's back, he applied more pressure than needed, and Tallen groaned loudly.

"If you don't scream, I won't gag you. Or cut your tongue out. For a man who likes to talk as much as you, it would be a shame for you to be unable to speak at all."

"Godsdammit, Stinton. Why?" Tallen's voice reached a higher pitch, almost a shriek.

"I'd love to kill you now. Take you back to your tent and end your miserable existence. The medics would assume you were weak and succumbed to your injuries. You simply expired."

"What about the children? The ones you chided me about saving as if you were the most noble man in Rosenfel."

"Oh, don't worry. You won't die. I made a promise to a friend. However, I require your disappearance. Once you're gone, I'll save the children, I assure you. I'll save Ezra, and receive Evalia's eternal gratitude, maybe even marry her."

"Godsdamn you."

"The gods won't help you now. Nor will anyone else. You underestimated me. You'll pay not only for that, but for all of your mistakes. All of your family's mistakes." He lifted Tallen off the ground and slung him over his shoulder. Gods, the man was heavy. "We'll be leaving now."

"Just kill me now, damn you. Don't leave me at the whims of your godsdamn games." Tallen kept his voice low; no doubt wishing to keep his tongue and avoid another jet of water down his throat, but the man's tone grew more imploring. Tight lines appeared on his forehead, making him look older and exhausted.

"No, I shan't kill you, but we do need to leave. Topper is waiting just to our north in the forest with a carriage."

"Why are you telling me this?"

"You can hardly do anything to stop it now, wounded as you are. I'll be drugging you in a moment to help you remain docile. I want you to know that I enjoy this feeling of triumph over you, as you and all of your complicated schemes unravel because I outsmarted you. It's glorious, really." With a lurch, he moved forward, taking Tallen out of the tent complex. He saw no one in the surrounding area, but he walked along the northern edge of the camp to be sure to avoid as much traffic as possible.

"You've grown silent, Tallen."

Tallen squirmed, but Tobias called upon the *Vida* and pressed the edge of a shard to Tallen's exposed lower back and dug into the wounds.

"I won't give you the satisfaction of speaking any longer." Tallen's resolute tone surprised him. The man wasn't as much of a coward as he thought.

"I doubt that very much. You enjoy hearing yourself speak too much for vows of silence." They reached the northernmost point of the camp, where Topper had left the carriage when he'd arrived earlier. Unlike the more exposed sections of the camp, the Obanni stationed no guards to the north, assuming the forest would keep out any invading armies. Thankfully, Tobias didn't need to invade, just make a quick trip into the forest.

He pushed Tallen through the flap and into the forested area outside the camp. Standing over him once again, Tobias pulled his hands up again into the *Vida*. "I can always coerce you to speak if I want to."

"Make up your damned mind. You want me silent. You want me to speak. You want me dead. You don't want me dead. It's exhausting."

"Yes, isn't it wonderful?"

"Why in Kirth's name are you doing this? I know we're not friends. I know I've been a prick, but killing me seems a bit much."

"Your father died before I could kill him."

"My father?" Tallen's brow furrowed.

"Coart Tallen ruined my life."

"My father was a man of the highest character."

Tobias burst into laughter. "Your father was a scoundrel and a criminal, and it seems his son isn't too far away."

"I don't know what you're talking about."

"No, I don't suppose your father would have told you all the gory details. I was nine when I left home to go to the Imperial Academy. That's when every young mage in Rosenfel leaves home. I barely had time to get to know my own father."

"How does that concern my father?"

"I'll get to that. I went off to the Academy, but when I left five years later, my parents were gone. My father imprisoned and my mother back to Piran."

"Piran?"

"Ah yes, I'm half Piranese myself."

And so, he told Tallen the story, his mother's suffering, Renedian's death, and Coart Tallen's place in it all.

Tallen sat quietly throughout. When Tobias finished, Tallen spoke in a soft voice, yet there was still a hint of a sneer. "This is all very touching, Stinton, but it has nothing to do with me."

"Blood is blood, Tallen. Your blood harmed mine. When I made it back to Rosenfel, I returned to the Academy, begging for a room. I had no family or friends left. Because of your father." He dug his boot into Tallen's skin, hoping he'd break a rib or two. "They gave me a cot in a small, drafty room, and a small stipend to help assist tutors with their lessons. I never heard from my mother again, though I found reports of an unnamed Rosenfellian spy, hanged for treason without a trial. My mother."

"I'm sorry, Stinton."

"I don't want your apologies. I want your blood, you bastard. For my mother *and* Renedian, the man who gave his life to help me. He was never mentioned in any of the reports. Just gone, never to be thought of again. When I traveled to Piran three years later, the inn was gone, destroyed in a fire. No one knew of Captain Tallen. I scoured Piranese records for information on your father and was disappointed to learn that he had died at sea six months after he killed my friends and family. But I read that Tallen had one son, a young man named Cordyn, who by twenty had graduated from one university and been kicked out of three." A kick to the stomach. "He was known as a rake and a scoundrel. And I vowed that young man would die."

"And here we are," Cordyn said, his voice thick. "Listen, Stinton, I'm sorry for what my father may have done—"

"No, I have no interest in your apologies or excuses. For now, you must only enjoy your drink."

Tobias extracted a thin glass vial of clear liquid from his coat pocket and forced Tallen's mouth open with two strategically placed shards, pouring the liquid down the bastard's throat. He placed his hands on Tallen's jaw and held the man's mouth closed, forcing him to swallow the liquid.

Once he confirmed the area outside the camp was still empty, Tobias picked up Tallen, grunting at the exertion. Gods knew where the man kept the extra weight. He was trim and fit, and yet he weighed Tobias down like an anvil, even more so now that he was sleeping.

Tobias tossed the unconscious bastard over his shoulder and moved through the dim light of the hazy morning. The two suns still gave enough light for him to see the path through the forest to the northwest, toward a small clearing Topper had found to wait in.

When Tobias arrived, Topper sat atop the carriage, the smallest coachmen Tobias had ever seen.

"We might need to get you lifted shoes, boy. Make sure you can see over the horses."

Topper, with an expansive flourish of his arms, more suited for the stage than the forest, gestured out into the forest.

"I see a lot of blasted trees. Horses can't hide that from me. Anyway, I can stand if I need to see. Won't be the first time I've driven horses on my feet."

"Head straight through to Wolstone. Stop for nothing except sleep until you reach the cottage I procured. Deposit Tallen in the cellars—you'll find a fine dungeon of sorts there—and stay at the cottage until I arrive."

"'Course, boss." Topper blinked in rapid succession and rubbed his fingers together, a sign of worry. Tobias had noticed Topper's tics whenever the boy felt anxious—rapid blinking, grinding teeth, and absent-minded hand gestures. "Will it just be me?"

So, he's afraid to be alone. Interesting. I'd not considered that before.

He smiled—a poor effort if Topper's lack of reassurance could be believed. "I've hired a manservant and a bodyguard. Paid them enough money to assist you however you need while not asking questions. I should be there within a few weeks." His smile vanished.

I have to tell the boy, even if it will cause him to worry.

"However, if affairs here take a negative turn, and I'm unable to join you, there's something you must do."

"Why wouldn't you be able to get there, boss?" Topper's lips trembled, and he blinked faster than before.

"If something happens to me. If I'm dead." Topper's eyes went wide. "In that case, do what you must with Tallen—free him, kill him, I don't care—but stay at the cottage. I've arranged for a sum of money each month to be deposited into your accounts. You won't be rich, but you'll be comfortable."

"Gods." Topper squeezed Tobias's hand. "Tobias, you've been like a father to me, and I...well, I love you."

Tobias hugged him. "I love you too, boy." Emotion overcame him. "I love you, my son."

And for a time, the world disappeared. It was just a man and his son, spending a few moments together before parting.

Finally, they broke off the embrace, and Tobias looked at the boy.

"Topper, I beg you, do not speak to Tallen. Don't go into the same room as him unless necessary. He has a way with words, and makes even the wisest, most determined man doubt himself. He's manipulated me, and he'll manipulate you. We cannot risk him using his wits to escape."

"What'll you do now, boss?"

Tobias ruffled Topper's hair. "What I must do."

"We've been betrayed," Tobias yelled, striding into Sword General Koston's chambers, where Koston and Wellise sat deep in conference, empty bottles of wine strewn about the tent.

Three Obanni pikemen raised their weapons at him, menacing snarls on their faces. Tobias stopped, holding his hands up to show he meant no harm. He had mussed his hair and arranged his jacket to look hastily thrown on, hanging off his left shoulder; a man who'd woke to horrific news.

Tobias locked eyes with the sword general. "Rennick was a spy," he said.

Koston instructed the men to lower their pikes. "What?"

Be like Tallen, as odious as that sounds. To lie convincingly, you must believe what you're saying.

"Rennick was not Rennick at all, but a man named Cordyn Tallen, hired to infiltrate this camp and unravel your plans."

"Kirth's boots," Wellise said, face scrunched in inebriation. "We're ruined!"

Koston twirled his sideburns. "How would Rennick—I mean, what did you say his name was, Tallen? How would he have known where our camp was?"

"I don't know, sir," Tobias admitted. "However, after my assistant told me he spotted Rennick leaving, I went to the medic tent and found these." He took out two parchments emblazoned with a gold seal and handed them to Koston.

Koston inspected the seal. "Kosellan," he muttered. He tore open the seal and scanned the contents. "Kirth buggering shit. The Winn."

"What?" Wellise shrieked.

Koston handed Wellise the parchment. "This is a letter from this Tallen man to Kosellan high command. As an envoy of the Winn, he's written to them pledging assistance." He pressed his unruly beard against his chin. "The Winn know where we are, and they're coming."

Wellise blubbered for a moment, then stood as tall as he could. "Koston, we must hurry. We must get to our destination immediately, before the Winn can overtake us. Wolstone is at least a week's march. We must go now."

Yes, yes, go to Wolstone. Right into my web.

Koston pondered. "It may be time to sever our partnership, Wellise. Oban gains nothing from traveling into Trunel and fighting the Winn."

"Your high command promised."

"We could travel faster without them, sir," Tobias told Wellise. "Hundreds of troops will require more rest than a few score mages."

"And a prison caravan," Koston added. "Don't forget your true purpose. I want nothing with what you're doing to those children."

"I will recall my mercenaries from your command, Koston," Wellise said. "I was kind enough to loan you a hundred men, but on my order, they will attack you without pause."

Koston stared off into the trees for a prolonged period, then turned back to Wellise. "We will stay with you as long as we remain unmolested by you or the Winn. However, if the Winn move to attack or you continue your threats, our partnership will end." He paused. "Don't make me regret this.

Tobias turned away. Tallen couldn't have done it better himself.

Part Three
The Rescue

I am not a martyr,

I shall not be remembered

if I help a few souls survive,

Spare a prayer once for me

The pain that I suffer

is done for a purpose

if my companions may live

Blessed will the gods ever be.

--Cordyn Tallen

TWENTY

THE TWO SUNS OF Sarakan rose in the north, casting an otherworldly glow on the snowy hills of Trunel, the northernmost country on the continent. By afternoon, the full brunt of both suns reflected off the snow, creating a blinding glare for anyone foolish enough to look directly at it. The mountains of western Trunel, with their snow-covered peaks, were uninhabited during the harsh light of day. In the evenings, the larger sun disappeared while the smaller sun lingered for a few hours, bathing the landscape in an ethereal twilight. This muted glow made it the only comfortable time to travel through the mountains.

During this extended dusk, the Obanni forces trudged through a frozen pass between two of the larger peaks, making their way west into Trunel and its deadly cold. The kind of cold that killed those who failed to dress for the weather.

Despite this, Gen wore sleeveless leather armor. Yes, she felt cold, but also invigorated. She'd put her coat back on when they stopped to rest, but while they trudged through the snow, she enjoyed the icy wind kissing her bare arms.

Gen, Cork, and Evalia traveled together, Gen and Cork assigned to dragging a ballista through the pass, a dreadful job in Gen's opinion, though Cork hummed an upbeat tune as they strained and pulled. The ballista legs had few places to grip, and they kept losing their hold of the wooden monstrosity.

"It would be a shame if this ballista accidentally fell off the mountainside," Gen said.

"Especially if the high mage fell with it," Evalia added.

They'd had to postpone their rescue until a later time. With the camp in uproar, the Rosenfellian mages buzzed around the mage encampment at all times, leaving little chance of sneaking in. Gen hoped there'd be confusion either along the road or as they approached wherever they were going, and they could use that to steal away with the children.

"Along with the rest of the bleedin' mages," Cork said.

"And Tobias," Gen said. "Bastard."

"Speaking of which," Evalia said, pointing in front of them, where Tobias stood with several other robed figures, arguing.

"Godsdamn him."

A sword lieutenant whistled, yelling that they'd stop to rest the horses. Only the senior officers and mages had horses, while the enlisted men enjoyed a brisk walk through the mountains.

Of course, they don't stop for us to rest, but for their horses. Aristocrats and commanders are the same. They worry only about their own needs.

Leaving the ballista on a flat stretch of ground, Gen stomped through an icy puddle, walking over to a tree stump, cut a half yard off the ground, jagged spikes of wood protruding from the sides.

Someone needs more lumberjack training.

Two swipes with Maralda removed most of the spikes, and Gen sat down.

"There's enough room for you, Evalia." She took up two-thirds of the stump's surface, but Evalia was small enough to fit in the remaining space. "Sorry, Cork. I don't think you'll fit."

Evalia sat next to her while Cork squatted in the snow.

"I'm used to this weather. Don't mind sittin' in a bit of snow, then. I've grown fond of it, by the gods. We ain't too far from home, and in Trunel, this is nearly summer." He spat onto the ground. "Balmy godsdamned weather."

Across the pass, Tobias shot a wave of water straight up into the air. Gen caught the phrase "Trunellic shit-stain bastards," which had a certain beauty to it. One to remember. Tobias waved his arms at his companions and continued yelling, but the wind picked up and Gen could no longer hear him over the gusts.

She shivered, remembering she hadn't put her coat on. After rummaging through her bag and finding her coat, she put it on and basked in the comfort of the Piranese sheep's wool lining. Her stomach grumbled, but the next meal was still hours away. She had eaten salted pork and biscuits for lunch, and the biscuits remained glued to her teeth—an unfortunate occurrence, as they'd tasted like salted dirt.

Things were odd with Cordyn gone. Evalia spoke little, often staring into the valley with a pinched look on her face. Cork was the same as always, but Gen couldn't shake the gnawing emptiness inside her. Cordyn was gone. Not only gone, but possibly off with the Winn. Had he been working for the Winn the whole time? Had he told her the truth about anything? She'd trusted him, and the betrayal destroyed her.

Perhaps Cordyn hadn't betrayed them, but if he hadn't, he was most likely dead. Kirth, there was no positive way to look at the situation. At least Tobias spent most of his time with the other mages; a blessing in disguise.

Where the mages sat drinking and stuffing their faces on pork and mutton bones, a bearded man and Tobias argued, arms gesturing wildly, almost as if the wind were blowing them. Watching them without hearing their argument amused Gen until she looked closer at the bearded man's face.

It was *him*. The mage who tried to kill her. She had only seen a glance of him in Rosenfel, but she had no doubt. Her pulse pounded against the stitches on her abdomen, and she couldn't decide whether to unsheathe Maralda or fall to the ground and cry.

She chose Maralda.

"Gen?" Cork hissed. "What the hell ya doin?"

"I have some business to attend to," she said, stepping forward. She'd cut the bastard's head off.

Cork gripped her arm, pulling her around to face him. "I hate the mages too," he said. "I's want to rip their bleedin' throats out, like. But we's got to wait for the right moment."

Gen tore her arm out of his grasp. "He almost killed me."

"And ya will be dead if ya kill 'em now, right?" He fixed fiery eyes on her. "Take a breath, calm down, and wait. We'll kill 'em together."

Gen sighed and followed his instructions. She knew he was right. Killing the mage now wouldn't solve anything. It'd make things worse. She couldn't save the children if she was dead, and Cordyn's triumphant reappearance to win the day seemed unlikely.

"Tobias knows him," she said. "He kept that from us."

"He's a right prick too, I'll wager. 'Course, he's a mage."

Tobias kicked a snow drift and stalked away from bearded mage, heading straight toward their stump.

No, turn around. I can't kill you in front of all these people, and gods know I don't want to talk.

"What did you do to Cordyn?" Gen asked once Tobias had arrived.

"What?" Tobias asked, confused. "He betrayed us, Gen." He spoke in a soft tone, as if speaking to a child.

"Cordyn wouldn't do that," she snapped. "Not to me. We were friends."

"I found the letters, Gen. Where he'd left them. I don't know how else to explain his absence other than betrayal."

"If he left for the Winn, that ain't even a betrayal," Cork said. "Hell, I can get word to the Winn, figure out where he is."

Gen kicked the ballista. Not her best idea: now her foot stung, and she felt just as upset. "No. He may not have exposed our true identities to the Obanni or the Rosenfellians, but it's still betrayal. He lied to us. To me."

"Perhaps he had a good reason," Evalia said. Gen had almost forgotten she was there. Evalia had been so quiet. And yet now she looked at them, jaw clenched, determined. "I don't think he would have left us otherwise."

"Tallen hasn't ever been forthcoming about his plans," Tobias said.

And dammit, Tobias had a point. Cordyn had never sought collaboration when planning. He schemed something up, and you followed along. With his success rate, Gen had found it hard to argue.

Not such a success now.

"I know you care for Tallen," Tobias said, "but in a way, this is the best turn of events regarding the rescue. There was no way to get through that many mages whenever we were in Rosenfel, the land of mages, with forests in every direction. The best chance at a rescue was to get the troops moving. When troops move, they're vulnerable to attacks from the outside. But I did not know how to make an army move until Tallen's, ahem, disappearance."

Gen opened her mouth to say something cutting and witty, but Evalia spoke first. "It seems like we have more freedom now that we're traveling, Gen. We all want to find Cordyn, but we should focus on the rescue." She pointed near the front of the line of marching troops. A monstrosity of wheels, ropes and leather clattered along the road like a drunken caterpillar, surrounded by a mix of mages and Obanni infantry. A prison caravan of sorts, which the mages and the soldiers in piecemeal armor had constructed by fastening several carriages together and covering it all in a dark leather tarp. Gen hadn't seen the children yet, but she knew they were inside.

"We need to make a plan," Tobias said.

Gen threw her hands out wildly. "What plan? Cordyn's gone."

"Shockingly, he's not the only one who can make a plan."

"What happened to Cordyn?" Gen bit down on her lip and tasted blood. This was the perfect time to take out Maralda and tell Tobias how she really felt. *Go away, Obanni, and let me severely wound this man in private, please.*

Tobias frowned. "What do you mean? He left."

"I don't believe you."

"I assure you I'm telling the truth." Tobias crossed his arms.

"Because you've been so truthful already. You knew the man who tried to kill me." She pointed toward the man, who stood a hundred years away, watching them. "I saw you arguing."

"I met him yesterday," Tobias explained. "There are terrible events on the horizon."

"Involving my sword and your head," Gen said.

The bastard had the gall to laugh. "Gen, I am not your enemy. Tallen's plan was doomed to failure, but we can work together." He pursed his lips. "And I'd prefer to keep my head."

"Hmph." Gen wrinkled her nose. Tobias's explanation made sense, at least a little.

"If you'd told us your plan beforehand, we could have been more prepared."

Tobias scoffed. "You think Tallen would have let me add anything to his glorious plan? He was too busy planning his self-sacrifice to consider anyone else might have ideas."

"Gen," Evalia said, as if she were talking to a child, "why would Tobias do something to Cordyn? It makes no sense." She squeezed Gen's arm. "We'll find him, I promise."

Gen gritted her teeth but said nothing.

"Right now," Evalia continued, "we have to focus. We can't afford to lose the time looking for him."

Tobias cleared his throat. "My plan—"

"Absolutely not—" Gen cut in.

Cork coughed, breaking them out of the argument. Gen had almost forgotten the big man was there. Cork pointed to the surrounding trees.

"Not to interrupt, but we're around four days' march from the coast. So, we don't got much time. You'd best be makin' yer plans quickly, like." He looked from Tobias to Gen. "Gen, I know you don't trust the man, but I reckon we need his help."

Gen reluctantly nodded her assent.

Tobias cleared his throat again, making eye contact with Gen, as if to say *I won this battle.*

"High Mage Wellise tells me our final destination is an inlet just north of Wolstone, which is the largest shipping port for the Winn in Trunel. They seem to think the Kosellans are actually working with the Winn after your reports." He motioned to Evalia. "You did an excellent job, Evalia."

Gods, was there anyone who wouldn't flirt with Evalia?

Gen had noticed Cork sneaking glances at the young woman whenever he thought no one was looking. Right now, he gnawed on an apple core, spitting seeds out as he went. He worked with aplomb, devouring the apple faster than Gen could.

Evalia nodded to Tobias, then looked at Gen ruefully. "Mr. Tallen wrote the letter. He deserves your praise. I just delivered it."

"And we appreciate you," Gen said.

Now let's stop talking about who did what and let's figure this shit out.

"And after Tallen's betrayal—"

"Stinton," an older mage called out. "Come conference with us."

Tobias bowed. "Of course, Your Excellency, I'll be there presently as soon as I finish my breakfast." He took a bite of apple.

Good, leave. We don't need you, anyway. I'm going to come up with the finest plan ever made.

Gen couldn't think of anything. Cork handed her an apple, pink with yellow streaks, probably not fully ripe but better than nothing. Anything to get the biscuit taste out of her mouth. She took a hesitant bite. Juice trickled onto her bottom lip as she chewed. It wasn't as sweet as some apples, but the tartness made her tongue tingle; she focused on chewing. Moving her teeth up and down, masticating the flesh and skin. No missions, no lost friends, only apples. She sighed. It was hopeless. She'd never push everything out of her mind with an apple. She needed to hit something with her sword, something more than a stump.

"Let's fight."

Cork perked up at that. "With pleasure. Just let me finish this." He took another bite of apple.

"Fighting won't help anything." Tobias pressed his boots into the snow, leaving deep, muddy tracks.

"I need something to do." Gen finished her own apple and tossed the core into the underbrush behind her. Food for birds, or Cork, if he wanted more apple and didn't mind scrounging through the grass.

"We need to contact the Winn," Tobias said. "Once they know of the situation at hand, they won't sit quietly."

Cork looked up from his apple. "Well, shit. I can help with that. The Winn are everywhere in Wolstone."

"And you think they'll help?" Gen asked.

Cork nodded. "The Winn hate two things. People who mistreat mages and assholes. We've got both right here, so the Winn should beg to help us after we tell them the situation."

"Stinton," the high mage bellowed, red-faced.

"On my way, Your Excellency!" Tobias walked toward the mages.

A whistle sounded, signaling their rest had ended all too soon. Gen and Cork moved back to their positions and dragged the ballista once more, though it seemed easier now. They pulled the ballista through the opening at the western end of the pass and onto the downward slope leading into the valley. It would be downhill for the rest of the journey, and the ballista would not cause as many problems for them. Now, if only they could solve the rest of their problems.

They had a plan. Not a well-thought-out one or even a complete one, but something.

"You can't piss without finding a Winn along the Trunellic coast," Cork stated.

"If you say so," Gen said, straining to pull her ballista leg over a stone. "I've never met one. Other than you, of course."

Cork nodded. "And I'm not a real one." Gen opened her mouth to protest, but Cork waved her off. "No, I'm Trunellic at this point. I'm proud of this icy shithole." He pointed to the forested hills to their north and the plains to the west.

It's not all that icy. Snowy, more like.

"Compared to Nazlin, it's beautiful here."

"Compared to Nazlin, my uncle's bloated corpse is beautiful."

"Such wonderful imagery. I thought my friend Cordyn was the poet, but perhaps it's you."

"Aye, all Winn have a way with words."

"But you're Trunellic."

"And you're too good of a listener." His laugh echoed against the receding mountains. Gen couldn't help but smile.

The smile faded as she felt a pang of sadness. If Cordyn ever reappeared, would he and Cork get along? Their wits were opposites: Cordyn's like a fencer dancing around an opponent, and Cork's like a war axe to the skull. Gen preferred war axes, but she'd grown to appreciate Cordyn, even if he'd never had patience for those he found less intelligent than himself.

Besides me. He's never told me I'm not as wise or witty as him, but it's obvious.

She let go of the ballista and rubbed her temples, willing the self-doubt away.

Well, I'll always be better at swords. War axes as well. Maybe even daggers, though it'd be a closer fight.

"So, we go to Wolstone, piss on bloated corpses, and that will call the Winn down upon us?"

"We'll get to the port, find the biggest buggerin' ship we can, have a polite chat with 'em, and then send five score angry mages after these Rosenfellians. Wipe the smirks off their faces."

"And save the children," Gen added.

Cork spat.

He's always coughing or spitting when he's not sure what to say.

"We're saving the children." She stared at him and refused to look away. "It's non-negotiable."

Cork looked sheepishly at the ground. "Of course, Gen, I wouldn't dream of not saving them. I just forgot about them, a little."

Evalia huffed. She'd been walking silently behind them. Gen assumed she'd been lost in thought.

Apparently, she was listening some, at least.

"How exactly could you forget?" Gen had

Cork shrugged. "I don't rightly know. Got sidetracked, ya know." A wet cough produced a clump of mucus that he spat out.

Lovely.

"Hmm," Evalia said.

"I got so caught up in sending the Winn after those arrogant Rosenfellians that I pushed the reason we was doing it outta my mind. Sorry, ladies. Of course, we're saving the kids."

"Glad to have your permission," Evalia said. She walked on ahead and refused to look back at them.

"The young lady's angry with me." Cork heaved his part of the ballista down a miniature stone bridge on the path, Gen struggling to hold on to her leg of the weapon. Traveling was so much easier without godsdamned siege weapons.

"Her brother is one of the children."

"Shit. If I'd have known that—" He paused to spit. "Well, I'd have done something different. Don't know what, though. Should I apologize?"

"Not now. Maybe in a bit. I don't think she'll hate you forever."

"I'm not smart, ya know, but I like to think I'm pleasant." He grinned. "And I can hit things. Hard."

After another hour of drudgery and cursing the ballista, a group of Obanni soldiers relieved them of ballista duty, leaving them to walk for the next few hours. Resting was not an option. Cork picked flowers as they went, handing the bouquets to any soldier who met his eyes. He gathered a larger bouquet and presented it to Evalia, whose glare softened as she took the flowers.

When Cork returned to her, Gen clapped him on the back.

"You may get her forgiveness yet."

"I enjoy spreading beauty," he said, and spat again. Gen narrowed her eyes at him. "And spitting. I bleedin' love spitting."

As they exited the deepest parts of the forest, Evalia rejoined their little group. She wasted little time in causing conflict once more.

"We should talk to Tobias about the plan."

"Don't mention him," Gen said.

"I know you don't trust him, but I believe he has the children's best interest at heart."

"When we were in Torrance, after he told us Topper had gone back to Dramin, I saw them together at the inn in town, having a secret meeting. Then Topper reappeared at the camp, and Tobias said he'd just returned from Dramin. If he were trustworthy, why would he lie about that? He's hiding something."

"Yes, I'm sure he is," Evalia said. "And we'll sit down later and confront him. Have a long chat with him about all the wrongs he's done. But for the moment, we need to trust him, at least a little."

"Gen," Cork said. "I don't knows the man, and ya know how I feel about them Rosenfellian mages, but it wouldn't hurt to have another ally, 'specially a mage on the inside."

Godsdammit.

Gen gave in.

"We need to move as quickly as possible," Tobias said.

They sat around a fire as darkness descended upon the hastily reconstructed camp. Only half a dozen tents stood on the cold ground of the valley. Tonight's focus was on sleeping somewhere sheltered from the harshest elements of the Trunellic evening, particularly the wind, which blew harder now than the torrential gusts of the daytime.

Huddled around the fire, they didn't feel the worst of the elements, though Gen wondered when it would be their turn to escape the wind and find refuge in one of the tents.

"With as far as we've traveled into the valley," Tobias continued, "the landscape is too open. A daytime desertion won't work. You'd be seen and captured. You need to move tonight, while it's dark."

"The question is, how do we get to the port?" Cork asked. "The Obanni aren't just going to let us have horses."

"Ever aspired to horse thievery?" Tobias asked.

"No, but I'm willing to learn."

"They hang horse thieves, you know," Gen said.

Cork tossed a branch into the fire, spraying sparks around the group. "They also hang deserters. Figure I may as well commit two hanging offenses if I'm committing one."

"There will be guards watching the outside of the camp. Mages and infantry. I'll distract them. Give me ten minutes, and then you go," Tobias said. "You can spend those ten minutes finding your horses. Then, the three of you—"

"I'm not going," Evalia said.

"What do you mean?" Gen asked.

"Ezra is here. I'm staying here too. I won't be swayed."

Tobias rubbed his eyes. "Evalia—"

"No. All of you, you can do whatever the hell you want, but I will not leave without my brother."

Seeing Evalia would stand firm on this, Gen hugged her. No point in leaving anyone angry.

"How ya gonna distract the guards?" Cork asked.

"Simple science," Tobias said, placing a sturdy branch into the fire and holding it there. "Nothing that will bother the mages much, but it will work the soldiers into hysteria."

"Can you give the less mysterious version?" Gen asked.

"Of course. I'm going to walk over to the supply carts, inspect the foodstuffs, and accidentally drop a torch on the sacks of grain Tallen brought."

"But that could burn everything," Gen said.

"Hardly. The troops are mobile, and they'd not camped close to the foodstuffs. The fire may destroy some supplies, but the bulk of the army will escape unscathed." Tobias lifted the burning branch from the fire. "It will, however, create a distraction."

TWENTY-ONE

FLAMES SURGED AND DANCED, lighting up the darkness of the camp at night, casting a fierce, flickering glow over the supply carts. The fire consumed the wood with insatiable greed, sending showers of sparks into the sky as the carts crumpled into ash. The snapping and hissing of the flames interspersed with the sharp pops of exploding containers and the dull thuds of collapsing structures. An acrid smell of burnt bread filled the air, mingling with the smoke that billowed upward in thick, black clouds.

Gen led a horse away into the forest, Cork following behind her. The only things they packed were weapons, food, and water skins. They needed to travel quickly and weighing down the horses with extra items would do the opposite.

It was four day's ride to Wolstone and the Winn ships in the harbor; four days of not knowing what was happening to Evalia or the children. Or Tobias. Perhaps he wasn't all bad.

Tobias had taken two blazing branches and snuck over the sup-ply carts, tossed the makeshift torches onto the oil-soaked grain, and the fire blazed.

Hopefully, he'd survived the inferno. Gen still didn't trust him, but the last thing she wanted was him dead.

Gen maneuvered through the trees in a semi-circle, arriving back at the road a few hundred paces away from the camp. She couldn't see anyone through the dark, so she'd have to assume it was safe. She motioned to Cork, and they set off at a brisk pace for Wol-stone.

Cork spent the first night of camping lamenting all the things he'd miss about the Obanni camp: the food, the liquor, and the friends he met there. He fell into morose silence, something Gen needed to fix as soon as possible. They had a meeting with the Winn and a rescue to organize, and they couldn't afford to waste time reminiscing on how things used to be. It would be easy for her to think of Cordyn and the times they'd spent together, but she had to push all that aside for now.

Still, she figured the way to get Cork talking was to talk him through his emotions.

"How are you feeling? This must be hard for you."

"It is. It's godsdamned hard, and I'm bleedin' shattered. I made friends there. They's treated me well. I'd found a home for the first time in a long damn time. But this shit with the mages and the kids? No, they've gone too far. Couldn't sit by and let that happen. Still gonna feel sad about it, though."

Over the next four days, they descended further into the val-ley, passing farms, livestock grazing on the verdant green grasses, quaint farmhouses struggling to hold up against the sweeping winds coming in from the mountains. It was a vast change from the snow of the mountains, though the temperature remained frigid, and crops—only the heartiest would survive in Trunel, the land of cabbages—dotted the landscape while farmers and their horse-drawn plows tilled the land. A few farmers waved to them, their wrinkled faces haggard underneath the large, brimmed hats they wore to block out some of the wind. It took a brave soul to live out here. Gen promised herself that she'd travel somewhere warmer after all this was over.

Assuming any of us are still alive.

They arrived at the coast near Wolstone after four days. They'd met no difficulties along the way beyond a slick spot of road here and there from the ice. Apparently, bandits avoided the cold here just like everyone else.

The port itself bustled with sailors from all over. Hulking ships sat moored along the docks, an assortment of Obanni and Rosen-fellian flags hanging from the masts, oscillating in the wind, which blew even harder along the water, something Gen didn't think possible. No Piranese here, not with the delicate situation in Trunel. Piranese or Kosellan ships risked being burned or taken during the night.

"I don't know what the Winn flag looks like," Gen admitted. They dropped off their horses at a stable at the northern edge of the port and headed down toward the water.

"I'd be surprised if ya did," Cork said. "On account of there's not one."

"You don't have a flag? I didn't know that was possible."

"What's a flag but a flimsy piece of art people hang from things? Don't mean nothin'." He pointed to a Rosenfellian merchant ship. "That flag, what does it say? We was born here, don't attack us if you was also born here? The Winn don't care where ya were born or what other allegiances ya might have. Ya make the choice to join, and ya respect your fellow Winn. Don't need no flags for that."

They walked past an Obanni sloop, its side riddled with cannon-ball-sized holes. Cannonballs were a relatively recent invention, and Gen had never seen a cannon fire in person—you needed several mages on duty to control enough water to propel the cannonballs forward—though she'd seen the damage on the ships that limped back into Mintar port after braving the seas.

"How do you know what ships are Winn? The ones with no flags?"

"No, we'll fly flags like all the other ships to fit in places. Rosenfellian in Rosenfel, Obanni in Oban, and so on. Don't pay to attract attention. Winn ships look like any other, but if yer Winn, ya know."

"Thanks for clearing that up." Gen scanned the harbor for any ships that screamed Winn, but they all looked the same. Oval shaped wooden vessels that floated on water and had terrible food.

They reached a gargantuan black ship in the harbor.

"That'll be my kind," Cork said.

"I'll take your word for it." Gen wanted to sit down, rest her weary legs, and close her eyes for a moment. It'd been so long since she'd slept more than a few hours. Not since her drunken night in Torrance, and that had not been the most restful sleep.

Cork went in alone. "They'll listen better if it's just me, to begin with. I'll come get ya soon."

She sat along the wharf, tossing rocks into the harbor, cursing herself for trusting Tobias. Yes, they were unwilling allies again, but she couldn't shake the feeling he was connected to Cordyn's disappearance.

She threw a thin smooth stone as hard as she could. It skipped through the water, reemerging twice before sinking to its watery grave. Unfortunately, she saw no suitable nap spots along the docks and had to postpone sleep once more. However, if she stayed still, she could reach the verge of unconsciousness, but could not hurdle the last barrier into slumber.

After what seemed like ages, Cork reemerged to invite Gen onto the ship.

"They'll see you now. Just don't say much and tell the truth. They'll know if you're lying."

Gen noticed after entering the Winn ship that it was empty. Not empty of sailors—they were everywhere aboard the ship, moving with brisk determination—but empty of clutter. She'd never been aboard ship, so she didn't know what it was supposed to look like, but she saw no boxes of supplies, no jackets thrown about, almost no furniture.

The sailors, covered in the dreamshapes like Cork, seemed not to notice Gen, as if tall sword-wielding women with no tattoos often tramped about their ship. Among the sailors stood wolves, bigger by half than any wolves Gen had seen in the wild, the size of warhorses, yet completely tame.

"Those wolves," Gen said. "Are they...?"

"The wolvinns are the mounts, yes." Cork said. "Faster and smarter than horses." He grinned. "And lots more vicious. Hell, I've seen wolvinns tear out more throats in battle than you've killed with that fancy sword."

Gen stared at the wolvinn's teeth; great white fangs hung down under the beast's jowls. "They're unnatural. But beautiful."

"Enhanced. Just the way of life on the isle. We always treat 'em well, though. Like family."

The wolvinn growled at Gen. "Family doesn't rip your throat out. And yet, I think they'd make excellent companions." Gen turned away from the beasts. She wanted to walk over and pet them, but that seemed like the best way to lose an arm.

"Just big bloody dogs, innit," Cork said.

"Do you think I could pet one?"

Cork let out a choked cough. "Gods, no. Ya don't pet a man's wolvinn without permission. Get us kicked off the ship."

"Fine," Gen said. "But one of these days, I'll ride one." She took one last lingering glance at the wolvinn.

As they walked across the deck, the deep charcoal-colored dark-wood glistened around them, soaking in the sun's light and reflecting it out, giving the entire deck an otherworldly shine. Gen had heard stories about the Winn never having to use lamps or candles, because the darkwood kept the surrounding areas illuminated.

Gods know why they call it darkwood, even with the color. They should call it lightwood.

"I've never seen darkwood up close before."

"Nah, the Winn don't like to share." Darkwood only grew on the Isle of Winn, and the Winn magically enhanced it somehow.

Wood doesn't glow like that without magic.

Gen felt the darkwood. Firm ridges moved up and down the seams, warm to the touch, even in the cold weather.

"I don't care if they share the darkwood, but hopefully they'll share reinforcements with us, at least."

"Like I said, let me do the talking."

The Winn never smiled. That was the first thing Gen noticed in the few minutes she spent among them. They sat stone-faced, listening to Cork describe where he had been over the past several years, and whether he had stayed loyal. There were two of them: a man and a woman. Both had close-cropped brown hair, ageless faces free of wrinkles, eyes that looked like they had seen far too much, and clear, tanned skin that should have been damaged from hours under the suns. The sailors in Piran had blackened spots all over their skin from sun damage, yet this man and woman had darker tans and flawless skin.

Cork answered their questions with a calmness Gen could only hope to have. When someone she cared about questioned her or seemed disappointed, her immediate reaction was to shut down and avoid the person confronting her. If she didn't know them, she would just get Maralda out and let her sword do the communicating.

"Do you then wish to return to us?" the male Winn asked.

Cork's calm facade faltered. "I don't—" He scratched at his nose for a moment.

Well, you wanted to do the talking. Do the talking.

"I suppose so," he said.

"Do you accept your penance?" the woman asked.

Cork swallowed. "Yes, I accept."

The male Winn put his hands on Cork's temples. "Your dreams are clouded. You must seek the wisdom of the Isle when you return."

"By the Winn, it shall be," Cork chanted.

The woman looked at Gen, as if seeing her for the first time. "Your companion's dreams are fractured. Young woman, you have seen great hardship?"

"That's an understatement," Gen said.

Cork glared at her.

"She asked me a question," she hissed at him.

"Why do you come among the Winn, child?" the man asked.

"Children," Gen said before Cork could interrupt. "Mage children. Rosenfellian mages have taken a large group of them, and they intend to experiment on them."

Shards crashed into the ceiling, shattering against the darkwood. Ice particles rained down on Gen, who had already begun unsheathing Maralda before realizing the Winn hadn't targeted her. Both Winn sat, mouths ajar, blinking rapidly, as if they had seen something horrific. The Winn man, bellowing in a high-pitched scream, turned to his companion and shook her. After a moment, she reached out and began shaking him as well.

They spoke in a gibberish that Gen decided must be Winn. Winnese? Winnellic?

Gods knew what they called their language.

"What are they saying?" she asked Cork.

He shushed her. "He's upset."

"I'd gathered that."

"They're deciding exactly how they'll dismember the Rosenfel."

"And the Obanni?"

"They haven't mentioned them yet, but I doubt they'll be friendly."

The two Winn stood up, bowed, and left the room, shutting the door behind them. Gen didn't hear the lock click.

"So, do we just sit here?" she asked.

"I'd recommend it. They'll come back, or at least someone will."

"What did they mean by your penance?"

Cork grimaced. "Well, when a Winn chooses to leave, they give up their Krooma—their birthright. I was a child, so my parents gave up my Krooma for me. That's the only reason they'll allow me back."

"What if you'd been an adult?"

"They pat me on the back, say it was nice to see me, and give me a meal, maybe even take me to where I wanted to travel, but they'd never let me back on the Isle permanently."

"So, how do you get your Krooma back?"

"I'm not sure, but it won't be easy. Nothing with the Winn ever is." He spat on the darkwood floor, and the spit sat on top of the wood, as if the wood refused to accept liquid into it. "That's a worry for a later time, though. It'll be weeks, maybe months, before I'd head back to the Isle. Lots of time to worry about that then."

With a screech of hinges, the door swung open, the two Winn returning with a plate of roasted meats. They were accompanied by a taller, younger Winn.

The new arrival bowed to Gen and Cork. "I am Unthed Winn. We welcome you, Gen of Piran and thank you for your visit. Corkelle Winn, we accept you back to our fold, pending your penance."

"Will you help us?" Gen asked.

"We will destroy the Rosenfellians and retrieve our young brethren." He frowned at the other two Winn. "We are undecided on the Obanni. Some of us believe they are an enemy, others just an annoyance. The dreams will speak to us when we encounter them."

"Piran will thank you," Gen stated.

"We care nothing for Piran. We would allow your nation to die as well if it meant the safety of our mage brethren. Do not assume we do anything for you."

And here I thought we were becoming boon companions.

"Well, then I thank you."

Unthed pressed his hands together in what Gen assumed was a gesture of thanks. "We do not do this for you either, but we will accept your gratitude more than Piran's. However, before we act, we ask you to lure our enemies closer to the water so we may draw upon our abilities to their fullest extent."

"Leave that to us," Cork said.

"But won't their mages also have heightened powers this close to the water?" Gen asked.

"Yes, but we have seventy of our brethren here. We cannot hope to defeat hundreds of infantry soldiers out in the grasslands, but along the coast, one mage is worth ten mere soldiers. If they do not come near the water, we shall still attack, but our chances will improve the closer to water we are."

Another Winn called over to Unthed, and he bowed to them. "I shall return momentarily."

After Unthed and his companion walked away, Gen turned to Cork, who was gnawing on a chicken leg. "How the hell are we going to bring them all closer to the water?" Gen asked. "Invite them to a soiree in the harbor?"

"I dunno." Cork picked at his teeth. "I hoped you'd come up with a plan."

"My friend Cordyn was the planner." She stroked Maralda. "I'm only comfortable with a sword, assuming we find someone to use it on."

"Oh," Cork said, grimacing. "Weapons is what I'm good at, too. I reckoned you'd make the plans. You did the planning to desert from the army."

"I wish Cordyn were here."

"Nothing to do but eat, then," Cork said, grabbing two chicken legs, biting into both of them at once.

Gen tried to imagine what Cordyn would do in a situation like this. He would talk incessantly, insulting whoever he spoke to, but in such flowery language that the person wouldn't even realize they were getting insulted. By the time they figured it out, they'd already be doing exactly what Cordyn wanted.

"Cordyn usually insults people," she said.

Cork placed his hands on his knees and shook his head. "I wouldn't insult the Winn, unless you dream of a life underwater."

Gen shook her head. "Drowning is not on my list of tasks to do today."

"I think we tell the Winn that we don't know if we'll be able to bring our enemies closer to the water, but there's no time to waste."

"Agreed."

Cork opened the door of their cabin and called out something in the Winn tongue. Unthed and his associates from before entered. After they sat, Cork spoke. "I dunno that we'll be able to get the Rosenfellian bastards closer to the coast. Can ya still help us?"

The Winn didn't yell or throw furniture, no swords drawn, no threats, not even looks of disappointment.

"Will you accept penance for each of those who perish?" Unthed asked, eyes burning into Cork, and Gen wanted to ask the man to stop staring.

After a moment's pause, Cork said, "I will."

"Then we will move within the hour. If you wish for rest, food, or drink, now is the time."

The two Winn swept out of the room.

"What the Kirth does that mean?"

Cork refused to meet her eye. "For each Winn who dies in the battle, I'll have more time added on to my penance."

"Gods, Cork. You'd do that?"

He slapped her back, connecting right below her shoulder blade, hitting several of the bruises from the Hillmen's bolts.

Harder than needed, that slap, but I suppose Cork doesn't know his own strength.

"Arggh," Gen said, taking a moment to regain her breath. "Thank you, Cork."

"Of course, Gen. I'm like you. I help my friends."

"Oh, I meant for the slap." She winked.

Gods, a wink? Cordyn was rubbing off on her.

"Friends who break ribs stay friends forever."

"I guess I've made a lot of friends, then." He snorted. "Come on, let's go make friends with those Rosenfellian and Obanni bastards. I reckon we's got a lot of head-crackin' and guts-spillin' in our future."

Gen had an idea. "Do you think they'd let me ride a wolvinn?"

TWENTY-TWO

WITHIN A WEEK OF Gen leaving, the plan went to shit.

Tobias tried to avoid Evalia as much as he could, but no matter what he did, his eyes always found their way back to her. Her proud, determined, jaw-clenched beauty was impossible to ignore.

Without Gen or even Tallen to keep her in check, Evalia's behavior had become reckless. She walked closer to the mages, attempting to get a view of the children. She no longer pretended to fulfill her duties as an Obanni officer and walked alone, ignoring the soldiers who should have been under her command. Worst of all, she kept looking at Tobias, too. Furtive glances, but he saw no longing in her eyes.

She didn't trust him; that much was obvious. He couldn't blame her. He'd struggle to trust himself, too.

She never would have loved you, anyway, you damned fool. Accept that, stop pining, and do what you must.

He watched the horizon, hoping to see an approaching force. The Winn, Gen, Cork, and anyone else who would fight. However, no one came. He'd started thinking of alternate plans, in case Gen failed, when Evalia joined him in his march, and ruined things even more.

"We've waited long enough," she said, arms crossed. "Gen may come back, but I have no hope in these Winn to be so selfless as well."

"They will come."

"Even so, I tire of waiting. I'm going to see my brother, no matter the consequences." She turned to march toward the prison caravan.

"Gods woman, no." He grabbed her arm, immediately letting go when he saw her imperious expression. "Wait for the Winn, I beg you." He clasped his hands together. "They don't allow mage mistreatment. As soon as they hear of the situation, they will come."

"You know this through your many experiences with them?"

"No, I've only met a few, and they were odd bastards. Didn't say much, didn't interact at all. Solemn, but the way they looked at you, it made you want to do everything in your power to avoid angering them. And what the Rosenfellians have done to the children will anger them."

"That does nothing to comfort me. Good day." She turned once more.

"I won't let you," he said, grabbing her arm again.

"Unhand me," she said. "When you go through a situation half as difficult in your miserable little life, then you can speak to me, but never touch me again."

"Evalia."

"No, I don't think we'll have this conversation." She stormed away, heading straight for the mages.

Tobias, you've well and truly buggered it all up.

Evalia walked right up to High Mage Wellise and, without bowing, kissing his hand, or any other sign of respect, said, "I'm here to inspect the prisoners. Sword General Koston's orders."

Wellise looked at her as if she were an ant. "I'm busy, girl."

"As is the sword general. He wishes me to make my report as soon as possible. If you'll excuse me." She moved to walk past him, toward the caravan of prisoners.

"I say, this is most intolerable." Wellise stamped his foot.

For a man of such power, he's a weak-willed prat.

"My apologies, sir. I'll just be a moment."

And she was in. Tobias cursed as Evalia opened the front hatch of the prison caravan and climbed in.

"I'll deal with this, sir," he said, nodding to Wellise. "This damned woman has been a thorn in my side for days now."

He raced after Evalia, ignoring Wellise's inquiring glance. Wellise would be fine wallowing in ignorance a while longer, but Tobias could not afford for Evalia to make a scene, reveal herself, and ruin everything.

As he opened the hatch and entered the prison caravan, he slipped, momentarily dizzy. The stench was abhorrent. Urine, feces, and sweat intermingled and left to fester for days.

Evalia walked among scores of children, all in varying stages of filth, sores festering on their hands and bare feet.

Gods, they look so much worse than just a few days ago.

He wanted to turn around, march over to Wellise, and slit the man's throat in front of the entire army. Wellise and his mages deserved to die. Before this, he'd found them obnoxious and had hoped someone would knock them down a peg.

He was now determined to kill any godsdamn mage that survived the Winn. He might even shoot a few shards into the faces of the dead ones.

Would these children grow up hating other mages, wanting them dead? The idea of one of those children growing up to become him—consumed by revenge, destroying any hope of a normal life—made him shudder. What if one of the children decided to hunt him down one day? He didn't deserve that. He hadn't been part of the original subjugation of the children. But then, Cordyn Tallen hadn't stuck a sword through Master Renedian's side or executed Tobias's mother either.

For the first time, he wondered if Tallen deserved it all. Perhaps Topper was right. Had he fallen so far into vengeance that he was punishing innocents?

No. Tallen was a bastard, and that was that. Tobias wouldn't kill him, but only because of his promise to Topper.

"What the Kirth are you doing, Evalia?" he asked. Better to argue with the woman in front of him than with himself. "Gods, we're risking everything just by being in here."

She ignored him, continuing her journey through the mass of limbs.

"Ezra," Evalia cried, rushing to a clump of children along the eastern wall of the caravan. "Ezra. It's me."

"Vale?" a boy asked. He was smaller than Tobias envisioned, with wavy auburn hair like Evalia, but shorter, falling just past his ears, framing his small mouth and nose. If Tobias had seen the boy on the street, he would have thought him no more than seven years old.

Evalia swept the boy up into a hug, while several other children stared on, no doubt wondering who this woman was.

"Vale, what are you doing here?"

"I came for you." Her voice broke into sobs. "It took too long, but I'm here now, and you look terrible. You all look terrible."

"I'm hungry," Ezra said. He looked at Tobias curiously, but devoid of emotion. "They don't give us enough food, and they won't take these off." He raised his arms, showing silver metal shackles clamped tightly around his wrists, red welts on his skin around where the shackles pressed.

Shit. Tobias knew those shackles. Not from experience, but he'd seen them at the Academy, locked away behind impenetrable mage-glass displays. Enhanced silver fused with iron to make unbreakable manacles, which also helped mute the wearer's mage abilities. Gods, they were an atrocity. A war crime anywhere in Sarakan, death to the person carrying them, or gods forbid, using them on a mage.

Yet here, the men who he'd trained under, who he'd thought of as a minor annoyance all these years. They were the worst criminals of all.

He looked at Ezra. The boy met his eye and didn't look away. "Do you know who put them on you, boy?" Tobias asked.

Ezra looked to Evalia, as if asking her silently if he should speak to Tobias or not. She nodded encouragement. "I don't feel like talking," Ezra said. "I want food."

"Ezra, you have to talk to this man," Evalia said. "It's important."

"No!" Ezra yelled. "I won't because I don't want to!"

Tobias winced. What in Kirth was wrong with the boy?

"Stop," he whispered through clenched teeth.

Evalia stroked Ezra's hair and whispered something to him. The boy's chest heaved, and he wheezed slightly, but he seemed to calm down.

"We're here to help," Evalia said.

"They knocked me out," Ezra said matter-of-factly. "When I woke up, the shackles were on my wrists." He wrung his hands. "They hurt, especially when you try to sleep."

"I'll see what I can do," Evalia said. "Maybe we can get them off."

"You can't," Tobias said. "No one can, except the mage who put them on originally. They're no mere shackles, Evalia. They restrict the wearer's magic, and over time, will kill them. That would take months at least, and I'd assume Wellise has no intention of killing the children that way. You can't experiment on the dead."

A loud groan escaped from Evalia's mouth, a mixture of moans and hisses. "I don't care if we have to torture every damn mage out there," Evalia said, her voice low. "I will find them."

"We're going to help you escape," Tobias said, turning in a circle so all the children in the caravan could see him. To look untroubled, he showed his teeth, trying his best to smile. Faking a smile was harder than faking anger. With anger, at least, you could remove all expression from your face. With happiness, you needed to put on a show.

The children scurried away from him in various states of terror.

"It's a bloody master," one boy screamed, pointing at Tobias's robes.

"He's come to kill us," a girl moaned, hiding her head in her hands.

"Shh," Evalia said. "No, he's not with the men who took you. He's working with me to free you." She hugged Ezra. "He's a good man who will help us." Her voice faltered, leaving Tobias with no doubt. Evalia no longer believed he was a good man.

Well, by Kirth, I may as well admit she's right.

"I won't hurt you," he said, showing his hands. "What's been done to you is abominable. I will personally take revenge on those who did this to you."

"Are you hurt? Have they done anything else to you?" Evalia asked, scanning Ezra's face.

The boy shook his head

"They haven't given you any odd tasting drinks or taken your blood?"

"No," Ezra said.

After the children murmured negatives or shook their heads, Tobias's tension eased. He massaged his neck, enjoying the pin pricks radiating on the base of his skull. Yes, the situation was still fraught, and he didn't know how they'd succeed if the Winn didn't arrive soon. But at least the children had undergone no experiments yet.

"It's not been that bad, except for the lack of food," a girl said.

A nearby boy added, "They've not been terrible to us, besides keeping us locked up in here."

Ezra wrinkled his nose. "It stinks."

"We'd noticed," Tobias said.

"You get used to it," a girl said. She took a deep breath in with no sign of disgust. "Most of the time, you can't even smell it anymore, unless it's really fresh."

"We're getting you out of here," Evalia said, looking at all the surrounding children. "Out of these horrid conditions."

Although Ezra just watched Evalia keenly, with no sign of excitement or concern, a few children began speaking loudly over one another. Tobias stepped in to calm them. It wouldn't do for them to make such a noise that the guards came closer to check out the situation.

"We will escape," Tobias told the children, "but we need to wait just a little longer. I promise you that you'll be free within the week, hopefully within a day or two."

Evalia hugged her brother once more—the boy did not return the embrace.

Tobias walked through the throng of expectant children, looking at him with a mixture of fear, admiration, and—in Ezra's case—indifference.

When Tobias exited the caravan, the plan went further to shit.

"Ah, welcome, friends," Sword General Koston said. "You have much to explain."

Koston, High Mage Wellise, Marston, and at least twenty Obanni troops—swords and crossbows out and at the ready—stood waiting for them.

Tobias put his hands out in a gesture of peace. "Sword General, Your Eminence, I'm honored by your presence. I was assisting the sword lieutenant with her inspection."

Koston gave him a wry smile. "Of course you were. What else could you be doing?" He motioned for the sword-wielding soldiers to move forward.

"Treason, that's what you were doing," Wellise said, stamping his foot and glaring at Tobias. Marston whispered in Wellise's ear. Wellise's jowls warbled as he listened. When Marston finished, Wellise stomped his foot a second time. "He's a Winn spy. I demand he be executed."

Koston glowered at Wellise. "Now, now, Wellise. You'll have your turn. For now, let me speak." He looked down at the ground, as if realizing for the first time that he stood in a half foot of muddy snow. "But first, let's retire to my quarters." He signaled something to an officer, and a whistle blew. The soldiers stopped their march and prepared to make camp.

Soldiers toiled for the next ten minutes, erecting tents and unpacking supplies for dinner. Tobias stood outside the tent, unshackled but watched carefully by ten guards. Evalia sat on a hay bale a few yards away. She'd said nothing since their capture, staring toward the prison caravan and refusing any of his attempts at conversation.

He watched a man roughly ten yards away who was unwrapping several legs of lamb, and his stomach rumbled. He doubted Koston would offer them refreshment during their upcoming meeting, which made the temptation to call upon the *Vida* even worse. A well-placed shard to the man's neck—or even his knee, if Tobias wanted to avoid murder—and the lamb's legs would be his. Of course, he'd certainly die soon after, but it might be worth it. His stomach rumbled again, and he forced himself to keep his hands down.

No shards right now. You've got too much at stake to throw it all away for some dinner.

He pushed the thoughts from his mind. He had to escape this.

Even with the distraction provided by the nearby food, the pit in his stomach grew bigger with every moment. He could eat all the lamb in the world, but if some of the children grew up hating him, making him their personal Coart Tallen, he would be shattered.

He needed to talk to someone. To confess. To fill the ever-growing pit. His options for confessor were limited: either the Obanni with the lamb or Evalia, and that assumed the Obanni would even look at him.

"Listen, Evalia, there's something I want to tell you." He rubbed his hands together, then moved one hand through his hair. It was easier to avoid women altogether than speak his feelings. He would not tell her of his hopeless infatuation with her, but he wanted her to know why he'd done what he did. "I kidnapped Tallen."

"What?" She looked like he'd struck her across the face.

"He deserved worse. That man's family ruined my life."

"His family ruined your life?" She looked at him as if he was insane.

"His father."

Hopefully now she'll understand that it's something I had to do.

"He's not his father."

"Close enough. They wear the same hat."

"Tobias." She said his name like a death knell. "You kidnapped a man because he wears the same hat as his father?"

"When you say it like that, it sounds all wrong." Godsdamn woman, twisting his words. "If you'd only let me tell you the complete story, I know you'd see—"

"Do you remember the reason we're here, Tobias?"

"Of course. I'm not stupid, Evalia."

"So, perhaps now you see why I have no sympathy for you." She turned away, moving back to her hay bale, and facing the opposite direction to where he stood.

"His father killed my friend, and probably my mother."

She didn't acknowledge his words for several moments. Finally, she spoke. "Unless Cordyn personally killed everyone you know, I don't want to hear another word."

"It was for the children," Tobias said. Evalia looked at him dubiously, but remained silent. Tobias pressed on. "I needed a way to get us closer to the coastline and the Winn, so I kidnapped Tallen and forged the notes." He placed a hand on his chest. "It was quite ingenious, I think."

Evalia turned away once more.

Well, that's the end of that. If the Winn would just get here, at least one thing might go right.

Once the soldiers finished pitching the command tent, Koston led Tobias, Evalia, and Wellise into the cramped space. Where was Marston? It was strange that he wasn't there considering how ever-present he'd been at Wellise's side.

Two flimsy wooden chairs lay propped up against the far side of the tent, next to a mahogany table, on which sat a pipe. Koston and Wellise took the chairs, and Koston picked up the pipe as if it were his most prized possession. Guards threw Tobias to the ground. His forearm connected with his skull and his world erupted into pain. Breathing to fight through the agony, Tobias maneuvered to a sitting position. Evalia sat next to him, red-faced but chin raised high. Brave in the face of the enemy.

After taking a deep puff from the pipe, Koston placed it on his lap and began. "Master Wellise's associate tells him that you are working to free those poor children from their imprisonment."

"I'm not sure what you mean, sir," Tobias said. He shifted his weight from side to side, trying to remain calm.

"Dammit," Wellise said. "Stinton, that Winn spy, the Nazlin cow and your Winn dog of a mercenary, Koston. They're all working together, along with whoever in Kirth this woman is." He pointed at Evalia.

Koston stroked his beard absentmindedly while holding the pipe to his lips. He took a puff and then fixated on Tobias. "What do you have to say for yourself, Stinton?"

"You'd have to ask the Winn spy or the Nazlin woman or this mercenary you speak of. I'm sure I know nothing of these affairs."

"Alas, they've disappeared in the night." Koston glanced at Wellise. "Not a bad idea, actually. I wish I'd thought of that before we packed up the entire camp and went on this mad journey toward the coast." Another puff, then Koston crushed the pipe between his fingers, snapping it in half. "And now we've received reports from our scouts of Winn traveling toward us."

"All part of your plan," Wellise spat.

"I hope they kill you all," Evalia said.

Wellise slapped her across the face. "Don't speak, woman."

Tobias sprang from his chair, launching himself toward Wellise, but found the path blocked by two Obanni guards, pikes in hand

"Stinton, sit down," Koston ordered. "Wellise," Koston said, his voice menacing, "This is your second warning. I have asked you not to interrupt me."

"Godsdammit, man—"

"No, you will not speak anymore." Koston fixed an imperious stare on Wellise. "This is my camp. You are my guest. I have allowed you to accompany me in this matter out of the goodness of my heart, and because of my duty to my nation, I have acquiesced to you traveling with us, and I have been an unwilling part of your nefarious deeds toward those children. But let us be clear. I am in charge. You are not. I do not give a damn about your goals, and I hope that, once we've parted ways, the children escape from you and live long, happy lives. You disgust me. You, your fellow mages, and your mercenaries have no honor. And if you persist in speaking, I will have you removed."

With a surprising temerity, Wellise accepted Koston's rebuke, slinking back into his chair.

Tobias went to make another attempt at Wellise, but Evalia shook her head at him.

"I'm fine," she whispered.

Tobias eased into a crouch, his focus on Koston.

"Where was I?" Koston asked. "Ah yes, your plan to send the Winn after us. They'll be here soon enough. I suppose this was your plan all along. Rennick fled the camp to pass information, and then your Nazlin friend also left. Perhaps she found out your plan and confronted you, so you killed her along with my fighter to hide your secret. What are you? Kosellan spies?"

"You have a fantastic imagination, Koston." Tobias said, but it was no use pretending at this point. Evalia had already given them away, but he didn't want to give Koston or Wellise the entire plan. "Unfortunately, you're mistaken. I've never even been to Kosel, nor do I know anything of Kosellan plots. I am a Rosenfellian mage, though not the most loyal to the Imperium, I confess." He nodded to Wellise. "I'm not impressed with the leadership there. And especially afraid of the men Wellise surrounds himself with."

"I can't argue with you there," Koston said. "Alas, I don't believe you. You may be a Rosenfellian mage, but I know you have connections to Kosel." He puffed at the pipe again. "You and your friend Rennick will be disappointed. We received word this morning that Kosel fell. Three days ago. I assume your Rosenfellian forces will soon take Piran as well."

"You must be pleased," Tobias said. Piran's fate meant nothing to him, nor Kosel's. What did he care if one nation subjugated another?

"Our troops march upon their capital now, liberating the people from the ignominy of Kosellan rule. We now control Trunel and

Kosel. It's high time we travel north to the Kosellan border to meet with high command, help with the occupation effort, and enjoy the victory celebrations." He regarded Wellise with disdain. "I believe it's time for our partnership to end."

"That's not what we agreed, dammit," Wellise said, sputtering.

"Affairs of more importance have arisen. You can play with your mages however you like, but you will do it without me or my men."

"Good," Tobias said. "Take your troops and go to Kosel. Burn it down for all I care."

Koston peered at him, a new look of understanding in his eyes. "Interesting." He pointed to Wellise, as if the high mage was a carcass ready for disposal. "You seek revenge against our mage friends, then?"

"Yes," Tobias said. There was no point in continuing the charade.

"What?" Wellise asked, jumping from his seat with such ferocity that he almost lost his balance and fell. "Stinton, you're an Academy man. I've known you since you were a boy."

"If you remember my boyhood, you'd know why I desire revenge."

Wellise's eyes moved to the tent ceiling. "I've always thought of you as a part of the family, like all the others who've come through the Academy."

"You were never my family," Tobias snarled. "You and your brethren destroyed my family."

"The business with your father was lamentable, but I had nothing to do with it. I don't even know what he was charged with. Whatever the issue, it came straight from the emperor."

"You lie. I know you for a craven wretch. Kidnapping children, experimenting on them. You deserve worse than death."

"The children are filthy," Evalia said, looking at Koston. "You say this is your camp, that you're in charge, but you let unspeakable things happen to children. Under your watch. You disgust me."

"Stinton is mine," Wellise said. "You can have the woman, Koston. She's pretty and will keep your men well entertained."

"My brother," Evalia said.

"What about him?" Wellise asked.

She lunged for him, a small knife appearing in her hand.

A fruit knife? Where in Kirth did she hide that?

It was barely larger than a finger. Evalia held it with determination as she launched toward Wellise. Tobias wasn't sure if the knife could kill a man, but it would hurt, and gods knew Wellise deserved the pain.

For an aging man used to the softer delicacies of rank, Wellise still possessed some agility. He stepped back, bringing his hands into the Vida with haste.

He began to speak the incantations. Soon shards would rip apart Evalia's skin, leaving ragged holes in the smooth curves of her neck and chest.

Tobias didn't have enough time to save her. He was faster than Wellise, but the older man had too much of a head start.

And so, I'll watch her die.

"Lower your hands or I'll chop them off," Koston said, watching both Wellise and Tobias, a longsword in his hands.

"This is not your fight, Koston," Tobias said.

"You can kill each other to your heart's content for all I care," Koston said. "But not in my tent."

"You're signing your death warrant, Koston," Wellise warned.

Three Obanni pikemen advanced on Wellise. He shot shards at the pikemen, killing one with a shard to the neck. The man gurgled and collapsed. Shards came from behind Tobias, striking Koston in the chest and legs. He fell with a muffled cry, and lay unconscious, but Tobias saw Koston's chest move in slow, ragged breaths. Death would soon follow without treatment.

"Thank you, Marston," Wellise said.

Tobias spun to see Marston standing in the doorway of the tent.

"Of course, your excellency." Marston turned to the group of mercenaries entering the tent. Seven of them against two Obanni pikemen. The skirmish lasted only seconds before the pikemen lay dead.

"Kill the woman," Marston ordered.

"No," Tobias cried. He stepped toward Marston.

"Oh, do shut up, Stinton," Marston said.

Tobias felt a sharp pain in the back of his head. His world flailed into a stream of colors: reds, blacks, and swirling blues, a harsh white driving through the colors and banishing them from existence.

Agony.

He tried to scream but couldn't.

He collapsed forward as whatever hit him drove further into his skull.

Everything went dark.

TWENTY-THREE

THE FIRST THING CORDYN noticed was the dampness. Second, the pain. His body ached and his head pounded with an intensity he'd never experienced, even after a night of uninhibited drinking.

He was in a carriage, that was for sure. It wasn't moving. A bench upholstered with some sort of sticky velvet and black wooden walls, scratched by years of passengers pressing their luggage against the doors when exiting, the telltale stench of body odor and horses. The merest hint of daylight snuck through the small window slits at the top of the door.

He was alone. Why in Kirth was he in a carriage and not his bed in the medic tent? It was damned confounding.

Then he remembered.

Stinton.

Betrayal.

He'd been drugged. Now he was godsdamned sure where he was.

After positioning himself to where he wasn't lying on his arms, he closed his eyes, hoping for sleep. But, alas, it did not come.

Cordyn pushed himself into a sitting position, peering out the window slit at the grassy plains of what could only be Trunel. No trees taller than him, the sheen of ice-covered grass reflecting in the light of the suns, and a tavern which had once been white, Cordyn guessed, but now was a mixture of grays and browns as the paint faded. The grounds were well-kept enough to not give off the impression of abandonment, yet dingy enough to keep any but the most desperate of travelers from sparing a second look.

A ramshackle barn sat behind the inn, along with two horses. No saddles, no reins. He would either have to escape via this carriage or by riding bareback. While the carriage would be slower, there was less chance of falling and dying.

He pushed the carriage door, but it did not budge. Swordsman's tears, Stinton must have done something to the door. But what? Kirth, mages were infuriating.

He removed the jacket of the Obanni uniform he still wore, leaving a thin cotton beige shirt and the uniform trousers, which he hoped, if he managed to escape, would be less recognizable.

But how the devil would he escape?

Rearing back, he kicked the door with all his strength. It shook but didn't break.

"Damn it," he called out. "I promise not to kill you if you just let me out."

"I've seen you fight," a voice Cordyn didn't recognize said. "I'm not all that worried about dying." There was a slight pause. "But I suppose I'll let you out." The carriage door opened, and there was Topper. The boy wore an amused grin. "You didn't think I could speak, did you?"

"You were always damned silent before," Cordyn said.

"Tobias taught me it was better to be underestimated." Topper's eyes looked out toward the forest, worried. "He's a good man, Tobias."

"And yet I find myself kidnapped."

"Well, good men sometimes do bad things, especially to those who deserve it."

"I hardly deserve it," Cordyn scoffed.

"Hmph," Topper said. He pointed toward the tavern. "Let's go get you some food. Wouldn't want you starving to death, would we?"

"I liked you better when you were silent."

The interior of the tavern was much like the outside. Drab and full of rotting wood. However, the inside smelled of piss and ale and had a roaring fire going in the hearth. Cordyn sat beside Topper at the bar, while the barkeep, an older man with a permanent scowl, poured their ales. They were the only customers, and yet Cordyn might as well have been alone. Topper sat in silence, staring at his hands, seemingly on the verge of tears.

"You seem rather dour, master Topper," Cordyn said. "I would have thought you'd be jubilant. You and your godfather have gotten what you've always wanted. I'm at your mercy." The barkeep placed their ales in front of them and moved the hearth, poking the fire with a long metal stick.

"You've never mattered," Topper said. He stared dolefully at his mug of ale. He was a bit young for ale, but the barkeep must have decided he needed cheering. That or the old man served everyone ale, no matter their age.

"And yet you're ferrying me away to parts unknown with a nefarious plan of vengeance in mind."

Topper blew his nose into his sleeve, then wiped his eyes. "We should have been much further along by now. You were asleep for over two days, and at the beginning, I traveled as fast as the carriage would go. But then I stopped at this tavern and started thinking."

Topper sipped his ale and frowned. "I'm running away when the person I care most about needs help. And I'm not sure I can do that."

"You care that much about Stinton?" It seemed ludicrous that anyone could care for that odious man.

Topper nodded earnestly. "He saved me. Several months ago, my parents were killed." Topper shifted in his seat, as if he struggled to think about the matter at hand. "I didn't have the strength to go on. I stopped eating. I didn't rise from bed for days. Tobias refused to let me give up on myself. He made meals and wouldn't leave the room until I'd eaten something. He talked me through the darkest moments and pushed me to move forward." Topper grimaced. "And he hunted down the men who killed my parents and avenged their death."

"I knew Stinton was a murderer," Cordyn said.

"He saved me," Topper repeated. "And now I need to save him."

Cordyn saw an opportunity. "Well, you could always free me. Once I'm on my merry way, you can save Stinton to your heart's content."

"You'd enjoy that, wouldn't you?" Topper gave a mirthless laugh.

"I do enjoy freedom." Cordyn took a drink of his own ale. Warm and bitter, but still refreshing. "I'm sure you and I could come to an arrangement."

Topper scoffed. "Look, I don't really care about you. You could rot in a cellar, and I'd still sleep at night. But Tobias? He's everything to me. The best man I know. And I'm willing to let you free if it means a better chance of helping him."

"Thank you. I—"

"To be clear, I don't think you'll do anything to help. I can just focus better on saving Tobias if I'm not worrying about you."

"As you wish." Cordyn cocked his head toward the barkeep, who sat by the fire, ignoring them. "Topper, do you have any idea where we are?"

"About three day's ride from Wolstone. Assuming things went as planned, the mages should be headed this way. Perhaps less than a day's ride from here. We're not far from the coast."

"What exactly was Tobias's plan?"

"He was going to unveil you as a Winn spy and attempt to get the Rosenfellians moving toward their final destination. Near Wolstone."

"A Winn spy?" Cordyn asked. He thought of the money the Winn sent him each month, the accusations of the Piranese leaders, and what they'd asked Gen to do. "That gives me an idea, Topper. Barkeep" Cordyn turned to the barkeep, who looked up from the hearth with tired eyes. "Do you have any Winn nearby?"

"Aye," the barkeep said. "Creepy buggers. There's a group of 'em about an hour's walk up the road." He grimaced. "They don't bother us much, but my wife is terrified of them.

Cordyn tossed the barkeep a crown. "Well," Cordyn said, turning back to Topper, "Shall we join forces one last time?"

Topper sighed. "If we must."

Within ten minutes of the cottage, they drove by a seaside village, empty except for a few white-bearded fishermen who gave them pouches of dried copperfish and pointed them toward the Winn encampment. Cordyn thanked the fishermen, forced the salty copperfish down, his lips puckering at the bitter aftertaste, and continued on, marveling at the rocky coastline. Trunel was prettier than Piran, with its craggy cliffs looming over the sea, giving way to impossibly green fields dotted with pink and purple flowers, which sheep and goats grazed upon. Even with its colder climate, Trunel made Piran seem drab, a land of plum trees, yes, but little else of beauty, unless you enjoyed wheat or dirt.

They rode for a while longer before arriving at a small village. Cordyn counted seven mud brick huts, all of which looked near collapse. He would have thought the village uninhabited if not for activity along the outskirts of the village, where a group of travelers stood. They wore sleeveless tunics, displaying arms covered in black and red markings. Based on how his father had described them, and from meeting Cork briefly, he knew these were the Winn.

"Hello," Cordyn called to the Winn as he approached. "Torr keep you, good people."

The Winn peered at him, expressionless, a few of them giving him a brief nod before continuing on their way.

"I say, would you be so kind as to help me? I've been waylaid by bandits and have lost all but this carriage. "

A gaunt man raised his hand, and the other Winn paused.

"We wish you well on your journey, traveler, but can provide nothing. Good day."

Cordyn cursed his misfortune. A few farmers, he could charm out of a meal or two, perhaps a change of clothing, but the Winn seemed unflappable, and thus, impervious to his charms.

Time to dispense with the bullshit, then. "There are captured mages nearby. Children. I intend to save them, but I need your help."

The gaunt Winn's expression remained the same. "Yes, we know of the children. Our brethren go to save them as we speak."

"Well, join me. Let's go help them. I just need a meal first. And perhaps a weapon."

"It is not our duty to assist our brethren." Several Winn shook their heads. "We can provide directions, food, and arms, however."

"Thank you," Cordyn said.

Well, that was easier than expected.

"We will, of course, need payment," the gaunt man said.

Ah, that's more what I expected.

"I have no money, currently, but I will repay you. I swear on Torr, Hurod, Kirth, and all—"

"We do not wish for coin. You will owe us a favor. We will call upon you when we wish you to repay that favor, and you will agree, or face the consequences."

And what are the consequences?

It didn't matter. He had to accept their terms. He hoped their request wouldn't be too ghastly.

"I accept."

"Blessings," all the Winn chanted.

Yes, gods, bless me. I'm going to need it.

With each passing moment, Gen wanted a wolvinn mount even more.

The Winn were majestic atop their wolvinn, saddled in with leather straps around the legs and waist to keep them firmly mounted. The wolvinn panted happily as they galloped along, and none of them had growled at Gen recently.

Gen, atop her horse, watched as the wolvinn passed her by, powerful leg muscles propelling the beasts forward. They moved faster than horses; she and Cork were at the rear of the group, with all twenty Winn ahead of them.

"They're fast," Gen told Cork.

"Aye, they're just trottin' right now, so they don't leave us behind."

"It'd be so much easier if they'd just let me ride one," Gen grumbled.

They'd traveled for two days along the road toward the mountains, where the Rosenfellian mages would be. They camped by night. The Winn slept in the open air under the stars. Apparently, the Winn were anti-tent. Gods, they were odd. By dusk of the second day, they noticed the telltale signs of dust in the air. An approaching army.

However, when they moved closer, they found themselves in the midst of battle. Rosenfellian robes and piecemeal armored soldiers fighting against the black and red of the Obanni. The Obanni soldiers had no chance. More than half of them lay dead, their bodies mangled and frozen. Gen wondered why Koston hadn't sounded the retreat. Perhaps he was dead as well.

The last remaining Obanni soldiers ran for the nearby forest, shards trailing them and claiming a few more victims before the Obanni made it into the relative safety of the forest.

"Shit," Cork said.

"I guess their relationship soured," Gen remarked.

"Let's go," Cork said. He turned to the Winn, who sat on their wolvinn, watching the battle dispassionately. "The children are in there." He pointed to the rear of the battle, where the prison caravan sat, seemingly unguarded.

"Many will die this day," a tall Winn woman with a blonde braid said. "We shall kill and die for our brethren." They intoned a rhythmic chant.

"Let's just get to the fighting," Gen whispered to Cork.

"Give them a moment," Cork said. "This won't take long."

After what seemed like an eternity, the chanting stopped, and the Winn charged. Gen struggled to keep up with them, which was okay for once. She'd never actually been in battle before. Yes, she'd fought brigands and thieves, but it was usually her and Cordyn against a small group of assailants. Large-scale battle made no sense to her. She knew nothing of tactics or how to fight in a sea of bodies, all intent on killing her.

Well, Maralda, it's time to learn.

Surely, swinging the massive blade would keep opponents from getting too close, and as long as she could keep from getting overwhelmed by enemies, she'd be fine.

The Winn called upon powers Gen hadn't known existed. Yes, they used ice weapons, but not the slender shards Tobias favored, but massive ice hammers, javelins, and raining barrages of icy death.

The Rosenfellian mages held their own, staving off the worst of the Winn attacks, but she'd seen four die; two via hammers to the skull, controlled by Winn hundreds of feet away, one from a javelin through the eye, and the fourth from tripping and impaling himself on a fallen soldier's pike.

She and Maralda joined the fray, cutting soldiers down with every swing. A few of the mercenaries wielded Obanni pikes, which were just as long as Maralda, but the soldiers lacked Gen's skill. They kept poking at her, an easy move to parry, and with each lunge forward, they left their guard open for her blade to breach their armor. She swung Maralda high and made continuous staggering cuts into any and all who dared oppose her. A big man with a bastard sword thrust his blade at her, but she parried it, then turned the parry into a thrust, stabbing the man through the shoulder just below his clavicle. He fell in a heap, blood spurting onto Gen's boots.

Lifting Maralda, she looked for her next victim.

A pike flew past her face.

Oh, we're playing that game?

She looked up at the soldier who'd just thrown the pike.

A true soldier would fight up close. One to one. None of this throwing stuff. If I threw Maralda, you'd laugh at me, too.

She stepped forward. The soldier turned and ran for the forest.

"Coward!" she yelled after him.

You're no fun at all.

Two more soldiers approached, hiding behind body-length rectangular shields, only their heads and their maces peeking out.

Well, this is more interesting. Let's see what you can do.

"You might as well surrender now," the soldier on her left said, his voice trembling. "We won't hurt you if you lay down your weapons now, and, uh, surrender."

"I'm getting the idea you'd like me to surrender." She bent her knees, preparing to lunge forward.

"Well, yes, that would be fantastic. Best for all of us, really."

Godsdamn, they were pitiful.

"First battle?" she asked.

"Uh, no. We've been in lots."

She sighed. "If you drop your shields and weapons and run away now, I won't hurt you."

Within seconds, both men threw the maces and shields to the ground and fled. One of them took an ice hammer to the skull moments later, his skull shattering and spraying blood on his companion, who screamed and ran even faster for the safety of the nearby lake. Gen hoped he'd make it. He was a piss-poor soldier, but after watching a friend die like that, he deserved a little good fortune.

She never got to see if he survived, as a mercenary cavalryman galloped toward her with his sword at the ready.

Killing a horse went against everything she stood for, but she knew if she could unhorse the man, she'd dispatch of him with ease. One blow to the horse's chest was all she needed. Unbidden, visions of Francois the horse entered her mind. She had no idea where he was, not since the Obanni had taken him, but she couldn't kill the horse; Francois would hate it. The Winn would never give her a wolvinn of her own.

Pulling a man off a horse. Easy, right?

The calvary man tore through the torrents of ice, somehow staying on his horse as several shards cut into his arms and legs.

He was less than ten yards away. No time to think now. She dove to her left, avoiding the charging horse, then jumped to her feet and reached for the rider. Her hand brushed against the man's sternum, but she couldn't grip him. The only options? Attempt to grab his arms or push him backward. She pushed.

There was no way to get much power behind the push, but thank the gods, it was enough. The rider fell, crashing to the ground at her feet. While the horse raced out of the fray, Gen brought Maralda down into where the man's gut should have been, but he'd rolled to the side, avoiding the quick death. With surprising agility, the man rose to his feet and took out an axe.

"You'll not kill me that easily," he said.

Gods, his accent.

Gen looked at him for the first time. *Really* looked at him. His repurposed Obanni Sword Corporal's jacket and torn leather trousers hung off him, he was so thin. Long, stringy black hair framed his thin face, a hawkish nose curving over his pale lips. He looked like a corpse speaking in a Nazlin accent.

"You're from Nazlin."

"Godsdamn right." He sneered, the slightest bit of red coming to his lips. He brought the axe back, either to throw it or to prepare a swing. "You Piranese shits irk me. You're not too popular with anyone back home. That's why we're joining up with anyone who promises to destroy you."

"You won't succeed."

"I won't," he agreed. "Gods, I'll be dead soon. I'm bleeding out as it is. But you'll be dead soon too, and Piran will burn."

"You talk too much." With a feint to the left, she moved right, launching a particularly successful swing that ripped his head and neck from his body.

Well, he's dead. That's good. The whole Piran burning, everyone hating us part? Not so much. Or the three mages looking at me.

A few yards in front of her, three Rosenfellian mages clumped together, attempting to stave off the Winn offensive. They'd seen her, and they were now aiming their incantations her way.

They had the power advantage, but she was pissed, and even haughty mages thought twice about going up against angry greatsword wielders.

Gen yelled something unintelligible; the mages hesitated. Just for a moment, but that brief moment was all she needed. A mage with no hands couldn't perform his spells. A quick strike to the biceps of two of the mages left them armless and no longer a threat. She kicked one in the skull and flung Maralda into the rib cage of the third mage. He cried out a woman's name—a lover, his mother?—and fell. She dispatched of the two armless mages, one with a slice to the neck and the other with a boot to the throat, his neck snapping.

Enjoy your time with Kirth.

She had a moment to breathe, and she used it to look for Tobias or Evalia. There was no sign of either of them.

Cork stood across the fray, war axe in hand, leaving a trail of death as he surged forward. Gen hoped none of the soldiers he killed were friends of his, but he could mourn fallen friends later.

Raising Maralda, she headed in the direction of Cork. The field had cleared, and there was more danger of tripping over bodies than facing enemy attacks. Yelling came from the west, where the Rosenfellian mages and the children were, though she could see little beyond a covered caravan and a few robed mages standing outside.

When they'd arrived at the camp, a group of Winn mages broke off and headed in that direction, leaving Gen, Cork, and fifteen other mages to confront the bulk of the enemy forces. She'd been convinced she'd die—they were so outnumbered—but the Winn mages cut through the soldiers so quickly, she felt a bit cheated. She'd barely got any action.

When she reached Cork, he'd just dispatched his last opponent with a strike to the temple. Blood trickled down his face, and from the carnage that used to be his left eye, she knew he allowed at least one strike through his guard. With the mangled mess of blood and skin, she couldn't tell if he still had an eye underneath.

"You're getting slow, old man."

He guffawed. At least he was still him, wounds and all. "Missed a pike. Deflected it at the last moment, but I was late."

"That you were. Glad you kept it from going any further."

"I'm fond of my brain, ya know. It ain't much, but it's somethin'."

From behind them came a high-pitched scream. A child?

"Come on," Gen said, raising Maralda. "Let's end this."

TWENTY-FOUR

The Winn were godsdamned insane, but Kirth, could they make an entrance.

When Cordyn rode up to where the Winn had said the Obanni had made camp, he saw Obanni corpses scattered about the road, in various stages of dismemberment. Topper's cheeks bulged at the sight of a headless pikeman and Cordyn turned away in time to avoid watching the boy retch.

Cordyn had witnessed war before, but always from the outskirts of the battlefield, delivering messages for generals and kings. His talents did not correlate with the brute force or the bloody accuracy needed for bows or daggers.

If only more of these battles could be fought with words. Throw in a few bottles of wine and a fetching barmaid. Gods, I'd love war, then.

His wounds didn't bother him nearly as much after Medic Thomos's yorn liquor treatment—hopefully the medic wouldn't die in the battle, even if he was a miserable bastard. All the other Obanni could die. Perhaps Thomos could just get slightly mutilated, unable to speak, but still able to treat the wounded. It would be best for everyone.

Cordyn forced those thoughts out of his mind and a stray shard flew perilously close to him, brushing the edge of the black wool jacket the Winn had given him. He looked like a fool, dressed all in black: leather boots, linen trousers and a silk shirt. The Winn had no fashion sense, sending a man out in three different materials, especially when there was a chance to see beautiful women along the way.

Hopefully, Evalia was still alive. Cordyn found it hard to believe anyone could kill Gen. She *had* to be alive. With her ferocity with her sword, her excellent defense technique, and most importantly, her kindness. She was the best person he'd ever met, and surely the gods wouldn't allow someone so good to die now, in bloody Trunel of all places?

Godsdamn it all. The war, the nations of Sarakan, mages. It all seemed pointless now. Piran had fallen or would soon fall. His mission was doomed from the beginning, and there was little he could do for Piran. Perhaps Gen was right. People mattered. He knew he'd choose Gen over any nation, and that scared him, caring enough about another person to put them before everything he'd lived for.

"Stay here with the horses," Cordyn told Topper, who'd finished vomiting and now sat on his horse, head in his hands. "I'll be back soon enough."

Or I'll be dead.

Cordyn urged his horse forward, not waiting for Topper's response. He could wait on the edge of the battle for hours, and while it would be safer, like everything else he'd done, it would accomplish nothing.

Time to swoop in and save the day. And stay alive doing so.

Cordyn shuddered. He'd rather be in a drawing room listening to a lecture on something tedious—Obanni poetry, perhaps?—but instead, he surged closer to the fray, hoping the Winn mages wouldn't kill him before he could introduce himself.

"Rennick," a low voice whispered from the trees.

Sword General Koston lay wounded, an ice spear sticking out of his left thigh, right below his waist. No vital organs damaged, in Cordyn's unprofessional opinion, but the man's blood flowed like a stream after the ice melted in the spring. Koston held a knife to his leg as if to saw it off.

Well, we meet again, sir. This time, you're unable to move, so I'll be the imperious prick.

"Koston," Cordyn snapped. "What in sweet Kirth are you doing?"

Koston gave him an inquiring look. "Sword General Rennick. Back to watch my demise, I presume?" His eyes flitted to the knife. "I hadn't decided whether I was going to cut at the ice, or—" He fell into a coughing fit.

"Or cut off your godsdamned leg."

Koston's lips curved into the slightest of smiles. "It hurts. Figured it might hurt less if it was gone." He reached to his shoulders and tore at his jacket. "Not thinking straight." He coughed and spat up blood. "I told the Rosenfellians I wouldn't help them anymore. We were going to retreat. Bastards attacked us."

Cordyn felt a pang of something—sympathy? He didn't hate Koston. He had no feeling at all about the man, but watching him writhe in a bloody pool pushed Cordyn to act.

A quick dismount, lifting Koston's arms to take off the man's jacket, then pressing the rags of the jacket to the gushing wound, and tying the sleeves into a tourniquet of sorts.

"You might live, assuming you can escape. Or find Thomos."

Koston watched him. "Why would you do this for me? Your enemy?"

"I have nothing against you, Koston. I don't love Oban, but right now, Oban is better than Rosenfel."

"But you're Kosellan."

"I'm Piranese," Cordyn gathered leaves and constructed a makeshift pillow for Koston. "I don't love Kosel either, even if they are Piran's ally."

"Were. Kosel fell yesterday."

"Ah well, that will be something for the diplomats and generals to worry about. I'm just a messenger, and not a very successful one at that, if recent events are anything to go by."

"Rennick—"

"Not Rennick. Tallen. The name's Cordyn Tallen. You won't have heard of me."

Koston's eyes clouded. "If I survive, I'll repay you."

"No need." Cordyn shook his head.

"I repay my debts. You will accept," Koston said, ever the commander.

"No debts, Koston. I don't care about you. I'm just too soft to watch another bleed to death." He helped Koston to his feet and pointed the man toward the forest. "You might want to exit the battlefield. Oh, but I'll take your sword." Cordyn put his hand out.

"An Obanni never gives up his sword," Koston said.

"Very well. I won't go stab mages and save the continent. Good day, sir."

Koston growled but tossed the sword to Cordyn. "I've no use for it, anyway. If the mages don't kill me, those damn Winn wolves will." He pursed his lips. "If you see Wellise, kill the bastard."

"That is my most ardent hope."

Cordyn walked through the trees, leaving Koston to figure out the rest by himself.

There's my good deed for the day, Torr, so maybe tell Kirth to let me live a bit longer.

It was carnage. Soldiers lay in varying degrees of dead or dying. Missing limbs, gaping wounds through the chest, at least two men who'd lost their heads altogether.

Near the clearing where the Winn and Rosenfellians battled, Cordyn found the remains of the Obanni army, only thirty strong, all of whom were hiding in the forest. Most looked wounded, and still breathing, though not for long. Not unless the situation changed drastically.

They looked at him with little interest as he approached. Only a few men half-heartedly lifted their pikes.

Cordyn glared at the men and did his best Koston impression. "What are you doing, men? Where is your honor? Are you not men? Are you not Obanni?"

"Who's askin'?"

"Sword General Rennick." He glared at the man, imitating the posture and expression Koston had been so fond of. "And you will address me as Your Eminence."

The soldiers glanced among themselves. "Who? You're that bloody Winn spy—"

"The Obanni army does not pay you to think, soldier. You have only your duty. And your duty today is to attack the Rosenfellian mages."

A confused murmur arose from the men. "But won't the Winn kill us too?"

The man had a point. Who knew what the Winn would do? But Cordyn was used to dealing with situations like this.

"The Winn attacked because of the Rosenfellians. They hate each other, but the Winn don't care overmuch about you." He waved an arm toward the battle. "We're caught in between warring factions, and when that happens, you choose the winning side. Can you tell who's winning?"

"The Winn," a thick-necked soldier said.

"Precisely. The Winn won't attack us if the Rosenfellians are defeated, I assure you. I've spent years as the Obanni emissary to the Winn."

"But what about—"

"You're thinking again, soldier."

After more confusion, the soldiers unsheathed their weapons and waited for Cordyn's command. "What shall we do?"

He liked dealing with soldiers. They were so used to following orders that they didn't ask too many questions. "Is Medic Thomos here?" Cordyn asked.

"Aye," Thomos's voice came from the back of the crowd of soldiers.

I suppose one more good deed is in order.

"Your friend Koston is dying a few hundred paces back through the woods. You may want to attend to him." Cordyn focused his attention on the men. "Have any of you seen a tall woman with a huge sword?"

"The Nazlin?" a soldier asked. "No, she left with Cork. Bastards deserted on us."

"When?"

"I dunno, days ago."

Good. Perhaps Gen is alive still. Though her abilities would come in handy right now.

"What about the captive children? Where are they?"

The soldier pointed out onto the battlefield to an enormous, covered caravan. Three Rosenfellian mages huddled together outside of it. He thought back to what Stinton had told him about experiments; dehumanizing stuff, all of it. But zealots who were willing to kidnap children and experiment on them were willing to fight to the death to protect their investment.

"We need to get to their leaders." He raised his voice and held a clenched fist out in front of him. "Head to the rear of the prison caravan. Kill any mages you see. Be men. Be Brave. For Oban!"

"For Oban!"

As the soldiers charged the caravan, Cordyn wondered if he had a future as a mercenary leader.

The troops—*his* troops?—hit the three mages with everything they had, swords slicing through ice attacks, blades finding their homes underneath Rosenfellian robes and relieving the miserable bastards of their lives. Several Obanni soldiers fell from shard wounds, but all three mages were put to the sword, and Cordyn walked unmolested to the back entrance of the prison caravan, which resembled a wooden carriage door.

Shit.

A heavy metal chain hung on the door, the mage kind. Something twenty soldiers couldn't break down. Presumably, one of the mages they'd just killed had been the one to lock the door. He scanned the outer layer of the caravan. There had to be another way in.

"Soldier," he called to the closest man. "Climb up onto the top of the caravan."

The soldier protested, but Cordyn's glare shut him up. After a brief struggle with the rope seams of the caravan exterior, the soldier pulled himself onto the top.

"What's it like up there?"

Cordyn heard a thump. Was it the soldier kicking the ceiling or preparing to die on the ceiling, if the mages on the other side of the caravan noticed him standing above them?

"Gods, man," Cordyn hissed. "Unless you want to kill us all, make less noise."

The man mouthed an apology. He disappeared on the top of the caravan for a moment, then returned, a triumphant smile across his pockmarked face.

"Sir, I reckon I found a way in."

Climbing a caravan quietly was more difficult than Cordyn expected. With each step upward, every grasp for the next leather rung, he felt he would lose his footing and fall back to the ground below.

If I can just make it to the top, we'll be in.

The soldier had found a weak spot in the heavy leather exterior of the caravan—a hole that they could cut bigger and slide through. Not the most flattering entrance, falling through the ceiling, but better than standing outside the doors waiting for a shard to the throat.

By the time Cordyn reached the top of the caravan, nine soldiers had passed him. With that many men sawing at the hole in the leather, the opening was almost big enough for a thin man to fit through. For the second time in the last hour, he thought of life as a mercenary leader. Having loyal troops ready to follow his every order sounded appealing, though spending his days in combat did not.

After a few more minutes of work, the opening was big enough for him.

"Keep toiling, men," he said, saluting in the Obanni fashion. "Then, once the opening is big enough for the largest of you, join me below. The children imprisoned here are what the Winn want. We release the children and get them to safety, and the battle ends."

He doubted the Rosenfellian mages would simply surrender if the children escaped, nor would the Winn allow the Rosenfellians to leave without punishment. The Obanni didn't need to know that.

Kirth, Torr, Hurod, I'll sing songs of your praises if you just let this work.

He shimmied through the opening and fell the five yards to the ground. His right knee erupted in pain, and he inhaled sharply, trying to keep from screaming. Holding his breath helped to ease the worst of it, and the pain further dulled as he surveyed the rest of his limbs. Nothing broken, several things bruised, though. Pushing against the wooden floor of the caravan, he got to his feet.

Across the room, a group of dirty and terrified children huddled together. As he walked toward them, they shrunk further.

"I'm here to save you, not hurt you."

The briefest glimpse of hope flashed across their faces.

"I need to know. Are there any men here in the caravan?"

The children watched him for a long moment before a small girl with matted brown hair spoke. "There's two in the front carriage. Master Marston and Master Tobias. Least that's what I heard. None of us have been up there."

"And Master Tobias, he's friendly with Master Marston?"

"Hurod, no. He's his prisoner. He was trying to save us and got captured."

"Marston's a nasty bastard," a dirty-faced boy said.

Cordyn pointed to the ceiling. "There will be some soldiers coming through there momentarily. They may look like the soldiers who captured you originally, but they're friends. They're going to help you to safety."

A few of the children spoke at once, thanking him, their voices were full of excitement though Cordyn noted an occasional tinge of fear.

"Cordyn?" Evalia's voice said from behind him. He jumped to his feet. She lay in a corner of the room, a tunic draped over her as a makeshift blanket, wiping sleep from her eyes. Gods, she was still radiant.

"Evalia," he said in a breathy voice. "You're imprisoned?"

"Yes, but you're alive!"

She threw off the tunic and got to her feet. She still wore her Obanni uniform, but now it was torn across the shoulders and threadbare at the knees. In mere moments, she crossed the room and embraced him tightly.

Gods, it was wonderful.

He hugged her back, breathing in her scent. Sweat and mildew had never smelled so good. "Barely, though our friend Stinton tried his best to change that."

She stepped back, and Cordyn reluctantly let her go.

"He told me he kidnapped you."

"Yes, he had Topper watch over me."

Evalia placed a hand on Cordyn's shoulder. "Is Topper still alive?"

He felt anger wash over him. If it were anyone but Evalia, he would have brushed her arm off and strode away. "Why does everyone assume I'd kill a child? Yes, the damned boy is still alive. He and I came to arrangement."

Evalia rubbed her eyes with her free hand. She looked haggard. Worry lines had emerged on her forehead and dark circles under her eyes suggested she hadn't slept recently.

"I'm sorry. I didn't mean—"

"No," he said, feeling pity toward her. Gods, she'd been through enough without him adding to her distress. "I apologize. I let anger get the best of me."

A small boy appeared at Evalia's side, a shorter, male version of her. The same curly auburn red hair, though his just peeked over his ears, instead of falling past the shoulder like Evalia's. He was thinner than her, with identical porcelain skin and wide lips that were too big for his face.

"You found your brother, then?"

"Ezra, this is Cordyn," Evalia said. The boy moved to shake Cordyn's hand, and Cordyn accepted; the boy's hands were scabbed over and bound by glass manacles.

"You're not that handsome," Ezra said, stone-faced.

Cordyn nodded somberly. "Indeed, I'm not. It's been a difficult fortnight."

"Vale said you were."

"Ezra!" Evalia snapped. She pulled absentmindedly at her uniform collar, pinkness cascading over her cheeks. "I never said that."

"Of course you didn't, madam." Cordyn placed a hand on her shoulder. "You are a woman of taste. We can talk more later about the events of these last days. Right now, I've got to find Stinton. Can you get the children out?"

Confusion shrouded her face. "How will we escape?"

"I enlisted the help of some Obanni soldiers. No, don't worry," he said, noticing the anger flashing across her face. "They're working with us now. They may still be the enemy to some extent, but currently, they also dislike Rosenfel more than us. They'll be following behind momentarily." Muffled thumps from the other end of the caravan reached their ears. "That's them now, I presume. Take the children and go."

"What will you do with Tobias?"

"I haven't decided." Which was the truth.

"Be careful," she said. She leaned forward and kissed him gently on the cheek.

"I'll do my best." He felt his cheeks warm, a welcome feeling. It had been years since anyone had aroused emotion in him.

A few of the children gave him furtive hugs as they passed. He responded with the best confident smile he could produce, which wasn't all that convincing.

"You'll most likely die," Ezra said, but there was no malice in the boy's voice. He was just stating a fact.

Cordyn saluted the boy. "Torr keep you, child."

Now, if you'll excuse me. Master Tobias and I have some unfinished business.

The journey from carriage to carriage was easier than anticipated. The Rosenfellians had placed wooden boards connecting the carriages, and Cordyn walked through three carriages, stopping in to tell the children to head to the back carriage and wait for the soldiers.

When he reached the entrance to the front carriage, he stopped. It would be easy to open the door and hurl insults at Stinton, but if this Marston was with him, he didn't fancy his chances against a mage who'd almost killed Gen.

So he waited, listening.

Nothing.

If anyone was in the room, they were asleep or dead.

With a sharp breath, he opened the door.

"Back so soon?" Stinton asked without turning around.

"Lovely to see you, old friend," Cordyn said.

If the situation were a happier one, he would've enjoyed the way Stinton reacted: almost jumping out of his skin and staring at Cordyn as if he were skinned alive and dripping blood.

"Gods," Stinton said.

Cordyn strode forward, placing the point of his dagger against Stinton's throat. "Where's Gen? I know she and Cork deserted."

Stinton ignored the dagger. "How did you escape? Did you kill Topper?"

"I told you once before that I'm not a monster. I'd appreciate if you'd believe me this time."

"Hmph." Stinton crossed his arms or did the closest thing possible when one had shackles on their wrists.

"Topper is alive. He's off in the woods, enjoying the company of our good friend Koston."

Stinton's posture relaxed, and he breathed. "As long as Topper is alive."

Cordyn gestured with the dagger to the shackles. "You've made some other enemies, I see. Kidnap them, too?"

Stinton remained silent.

"I asked you where Gen was once. I will not ask again."

Stinton laughed. *The bastard.* "You're not a killer, Tallen."

Cordyn nudged the blade against Stinton's skin, a pearl of blood leaking out from Stinton's neck. "How confident are you in that assumption?"

And yet Stinton was correct. Cordyn had killed in combat when necessary, but he'd never taken a defenseless life. No matter how much Stinton deserved it, Cordyn wouldn't kill him. Not today.

"I assume she's somewhere out there in the fray. She and her Winn friend left to gather Winn reinforcements. I set fire to the camp to help them escape. You know, kidnapping you did wonders for our planning. We suddenly saw much clearer."

Cordyn bit his lip to suppress an angry retort. There would be time for anger later. "As much as I hate to say this, Stinton, we could use another man on our side in the battle. A mage. I know you hate me, but if you can refrain from killing me for a bit, I'll promise to do the same. After the children are free, you can hunt me down to your heart's content. Now, how do we get those damned shackles off?"

"That would ruin all the fun," a voice said from behind him.

Cordyn turned to see a bearded man standing in the doorway, his eyes fixed on Tobias.

"Who in Kirth are you?" Cordyn asked. He was relatively sure this was Marston.

"Your better," the man sneered.

"That's where you're wrong. I'm not torturing children. I'll always be your better."

The man raised a hand and flicked it at Cordyn.

Cordyn reeled back. A stream of water smashed against his chest, flinging him against the carriage wall; his head connected with a wooden beam, and he crashed to the floor, his skull pounding. He wanted to scream, but his mouth wouldn't move.

Marston's boot crept closer, then crushed down on Cordyn's face.

Blood soaked the ground.

The snow turned pink; rivers of red flowed down the icy paths.

Gen swung Maralda in towering cuts, breaking the guard of mercenary infantrymen, then thrusting through their useless chainmail. Bodies littered the ground. Gen had to watch below her as she charged toward two mages to avoid stepping on corpses or fallen weapons.

The mages raised their hands, preparing their assault. One of them never got his hands into position. Cork's axe cleaved through his temple, splashing blood on the other mage's face, breaking his concentration for a moment.

That moment was all Gen needed.

Maralda sliced through smoky air, separating flesh from bone.

Gen looked at the field in front of them. Winn and Rosenfellian mages battled, the Winn ice axes crushing through the barriers of their enemies, sending the bastards sprawling into the earth, many for the last time. Those Rosenfellians who managed to avoid the first round of ice axes then had to weather a storm of ice spears that descended from the skies, impaling anyone unfortunate enough to be in their path.

It wouldn't be long now. The prison caravan sat a few hundred paces from Gen and Cork. One last charge.

"Cork," Gen said. "Would you tell your countrymen to give us some cover?"

Cork bellowed something in the Winn language. The barrage of axes and spears eased, but a layer of ice appeared inches above Gen and Cork. Gen could almost reach up to touch it.

"How's that for protection?" Cork asked.

"I could get used to it."

With Cork by her side, Gen led the charge. The airborne attacks from the Rosenfellians couldn't penetrate the ice barrier, so the Rosenfellians converged on the caravan, switching to close combat. This was Gen's domain.

She roared as she brought Maralda down, thrusting it through the shoulder of a mage, then kicked his body to the ground. The mage moaned in pain for a moment before the sound of metal on bone silenced him. Out of the corner of her eye, Gen saw Cork pull his axe from the mage's lifeless body.

"He was loud," Cork said.

Gen opened her mouth to say something, but never got the chance.

Cork took a shard to the chest, looking at Gen in disbelief. Time slowed; Gen's heart hammered in her chest, waiting for her friend to fall to the ground.

However, Cork continued as if he'd not been hit, swinging his axe through the torso of a mercenary.

Gen thundered forward, flailing her blade through any and everyone in her way. She was the blade, and this was her vengeance. No one tried to kill her friends and lived.

Within minutes, Gen and Cork stood in front of the caravan.

"You're not dead," she said, panting.

"I got hit," Cork admitted, pointing at a puncture wound on the right side of his chest. "It'll take more than that to kill me." He wiped a thin stream of blood running down his chest and lifted his axe again.

Unthed and two other Winn headed in their direction.

"Might as well finish this," Gen said. She stepped to the caravan and opened the door.

There Cordyn was, lying unconscious on the floor of the caravan, blood gushing from his head.

TWENTY-FIVE

"Cordyn?" Gen asked, rushing to his side to check for a pulse, a breath, anything. After a torturous few seconds, she felt his ribs expand.

He was alive.

"Swordsman's tears, Cordyn."

Cordyn opened his eyes, staring at Gen, blinking and confused. "It's good to see you, Gen," Cordyn whispered.

"Where were you?"

"Stinton kidnapped me."

"He kidnapped you?" Rage welled inside Gen. When she found Tobias, she would...what? Save him, and then tell him exactly what she thought of his actions? "Why?"

"To make the mages move their camp closer to the Winn. Ingenious really. Oh, I should tell you I've come to an agreement with the Obanni. They aren't our enemies anymore."

"They never were mine," Cork said in a low voice.

Gen paused to look at Cordyn. "As long as they fight the Rosenfellians, they're not my enemy either. Come on." Gen started to move further into the caravan.

"Wait," Cordyn hissed. "Evalia, Stinton, and the children should all be back there, along with some Obanni soldiers."

"It's too quiet," Cork said. "If there were that many people in one carriage, it'd be louder."

"I'll go look," Gen said.

She moved back through the carriages, finding nobody until she reached the last one. Propped up against the back wall were two bodies. Obanni soldiers, shards embedded in their throats and eyes. There was no way they could have survived that.

Gods. A macabre thought rose unbidden into Gen's mind: what if Evalia, Tobias, and all the children were dead too?

When Gen returned to her companions, Cordyn stood, one arm over Cork's shoulder. Unthed and one of his compatriots had entered the carriage too, standing off to the side, watching the scene dispassionately.

"Well?" Cordyn asked.

"Empty."

"Shit," Cork said.

"Come on," Gen said. "They can't be far. Probably heading for the woods."

"Let's hope so." Cordyn let go of Cork's shoulder and hobbled toward the exit. "I have some friends in the woods."

At the edge of the forest, a battle raged. The remaining Obanni struggled in vain against the superior abilities of the small group of Rosenfellian mages. Gen ran for the forest. By the time she arrived among the carnage, all but a few Obanni were wounded or dead.

"Swordsman's bloody bollocks," Gen cursed.

The children lay strewn across the ground. At first, Gen thought they were dead, but there was no blood, and some of their chests moved with the steady rhythm of breath. Asleep? Sword General

Koston and a few of his Obanni soldiers were also in a slumber, their heavy red and black uniforms clashing with the dirty white tunics the children wore. It was a harrowing sight—so many children unconscious or dead. Gen fought to stay calm. She wanted to rush the mages and kill them all, lop their heads off, stab them through their godsdamn eyes until their skulls were shattered.

"Shit," Cordyn said.

Among the mages stood Evalia, eyes and hair wild, while Wellise stood next to her, hands pointed at her skull. Marston stood next to them, with Tobias kneeling before him, shackled. Marston had a boot resting against Tobias's back, ready to put him face down into the dirt if needed. A few children stood, swaying and staring out at the fray with glassy eyes, as if they were asleep standing up. Two other mages stood by the children, holding their hands out, ready to end the children's lives with a flick of their wrists.

Gen lifted Maralda, Cork to her left with an axe at the ready, Cordyn standing to her right. She heard the steady breathing of Unthed and his two companions behind her. Five mages against three mages, two warriors, and Cordyn.

We're outnumbered.

"Welcome, friends," Marston said, tipping an imaginary hat to Gen. "You survived somehow, even with the gift I gave you." His lips curled. "No matter, I can just do it again. Perhaps to your friend this time?" He pointed to Cork.

"You bastard," Gen said. She felt the wound in her abdomen ache for the first time in days. The tonic had mostly healed it, and she'd all but forgotten how it felt, but seeing the man who'd done it to her brought all the pain, anger, and helplessness back. "What did you do to them?" Gen pointed her blade toward the children.

"Swirled the liquid in their brains a little," Marston said with glee. "Nothing that will harm them permanently, unless I choose to."

"This is the bastard who tried to kill you?" Cordyn asked.

"I say we kill the prick," Cork added, shaking his axe as if to say, 'run away now, mage, or I will slice your head off.'

Gods. I don't stand a chance. He can end my life before I even lift my blade. Gen pushed the helplessness away. Today, she would defeat him. Revenge would be hers.

"Alas, Stinton here was too soft-hearted and saved you." Marston pushed his fingers against Tobias's back. "No matter, he'll be dead soon, too." Marston turned to Cork. "I recognize you," he said with a smirk. "Koston's favorite fighter. The big Winn who couldn't lose." He cackled. "Well, you'll enjoy losing today. Dying, too." He eyed the sleeping Koston. "I've kept our friend Koston alive so that he can see just how much he failed. Then I'll kill him too."

"You'll not defeat us with your taunts," Gen said. "We're taking the children. You can either surrender or you can die."

Marston stroked his beard. "I choose neither."

Wellise glared at his companion. "Marston, stop playing with them." He looked warily toward Unthed. "Focus on the Winn. They're the real threat here, not these idiots with their blades."

"Fine," Marston said. "*Trescarrus!*"

He raised his arms above his head and rained shards upon them. Gen dove to the ground, avoiding a shard that would have taken off her ear. She lost her grip on Maralda, the blade thudding against the ground.

Even with their superior abilities, the Winn couldn't contain the barrage. Gen was unable to see any Winn fall, but they were distracted, focusing their attention on protecting themselves. Cork grunted and fell.

Let him live, Kirth.

Unthed yelled something incoherent from behind Gen, and another barrier of ice appeared, stopping most of the projectiles. Gen took a breath, picking up Maralda from the ground as she stood. Cork was alive and climbing unsteadily to his feet, but his legs were riddled with puncture wounds, causing him to bleed. He'd need further medical attention, but there was no time for that now.

"Gods," Gen said. She had so much she wanted to say to Marston, so many curses to hurl at him, and yet she couldn't think of anything. "Gods."

"As I said, I don't intend to die today," Marston said. "The children and your friends, though? I'm unconcerned. Attempt to save them, if you will, but I will be victorious."

Gen squeezed Maralda's hilt.

"You've made quite an error," Cordyn said. "See, these children you've attacked? I've spent quite some time with them now, and I consider many of them close friends."

"You bore me." Marston wiggled a finger against Tobias's skull. "I don't wish to kill you," Marston said, silken yet deadly. "I just wish to exit with my friends here." He pointed to the swaying children. "I would hate to have to kill the other children, as well as Master Stinton and this very beautiful young woman." He leered at Evalia.

"You'll let the woman go," Cordyn said. "Or I will cut your bollocks off. Stinton, well, he probably deserves this."

"You bastard," Tobias muttered.

Kirth, even in battle, Cordyn can't learn when to stop talking.

Unthed cleared his throat. "Casualties are a part of war. We will accept the death of these people for the good of the cause."

"What?" Gen combated. "Cork, do something."

"There's nothing I can do," Cork said. "When the Winn decide something, they don't change their minds."

"My dear fellow," Cordyn said to Unthed, "if you give me a few moments, I'll undoubtedly come up with a plan."

"That's what I'm afraid of," Gen sighed.

"Fine, I'll kill the woman," Marston said. "A pity. She would have made an excellent whore."

Cordyn stepped forward, a dagger in hand. Gen reached to hold him back. Getting killed before the fight wouldn't solve anything.

Marston looked bemused, tapping his foot as if enjoying himself. "Ah, an excellent plan: charge the enemy and die. I've found a sore spot, haven't I? You have feelings for the young woman. Not surprising, considering her loveliness. Imagine your distress if you lost her. It would be a shame if I had to put a hole in her pretty head."

"Godsdamn you," Cordyn cursed.

"I'm sure the gods do damn me, but I have little concern for them. I am as powerful as I wish to be, whether the gods approve or not." He wagged his finger from his free hand at Cork, who'd started inching toward him. "Oh, that will not do. If you move again, I will kill a child for each step you take. Killing children is easy. I've done it before, and I'll do it again. They're so weak, they barely fight back. Not very fulfilling, but not hard at all."

He twitched his right thumb and pointer finger, shooting a shard into the leg of a sleeping child. Blood seeped from the wound, but the child did not awaken or make a sound.

"The next one," Marston said, "will go through his heart." His gaze wandered to Evalia. "And through her as well."

"You will die, Marston," Gen said. "My sword will kill you. I vow it."

They needed to act. This talking and waiting accomplished nothing.

"We have to strike," Gen whispered to Cordyn. "He's going to kill us. No matter what. Perhaps some of the children as well. There's no way we walk away from this unless we move."

Cordyn gave Gen the slightest nod.

"Cork?" Gen looked at Cork, who had pulled himself to his feet. He limped and gritted his teeth in agony, but he held his axe high.

"Aye."

"On my signal. Now!" Gen roared.

Before Gen could take a step forward, Marston sent shards into Tobias's back, causing him to crash to the ground.

A small knife flew from the forest, crashing off Marston's leg but not piercing skin. Topper stood between two trees, eyes blazing.

Marston's attention shifted to Topper. "That was silly, boy. Now you must die too." He reached down to scoop the dagger off the ground, and for a moment, he was distracted.

Gen charged.

The situation at hand had gone to shit. Cordyn searched for a way to remedy things, but combat appeared to be the only way forward. *Damn.*

"Save him," Topper yelled from the trees.

Gods, the boy wanted him to save Tobias? That was the farthest thing from Cordyn's mind.

Gen and Cork charged. It seemed silly to stand back with a dagger, while his companions fought bravely and died. The Winn sent their ice axes toward the Rosenfellians, and the Rosenfellians didn't seem to notice Cordyn standing there.

He could sneak in.

Free Evalia.

Perhaps save Gen?

Cordyn was brought from his daydream when Marston brought his hands up violently, sending a rush of water at Topper, flinging the boy into the trunk of a nearby tree. The boy's body cracked and fell motionless to the ground.

Shit.

Cordyn ran for Evalia, weaving in and out of the path of shards, axes, and Gen's massive sword. Evalia shook her head *no,* but it was too late. Cordyn had made up his mind. There was nothing else to do.

Wellise, focused on the Winn attacks, never saw Cordyn coming. Cordyn sunk his dagger into Wellise's neck, blood spraying from the wound. Wellise sucked at air, blinking frantically as his blood splattered against Cordyn's chest. He tore the dagger across Wellise's neck, severing the arteries. Cordyn let the corpse fall.

"That was stupid," Evalia said. She had a halo of Wellise's splattered blood across her forehead, the dripping red intermingling with freckles. Bloody *and* bloody appealing.

"Why?"

"You could have died."

"I didn't know you cared." Cordyn frowned with mock seriousness. "I fear you might be growing fond of me."

Evalia scoffed and looked away, but Cordyn saw a slight smile cross her face.

Gen, Cork, and the Winn continued to press through the Rosenfellian defenses. An ice axe beheaded one mage and Cork cut the legs off another, after which Gen stuck her sword through the man's throat.

It was just Marston left.

Marston shot out a wave of water, turning to flee into the forest.

Cordyn moved to Topper, who thankfully breathed. The boy stirred, opening his eyes for a brief second, before falling out of consciousness again. Cordyn picked Topper up, carrying him over to Gen and Cork. The big man kneeled by Stinton, examining him. Stinton's eyes were open.

Nearby, The Winn attended to the children. Cordyn had little hope for them, but if anyone could save them, it would be the Winn.

"Cork, how is he?" Cordyn asked.

"Don't look good," Cork said, leaning down to inspect the wound. A fountain of blood poured. "I ain't no doctor, but I don't see how he could survive."

"Topper's going to kill me."

"We need to deal with Marston," Gen said, peering down at Tobias. "We'll come back for you, Tobias. Keep breathing."

"Kill Marston," Stinton said, his voice a mere whisper. "Leave me here. It doesn't matter what happens to me now. I'm dead anyway." Cordyn could still hear his labored breaths.

Gen's eyes flitted between Stinton and the forest.

"Gen," Cordyn said. "We've got to move." He looked to the Winn. "Are you ready?"

Unthed looked at Cordyn like he was on the verge of sleep. "We have done what we came to do. That man no longer matters. We shall not pursue him."

Gods, the Winn were infuriating.

Cordyn grabbed at his hair in frustration. He would have torn it out if his curls remained. As it was, he just ran a hand over what was left. "Perhaps you could attend to Master Stinton and the boy?"

Unthed nodded his assent.

Cordyn turned to Gen. "Looks like it's just us."

"Just the way it should be." Gen helped Cork back to his feet, and the big man beamed at Cordyn.

"Let's go kill us a bastard," Cork said.

Cordyn laughed mirthlessly. "I like you, Cork."

They rushed into the forest. Tree branches hung low, blocking any straight path, forcing them to weave around branches, boulders, and fallen trunks. It took ages to get even a few hundred paces into the forest.

Cordyn expected an attack at any moment, but none came. They were about to give up hope of finding Marston when Gen motioned for them to pause.

"Blood," she whispered, pointing to a trail of red dots leading toward a large tree.

"We've caught us a wanker," Cork said.

As Gen stepped forward, a towering wave of water suddenly appeared from beside the tree. It crashed into Cork and Gen, knocking them over. Cork landed with a sickening thud, unmoving. Gen raised herself to her knees, reaching for the back of her neck.

The wave flowed back toward Marston, where the water swirled into a whirlpool.

Gen had time to stand and pick up Cork's war axe. Beside her, Cork stirred, but he was in no shape to fight.

Gen handed the war axe to Cordyn, who stared at her. The last thing he needed was a kirthed axe. "I don't know how to use this," he said.

"You pick it up and swing."

He did as he was told, taking the war axe and raising it above his head. "I have a feeling this won't end well."

"One final charge," Gen said.

I just hope I don't trip.

"One final charge," he repeated.

They rushed Marston. Well, *Gen* rushed Marston. Cordyn, unfamiliar with heavy weapons, walked quickly, the best he could do while wielding a war axe.

Gen swung her sword with a fury Cordyn rarely witnessed, slicing into Marston's arm, above the elbow. Marston winced, keeping his focus to call forth another wave.

Cordyn reached Marston and swung at the bastard, hitting only air and a stray tree branch. He saw Gen lift her sword, and the killing blow came down.

It wasn't enough. A wave of water stopped Gen's sword just as it should have entered Marston's skull. The water exploded, throwing Cordyn to the ground. With unexpected dexterity, he rolled onto one knee and sprang to his feet.

But it was too late.

Cordyn watched as Marston fled through the trees. Gen was on the ground, face down, a trickle of blood down her neck. Cordyn was helpless to stop Marston, the wave still blocking his path, and he had no weapon but a dagger and the damnable war axe.

Gen pulled herself up onto one knee and gripped her sword, staring into the wave, as if thinking of how to find a way through. Her nose bled, but she seemed fine otherwise. Without checking himself for wounds, Cordyn hugged Gen.

"Gen," Cordyn said into Gen's shoulder.

Nothing.

"Gen."

Cordyn leaned back and saw that she still gazed through the wave of water. Beside them, Cork stirred, grunting.

Cordyn grabbed Gen by the shoulders and shook her. "Gen, I'll buy you so much wine if you just say something."

Her eyes moved to him. "I *am* thirsty," she said, her voice weak and raspy. "I don't know if I can walk." Gen pointed to her swollen ankle. "I'm so tired."

With a strength Cordyn didn't know he had, he picked Gen up, carrying her out of the forest. Cordyn heard Gen's soft snores as he maneuvered through the trees and out into the clearing, where Evalia sat beside her unconscious brother. One of the Winn hovered over Stinton, while the others were still attending to the sleeping children, swirling their hands feverishly over the shackles that bound the children.

"Cork's in the forest," Cordyn told the Winn. "He's wounded but alive, if you'd like to retrieve him." Unthed motioned to his two companions, who headed into the forest.

Cordyn laid Gen down and sat beside her, making sure she was still breathing. Gen opened her eyes again, smiling with the little strength she had left.

"What next?" Gen asked. "We didn't win."

Cordyn rubbed his eyes, trying to think of what to say. "I don't know. At least we didn't lose."

TWENTY-SIX

ONE BY ONE, THE sleeping children woke until only two were left.

Two children who might go into eternal slumber.

The Winn set up a makeshift camp on the outskirts of the battlefield, and everyone huddled around fires eating mutton and roasted vegetables. Despite her gloom, Gen had to admit the Winn had culinary skills. She sat with Cordyn, Cork, Topper, Evalia, and Ezra at the smallest fire, while at the larger fires children sat laughing and eating while the Winn monitored them. The Winn had removed the children's shackles, even though Cork swore it should have been impossible to remove the mage-glass. Just one more mystery of the Winn.

The Winn said little in the aftermath of the battle, but Gen appreciated their willingness to share supplies and concern for the children. Evalia, arm around her brother, glowed in the fire's light; Gen had never seen her this happy.

Gen glowered at the fire, gritting her teeth. Marston's escape gnawed at her. If only she'd been faster, better with Maralda. This was her fault. Marston would pay for this. She'd find him and kill him. It wouldn't change the trauma he'd inflicted on the children or bring back the ones still asleep, but chopping his head off would be so cathartic.

Cordyn said they hadn't lost, but to Gen, it felt like a loss. Marston escaped, Cork lost an eye, Topper broke his leg, and Tobias was fighting for his life in a coma. Tobias, along with two sleeping children, had already been taken back toward Wolstone on wolvinn, so that Winn doctors could attend to them. The Winn who rode to Wolstone would ask for wolvinn-drawn carts to be sent to help gather the remaining children.

Unthed and his companions watched over the camp, keeping an especially close eye on Koston and the few surviving Obanni soldiers, who sat alone on the edge of camp, without the comfort of a fire. Koston and the soldiers weren't prisoners as far as Gen could tell, but they weren't trusted allies, either.

Cordyn was more cheerful than he had the right to be, laughing as he spoke with Evalia and Ezra. Cordyn and Evalia were stealing glances at each other. Every time Evalia laughed, Gen saw a hint of a smile on Cordyn's face; he looked shyer than she'd ever seen him.

"We make for a sorry-looking group," Cordyn said, gnawing on a parsnip.

"There's nothing to celebrate." Gen tossed her mutton bone into the fire. The flames rose, dancing in the Trunellic dusk. The suns had set, and an eerie light emanated from the three moons. "We need to find Marston. And when we do, Maralda is going to have a lot to say."

"That's a fight for another day."

Gen pushed her plate of vegetables away, her appetite gone. "Cordyn, how can you dismiss this? After what Marston did?"

"We saved the children."

"Not all of them," Gen replied.

"We saved the children," Cordyn reiterated. "They'll go to stay with the Winn and live a better life than they could have hoped." He bit viciously into the remaining bit of parsnip. "When we find Marston, we'll get vengeance. But tonight, let's enjoy victory."

"I wonder if Tobias will live?" Cork asked. "The Winn are good healers, but he took a knife to the back."

Topper took a sharp breath and turned away, rubbing his eyes.

"A few hours ago, I would have hoped he was dead, his corpse rotting somewhere in the forest." Cordyn took a bite of mutton, then wiped the grease from his lips. "Now," he said, showing his food as he spoke, "I sort of hope the bastard lives."

A week later, they were in Wolstone, staying at an inn by the harbor. The Winn were preparing to set sail for the Isle, bringing the children with them, as well as Evalia and Cork. As far as Gen knew, Tobias was already on the Isle, assuming he was still alive. Topper stayed with Gen and Cordyn, making progress walking on his recently broken leg with the help of Winn medicine.

However, Winn medicine couldn't bring back Cork's missing eye. He'd taken the loss in stride and seemed to think of the wound as an excellent conversation starter, telling anyone who asked the whole story, though the story grew more and more exaggerated each time Cork brought it up.

They'd parted ways with Koston and the Obanni before leaving the battle site. Koston thanked the Winn somberly. Unthed told him it would be best for them to never meet again, lest the Winn decide to declare war on the Obanni as well.

Gen and Cordyn sat together drinking ale at a table in the inn's dining hall, a long, rectangular room with rough wooden tables and a nautical theme. The walls were covered in anchors, compasses, and paintings of mage-captains taming the Sea of Dread.

Topper sat at a nearby table, picking at a bowl of porridge. The boy had been their shadow ever since the battle ended, but still sat alone, even after Gen had invited him several times to sit with them.

"The children will be traveling to the Isle of Winn soon, and thus, our duties to them end," Cordyn said. He poked a finger into the head of his light ale, absentmindedly swirling. "What shall we do now?"

Gen sipped her own dark ale in front of her, wishing it was sweet wine. "If you want, we can travel home to Piran. Look for survivors, start a resistance movement." It had been a shock when Cordyn first told her of the Rosenfellian occupation of Piran, but after the events of the last fortnight, she found it difficult to care.

Cordyn shook his head. "No, we don't even know what's left. There's not much that the two of us could do."

The residents of Piran were either dead or living under Rosenfellian rule. Gen wondered about Ned. Would he be recognized as a Rosenfellian mage? Was he even still alive? She pushed the thoughts from her mind. There would be time later to look for him. She wouldn't be able to save Ned if horrible things had happened, but she wanted to know where he was, and do what she could to help, if anything.

"I know what we should do next." She favored Cordyn with a mysterious smile. "You could say I have a plan."

"A plan?" Cordyn placed a hand to his temple. "And so, the student becomes the master." He slapped her on the back, mimicking her favorite sign of affection.

"I didn't even feel that. You should get stronger."

"Stop stalling and tell me the plan, Master Gen."

She was shy all of a sudden. What if he hated it? And then she found it didn't matter. She cared about him and wanted his approval, but not enough to be someone she wasn't. If he didn't like the plan, well, he'd just have to get over it.

"When someone has a problem, we can help. It's a beautiful life. Traveling the continent and helping people. What do you think?"

He considered the idea for a moment. "A purpose would be nice. I've grown to enjoy traveling."

"More importantly, Maralda will still get a lot of action."

"Oh, I have a feeling you'll be using your sword more than ever."

Topper stood from his table. "I want to go too." He spoke with a firmness that belied his years."

Cordyn eyed Topper. "You're only a boy."

Topper met with Cordyn's eyes. "Just until Tobias heals. I can't go to the Isle. I can't sit and stare at his body, hoping he'll wake up. I need to stay busy. Please let me stay with you."

Cordyn looked at Gen. "Well, it's your plan. What say you?"

Their journeys would be dangerous, but Topper had proven his bravery in the battle against the mages.

I wouldn't be able to sit and wait, either.

"On one condition," Gen told Topper. "You always listen to what I say."

Topper hesitated. "As long as I don't have to listen to everything Cordyn says."

Gen laughed. "No, just me."

"I'm sitting right here," Cordyn said.

"First thing you have to do, Topper." Gen looked at the empty seat next to her. "Come sit with us."

Topper claimed the seat by Gen. "You know, Tobias and I were hired to waylay Tallen in Dramin. Keep him from ever returning to Piran. You've made some enemies, eh?"

"What?" Cordyn blinked. "By whom?"

"Dunno, Tobias said he's dead now."

"Not surprising," Gen said. "You did sleep with half the women in Mintar. There were countless angry husbands."

"And you know nothing else?" Cordyn asked Topper.

"Not a thing," Topper said. "Maybe the boss will help you when he wakes."

"Assuming—" Cordyn began.

"We can always hope," Gen cut in. She kicked Cordyn under the table. There was no need to remind Topper that Tobias might not wake up. The boy surely knew that already.

The door to the inn swung open, revealing Unthed, Cork, and Evalia. Cork, with his missing eye, looked perpetually angry now, even if he was still the same old Cork. He spoke less now as his penance drew near, but Gen still shared a bottle or three with him most nights. Evalia wore a green dress which complemented her flushed cheeks. Evalia was so much different now: bright and gregarious, taking it upon herself to provide mirth and song whenever anyone felt pangs of sadness or—in Gen's case—guilt. Evalia had borrowed a lute from the innkeep and played and sang for the group nightly.

While Cork and Evalia spoke with the innkeep, Unthed approached Gen and Cordyn, his face a stone.

"You have done well." Unthed sat beside them and peered at the fire, as if surprised to see it there. "The Winn appreciate your sacrifice. The council has spoken, and we have decided to provide you with further opportunities to serve."

Cordyn placed a hand on his chin. "I wasn't aware there was a council, nor that anyone had met to discuss anything."

"What opportunities?" Topper asked. He watched Unthed with intensity, as if he was on the verge of yelling at the man.

Unthed pinched his lips together, looking beyond them toward the hearth. After a long moment, he looked back at Cordyn. "Apologies. What was your question?"

So, Winn do have emotions. Good to know.

"The council," Cordyn said. "May I speak with them?"

"The council is not here," Unthed said. "However, they *are* here, within all Winn."

"Of course, how silly of me," Cordyn said. "How could I have not known?" He cocked his head to Cork, who approached. "Cork, how does it feel having the council inside you?"

"Hmm," Cork murmured.

"The council has declared war on Rosenfel," Unthed continued, as if Cordyn had not spoken.

"Well, shit," Gen said. "No more than they deserve."

Cordyn tapped his foot, scowling at Unthed. "And what do I care? How is this an opportunity for me?"

"We wish to hire you," Unthed said. "Your father was an excellent servant to us, and we wish you to be the same."

"I'm not my father."

"Do you trust us?" Gen asked Unthed. "All of us?" She gestured to herself and Topper.

Unthed weighed this for a moment. "Yes."

"What would this entail?" Gen looked to Cork for advice, but he wouldn't meet her eye. Working for the Winn, as odd as they were, wasn't the worst idea. The Winn paid well at least.

"You would travel to Rosenfel," Unthed said. "And infiltrate the Imperial Academy."

Cordyn snorted. "Would you also like us to take over Oban with a snap of the fingers, or go home to Piran and order the people to make us king and queen?"

"That would be difficult." Unthed showed no signs of recognizing Cordyn's sarcasm.

"I'm in," Topper said. "Tobias will be too when he wakes."

"We're not mages," Cordyn protested.

"We'll do it," Gen said.

"You will do what you must. We will provide all that you need." Unthed bowed and exited, past Cork.

"This is ludicrous," Cordyn said.

Gen gave a wide smile. "Think about the money."

"I know Dramin well," Topper said. "I'll find a way into the Academy."

"It's not the finding a way in that frightens me," Cordyn said. "It's the leaving once we've made it inside."

"I believe in us," Gen said. "We'll figure it out."

Evalia, finished with her conversation with the innkeep, strolled over to them, cradling a package wrapped in brown paper. She placed the package on the table and made to sit down.

"Milady," Cordyn said, taking Evalia's hand and kissing it.

Evalia giggled. "I can't stay long. We depart on the hour. However, the innkeep here has volunteered to house my unneeded luggage while I travel to the Isle."

"I wish that I could travel with you." Cordyn released her hand, though his fingers lingered as he pulled them away. "Alas, Gen and I have matters that we must attend to. I will keep you in my thoughts."

"And I you," Evalia said.

Gen squirmed in her seat. This felt too personal, like she was eavesdropping on a conversation not meant for her. "Yes, we'll all miss you, Evalia. How long do you think you'll stay on the Isle?"

"I want to get Ezra settled. He'll be staying there. It's not safe for him or the other mage children in Rosenfel any longer. But once I feel he no longer needs my care, I'll return to the continent." Her eyes flitted to Cordyn's. "And I hope to travel with you—all of you—once again."

"Nothing would please me more." Cordyn reached into his waistcoat pocket and brought forth a letter, sealed with red wax. "I wrote you something, Evalia." He held the letter just out of Evalia's reach. "I ask that you don't open it until we say our goodbyes."

"Of course." Cordyn handed her the note, and she held it between her gloved hands.

"What's that?" Gen asked, pointing to Evalia's parcel. She desperately needed a change of subject. She was happy Cordyn and Evalia seemed to have feelings for one another, but couldn't they save moments like this for when she wasn't around to watch?

Evalia unwrapped the parcel, revealing a lute of pitch-black wood, though it shimmered in the room as if it had a torch inside it.

"It's darkwood," Evalia said. "Unthed gave it to me. He's quite nice, don't you think?"

"That's one way to describe him," Gen said.

"Quite an odd bugger," Cordyn said. "Will I need to purchase head protection once more? My hat is sadly still with Mother Tull."

"That all depends," Evalia said, winking. Cordyn's cheeks were pink.

Evalia wrapped the lute in the paper once more. "I must go upstairs to retrieve my bags from my rooms and head to the ship. Will you still be here when I return?"

Cordyn's hand brushed against Evalia and lingered. "I wouldn't dream of being anywhere else, madam."

"I'll help you with your bags," Topper said.

"She's even more beautiful when she's happy," Gen said as Evalia and Topper left.

"She is. More beautiful than any woman I've known before." Cordyn looked back at his ale, pursing his lips in a sour expression.

"What's wrong?"

His face cycled through several emotions in the span of a few seconds. Fear, sadness, joy, and finally resignation. "She deserves a better man than I can ever be. How could I ask her or anyone to join me when my life is so uncertain?"

Gen scoffed. "Too bad. You're stuck with me."

"Gen—"

"No." She willed herself to stay firm. "You can self-deprecate, if you wish, and avoid things that will make you happy, but you'll not get rid of me. We're a team."

"As long as you know I'm going to continue to fail."

"Then we'll fail together."

Cork strayed from his own ale, speaking finally. "I'm good at failing too, if you ever need a third. I've got to go back to the Isle for a bit, do my penance, but when I'm done...Well, it's nice to have friends."

"And, speaking of my friend, Evalia," Gen said. "I'm not letting you off the hook so easily. You may say you don't deserve her, but what about what she wants? Had you considered that?"

For a moment, Cordyn's resolve broke. "Maybe later. We've got time."

Gen swallowed her last swig of ale. "I'll accept that, for now. I hope Evalia and Ezra are happy." She sighed. "I tried my best."

"Not to be a bother," Cork said, "But I wonder if you'd do somethin' fer me." For a big man, he seemed almost small as he asked, like he expected to be rebuffed.

"Of course. What do you need?" Gen asked.

"My mam, see. I send all my money back to her." Cork took a purse from his trouser pocket, lifting it in front of him. "She's sick, and the money I send helps pay for treatment. I'll be on the Isle for several months, doin' my penance and the like, but I need this money to get to her. She lives up in Kilnic, 'bout six days' ride from here." He paused, sheepish. "It's the opposite direction from Rosenfel, I know." He hung his head, waiting for rejection.

"Of course we'll do it," Gen said. She heard Cordyn groan beside her. "Cork has done so much for us," she muttered. "It's only fair we do this for him."

"I didn't say anything," Cordyn protested.

"Tell her any supplies ya need for your journey back to Rosenfel, and she'll find something for ya. Might not be fancy, but it'll do."

Evalia and Topper descended the stairs with Evalia's luggage, Topper carrying all three bags while Evalia held only Cordyn's note. The seal had been broken; Evalia's cheeks were flushed.

Impatient aren't you, Evalia? I would have done the same thing if someone told me to wait.

Cordyn nodded, then grabbed Evalia's hand, kissing it once more. "Farewell, milady."

Gen pulled Cork in a hug, squeezing his arms until she heard him take in a sharp breath. "Don't let the Winn change you," she said. "We'll be waiting for you when your penance is done."

"Aye, I'll still be the big bastard, no matter what." Cork squeezed her back.

Next, she hugged Evalia, though she attempted to be less violent this time. Evalia placed her forehead on Gen's shoulder and whispered, "Thank you. For everything."

"I help my friends," Gen said. "And kill those who hurt them." She wrapped her arms around Evalia's back and gave her a softer squeeze.

After the farewells concluded, Cork and Evalia left the inn, heading for the harbor. Gen, Cordyn, and Topper sat down at the table, ordering another round of ale, beginning to plan their journey; first to Kilnic, then back to Dramin from there. There were many hours of travel ahead of them and dangers they'd not yet conceived. Yet, all was well.

Gen had one question. "Cordyn, what exactly did you write in that note to Evalia?"

"Oh, nothing," Cordyn replied with a rakish smile. "Just a poem."

Evalia, an Ode

Auburn tresses dance past her ivory skin,
Any soul not entranced by her visage, a brute
She floats through halls, a vision, with peerless grace
I pray that I shall not be attacked by her lute

Radiant in gowns and finery, she is
Such beauty no queen could hope to compare
But when upon her she wears the garments of war
A man cannot help but watch her, to stare

I cannot hope to win her love, a wastrel cur
And mere mortal I dare not have such a design
But perchance when we meet again, I may
Kiss your hand in servitude, O Evalia mine.

Your Servant, Cordyn Tallen

Afterword

I've had some amazing help along the way as I wrote Envoys, and there are some people who deserve a shout out.

First and foremost, Audrie Hopper. Without Audrie, this book would be completely different and not as good. Audrie fell in love with the characters, especially Tobias, and was an invaluable resource throughout the entire process. She's the best hype squad, she's always willing to chat about the plot and characters, and she comes up with some fantastic ideas. She started as a beta reader but soon became my go to source for all my story questions as I revised the novel. She's starting her journey toward developmental editing and I know she'll do amazing things. She's also just super cool and a great friend. I'll never forget the Dungeons & Dragons session where her character went full Cordyn Tallen with her schemes...and somehow it worked. So, thanks Audrie! You're the best!

I'd also like to thank Rach, who did an editorial assessment for me and has also been a champion of the book. She shipped Cordyn and Tobias as enemies to lovers, but sadly for her, I don't see that happening.

Next, I'd like to thank Eilidh, my line and copy editor, who helped me with a lot of the nitty gritty aspects of the novel and became a friend in the process. She's been a great sounding board and a helpful resource. Style guides are complicated!

I'd also like to thank my crew, the Secret Scribes: Greg, Bill, Alex, Lamia, Rach, Bella, Lorraine, Rob, Sean, Tom, Damien, and Eamonn. Y'all are the best, and I can't wait to take over the world with you—aka read all of your books. Onward and upward!

Within the indie fantasy community, I'd like to thank Boe, Nick, Jon P, and the other cool people I've met via the SFFinsiders discord, as well as the writers and readers I've connected with on social media.

This novel began with a short story for my dnd campaign, so I'd be remiss to not thank Robert--our fearless DM--Mike, Ali, Audrie, Erin, and Larry. Y'all are crazy, and I look forward to Mondays.

In my personal life, I'd like to thank my parents—Russ and Linda—and my brothers—Riley and Ben. Also, my best friend Justin, all my other friends, and all the pups in my life, past and present: Rowena, Charlie, Princess, Abby, Hanny, Teddy, Buzzy, Dyson, and Baxter.

And last but not least, my wife Caitlin. She's smart, dedicated, and sweet, and she puts up with me day after day, even when I'm just as chaotic as my characters—seriously, I'm a certified pot-stirrer. I love you, Caitlin, and yes, I'll mow the lawn.

About the Author

Dave Lawson is an Oklahoma-based fantasy novelist. He received an MFA in Fiction Writing from The New School in 2009 and published some contemporary literary fiction, before spending several years doing absolutely nothing with his degree. Now, he's returned to his first love--and what he enjoys reading--fantasy. His first fantasy novel, The Envoys of War, will be published in October of 2024. He enjoys writing about conniving rakes and creative liars who do whatever they must to get what they desire. However, Dave's not like his characters. Pinky swear.

When he's not writing, he teaches high school English and Drama. He lives with his wife and their dog, Rowena, who is a ball of energy. In a past life, Dave was surely a pirate.

The Secret Scribes are a collective of thirteen indepedent fantasy authors. If you've enjoyed this book, check out these other great reads!

Bill Adams: The Godsblood Tragedy
The Tenacious Tale of Tanna the Tendersword

L.N. Bayen: Wingspan of Treason

Tom Bookbeard: The Corsair

E.H. Bradley: The Ranger

L.M. Douglas: Gharantia's Guardian
Gharantia's Fury

Bella Dunn: The Dream's Thief

Damien Francis: Tome of Haren

Dave Lawson: The Envoys of War

Sean O'Boyle: The Ballad of Sprikit the Bard (and Company)

R.A. Sandpiper: A Pocket of Lies
A Promise of Blood

Alex Scheuermann: The Odyllic Stone

G.J. Terral: Bloodwoven